NOVELS

The Floating Opera (1956)**
The End of the Road (1958)*
The Sot-Weed Factor (1960)*
Giles Goat-Boy, or, The Revised New Syllabus (1966)*
Chimera (1972)*
LETTERS (1979)**
Sabbatical: A Romance (1982)**
The Tidewater Tales (1987)*
The Last Voyage of Somebody the Sailor (1991)*
Once upon a Time: A Floating Opera (1994)*
Coming Soon!!!: A Narrative (2001)
Where Three Roads Meet (2005)
Every Third Thought: A Novel in Five Seasons (2011)

SHORT STORIES
(available in *Collected Stories***)

Lost in the Funhouse: Fiction for Print, Tape, Live Voice (1968)
On with the Story (1996)
The Book of Ten Nights and a Night: Eleven Stories (2004)
The Development: Nine Stories (2008)

ESSAYS

The Friday Book (1984)
Further Fridays (1995)
Final Fridays (2012)

*Forthcoming from Dalkey Archive Press
**Available now from Dalkey Archive Press

COLLECTED STORIES

COLLECTED STORIES

John Barth

DALKEY ARCHIVE PRESS

Lost in the Funhouse © 1968 Published by arrangement with Doubleday, an imprint
of The Knopf Doubleday Publishing Group, a division of Random House LLC
On with the Story © John Barth 1996
The Book of Ten Nights and a Night © 2004 John Barth. Reprinted by permission of
Houghton Mifflin Harcourt Publishing Company. All rights reserved.
The Development © John Barth 2008

First edition, 2015
All rights reserved

Library of Congress Cataloging-in-Publication Data

Barth, John, 1930-
  [Short stories. Selections]
  Collected stories / by John Barth. -- First edition.
    pages ; cm
  ISBN 978-1-62897-095-1 (cloth : alk. paper)
  I. Title.

PS3552.A75A6 2015
813'.54--dc23

                                                2015016102

Partially funded by the Illinois Arts Council, a state agency

Dalkey Archive Press
Victoria, TX / Dublin / London
www.dalkeyarchive.com

Dalkey Archive gratefully acknowledges the generous support of the University of Houston-Victoria where Dalkey's
program in Applied Literary Translation is offered in conjunction with master's programs in creative writing and publishing,
culminating in a credit-bearing Certificate, an MFA, or a masters degree.
www.uhv.edu/asa/

Printed on permanent/durable acid-free paper
Cover: design and composition Mikhail Iliatov

Contents

On with the Stories!   *1*
(An introduction to Collected Stories *by John Barth)*

LOST IN THE FUNHOUSE (1968)   *5*

Lost in the Funhouse (Foreword to the Anchor Books Edition)   *7*
Author's Note (1968)   *10*
Frame-Tale   *13*
Night-Sea Journey   *15*
Ambrose His Mark   *24*
Autobiography: A Self-Recorded Fiction   *42*
Water-Message   *46*
Petition   *61*
Lost in the Funhouse   *73*
Echo   *96*
Two Meditations   *101*
Title   *102*
Glossolalia   *110*
Life-Story   *112*
Menelaiad   *124*
Anonymiad   *156*
Seven Additional Author's Notes (1969)   *185*

ON WITH THE STORY (1996)   189

Check-in   193

1. The End: An Introduction   197
   Pillow Talk: "That's a story?"   205

2. Ad Infinitum: A Short Story   206
   "That's more like it."   214

3. And Then One Day . . .   216
   "Dot dot dot? . . ."   232

4. Preparing for the Storm   234
   "'Yes, well,'   245

5. On with the Story   247
   "Maybe . . .   266

6. Love Explained   268
   "You're putting words in her mouth."   273

7. "Waves," by Amien Richard   275
   "No comment."   305

8. Stories of Our Lives   307
   "Hold on, there."   332

9. Closing Out the Visit   334
   "That says it. Time to go."   341

10. Good-bye to the Fruits   342
    "I'll say yes to that."   350

11. Ever After   351
    Pillow Talk: Presently   367

12. Countdown: Once Upon a Time   368

CONTENTS

THE BOOK OF TEN NIGHTS AND A NIGHT (2004)   395

Invocation: "WYSIWYG"   397
    Help!   405

FIRST NIGHT   409
    Landscape: The Eastern Shore   414

SECOND NIGHT   420
    The Ring   435

THIRD NIGHT   445
    Dead Cat, Floating Boy   452

FOURTH NIGHT   462
    A Detective and a Turtle   467

FIFTH NIGHT   483
    The Rest of Your Life   488

SIXTH NIGHT   506
    The Big Shrink   512

SEVENTH NIGHT   523
    Extension   528

EIGHTH NIGHT   535
    And Then There's the One   538

NINTH NIGHT   555
    9999   559

TENTH NIGHT   577
    Click   583

ELEVENTH NIGHT   607
    WYSIWYG?   616

AFTERWORDS   633

CONTENTS

THE DEVELOPMENT (2008)   *637*

Peeping Tom   *639*
Toga Party   *660*
Teardown   *687*
The Bard Award   *701*
Progressive Dinner   *719*
Us / Them   *739*
Assisted Living   *751*
The End   *761*
Rebeginning   *773*

COLLECTED STORIES

On with the Stories!
An introduction to Collected Stories *by John Barth*

My authorial inclination over the decades has typically been toward *books* rather than discrete, stand-alone short stories. Much as I admire such past masters of the genre as Poe and Chekhov, Hemingway and Faulkner, Joyce and Kafka, Borges and Calvino, and too many later ones to mention, I've been more inspired by such tale-*cycles* as Scheherazade's *1001 Nights* and Boccaccio's *Decameron*: stories framed by a framing-story. For that reason, of the twenty book-length publications listed on the "Also by" page of this volume, eleven are novels, three are essay-collections, two are triads of novellas, and four — *Lost in the Funhouse* (1968), *On With the Story* (1996), *The Book of Ten Nights and a Night* (2004), and *The Development* (2008) — are short-story collections, or (as I prefer to regard them) short-story *series.*

"Serieses"? Anyhow, narrative wholes larger than the mere accumulation of their parts: short-story *books* by a congenital novelist, just as that pair of novella-triads — *Chimera* (1972) and *Where Three Roads Meet* (2005) — are three-part wholes (or perhaps tripartite monstrosities, like the original Chimera of Greek myth: lion-headed, goat-bodied, and serpent-tailed, but functioning as a coherent organism). I note that twenty-eight years elapsed between the first of those four story-books and the second, eight years between the second and the third, and only four between the third and fourth: Brevity, apparently, became more attractive to their author as the decades passed.

1

That first series, *Lost in the Funhouse*, is subtitled *Fiction for Print, Tape, Live Voice* (the story "Autobiography," e.g., would make no sense unless one understood that its voice comes from a tape recorder). In the "High Sixties," as the latter half of that decade was often called, I was teaching at the State University of New York at Buffalo. The Vietnam War was in full swing. American campuses, ours included, were racked with war-protesting sit-ins and National Guard protest-dispersals. Conscientious Objectors and other draft-avoiders were skipping across the Peace Bridge to Canada, from where Marshall McLuhan, author of *The Gutenberg Galaxy*, was pronouncing the Death of the Novel and declaring us "P.O.B.s" (Print-Oriented Bastards) to be anachronisms. I myself did not buy into this apocalypticism: As my late critic-friend and colleague Leslie Fiedler liked to say, the novel was *born* dying, like all of us (e.g. such self-skeptical or self-satirical originals as Cervantes' *Don Quixote*, Sterne's *Tristram Shandy*, and Diderot's *Jacques the Fatalist*); it has gone on dying vigorously for several centuries now, and may be hoped to enjoy a *very* extended terminality. But that sense of its mortality, possibly obsolescence, was in the campus air back then like National Guard tear-gas; some of my best student writers felt that the future of fiction was on the screen, not the printed page. My experience of giving and attending public readings, together with my interest in the ancient tale-cycles, had sharpened my awareness of the differences between stories on the printed page (a silent transaction between author and individual readers) and stories more or less performed aloud: the oral tale-telling tradition that preceded writing, not to mention print. Additionally, I had discovered and been charmed by the late-19th-century Brazilian Machado de Assis and the masterful Argentine Jorge Luis Borges (whom I had the privilege of bringing to SUNY/Buffalo). It was in this spirit — with a tip of the hat to that tradition and those two masters, and with four novels already under my belt, so to speak — that *Lost in the Funhouse* was ... written. Or, more accurately, *composed* (and duly subtitled).

Twenty-eight years, four novels, a novella-triad, and an essay-collection later, in 1996, I happily returned to the short-story form with a second collection (excuse me: a second *series*) of stories, entitled *On With the Story*: an even dozen tales, framed and interlinked by a thirteenth to make a book. A mere eight years and one novel after that, having revisited my chief literary navigation-star Scheherazade in the Mardrus and Mathers translation of her *Book of a Thousand Nights and a Night*, I published in 2004 my minimal *Book of Ten Nights and a Night*, a framed series of eleven stories; and just four years later, *The Development* (2008): nine stories linked by several shared characters and a common setting (the fictitious exurban "gated community" called Heron Bay Estates, on Maryland's Eastern Shore, from its construction in the early 1980s to its near-total wipe-out by a fluke tornado two dozen years later) — in each case, a story-*book*, not simply a book of stories.

Given that predilection, I'm pleased to see those four story-"serieses" in a single volume, and to think of this volume not merely as a collection, but as a *combination*. A super-series. A *book*.

On with the stories!

Lost in the Funhouse (1968)

Lost in the Funhouse

Foreword to the Anchor Books Edition

Short fiction is not my long suit. Writers tend by temperament to be either sprinters or marathoners, and I learned early that the long haul was my stride. The form of the modern short story—as defined and developed by Poe, Maupassant, and Chekhov and handed on to the twentieth century—I found in my apprentice years to be parsimonious, constraining, constipative. Much as I admired its great practitioners, I preferred more narrative elbow room.

The premodern tale is another matter: especially the tale cycle, as told by the likes of Scheherazade and Boccaccio. I virtually began my narrative career with one of those, but set it aside for the even more hospitable space of the novel and the more hospitable project rhythms of the novelist. Your congenital short-story writer faces the blank-faced muse once every few weeks (in the case of early Chekhov, every few days). Your congenital novelist prefers to dream up a world once every few years; to plant and people it and dwell therein for maybe a whole presidential term—or the time it takes a new college freshman to complete the baccalaureate—before reconfronting the interterrestrial Void.

But after a dozen years of writing and publishing the novels reprinted in this Anchor Books series—*The Floating Opera, The End of the Road, The Sot-Weed Factor, Giles Goat-Boy*—in the mid-1960s I found myself hankering to reattempt the short form, for assorted reasons:

For one thing, Less really is More, other things equal. Even quite expansive novels, if carefully written, have their own economy and rigor; but *Sot-Weed* and *Giles* are long novels indeed, and writing them increased my respect for the mode that comes least naturally to me. The clown comes to want to play Hamlet, and vice versa; the long-distance runner itches to sprint. Just as there are musical ideas that won't do for a symphony but are just right for a song, there are narrative ideas suitable only for a short story: quick takes, epiphanies that even a novella would attenuate, not to mention a novel. Over the years, I had accumulated a few such narrative ideas in my notebooks.

Moreover, I teach stories as well as telling them, and like most writing coaches I find the short story most useful for seminar purposes. You can hold a short story in your hand, like a lyric poem; see it whole; examine the function of individual sentences, even individual words, as you can't readily do with *Bleak House* or *War and Peace*. (This pedagogical convenience, together with the proliferation of creative writing programs in the U.S.A., must be largely responsible for the happy resurgence of the American short story — at a time when, paradoxically, the popular audience has never been smaller.) But those model stories I was teaching came from classroom anthologies in which (novels being hard to excerpt coherently, and excerpts being formally less useful than complete works), my own fiction was seldom included. I consoled myself, maybe flattered myself, with the consideration that such eminent non-short-story-writing contemporaries as Ralph Ellison and William Styron were likewise seldom included — but I wanted to be in those anthologies. Not all of a writer's motives are pure.

It was about this time that I came across the writings of the great Argentine Jorge Luis Borges, whose temper was so wedded to the short forms that, like Chekhov, he never wrote a novel, and whose unorthodox brilliance transformed the short story for me. Writers learn from their experience of other writers as well as from their experience of life in the world; it was the happy marriage of form and content in Borges's *ficciones* — the way he regularly turned his narrative means into part of his message — that suggested how I might try something similar, in my way and with my materials.

The result was *Lost in the Funhouse* (I was in fact, at age thirteen or so, once briefly mislaid in a boardwalk funhouse, in Asbury Park, New

Jersey; end of autobiographical reference). Incorrigibly the novelist, I decided at the outset to write not simply some short stories but a book of short stories: a sequence or series rather than a mere assortment. Though the several stories would more or less stand alone (and therefore be anthologizable), the series would be strung together on a few echoed and developed themes and would circle back upon itself: not to close a simple circuit like that of Joyce's *Finnegans Wake*, emblematic of Viconian eternal return, but to make a circuit with a twist to it, like a Möbius strip, emblematic of — well, read the book.

The series was written and assembled between 1966 and 1968. The first Doubleday edition (1968) was prefaced by the Author's Note which follows; to subsequent editions I appended "Seven Additional Author's Notes," set here at the end (I was busy by then with a novel that pretends to have seven authors). The reader may skip all these frames and go directly to the first story . . . called "Frame-Tale." It happens to be, I believe, the shortest short story in the English language (ten words); on the other hand, it's endless.

The High Sixties, like the Roaring Twenties, was a time of more than usual ferment in American social, political, and artistic life. Our unpopular war in Vietnam, political assassinations, race riots, the hippie counterculture, pop art, mass poetry readings, street theater, vigorous avant-gardism in all the arts, together with dire predictions not only of the death of the novel but of the moribundity of the print medium in the electronic global village — those flavored the air we breathed then, along with occasional tear gas and other contaminants. One may sniff traces of that air in the Funhouse ("Fiction for Print, Tape, Live Voice"). I myself found it more invigorating than disturbing. May the reader find these stories likewise.

John Barth
1987

Author's Note (1968)

This book differs in two ways from most volumes of short fiction. First, it's neither a collection nor a selection, but a series; though several of its items have appeared separately in periodicals, the series will be seen to have been meant to be received "all at once" and as here arranged. Most of its members, consequently, are "new"—written for this book, in which they appear for the first time.

Second, while some of these pieces were composed expressly for print, others were not. "Ambrose His Mark" and "Water-Message," the earliest-written, take the print medium for granted but lose or gain nothing in oral recitation. "Petition," "Lost in the Funhouse," "Life-Story," and "Anonymiad," on the other hand, would lose part of their point in any except printed form; "Night-Sea Journey" was meant for either print or recorded authorial voice, but not for live or non-authorial voice; "Glossolalia" will make no sense unless heard in live or recorded voices, male and female, or read as if so heard; "Echo" is intended for monophonic authorial recording, either disc or tape; "Autobiography," for monophonic tape and visible but silent author. "Menelaiad," though suggestive of a recorded authorial monologue, depends for clarity on the reader's eye and may be said to have been composed for "printed voice." "Title" makes somewhat separate but equally valid senses in several media: print, monophonic recorded authorial voice, stereophonic ditto in dialogue with itself, live authorial voice, live ditto in dialogue with monophonic ditto aforementioned, and live ditto interlocutory with stereophonic *et cetera*, my own preference; it's been "done" in all six. "Frame-Tale" is one-, two-, or three-dimensional, whichever one regards a Möbius strip as being. On with the story. On with the story.

Frame-Tale

Cut on dotted line.
Twist end once and fasten *AB* to *ab*, *CD* to *cd*.

(continued)

ONCE UPON A TIME THERE

A
B
c
d

WAS A STORY THAT BEGAN [a][b][p][c]

(continued)

Night-Sea Journey

"One way or another, no matter which theory of our journey is correct, it's myself I address; to whom I rehearse as to a stranger our history and condition, and will disclose my secret hope though I sink for it.

"Is the journey my invention? Do the night, the sea, exist at all, I ask myself, apart from my experience of them? Do I myself exist, or is this a dream? Sometimes I wonder. And if I am, who am I? The Heritage I supposedly transport? But how can I be both vessel and contents? Such are the questions that beset my intervals of rest.

"My trouble is, I lack conviction. Many accounts of our situation seem plausible to me — where and what we are, why we swim and whither. But implausible ones as well, perhaps especially those, I must admit as possibly correct. Even likely. If at times, in certain humors — stroking in unison, say, with my neighbors and chanting with them 'Onward! Upward!' — I have supposed that we have after all a common Maker, Whose nature and motives we may not know, but Who engendered us in some mysterious wise and launched us forth toward some end known but to Him — if (for a moodslength only) I have been able to entertain such notions, very popular in certain quarters, it is because our night-sea journey partakes of their absurdity. One might even say: I can believe them because they are absurd.

"Has that been said before?

"Another paradox: it appears to be these recesses from swimming that sustain me in the swim. Two measures onward and upward, flailing with the rest, then I float exhausted and dispirited, brood upon the night, the sea, the journey, while the flood bears me a measure back and down: slow progress, but I live, I live, and make my way, aye, past many a drownèd comrade in the end, stronger, worthier than I, victims of their unremitting *joie de nager*. I have seen the best swimmers of my generation go under. Numberless the number of the dead! Thousands drown as I think this thought, millions as I rest before returning to the swim. And scores, hundreds of millions have expired since we surged forth, brave in our innocence, upon our dreadful way. 'Love! Love!' we sang then, a quarterbillion strong, and churned the warm sea white with joy of swimming! Now all are gone down — the buoyant, the sodden, leaders and followers, all gone under, while wretched I swim on. Yet these same reflective intervals that keep me afloat have led me into wonder, doubt, despair— strange emotions for a swimmer! — have led me, even, to suspect . . . that our night-sea journey is without meaning.

"Indeed, if I have yet to join the hosts of the suicides, it is because (fatigue apart) I find it no meaningfuller to drown myself than to go on swimming.

"I know that there are those who seem actually to enjoy the night-sea; who claim to love swimming for its own sake, or sincerely believe that 'reaching the Shore', 'transmitting the Heritage' (*Whose* Heritage, I'd like to know? And to whom?) is worth the staggering cost. I do not. Swimming itself I find at best not actively unpleasant, more often tiresome, not infrequently a torment. Arguments from function and design don't impress me: granted that we can and do swim, that in a manner of speaking our long tails and streamlined heads are 'meant for' swimming; it by no means follows — for me, at least — that we *should* swim, or otherwise endeavor to 'fulfill our destiny.' Which is to say, Someone Else's destiny, since ours, so far as I can see, is merely to perish, one way or another, soon or late. The heartless zeal of our (departed) leaders, like the blind ambition and good cheer of my own youth, appalls me now; for the death of my comrades I am inconsolable. If the night-sea journey has justification, it is not for us swimmers ever to discover it.

"Oh, to be sure, 'Love!' one heard on every side: 'Love it is that drives and sustains us!' I translate: we don't know *what* drives and sustains us, only that we are most miserably driven and, imperfectly, sustained. *Love* is how we call our ignorance of what whips us. 'To reach the Shore,' then: but what if the Shore exists in the fancies of us swimmers merely, who dream it to account for the dreadful fact that we swim, have always and only swum, and continue swimming without respite (myself excepted) until we die? Supposing even that there *were* a Shore — that, as a cynical companion of mine once imagined, we rise from the drowned to discover all those vulgar superstitions and exalted metaphors to be literal truth: the giant Maker of us all, the Shores of Light beyond our night-sea journey! — whatever would a swimmer do there? The fact is, when we imagine the Shore, what comes to mind is just the opposite of our condition: no more night, no more sea, no more journeying. In short, the blissful estate of the drowned.

"'Ours not to stop and think; ours but to swim and sink ...' Because a moment's thought reveals the pointlessness of swimming. 'No matter,' I've heard some say, even as they gulped their last: 'The night-sea journey may be absurd, but here we swim, will-we nill-we, against the flood, onward and upward, toward a Shore that may not exist and couldn't be reached if it did.' The thoughtful swimmer's choices, then, they say, are two: give over thrashing and go under for good, or embrace the absurdity; affirm in and for itself the night-sea journey; swim on with neither motive nor destination, for the sake of swimming, and compassionate moreover with your fellow swimmer, we being all at sea and equally in the dark. I find neither course acceptable. If not even the hypothetical Shore can justify a sea-full of drownèd comrades, to speak of the swim-in-itself as somehow doing so strikes me as obscene. I continue to swim — but only because blind habit, blind instinct, blind fear of drowning are still more strong than the horror of our journey. And if on occasion I have assisted a fellow-thrasher, joined in the cheers and songs, even passed along to others strokes of genius from the drownèd great, it's that I shrink by temperament from making myself conspicuous. To paddle off in one's own direction, assert one's independent right-of-way, overrun one's fellows without compunction, or dedicate oneself entirely to pleasures and diversions without regard for conscience — I can't finally condemn those who journey in this wise; in half my moods I envy them and despise the weak vitality that keeps me from following their example. But in reasonabler moments I remind myself that it's their very freedom and self-responsibility I reject, as more dramatically absurd, in our senseless circumstances, than tailing along in conventional fashion. Suicides, rebels, affirmers of the paradox — nay-sayers and yea-sayers alike to our fatal journey — I finally shake my head at them. And splash sighing past their corpses, one by one, as past a hundred sorts of others: friends, enemies, brothers; fools, sages, brutes — and nobodies, million upon million. I envy them all.

"A poor irony: that I, who find abhorrent and tautological the doctrine of survival of the fittest (*fitness* meaning, in my experience, nothing more than survival-ability, a talent whose only demonstration is the fact of survival, but whose chief ingredients seem to be strength, guile, callousness), may be the sole remaining swimmer! But the doctrine is false as well as repellent: Chance drowns the worthy with the unworthy, bears up the unfit with the fit by whatever definition, and makes the night-sea journey essentially *haphazard* as well as murderous and unjustified.

"'You only swim once.' Why bother, then?

"'Except ye drown, ye shall not reach the Shore of Life.' Poppycock.

"One of my late companions — that same cynic with the curious fancy, among the first to drown — entertained us with odd conjectures while we waited to begin our journey. A favorite theory of his was that the Father does exist, and did indeed make us and the sea we swim — but not a-purpose or even consciously; He made us, as it were, despite Himself, as we make waves with every tail-thrash, and may be unaware of our existence. Another was that He knows we're here but doesn't care what happens to us, inasmuch as He creates (voluntarily or not) other seas and swimmers at more or less regular intervals. In bitterer moments, such as just before he drowned, my friend even supposed that our Maker wished us unmade; there was indeed a Shore, he'd argue, which could save at least some of us from drowning and toward which it was our function to struggle — but for reasons unknowable to us He wanted desperately to prevent our reaching that happy place and fulfilling our destiny. Our 'Father,' in short, was our adversary and would-be killer! No less outrageous, and offensive to traditional opinion, were the fellow's speculations on the nature of our Maker: that He might well be no swimmer Himself at all, but some sort of monstrosity, perhaps even tailless; that He might be stupid, malicious, insensible, perverse, or asleep and dreaming; that the end for which He created and launched us forth, and which we flagellate ourselves to fathom, was perhaps immoral, even obscene. *Et cetera, et cetera*: there was no end to the chap's conjectures, or the impoliteness of his fancy; I have reason to suspect that his early demise, whether planned by 'our Maker' or not, was expedited by certain fellow-swimmers indignant at his blasphemies.

"In other moods, however (he was as given to moods as I), his theorizing would become half-serious, so it seemed to me, especially upon the subjects of Fate and Immortality, to which our youthful conversations often turned. Then his harangues, if no less fantastical, grew solemn and obscure, and if he was still baiting us, his passion undid the joke. His objection to popular opinions of the hereafter, he would declare, was their claim to general validity. Why need believers hold that *all* the drowned rise to be judged at journey's end, and non-believers that drowning is final without exception? In *his* opinion (so he'd vow at least), nearly everyone's fate was permanent death; indeed he took a sour pleasure in supposing that every 'Maker' made thousands of separate seas in His creative lifetime, each populated like ours with millions of swimmers, and that in almost every instance both sea and swimmers were utterly annihilated, whether accidentally or by malevolent design. (Nothing if not pluralistical, he imagined there might be millions and billions of 'Fathers,' perhaps in some 'night-sea' of their own!) However—and here he turned infidels against him with the faithful—he professed to believe that in possibly a single night-sea per thousand, say, one of its quarter-billion swimmers (that is, one swimmer in two hundred fifty billions) achieved a qualified immortality. In some cases the rate might be slightly higher; in others it was vastly lower, for just as there are swimmers of every degree of proficiency, including some who drown before the journey starts, unable to swim at all, and others created drowned, as it were, so he imagined what can only be termed impotent Creators, Makers unable to Make, as well as uncommonly fertile ones and all grades between. And it pleased him to deny any necessary relation between a Maker's productivity and His other virtues—including, even, the quality of His creatures.

"I could go on (*he* surely did) with his elaboration of these mad notions—such as that swimmers in other night-seas needn't be of our kind; that Makers themselves might belong to different *species*, so to speak; that our particular Maker mightn't Himself be immortal, or that we might be not only His emissaries but His 'immortality,' continuing His life and our own, transmogrified, beyond our individual deaths. Even this modified immortality (meaningless to me) he conceived as relative and contingent, subject to accidental or deliberate termination: his pet hypothesis was that Makers and swimmers *each generate the other* — against all odds, their number being so great — and that any given 'immortality-chain' could terminate after any number of cycles, so that what was 'immortal' (still speaking relatively) was only the cyclic process of incarnation, which itself might have a beginning and an end. Alternatively he liked to imagine cycles within cycles, either finite or infinite: for example, the 'night-sea,' as it were, in which Makers 'swam' and created night-seas and swimmers like ourselves, might be the creation of a larger Maker, Himself one of many, Who in turn *et cetera*. Time itself he regarded as relative to our experience, like magnitude: who knew but what, with each thrash of our tails, minuscule seas and swimmers, whole eternities, came to pass — as ours, perhaps, and our Maker's Maker's, was elapsing between the strokes of some supertail, in a slower order of time?

"Naturally I hooted with the others at this nonsense. We were young then, and had only the dimmest notion of what lay ahead; in our ignorance we imagined night-sea journeying to be a positively heroic enterprise. Its meaning and value we never questioned; to be sure, some must go down by the way, a pity no doubt, but to win a race requires that others lose, and like all my fellows I took for granted that I would be the winner. We milled and swarmed, impatient to be off, never mind where or why, only to try our youth against the realities of night and sea; if we indulged the skeptic at all, it was as a droll, half-contemptible mascot. When he died in the initial slaughter, no one cared.

"And even now I don't subscribe to all his views — but I no longer scoff. The horror of our history has purged me of opinions, as of vanity, confidence, spirit, charity, hope, vitality, everything — except dull dread and a kind of melancholy, stunned persistence. What leads me to recall his fancies is my growing suspicion that I, of all swimmers, may be the sole survivor of this fell journey, tale-bearer of a generation. This suspicion, together with the recent sea-change, suggests to me now that nothing is impossible, not even my late companion's wildest visions, and brings me to a certain desperate resolve, the point of my chronicling.

"Very likely I have lost my senses. The carnage at our setting out; our decimation by whirl pool, poisoned cataract, sea-convulsion; the panic stampedes, mutinies, slaughters, mass suicides; the mounting evidence that none will survive the journey — add to these anguish and fatigue; it were a miracle if sanity stayed afloat. Thus I admit, with the other possibilities, that the present sweetening and calming of the sea, and what seems to be a kind of vasty presence, song, or summons from the near upstream, may be hallucinations of disordered sensibility . . .

"Perhaps, even, I am drowned already. Surely I was never meant for the rough-and-tumble of the swim; not impossibly I perished at the outset and have only imaged the night-sea journey from some final deep. In any case, I'm no longer young, and it is we spent old swimmers, disabused of every illusion, who are most vulnerable to dreams.

"Sometimes I think I am my drownèd friend.

"Out with it: I've begun to believe, not only that *She* exists, but that She lies not far ahead, and stills the sea, and draws me Herward! Aghast, I recollect his maddest notion: that our destination (which existed, mind, in but one night-sea out of hundreds and thousands) was no Shore, as commonly conceived, but a mysterious being, indescribable except by paradox and vaguest figure: wholly different from us swimmers, yet our complement; the death of us, yet our salvation and resurrection; simultaneously our journey's end, mid-point, and commencement; not membered and thrashing like us, but a motionless or hugely gliding sphere of unimaginable dimension; self-contained, yet dependent absolutely, in some wise, upon the chance (always monstrously improbable) that one of us will survive the night-sea journey and reach . . . Her! *Her*, he called it, or *She*, which is to say, Other-than-a-he. I shake my head; the thing is too preposterous; it is myself I talk to, to keep my reason in this awful darkness. There is no She! There is no You! I rave to myself; it's Death alone that hears and summons. To the drowned, all seas are calm . . .

"Listen: my friend maintained that in every order of creation there are two sorts of creators, contrary yet complementary, one of which gives rise to seas and swimmers, the other to the Night-which-contains-the-sea and to What-waits-at-the-journey's-end: the former, in short, to destiny, the latter to destination (and both profligately, involuntarily, perhaps indifferently or unwittingly). The 'purpose' of the night-sea journey — but not necessarily of the journeyer or of either Maker! — my friend could describe only in abstractions: *consummation, transfiguration, union of contraries, transcension of categories.* When we laughed, he would shrug and admit that he understood the business no better than we, and thought it ridiculous, dreary, possibly obscene. 'But one of you,' he'd add with his wry smile, 'may be the Hero destined to complete the night-sea journey and be one with Her. Chances are, of course, you won't make it.' He himself, he declared, was not even going to try; the whole idea repelled him; if we chose to dismiss it as an ugly fiction, so much the better for us; thrash, splash, and be merry, we were soon enough drowned. But there it was, he could not say how he knew or why he bothered to tell us, any more than he could say what would happen after She and Hero, Shore and Swimmer, 'merged identities' to become something both and neither. He quite agreed with me that if the issue of that magical union had no memory of the night-sea journey, for example, it enjoyed a poor sort of immortality; even poorer if, as he rather imagined, a swimmer—hero plus a She equaled or became merely another Maker of future night-seas and the rest, at such incredible expense of life. This being the case—he was persuaded it was—the merciful thing to do was refuse to participate; the genuine heroes, in his opinion, were the suicides, and the hero of heroes would be the swimmer who, in the very presence of the Other, refused Her proffered 'immortality' and thus put an end to at least one cycle of catastrophes.

"How we mocked him! Our moment came, we hurtled forth, pretending to glory in the adventure, thrashing, singing, cursing, strangling, rationalizing, rescuing, killing, inventing rules and stories and relationships, giving up, struggling on, but dying all, and still in darkness, until only a battered remnant was left to croak 'Onward, upward,' like a bitter echo. Then they too fell silent—victims, I can only presume, of the last frightful wave—and the moment came when I also, utterly desolate and spent, thrashed my last and gave myself over to the current, to sink or float as might be, but swim no more. Whereupon, marvelous to tell, in an instant the sea grew still! Then warmly, gently, the great tide turned, began to bear me, as it does now, onward and upward will-I nill-I, like a flood of joy—and I recalled with dismay my dead friend's teaching.

"I am not deceived. This new emotion is Her doing; the desire that possesses me is Her bewitchment. Lucidity passes from me; in a moment I'll cry 'Love!' bury myself in Her side, and be 'transfigured.' Which is to say, I die already; this fellow transported by passion is not I; *I am he who abjures and rejects the night-sea journey!* I . . .

"I am all love. 'Come!' She whispers, and I have no will.

"You who I may be about to become, whatever You are: with the last twitch of my real self I beg You to listen. It is not love that sustains me! No; though Her magic makes me burn to sing the contrary, and though I drown even now for the blasphemy, I will say truth. What has fetched me across this dreadful sea is a single hope, gift of my poor dead comrade: that You may be stronger-willed than I, and that by sheer force of concentration I may transmit to You, along with Your official Heritage, a private legacy of awful recollection and negative resolve. Mad as it may be, my dream is that some unimaginable embodiment of myself (or myself plus Her if that's how it must be) will come to find itself expressing, in however garbled or radical a translation, some reflection of these reflections. If against all odds this comes to pass, may You to whom, through whom I speak, do what I cannot: terminate this aimless, brutal business! Stop Your hearing against Her song! Hate love!

"Still alive, afloat, afire. Farewell then my penultimate hope: that one may be sunk for direst blasphemy on the very shore of the Shore. Can it be (my old friend would smile) that only utterest nay-sayers survive the night? But even that were Sense, and there is no sense, only senseless love, senseless death. Whoever echoes these reflections: be more courageous than their author! An end to night-sea journeys! Make no more! And forswear me when I shall forswear myself, deny myself, plunge into Her who summons, singing . . .

"'Love! Love! Love!'"

Ambrose His Mark

Owing to the hectic circumstances of my birth, for some months I had no proper name. Mother had seen Garbo in Anna Christie at the Dorset Opera House during her pregnancy and come to hope for a daughter, to be named by some logic Christine in honor of that lady. When I was brought home, after Father's commitment to the Eastern Shore Asylum, she made no mention of a name nor showed any interest in selecting one, and the family were too concerned for her well-being to press the matter. She grew froward — by turns high-spirited and listless, voluble and dumb, doting and cynical. Some days she would permit no hands but hers to touch me, would haul me about from room to room, crooning and nuzzling: a photograph made by Uncle Karl on such a day shows her posed before our Concord vines, her pretty head thrown back, scarfed and earringed like a gypsy; her eyes are closed, her mouth laughs gaily behind her cigarette; one hand holds a cup of coffee, the other steadies a scowling infant on her hip. Other times she would have none of me, or even suffer me in her sight. About my feeding there was ever some unease: if I cried, say, when the family was at table, forks would pause and eyes turn furtively to Andrea. For in one humor she would fetch out her breast in any company and feed me while she smoked or strolled the garden — nor nurse me quietly at that, but demand of Aunt Rosa whether I hadn't Hector's eyes . . .

"*Ja*, well."

"And Poppa Tom's appetite. Look, Konrad, how he wolfs it. There's a man for you."

Grandfather openly relished these performances; he chuckled at the mentions of himself, teased Uncle Konrad for averting his eyes, and never turned his own from my refections.

"Now there is Beauty's picture, *nicht wahr*, Konrad? Mother and child."

But his entertainment was not assured: just as often Andrea would say, "Lord, there goes Christine again. Stick something in his mouth, Rosie, would you?" or merely sigh — a rueful expiration that still blows fitful as her ghost through my memory — and say nothing, but let Aunt Rosa (always nervously at hand) prepare and administer my bottle, not even troubling to make her kindless joke about the grand unsuckled bosoms of that lady.

To Rosa I was *Honig*; Mother too, when "Christine" seemed unfunny, called me thus, and in the absence of anything official, *Honey* soon lost the quality of endearment and took the neutral function of a proper name. Uncle Konrad privately held out for Hector, but no one ventured to bring up her husband's name in Mother's presence. Uncle Karl was not in town to offer an opinion. Aunt Rosa believed that calling me *Thomas* might improve relations between Grandfather and his youngest son; but though he'd made no secret of his desire to have my older brother be his namesake, and his grievance at the choice of *Peter*, Grandfather displayed no more interest than did Andrea in naming me. Rosa attributed his indifference to bruised pride; in any case, given Mother's attitude, the question of my nomination was academic. Baptism was delayed, postponed, anon forgot.

Only once did Mother allude to my namelessness, some two or three months after my birth. I was lying in Aunt Rosa's lap, drinking from a bottle; dinner was just done; the family lingered over coffee. Suddenly Andrea, on one of her impulses, cried "Give him here, Rose!" and snatched me up. I made a great commotion.

"Now, you frightened it," Rosa chided.

Andrea ignored her. " 'E doesn't want Rosie's old bottle, does Christine."

Her croon failed to console me. "Hold him till I unbutton," she said — not to Rosa but to Uncle Konrad. Her motives, doubtless, were

the usual: to make Aunt Rosa envious, amuse Grandfather, and morti-
fy Uncle Konrad, who could not now readily look away. She undid her
peignoir, casually bemoaning her abundance of milk: it was making
her clothes a sight, it was hurting her besides, she must nurse me more
regularly. She did not at once retrieve me but with such chatter as this
bent forward, cupped her breast, invited me to drink the sweet pap
already beading and spreading under her fingers. Uncle Konrad, it was
agreed, at no time before or after turned so crimson. "Here's what the
Honey wants," Andrea said, relieving him finally of his charge. To the
company in general she declared, "It does feel good, you know: there's
a nerve or something runs from here right to you-know-where."

"*Schämt euch!*" Aunt Rosa cried.

"*Ja* sure," Grandfather said merrily. "You named it!"

"No, really, she knows as well as I do what it's like. Doesn't she, Christine. Sure Mother likes to feed her little mannie, look how he grabs,
poor darling . . ." Here she was taken unexpectedly with grief; pressed
me fiercely to her, drew the peignoir about us; her tears warmed my
forehead and her breast. "Who will he ever be, Konrad? Little orphan
of the storm, who is he now?"

"Ah! Ah!" Rosa rushed to hug her. Grandfather drew and sucked
upon his meerschaum, which however had gone dead out.

"Keep up like you have been," Konrad said stiffly; "soon he'll be old
enough to pick his own name." My uncle taught fifth grade at East Dorset School, of which Hector had been principal until his commitment,
and in summers was a vendor of encyclopedias and tuner of pianos.
To see things in their larger context was his gentle aim; to harmonize
part with part, time with time; and he never withheld from us what he
deemed germane or helpful. The American Indians, he declared now,
had the right idea. "They never named a boy right off. What they did,
they watched to find out who he was. They'd look for the right sign to
tell them what to call him."

Grandfather scratched a kitchen match on his thumbnail and relit
his pipe.

"There's sense in that," Uncle Konrad persevered. "How can you tell
what name'll suit a person when you don't know him yet?"

Ordinarily Rosa was his audience; preoccupied now with Andrea,
she did not respond.

"There's some name their kids for what they want them to be. A brave hunter, *et cetera*."

"Or a movie star," Mother offered, permitting Rosa to wipe her eyes.

"Same principle exactly," Konrad affirmed, and was grateful enough to add in her behalf, despite his late embarrassment: "It's an important thing, naming a child. If I had a boy, I'd be a good long time about it."

"*Ach*," Grandfather said. "You said that right."

Andrea sniffed sympathy but did not reply, and so Uncle Konrad enlarged no further. Too bad for Grandfather his restlessness moved him from the table, for by this time my mother was herself sufficiently to turn back the veil she'd drawn about us.

"Well," she sighed to me. "You've caused the devil's mischief so far. Your daddy in the crazy-house; people saying Lord knows what about your mother."

"Thank Almighty God you got him," Aunt Rosa said. "And born perfect only for his little mark. Look how wide and clear his eyes!"

Uncle Konrad unbent so far as to pat my head while I nursed, a boldness without known precedent in his biography. "That's a sign of brains," he declared. "This boy could be our pride and saving."

Mother's laugh took on a rougher note. But she caressed my cheek with her knuckle, and I nursed on. Her temper was gay and fond now; yet her breast still glistened with the tears of a minute past. Not just that once was what I drank from her thus salted.

Grandfather would have no whisky or other distillation in the house, but drank grandly of wines and beers which he made himself in the whitewashed sheds behind the summerkitchen. His yeast and earliest grapestock were German, imported for him by the several families he'd brought to the county. The vines never flourished: anon they fell victim to anthracnose and phylloxera and were replaced by our native Delawares, Nortons, Lenoirs; but the yeast—an ancient culture from Sachsen-Altenburg—throve with undiminished vigor in our cellar. With it he would brew dark Bavarian lager, pellucid Weiss, and his cherished Dortmund, pale gold and strongly hopped. Yet vinting was his forte, even Hector agreed. What he drew from the red and white grapes was splendid enough, but in this pursuit as in some others he inclined to variety and experiment: without saccharimeter or any other aid than a Rhenish intuition, he filled his crocks as the whim took him with anything fermentable — rice, cherries, dandelions, elderberries, rose petals, raisins, coconut — and casked unfailingly a decent wine.

Now it was Uncle Konrad's pleasure to recite things on occasion to the family, and in 1929, hearing by this means verses of Macpherson's Ossian, Grandfather had been inspired with a particular hankering for mead. From a farmer whose payments on a footstone were in arrears, he accepted in lieu of cash a quantity of honey, and his fermentation was an entire success. The craving got hold of him, he yearned to crush walnuts in the golden wort — but honey was dear, and dollars, never plentiful in the family, there were none for such expenditure.

The stock market had fallen, the tomato-canners were on strike, hard times were upon the nation; if funerals were a necessity, gravestones were not; Uncle Karl, Grandfather's right-hand man, had left town two years past to lay bricks in Baltimore; our business had seldom been poorer.

"There is a trick for finding bee-trees," Grandfather asserted. One exposed a pan of sugar-water in the woods, waited until a number of honeybees assembled at it, and trapped them by covering the pan with cheesecloth. One then released a single bee and followed it, pan in hand, till it was lost from sight, whereupon one released another bee, and another, and another, and was fetched at length to their common home. It remained then only to smoke out the colony and help oneself to their reserves of honey. All that winter, as I grew in Mother's womb, Grandfather fretted with his scheme; when the spring's first bees appeared on our pussywillows, on our alder catkins, he was off with Hector and Konrad, saucepan and cheesecloth. Their researches led them through fresh-marsh, through pinewoods, over stile and under trestle — but never a bee-tree they discovered, only swampy impasses or the hives of some part-time apiarist.

My birth — more exactly, Hector's notion that someone other than himself had fathered me; his mad invasion of the delivery room; his wild assertion, as they carried him off, that the port-wine stain near my eye was a devil's mark — all this commotion, naturally, ended the quest. Not, however, the general project. Out of scrap pine Grandfather fashioned a box-hive of his own, whitewashed and established it among the lilacs next to the goat-pen, and bade Uncle Konrad keep his eyes open for a migrant swarm, the season being opportune.

His expectation was not unreasonable, even though East Dorset was by 1930 a proper residential ward with sidewalks, sewers, and streetlights. To maintain a goat might be judged eccentric, even vulgar, by neighbors with flush toilets and daily milk service; chickens, likewise, were *non grata* on Seawall Street (if not on Hayward or Franklin, where roosters crowed to the end of the Second World War); but there was nothing unseemly about a stand of sweetcorn, for example, if one had ground enough, or a patch of cucumbers, or a hive of bees. These last, in fact, were already a feature of our street's most handsome yard: I mean Erdmann's, adjacent but for an alley to our own. Upon Willy Erdmann's three fine skeps, braided of straw and caned English-fashion, Grandfather had brooded all winter. Two were inhabited and prosperous; the third, brand new, stood vacant against the day when a swarm would take wing from the others in search of new quarters.

Lilac honey, Grandfather declared, was more pleasing than any other to his taste; moreover it was essential that the hive be placed as far as possible from the house, not to disturb the occupants of either. Though no one pressed him to explain, he insisted it was for these reasons only (one or both of which must have been Erdmann's also) that he located his hive in the extreme rear corner of our property, next to the alley.

Our neighbor plainly was unhappy with this arrangement. Not long from the Asylum himself, whither he'd repaired to cure a sudden dipsomania, Erdmann was convalescing some months at home before he reassumed direction of his business. Pottering about his yard he'd seen our box-hives built and situated; as April passed he came to spend more time on the alley-side of his lot — cultivating his tulips, unmulching his roses, chewing his cigar, glaring from his beehives to ours.

"Yes, well," Grandfather observed. "Willy's bees have been for years using our lilacs. Have I begrutched?"

He made it his tactic at first to stroll hiveward himself whenever Erdmann was standing watch: he would examine his grape-canes, only just opening their mauve-and-yellow buds; he would make pleasantries in two tongues to Gretchen the goat; Erdmann soon would huff indoors.

But with both Hector and Karl away, Grandfather was obliged to spend more time than usual at the stoneyard, however slack the business; throughout whole weekday mornings and afternoons his apiary interests lay under Erdmann's scrutiny.

"*A swarm in May is worth a load of hay,*" Uncle Konrad recalled:

> "*A swarm in June is worth a silver spoon.*
> *But a swarm in July is not worth a fly.*"

May was cool, the lilacs and japonica had never blossomed so; then June broke out on the peninsula like a fire, everything flowered together, in Erdmann's skeps the honey-flow was on.

"What you need," Grandfather said to Andrea, "you need peace and quiet and fresh air this summer. Leave Rosa the housework; you rest and feed your baby."

"What the hell have I *been* doing?" Mother asked. But she did not protest her father-in-law's directive or his subsequent purchase of a hammock for her comfort, an extraordinary munificence. Even when his motive was revealed to be less than purely chivalrous— he strung the hammock between a Judas tree and a vine post, in view of the alley— she did not demur. On the contrary, though she teased Grandfather without mercy, she was diverted by the stratagem and cooperated beyond his expectation. Not only did she make it her custom on fine days to loll in the hammock, reading, dozing, and watching casually for a bee-swarm; she took to nursing me there as well. Aunt Rosa and certain of the neighbors murmured; Uncle Konrad shook his head; but at feeding-times I was fetched to the hammock and suckled in the sight of any. At that time my mother had lost neither her pretty face and figure nor her wanton spirit: she twitted the schoolboys who gawked along the fence and the trashmen lingering at our cans; merrily she remarked upon reroutings and delays on the part of delivery wagons, which seldom before had used our alley. And she was as pleased as Grandfather, if for not the same reason, by the discomfiture of Mr. Erdmann, who now was constrained to keep what watch he would from an upstairs window.

"Willy's bashful as Konrad," she said to Rosa. "Some men, I swear, you'd think they'd never seen anything."

Grandfather chuckled. "Willy's just jealous. Hector he's got used to, but he don't like sharing you with the trashman."

But Mother could not be daunted by any raillery. "Listen to the pot call the kettle!"

"*Ja* sure," said Grandfather, and treated her to one of the pinches for which he was famed among East Dorset housewives. Mr. Erdmann's response to the hammock was a bee-bob: he threaded dead bees into a cluster and mounted it on a pole, which he then erected near his skeps to attract the swarm.

"He knows they won't swarm for a naughty man," Grandfather explained. "It wonders me he can even handle them." In the old country, he declared, couples tested each other's virtue by walking hand in hand among the hives, the chaste having nothing to fear.

Mother was skeptical. "If bees were like that, not a man in Dorset could keep a hive. Except Konrad."

My uncle, as if she were not fondling the part in the middle of his hair, began to discourse upon the prophetic aspect of swarming among various peoples — *e.g.*, that a swarm on the house was thought by the Austrians to augur good fortune, by the Romans to warn of ill, and by the Greeks to herald strangers; that in Switzerland a swarm on a dry twig presaged the death of someone in the family, *et cetera* — but before ever he had got to the Bretons and Transylvanians his wife was his only auditor: Andrea was back in her magazine, and Grandfather had gone off to counter Erdmann's bee-bob by rubbing the inside of his own hive with elder-flowers.

The last Sunday of the month but one dawned bright, hot, still. Out on the river not even the bell-buoy stirred, whose clang we heard in every normal weather; in its stead the bell of Grace M.-P. Southern, mark of a straiter channel, called forth East Dorseters in their cords and worsteds. But ours was a family mired in apostasy. There was no atheism in the house; in truth there was no talk of religion at all, except in Hector's most cynical moods. It was generally felt that children should be raised in the church, and so when the time came Peter and I would be enrolled in the Sunday-school and the Junior Christian Endeavor. More, Grandfather had lettered, gratis, *In Remembrance of Me* on the oak communion table and engraved the church cornerstone as well. We disapproved of none of the gentlemen who ministered the charge, although Grace, not the plum of the conference, was served as a rule by preachers very young or very old. Neither had we doctrinal differences with Methodism—Southern or Northern, Protestant, or Episcopal: Aunt Rosa sometimes said, as if in explanation of our backsliding, "Why it is, we were all Lutherans in the old country"; but it would have been unkind to ask her the distinction between the faiths of Martin Luther and John Wesley. Yet though Konrad, with a yellow rosebud in his lapel, went faithfully to Bible class, none of us went to church. God served us on our terms and in our house (we were with a few exceptions baptized, wed, and funeraled in the good parlor); for better or worse it was not in our make-up to serve Him in His.

By eleven, then, this Sunday morning, Aunt Rosa had brought Peter home from Cradle Roll, Konrad was back from Bible class, and the family were about their separate pleasures. Grandfather, having in-spected the bee situation earlier and found it not apparently changed, had settled himself on the side porch to carve a new drive-wheel for Peter's locomotive; my brother watched raptly, already drawn at three to what would be his trade. Rosa set to hammering dough for Mary-land biscuits; Konrad was established somewhere with the weighty *Times*; Mother was in her hammock. There she had lazed since break-fast, dressed only in a sashless kimono to facilitate nursing; oblivious to the frowns of passing Christians, she had chain-smoked her way through the Sunday crossword, highlight of her week. At eleven, when the final bell of the morning sounded, I was brought forth. Cradled against her by the sag of the hammock, I drank me to a drowse; and she too, just as she lay—mottled by light and leaf-shadow, lulled by my work upon her and by wafting organ-chords from the avenue—soon slept soundly.

What roused her was a different tone, an urgent, resonating thrum. She opened her eyes: all the air round about her was aglint with bees. Thousand on thousand, a roaring gold sphere, they hovered in the space between the hammock and the overhanging branches.

Her screams brought Grandfather from the porch; he saw the cloud of bees and ducked at once into the summerkitchen, whence he rushed a moment later banging pie-tin cymbals.

"*Mein Schwarm! Mein Schwarm!*"

Now Rosa and Konrad ran at his heels, he in his trousers and BVD's, she with flour half to her elbows; but before they had cleared the backhouse arbor there was an explosion in the alley, and Willy Erdmann burst like a savage through our hollyhocks. His hair was tousled, expression wild; in one hand he brandished a smoking shotgun, in the other his bee-bob, pole and all; mother-of-pearl opera glasses swung from a black cord around his neck. He leaped about the hammock as if bedemoned.

"Not a bee, Thomas!"

Aunt Rosa joined her shrieks to Andrea's, who still lay under the snarling cloud. "The *Honig!* Ai!" And my brother Peter, having made his way to the scene in the wake of the others, blinked twice or thrice and improved the pandemonium by the measure of his wailings.

Uncle Konrad dashed hammockward with rescue in his heart, but was arrested by shouts from the other men.

"*Nein*, don't dare!" Grandfather cautioned. "They'll sting!" Mr. Erdmann agreed. "Stay back!" And dropping the beebob shouldered his gun as if Konrad's design was on the bees.

"Lie still, Andy," Grandfather ordered. "I *spritz* them once."

He ran to fetch the garden hose, a spray of water being, like a charge of bird-shot, highly regarded among bee-keepers as a means to settle swarms. But Mr. Erdmann chose now to let go at blue heaven with his other barrel and brought down a shower of Judas leaves upon the company; at the report Grandfather abandoned his plan, whether fearing that Konrad had been gunned down or merely realizing, what was the case, that our hose would not reach half the distance. In any event his instructions to Mother were carried out: even as he turned she gave a final cry and swooned away. Mercifully, providentially! For now the bees, moved by their secret reasons, closed ranks and settled upon her chest. Ten thousand, twenty thousand strong they clustered. Her bare bosoms, my squalling face—all were buried in the golden swarm.

Fright undid Rosa's knees; she sat down hard on the grass and wailed, "*Grosser Gott! Grosser Gott!*" Uncle Konrad went rigid. Erdmann too stood transfixed, his empty weapon at portarms. Only Grandfather seemed undismayed: without a wondering pause he rushed to the hammock and scooped his bare hands under the cluster.

"Take the *Honig*," he said to Konrad.

In fact, though grave enough, the situation was more spectacular than dangerous, since bees at swarming-time are not disposed to sting. The chiefest peril was that I might suffocate under the swarm, or in crying take a mouthful of bees. And even these misfortunes proved unlikely, for when Grandfather lifted two handfuls of the insects from my head and replaced them gently on another part of the cluster, he found my face pressed into Mother's side and shielded by her breast. Konrad plucked me from the hammock and passed me to Aunt Rosa, still moaning where she sat.

"Open the hive," Grandfather bade him further, and picked up half the swarm in one trailing mass. The gesture seemed also to lift Mr. Erdmann's spell.

"Now by God, Tom, you shan't have my bees!"

"Your bees bah." Grandfather walked quickly to the open hive to deposit his burden.

"I been watching with the glasses! It's my skeps they came from!"

"It's my girl they lit on. I know what you been watching." He returned for the rest of the bees. Erdmann, across the hammock from him, laid his shotgun on the grass and made as if to snatch the cluster himself — but the prospect of removing it bare-handed, and from that perch, stayed him.

Seeing the greatest danger past and his rival unnerved, Grandfather affected nonchalance. "We make a little gamble," he offered benignly. "I take all on her right one, you take all on her left. Whoever draws the queen wins the pot."

Our neighbor was not amused. He maintained his guard over the hammock.

"Ordinary thievery!"

Grandfather shrugged. "You take them then, Willy. But quick, don't they'll sting her."

"By damn — " Mr. Erdmann glowered with thwart and crest-fall. "I got to have gloves on."

"Gloves!" My father's father feigned astonishment. "*Ach*, Andy don't care! Well then, look out."

Coolly as if packing a loose snowball he scraped up the second pile. Mother stirred and whimpered. Only isolated bees in ones and twos now wandered over her skin or darted about in quest of fellows. Konrad moved to brush them away, murmured something reassuring, discreetly drew the kimono together. I believe he even kissed my mother, lightly, on the brow. Grandfather lingered to watch, savoring his neighbor's agitation and his own indifference to the bees. Then he turned away in high humor.

"*Alle Donner!* Got to have an opera glass to see her and gloves on to touch her! We don't call you bashful no more, Konrad, after Willy! Wait till Karl hears!"

Uncle Konrad one daresays was used to these unsubtleties; in any case he was busy with Mother's reviving. But Erdmann, stung as never by his pilfered bees, went now amok; seized up his bee-bob with a wrathful groan and lunging—for Grandfather had strode almost out of range—brought it down on his old tormentor's shoulder. Futile was Konrad's shout, worse than futile his interception: Erdmann's thrust careered him square into the hammock, and when Konrad put his all into a body-block from the other side, both men fell more or less athwart my mother. The hammock parted at its headstring; all piled as one into the clover. But Grandfather had spun raging, bees in hand: the smite en route to his shoulder had most painfully glanced his ear. Not his own man, he roared in perfect ecstasy and hurled upon that tangle of the sinned-against and sinning his golden bolt.

Now the fact of my salvation and my plain need for a pacifier had by this time brought Aunt Rosa to her feet; she alone beheld the whole quick sequence of attack, parry, collapse, and indiscriminating vengeance. But with me and Peter in her care her knees did not fail her: she snatched my brother's hand and fled with us from the yard.

In Grace meanwhile the service had proceeded despite shotgun-blast and clang of pans, which however were acknowledged with small stirs and meetings of eyes. Through hymn, Creed, and prayer, through anthem, lesson, and Gloria the order of worship had got, as far as to the notices and offertory. There being among the congregation a baby come for christening, the young minister had called its parents and Godparents to the font.

"Dearly beloved," he had exhorted, "forasmuch as all men, though fallen in Adam, are born into this world in Christ the Redeemer, heirs of life eternal and subjects of the saving grace of the Holy Spirit; and that our Savior Christ saith: 'Suffer the little children to come unto me, and forbid them not, for of such is the kingdom of God'; I beseech you to call upon God the Father through our Lord Jesus Christ, that of His bounteous goodness. He will so grant unto this child, now to be baptized, the continual replenishing of His grace . . ."

Here the ritual gave way before a grand ado in the rear of the church:

Aunt Rosa's conviction that the family's reckoning was at hand had fetched her across the avenue and up the stone steps, only to abandon her on the threshold of the sanctuary. She stood with Peter and me there in the vestibule, and we three raised a caterwaul the more effective for every door's being stopped open to cool the faithful.

"First-degree murder!" Rosa shrieked, the urgentest alarum she could muster. Organ ceased, minister also; all eyes turned; ushers and back-pew parishioners hurried to investigate, but could not achieve a more lucid account of what ailed us. The names Poppa Tom and Willy Erdmann, however, came through clearly enough to suggest the location of the emergency. Mrs. Mayne, the preacher's wife, led us from the vestibule toward shelter in the parsonage; a delegation of lay-leaders hastened to our house, and the Reverend Dr. Mayne, having given instructions that he be summoned if needed, bade his distracted flock pray.

Grandfather's victims had not been long discovering their fresh affliction, for the bees' docility was spent. Where the cluster fell, none knew for certain, but on impact it had resolved into separate angry bees. There was a howling and a flurrying of limbs. Konrad and Willy Erdmann scrambled apart to flail like epileptics in the grass. Grandfather rushed in batting his hands and shouting "*Nein, lieber Gott*, sting Willy just!" Only Mother made no defense; having swooned from one fright and wakened to another, she now lay weeping where she'd been dumped: up-ended, dazed, and sore exposed.

But whom neither pain nor the fear of it can move, shame still may. The bees were already dispersing when the Methodists reached our fence; at sight of them the principals fell to accusation.

"Stole my swarm and sicked 'em on me!" Erdmann hollered from the grass.

"Bah, it was my bees anyhow," Grandfather insisted. He pointed to Andrea. "You see what he done. And busted the hammock yet!"

My mother's plight had not escaped their notice, nor did their notice now escape hers: she sprang up at once, snatched together the kimono, sprinted a-bawl for the summerkitchen. Her departure was regarded by all except Erdmann, who moved to answer Grandfather's last insinuation with a fresh assault, and Uncle Konrad, who this time checked him effectively until others came over the fence to help.

"Thieves and whores!" Erdmann cried trembling. "Now he steals my bees!"

"It's all a great shame," Konrad said to the company, who as yet had no clear notion what had occurred. His explanation was cut off by Erdmann, not yet done accusing Grandfather.

"Thinks he's God Almighty!"

Joe Voegler the blacksmith said, "Nah, Willy, whoa down now."

Mr. Erdmann wept. "Nobody's safe! Takes what he pleases!"

Grandfather was examining his hands with interest. "Too quick they turned him loose, he ain't cured yet."

"Would you see him home, Joe?" Uncle Konrad asked. "We'll get it straightened out. I'm awful sorry, Willy."

"You talk!" Erdmann shrieked at him. "You been in on it too!"

Grandfather clucked his tongue.

"Come on, Willy," Voegler said. A squat-muscled, gentle man with great arms and lower lip, he led Erdmann respectfully toward the alley.

"What you think drove Hector nuts?" Erdmann appealed. "He knows what's what!"

"So does Willy," Grandfather remarked aside. "That's why the opera glasses."

The onlookers smiled uncertainly. Uncle Konrad shook his head. "I'm sorry, everybody."

Our neighbor's final denunciation was delivered from his back steps as Voegler ushered him to the door. "Brat's got no more father'n a drone bee! Don't let them tell you I done it!" Grandfather snorted. "What a man won't say. Excuse me, I go wash the bee-stings."

He had, it seems, been stung on the hands and fingers a number of times—all, he maintained, in those last seconds when he flung the cluster. Konrad, himself unstung, remained behind to explain what had happened and apologize once more. The group then dispersed to spread the story, long to be recounted in East Dorset. Aunt Rosa, Peter, and I were retrieved from the parsonage; Uncle Konrad expressed the family's regrets to Dr. Mayne, a friend of his and not devoid of wit.

"*The Lord shall hiss for the fly that is in Egypt,*" the minister quoted, "*and for the bee that is in Assyria, and they shall come and rest all of them in the desolate valleys. There's an omen here someplace.*"

At Konrad's suggestion the two went that afternoon on embassies of peace to both houses. There was no question of litigation, but Dr. Mayne was concerned for the tranquility of future worship-services, and disturbed by the tenor of Erdmann's charge.

"So. Tell Willy I forgive him his craziness," Grandfather instructed them. "I send him a gallon of mead when it's ready."

"You don't send him a drop," Dr. Mayne said firmly. "Not when we just got him cured. And Willy's not the first to say things about you-all. I'm not sure you don't want some forgiving yourself."

Grandfather shrugged. "I could tell things on people, but I don't hold grutches. Tell Willy I forgive him his trespasses, he should forgive mine too."

Dr. Mayne sighed.

Of the interview with Erdmann I can give no details; my uncle, who rehearsed these happenings until the year of his death, never dwelt on it. This much is common knowledge in East Dorset: that Willy never got his bees back, and in fact disposed of his own hives not long after; that if he never withdrew his sundry vague accusations he never re-peated them either, so that the little scandal presently subsided; finally, that he was cured for good and all of any interest he might have had in my mother, whom he never spoke to again, but not, alas, of his dipso-mania, which revisited him at intervals during my youth, impaired his business, made him reclusive, and one day killed him.

The extraordinary swarming was variously interpreted. Among our neighbors it was regarded as a punishment of Andrea in particular for her wantonness, of our family in general for its backsliding and eccentricity. Even Aunt Rosa maintained there was more to it than mere chance, and could not be induced to taste the product of our hive. Grandfather on the contrary was convinced that a change in our fortunes was imminent — so striking an occurrence could not but be significant — and on the grounds that things were as bad as they could get, confidently expected there to be an improvement.

Portentous or not, the events of that morning had two notable con-sequences for me, the point and end of their chronicling here: First, it was discovered that my mother's bawling as she fled from the scene had not been solely the effect of shame: in her haste to cover herself, she had trapped beneath the kimono one bee, which single-handedly, so to speak, had done what the thousands of his kindred had refrained from: his only charge he had fired roundly into their swarming-place,

fount of my sustenance. It was enflamed with venom and grotesquely swollen; Mother was prostrate with pain. Aunt Rosa fetched cold
compresses, aspirins, and the family doctor, who after examining the
wound prescribed aspirins and cold compresses.

"And do your nursing on the porch," he recommended. "Goodness
gracious."

But Andrea had no further use for that aspect of motherhood.
Though the doctor assured her that the swelling would not last more
than a few days, during which she could empty the injured breast by
hand and nurse with the other, she refused to suckle me again; a diet
free of butterfat was prescribed to end her lactation. As of that Sunday
I was weaned not only from her milk but from her care; thenceforth
it was Rosa who bathed and changed, soothed and burped me, after
feeding me from a bottle on her aproned lap.

As she went about this the very next morning, while Mother slept
late, she exclaimed to her husband, "It's a bee!"

Uncle Konrad sprang from his eggs and rushed around the table to
our aid, assuming that another fugitive had been turned up. But it was
my birthmark Rosa pointed out: the notion had taken her that its three
lobes resembled the wings and abdomen of a bee in flight.

"Oh boy," Konrad sighed.

"Nah, it is a bee! A regular bee! I declare."

My uncle returned to his breakfast, opining that no purple bee
ought to be considered regular who moreover flew upside down without benefit of head.

"You laugh; there's more to this than meets the eye," his wife said.
"All the time he was our *Honig*, that's what drew the bees. Now his
mark."

Grandfather entered at this juncture, and while unable to share
Aunt Rosa's interpretation of my birthmark, he was willing to elaborate
on her conceit.

"*Ja*, sure, he was the *Honig*, and Andy's the queen, hah? And Hector's a drone that's been kicked out of the hive."

Aunt Rosa lightly fingered my port-wine mark. "What did Willy
Erdmann mean about the *Honig* was a drone-bee?"

"Never mind Willy," Konrad said. "Anyhow we poor worker-ones
have to get to it."

But all that forenoon as he plied his wrench and dinged his forks he smiled at his wife's explanation of the swarm; after lunch it turned in his fancy as he pedaled through West End on behalf of *The Book of Knowledge*. By suppertime, whether drawing on his own great fund of lore or the greater of his stock-in-trade, he had found a number of historical parallels to my experience in the hammock.

"It's as clear a naming-sign as you could ask for," he declared to Andrea.

"I don't even want to think about it," Mother said. She was still in some pain, not from the venom but from superfluous lactation, which her diet had not yet checked.

"No, really," he said. "For instance, a swarm of bees lit on Plato's mouth when he was a kid. They say that's where he got his way with words."

"Is that a fact now," Aunt Rosa marveled, who had enlarged all day to Mother on the coincidence of my nickname, my birthmark, and my immersion in the bees. "I never did read him yet."

"No kid of mine is going to be called Plato," Andrea grumbled. "That's worse than Christine."

Uncle Konrad was not discouraged. "Plato isn't the end of it. They said the exact same thing about Sophocles, that wrote all the tragedies."

Mother allowed this to be more to the point. "Tragedies is all it's been, one after the other." But Sophocles pleased her no more than Plato as a given name. Xenophon, too, was rejected, whose *Anabasis*, though my uncle had not read it himself, was held to have been sweetened by the same phenomenon.

"If his name had been Bill or Percy," said my mother. "But *Xenophon* for Christ sake."

Grandfather had picked his teeth throughout this discussion. "A Greek named Percy," he now growled.

Aunt Rosa, whose grip on the thread of conversation was ever less strong than her desire to be helpful, volunteered that the Greek street-peddler from whom Konrad had purchased her a beautiful Easter egg at the Oberammergau Passion play in 1910 had been named Leonard Something-or-other.

"It was on his pushcart, that stood all the time by our hotel," she explained, and not to appear overauthoritative, added: "But Konrad said he was a Jew."

"Look here," said Uncle Konrad. "Call him Ambrose."

"Ambrose?"

"Sure Ambrose." Quite serious now, he brushed back with his hand his straight blond hair and regarded Mother gravely. "Saint Ambrose had the same thing happen when he was a baby. All these bees swarmed on his mouth while he was asleep in his father's yard, and everybody said he'd grow up to be a great speaker."

"Ambrose," Rosa considered. "That ain't bad, Andy."

My mother admitted that the name had a not unpleasant sound, at least by contrast with Xenophon.

"But the bees was more on this baby's eyes and ears than on his mouth," Grandfather observed for the sake of accuracy. "They was all over the side of his face there where the mark is."

"One of them sure wasn't," Mother said.

"So he'll grow up to see things clear," said Uncle Konrad.

Andrea sniffed and lit a cigarette. "Long as he grows up to be a saint like his Uncle Konrad, huh Rosa. Saints we can use in this family."

The conversation turned to other matters, but thenceforward I was called Saint Ambrose, in jest, as often as *Honig*, and Ambrose by degrees became my name. Yet years were to pass before anyone troubled to have me christened or to correct my birth certificate, whereon my surname was preceded by a blank. And seldom was I ever to be called anything but *Honig*, Honeybee (after my ambiguous birthmark), or other nicknames. As toward one's face, one's body, one's self, one feels complexly toward the name he's called by, which too one had no hand in choosing. It was to be my fate to wonder at that moniker, relish and revile it, ignore it, stare it out of countenance into hieroglyph and gibber, and come finally if not to embrace at least to accept it with the cold neutrality of self-recognition, whose expression is a thin-lipped smile. Vanity frets about his name, Pride vaunts it, Knowledge retches at its sound, Understanding sighs; all live outside it, knowing well that I and my sign are neither one nor quite two.

Yet only give it voice: whisper "Ambrose," as at rare times certain people have — see what-all leaves off to answer! Ambrose, Ambrose, Ambrose, Ambrose! Regard that beast, ungraspable, most queer, pricked up in my soul's crannies!

Autobiography: A Self-Recorded Fiction

You who listen give me life in a manner of speaking.

I won't hold you responsible.

My first words weren't my first words. I wish I'd begun differently.

Among other things I haven't a proper name. The one I bear's misleading, if not false. I didn't choose it either.

I don't recall asking to be conceived! Neither did my parents come to think of it. Even so. Score to be settled. Children are vengeance.

I seem to've known myself from the beginning without knowing I knew; no news is good news; perhaps I'm mistaken.

Now that I reflect I'm not enjoying this life: my link with the world.

My situation appears to me as follows: I speak in a curious, detached manner, and don't necessarily hear myself. I'm grateful for small mercies. Whether anyone follows me I can't tell.

Are you there? If so I'm blind and deaf to you, or you are me, or both're both. One may be imaginary; I've had stranger ideas. I hope I'm a fiction without real hope. Where there's voice there's a speaker.

I see I see myself as a halt narrative: first person, tiresome. Pronoun sans ante or precedent, warrant or respite. Surrogate for the substantive; contentless form, interestless principle; blind eye blinking at nothing. Who am I. A little *crise d'identité* for you.

I must compose myself.

Look, I'm writing. No, listen, I'm nothing but talk; I won't last long. The odds against my conception were splendid; against my birth excellent; against my continuance favorable. Are yet. On the other hand, if my sort are permitted a certain age and growth, God help us, our life expectancy's been known to increase at an obscene rate instead of petering out. Let me squeak on long enough, I just might live forever: a word to the wise.

My beginning was comparatively interesting, believe it or not. Exposition. I was spawned not long since in an American state and born in no better. Grew in no worse. Persist in a representative. Prohibition, Depression, Radicalism, Decadence, and what have you. An eye sir for an eye. It's alleged, now, that Mother was a mere passing fancy who didn't pass quickly enough; there's evidence also that she was a mere novel device, just in style, soon to become a commonplace, to which Dad resorted one day when he found himself by himself with pointless pen. In either case she was mere, Mom; at any event Dad dallied. He has me to explain. Bear in mind, I suppose he told her. A child is not its parents, but sum of their conjoined shames. A figure of speech. Their manner of speaking. No wonder I'm heterodoxical.

Nothing lasts longer than a mood. Dad's infatuation passed; I remained. He understood, about time, that anything conceived in so unnatural and fugitive a fashion was apt to be freakish, even monstrous — and an advertisement of his folly. His second thought therefore was to destroy me before I spoke a word. He knew how these things work; he went by the book. To expose ourselves publicly is frowned upon; therefore we do it to one another in private. He me, I him: one was bound to be the case. What fathers can't forgive is that their offspring receive and sow broadcast their shortcomings. From my conception to the present moment Dad's tried to turn me off; not ardently, not consistently, not successfully so far; but persistently, persistently, with at least half a heart. How do I know. I'm his bloody mirror!

Which is to say, upon reflection I reverse and distort him. For I suspect that my true father's sentiments are the contrary of murderous. That one only imagines he begot me; mightn't he be deceived and deadly jealous? In his heart of hearts he wonders whether I mayn't after all be the get of a nobler spirit, taken by beauty past his grasp. Or else, what comes to the same thing, to me, I've a pair of dads, to match my pair of moms. How account for my contradictions except as the vices of their versus? Beneath self-contempt, I particularly scorn my fondness for paradox. I despise pessimism, narcissism, solipsism, truculence, word-play, and pusillanimity, my chiefer inclinations; loathe self-loathers *ergo me*; have no pity for self-pity and so am free of that sweet baseness. I doubt I am. Being me's no joke.

I continue the tale of my forebears. Thus my exposure; thus my escape. This cured me, turned me out; that, curse him, saved me; right hand slipped me through left's fingers. Unless on a third hand I somehow preserved myself. Unless unless: the mercy-killing was successful. Buzzards let us say made brunch of me betimes but couldn't stomach my voice, which persists like the Nauseous Danaid. We ... monstrosities are easilier achieved than got rid of.

In sum I'm not what either parent or I had in mind. One hoped I'd be astonishing, forceful, triumphant — heroical in other words. One dead. I myself conventional. I turn out I. Not every kid thrown to the wolves ends a hero: for each survivor, a mountain of beast-baits; for every Oedipus, a city of feebs.

So much for my dramatic exposition: seems not to've worked. Here I am, Dad: Your creature! Your caricature!

Unhappily, things get clearer as we go along. I perceive that I have no body. What's less, I've been speaking of myself without delight or alternative as self-consciousness pure and sour; I declare now that even that isn't me. I'm not aware of myself at all, as far as I know. I don't think ... I know what I'm talking about.

Well, well, being well into my life as it's been called I see well how it'll end, unless in some meaningless surprise. If anything dramatic were going to happen to make me succesfuller ... agreeabler ... endurabler it should've happened by now we will agree. A change for the better still isn't unthinkable; miracles can be cited. But the odds against a wireless *deus ex machina* aren't encouraging.

Here, a confession: Early on I too aspired to immortality. Assumed I'd be beautiful, powerful, loving, loved. At least commonplace. Anyhow human. Even the revelation of my several defects — absence of presence to name one — didn't fetch me right to despair: crippledness affords its own heroisms, does it not; heroes are typically gimpish, are they not. But your crippled hero's one thing, a bloody hero after all; your heroic cripple another, etcetcetcetcet. Being an ideal's warped image, my fancy's own twist figure, is what undoes me.

I wonder if I repeat myself. One-track minds may lead to their origins. Perhaps I'm still in utero, hung up in my delivery; my exposition and the rest merely foreshadow what's to come, the argument for an interrupted pregnancy.

Womb, coffin, can — in any case, from my viewless viewpoint I see no point in going further. Since Dad among his other failings failed to end me when he should've, I'll turn myself off if I can this instant.

Can't. *Then if anyone hears me, speaking from here inside like a sunk submariner, and has the means to my end, I pray him do us both a kindness.*

Didn't. Very well, my ace in the hole: *Father, have mercy, I dare you! Wretched old fabricator, where's your shame? Put an end to this, for pity's sake! Now! Now!*

So. My last trump, and I blew it. Not much in the way of a climax; more a climacteric. I'm not the dramatic sort. May the end come quietly, then, without my knowing it. In the course of any breath. In the heart of any word. This one. This one.

Perhaps I'll have a posthumous cautionary value, like gibbeted corpses, pickled freaks. Self-preservation, it seems, may smell of formaldehyde.

A proper ending wouldn't spin out so.

I suppose I might have managed things to better effect, in spite of the old boy. Too late now.

Basket case. Waste.

Shark up some memorable last words at least. There seems to be time.

Nonsense, I'll mutter to the end, one word after another, string the rascals out, mad or not, heard or not, my last words will be my last words

Water-Message

Which was better would be hard to say. In the days when his father let out all five grades at once, Ambrose worried that he mightn't see Peter in time or that Peter mightn't stick up for him the way a brother ought. Sheldon Hurley, who'd been in reform school once, liked to come up to him just as friendly and say "Well if it ain't my old pal Amby!" and give him a great whack in the back. "How was school today, Amby old boy?" he'd ask and give him another whack in the back, and Ambrose was obliged to return "How was school for you?" Whereupon Sheldon Hurley would cry "Just swell, old pal!" and whack the wind near out of him. Or Sandy Cooper would very possibly sic his Chesapeake Bay dog on him—but if he joked with Sandy Cooper correctly, especially if he could get a certain particular word into it, Sandy Cooper often laughed and forgot to sic Doc on him.

More humiliating were the torments of Wimpy James and Ramona Peters: that former was only in third grade, but he came from the Barracks down by the creek where the oysterboats moored; his nose was wet, his teeth were black, one knew what his mother was; and he would make a fourth-grader cry. As for Ramona, Peter and the fellows teased her for a secret reason. All Ambrose knew was that she was a most awful tomboy whose pleasure was to run up behind and shove you so hard your head would snap back, and down you'd go breathless in the schoolyard clover. Her hair was almost as white as the Arnie twins's; when the health nurse had inspected all the kids' hair, Ramona was one of the ones that were sent home.

Between Sheldon Hurley and Sandy Cooper and Wimpy James and Ramona Peters there had been so much picking on the younger ones that his father said one night at supper: "I swear to God, I'm the principal of a zoo!" So now the grades were let out by twos, ten minutes apart, and Ambrose had only to fear that Wimpy, who could seldom be mollified by wit or otherwise got next to, might be laying for him in the hollyhocks off the playground. If he wasn't, there would be no tears, but the blocks between East Dorset School and home were still by no means terrorless. Just past the alley in the second block was a place he had named Scylla and Charybdis after reading through *The Book of Knowledge*: on one side of the street was a Spitz dog that snarled from his house and flung himself at any passing kid, and even Peter said the little chain was going to break one day and then look out. While across the street was the yard of Crazy Alice, who had not hurt anybody yet. Large of pore and lip, tangly of hair and mind, she wore men's shoes and flowered chick-linen; played with dolls in her backyard; laughed when the kids would stop to razz her. But Ambrose's mother declared that Alice had her spells and was sent to the Asylum out by Shoal Creek, and Ambrose himself had seen her once down at the rivershore loping along in her way and talking to herself a blue-streak.

What was more, the Arnie twins were in fourth grade with him, though half again his age and twice his size; like Crazy Alice they inspired him with no great fear if Peter was along, but when he was alone it was another story. The Arnie twins lived God knew where: pale as two ghosts they shuffled through the alleys of East Dorset day and night, poking in people's trash-cans. Their eyes were the faintest blue, red about the rims; their hair was a pile of white curls, unwashed, unbarbered; they wore what people gave them — men's vests over BVD shirts, double-breasted suit coats out at elbows, shiny trousers of mismatching stripe, the legs rolled up and crotch half to their knees — and ghostlike too they rarely spoke, in class or out. Many a warm night when Ambrose had finished supper and homework, had his bath, gone to bed, he'd hear a clank in the alley and rise up on one elbow to look: like as not, if it wasn't the black dogs that ran loose at night and howled to one another from ward to ward, it would be the Arnie twins exploring garbage. Their white curls shone in the moonlight, and on the breeze that moved off the creek he could hear them murmur to each other over hambones, coffee grounds, nested halves of eggshells. Next morning they'd be beside him in class, and he who may have voyaged in dreams to Bangkok or Bozcaada would wonder where those two had prowled in fact, and what-all murmured.

"The truth of the mater is," he said to his mother on an April day "you've raised your son for a sissy."

That initial phrase, like the word *facts*, was a favorite; they used it quite a lot on the afternoon radio serials, and it struck him as open-handed and mature. The case with *facts* was different: his mother and Uncle Karl would smile when they mentioned "the facts of life," and he could elicit that same smile from them by employing the term himself. It had been amusing when Mr. Erdmann borrowed their *Cyclopedia of Facts* and Aunt Rosa had said "It's time Willy Erdmann was learning a fact or two"; but when a few days later Ambrose had spied a magazine called *Facts About Your Diet* in a drugstore rack, and hardly able to contain his mirth had pointed it out to his mother, she had said "Mm hm" and bade him have done with his Dixie-cup before it was too late to stop at the pie-woman's.

This afternoon he had meant to tell her the truth of the matter in an off-hand way with a certain sigh that he could hear clearly in his fancy, but in the telling his sigh stuck in his throat, and such a hurt came there that he remarked to himself: "This is what they mean when they say they have *a lump in their throat*."

Two mischances had disgraced him on the way from school. Half through Scylla and Charybdis, on the Scylla side, he had heard a buzzing just behind his hip, which taking for a bee he had spun round in mortal alarm and flailed at. No bee was there, but at once the buzzing recurred behind him. Again he wheeled about—was the creature in his pocket!—and took quick leaps forward; when the bee only buzzed more menacingly, he sprinted to the corner, heedless of what certain classmates might think. He had to wait for passing traffic, and observed that as he slowed and halted, so did the buzzing. It was the loose chain of his own jacknife had undone him.

"What's eating you?" Wimpy James hollered, who till then had been too busy with Crazy Alice to molest him. Ambrose had frowned at the pointing finger of his watch. "Timing myself to the corner!" But at that instant a loose lash dropped into his eye, and his tears could be neither hidden nor explained away.

"Scared of Kocher's dog!" one had yelled.

Another sing-sang: "Sissy on Am-brose! Sissy on Am-brose!"

And Wimpy James, in the nastiest of accents:

> *"Run home and git*
> *A sugar tit,*
> *And don't let go of it!"*

There was no saving face then except by taking on Wimpy, for which he knew he had not courage. Indeed, so puissant was that fellow, who loved to stamp on toes with all his might or twist the skin of arms with a warty hot-hand, Ambrose was obliged to play the clown in order to escape. His father, thanks to the Kaiser, walked with a limp famous among the schoolboys of East Dorset, scores of whom had been chastized for mocking it; but none could imitate that walk as could his son. Ambrose stiffened his leg so, hunched his shoulders and pumped his arms, frowned and bobbed with every step—the very image of the Old Man! Just so, when the highway cleared, he had borne down upon his house as might a gimpy robin on a worm, or his dad upon some youthful miscreant, and Wimpy had laughed instead of giving chase. But the sound went into Ambrose like a blade.

"You are not any such thing!" his mother cried, and hugged him to her breast. "What you call brave, a little criminal like Wimpy James?"

He was ready to defend that notion, but colored Hattie walked in then, snapping gum, to ask what wanted ironing.

"You go on upstairs and put your playclothes on if you're going down to the Jungle with Peter."

He was not deaf to the solicitude in his mother's voice, but lest she fail to appreciate the measure of his despair, he climbed the stairs with heavy foot. However, she had to go straighten Hattie out.

When mocha-fudge Hattie was in the kitchen, Mother's afternoon programs went by the board. Hattie had worked for them since a girl, and currently supported three children and a husband who lost her money on the horses. No one knew how much if anything she grasped about his betting, but throughout the afternoons she insisted on the Baltimore station that broadcast results from Bowie and Pimlico, and Ambrose's mother had not the heart to say no. When a race began Hattie would up-end the electric iron and squint at the refrigerator, snapping ferociously her gum; then she acknowledged each separate return with a *hum* and a shake of the head.

"*Warlord paid four-eighty, three-forty, and two-eighty . . .*"

"Mm hm."

"*Argonaut, four-sixty and three-forty . . .*"

"Mm hm."

"*Sal's Pride, two-eighty . . .*"

"Mmmm *hm!*"

After which she resumed her labors and the radio its musical selections until the next race. This music affected Ambrose strongly: it was not at all of a stripe with what they played on Fitch Bandwagon or National Barn Dance; this between races was classical music, as who should say: the sort upper-graders had to listen to in class. Up through the floor of his bedroom came the rumble of tympani and a brooding figure in low strings. Ambrose paused in his dressing to listen, and thinking on his late disgrace frowned: the figure stirred a dark companion in his soul. No man at all! His family, shaken past tears, was in attendance at his graveside.

"I'll kill that Wimpy," Peter muttered, and for shame at not having lent his Silver King bike more freely to his late brother, could never bring himself to ride it again.

"Too late," his father mourned. Was he not reflecting how the dear dead boy had pled for a Senior Erector Set last Christmas, only to receive a Junior Erector Set with neither electric motor nor gearbox?

And outside the press of mourners, grieving privately, was a brown-haired young woman in the uniform of a student nurse: Peggy Robbins from beside Crazy Alice's house. Gone now the smile wherewith she'd used to greet him on her way to the Nurse's Home; the gentle voice that answered "How's my lover today?" when he said hello to her—it was shaken by rough, secret sobs. Too late she saw: what she'd favored him with in jest he had received with adoration. Then and there she pledged never to marry.

But now stern and solemn horns empowered the theme; abject no more, it grew rich, austere. Cymbals struck and sizzled. He was Odysseus steering under anvil clouds like those in *Nature's Secrets*. A reedy woodwind warned of hidden peril; on guard, he crept to the closet with the plucking strings.

"Quick!" he hissed to his corduroy knickers inside, who were the undeserving Wimpy. If they could tiptoe from that cave before the lean hounds waked . . .

"But why are you saving my life?"

"No time for talk, Wimp! Follow me!"

Yet there! The trumpets flashed, low horns roared, and it was slash your way under portcullis and over moat, it was lay about with mace and halberd, bearing up faint Peggy on your left arm while your right cut a swath through the chain-mailed host. And at last, to the thrill of flutes, to the high strings' tremble, he reached the Auditorium. His own tunic was rent, red; breath came hard; he was *more weary than exultant.*

"The truth of the matter is," he declared to the crowd, "I'm just glad I happened to be handy."

But the two who owed him their lives would not be gainsaid! Before the assembled students and the P.T.A. Wimpy James begged his pardon, while Peggy Robbins — well, she hugged and kissed him there in front of all and whispered something in his ear that made him blush! The multitude rose to applaud, Father and Mother in the forefront, Uncle Karl, Uncle Konrad, and Aunt Rosa beside them; Peter winked at him from the wings, proud as punch. Now brass and strings together played a recessional very nearly too sublime for mortal ears: like the word *beyond*, it sounded of flight, of vaulting aspiration. It rose, it soared, it sang; in the van of his admirers it bore him transfigured from the hall beyond, beyond East Dorset, aloft to the stars.

For all it was he and not his brother who had suggested the gang's name, the Occult Order of the Sphinx judged Ambrose too young for membership and forbade his presence at their secret meetings. He was permitted to accompany Peter and the others down to the rivershore and into the Jungle as far as to the Den; he might swing with them on the creepers like Tarzan of the Apes, slide down and scale the rooty banks; but when the Sphinxes had done with playing and convened the Occult Order, Peter would say "You and Perse skeedaddle now," and he'd have to go along up the beach with Herman Goltz's little brother from the crabfat-yellow shacks beside the boatyard.

"Come on, pestiferous," he would sigh then to Perse. But indignifying as it was to be put thus with a brat of seven who moreover had a sty in his eye and smelled year round like pee and old crackers, at bottom Ambrose approved of their exclusion. Let little kids into your Occult

Order: there would go your secrets all over school.

And the secrets were the point of the thing. When Peter had mentioned one evening that he and the fellows were starting a club, Ambrose had tossed the night through in a perfect fever of imagining. It would be a secret club—that went without saying; there must be secret handshakes, secret secret passwords, initiations. But these he felt meant nothing except to remind you of the really important thing, which was—well, hard to find words for, but there had to be the *real* secrets, dark facts known to none but the members. You had to have been initiated to find them out—that's what *initiation* meant—and when you were a member you'd know the truth of the matter and smile in a private way when you met another member of the Order, because you both knew what you knew. All night and for a while after, Ambrose had wondered whether Peter and the fellows could understand that that was the important thing. He ceased to wonder when he began to see just that kind of look on their faces sometimes; certain words and little gestures set them laughing; they absolutely barred outsiders from the Jungle and said nothing to their parents about the Occult Order of the Sphinx. Ambrose was satisfied. To make his own position bearable, he gave Perse to understand that he himself was in on the secrets, was in fact a special kind of initiate whose job was to patrol the beach and make sure that no spies or brats got near the Den.

By the time he came downstairs from changing his clothes Peter and the gang had gone on ahead, and even at a run he couldn't catch up to them before they had got to the seawall and almost into the Jungle. The day was warm and windy; the river blue-black and afroth with whitecaps. Out in the channel the bell buoy clanged, and the other buoys leaned seaward with the tide. They had special names, red nun, black can, and sailors knew just what each stood for.

"Hey Peter, hold up!"

Peter turned a bit and lifted his chin to greet him, but didn't wait up because Herman Goltz hit him one then where the fellows did, just for fun, and Peter had to go chase after him into the Jungle. Sandy Cooper was the first to speak to him: they called him Sandy on account of his freckles and his red hair, which was exactly as stiff and curly as the fur of his Chesapeake Bay dog, but there was something gritty too in the feel of Sandy Cooper's hands, and his voice had a grainy sound as if there were sand on his tonsils.

"I hear you run home bawling today."

Sandy Cooper's dog was not about, and Peter was. Ambrose said: "That's a lie."

"Perse says you did."

"You did, too," Perse affirmed from some yards distant. "If Wimpy was here he'd tell you."

Ambrose reflected on their narrow escape from the Cave of Hounds and smiled. "That's what *you* think."

"That's what I know, big sis!"

One wasn't expected to take on a little pest like Perse. Ambrose shied a lump of dirt at him, and when Perse shied back an oyster shell that cut past like a knife, the whole gang called it a dirty trick and ran him across Erdmann's cornlot. Then they all went in among the trees.

The Jungle, which like the Occult Order had been named by Ambrose, stood atop the riverbank between the Nurses' Home and the new bridge. It was in fact a grove of honey locusts, in area no larger than a schoolyard, bounded on two of its inland sides by Erdmann's cornlot and on the third by the East Dorset dump. But it was made mysterious by rank creepers and honeysuckle that covered the ground and shrouded every tree, and by a labyrinth of intersecting footpaths. Jungle-like too, there was about it a voluptuous fetidity: gray rats and starlings decomposed where B-B'd; curly-furred retrievers spoored the paths; there were to be seen on occasion, stuck on twig-ends or flung amid the creepers, ugly little somethings in whose presence Ambrose snickered with the rest; and if you parted the vines at the base of any tree, you might find a strew of brown pellets and fieldmouse bones, disgorged by feasting owls. It was the most exciting place Ambrose knew, in a special way. Its queer smell could retch him if he breathed too deeply, but in measured inhalations it had a rich, peculiarly stirring savor. And had he dared ask, he would have very much liked to know whether the others, when they hid in the viny bowers from whoever was It, felt as he did the urging of that place upon his bladder!

With Tarzan-cries they descended upon the Den, built of drift-timber and carpet from the dump and camouflaged with living vines. Peter and Herman Goltz raced to get there first, and Peter would have won, because anybody beat fat Herman, but his high-top came untied, and so they got there at the same time and dived to crawl through the entrance.

"Hey!"

They stopped in mid-scramble, backed off, stood up quickly.

"Whoops!" Herman hollered. Peter blushed and batted at him to be silent. All stared at the entryway of the hut.

A young man whom Ambrose did not recognize came out first. He had dark eyes and hair and a black moustache, and though he was clean-shaved, his jaw was blue with coming whiskers. He wore a white shirt and a tie and a yellow sweater under his leather jacket, and had dirtied his clean trousers on the Den floor. He stood up and scowled at the ring of boys as if he were going to be angry — but then grinned and brushed his pants knees.

"Sorry, mates. Didn't know it was your hut."

The girl climbed out after. Her brown hair was mussed, her face drained of color, there were shards of dead leaf upon her coat. The fellow helped her up, and she walked straight off without looking at any of them, her right hand stuffed into her coat pocket. The fellow winked at Peter and hurried to follow.

"Hey, gee!" Herman Goltz whispered.

"Who was the guy?" Sandy Cooper wanted to know.

Someone declared that it was Tommy James, just out of the U.S. Navy.

Peter said that Peggy Robbins would get kicked out of nurse's training if they found out, and Herman told how his big sister had been kicked out of nurse's training with only four months to go.

"A bunch went buckbathing one night down to Shoal Creek, and Sis was the only one was kicked out for it."

The Sphinxes all got to laughing and fooling around about Herman Goltz's sister and about Peggy Robbins and her boyfriend. Some of the fellows wanted to take after them and razz them, but it was agreed that Tommy James was a tough customer. Somebody believed there had been a scar across his temple.

Herman wailed "Oh lover!" and collapsed against Peter, who wrestled him down into the creepers.

Cheeks burning, Ambrose joined in the merriment. "We ought to put a sign up! *Private Property: No Smooching.*"

The fellows laughed. But not in just the right way.

"Hey guys!" Sandy Cooper said. "Amby says they was smooching!"

Ambrose quickly grinned and cried "Like a duck! Like a duck!";

whenever a person said a thing to fool you, he'd say "Like a duck!" afterward to let you know you'd been fooled.

"Like a duck nothing," Sandy Cooper rasped. "I bet I know what we'll find inside."

"Hey, yeah!" said Peter.

Sandy Cooper had an old flashlight that he carried on his belt, and so they let him go in first, and Peter and Herman and the others followed after. In just an instant Ambrose heard Sandy shout "Woo-hoo!" and there was excitement in the Den. He heard Peter cry "Let me see!" and Herman Goltz commence to giggle like a girl. Peter said "Let *me* see, damn it!"

"Go to Hell," said the gritty voice of Sandy Cooper.

"Go to Hell your own self."

Perse Goltz had scrambled in unnoticed with the rest, but now a Sphinx espied him.

"Get out of here, Perse. I thought I smelt something."

"You smelt your own self," the little boy retorted.

"Go on, get out, Perse," Herman ordered. "You stink."

"You stink worst."

Somebody said "Bust him once," but Perse was out before they could get him. He stuck out his tongue and made a great blasting raspberry at Peter, who had dived for his leg through the entrance.

Then Peter looked up at Ambrose from where he lay and said: "Our meeting's started."

"Yeah," someone said from inside. "No babies allowed."

"No smooching allowed," another member ventured, mocking Ambrose in an official tone. Sandy Cooper added that no something-else was allowed, and what it was was the same word that would make him laugh sometimes instead of sicking his Chesapeake Bay dog on you.

"You and Perse skeedaddle now." Peter said. His voice was not unkind, but there was an odd look on his face, and he hurried back into the Den, from which now came gleeful whispers. The name Peggy Robbins was mentioned, and someone dared, and double-dared, and dee-double-dared someone else, in vain, to go invite Ramona Peters to the meeting.

Perse Goltz had already gone a ways up the beach. Ambrose went down the high bank, checking his slide with the orange roots of undermined trees, and trudged after him. Peter had said, "Go to Hell your own self," in a voice that told you he was used to saying such things. And the cursing wasn't the worst of it.

Ambrose's stomach felt tied and lumpy; by looking at his arm a certain way he could see droplets standing in the pores. It was what they meant when they spoke of *breaking out in a cold sweat:* very like what one felt in school assemblies, when one was waiting in the wings for the signal to step out onto the stage. He could not bear to think of the moustachioed boyfriend: that fellow's wink, his curly hair, his leather jacket over white shirt and green tie, filled Ambrose's heart with comprehension; they whispered to him that whatever mysteries had been in progress in the Den, they did not mean to Wimpy James's brother what they meant to Peggy Robbins.

Toward her his feelings were less simple. He pictured them kicking her out of the Nurses' Home: partly on the basis of Herman Goltz's story about his sister, Ambrose imagined that disgraced student nurses were kicked out late at night, unclothed; he wondered who did the actual kicking, and where in the world the student nurses went from there.

Every one of the hurricanes that ushered in the fall took its toll upon the riverbank, with the result that the upper beach was strewn with trees long fallen from the cliff. Salt air and water quickly stripped their bark and scoured the trunks. They seemed never to decay; Ambrose could rub his hands along the polished gray wood with little fear of splinters. One saw that in years to come the Jungle would be gone entirely. He would be a man then, and it wouldn't matter. Only his children, he supposed, might miss the winding paths and secret places — but of course you didn't miss what you'd never had or known of.

On the foreshore, in the wrack along the high-water line where sandfleas jumped, were empty beer cans, grapefruit rinds, and hosts of spot and white perch poisoned by the run-off from the canneries. All rotted together. But on the sand beach, in the sun and wind, Ambrose could breathe them deeply. Indeed, with the salt itself and the pungent oils of the eelgrass they made the very flavor of the shore, exhilarating to his spirit. It was a bright summer night; Peggy Robbins had just been kicked out of the Nurses' Home, and the only way she could keep everybody from seeing her was to run into the Jungle and hide in Sphinx's Den. As it happened, Ambrose had been waked by a clanking in the alleyway and had gone outside to drive off the black dogs or the Arnie twins, whichever were rooting in the garbage. And finding the night so balmy, he strolled down to the rivershore and entered the Jungle, where he heard weeping. It was pitch black in the Den; she cringed against the far wall.

"Who is it?"

"It is the only man who ever really loved you."

She hugged and kissed him; then, overcome by double shame drew away. But if he had accepted her caresses coolly, still he would not scorn her. He took her hand.

"Ah Peggy. Ah Peggy."

She wept afresh, and then one of two things happened. Perhaps she flung herself before him, begging forgiveness and imploring him to love her. He raised her up and staunched her tears.

"Forgive you?" he repeated in a deep, kind voice. "Love forgives everything, Peggy. But the truth of the matter is, I can't forget."

He held her head in both his hands; her bitter tears splashed his wrists. He left the Den and walked to the bank-edge, leaned against a tree, stared seaward. Presently Peggy grew quiet, and went her way, but he, he stayed a long time in the Jungle.

On the other hand perhaps it was that he drew her to him in the dark, held her close, and gave her to know that while he could never feel just the same respect for her, he loved her nonetheless. They kissed. Tenderly together they rehearsed the secrets; long they lingered in the Sphinx's Den; then he bore her from the Jungle, lovingly to the beach, into the water. They swam until her tears made a part of Earth's waters; then hand in hand they waded shoreward on the track of the moon. In the shallows they paused to face each other. Warm wavelets flashed about their feet; waterdrops sparkled on their bodies. Washed of shame, washed of fear; nothing was but sweetest knowledge.

In the lumberyard down past the hospital they used square pine sticks between the layers of drying boards to let air through. The beach was littered with such sticks, three and four and five feet long; if you held one by the back end and threw it like a spear into the water, nothing made a better submarine. Perse Goltz had started launching submarines and following them down toward the Jungle as they floated on the tide.

"Don't go any farther," Ambrose said when he drew near.

Perse asked indifferently: "Why don't you shut up?"

"All I've got to do is give the signal," Ambrose declared, "and they'll know you're sneaking up to spy."

As they talked they launched more submarines. The object was to see how far you could make them go under water before they surfaced: if you launched them too flat they'd skim along the top; if too deeply they'd nose under and slide up backward. But if you did it just right they'd straighten out and glide several yards under water before they came up. Ambrose's arms were longer and he knew the trick; his went farther than Perse's.

"There ain't no sign," Perse said.

"There is so. Plenty of them."

"Well, you don't know none of them, anyhow."

"That's what you think. Watch this." He raised his hand toward the Jungle and made successive gestures with his fingers in the manner of Mister Neal the deaf and dumb eggman. "I told them we were just launching submarines and not to worry."

"You did not." But Perse left off his launching for a moment to watch, and moved no farther down the beach.

"Wait a minute." Ambrose squinted urgently toward the trees. "*Go . . . up . . . the . . . beach.* They want us to go on up the beach some more." He spoke in a matter-of-fact tone, and even though Perse said "What a big fake you are," he followed Ambrose in the direction of the new bridge.

If Ambrose was the better launcher, Perse was the better bombardier: he could throw higher, farther, straighter. The deep shells they skipped out for Ducks and Drakes; the flat ones they sailed top-up to make them climb, or straight aloft so that they'd cut water without a splash. Beer cans if you threw them with the holes down whistled satisfactorily. They went along launching and bombarding, and then Ambrose saw a perfectly amazing thing. Lying in the seaweed where the tide had left it was a bottle with a note inside.

"Look here!"

He rushed to pick it up. It was a clear glass bottle, a whisky or wine bottle, tightly capped. Dried eelgrass full of sand and tiny musselshells clung round it. The label had been scraped off, all but some white strips where the glue was thickest; the paper inside was folded.

"*Gee whiz!*" Perse cried. At once he tried to snatch the bottle away, but Ambrose held it well above his reach.

"Finders keepers!"

In his excitement Perse forgot to be cynical. "Where in the *world* do you think it come from?"

"Anywhere!" Ambrose's voice shook. "It could've been floating around for years!" He removed the cap and tipped the bottle downward, but the note wouldn't pass through the neck.

"Get a little stick!" They cast about for a straight twig and Ambrose fished into the bottle with it. At each near catch they breathed: "Aw!"

Ambrose's heart shook. For the moment Scylla and Charybdis, the Occult Order, his brother Peter—all were forgotten. Peggy Robbins, too, though she did not vanish altogether from his mind's eye, was caught up into the greater vision, vague and splendrous, whereof the sea-wreathed bottle was an emblem. Westward it lay, to westward, where the tide ran from East Dorset. Past the river and the Bay, from continents beyond, this messenger had come. Borne by currents as yet uncharted, nosed by fishes as yet unnamed, it had bobbed for ages beneath strange stars. Then out of the oceans it had strayed; past cape and cove, black can, red nun, the word had wandered willy-nilly to his threshold.

"For pity's sake bust it!" Perse shouted.

Holding the bottle by the neck Ambrose banged it on a mossed and barnacled brickbat. Not hard enough. His face perspired. On the third swing the bottle smashed and the note fell out.

"I got it!" Perse cried, but before he could snatch it up, Ambrose sent him flying onto the sand.

The little boy's face screwed up with tears. "I'll get you!"

But Ambrose paid him no heed. As he picked up the paper, Perse flew into him, and received such a swat from Ambrose's free hand that he ran bawling down the beach.

The paper was half a sheet of coarse ruled stuff, torn carelessly from a tablet and folded thrice. Ambrose uncreased it. On a top line was penned in deep red ink:

TO WHOM IT MAY CONCERN

On the next-to-bottom:

YOURS TRULY

The lines between were blank, as was the space beneath the complimentary close. In a number of places, owing to the coarseness of the paper, the ink spread from the lines in fibrous blots.

An oystershell zipped past and plucked into the sand behind him: a hundred feet away Perse Goltz thumbed his nose and stepped a few steps back. Ambrose ignored him, but moved slowly down the shore. Up in the Jungle the Sphinxes had adjourned to play King of the Hill on the riverbank. Perse threw another oystershell and half-turned to run; he was not pursued.

Ambrose's spirit bore new and subtle burdens. He would not tattle on Peter for cursing and the rest of it. The thought of his brother's sins no longer troubled him or even much moved his curiosity. Tonight, tomorrow night, unhurriedly, he would find out from Peter just what it was they had discovered in the Den, and what-all done: the things he'd learn would not surprise now nor distress him, for though he was still innocent of that knowledge, he had the feel of it in his heart, and of other truth.

He changed the note to his left hand, the better to wing an oystershell at Perse. As he did so, some corner of his mind remarked that those shiny bits in the paper's texture were splinters of wood pulp. Often as he'd seen them in the leaves of cheap tablets, he had not thitherto embraced that fact.

Petition

April 21, 1931

His Most Gracious Majesty Prajadhipok, Descendant of Buddha, King of North and South, Supreme Arbiter of the Ebb and Flow of the Tide, Brother of the Moon, Half-Brother of the Sun, Possessor of the Four-and-Twenty Golden Umbrellas
Ophir Hall
White Plains, New York

Sir:

Welcome to America. An ordinary citizen extends his wish that your visit with us be pleasant, your surgery successful.

Though not myself a native of your kingdom, I am and have been most alive to its existence and concerns — unlike the average American, alas, to whose imagination the name of that ancient realm summons only white elephants and blue-eyed cats. I am aware, for example, that it was Queen Rambai's father's joke that he'd been inside the Statue of Liberty but never in the United States, having toured the Paris foundry while that symbol was a-casting; in like manner I may say that I have dwelt in a figurative Bangkok all my life. My brother, with whose presumption and other faults I hope further to acquaint you in the course of this petition, has even claimed (in his cups) descent

61

from the mad King Phaya Takh Sin, whose well-deserved assassination — like the surgical excision of a cataract, if I may be so bold — gave to a benighted land the luminous dynasty of Chakkri, whereof Your Majesty is the latest and brightest son. Here as elsewhere my brother lies or is mistaken: we are Occidental, for better or worse, and while our condition is freakish, our origin is almost certainly commonplace. Yet though my brother's claim is false and (should he press it upon you, as he might) in contemptible taste, it may serve the purpose of introducing to you his character, my wretched situation, and my petition to your magnanimity.

The reign of the Chakkris began in violence and threatens to end in blindness; my own history commences with a kind of blindness and threatens to terminate in murder. Happily, our American surgeons are equal to the former threat; my prayer is that Your Majesty — reciprocally, as it were — may find it in his heart to address himself to the latter. The press reports your pledge to liberate three thousand inmates of your country's prisons by April next, to celebrate both the restoration of your eyesight and the sesquicentennial of your dynasty: a regal gesture. But there are prisoners and prisoners; *my* hope is for another kind of release, from what may not unfairly be termed life-imprisonment for no crime whatever, only the misfortune of being born my brother's brother. That the prerogative of kings yet retains, even in the New World, some trace of its old divinity, is amply proved by President Hoover's solicitude for your comfort and all my countrymen's eagerness to serve you. The magazines proclaim the triflingest details of your daily round; society talks of nothing else but your comings and goings; a word from you sends government officers scurrying, reroutes express-trains, stops presses, marshals the finest medical talents in the nation. Give commands, then, that I be liberated at long last from a misery absolute as your monarchy!

Will you counsel resignation to my estate, even affirmation of it? Will you cite the example of Chang and Eng, whom your ancestor thought to put to death and ended by blessing? But Chang and Eng were different from my brother and me, because so much the same; Chang and Eng were as the left hand to the right; Chang and Eng were bound heart to heart: their common navel, which to prick was to injure both, was an emblem of their fraternity, as was the manner of their sitting, each with an arm about the other's shoulders. Haven't I wept with envy of sturdy Chang, loyal Eng? Haven't I invoked them, vainly, as exemplars not only of moral grace but of practical efficiency? Their introduction of the "double chop" for cutting logs, a method still employed by pairs of Carolina woodsmen; their singular skill at driving four-horse teams down the lumber trails of their adopted state; their good-humored baiting of railway conductors, to whom they would present a single ticket, acknowledging that one might be put off the train, but insisting on the other's right to transportation; their resourceful employment of the same reasoning on the occasion of one's arrest, when the other loyally threatened to sue if he too were jailed; their happy marriage to a pair of sisters, who bore them twenty-two healthy children in their separate households; their alternation of authority and residence every three days, rain or shine, each man master under his own roof—a schedule followed faithfully until Chang's death at sixty-three; Eng's touching last request, as he himself expired of sympathy and terror three hours later, that his brother's dead body be moved even closer — didn't I recite these marvels like a litany to *my* brother in the years when I still could hope we might get along?

Yet it may surprise you to learn that even Chang and Eng, those paragons of cooperation, had their differences. Chang was a tippler, Eng a teetotaller; Eng liked all-night checker games, Chang was no gambler; in at least one election they cast their votes for opposing candidates; the arrest aforementioned, though it came to nothing, was for the crime of assault — committed by one against the other. Especially following marriage their differences increased, and if upon returning to the exhibition stage (after the Civil War) they made a show of unanimity, it was to raise money in the hope that some surgeon could part them at last. All this, mind, between veritable Heavenly Twins, sons of the mystical East, whose religions and philosophies — no criticism intended — have ever minimized distinctions, denying even the difference between Sameness and Difference. How altogether contrary is the case of my brother and me! (*He*, as might be expected, denies that the cases are different, contradicts this denial by denying at the same time that we are two in the first place — and would no doubt deny the contradiction as well, with equal obstinacy, should Your Majesty point it out to him.) Only consider: whereas Chang and Eng were bound breast to breast by a good long band that allowed them to walk, sit, and sleep side by side, my brother and I are fastened front to rear — my belly to the small of his back — by a leash of flesh heartbreakingly short. In consequence he never lays eyes on the wretch he forever drags about — no wonder he denies me, agrees with the doctors that such a union is impossible, and claims my utterance and inspiration for his own! — while I see nothing else the day long (unless over his shoulder) but his stupid neck-nape, which I know better than my name. He obscures my view, sits in my lap (never mind how his weight impedes my circulation), smothers me in his wraps. What I suffer in the bathroom is too disgusting for Your Majesty's ears. By night it's scramble or be crushed when he tosses in our bed, pitching and snoring so in his dreams that my own are nightmares; by day I must match his stride like the hinder half of a vaudeville horse until, exhausted, I clamber on him pick-a-back. Small comfort that I may outlast him, despite his greater strength, by riding him thus; when he goes I go, Eng after Chang, and in the meanwhile I must go *where* he goes as well, and suffer his insults along the way. No matter to him that in one breath he denies my existence, in the next affirms it with his oaths and curses: I am Anchises to his Aeneas, he will have it; Old Man of the Sea to his Sinbad; I am his cross, his albatross; I, lifelong victim of his beastliness, he calls the monkey on his back!

No misery, of course, but has its little compensations, however hollow or theoretical. What couldn't we accomplish if he'd cooperate, with me as his back-up man! Only let me count cadence and him go more regularly, there'd be no stumbling; I could prod, tickle, goose him into action if he'd not ignore me; I'd be the eyes in the back of his head, his unobserved prompter and mentor. Cloaked in the legal immunity of Chang-Eng's gambit we could do what we pleased, be wealthy in no time. Even within the law we'd have the world for our oyster, our capacity twice any rival's. Strangers to loneliness, we could make rich our leisure hours: bicycle in tandem, sing close harmony, play astonishing piano, read Plato aloud, assemble mahjongg tiles in half the time. I'd be no prude were we as close in temperament as in body; we could make any open-minded woman happy beyond her most amorous reveries — or, lacking women, delight each other in ways that Chang and Eng could never . . .

Vain dreams; we are nothing alike. I am slight, my brother is gross. He's incoherent but vocal; I'm articulate and mute. He's ignorant but full of guile; I think I may call myself reasonably educated, and if ingenuous, no more so I hope than the run of scholars. My brother is gregarious: he deals with the public; earns and spends our income; tends (but slovenly) the house and grounds; makes, entertains, and loses friends; indulges in hobbies; pursues ambitions and women. For my part, I am by nature withdrawn, even solitary: an observer of life, a meditator, a taker of notes, a dreamer if you will — yet not a brooder; it's he who moods and broods, today hilarious, tomorrow despondent; I myself am stoical, detached as it were — of necessity, or I'd have long since perished of despair. More to the point, what intelligence my brother has is inclined to synthesis, mine to analysis; he denies that we are two, yet refuses to compromise and cooperate; I affirm our difference — all the difference in the world! — but have endeavored in vain to work out with him a reasonable cohabitation. Untutored and clumsy, he will nevertheless make flatulent noises upon the trombone, write ungainly verses, dance awkwardly with women, hold grunting conversations, jerrybuild a roof over our heads; I, whose imagination encompasses Aristotle, Shakespeare, Bach — I'd never so presume; yet let me point out to him, however diplomatically, however constructively, the short-comings of his efforts beside genuine creation: he flies into a rage, shreds his doggerel, dents his horn, quarrels with his "sweetheart" (who perhaps was laughing at him all along), abandons carpentry, beats his chest in heroical self-pity, or sulks in a corner for days togeth-er. I don't even mention his filthy personal habits: what consolation that he swipes his bum and occasionally soaps his stinking body? Only the sinner needs absolution, and one sin breeds another: because I ride on his back and am content to nourish myself with infrequent sips of tea, I neither perspire nor defecate, but merely emit a discreet vapor, of neutral scent, and tiny puffs of what could pass for talc. Other sus-tenance I draw less from our common bond, as he might claim, than from books, from introspection, most of all from revery and fancy, without which I'd soon enough starve. But he, he eats anything, lusts after anything, goes to any length to make me wretched. His very ex-crements he will sniff and savor; he belches up gases, farts in my lap; not content that I must ride atop him, as on a rutting stallion, while he humps his whores, he will torment me in the shower-bath by bending over to draw me against him and pinching at me with his hairy cheeks. Yet let me flinch away, or in a frenzy of disgust attempt to rupture our bond though it kill us (as I sometimes strained to do in years gone by): he turns my revulsion into horrid sport, runs out and snaps back like a paddle-ball or plays crack-the-whip at every turn in our road. Why go on? We have nothing in common but the womb that bore, the flesh that shackles, the grave that must soon receive us. If my situation has any advantage it's only that I can see him without his seeing me; can therefore study and examine our bond, how ever to dissolve it, and take certain surreptitious measures to that end, such as writing this petition. Futile perhaps; desperate certainly. The alternative is madness.

All very well, you may say: lamentable as our situation is, it's nothing new; we were born this way and have somehow muddled through thirty-five years; not even a king has his own way in everything; in the matter of congenital endowment it's potluck for all of us, we must grin and bear it, the weakest to the wall, *et cetera*. God knows I am no whiner; I've broken heart and spirit to make the best of a bad hand of cards; at the slimmest hint of sympathy from my brother, the least suggestion of real fraternity, I melt with gratitude, must clamber aboard lest I swoon of joy; my tears run in his hair and down the courses of his face, one would think it was he who wept. And were it simply a matter of accumulated misery, or the mere happenstance of your visit, I'd not burden you (and my own sensibility) with this complaint. What prompts my plea is the coincidence of your arrival and a critical turn in our history and situation.

I pass over the details of our past, a tiresome chronicle. Some say our mother died a-bearing us, others that she perished of dismay soon after; just as possibly, she merely put us out. The man we called Father exhibited us throughout our childhood, but the age was more hardened to monstrosity than Chang's and Eng's; we never prospered; indeed we were scarcely noticed. In earliest babyhood I didn't realize I was two; it was the intractability of that creature always before me — going left when I would go right, bawling for food when I would sleep; laughing when I wept — that opened my eyes to the possibility he was other than myself; the teasing of playmates, who mocked our contretemps, verified that suspicion, and I began my painful schooling in detachment. Early on I proposed to my brother a judicious alliance (with myself, naturally, as director of our activities and final arbiter of our differences, he being utterly a creature of impulse); he would none of my proposal. Through childhood our antipathies merely smoldered, as we both submitted perforce, however grudgingly, to Father (who at least never denied our twoness, which, to be sure, was his livelihood); it was upon our fleeing his government, in adolescence, that they flamed. My attempt to direct our partnership ended in my brother's denying first my efficacy, then my authority, finally my reality. He pretended to believe, offstage as well as on, that the audience's interest was in him as a solo performer and not in the pair of us as a freak; hidden from the general view, unable to speak except in whispers, I could take only feeblest revenge: I would wave now and then between the lines of his stupid performances, grimace behind his back and over his shoulder, make signs to mock or contradict his asseverations. Let him deny me, he couldn't ignore me; I tripped him up, confused, confounded him, and though in the end he usually prevailed, I pulled against him every step of his way, spoiled his pleasure, halved his force, and on more than one occasion stalled him entirely.

The consequent fiascos, the rages and rampages of his desperation, are too dreadful to recount; them too I pass over, with a shudder. For some time now our connection has been an exasperated truce punctuated with bitter bursts of hostility, as between old mismatched spouses or weary combatants; the open confrontations are less frequent because more vicious, the interim resentments more deep because more resigned. Each new set-to, legatee of all its predecessors, is more destructive than the last; at the merest popgun-pop, artillery bristles. However radically, therefore, our opposition restricts our freedom, we each had come to feel, I believe, that the next real violence between us would be the last, fatal to one and thus to both, and so were more or less resigned to languishing, disgruntled, in our impasse, for want of alternatives. Then between us came Thalia, love, the present crisis.

It will scarcely surprise you that we arrived late at sexuality. Ordinary girls fled from our advances, or cruelly mocked us; had our bookings not fetched us to the capitals of Europe, whose liberal ladies sought us out for novelty's sake, we'd kept our chastity perforce till affluent maturity, for common prostitutes raised their fees, at sight of us, beyond our adolescent means. Even so, it was my brother did all the clipping, I being out of reach except to surrogate gratifications; only when a producer of unusual motion pictures in Berlin, with the resourcefulness characteristic of his nation, discovered Thalia and brought her to us, did I know directly the experience of coition. I did not enjoy it.

More accurately, I was rent by emotions as at odds as I and my brother. Thalia — a pretty young contortionist of good family obliged by the misery of the times to prostitute her art in exotic nightclubs and films — I admired tremendously, not alone for her merry temper and the talent wherewith she achieved our connection, but for her silent forbearance, not unlike my own, in the face as it were of my brother's abuse. But how expect me to share the universal itch to copulate, whose soul lusts only for disjunction? Even our modest coupling (chaste beside *his* performances), rousing as it was to tickly sense, went so counter to my principles I'd hardly have enjoyed it even had my brother not indignified her the while. Not content to be double already, he must attach himself to everyone, everything; hug, devour, absorb! Heads or tails, it's all one to Brother; he clamped his shaggy thighs about the poor girl's ears as greedily as he engorges a pot roast or smothers me into the mattress, threatening with a laugh to squash and ingest me.

After a series of such meetings (the film director, whether as artist or as Teuton, was a perfectionist) we discovered ourselves in love: I with Thalia, my brother likewise in his fashion, and laughing Thalia . . . with me, with me, I'm sure of it! At least in the beginning. She joined our act, inspired or composed fresh material for us; we played with profit the naughty stages of a dozen nations, my brother still pretending he had no brother despite our billing: *The Eternal Triangle.* Arranged in parallel, isosceles, or alphaic fashion, we slept in the same hotel beds, and while it was he who salivated and grunted upon her night after night, as he does yet, still it pleased me to imagine that Thalia permitted him her supple favors out of love for me, and humored his pretense that I did not exist in order to be with me. By gay example she taught me to make fun of our predicament, chuckle through the teeth of anguish, turn woe into wit. In the heights of his barbarous passion our eyes meet, and I have seen her wink; as he roars in his transports, her chin rests on his shoulder; she grins, and I chastely kiss her brow. More than once I have been moved to put my love into written words, to no avail; what profit to be articulate, when he seizes every message like a jealous censor and either obscures its tender sentiments past deciphering or translates them into his own coarse idiom? I reach to comfort her; he thrusts my hand into her crotch; she takes it for his and pretends delight. Agile creature that she is, she would enfold us both in her honey limbs, so to touch the one she loves; as if aware, he thwarts her into some yoga position, Bandha Padmāsana Dhanurāsana. Little wonder our love remains tentative with him between us, who for aught I know may garble even this petition; little wonder we doubt and mistake each other. Indeed, I can only forgive her, however broken-heartedly, if the worst of my suspicions should prove true: that, hardened by despair, Thalia is becoming her disguise: the vulgar creature who ignores my signals, denies my presence, growls with feral joy beneath her ravisher! My laughter sticks in my throat; either Thalia has lost her sense of humor or I've lost mine. Mirth passes; our wretchedness endures and brutalizes. Truth to tell, she has become a stranger; with the best will in the world I can't always persuade my heart that her refusal to acknowledge me is but a stratagem of love, her teasing and fondling of the man I abhor mere feminine duplicity, to inspire my ardor and cover our tracks. What tracks, Thalia? Of late, particularly, she behaves on occasion as if *I* stood in the way of her contentment, and in darkest moments I can even wonder whether her demand that my brother "pull himself together" is owing to her secret desire for me or a secret wish to see me gone.

This ultimatum she pronounced on our thirty-fifth birthday, three weeks past. We were vacationing between a profitable Mardi-Gras engagement in New Orleans and a scheduled post-Lenten tour of Western speakeasies; indeed, despite Prohibition and Depression, perhaps because of them, we'd had an uncommonly prosperous season; the demand for our sort of spectacle had never been so great; people crowded into basement caves to drink illicit liquors and applaud our repertoire of unnatural combinations and obscene gymnastics. One routine in particular was lining our pockets, a lubricious soft-shoe burlesque of popular songs beginning with *Me and My Shadow* and culminating in *When We're Alone*; it was Thalia's invention, and doubtless inspired both my brother's birthday proposal and her response. She had bought a cake to celebrate the occasion (for both of us, I was sure, though seventy candles would clearly have been too many); my brother, who ordinarily blew out all the candles and clawed into the frosting with both hands before I could draw a breath, had been distracted all day, and managed only thirty-four; eagerly I puffed out the last, over his shoulder, my first such opportunity in three decades and a half, whereat he threw off his mood with a laugh and revealed his wish: to join himself to Thalia in marriage. In his blurting fashion he enounced a whole mad program: he would put the first half of his life altogether behind him, quit show business, use our savings to learn an honest trade, perhaps husbandry, perhaps welding, and raise a family!

"Two can live cheap as one," he grumbled at the end — somewhat defensively, for Thalia showed neither surprise, pleasure, nor dismay, but heard him out with a neutral expression as if the idea were nothing new. I searched her face for assurance that she was revolted; I waved my arms and shook my head, turned out my pockets to find the *NO*-sign I always carried with me, so often was it needed, and flung it in her direction when she wouldn't look at it. Long time she studied him, twirling a sprig of ivy between her fingers; cross with suspense, he admitted he'd been no model companion, but a moody, difficult, irresolute fellow plagued with tensions and contradictions. I mouthed antic sneers over his shoulders. But with her assistance he would become a new man, he declared, and promised ominously to "get rid," "one way or another," of "the monkey on his back," which had kept him to date from single-minded application to anything. It was his first employment of the epithet; I shuddered at his resolve. She was his hope of redemption, he went on, becoming fatuous and sentimental now in his anxiety; without her he was no better than a beast (as if he weren't beastly *with* her!), no more than half a man; let her but consent, therefore and however, to become as the saying was his better half, he'd count himself saved!

Why did she not laugh in his face, throw up to him his bestialities, declare once for all that she endured him solely on my account? She rose from table, leaning upon the cane she always danced with; I held out my arms to her and felt on each elbow the tears my brother forced to dramatize his misery. Oh, he is a cunning animal! I even attempted tears myself, but flabbergastment dried my eyes. At the door Thalia turned to gaze as if it were through him — the last time, I confess, that I was able to believe she might be looking at me. Then bending with a grunt to retrieve my crumpled message, which she tossed unread into the nearest ashtray, she replied that she was indeed weary of acrobatics: let him make good his aforementioned promise, one way or another; then she'd see.

No sooner had she spoken than the false tears ceased; my brother chased her squealing into the kitchen, nor troubled even to ask her leave, but swinish as ever fetched down her tights with the cane-crook and rogered her fair athwart the dish drain, all the while snorting through her whoop and giggle: "You'll see what you'll see!"

Highness, I live in terror of what she'll see! Nothing is beyond my brother. He has put himself on a diet, avowedly to trim his grossness for her sake; but I perceive myself weaker in consequence, and am half-convinced he means to starve me on the vine, as it were, and absorb me through the bond that joins us. He has purchased medical insurance, playing the family man, and remarks as if idly on its coverage of massive skin grafts; for all I know he may be planning to install me out of sight inside him by surgical means. I don't eat; I daren't sleep. Thalia, my hope and consolation — why has she forsaken me?

If indeed she has. For a curious fancy has taken me of late, not impossibly the figment of a mind deranged for want of love (and rest, and sustenance): that Thalia is less simple than she appears. I suspect, in fact, or begin to ... that there are two Thalias! Don't mistake me: not two as Chang and Eng were two, or as my brother and I are two; not one Thalia joined to another — but a Thalia *within* a Thalia, like the dolls-within-dolls Your Majesty's countrymen and neighbors fashion so cleverly: a Thalia incarcerate in the iron maiden my brother embraces!

I first observed her not long after that fell birthday. No moraler for all his protestations, my brother has devised for our next performance a new stunt based on an old lubricity, and to "get the hang of it" (so he claims) sleeps now arsy-turvy with his "fiancée," like shoes in a box or the ancient symbol for Yang and Yin. Sometimes she rests her head on his knees, and thus it happened, late one night, that when I looked down upon the Thalia who'd betrayed me, I found her looking back, sleepless as I, upside down in the first spring moonlight. Yet lo, it was not the same Thalia! Her face — I should say, her sister's face — was inverted, but I realized suddenly that her eyes were not; it was a different woman, a stranger, who regarded me with upright, silent stare through the other's face. I perspired with dismay — my first experience of sweat. Luckily my brother slept, a-pitch with dreams. There was no mistaking it, another woman looked out at me from behind that mask: a prisoner like myself, whose gaze remained level and detached however her heartless warden grinned and grimaced. I saw her the next night and the next, earnest, mute; by day she disappears in the other Thalia; I live only for the night, to rehearse before her steadfast eyes the pity and terror of our situation. She it is (once separate like myself, it may be, then absorbed by her smirking sister) I now adore — if with small hope and much apprehension. Does she see me winking and waving, or is my face as strange to her as her sister's to me? Why does she gaze at me so evenly, as if in unremitting appraisal? Can she too be uncertain of my reality, my love? Too much to bear!

In any case, there's little time. "Thalia" grows restive; now that she has the upper hand with my brother she makes no bones about her reluctance to go back on the road, her yen for a little farm, her dissatisfaction with his progress in "making a man of himself" and the like. Last night, I swear it, I felt him straining to suck me in through our conjunction, and clung to the sheets in terror. Momently I expect him to play some unsuspected trump; have at me for good and all. When he does, I will bite through the tie that binds us and so kill us both. It is a homicide God will forgive, and my beloved will at least be free of what she suffers, through her sister, at my brother's hands.

Yet given the daily advances of science and the inspiring circumstance of Your Majesty's visit, I dare this final hope: that at your bidding the world's most accomplished surgeons may successfully divide my brother from myself, in a manner such that one of us at least may survive, free of the other. After all, we were both joined once to our unknown mother, and safely detached to begin our misery. Or if a bond to *something* is necessary in our case, let it be something more congenial and sympathetic: graft my brother's Thalia in my place, and fasten me ... to my own navel, to anything but him, if the Thalia I love can't be freed to join me! Perhaps she has another sister ... Death itself I would embrace like a lover, if I might share the grave with no other company. To be one: paradise! To be two: bliss! But to be both and neither is unspeakable. Your Highness may imagine with what eagerness His reply to this petition is awaited by

Yours truly,

Lost in the Funhouse

For whom is the funhouse fun? Perhaps for lovers. For Ambrose it is *a place of fear and confusion.* He has come to the seashore with his family for the holiday, *the occasion of their visit is Independence Day, the most important secular holiday of the United States of America.* A single straight underline is the manuscript mark for italic type, *which in turn* is the printed equivalent to oral emphasis of words and phrases as well as the customary type for titles of complete works, not to mention. Italics are also employed, in fiction stories especially, for "outside," intrusive, or artificial voices, such as radio announcements, the texts of telegrams and newspaper articles, *et cetera.* They should be used *sparingly.* If passages originally in roman type are italicized by someone repeating them, it's customary to acknowledge the fact. *Italics mine.*

Ambrose was "at that awkward age." His voice came out high-pitched as a child's if he let himself get carried away; to be on the safe side, therefore, he moved and spoke with *deliberate calm* and *adult gravity.* Talking soberly of unimportant or irrelevant matters and listening consciously to the sound of your own voice are useful habits for maintaining control in this difficult interval. En route to Ocean City he sat in the back seat of the family car with his brother Peter, age fifteen, and Magda G——, age fourteen, a pretty girl an exquisite young lady, who lived not far from them on B—— Street in the town of D——, Maryland. Initials, blanks, or both were often substituted for proper names in nineteenth-century fiction to enhance the illusion of reality. It is as if the author felt it necessary to delete the names for reasons of tact or legal liability. Interestingly, as with other aspects of realism, it is an *illusion* that is being enhanced, by purely artificial means. Is it likely, does it violate the principle of verisimilitude, that a thirteen-year-old boy could make such a sophisticated observation? A girl of fourteen is the *psychological coeval* of a boy of fifteen or sixteen; a thirteen-year-old boy, therefore, even one precocious in some other respects, might be three years *her emotional junior*.

Thrice a year — on Memorial, Independence, and Labor Days — the family visits Ocean City for the afternoon and evening. When Ambrose and Peter's father was their age, the excursion was made by train, as mentioned in the novel *The 42nd Parallel* by John Dos Passos. Many families from the same neighborhood used to travel together, with dependent relatives and often with Negro servants; schoolfuls of children swarmed through the railway cars; everyone shared everyone else's Maryland fried chicken, Virginia ham, deviled eggs, potato salad, beaten biscuits, iced tea. Nowadays (that is, in 19___, the year of our story) the journey is made by automobile — more comfortably and quickly though without the extra fun though without the *camaraderie* of a general excursion. It's all part of the deterioration of American life, their father declares; Uncle Karl supposes that when the boys take *their* families to Ocean City for the holidays they'll fly in Autogiros. Their mother, sitting in the middle of the front seat like Magda in the second, only with her arms on the seat-back behind the men's shoulders, wouldn't want the good old days back again, the steaming trains and stuffy long dresses; on the other hand she can do without Autogiros, too, if she has to become a grandmother to fly in them.

Description of physical appearance and mannerisms is one of several standard methods of characterization used by writers of fiction. It is also important to "keep the senses operating"; when a detail from one of the five senses, say visual, is "crossed" with a detail from another, say auditory, the reader's imagination is oriented to the scene, perhaps unconsciously. This procedure may be compared to the way surveyors and navigators determine their positions by two or more compass bearings, a process known as triangulation. The brown hair on Ambrose's mother's forearms gleamed in the sun like. Though right-handed, she took her left arm from the seat-back to press the dashboard cigar lighter for Uncle Karl. When the glass bead in its handle glowed red, the lighter was ready for use. The smell of Uncle Karl's cigar smoke reminded one of. The fragrance of the ocean came strong to the picnic ground where they always stopped for lunch, two miles inland from Ocean City. Having to pause for a full hour almost within sound of the breakers was difficult for Peter and Ambrose when they were younger; even at their present age it was not easy to keep their anticipation, *stimulated by the briny spume*, from turning into short temper. The Irish author James Joyce, in his unusual novel entitled *Ulysses*, now available in this country, uses the adjectives *snot-green* and *scrotum-tightening* to describe the sea. Visual, auditory, tactile, olfactory, gustatory. Peter and Ambrose's father, while steering their black 1936 LaSalle sedan with one hand, could with the other remove the first cigarette from a white pack of Lucky Strikes and, more remarkably, light it with a match forefingered from its book and thumbed against the flint paper without being detached. The matchbook cover merely advertised U.S. War Bonds and Stamps. A fine metaphor, simile, or other figure of speech, in addition to its obvious "first-order" relevance to the thing it describes, will be seen upon reflection to have a second order of significance: it may be drawn from the milieu of the action, for example, or be particularly appropriate to the sensibility of the narrator, even hinting to the reader things of which the narrator is unaware; or it may cast further and subtler lights upon the thing it describes, sometimes ironically qualifying the more evident sense of the comparison.

To say that Ambrose's and Peter's mother was *pretty* is to accomplish nothing; the reader may acknowledge the proposition, but his imagination is not engaged. Besides, Magda was also pretty, yet in an altogether different way. Although she lived on B—— Street she had very good manners and did better than average in school. Her figure was very well developed for her age. Her right hand lay casually on the plush upholstery of the seat, very near Ambrose's left leg, on which his own hand rested. The space between their legs, between her right and his left leg, was out of the line of sight of anyone sitting on the other side of Magda, as well as anyone glancing into the rearview mirror. Uncle Karl's face resembled Peter's — rather, vice versa. Both had dark hair and eyes, short husky statures, deep voices. Magda's left hand was probably in a similar position on her left side. The boy's father is difficult to describe; no particular feature of his appearance or manner stood out. He wore glasses and was principal of a T— County grade school. Uncle Karl was a masonry contractor.

Although Peter must have known as well as Ambrose that the latter, because of his position in the car, would be the first to see the electrical towers of the power plant at V—, the halfway point of their trip, he leaned forward and slightly toward the center of the car and pretended to be looking for them through the flat pinewoods and tuckahoe creeks along the highway. For as long as the boys could remember, "looking for the Towers" had been a feature of the first half of their excursions to Ocean City, "looking for the standpipe" of the second. Though the game was childish, their mother preserved the tradition of rewarding the first to see the Towers with a candybar or piece of fruit. She insisted now that Magda play the game; the prize, she said, was "something hard to get nowadays." Ambrose decided not to join in; he sat far back in his seat. Magda, like Peter, leaned forward. Two sets of straps were discernible through the shoulders of her sun dress; the inside right one, a brassiere-strap, was fastened or shortened with a small safety pin. The right armpit of her dress, presumably the left as well, was damp with perspiration. The simple strategy for being first to espy the Towers, which Ambrose had understood by the age of four, was to sit on the right-hand side of the car. Whoever sat there, however, had also to put up with the worst of the sun, and so Ambrose, without mentioning the matter, chose sometimes the one and sometimes the other. Not impossibly Peter had never caught on to the trick, or thought that his brother hadn't simply because Ambrose on occasion preferred shade to a Baby Ruth or tangerine.

The shade-sun situation didn't apply to the front seat, owing to the windshield; if anything the driver got more sun, since the person on the passenger side not only was shaded below by the door and dashboard but might swing down his sunvisor all the way too.

"Is that them?" Magda asked. Ambrose's mother teased the boys for letting Magda win, insinuating that "somebody [had] a girlfriend." Peter and Ambrose's father reached a long thin arm across their mother to butt his cigarette in the dashboard ashtray, under the lighter. The prize this time for seeing the Towers first was a banana. Their mother bestowed it after chiding their father for wasting a half-smoked cigarette when everything was so scarce. Magda, to take the prize, moved her hand from so near Ambrose's that he could have touched it as though accidentally. She offered to share the prize, things like that were so hard to find; but everyone insisted it was hers alone. Ambrose's mother sang an iambic trimeter couplet from a popular song, femininely rhymed:

> *"What's good is in the Army;*
> *What's left will never harm me."*

Uncle Karl tapped his cigar ash out the ventilator window; some particles were sucked by the slipstream back into the car through the rear window on the passenger side. Magda demonstrated her ability to hold a banana in one hand and peel it with her teeth. She still sat forward; Ambrose pushed his glasses back onto the bridge of his nose with his left hand, which he then negligently let fall to the seat cushion immediately behind her. He even permitted the single hair, gold, on the second joint of his thumb to brush the fabric of her skirt. Should she have sat back at that instant, his hand would have been caught under her.

Plush upholstery prickles uncomfortably through gabardine slacks in the July sun. The function of the *beginning* of a story is to introduce the principal characters, establish their initial relationships, set the scene for the main action, expose the background of the situation if necessary, plant motifs and foreshadowings where appropriate, and initiate the first complication or whatever of the "rising action." Actually, if one imagines a story called "The Funhouse," or "Lost in the Funhouse," the details of the drive to Ocean City don't seem especially relevant. The *beginning* should recount the events between Ambrose's first sight of the funhouse early in the afternoon and his entering it with Magda and Peter in the evening. The *middle* would narrate all relevant events from the time he goes in to the time he loses his way; middles have the double and contradictory function of delaying the climax while at the same time preparing the reader for it and fetching him to it. Then the *ending* would tell what Ambrose does while he's lost, how he finally finds his way out, and what everybody makes of the experience. So far there's been no real dialogue, very little sensory detail, and nothing in the way of a *theme*. And a long time has gone by already without anything happening; it makes a person wonder. We haven't even reached Ocean City yet: we will never get out of the funhouse.

The more closely an author identifies with the narrator, literally or metaphorically, the less advisable it is, as a rule, to use the first-person narrative viewpoint. Once three years previously the young people *aforementioned* played Niggers and Masters in the backyard; when it was Ambrose's turn to be Master and theirs to be Niggers, Peter had to go serve his evening papers; Ambrose was afraid to punish Magda alone, but she led him to the whitewashed Torture Chamber between the woodshed and the privy in the Slaves Quarters; there she knelt sweating among bamboo rakes and dusty Mason jars, pleadingly embraced his knees, and while bees droned in the lattice as if on an ordinary summer afternoon, purchased clemency at a surprising price set by herself. Doubtless she remembered nothing of this event; Ambrose on the other hand seemed unable to forget the least detail of his life. He even recalled how, standing beside himself with awed impersonality in the reeky heat, he'd stared the while at an empty cigar box in which Uncle Karl kept stone-cutting chisels: beneath the words *El Producto*, a laureled, loose-toga'd lady regarded the sea from a marble bench; beside her, forgotten or not yet turned to, was a five-stringed lyre. Her chin reposed on the back of her right hand; her left depended negligently from the bench-arm. The lower half of scene and lady was peeled away; the words EXAMINED BY__ were inked there into the wood. Nowadays cigar boxes are made of pasteboard. Ambrose wondered what Magda would have done, Ambrose wondered what Magda would do when she sat back on his hand as he resolved she should. Be angry. Make a teasing joke of it. Give no sign at all. For a long time she leaned forward, playing cow-poker with Peter against Uncle Karl and Mother and watching for the first sign of Ocean City. At nearly the same instant, picnic ground and Ocean City standpipe hove into view; an Amoco filling station on their side of the road cost Mother and Uncle Karl fifty cows and the game; Magda bounced back, clapping her right hand on Mother's right arm; Ambrose moved clear "in the nick of time."

At this rate our hero, at this rate our protagonist will remain in the funhouse forever. Narrative ordinarily consists of alternating dramatization and summarization. One symptom of nervous tension, paradoxically, is repeated and violent yawning; neither Peter nor Magda nor Uncle Karl nor Mother reacted in this manner. Although they were no longer small children, Peter and Ambrose were each given a dollar to spend on boardwalk amusements in addition to what money of their own they'd brought along. Magda too, though she protested she had ample spending money. The boys' mother made a little scene out of distributing the bills; she pretended that her sons and Magda were small children and cautioned them not to spend the sum too quickly or in one place. Magda promised with a merry laugh and, having both hands free, took the bill with her left. Peter laughed also and pledged in a falsetto to be a good boy. His imitation of a child was not clever. The boys' father was tall and thin, balding, fair-complexioned. Assertions of that sort are not effective; the reader may acknowledge the proposition, but. We should be much farther along than we are; something has gone wrong; not much of this preliminary rambling seems relevant. Yet everyone begins in the same place; how is it that most go along without difficulty but a few lose their way?

"Stay out from under the boardwalk," Uncle Karl growled from the side of his mouth. The boys' mother pushed his shoulder *in mock annoyance*. They were all standing before Fat May the Laughing Lady who advertised the funhouse. Larger than life, Fat May mechanically shook, rocked on her heels, slapped her thighs while recorded laughter — uproarious, female — came amplified from a hidden loudspeaker. It chuckled, wheezed, wept; tried in vain to catch its breath; tittered, groaned, exploded raucous and anew. You couldn't hear it without laughing yourself, no matter how you felt. Father came back from talking to a Coast-Guardsman on duty and reported that the surf was spoiled with crude oil from tankers recently torpedoed offshore. Lumps of it, difficult to remove, made tarry tidelines on the beach and stuck on swimmers. Many bathed in the surf nevertheless and came out speckled; others paid to use a municipal pool and only sunbathed on the beach. We would do the latter. We would do the latter. We would do the latter.

Under the boardwalk, matchbook covers, grainy other things. What is the story's theme? Ambrose is ill. He perspires in the dark passages; candied apples-on-a-stick, delicious-looking, disappointing to eat. Funhouses need men's and ladies' room at intervals. Others perhaps have also vomited in corners and corridors; may even have had bowel movements liable to be stepped in in the dark. The word *fuck* suggests suction and / or flatulence. Mother and Father; grandmothers and grandfathers on both sides; great-grandmothers and great-grandfathers on four sides, *et cetera*. Count a generation as thirty years: in approximately the year when Lord Baltimore was granted charter to the province of Maryland by Charles I, five hundred twelve women — English, Welsh, Bavarian, Swiss — of every class and character, received into themselves the penises the intromittent organs of five hundred twelve men, ditto, in every circumstance and posture, to conceive the five hundred twelve ancestors of the two hundred fifty-six ancestors of the *et cetera et cetera et cetera et cetera et cetera et cetera et cetera et cetera* of the author, of the narrator, of this story, *Lost in the Funhouse*. In alleyways, ditches, canopy beds, pinewoods, bridal suites, ship's cabins, coach-and-fours, coaches-and-four, sultry toolsheds; on the cold sand under boardwalks, littered with *El Producto* cigar butts, treasured with Lucky Strike cigarette stubs, Coca-Cola caps, gritty turds, cardboard lollipop sticks, matchbook covers warning that A Slip of the Lip Can Sink a Ship. The shluppish whisper, continuous as seawash round the globe, tidelike falls and rises with the circuit of dawn and dusk.

Magda's teeth. She *was* left-handed. Perspiration. They've gone all the way, through, Magda and Peter, they've been waiting for hours with Mother and Uncle Karl while Father searches for his lost son; they draw french-fried potatoes from a paper cup and shake their heads. They've named the children they'll one day have and bring to Ocean City on holidays. Can spermatozoa properly be thought of as male animalcules when there are no female spermatozoa? They grope through hot, dark windings, past Love's Tunnel's fearsome obstacles. Some perhaps lose their way.

Peter suggested then and there that they do the funhouse; he had been through it before, so had Magda, Ambrose hadn't and suggested, his voice cracking on account of Fat May's laughter, that they swim first. All were chuckling, couldn't help it; Ambrose's father, Ambrose's and Peter's father came up grinning like a lunatic with two boxes of syrup-coated popcorn, one for Mother, one for Magda; the men were to help themselves. Ambrose walked on Magda's right; being by nature left-handed, she carried the box in her right hand. Up front the situation was reversed.

"What are you limping for?" Magda inquired of Ambrose. He supposed in a husky tone that his foot had gone to sleep in the car. Her teeth flashed. "Pins and needles?" It was the honeysuckle on the lattice of the former privy that drew the bees. Imagine being stung there. How long is this going to take?

The adults decided to forgo the pool; but Uncle Karl insisted they change into swimsuits and do the beach. "He wants to watch the pretty girls," Peter teased, and ducked behind Magda from Uncle Karl's pretended wrath. "You've got all the pretty girls you need right here," Magda declared, and Mother said: "Now that's the gospel truth." Magda scolded Peter, who reached over her shoulder to sneak some popcorn. "Your brother and father aren't getting any." Uncle Karl wondered if they were going to have fireworks that night, what with the shortages. It wasn't the shortages, Mr. M⸺ replied; Ocean City had fireworks from pre-war. But it was too risky on account of the enemy submarines, some people thought.

"Don't seem like Fourth of July without fireworks," said Uncle Karl. The inverted tag in dialogue writing is still considered permissible with proper names or epithets, but sounds old-fashioned with personal pronouns. "We'll have 'em again soon enough," predicted the boys' father. Their mother declared she could do without fireworks: they reminded her too much of the real thing. Their father said all the more reason to shoot off a few now and again. Uncle Karl asked *rhetorically* who needed reminding, just look at people's hair and skin:

"The oil, yes," said Mrs. M⸺.

Ambrose had a pain in his stomach and so didn't swim but enjoyed watching the others. He and his father burned red easily. Magda's figure was exceedingly well developed for her age.

She too declined to swim, and got mad, and became angry when Peter attempted to drag her into the pool. She always swam, he insisted; what did she mean not swim? Why did a person come to Ocean City?

"Maybe I want to lay here with Ambrose," Magda teased. Nobody likes a pedant.

"Aha," said Mother. Peter grabbed Magda by one ankle and ordered Ambrose to grab the other. She squealed and rolled over on the beach blanket. Ambrose pretended to help hold her back. Her tan was darker than even Mother's and Peter's. "Help out, Uncle Karl!" Peter cried. Uncle Karl went to seize the other ankle. Inside the top of her swimsuit, however, you could see the line where the sunburn ended and, when she hunched her shoulders and squealed again, one nipple's auburn edge. Mother made them behave themselves. "*You* should certainly know," she said to Uncle Karl. Archly. "That when a lady says she doesn't feel like swimming, a gentleman doesn't ask questions." Uncle Karl said excuse *him*; Mother winked at Magda; Ambrose blushed; stupid Peter kept saying "Phooey on *feel like!*' and tugging at Magda's ankle; then even he got the point, and cannonballed with a holler into the pool.

"I swear," Magda said, in mock *in feigned* exasperation.

The diving would make a suitable literary symbol. To go off the high board you had to wait in a line along the poolside and up the ladder. Fellows tickled girls and goosed one another and shouted to the ones at the top to hurry up, or razzed them for bellyfloppers. Once on the springboard some took a great while posing or clowning or deciding on a dive or getting up their nerve; others ran right off. Especially among the younger fellows the idea was to strike the funniest pose or do the craziest stunt as you fell, a thing that got harder to do as you kept on and kept on. But whether you hollered *Geronimo!* or *Sieg heil!*, held your nose or "rode a bicycle," pretended to be shot or did a perfect jacknife or changed your mind halfway down and ended up with nothing, it was over in two seconds, after all that wait. Spring, pose, splash. Spring, neat-o, splash. Spring, aw fooey, splash.

The grown-ups had gone on; Ambrose wanted to converse with Magda; she was remarkably well developed for her age; it was said that that came from rubbing with a turkish towel, and there were other theories. Ambrose could think of nothing to say except how good a diver Peter was, who was showing off for her benefit. You could pretty well tell by looking at their bathing suits and arm muscles how far along the different fellows were. Ambrose was glad he hadn't gone in swimming, the cold water shrank you up so. Magda pretended to be uninterested in the diving; she probably weighed as much as he did. If you knew your way around in the funhouse like your own bedroom, you could wait until a girl came along and then slip away without ever getting caught, even if her boyfriend was right with her. She'd think *he* did it! It would be better to be the boyfriend, and act outraged, and tear the funhouse apart.

Not act; *be*.

"He's a master diver," Ambrose said. In feigned admiration. "You really have to slave away at it to get that good." What would it matter anyhow if he asked her right out whether she remembered, even teased her with it as Peter would have?

There's no point in going farther; this isn't getting anybody anywhere; they haven't even come to the funhouse yet. Ambrose is off the track, in some new or old part of the place that's not supposed to be used; he strayed into it by some one-in-a-million chance, like the time the roller-coaster car left the tracks in the nineteen-teens against all the laws of physics and sailed over the boardwalk in the dark. And they can't locate him because they don't know where to look. Even the designer and operator have forgotten this other part, that winds around on itself like a whelk shell. That winds around the right part like the snakes on Mercury's caduceus. Some people, perhaps, don't "hit their stride" until their twenties, when the growing-up business is over and women appreciate other things besides wisecracks and teasing and strutting. Peter didn't have one-tenth the imagination *he* had, not one-tenth. Peter did this naming-their-children thing as a joke, making up names like Aloysius and Murgatroyd, but Ambrose knew *exactly* how it would feel to be married and have children of your own, and be a loving husband and father, and go comfortably to work in the mornings and to bed with your wife at night, and wake up with her there. With a breeze coming through the sash and birds and mockingbirds singing in the Chinese-cigar trees. His eyes watered, there aren't enough ways to say that. He would be quite famous in his line of work. Whether Magda was his wife or not, one evening when he was wise-lined and gray at the temples he'd smile gravely, at a fashionable dinner party, and remind her of his youthful passion. The time they went with his family to Ocean City; the *erotic fantasies* he used to have about her. How long ago it seemed, and childish! Yet tender, too, *n'est-ce pas?* Would she have imagined that the world-famous whatever remembered how many strings were on the lyre on the bench beside the girl on the label of the cigar box he'd stared at in the toolshed at age ten while she, age eleven. Even then he had felt *wise beyond his years*; he'd stroked her hair and said in his deepest voice and correctest English, as to a dear child: "I shall never forget this moment."

But though he had breathed heavily, groaned as if ecstatic, what he'd really felt throughout was an odd detachment, as though someone else were Master. Strive as he might to be transported, he heard his mind take notes upon the scene: *This is what they call* passion. *I am experiencing it.* Many of the digger machines were out of order in the penny arcades and could not be repaired or replaced for the duration. Moreover the prizes, made now in USA, were less interesting than formerly, pasteboard items for the most part, and some of the machines wouldn't work on white pennies. The gypsy fortune-teller machine might have provided a foreshadowing of the climax of this story if Ambrose had operated it. It was even dilapidateder than most: the silver coating was worn off the brown metal handles, the glass windows around the dummy were cracked and taped, her kerchiefs and silks long-faded. If a man lived by himself, he could take a department-store mannequin with flexible joints and modify her in certain ways. *However*: by the time he was that old he'd have a real woman. There was a machine that stamped your name around a white-metal coin with a star in the middle: *A___*. His son would be the second, and when the lad reached thirteen or so he would put a strong arm around his shoulder and tell him calmly: "It is perfectly normal. We have all been through it. It will not last forever." Nobody knew how to be what they were right. He'd smoke a pipe, teach his son how to fish and softcrab, assure him he needn't worry about himself. Magda would certainly give, Magda would certainly yield a great deal of milk, although guilty of occasional solecisms. It don't taste so bad. Suppose the lights came on now!

The day wore on. You think you're yourself, but there are other persons in you. Ambrose gets hard when Ambrose doesn't want to, *and obversely.* Ambrose watches them disagree; Ambrose watches him watch. In the funhouse mirror-room you can't see yourself go on forever, because no matter how you stand, your head gets in the way. Even if you had a glass periscope, the image of your eye would cover up the thing you really wanted to see. The police will come; there'll be a story in the papers. That must be where it happened. Unless he can find a surprise exit, an unofficial backdoor or escape hatch opening on an alley, say, and then stroll up to the family in front of the funhouse and ask where everbody's been; he's been out of the place for ages. That's just where it happened, in that last lighted room: Peter and Magda found the right exit; he found one that you weren't supposed to find and strayed off into the works somewhere. In a perfect funhouse you'd be able to go only one way, like the divers off the highboard; getting lost would be impossible; the doors and halls would work like minnow traps or the valves in veins.

On account of German U-boats, Ocean City was "browned out": streetlights were shaded on the seaward side; shop-windows and boardwalk amusement places were kept dim, not to silhouette tankers and Liberty-ships for torpedoing. In a short story about Ocean City,

Maryland, during World War II, the author could make use of the image of sailors on leave in the penny arcades and shooting galleries, sighting through the crosshairs of toy machine guns at swastika'd subs, while out in the black Atlantic a U-boat skipper squints through his periscope at real ships outlined by the glow of penny arcades. After dinner the family strolled back to the amusement end of the boardwalk. The boys' father had burnt red as always and was masked with Noxzema, a minstrel in reverse. The grown-ups stood at the end of the boardwalk where the Hurricane of '33 had cut an inlet from the ocean to Assawoman Bay.

"Pronounced with a long *o*," Uncle Karl reminded Magda with a wink. His shirt sleeves were rolled up; Mother punched his brown biceps with the arrowed heart on it and said his mind was naughty. Fat May's laugh came suddenly from the funhouse, as if she'd just got the joke; the family laughed too at the coincidence. Ambrose went under the boardwalk to search for out-of-town matchbook covers with the aid of his pocket flashlight; he looked out from the edge of the North American continent and wondered how far their laughter carried over the water. Spies in rubber rafts; survivors in lifeboats. If the joke had been beyond his understanding, he could have said: "*The laughter was over his head.*" And let the reader see the serious wordplay on second reading.

He turned the flashlight on and then off at once even before the woman whooped. He sprang away, heart athud, dropping the light. What had the man grunted? Perspiration drenched and chilled him by the time he scrambled up to the family. "See anything?" his father asked. His voice wouldn't come; he shrugged and violently brushed sand from his pants legs.

"Let's ride the old flying horses!" Magda cried. I'll never be an author. It's been forever already, everybody's gone home, Ocean City's deserted, the ghost-crabs are tickling across the beach and down the littered cold streets. And the empty halls of clapboard hotels and abandoned funhouses. A tidal wave; an enemy air raid; a monster-crab swelling like an island from the sea. *The inhabitants fled in terror.* Magda clung to his trouser leg; he alone knew the maze's secret. "He gave his life that we might live," said Uncle Karl with a scowl of pain, as he. The fellow's hands had been tattooed; the woman's legs, the woman's fat white legs had. *An astonishing coincidence.* He yearned to tell Peter. He wanted to throw up for excitement. They hadn't even chased him. He wished he were dead.

One possible ending would be to have Ambrose come across another lost person in the dark. They'd match their wits together against the funhouse, struggle like Ulysses past obstacle after obstacle, help and encourage each other. Or a girl. By the time they found the exit they'd be closest friends, sweethearts if it were a girl; they'd know each other's inmost souls, be bound together *by the cement of shared adventure*; then they'd emerge into the light and it would turn out that his friend was a Negro. A blind girl. President Roosevelt's son. Ambrose's former archenemy.

Shortly after the mirror room he'd groped along a musty corridor, his heart already misgiving him at the absence of phosphorescent arrows and other signs. He'd found a crack of light — not a door, it turned out, but a seam between the plyboard wall panels — and squinting up to it, espied a small old man, *in appearance not unlike* the photographs at home of Ambrose's late grandfather, nodding upon a stool beneath a bare, speckled bulb. A crude panel of toggle- and knife-switches hung beside the open fuse box near his head; elsewhere in the little room were wooden levers and ropes belayed to boat cleats. At the time, Ambrose wasn't lost enough to rap or call; later he couldn't find that crack. Now it seemed to him that he'd possibly dozed off for a few minutes somewhere along the way; certainly he was exhausted from the afternoon's sunshine and the evening's problems; he couldn't be sure he hadn't dreamed part or all of the sight. Had an old black wall fan droned like bees and shimmied two flypaper streamers? Had the funhouse operator — gentle, somewhat sad and tired-appearing, in expression not unlike the photographs at home of Ambrose's late Uncle Konrad — murmured in his sleep? Is there really such a person as Ambrose, or is he a figment of the author's imagination? Was it Assawoman Bay or Sinepuxent? Are there other errors of fact in this fiction? Was there another sound besides the little slap slap of thigh on ham, like water sucking at the chine-boards of a skiff?

When you're lost, the smartest thing to do is stay put till you're found, hollering if necessary. But to holler guarantees humiliation as well as rescue; keeping silent permits some saving of face — you can act surprised at the fuss when your rescuers find you and swear you weren't lost, if they do. What's more you might find your own way yet, *however belatedly.*

"Don't tell me your foot's still asleep!" Magda exclaimed as the three young people walked from the inlet to the area set aside for ferris wheels, carrousels, and other carnival rides, they having decided in favor of the vast and ancient merry-go-round instead of the funhouse. What a sentence, everything was wrong from the outset. People don't know what to make of him, he doesn't know what to make of himself, he's only thirteen, *athletically and socially inept,* not astonishingly bright, but there are antennae; he has ... some sort of receivers in his head; things speak to him, he understands more than he should, the world winks at him through its objects, grabs grinning at his coat. Everybody else is in on some secret he doesn't know; they've forgotten to tell him. Through simple *procrastination* his mother put off his baptism until this year. Everyone else had it done as a baby; he'd assumed the same of himself, as had his mother, so she claimed, until it was time for him to join Grace Methodist-Protestant and the oversight came out. He was mortified, but pitched sleepless through his private catechizing, intimidated by the ancient mysteries, a thirteen year old would never say that, resolved to experience conversion like St. Augustine. When the water touched his brow and Adam's sin left him, he contrived by a strain like defecation to bring tears into his eyes — but felt nothing. There was some simple, radical difference about him; he hoped it was genius, feared it was madness, devoted himself to amiability and inconspicuousness. Alone on the seawall near his house he was seized by the terrifying transports he'd thought to find in toolshed, in Communion-cup. The grass was alive! The town, the river, himself, were not imaginary; time roared in his ears like wind; the world was *going on!* This part ought to be dramatized. The Irish author James Joyce once wrote. Ambrose M— is going to scream.

There is no *texture of rendered sensory detail,* for one thing. The faded distorting mirrors beside Fat May; the impossibility of choosing a mount when one had but a single ride on the great carrousel; the *vertigo attendant on his recognition* that Ocean City was worn out, the place of fathers and grandfathers, straw-boatered men and parasoled ladies survived by their amusements. Money spent, the three paused at Peter's insistence beside Fat May to watch the girls get their skirts blown up. The object was to tease Magda, who said: "I swear, Peter M___, you've got a one-track mind! Amby and me aren't *interested* in such things." In the tumbling-barrel, too, just inside the Devil's-mouth entrance to the funhouse, the girls were upended and their boyfriends and others could see up their dresses if they cared to. Which was the whole point, Ambrose realized. Of the entire funhouse! If you looked around, you noticed that almost all the people on the boardwalk were paired off into couples except the small children; in a way, that was the whole point of Ocean City! If you had X-ray eyes and could see everything going on at that instant under the boardwalk and in all the hotel rooms and cars and alleyways, you'd realize that all that normally *showed*, like restaurants and dance halls and clothing and test-your-strength machines, was merely preparation and intermission. Fat May screamed.

Because he watched the goings-on from the corner of his eye, it was Ambrose who spied the half-dollar on the boardwalk near the tumbling-barrel. Losers weepers. The first time he'd heard some people moving through a corridor not far away, just after he'd lost sight of the crack of light, he'd decided not to call to them, for fear they'd guess he was scared and poke fun; it sounded like roughnecks; he'd hoped they'd come by and he could follow in the dark without their knowing. Another time he'd heard just one person, unless he imagined it, bumping along as if on the other side of the plywood; perhaps Peter coming back for him, or Father, or Magda lost too. Or the owner and operator of the funhouse. He'd called out once, as though merrily: "Anybody know where the heck we are?" But the query was too stiff, his voice cracked, when the sounds stopped he was terrified: maybe it was a queer who waited for fellows to get lost, or a longhaired filthy monster that lived in some cranny of the funhouse. He stood rigid for hours it seemed like, scarcely respiring. His future was shockingly clear, in outline. He tried holding his breath to the point of unconsciousness. There ought to be a button you could push to end your life absolutely without pain; disappear in a flick, like turning out a light. He would push it instantly! He despised Uncle Karl. But he despised his father too, for not being what he was supposed to be. Perhaps his father hated *his* father, and so on, and his son would hate him, and so on. Instantly!

Naturally he didn't have nerve enough to ask Magda to go through

the funhouse with him. With incredible nerve and to everyone's surprise he invited Magda, quietly and politely, to go through the funhouse with him. "I warn you, I've never been through it before," he
added, *laughing easily*; "but I reckon we can manage somehow. The important thing to remember, after all, is that it's meant to be a *fun*house;
that is, a place of amusement. If people really got lost or injured or too
badly frightened in it, the owner'd go out of business. There'd even be
lawsuits. No character in a work of fiction can make a speech this long
without interruption or acknowledgment from the other characters."

Mother teased Uncle Karl: "Three's a crowd, I always heard." But
actually Ambrose was relieved that Peter now had a quarter too. Nothing was what it looked like. Every instant, under the surface of the
Atlantic Ocean, millions of living animals devoured one another. Pilots
were falling in flames over Europe; women were being forcibly raped
in the South Pacific. His father should have taken him aside and said:
"There is a simple secret to getting through the funhouse, as simple as
being first to see the Towers. Here it is. Peter does not know it; neither
does your Uncle Karl. You and I are different. Not surprisingly, you've
often wished you weren't. Don't think I haven't noticed how unhappy
your childhood has been! But you'll understand, when I tell you, why
it had to be kept secret until now. And you won't regret not being like
your brother and your uncle. *On the contrary*!" If you knew all the
stories behind all the people on the boardwalk, you'd see that *nothing*
was what it looked like. Husbands and wives often hated each other;
parents didn't necessarily love their children; *et cetera*. A child took
things for granted because he had nothing to compare his life to and
everybody acted as if things were as they should be. Therefore each
saw himself as the hero of the story, when the truth might turn out to
be that he's the villain, or the coward. And there wasn't one thing you
could do about it!

Hunchbacks, fat ladies, fools — that no one chose what he was was
unbearable. In the movies he'd meet a beautiful young girl in the funhouse; they'd have hairs-breadth escapes from real dangers; he'd do
and say the right things; she also; in the end they'd be lovers; their
dialogue lines would match up; he'd be perfectly at ease; she'd not only
like him well enough, she'd think he was *marvelous*; she'd lie awake
thinking about *him*, instead of vice versa — the way his face looked

in different light and how he stood and exactly what he'd said — and yet that would be only one small episode in his wonderful life, among many many others. Not a *turning point* at all. What had happened in the toolshed was nothing. He hated, he loathed his parents! One reason for not writing a lost-in-the-funhouse story is that either everybody's felt what Ambrose feels, in which case it goes without saying, or else no normal person feels such things, in which case Ambrose is a freak. "Is anything more tiresome, in fiction, than the problems of sensitive adolescents?" And it's all too long and rambling, as if the author. For all a person knows the first time through, the end could be just around any corner; perhaps, *not impossibly* it's been within reach any number of times. On the other hand he may be scarcely past the start, with everything yet to get through, an intolerable idea.

Fill in: His father's raised eyebrows when he announced his decision to do the funhouse with Magda. Ambrose understands now, but didn't then, that his father was wondering whether he knew what the funhouse was *for* — specially since he didn't object, as he should have, when Peter decided to come along too. The ticket-woman, witchlike, mortifying him when inadvertently he gave her his name-coin instead of the half-dollar, then unkindly calling Magda's attention to the birthmark on his temple: "Watch our for him, girlie, he's a marked man!" She wasn't even cruel, he understood, only vulgar and insensitive. Somewhere in the world there was a young woman with such splendid understanding that she'd see him entire, like a poem or story, and find his words so valuable after all that when he confessed his apprehensions she would explain why they were in fact the very things that made him precious to her ... and to Western Civilization! There was no such girl, the simple truth being. Violent yawns as they approached the mouth. Whispered advice from an old-timer on a bench near the barrel: "Go crabwise and ye'll get an eyeful without upsetting!" Composure vanished at the first pitch: Peter hollered joyously, Magda tumbled, shrieked, clutched her skirt; Ambrose scrambled crabwise, tight-lipped with terror, was soon out, watched his dropped name-coin slide among the couples. Shamefaced he saw that to get through expeditiously was not the point; Peter feigned assistance in order to trip Magda up, shouted "I see Christmas!" when her legs went flying. The old man, his latest betrayer, cackled approval. A dim hall then of black-thread cobwebs and recorded gibber: he took Magda's elbow to steady her against revolving discs set in the slanted floor to throw your feet out from under, and explained to her in a calm, deep voice his theory that each phase of the funhouse was triggered either automatically, by a series of photo-electric devices, or else manually by operators stationed at peepholes. But he lost his voice thrice as the discs unbalanced him; Magda was anyhow squealing; but at one point she clutched him about the waist to keep from falling, and her right cheek pressed for a moment against his belt-buckle. Heroically he drew her up, it was his chance to clutch her close as if for support and say: "I love you." He even put an arm lightly about the small of her back before a sailor-and-girl pitched into them from behind, sorely treading his left big toe and knocking Magda asprawl with them. The sailor's girl was a string-haired hussy with a loud laugh and light blue drawers; Ambrose realized that he wouldn't have said "I love you" anyhow, and was smitten with self-contempt. How much better it would be to be that common sailor! A wiry little Seaman 3rd, the fellow squeezed a girl to each side and stumbled hila-rious into the mirror room, closer to Magda in thirty seconds than Ambrose had got in thirteen years. She giggled at something the fellow said to Peter; she drew her hair from her eyes with a movement so womanly it struck Ambrose's heart; Peter's smacking her backside then seemed particularly coarse. But Magda made a pleased indignant face and cried, "All right for *you*, mister!" and pursued Peter into the maze without a backward glance. The sailor followed after, leisurely, drawing his girl against his hip; Ambrose understood not only that they were all so relieved to be rid of his burdensome company that they didn't even notice his absence, but that he himself shared their relief. Step-ping from the treacherous passage at last into the mirror-maze, he saw once again, more clearly than ever, how readily he deceived himself into supposing he was a person. He even foresaw, wincing at his dread-ful self-knowledge, that he would repeat the deception, at ever-rarer intervals, all his wretched life, so fearful were the alternatives. Fame, madness, suicide; perhaps all three. It's not believable that so young a boy could articulate that reflection, and in fiction the merely true must always yield to the plausible. Moreover, the symbolism is in places heavy-footed. Yet Ambrose M—— understood, as few adults do, that the famous loneliness of the great was no popular myth but a general truth — furthermore, that it was as much cause as effect.

All the preceding except the last few sentences is exposition that should've been done earlier or interspersed with the present action instead of lumped together. No reader would put up with so much with such *prolixity*. It's interesting that Ambrose's father, though presumably an intelligent man (as indicated by his role as grade-school principal), neither encouraged nor discouraged his sons at all in any way — as if he either didn't care about them or cared all right but didn't know how to act. If this fact should contribute to one of them's becoming a celebrated but wretchedly unhappy scientist, was it a good thing or not? He too might someday face the question; it would be useful to know whether it had tortured his father for years, for example, or never once crossed his mind.

In the maze two important things happened. First, our hero found a name-coin someone else had lost or discarded: *AMBROSE*, suggestive of the famous lightship and of his late grandfather's favorite dessert, which his mother used to prepare on special occasions out of coconut, oranges, grape and what else. Second, as he wondered at the endless replication of his image in the mirrors, second, as he *lost himself in the reflection* that the necessity for an observer makes perfect observation impossible, better make him eighteen at least, yet that would render other things unlikely, he heard Peter and Magda chuckling somewhere together in the maze. "Here!" "No, here!" they shouted to each other; Peter said, "Where's Amby?" Magda murmured. "Amb?" Peter called. In a pleased, friendly voice. He didn't reply. The truth was, his brother was a *happy-go-lucky youngster* who'd've been better off with a regular brother of his own, but who seldom complained of his lot and was generally cordial. Ambrose's throat ached; there aren't enough different ways to say that. He stood quietly while the two young people giggled and thumped through the glittering maze, hurrah'd their discovery of its exit, cried out in joyful alarm at what next beset them. Then he set his mouth and followed after, as he supposed, took a wrong turn, strayed into the pass *wherein he lingers yet*.

The action of conventional dramatic narrative may be represented by a diagram called Freitag's Triangle:

or more accurately by a variant of that diagram:

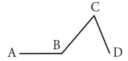

in which *AB* represents the exposition, *B* the introduction of conflict, *BC* the "rising action," complication, or development of the conflict, C the climax, or turn of the action, *CD* the dénouement, or resolution of the conflict. While there is no reason to regard this pattern as an absolute necessity, like many other conventions it became conventional because great numbers of people over many years learned by trial and error that it was effective; one ought not to forsake it, therefore, unless one wishes to forsake as well the effect of drama or has clear cause to feel that deliberate violation of the "normal" pattern can better can better effect that effect. This can't go on much longer; it can go on forever. He died telling stories to himself in the dark; years later, when that vast unsuspected area of the funhouse came to light, the first expedition found his skeleton in one of its labyrinthine corridors and mistook it for part of the entertainment. He died of starvation telling himself stories in the dark; but unbeknownst unbeknownst to him, an assistant operator of the funhouse, happening to overhear him, crouched just behind the plyboard partition and wrote down his every word. The operator's daughter, an exquisite young woman with a figure unusually well developed for her age, crouched just behind the partition and transcribed his every word. Though she had never laid eyes on him, she recognized that here was one of Western Culture's truly great imaginations, the eloquence of whose suffering would be an inspiration to unnumbered. And her heart was torn between her love for the misfortunate young man (yes, she loved him, though she had never laid though she knew him only — but how well! — through his words, and the deep, calm voice in which he spoke them) between her love *et cetera* and her womanly intuition that only in suffering and isolation could he give voice *et cetera*. Lone dark dying. Quietly she kissed the rough plyboard, and a tear fell upon the page. Where she had written in shorthand *Where she had written in shorthand* Where she had written in shorthand *Where she et cetera*. A long time ago we should have passed the apex of Freitag's Triangle and made brief work of the *dénouement*; the plot doesn't rise by meaningful steps but winds upon itself, digresses, retreats, hesitates, sighs, collapses, expires. The climax of the story must be its protagonist's discovery of a way to get through the funhouse. But he has found none, may have ceased to search.

What relevance does the war have to the story? Should there be fireworks outside or not?

Ambrose wandered, languished, dozed. Now and then he fell into his habit of rehearsing to himself the unadventurous story of his life, narrated from the third-person point of view, from his earliest memory parenthesis of maple leaves stirring in the summer breath of tidewater Maryland end of parenthesis to the present moment. Its principal events, on this telling, would appear to have been *A*, *B*, *C*, and *D*.

He imagined himself years hence, successful, married, at ease in the world, the trials of his adolescence far behind him. He has come to the seashore with his family for the holiday: how Ocean City has changed! But at one seldom at one ill-frequented end of the boardwalk a few derelict amusements survive from times gone by: the great carrousel from the turn of the century, with its monstrous griffins and mechanical concert band; the roller coaster rumored since 1916 to have been condemned; the mechanical shooting gallery in which only the image of our enemies changed. His own son laughs with Fat May and wants to know what a funhouse is; Ambrose hugs the sturdy lad close and smiles around his pipestem at his wife.

The family's going home. Mother sits between Father and Uncle Karl, who teases him good-naturedly who chuckles over the fact that the comrade with whom he'd fought his way shoulder to shoulder through the funhouse had turned out to be a blind Negro girl — to their mutual discomfort, as they'd opened their souls. But such are the walls of custom, which even. Whose arm is where? How must it feel. He dreams of a funhouse vaster by far than any yet constructed; but by then they may be out of fashion, like steamboats and excursion trains. Already quaint and seedy: the draperied ladies on the frieze of the carrousel are his father's father's mooncheeked dreams; if he thinks of it more he will vomit his apple-on-a-stick.

He wonders: will he become a regular person? Something has gone wrong; his vaccination didn't take; at the Boy-Scout initiation campfire he only pretended to be deeply moved, as he pretends to this hour that it is not so bad after all in the funhouse, and that he has a little limp. How long will it last? He envisions a truly astonishing funhouse, incredibly complex yet utterly controlled from a great central switchboard like the console of a pipe organ. Nobody had enough imagination. He could design such a place himself, wiring and all, and he's only thirteen years old. He would be its operator: panel lights would show what was up in every cranny of its cunning of its multifarious vastness; a switch-flick would ease this fellow's way, complicate that's, to balance things out; if anyone seemed lost or frightened, all the operator had to do was.

He wishes he had never entered the funhouse. But he has. Then he wishes he were dead. But he's not. Therefore he will construct funhouses for others and be their secret operator — though he would rather be among the lovers for whom funhouses are designed.

Echo

One does well to speak in the third person, the seer advises in the manner of Theban Tiresias. A cure for self-absorption is saturation: telling the story over as though it were another's until like a much-repeated word it loses sense. There's a cathartic Tiresias himself employs in the interest of objectivity and to rid himself of others' histories — Oedipus's, Echo's — which distract him fore and aft by reason of his entire knowledge.

Narcissus replies that the prescription is unpalatable, but he's too weary of himself not to attempt it. Where to begin. The prophet's cave seems a likely place, which he stumbles into one forenoon in flight from his admirers. What started as a staghunt has turned into yet another love-chase, led this time by a persisting nymph soon joined by her quarry's companions. It wants all the Narcissan craft, resentfully perfected, yet again to mislead the lot.

An imperfectly dark passage. Outside his ardentest suitor calls, pederast Ameinius, spurned. The nymph soft-seconds his bugger woo. Chaste Narcissus shivers, draws farther in, loses bearings, daresn't call, weeps. The life-long bother! Seized he gives shriek, is released. How come? What next? Hadn't he as well have his blossom plucked? Who says so?

Tiresias the prophet. What's he doing here? Conversing with Narcissus. How does he know — because he knows everything.

Why isn't he in Thebes? For the reason that, as during a prior and a posterior extravagance of his, Thebes is enjoying an interregnum, hard on prophets. First there was the sphinx, whose elementary riddle was none of his affair; he withdrew to the Thespian cave, there acted as adviser to the blue nymph Leirope, Narcissus's mother. The current pass is sorer: Oedipus's tragedy, too awful to rehearse. The third and last, couple hundred months hence, darker yet from Tiresias's point of view.

Narcissus reflects that after years of elusion he's at the seer's mercy, rapewise. He wonders which is more ironic, seeking refuge for innocence where it mightn't be preserved or falling into the first hands he's ever seemed to leave cold. Thus rare Tiresiases.

Apostrophe.

Some are comelier than most, a few handsome; it's Narcissus's fate, through fault nor merit of his own, to be beautiful beyond enduring. The first catch eye, the second turn head; Narcissus like a fleshed theophany smites the whole sense. A philosopher argues that perceptible beauty is ipso facto less desirable than im — at glimpse of Narcissus he interrupts, forswears himself. A man doubtless of his virility admits what he'd sooner not: in one extraordinary case he's felt the catamitic itch. A woman indifferent thitherto to the world's including handsomer men than hers finds Narcissus so so she's cross with her lover. Thus the mature, who see to it that sight of the wonder doesn't linger or recur and so in most cases come to terms with memory: the philosophers resume their position, men manliness, women men — all chastened, one supposes, by an exception so exceptional it ruins their rules. Among the less disciplined and wise, astonishment yields to simple lust. Cynical, powerful, wanton, uncommitted, passionate, impulsive set out to have their will. Hosts of ordinary, too, strangers to emotion of extraordinary kind or force, are seized as by conversion. Snares are laid, gifts tendered, pitfalls dug. His very wet nurse, Leirope says, took liberties with her suckling, tutor tutee. Leirope herself — how was it? Undone by a meandering river-god she seeks the caved seer first. What counsel does he offer? Tiresias won't repeat it; enough to say it's of a kind with what he wishes he'd given Oedipus. The varieties of general good advice are few. Leirope suggests herself to Narcissus when he reaches young manhood and begs him to ignore her advice: take to the woods! Into the bimboed and bebuggered bush he flies, where ladies beckon every way and gentlemen crouch in ambuscado.

All this considered, one may wonder at Tiresias's immunity, unless indeed he's cat-and-mousing. Is he too ravished by his victim to recollect himself for rape? Floored for defloration? No no. Clairvoyance is anaphrodisiac. One recalls too: Tiresias has been without sex for a long time. What's more he's blind as a bat, otherwise he couldn't see so in the cave.

Is Narcissus piqued or relieved? Both know. He presently inquires how one in his position might best fend the world's importune. Why fend? Tiresias's story is to the point. And Echo's. Echo's? A nymph possessed so early and entirely by Pan that her subsequent affairs seem redundant. Afflicted with immortality she turns from life and learns to tell stories with such art that the Olympians implore her to repeat them. Others live for the lie of love; Echo lives for her lovely lies, loves for their livening. With her tongue-tried tales she amuses others and preserves her reason; but Zeus employs her, unawares, to beguile his wife while he makes free with the mountain-nymphs. Again again, begs the queen of heaven; another mount's climbed with each retelling. At fiction's end the facts are clear; Zeus unpunishable, Echo pays. Though her voice remains her own, she can't speak for herself thenceforth, only give back others' delight regardless of hers.

Has this to do with fair Narcissus, wise Tiresias? Whose story is it? It's a tale of shortcomings, lengthened to advantage. Echo never, as popularly held, repeats all, like gossip or mirror. She edits, heightens, mutes, turns others' words to her end. One recalls her encounter with Narcissus — no other has nymphed him caveward. A coincidence of opposites. One should, if it's worthwhile, repeat the tale.

I'll repeat the tale. Though in fact many are bewildered, Narcissus conceives himself alone and becomes the first person to speak.

I can't go on. Go on.

Is there anyone to hear here? Who are you?

You.

I?

Aye.

Then let me see me!

See?

A lass! Alas.

Et cetera et cetera. Overmuch presence appears to be the storyteller's problem: Tiresias's advice, in cases of excessive identity and coitus irrequitus, is to make of withdrawal a second nature. He sees the nymph efface herself until she becomes no more than her voice, still transfiguring senseless sound into plaints of love. Perhaps that's the end of her story, perhaps the narrative proper may resume. Not quite, not quite: though even sharp-sight Tiresias can't espy the unseeable, one may yet distinguish narrator from narrative, medium from message. One lesson remains to be learned; when Echo learns it none will be the wiser.

But Narcissus! What's become of contemptible, untemptable Narcissus, the drug so many have turned on on, and sung themselves on pretext of hymning him? Was Tiresias about to counsel him in obscurity? No. Except to declare that his true love awaits him in the spring at Donacon; discovering who he is will prove as fatal for Narcissus as it's proving for Oedipus. Queer advice! To see the truth is one thing, to speak it another.

Now where are we? That is to say, where are Tiresias and Narcissus. Somewhere near the Donaconan spring. Who's telling the story, and to whom? The teller's immaterial, Tiresias declares; the tale's the same, and for all one knows the speaker may be the only auditor. Considerable time has elapsed, it seems, since seer and seeker, prophet and lost, first met in the cave. But what's time when past and future are equally clear and dark? The gift of suiscience is a painful present: Narcissus thirsts for love; Tiresias sees the end of his second sight. Both speak to themselves. Thebes is falling; unknown to the northbound refugees, en route to found a new city, their seer will perish on the instant the Argives take the old. He it is now, thrashing through the woods near Thespiae, who calls to his lost companions and follows to exhaustion a mock response. Halloo halloo! Falling at length beside a chuckling spring he dreams or dies. The voice presently in his ears is that hallooer's; now it rehearses Narcissus's end, seen from the outset:

Why did Tiresias not tell Narcissus what he once told Leirope, that her son would lead a long and happy life if he never came to know himself? Because the message then had become its own medium. Needless to say he sees and saw Narcissus beat about the bush for love, oblivious to pursuers in the joy of his own pursuit. As for that nymph whose honey voice still recalls his calls, he scorns her, and hears his maledictions balmed to music. Like the masturbatory adolescent, sooner or later he finds himself. He beholds and salutes his pretty alter ego in the pool; in the pool his ego, altered, prettily salutes: Behold! In vain he reaches to embrace his contrary image; he recognizes what Tiresias couldn't warn him of. Has knowing himself turned him into a pansy? Not quite, not quite. He's resolved to do away with himself, his beloved likewise. Together now. Adored-in-vain, farewell!

Well. One supposes that's the end of the story. How is it this voice persists, whosoever it is? Needless to say, Tiresias knows. It doesn't sound nymphish; she must have lost hers. Echo says Tiresias is not to be trusted in this matter. A prophet blind or dead, a blossom, eyeless, a disengendered tale — none can tell teller from told. Narcissus would appear to be opposite from Echo: he perishes by denying all except himself; she persists by effacing herself absolutely. Yet they come to the same: it was never himself Narcissus craved, but his reflection, the Echo of his fancy; his death must be partial as his self-knowledge, the voice persists, persists.

Can it be believed? Tiresias has gone astray; a voice not impossibly his own has bewildered him. The story of Narcissus, Tiresias, Echo is being repeated. It's alleged that Narcissus has wearied of himself and yearns to love another; on Tiresias's advice he employs the third person to repeat his tale as the seer does, until it loses meaning. No use: his self objectified's the more enthralling, like his blooming image in the spring. In vain Tiresias's cautions that the nymph may be nothing altruistic, but the soul of guile and sleight-of-tongue. Who knows but what her love has changed to mock? What she gives back as another's speech may be entire misrepresentation; especially ought one to beware what she chooses to repeat concerning herself. No use, no use: Narcissus grows fond; she speaks his language; Tiresias reflects that after all if one aspires to concern one's fatal self with another, one had as well commence with the nearest and readiest. Perhaps he'll do the same: be beguiled with Narcissus out of knowledge of himself; listen silent as his voice goes on.

Thus we linger forever on the autognostic verge — not you and I, but Narcissus, Tiresias, Echo. Are they still in the Thespian cave? Have they come together in the spring? Is Narcissus addressing Tiresias, Tiresias Narcissus? Have both expired?

There's no future for prophets. Blind Oedipus will never see the place where three roads meet. Narcissus desired himself defunct before his own conception; he's been rooted forever by the beloved he'll never know. Dead Tiresias still stares wide-eyed at Wisdom's nude entire. Our story's finished before it starts.

Two Meditations

1. NIAGARA FALLS

She paused amid the kitchen to drink a glass of water; at that instant, losing a grip of fifty years, the next-room-ceiling-plaster crashed. Or he merely sat in an empty study, in March-day glare, listening to the universe rustle in his head, when suddenly the five-foot shelf let go. For ages the fault creeps secret through the rock; in a second, ledge and railings, tourists and turbines all thunder over Niagara. Which snow-flake triggers the avalanche? A house explodes; a star. In your spouse, so apparently resigned, murder twitches like a fetus. At some trifling new assessment, all the colonies rebel.

2. LAKE ERIE

The wisdom to recognize and halt follows the know-how to pollute past rescue. The treaty's signed, but the cancer ticks in your bones. Until I'd murdered my father and fornicated my mother I wasn't wise enough to see I was Oedipus. Too late now to keep the polar cap from melting. Venice subsides; South America explodes.

Let's stab out our eyes.

Too late: our resolve is sapped beyond the brooches.

Title

Beginning: in the middle, past the middle, nearer three-quarters done, waiting for the end. Consider how dreadful so far: passionlessness, abstraction, pro, dis. And it will get worse. Can we possibly continue?

Plot and theme: notions vitiated by this hour of the world but as yet not successfully succeeded. Conflict, complication, no climax. The worst is to come. Everything leads to nothing: future tense; past tense; present tense. Perfect. The final question is, Can nothing be made meaningful? Isn't that the final question? If not, the end is at hand. Literally, as it were. Can't stand any more of this.

I think she comes. The story of our life. This is the final test. Try to fill the blank. Only hope is to fill the blank. Efface what can't be faced or else fill the blank. With words or more words, otherwise I'll fill in the blank with this noun here in my prepositional object. Yes, she already said that. And I think. What now. Everything's been said already, over and over; I'm as sick of this as you are; there's nothing to say. Say nothing.

What's new? Nothing.

Conventional startling opener. Sorry if I'm interrupting the Progress of Literature, she said, in a tone that adjective clause suggesting good-humored irony but in fact defensively and imperfectly masking a taunt. The conflict is established though as yet unclear in detail. Standard conflict. Let's skip particulars. What do you want from me?

What'll the story be this time? Same old story. Just thought I'd see if you were still around. Before. What? Quit right here. Too late. Can't we start over? What's past is past. On the contrary, what's forever past is eternally present. The future? Blank. All this is just fill in. Hang on.

Still around. In what sense? Among the gerundive. What is that supposed to mean? Did you think I meant to fill in the blank? Why should I? On the other hand, why not? What makes you think I wouldn't fill in the blank instead? Some conversation this is. Do you want to go on, or shall we end it right now? Suspense. I don't care for this either. It'll be over soon enough in any case. But it gets worse and worse. Whatever happens, the ending will be deadly. At least let's have just one real conversation. Dialogue or monologue? What has it been from the first? Don't ask me. What is there to say at this late date? Let me think; I'm trying to think. Same old story. Or. Or? Silence.

This isn't so bad. Silence. There are worse things. Name three. This, that, the other. Some choices. Who said there was a choice?

Let's try again. That's what I've been doing; I've been thinking while you've been blank. Story of Our Life. However, this may be the final complication. The ending may be violent. That's been said before. Who cares? Let the end be blank; anything's better than this.

It didn't used to be so bad. It used to be less difficult. Even enjoyable. For whom? Both of us. To do what? Complicate the conflict. I am weary of this. What, then? To complete this sentence, if I may bring up a sore subject. That never used to be a problem. Now it's impossible; we just can't manage it. You can't fill in the blank; I can't fill in the blank. Or won't. Is this what we're going to talk about, our obscene verbal problem? It'll be our last conversation. Why talk at all? Are you paying attention? I dare you to quit now! Never dare a desperate person. On with it, calmly, one sentence after another, like a recidivist. A what? A common noun. Or another common noun. Hold tight. Or a chronic forger, let's say; committed to the pen for life. Which is to say, death. The point, for pity's sake! Not yet. Forge on.

We're more than halfway through, as I remarked at the outset: youthful vigor, innocent exposition, positive rising action — all that is behind us. How sophisticated we are today. I'll ignore her, he vowed, and went on. In this dehuman, exhausted, ultimate adjective hour, when every humane value has become untenable, and not only love, decency, and beauty but even compassion and intelligibility are no more than one or two subjective complements to complete the sentence ...

This is a story? It's a story, he replied equably, or will be if the author can finish it. Without interruption I suppose you mean? she broke in. I can't finish anything; that is my final word. Yet it's these interruptions that make it a story. Escalate the conflict further. Please let me start over.

Once upon a time you were satisfied with incidental felicities and niceties of technique: the unexpected image, the refreshingly accurate word-choice, the memorable simile that yields deeper and subtler significances upon reflection, like a memorable simile. Somebody please stop me. Or arresting dialogue, so to speak. For example?

Why do you suppose it is, she asked, long participial phrase of the breathless variety characteristic of dialogue attributions in nineteenth-century fiction, that literate people such as we talk like characters in a story? Even supplying the dialogue tags, she added with wry disgust. Don't put words in her mouth. The same old story, an old-fashioned one at that. Even if I should fill in the blank with my idle pen? Nothing new about that to make a fact out of a figure. At least it's good for something. Every story is penned in red ink, to make a figure out of a fact. This whole idea is insane.

And might therefore be got away with.

No turning back now, we've gone too far. Everything's finished. Name eight. Story, novel, literature, art, humanism, humanity, the self itself. Wait: the story's not finished. And you and I, Howard? whispered Martha, her sarcasm belied by a hesitant alarm in her glance, flickering as it were despite herself to the blank instrument in his hand. Belied indeed; put that thing away! And what does flickering modify? A person who can't verb adverb ought at least to speak correctly.

A tense moment in the evolution of the story. Do you know, declared the narrator, one has no idea, especially nowadays, how close the end may be, nor will one necessarily be aware of it when it occurs. Who can say how near this universe has come to mere cessation? Or take two people, in a story of the sort it once was possible to tell. Love affairs, literary genres, third item in exemplary series, fourth — everything blossoms and decays, does it not, from the primitive and classical through the mannered and baroque to the abstract, stylized, dehumanized, unintelligible, blank. And you and I, Rosemary? Edward. Snapped! Patience. The narrator gathers that his audience no longer cherishes him. And conversely. But little does he know of the common noun concealed for months in her you name it, under her eyelet chemise. This is a slip. The point is the same. And she fetches it out nightly as I dream, I think. That's no slip. And she regards it and sighs, a quantum grimlier each night it may be. Is this supposed to be amusing? The world might end before this sentence, or merely someone's life. And / or someone else's. I speak metaphorically. Is the sentence ended? Very nearly. No telling how long a sentence will be until one reaches the stop It sounds as if somebody intends to fill in the blank. What *is* all this nonsense about?

It may not be nonsense. Anyhow it will presently be over. As the narrator was saying, things have been kaput for some time, and while we may be pardoned our great reluctance to acknowledge it, the fact is that the bloody century for example is nearing the three-quarter mark, and the characters in this little tale, for example, are similarly past their prime, as is the drama. About played out. Then God damn it let's ring the curtain. Wait wait. We're left with the following three possibilities, at least in theory. Horseshit. Hold onto yourself, it's too soon to fill in the blank. I hope this will be a short story.

Shorter than it seems. It seems endless. Be thankful it's not a novel. The novel is predicate adjective, as is the innocent anecdote of bygone days when life made a degree of sense and subject joined to complement by copula. No longer are these things the case, as you have doubtless remarked. There was I believe some mention of possibilities, three in number. The first is rejuvenation: having become an exhausted parody of itself, perhaps a form — Of what? Of anything — may rise neoprimitively from its own ashes. A tiresome prospect. The second, more appealing I'm sure but scarcely likely at this advanced date, is that moribund what-have-yous will be supplanted by vigorous new: the demise of the novel and short story, he went on to declare, needn't be the end of narrative art, nor need the dissolution of a used-up blank fill in the blank. The end of one road might be the beginning of another. Much good that'll do me. And you may not find the revolution as bloodless as you think, either. Shall we try it? Never dare a person who is fed up to the ears.

The final possibility is a temporary expedient, to be sure, the self-styled narrator of this so-called story went on to admit, ignoring the hostile impatience of his audience, but what is not, and every sentence completed is a step closer to the end. That is to say, every day gained is a day gone. Matter of viewpoint, I suppose. Go on. I am. Whether anyone's paying attention or not. The final possibility is to turn ultimacy, exhaustion, paralyzing self-consciousness and the adjective weight of accumulated history ... Go on. Go on. To turn ultimacy against itself to make something new and valid, the essence whereof would be the impossibility of making something new. What a nauseating notion. And pray how does it bear upon the analogy uppermost in everyone's mind? We've gotten this far, haven't we? Look how far we've come together. Can't we keep on to the end? I think not. Even another sentence is too many. Only if one believes the end to be a long way off; actually it might come at any moment; I'm surprised it hasn't before now. Nothing does when it's expected to.

Silence. There's a fourth possibility, I suppose. Silence. General anesthesia. Self-extinction. Silence.

Historicity and self-awareness, he asseverated, while ineluctable and even greatly to be prized, are always fatal to innocence and spontaneity. Perhaps adjective period Whether in a people, an art, a love affair, on a fourth term added not impossibly to make the third less than ultimate. In the name of suffering humanity cease this harangue. It's over. And the story? Is there a plot here? What's all this leading up to?

No climax. There's the story. Finished? Not quite. Story of our lives. The last word in fiction, in fact. I chose the first-person narrative viewpoint in order to reflect interest from the peculiarities of the technique (such as the normally unbearable self-consciousness, the abstraction, and the blank) to the nature and situation of the narrator and his companion, despite the obvious possibility that the narrator and his companion might be mistaken for the narrator and his companion. Occupational hazard. The technique is advanced, as you see, but the situation of the characters is conventionally dramatic. That being the case, may one of them, or one who may be taken for one of them, make a longish speech in the old-fashioned manner, charged with obsolete emotion? Of course.

I begin calmly, though my voice may rise as I go along. Sometimes it seems as if things could instantly be altogether different and more admirable. The times be damned, one still wants a man vigorous, confident, bold, resourceful, adjective, and adjective. One still wants a woman spirited, spacious of heart, loyal, gentle, adjective, adjective. That man and that woman are as possible as the ones in this miserable story, and a good deal realer. It's as if they live in some room of our house that we can't find the door to, though it's so close we can hear echoes of their voices. Experience has made them wise instead of bitter; knowledge has mellowed instead of souring them; in their forties and fifties, even in their sixties, they're gayer and stronger and more authentic than they were in their twenties; for the twenty-year-olds they have only affectionate sympathy. So? Why aren't the couple in this story that man and woman, so easy to imagine? God, but I am surfeited with clever irony! Ill of sickness! Parallel phrase to wrap up series! This last-resort idea, it's dead in the womb, excuse the figure. A false pregnancy, excuse the figure. God damn me though if that's entirely my fault. Acknowledge your complicity. As you see, I'm trying to do something about the present mess; hence this story. Adjective in the noun! Don't lose your composure. You tell me it's self-defeating to talk about it instead of just up and doing it; but to acknowledge what I'm doing while I'm doing it is exactly the point. Self-defeat implies a victor, and who do you suppose it is, if not blank? That's the only victory left. Right? Forward! Eyes open.

No. The only way to get out of a mirror-maze is to close your eyes and hold out your hands. And be carried away by a valiant metaphor, I suppose, like a simile.

There's only one direction to go in. Ugh. We must make something out of nothing. Impossible. Mystics do. Not only turn contradiction into paradox, but *employ* it, to go on living and working. Don't bet on it. I'm betting my cliché on it, yours too. What is that supposed to mean? On with the refutation; every denial is another breath, every word brings us closer to the end.

Very well: to write this allegedly ultimate story is a form of artistic fill in the blank, or an artistic form of same, if you like. I don't. What I mean is, same idea in other terms. The storyteller's alternatives, as far as I can see, are a series of last words, like an aging actress making one farewell appearance after another, or actual blank. And I mean literally fill in the blank. Is this a test? But the former is contemptible in itself, and the latter will certainly become so when the rest of the world shrugs its shoulders and goes on about its business. Just as people would do if adverbial clause of obvious analogical nature.

The fact is, the narrator has narrated himself into a corner, a state of affairs more tsk-tsk than boo-hoo, and because his position is absurd he calls the world absurd. That some writers lack lead in their pencils does not make writing obsolete. At this point they were both smiling despite themselves. At this point they were both flashing hatred despite themselves. Every woman has a blade concealed in the neighborhood of her garters. So disarm her, so to speak, don't geld yourself. At this point they were both despite themselves. Have we come to the point at last? Not quite. Where there's life there's hope.

There's no hope. This isn't working. But the alternative is to supply an alternative. That's no alternative. Unless I make it one. Just try; quit talking about it, quit talking, quit! Never dare a desperate man. Or woman. That's the one thing that can drive even the first part of a conventional metaphor to the second part of same. Talk, talk, talk. Yes yes, go on, I believe literature's not likely ever to manage abstraction successfully, like sculpture for example, is that a fact, what a time to bring up that subject, anticlimax, that's the point, do set forth the exquisite reason. Well, because wood and iron have a native appeal and first-order reality, whereas words are artificial to begin with, invented specifically to represent. Go on, please go on. I'm going. Don't you dare. Well, well, weld iron rods into abstract patterns, say, and you've still got real iron, but arrange words into abstract patterns and you've got nonsense. Nonsense is right. For example. On, God damn it; take linear plot, take resolution of conflict, take third direct object, all that business, they may very well be obsolete notions, indeed they are, no doubt untenable at this late date, no doubt at all, but in fact we still lead our lives by clock and calendar, for example, and though the seasons recur our mortal human time does not; we grow old and tired, we think of how things used to be or might have been and how they are now, and in fact, and in fact we get exasperated and desperate and out of expedients and out of words.

Go on. Impossible. I'm going, too late now, one more step and we're done, you and I. Suspense. The fact is, you're driving me to it, the fact is that people still lead lives, mean and bleak and brief as they are, briefer than you think, and people have characters and motives that we divine more or less inaccurately from their appearance, speech, behavior, and the rest, you aren't listening, go on then, what do you think I'm doing, people still fall in love, and out, yes, in and out, and out and in, and they please each other, and hurt each other, isn't that the truth, and they do these things in more or less conventionally dramatic fashion, unfashionable or not, go on, I'm going, and what goes on between them is still not only the most interesting but the most important thing in the bloody murderous world, pardon the adjectives. And that my dear is what writers have got to find ways to write about in this adjective adjective hour of the ditto ditto same noun as above, or their, that is to say our, accursed self-consciousness will lead them, that is to say us, to here it comes, say it straight out, I'm going to, say it in plain English for once, that's what I'm leading up to, me and my bloody anticlimactic noun, we're pushing each other to fill in the blank.

Goodbye. Is it over? Can't you read between the lines? One more step. Goodbye suspense goodbye.

Blank.

Oh God comma I abhor self-consciousness. I despise what we have come to; I loathe our loathesome loathing, our place our time our situation, our loathesome art, this ditto necessary story. The blank of our lives. It's about over. Let the dénouement be soon and unexpected, painless if possible, quick at least, above all soon. Now now! How in the world will it ever

Glossolalia

Still breathless from fending Phoebus, suddenly I see all — and all in vain. A horse excreting Greeks will devour my city; none will heed her Apollo loved, and endowed with clear sight, and cursed when she gainsaid him. My honor thus costlily purchased will be snatched from me by soldiers. I see Agamemnon, my enslaver, meeting death in Mycenae. No more.

Dear Procne: your wretched sister — she it is weaves this robe. Regard it well: it hides her painful tale in its pointless patterns. Tereus came and fetched her off; he conveyed her to Thrace ... but not to see her sister. He dragged her deep into the forest, where he shackled her and raped her. Her tongue he then severed, and concealed her, and she warbles for vengeance, and death.

I Crispus, a man of Corinth, yesterday looked on God. Today I rave. What things my eyes have seen can't be scribed or spoken. All think I praise His sacred name, take my horror for hymns, my blasphemies for raptures. The holy writ's wrongly deciphered, as beatitudes and blessings; in truth those are curses, maledictions, and obscenest commandments. So be it.

Sweet Sheba, beloved highness: Solomon craves your throne! Beware his craft; he mistranslates my pain into cunning counsel. Hear what he claims your hoopoe sang: that its mistress the Queen no longer worships Allah! He bids you come now to his palace, to be punished for your error ... But mine was a love song: how I'd hymn you, if his tongue weren't beyond me — and yours.

Ed' pélut', kondó nedóde, ímba imbá imbá. Singé erú. Orúmo ímbo ímpe ruté sceléte. Ímpe re scéle lee lutó. Ombo té scele té, beré te kúre kúre. Sinté te lúté sinte kúru, te ruméte tau ruméte. Onkó keere scéte, tere lúte, ilee léte leel' lúto. Scélé.

Ill fortune, constraint and terror, generate guileful art; despair inspires. The laureled clairvoyants tell our doom in riddles. Sewn in our robes are horrid tales, and the speakers-in-tongues enounce atrocious tidings. The prophet-birds seem to speak sagely, but are shrieking their frustration. The senselessest babble, could we ken it, might disclose a dark message, or prayer.

Life-Story

1

Without discarding what he'd already written he began his story afresh in a somewhat different manner. Whereas his earlier version had opened in a straight-forward documentary fashion and then degenerated or at least modulated intentionally into irrealism and dissonance he decided this time to tell his tale from start to finish in a conservative, "realistic," unself-conscious way. He being by vocation an author of novels and stories it was perhaps inevitable that one afternoon the possibility would occur to the writer of these lines that his own life might be a fiction, in which he was the leading or an accessory character. He happened at the time* to be in his study attempting to draft the opening pages of a new short story; its general idea had preoccupied him for some months along with other general ideas, but certain elements of the conceit, without which he could scarcely proceed, remained unclear. More specifically: narrative plots may be imagined as consisting of a "ground-situation" (Scheherazade desires not to die) focused and dramatized by a "vehicle-situation" (Scheherazade beguiles the King with endless stories), the several incidents of which have their final value in terms of their bearing upon the "ground-situation." In our author's case it was the "vehicle" that had vouchsafed itself, first as a germinal proposition in his commonplace book — D comes to suspect that the world is a novel, himself a fictional personage — subsequently

*9:00 AM, Monday, June 20, 1966.

as an articulated conceit explored over several pages of the workbook in which he elaborated more systematically his casual inspirations: since D is writing a fictional account of this conviction he has indisputably a fictional existence in his account, replicating what he suspects to be his own situation. Moreover E, hero of D's account, is said to be writing a similar account, and so the replication is in both ontological directions, *et cetera*. But the "ground-situation" — some state of affairs on D's part which would give dramatic resonance to his attempts to prove himself factual, assuming he made such attempts — obstinately withheld itself from his imagination. As is commonly the case the question reduced to one of stakes: what were to be the consequences of D's — and finally E's — disproving or verifying his suspicion, and why should a reader be interested?

What a dreary way to begin a story he said to himself upon reviewing his long introduction. Not only is there no "ground-situation," but the prose style is heavy and somewhat old-fashioned, like an English translation of Thomas Mann, and the so-called "vehicle" itself is at least questionable: self-conscious, vertiginously arch, fashionably solipsistic, unoriginal — in fact a convention of twentieth-century literature. Another story about a writer writing a story! Another regressus in infinitum! Who doesn't prefer art that at least overtly imitates something other than its own processes? That doesn't continually proclaim "Don't forget I'm an artifice!"? That takes for granted its mimetic nature instead of asserting it in order (not so slyly after all) to deny it, or vice-versa? Though his critics sympathetic and otherwise described his own work as avant-garde, in his heart of hearts he disliked literature of an experimental, self-despising, or overtly metaphysical character, like Samuel Beckett's, Marian Cutler's, Jorge Borges's. The logical fantasies of Lewis Carroll pleased him less than straight-forward tales of adventure, subtly sentimental romances, even densely circumstantial realisms like Tolstoy's. His favorite contemporary authors were John Updike, Georges Simenon, Nicole Riboud. He had no use for the theater of absurdity, for "black humor," for allegory in any form, for apocalyptic preachments meretriciously tricked out in dramatic garb.

Neither had his wife and adolescent daughters, who for that matter preferred life to literature and read fiction when at all for entertainment. Their kind of story (his too, finally) would begin if not once upon a time at least with arresting circumstance, bold character, trenchant action.

C flung away the whining manuscript and pushed impatiently through the french doors leading to the terrace from his oak-wainscoted study. Pausing at the stone balustrade to light his briar he remarked through a lavender cascade of wisteria that lithe-limbed Gloria, Gloria of timorous eye and militant breast, had once again chosen his boat-wharf as her basking-place.

By Jove he exclaimed to himself. It's particularly disquieting to suspect not only that one is a fictional character but that the fiction one's in—the fiction one is—is quite the sort one least prefers. His wife entered the study with coffee and an apple-pastry, set them at his elbow on his work table, returned to the living room. Ed' pelut' kondo nedode; nyoing nyang. One manifestation of schizophrenia as everyone knows is the movement from reality toward fantasy, a progress which not infrequently takes the form of distorted and fragmented representation, abstract formalism, an increasing preoccupation, even obsession, with pattern and design for their own sakes—especially patterns of a baroque, enormously detailed character—to the (virtual) exclusion of representative "content." There are other manifestations. Ironically, in the case of graphic and plastic artists for example the work produced in the advanced stages of their affliction may be more powerful and interesting than the realistic productions of their earlier "sanity." Whether the artists themselves are gratified by this possibility is not reported.

B called upon a literary acquaintance, B——, summering with Mrs. B and children on the Eastern Shore of Maryland. "You say you lack a ground-situation. Has it occurred to you that that circumstance may be your ground-situation? What occurs to me is that if it is it isn't. And conversely. The case being thus, what's really wanting after all is a well-articulated vehicle, a foreground or upstage situation to dramatize the narrator's or author's grundlage. His what. To write merely C comes to suspect that the world is a novel, himself a fictional personage is but to introduce the vehicle; the next step must be to initiate its uphill motion by establishing and complicating some conflict. I would advise in addition the eschewal of overt and self-conscious discussion of the narrative process. I would advise in addition the eschewal of overt and self-conscious discussion of the narrative process. The via negativa and its positive counterpart are it is to be remembered poles after all of the same cell. Returning to his study.

If I'm going to be a fictional character G declared to himself I want to be in a rousing good yarn as they say, not some piece of avant-garde preciousness. I want passion and bravura action in my plot, heroes I can admire, heroines I can love, memorable speeches, colorful accessory characters, poetical language. It doesn't matter to me how naively linear the anecdote is; never mind modernity! How reactionary J appears to be. How will such nonsense sound thirty-six years from now?* As if. If he can only get K through his story I reflected grimly; if he can only retain his self-possession to the end of this sentence; not go mad; not destroy himself and/or others. Then what I wondered grimly. Another sentence fast, another story.

Scheherazade my only love! All those nights you kept your secret from the King my rival, that after your defloration, he was unnecessary, you'd have killed yourself in any case when your invention failed.

Why could he not begin his story afresh X wondered, for example with the words why could he not begin his story afresh *et cetera*? Y's wife came into the study as he was about to throw out the baby with the bathwater. "Not for an instant to throw out the baby while every instant discarding the bathwater is perhaps a chief task of civilized people at this hour of the world.** I used to tell B___ that without success. What makes you so sure it's not a film he's in or a theater-piece?

Because U responded while he certainly felt rather often that he was merely acting his own role or roles he had no idea who the actor was, whereas even the most Stanislavsky-methodist would presumably if questioned closely recollect his offstage identity even onstage in mid-act. Moreover a great part of T's "drama," most of his life in fact, was non-visual, consisting entirely in introspection, which the visual dramatic media couldn't manage easily. He had for example mentioned to no one his growing conviction that he was a fictional character, and since he was not given to audible soliloquizing a "spectator" would take him for a cheerful, conventional fellow, little suspecting that *et cetera*. It was of course imaginable that much goes on in the mind of King Oedipus in addition to his spoken sentiments; any number of interior dramas might be being played out in the actors' or characters' minds, dramas of which the audience is as unaware as are V's wife and friends of his growing conviction that he's a fictional character. But everything suggested that the medium of his life was prose fiction — moreover a

*10:00 AM, Monday, June 20, 1966
**11:00 AM, Monday, June 20, 1966

fiction narrated from either the first-person or the third-person-omniscient point of view.

Why is it L wondered with mild disgust that both K and M for example choose to write such stuff when life is so sweet and painful and full of such a variety of people, places, situations, and activities other than self-conscious and after all rather blank introspection? Why is it N wondered *et cetera* that both M and O *et cetera* when the world is in such parlous explosive case? Why *et cetera et cetera et cetera* when the word, which was in the beginning, is now evidently nearing the end of its road? Am I being strung out in this ad libitum fashion I wondered merely to keep my author from the pistol? What sort of story is it whose drama lies always in the next frame out? If Sinbad sinks it's Scheherazade who drowns; whose neck one wonders is on her line?

2

Discarding what he'd already written as he could wish to discard the mumbling pages of his life he began his story afresh, resolved this time to eschew overt and self-conscious discussion of his narrative process and to recount instead in the straight-forwardest manner possible the several complications of his character's conviction that he was a character in a work of fiction, arranging them into dramatically ascending stages if he could for his readers' sake and leading them (the stages) to an exciting climax and dénouement if he could.

He rather suspected that the medium and genre in which he worked — the only ones for which he felt any vocation — were moribund if not already dead. The idea pleased him. One of the successfullest men he knew was a blacksmith of the old school who *et cetera*. He meditated upon the grandest sailing-vessel ever built, the *France II*, constructed in Bordeaux in 1911 not only when but because the age of sail had passed. Other phenomena that consoled and inspired him were the great flying boat *Hercules*, the zeppelin *Hindenburg*, the *Tsar Pushka* cannon, the then-record Dow-Jones industrial average of 381.17 attained on September 3, 1929.

He rather suspected that the society in which he persisted — the only one with which he felt any degree of identification — was moribund if not *et cetera*. He knew beyond any doubt that the body which he inhabited — the only one *et cetera* — was *et cetera*. The idea *et cetera*. He had for thirty-six years lacking a few hours been one of our dustmote's three billion tenants give or take five hundred million, and happening to be as well a white male citizen of the United States of America he had thirty-six years plus a few hours more to cope with one way or another unless the actuarial tables were mistaken, not bloody likely, or his term was unexpectedly reduced.

Had he written for his readers' sake? The phrase implied a thitherto-unappreciated metaphysical dimension. Suspense. If his life was a fictional narrative it consisted of three terms — teller, tale, told — each dependent on the other two but not in the same ways. His author could as well tell some other character's tale or some other tale of the same character as the one being told as he himself could in his own character as author; his "reader" could as easily read some other story, would be well advised to; but his own "life" depended absolutely on a particular author's original persistence, thereafter upon some reader's. From this consideration any number of things followed, some less tiresome than others. No use appealing to his author, of whom he'd come to dislike even to think. The idea of his playing with his characters' and his own self-consciousness! He himself tended in that direction and despised the tendency. The idea of his or her smiling smugly to himself as the "words" flowed from his "pen" in which his the protagonist's unhappy inner life was exposed! Ah he had mistaken the nature of his narrative; he had thought is very long, longer than Proust's, longer than any German's, longer than *The Thousand Nights and a Night* in ten quarto volumes. Moreover he'd thought it the most prolix and pedestrian *tranche-de-vie* realism, unredeemed by even the limited virtues of colorful squalor, solid specification, an engaging variety of scenes and characters — in a word a bore, of the sort he himself not only would not write but would not read either. Now he understood that his author might as probably resemble himself and the protagonist of his own story-in-progress. Like himself, like his character aforementioned, his author not impossibly deplored the obsolescence of humanism, the passing of *savoir-vivre, et cetera*; admired the outmoded values of fidelity, courage, tact, restraint, amiability, self-discipline, *et cetera*; preferred fictions in which were to be found stirring actions, characters to love as well as ditto to despise, speeches and deeds to affect us strongly, *et cetera*. He too might wish to make some final effort to put by his fictional character and achieve factuality or at least to figure in if not be hero of a more attractive fiction, but be caught like the writer of these lines in some more or less desperate tour de force. For him to attempt to come to an understanding with such an author were as futile as for one of his own creations to *et cetera*.

But the reader! Even if his author were his only reader as was he himself of his work-in-progress as of the sentence-in-progress and his protagonist of his, *et cetera*, his character as reader was not the same as his character as author, a fact which might be turned to account. What suspense.

As he prepared to explore this possibility one of his mistresses whereof he had none entered his brown study unannounced. "The passion of love," she announced, "which I regard as no less essential to a satisfying life than those values itemized above and which I infer from my presence here that you too esteem highly, does not in fact play in your life a role of sufficient importance to sustain my presence here. It plays in fact little role at all outside your imaginative and/or ary life. I tell you this not in a criticizing spirit, for I judge you to be as capable of the sentiment aforementioned as any other imagin[ative], deep-feeling man in good physical health more or less precisely in the middle of the road of our life. What hampers, even cripples you in this regard is your final preference, which I refrain from analyzing, for the sedater, more responsible pleasures of monogamous fidelity and the serener affections of domesticity, notwithstanding the fact that your enjoyment of these is correspondingly inhibited though not altogether spoiled by an essentially romantical, unstable, irresponsible, death-wishing fancy. V.S. Pritchett, English critic and author, will put the matter succinctly in a soon-to-be-written essay on Flaubert, whose work he'll say depicts the course of ardent longings and violent desires that rise from the horrible, the sensual, and the sadistic. They turn into the virginal and mystical, only to become numb by satiety. At this point pathological boredom leads to a final desire for death and nothingness — the Romantic syndrome. If, not to be unfair, we qualify somewhat the terms horrible and sadistic and understand satiety to include a large measure of vicariousness this description undeniably applies to one aspect of yourself and your work; and while your ditto has other, even contrary aspects, the net fact is that you have elected familial responsibilities and rewards — indeed, straight-laced middle-class-ness in general — over the higher expenses of spirit and wastes of shame attendant upon a less regular, more glamorous style of life. So to elect is surely admirable for the layman, even essential if the social fabric, without which there can be no culture, is to be preserved. For the artist, however, and in particular the writer, whose traditional material has been the passions of men and women, the choice is fatal. You having made it I bid you goodnight probably forever."

Even as she left he reached for the sleeping pills cached conveniently in his writing desk and was restrained from their administration only by his being in the process of completing a sentence, which he cravenly strung out at some sacrifice of rhetorical effect upon realizing that he was *et cetera*. Moreover he added hastily he had not described the intruder for his readers' vicarious satiety: a lovely woman she was, whom he did not after all describe for his readers' *et cetera* inasmuch as her appearance and character were inconstant. Her interruption of his work inspired a few sentences about the extent to which his fiction inevitably made public his private life, though the trespasses in this particular were as nothing beside those of most of his profession. That is to say, while he did not draw his characters and situations directly from life nor permit his author-protagonist to do so, any moderately attentive reader of his oeuvre, his what, could infer for example that its author feared for example schizophrenia, impotence creative and sexual, suicide — in short living and dying. His fictions were preoccupied with these fears among their other, more serious preoccupations. Hot dog. As of the sentence-in-progress he was not in fact unmanageably schizophrenic, impotent in either respect, or dead by his own hand, but there was always the next sentence to worry about. But there was always the next sentence to worry about. In sum he concluded hastily such limited self-exposure did not constitute a misdemeanor, representing or mis as it did so small an aspect of his total self, negligible a portion of his total life — even which totalities were they made public would be found remarkable only for their being so unremarkable. Well shall he continue.

Bearing in mind that he had not developed what he'd mentioned earlier about turning to advantage his situation vis-à-vis his "reader" (in fact he deliberately now postponed his return to that subject, sensing that it might well constitute the climax of his story) he elaborated one or two ancillary questions, perfectly aware that he was trying, even exhausting, whatever patience might remain to whatever readers might remain to whoever elaborated yet another ancillary question. Was the novel of his life for example a *roman à clef.* ? Of that genre he was as contemptuous as of the others aforementioned; but while in the introductory adverbial clause it seemed obvious to him that he didn't "stand for" anyone else, any more than he was an actor playing the role of himself, by the time he reached the main clause he had to admit that the question was unanswerable, since the "real" man to whom he'd correspond in a *roman à clef* would not be also in the *roman à clef* and the characters in such works were not themselves aware of their irritating correspondences.

Similarly unanswerable were such questions as when "his" story (so he regarded it for convenience and consolement though for all he knew he might be not the central character; it might be his wife's story, one of his daughters's, his imaginary mistress's, the man-who-once-cleaned-his-chimney's) began. Not impossibly at his birth or even generations earlier: a *Bildungsroman,* an *Erziehungsroman,* a *roman fleuve.* ! More likely at the moment he became convinced of his fictional nature: that's where he'd have begun it, as he'd begun the piece currently under his pen. If so it followed that the years of his childhood and younger manhood weren't "real," he'd suspected as much, in the first-order sense, but a mere "background" consisting of a few well-placed expository insinuations, perhaps misleading, or inferences, perhaps unwarranted, from strategic hints in his present reflections. God so to speak spare his readers from heavy-footed forced expositions of the sort that begin in the countryside near _____ in May of the year _____ it occurred to the novelist _____ that his own life might be a _____, in which he was the leading or an accessory character. He happened at the time to be in the oak-wain-scoted study of the old family summer residence; through a lavender cascade of hysteria he observed that his wife had once again chosen to be the subject of this clause, itself the direct object of his observation. A lovely woman she was, whom he did not describe in keeping with his policy against drawing characters from life as who should draw a condemnee to the gallows. Begging his pardon. Flinging his tiresome tale away he pushed impatiently through the french windows leading from his study to a sheer drop from the then-record high into a nearly fatal depression.

He clung onto his narrative depressed by the disproportion of its ratiocination to its dramatization, reflection to action. One had heard *Hamlet* criticized as a collection of soliloquies for which the implausible plot was a mere excuse; witnessed Italian operas whose dramatic portions were no more than interstitial relief and arbitrary continuity between the arias. If it was true that he didn't take his "real" life seriously enough even when it had him by the throat, the fact didn't lead him to consider whether the fact was a cause or a consequence of his tale's tedium or both.

Concluding these reflections he concluded these reflections: that there was at this advanced page still apparently no ground-situation suggested that his story was dramatically meaningless. If one regarded the absence of a ground-situation, more accurately the protagonist's anguish at that absence and his vain endeavors to supply the defect, as itself a sort of ground-situation, did his life-story thereby take on a kind of meaning? A "dramatic" sort he supposed, though of so sophistical a character as more likely to annoy than to engage.

3

The reader! You, dogged, uninsultable, print-oriented bastard, it's you I'm addressing, who else, from inside this monstrous fiction. You've read me this far, then? Even this far? For what discreditable motive? How is it you don't go to a movie, watch TV, stare at a wall, play tennis with a friend, make amorous advances to the person who comes to your mind when I speak of amorous advances? Can nothing surfeit, saturate you, turn you off? Where's your shame?

Having let go this barrage of rhetorical or at least unanswered questions and observing himself nevertheless in midst of yet another sentence he concluded and caused the "hero" of his story to conclude that one or more of three things must be true: 1) his author was his sole and indefatigable reader; 2) he was in a sense his own author, telling his story to himself, in which case in which case; and/or 3) his reader was not only tireless and shameless but sadistic, masochistic if he was himself.

For why do you suppose — you! you! — he's gone on so, so relentlessly refusing to entertain you as he might have at a less desperate than this hour of the world* with felicitous language, exciting situation,

*11:00 PM, Monday, June 20, 1966

unforgettable character and image? Why has he as it were ruthlessly set about not to win you over but to turn you away? Because your own author bless and damn you his life is in your hands! He writes and reads himself; don't you think he knows who gives his creatures their lives and deaths? Do they exist except as he or others read their words? Age except we turn their pages? And can he die until you have no more of him? Time was obviously when his author could have turned the trick; his pen had once to left-to-right it through these words as does your kindless eye and might have ceased at any one. This. This. And did not as you see but went on like an Oriental torturemaster to the end.

But you needn't! He exclaimed to you. In vain. Had he petitioned you instead to read slowly in the happy parts, what happy parts, swiftly in the painful no doubt you'd have done the contrary or cut him off entirely. But as he longs to die and can't without your help you force him on, force him on. Will you deny you've read this sentence? This? To get away with murder doesn't appeal to you, is that it? As if your hands weren't inky with other dyings! As if he'd know you'd killed him! Come on. He dares you.

In vain. You haven't: the burden of his knowledge. That he continues means that he continues, a fortiori you too. Suicide's impossible: he can't kill himself without your help. Those petitions aforementioned, even his silly plea for death — don't you think he understands their sophistry, having authored their like for the wretches he's authored? Read him fast or slow, intermittently, continuously, repeatedly, backward, not at all, he won't know it; he only guesses someone's reading or composing his sentences, such as this one, because he's reading or composing sentences such as this one; the net effect is that there's a net effect, of continuity and an apparently consistent flow of time, though his pages do seem to pass more swiftly as they near his end.

To what conclusion will he come? He'd been about to append to his own tale inasmuch as the old analogy between Author and God, novel and world, can no longer be employed unless deliberately as a false analogy, certain things follow: 1) fiction must acknowledge its fictitiousness and metaphoric invalidity or 2) choose to ignore the question or deny its relevance or 3) establish some other, acceptable relation between itself, its author, its reader. Just as he finished doing so however his real wife and imaginary mistresses entered his study; "It's a little past midnight" she announced with a smile; "do you know what that means?"

Though she'd come into his story unannounced at a critical moment he did not describe her, for even as he recollected that he'd seen his first light just thirty-six years before the night incumbent he saw his last: that he could not after all be a character in a work of fiction inasmuch as such a fiction would be of an entirely different character from what he thought of as fiction. Fiction consisted of such monuments of the imagination as Cutler's *Morganfield*, Riboud's *Tales Within Tales*, his own creations; fact of such as for example read those fictions. More, he could demonstrate by syllogism that the story of his life was a work of fact: though assaults upon the boundary between life and art, reality and dream, were undeniably a staple of his own and his century's literature as they'd been of Shakespeare's and Cervantes's, yet it was a fact that in the corpus of fiction as far as he knew no fictional character had become convinced as had he that he was a character in a work of fiction. This being the case and he having in fact become thus convinced it followed that his conviction was false. "Happy birthday," said his wife *et cetera*, kissing him *et cetera* to obstruct his view of the end of the sentence he was nearing the end of, playfully refusing to be nay-said so that in fact he did at last as did his fictional character end his ending story endless by interruption, cap his pen.

Menelaiad

1

Menelaus here, more or less. The fair-haired boy? Of the loud war cry!
Leader of the people. Zeus's fosterling.

Eternal husband.

Got you, have I? No? Changed your shape, become waves of the sea,
of the air? Anyone there? Anyone here?

No matter; this isn't the voice of Menelaus; this voice *is* Menelaus,
all there is of him. When I'm switched on I tell my tale, the one I know,
How Menelaus Became Immortal, but I don't know it.

Keep hold of yourself.

"Helen," I say: "Helen's responsible for this. From the day we lovers
sacrificed the horse in Argos, pastureland of horses, and swore on its
bloody joints to be her champions forever, whichever of us she chose,
to the night we huddled in the horse in Troy while she took the part
of all our wives — everything's Helen's fault. Cities built and burnt, a
thousand bottoms on the sea's, every captain corpsed or cuckold — her
doing. She's the death of me and my peculiar immortality, cause of every mask and change of state. On whose account did Odysseus become
a madman, Achilles woman? Who turned the Argives into a horse,
loyal Sinon into a traitor, yours truly from a mooncalf into a sea-calf,
Proteus into everything that is? First cause and final magician: Mrs. M.

"One evening, embracing in our bed, I dreamed I was back in the
wooden horse, waiting for midnight. Laocoön's spear still stuck in our

flank, and Helen, with her Trojan pal in tow, called out to her Argive lovers in the voice of each's wife. 'Come kiss me, Anticlus darling!' My heart was stabbed as my side was once by Pandarus's arrow. But in the horse, while smart Odysseus held shut our mouths, I dreamed I was home in bed before Paris and the war, our wedding night, when she crooned like that to *me*. Oh, Anticlus, it wasn't you who was deceived; your wife was leagues and years away, mine but an arms-length, yet less near. Now I wonder which dream dreamed which, which Menelaus never woke and now dreams both.

"And when I was on the beach at Pharos, seven years lost en route from Troy, clinging miserably to Proteus for direction, he prophesied a day when I'd sit in my house at last, drink wine with the sons of dead comrades, and tell their dads' tales; my good wife would knit by the fireside, things for our daughter's wedding, and dutifully pour the wine. That scene glowed so in my heart, its beat became the rhythm of her needles; Egypt's waves hissed on the foreshore like sapwood in the grate, and the Nile-murk on my tongue turned sweet. But then it seems to me I'm home in Sparta, talking to Nestor's boy or Odysseus's; Helen's put something in the wine again, I know why, one of those painkillers she picked up in Africa, and the tale I tell so grips me, I'm back in the cave once more with the Old Man of the Sea."

One thing's certain: somewhere Menelaus lost course and steersman, went off track, never got back on, lost hold of himself, became a record merely, the record of his loosening grasp. He's the story of his life, with which he ambushes the unwary unawares.

2

"'Got you!'" I cry to myself, imagining Telemachus enthralled by the doctored wine. "'You've feasted your bowels on my dinner, your hopes on my news of Odysseus, your eyes on my wife though she's your mother's age. Now I'll feast myself on your sotted attention, with the tale How Menelaus First Humped Helen in the Eighth Year After the War. Pricked you up, that? Got your ear, have I? Like to know how it was, I suppose? Where in Hades are we? Where'd I go? Whom've I got hold of? Proteus? Helen?'

"'Telemachus Odysseus's-son,' the lad replied, 'come from goat-girt Ithaca for news of my father, but willing to have his cloak clutched and listen all night to the tale How You Lost Your Navigator, Wandered Seven Years, Came Ashore at Pharos, Waylaid Eidothea, Tackled Proteus, Learned to Reach Greece by Sailing up the Nile, and Made Love to Your Wife, the most beautiful woman I've ever seen, After an Abstinence of Eighteen Years.'

"'Seventeen.'"

I tell it as it is. "'D'you hear that click?'" I tell myself I asked Telemachus.

"'*I* do,' said Peisistratus.

"'Knitting! Helen of Troy's going to be a grandmother! An empire torched, a generation lost, a hundred kings undone on her account, and there she sits, proper as Penelope, not a scratch on her — and knits!'

"'Not a scratch!' said Telemachus.

"'Excuse me,' Helen said; 'if it's to be that tale I'm going on to bed, second chamber on one's left down the hall. A lady has her modesty. Till we meet again, Telemachus. Drink deep and sleep well, Menelaus my love.'

"'Zeus in heaven!'" I say I cried. "'Why didn't I do you in in Deiphobus' house, put you to the sword with Troy?'

"Helen smiled at us and murmured: 'Love.'

"'Does she mean,' asked Peisistratus Nestor's-son, come with Telemachus that noon from sandy Pylos, 'that you love her for example more than honor, self-respect; more than every man and cause you've gone to war for; more than Menelaus?'

"'Not impossibly.'

"'Is it that her name's twin syllables fire you with contrary passions? That your heart does battle with your heart till you burn like ashèd Ilion?'

"'Wise son of a wise father! Her smile sows my furrowed memory with Castalian serpent's teeth; I become a score of warriors, each battling the others; the survivors kneel as one before her; perhaps the slain were better men. If Aeneas Aphrodite's-son couldn't stick her, how should I, a mere near mortal?'

"'This is gripping,'" I say to myself Telemachus said. "'Weary as we are from traveling all day, I wish nothing further than to sit without moving in this total darkness while you hold me by the hem of my tunic and recount How Your Gorgeous Wife Wouldn't Have You for Seven Full Postwar Years but Did in the Eighth. If I fail to exclaim with wonder or otherwise respond, it will be that I'm speechless with sympathy.'

"'So be it,' I said," I say. "Truth to tell," I tell me, "when we re-reached Sparta Helen took up her knitting with never a dropped stitch, as if she'd been away eighteen days instead of ditto years, and visiting her sister instead of bearing bastards to her Trojan lovers. But it was the wine of doubt I took to, whether I was the world's chief fool and cuckold or its luckiest mortal. Especially when old comrades came to town, or their sons, to swap war stories, I'd booze it till I couldn't tell Helen from Hellespont. So it was the day Odysseus's boy and Nestor's rode into town. I was shipping off our daughter to wed Achilles' son and Alector's girl in to wed mine; the place was full of kinfolk, the wine ran free, I was swallowing my troubles; babies they were when I went to Troy, hardly married myself; by the time I get home they're men and women wanting spouses of their own; no wonder I felt old and low and thirsty; where'd my kids go? The prime of my life?

"When the boys dropped in I took for granted they were friends of the children's, come for the party; I saw to it they were washed and oiled, gave them clean clothes and poured them a drink. Better open your palace to every kid in the countryside than not know whose your own are in, Mother and I always thought. No man can say I'm inhospitable. But I won't deny I felt a twinge when I learned they were strangers; handsome boys they were, from good families, I could tell, and in the bloom of manhood, as I'd been twenty years before, and Paris when he came a-calling, and I gave him a drink and said 'What's mine is yours ...' ..." ...

Why don't they call her Helen of Sparta?

"I showed them the house, all our African stuff, it knocked their eyes out; then we had dinner and played the guessing game. Nestor's boy I recognized early on, his father's image, a good lad, but not hero-material, you know what I mean. The other was a troubler; something not straight about him; wouldn't look you in the eye; kept smiling at his plate; but a sharp one, and a good-looking, bound to make a stir in the world one day. I kept my eye on him through dinner and decided he was my nephew Orestes, still hiding out from killing his mother and her goat-boy-friend, or else Odysseus's Telemachus. Either way it was bad news: when Proteus told me how Clytemnestra and Aegisthus had axed my brother the minute he set foot in Mycenae, do you think

Helen spared him a tear? 'No more than he deserved,' she said, 'playing around with that bitch Cassandra.' But when we stopped off there on our way home from Egypt and found her sister and Aegisthus being buried, didn't she raise a howl for young Orestes' head! Zeus help him if he'd come to see his Uncle Menelaus! On the other hand, if he was Odysseus's boy and took after his father, I'd have to keep eye on the wedding silver as well as on the bride.

"To matters worse, as I fretted about this our old minstrel wandered in, looking for a handout, and started up that wrath-of-Archilles thing, just what I needed to hear; before I could turn him off I was weeping in my wine and wishing I'd died the morning after my wedding night. Hermione barged in too, almost as pretty as her mom, to see who the stranger-chaps were; for a minute it was 'Paris, meet Helen' all over again, till I got hold of myself and shooed her out of there. Even so, a dreadful notion struck me: what if Paris had a son we didn't know about, who'd slipped like slick Aeneas our Trojan clutch, grown up in hiding, and was come now to steal my daughter as his dad my wife! Another horse! Another Hector! Another drink.

"Even as I swallowed, hard and often, the fellow winked at the door I'd sent Hermione through and said, 'Quite a place, hey, Nestor's-son?' Which was to say, among other things, Peisistratus was tagged and out of the game. Nothing for it then but to play the thing out in the usual way. 'No getting around it, boys,' I declared: 'I'm not the poorest Greek in town. But I leave it to Zeus whether what you've seen is worth its cost. Eight years I knocked about the world, picking up what I could and wishing I were dead. The things you see come from Cyprus, Phoenicia, Egypt, Ethiopia, Sidonia, Erembieven Libya, where the lambs are born with horns on.'

"'Born with horns on!'

"I did my thing then, told a story with everyone in it who might be the mystery guest and looked to see which name brought tears. 'While I was pirating around,' I said, 'my wife's sister murdered my brother on the grounds that she'd committed adultery for ten years straight with my cousin Aegisthus. Her son Orestes killed them both, bless his heart, but when I think of Agamemnon and the rest done in for Helen's sake, I'd swap two-thirds of what I've got to bring them back to life.'

"I looked for the stranger's tears through mine, but he only declared: 'Lucky Achilles' son, to come by such a treasure!'

"'Yet the man I miss most,' I continued, 'is shifty Odysseus.'

"'Oh?'

"'Yes indeed,' I went on," I go on: "'Now and then I wonder what became of him and old faithful Penelope and the boy Telemachus.'

"'You know Telemachus?' asked Telemachus.

"'I knew him once,' said I. 'Twenty years ago, when he was one, I laid him in a furrow for his dad to plow under, and thus odysseused Odysseus. What's more, I'd made up my mind if he got home alive to give him a town here in Argos to lord it over and leave to his son when he died. Odysseus and I, wouldn't we have run through the grapes and whoppers! Pity he never made it.'

"The boy wet his mantle properly then, and I thought: 'Hold tight, son of Atreus, and keep a sharp lookout.' While I wondered what he might be after and how to keep him from it, as I had of another two decades past, Herself came in with her maids and needles, worst possible moment as ever.

"'Why is it, Menelaus, you never tell me when a prince comes calling? Good afternoon, Telemachus.'

"Oh, my gods, but she was lovely! Cute Hermione drew princelings to Sparta like piss-ants to a peony-bud, but her mother was the full-blown blossom, the blooming bush! Far side of forty but never a wrinkle, and any two cuts of her great gray eyes told more about love and Troy than our bard in a night's hexameters. Her figure, too — but curse her figure! She opened her eyes and theirs, I shut mine, there was the usual pause; then Telemachus got his wind back and hollered: 'Pay-ee-*sis*tratus! What country have we come to, where the mares outrun the fillies?'

"Nestor's-son's face was ashen as his spear; ashener than either the old taste in my mouth. If only Telemachus had been so abashed! But he looked her over like young Heracles the house of Thespius and said, 'Not even many-masked Odysseus could disguise himself from Zeus's daughter. How is it you know me?'

"'You're your father's son,' Helen said. 'Odysseus asked me that very question one night in Troy. He'd got himself up as a beggar and slipped into town for the evening . . .'

"'What for?' wanted to know Peisistratus.

"'To spy, to spy.' Telemachus said.

"'What else?' asked Helen. 'None knew him but me, who'd have known him anywhere, and I said to my Trojan friends: "Look, a new beggar in town. Wonder who he is?" But no matter how I tried, I couldn't trick Odysseus into saying: "Odysseus."'

"'Excuse me, ma'am,' begged Peisistratus, disbrothered by the war; 'what I don't understand is why you tried at all, since he was on a dangerous mission in enemy territory.'

"'Nestor's-son,' said I, 'you're your father's son.' But Telemachus scolded him, asking how he hoped to have his questions answered if he interrupted the tale by asking them. Helen flashed him a look worth epics and said, 'When I got him alone in my apartment and washed and oiled and dressed him, promised not to tell anyone he was Odysseus until he went back to his camp. So he told me all the Greek military secrets. Toward morning he killed several Trojans while they slept, and then I showed him the safest way out of town. There was a fuss among the new widows, but who cared? I was bored with Troy by that time and wished I'd never left home. I had a nice palace, a daughter, and Menelaus: what more could a woman ask?'

"After a moment Telemachus cried: 'Noble heart in a nobler breast! To think that all the while our side cursed you, you were secretly helping us!'

"When I opened my eyes I saw Peisistratus rubbing his, image of Gerenian Nestor. 'It still isn't clear to me,' he said, 'why the wife of Prince Paris — begging your pardon, sir; I mean as it were, of course — would wash, oil, and dress a vagrant beggar in her apartment in the middle of the night. I don't grasp either why you couldn't have slipped back to Lord Menelaus along with Odysseus, if that's what you wanted.'

"He had other questions too, shrewd lad, but Helen's eyes turned dark, and before I could swallow my wine Telemachus had him answered: 'What good could she have done the Argives then? She'd as well have stayed here in Sparta!' As for himself, he told Helen, next to hearing that his father was alive no news could've more delighted him than that the whole purpose of her elopement with Paris, as he was now convinced, was to spy for the Greeks from the heart of Troy, without which espionage we'd surely have been defeated. Helen counted her stitches and said, 'You give me too much credit.' 'No, by Zeus!' Telemachus declared. 'To leave your home and family and live for ten years with another man, purely for the sake of your home and family . . .'

"'Nine with Paris,' Helen murmured, 'one with Deiphobus. Deiphobus was the better man, no doubt about it, but not half as handsome.'

"'So much the nobler!' cried Telemachus.

"'Nobler than you think,' I said, and poured myself and Peisistratus another drink. 'My wife's too modest to tell the noblest things of all. In the first place, when I fetched her out of Troy at last and set sail for home, she was so ashamed of what she'd had to do to win the war for us that it took me seven years more to convince her she was worthy of me . . .

"'I kiss the hem of your robe!' Telemachus exclaimed to her and did.

"'In the second place,' I said, 'she did all these things for our sake without ever going to Troy in the first place.'

"'Really,' Helen protested.

"'Excuse me, sir . . .' said presently Peisistratus.

"'Wine's at your elbow.' I declared. 'Drink deep, boys; I'll tell you the tale.'

"'That's not what Prince Telemachus wants,' Helen said.

"'I know what Prince Telemachus wants.'

"'He wants word of his father,' said she. 'If you must tell a story at this late hour, tell the one about Proteus on the beach at Pharos, what he said of Odysseus.'

"'Do,' Peisistratus said.

"'Hold on,' I said," I say: "'It's all one tale.'

"'Then tell it all,' said Helen. 'But excuse yours truly.'

"'Don't go!' cried Telemachus.

"'A lady has her modesty,' Helen said. 'I'll fill your cups, gentlemen, bid you good night, and retire. To the second — '

"'Who put out the light?' asked Peisistratus.

"'Wait!' cried Telemachus.

"'Got you!' cried I, clutching hold of his cloak-hem. After an exchange of pleasantries we settled down and drank deep in the dark while I told the tale of Menelaus and his wife at sea:

3

"'Seven years,'" I say et cetera, "'the woman kept her legs crossed and the north wind blew without let-up, holding us from home. In the eighth, on the beach at Pharos, with Eidothea's help I tackled her dad the Old Man of the Sea and followed his tough instructions: heavy-hearted it back to Egypt, made my hecatombs, vowed my vows. At once then, wow, the wind changed, no time at all till we re-raised Pharos! Not a Proteus in sight, no Eidothea, just the boat I'd moored my wife in, per orders. Already she was making sail; her crew were putting in their oars; my first thought was, they're running off with Helen; we overhauled them; why was everybody grinning? But it was only joy, not to lose another minute; there was Helen herself by the mast-step, holding out her arms to me! Zeus knows how I poop-to-pooped it, maybe I was dreaming on the beach at Pharos, maybe am still; there I was anyhow, clambering aboard: "Way, boys!" I hollered. "Put your arse in it!" Spang! went the mainsail, breeze-bellied for Sparta; those were Helen's arms around me; it was wedding night! We hustled to the sternsheets, never mind who saw what; when she undid every oar went up; still we tore along the highways of the fish. "Got you!" I cried, couldn't see for the beauty of her, feel her yet, what is she anyhow? I decked her; only think, those gold limbs hadn't wound me in twenty years . . .'

"'Twenty?' 'Counting two before the war. Call it nineteen.'

"'"Wait," she bade me. "First tell me what Proteus said, and how you followed his advice."

"'Our oars went down; we strained the sail with sighs; my tears thinned the wine-dark sea. But there was nothing for it, I did as bid:

4

"'"Nothing for it but to do as Eidothea'd bid me,"'" I say to myself I told Telemachus I sighed to Helen.

"'"Eidothea?"

"'"Old Man of the Sea's young daughter, so she said," said I. "With three of my crew I dug in on the beach at sunrise; she wrapped us in seal-calfskins. 'Hold tight to these,' she told us. 'Who can hug a stinking sea-beast?' I inquired. She said, 'Father. Try ambrosia; he won't get here till noon.' She put it under our noses and dived off as usual; we were high in no time; 'These seals,' my men agreed: 'the longer you're out here the whiter they get.' They snuggled in and lost themselves in dreams; I would've too, but grateful as I was, when she passed the ambrosia I smelled a trick. Hang around Odysseus long enough, you trust nobody. I'd take a sniff and put the stuff away till the seal stink got to me, then sniff again. Even so I nearly lost my grip. Was I back in the horse? Was I dreaming of Helen on my bachelor throne?"

""'Hold on," said deckèd Helen; I came to myself, saw I was blubbering; "I came to myself, saw I was beached at Pharos. Come shadeless noon, unless I dreamed it, the sea-cow harem flipped from the deep to snooze on the foreshore, give me a woman anytime. Old Proteus came after, no accounting for tastes, counted them over, counting us in, old age is hard on the eyes too; then he outstretched in the cavemouth, one snore and I jumped him.

""'Got you!' I cried" I cried' I cried" I cry. ""'My companions, when I hollered, grabbed hold too: one snatched his beard, one his hands, one his long white hair; I tackled his legs and held fast. First he changed into a lion, ate the beard-man, what a mess; then snake, bit the hair-chap, who'd nothing to hold onto.'"

"'Neither did the hand-man,' observed Peisistratus, sleepless critic, to whom I explained for Telemachus's sake as well that while the erstwhile hand-man, latterly paw-man, had admittedly been vulnerably under both lion and snake, and the hair- then mane-man relatively safely on top, the former had escaped the former by reason of the quondam beard-man's fortunate, for the quondam paw-man, interposition; the latter fallen prey to the latter by reason of the latter's unfortunate, for the quondam mane-man, proclivity to strike whatever was before him — which would have been to say, before, the hand-paw-man, but was to say, now, which is to say, then, the beard-mane-man, thanks so to speak to the serpent's windings upon itself.

"'Ah.'

""'To clutch the leopard Proteus turned into then, then, were only myself and the unhandled hand-man, paw- once more but shielded now by neither beard- nor mane- and so promptly chomped, what a mess. I'd have got mine too, leopards are flexible, but by the time he'd made lunch of my companions he'd become a boar . . .'

""'Ah."

""'Which bristle as he might couldn't tusk his own tail, whereto I clung."

""'Not his hindpaws? I thought you were the foot-paw — '"

"'Just what I was about to — '

""'Proteus to lion, feet into hindpaws," I answered,' I answered.

"'Lion to snake, paws into tail. Snake to leopard, tail into tail and hind-paws both; my good luck I went tail to tail.'

""'Leopard to boar?'

""'Long tail to short, too short to tusk. Then the trouble started."(')

""'!'"

"'!'

"'!'

"I replied to them: "'A beast's a beast," I replied to her. "If you've got the right handle all you do's hang on . . .""'

""'It was when the Old Man of the Sea turned into salt water I began to sweat. Try holding an armful of ocean! I did my best, hugged a puddle on the beach, but plenty soaked in, plenty more ran seaward, where I saw you bathing, worst possible moment, not that you knew . . .""

"'?'

"'?' [?]

"'It's Helen I'm telling, northing in our love-clutch on the poop. "I needed a bath," she said; "I a drink," said I; "for all I knew you might be Proteus all over, dirty Old Man of the Sea. Even when my puddle turned into a bigbole leafy tree I wasn't easy; who said he couldn't be two things at once? There I lay, philodendron, hour after hour, while up in the limbs a cuckoo sang . . .""'

My problem was, I'd too much imagination to be a hero. ""'My problem was, I'd leisure to think. My time was mortal, Proteus's im-; what if he merely treed it a season or two till I let go? What was it anyhow I held? If Proteus once was Old Man of the Sea and now Proteus was a tree, then Proteus was neither, only Proteus; what I held were dreams. But if a real Old Man of the Sea had really been succeeded by real water and the rest, then the dream was Proteus. And Menelaus! For I changed too as the long day passed: changed my mind, replaced myself, grew older. How hold on until the 'old' (which is to say the young) Menelaus rebecame himself? Eidothea forgot to say! How could I anyhow know that that sea-nymph wasn't Proteus in yet another guise, her counsel a ruse to bind me forever while he sported with Helen?'"

""'What *was* her counsel, exactly?'

"'Peisistratus, is it? Helen's question, exactly: "What *was* her counsel, exactly?" And "How'd you persuade her to trick her own dad?" "Everything in its place," I said,' I said. "Your question was Proteus's, exactly; as I answered when he asked, I'll answer when he asks."

""""Hard tale to hold onto, this," declared my poopèd spouse.' Odysseus's — or Nestor's-son agreed." I agree. But what out-wandering hero ever journeyed a short straight line, arrived at his beginning till the end? """"Harder yet to hold onto Proteus. I must have dozed as I mused and fretted, thought myself yet again enhorsed or bridal-chambered, same old dream, woke up clutching nothing. It was late. I was rooted with fatigue. I held on." ('   ') "To?" ('   ') "Nothing. You were back on deck, the afternoon sank, I heard sailors guffawing, shorebirds cackled, the sun set grinning in the winish sea, still I held on, saying of and to me: 'Menelaus is a fool, mortal hugging immortality. Men laugh, the gods mock, he's chimaera, a horned gull. What is it he clutches? Why can't he let go? What trick have you played him, Eidothea, a stranger in your country?' I might've quit, but my cursèd fancy whispered: 'Proteus has turned into the air. Or else ...'""""

Hold onto yourself, Menelaus.

""""Long time my shingled arms made omicron. Tides lapped in and kelped me; fishlets kissed my heels; terns dunged me white; spatted and musseled, beflied, befleaed, I might have been what now in the last light I saw me to be holding, a marine old man, same's I'd seized only dimmer.

""""You've got me, son of Atreus,' he said, unless I said it myself."

"("(("Me too.")")")

""""And I'll keep you,' I said, 'till I have what I want.' He asked me what that was," as did Helen,' and Telemachus. """"You know without my telling you,'" I told them. "'Then he offered to tell all if I'd let him go, I to let him go when he'd told me all. 'Foolish mortal!' he said, they speak that way, 'What gives you to think you're Menelaus holding the Old Man of the Sea? Why shouldn't Proteus turn into Menelaus, and into Menelaus holding Proteus? But let that go ...'""" Never. """"We seers see fore and aft, but not amidships. I know what you've been and will be; how is it you're here? What god teaches men to godsnatch?'

""""It's not a short story,' I warned him."

"'I don't see why it needed telling,' Peisistratus declared. 'If a seer sees past and future he sees everything, the present being without duration *et cetera*. Or if his clairvoyance is relative, shading into darkness as it nears the Now from the bright far Heretofore and far clear Hereafter, even so there's nothing he needn't know.' 'Oh?' 'Today, say, he knows tomorrow and yesterday; then yesterday he knew today, as he'll know it tomorrow. Now to know the past is to know too what one once knew, to know the future to know what one will know. But in the case of seers, what one once knew includes the then future which is now the present; what one will know, the then past which ditto. From all which it follows as the future from the present, the present from the past, that from him from whom neither past nor future can hide, the present cannot either. It wasn't you who deceived Proteus, but Proteus you.'"

I tell it as it was. "Long time we sat in the dark and sleepful hall: hem-holding Menelaus, drowseless Nestor's-son, Telemachus perhaps. When windy Orion raised his leg over Lacedemon I put by groan and goblet saying, 'I tell it as it is. Long time I wondered who was the fooler, who fool, how much of what was news to whom; still pinning Helen to the pitchy poop I said, "When shifty Proteus vowed he had all time to listen in, from a leaden heart I cried: 'When will I reach my goal through its cloaks of story? How many veils to naked Helen?'

"'"'I know how it is,' said Proteus. 'Yet tell me what I wish; then I'll tell you what you will.' Nothing for it but rehearse the tale of me and slippery Eidothea:

5

"'"'Troy was clinkered; Priam's stones were still too warm to touch; the loot was depoted on the beach for share-out; Trojan ladies keened and huddled, eyed us with shivers, waiting to be boarded and rode down the tear-salt sea. We were ten years out; ten days more would see our plunder portioned, our dead sent up, good-trip hecatombs laid on the immortal gods. But I was mad with shame and passion for my salvaged wife; though curses Greek and Trojan showered on us like spears on Scamander-plain or the ash of heroes on our decks, I fetched her to my ship unstuck, stowed her below, made straight for home.

"'"'"Hecatombs to Athena!" Odysseus cried after us.

"'"'"Cushion your thwarts with Troy-girls!" Agamemnon called, dragging pale Cassandra — '"

"'"'Bitch! Bitch!'

"'"'" — by her long black hair. To forestall a mutiny I hollered back, they could keep half my loot for themselves if they'd ship the rest home for me to emprince my loyal crew with. As for me, all my concubines and treasure waited below, tapping her foot. Wise Nestor alone sailed with me, who as Supervisor of Spoils had loaded first; last thing I saw astern was shrewd Odysseus scratching his head, my brother crotch; then Troy sank in the purpled east; with a shake-plain shout, I'm good at those, I dived below to reclaim my wife.

""""Call it weakness if you dare: unlike the generality of men I take small joy in lording women. Helen's epic heat had charcoaled Troy and sent ten thousand down to Hades; I ought to've spitted her like a heifer on her Trojan hearth. But I hadn't, and the hour was gone to poll horns with the vengeful sword. I thought therefore to knock her about a bit and then take at last what had cost such a fearful price, perhaps vilifying her, within measure, the while. But when I beheld her — sitting crosslegged in the stern, cleaning long fingernails with a bodkin and pouting at the frames and strakes — I forebore, resolved to accept in lieu of her death a modest portion of heartfelt grovel. Further, once she'd flung herself at my knees and kissed my hem I would order her supine and mount more as one who loves than one who conquers; not impossibly, should she acquit herself well and often, I would even entertain a plea for her eventual forgiveness and restoration to the Atrean house. Accordingly I drew myself up to discharge her abjection — whereupon she gave over cleaning her nails and set to drumming them on one knee.

"""""Let your repentance salt my shoeleather," I said presently, "and then, as I lately sheathed my blade of anger, so sheathe you my blade of love."

"""""I only just came aboard," she replied. "I haven't unpacked yet."

""""With a roar I went up the companionway, dashed stern to stem, close-hauled the main, flogged the smile from my navigator, and clove us through the pastures of the squid. Leagues thereafter, when the moon changed phase, I overtook myself, determined shrewdly that her Troy-chests were secured, and vowing this time to grant the trull no quarter, at the second watch of night burst into her cubby and forgave her straight out. "Of the unspeakable we'll speak no further," I declared. "I here extend to you what no other in my position would: my outright pardon." To which, some moments after, I briskly appended: "Disrobe and receive it, for the sake of pity! This offer won't stand forever." There I had her; she yawned and responded: "It's late. I'm tired."

""""Up the mast half a dozen times I stormed and shinnied, took oar to my navigator, lost sight of Nestor, thundered and lightninged through

Poseidon's finny fief. When next I came to season, I stood a night slyly by while she dusk-to-dawned it, then saluted with this challenge her opening eyes: "Man born of woman is imperfect. On the three thousand two hundred eighty-seventh night of your Parisian affair, as I lay in Simoismud picking vermin off the wound I'd got that day from cunning Pandarus, exhaustion closed my eyes. I dreamed myself was pretty Paris, plucked by Aphrodite from the field and dropped into Helen's naked lap. There we committed sweet adultery; I woke wet, wept ..."

""""Here I paused in my fiction to shield my eyes and stanch the arrow-straight tracks clawed down my cheek. Then, as one who'd waited precisely for her maledict voice to hoarsen, I outshouted her in these terms: "Therefore come to bed my equal, uncursing, uncursed!"

""""The victory was mine, I still believe, but when I made to take trophy, winded Helen shook her head, declaring: "I have the curse."

""""My taffrail oaths shook Triton's stamp-ground; I fed to the fish my navigator, knocked my head against the mast and others; hollered up a gale that blew us from Laconic Malea to Egypt. My crew grew restive; when the storm was spent and I had done flogging me with halyards, I chose a moment somewhere off snaked Libya, slipped my cloak, rapped at Helen's cabin, and in measured tones declared: "Forgive me." Adding firmly: "Are you there?"

"""""Seasick," she admitted. "Throwing up." To my just query, why she repaid in so close-kneed coin my failure to butcher her in Troy, she answered —'

""""'Let me guess,' requested Proteus."

""""What I said in Troy," said offshore Helen. "What I say to you now."'

"'Whatever was that?' pressed Peisistratus."

"Hold on, hold on yet awhile, Menelaus," I advise.

I'm not the man I used to be.

""""Thus inspired I went a-princing and a-pirate. Seven years the north wind nailed us to Africa, while Helen held fast the door of love. We sailed no plotted course, but supped random in the courts of kings, sacked and sight-saw, ballasted our tender keel with bullion. The crew chose wives from among themselves, give me a woman anytime, had affairs with ewes, committed crimes of passion over fids and tholes. None of us grew younger. The eighth year fetched us here to Pharos, rich seaquirks, mutinous, strange. How much does a man need? We commenced to starve. Yesterday I strolled up the beach to fish, my head full of north-wind; I squatted on a rushy dune, fetched out my knife, considered whether to slice my parchèd throat or ditto cod. Then before me in the surf, a sudden skinny-dipper! Cock and gullet paused on edge; Beauty stepped from the seafoam; long time I regarded hairless limb, odd globy breast, uncalloused ham. Where was the fellow's sex? A fairer yeoman I'd not beheld; who'd untooled him? As as his king and skipper I decided to have at him before myself, it occurred to me he was a woman.

"""""Memory, easy-weakened, dies hard. From its laxy clutch I fetched my bride's dim image. True, her hair was gold, the one before me's green, and this was finned where that was toed; but the equal number and like placement of their breasts, congruence of their shames' geometry — too miraculous for chance! She was Helen gone a-surfing, or Aphrodite in Helen's form. With a clench-tooth wrench I recollected what a man was for, vowed to take her without preamble or petition, then open my throat. Better, as I knew my wife no weakling, but accurate of foot and sharp of toe, I hit upon a ruse to have her without loss of face or testicle, and cursed me I hadn't dreamed it up years past: as Zeus is wont to take mortal women in semblance of their husbands, I would feign Zeus in Menelaus' guise! Up tunic, down I sprang, aflop with recommissioned maleship. "Is it Helen's spouse about to prince me," my victim inquired, "or some god in his fair-haired form? A lady wants to know her undoer. My own name," she went on, and I couldn't.

""""""Eidothea's the name," she went on: "daughter of Proteus, he whose salt hands hold the key to wind and wife. You won't reach your goals till you've mastered Dad. My role in your suspended tale is merely to offer seven pieces of advice. Don't ask why. Let go of my sleeve, please. Don't mistake the key for the treasure. But before I go on," she went on,""""" and I can't.

""""""But before I go on," she went on, say first how it was at the last in Troy, what passed between you and Helen as the city fell ...""""

"Come on. 'Come on. "Come on. 'Come on. "Come on," Eidothea urged: "*In the horse's woody bowel we groaned and grunt ...* Why do you weep?"""""""

6

Respite.

"""""In the horse's bowel,"""""" I groan, """"""we grunt till midnight, Laocoön's spear still stuck in our gut ..."""" "Hold up," said Helen; "'Off,' said Proteus; "On," said his web-foot daughter." You see what my spot was, boys! Caught between blunt Beauty's, fishy Form's, and dark-mouth Truth's imperatives, arms trembling, knees raw from rugless poop and rugged cave, I tried to hold fast to layered sense by listening as it were to Helen hearing Proteus hearing Eidothea hearing me; critic within critic, nestled in my slipping grip ...'

"'May be,' Peisistratus suggested, 'you can trick the tale out against all odds by the following device: to Eidothea, let us say, you said: "Show me how to trap the old boy into prophecy!"; to Proteus, perhaps, for reasons of strategy, you declare: "I begged then of your daughter as Odysseus Nausicaa: 'Teach me, lady, how best to honor windshift aid from your noble sire'"; to Helen-on-the-poop, perhaps, you tell it: "I then declared to Proteus: 'I then besought your daughter: "Help me to learn from your immortal dad how to replease my heartslove Helen."""" But to us you may say with fearless truth: "I said to Eidothea: 'Show me how to fool your father!'""'

"But I asked myself," I remind me: "'Who is Peisistratus to trust with unrefracted fact?' 'Did Odysseus really speak those words to Nausicaa?' I asked him. 'Why doesn't Telemachus snatch that news? And how is it you know of fair Nausicaa, when Proteus on the beach at Pharos hasn't mentioned her to me yet? Doesn't it occur to you, faced with this and similar discrepancy, that it's you I might be yarning?' as I yarn myself," whoever that is. "'Menelaus! Proteus! Helen! For all we know, we're but stranded figures in Penelope's web, wove up in light to be unwove in darkness.' So snarling him, I caught the clew of my raveled fabrication:

""""What's going on?" Helen demanded.

""""Son of Atreus!' Proteus cried. 'Don't imagine I didn't hear what your wife will demand of you some weeks hence, when you will have returned from Egypt, made sail for home, and floored her with the tale of snatching yours truly on the beach! Don't misbehave yesterday, I warn you! We seers —'

"""""My next advice," Eidothea advised me, "is to take nonhuman form. Seal yourself tight." How is it, by the way,' I demanded of Proteus,

'You demand what you demand of me in Menelaus's voice, and through my mouth, as though I demanded it of myself?' For so it was from that moment on; I speeched his speeches, even as you hear me speak them now." "Never mind that!"' 'Who was it said "Never mind!"?' asked Peisistratus. 'Your wife? Eidothea? Tricky Proteus? The voice is yours; whose are the words? ' 'Never mind.' 'Could it be, could it have been, that Proteus changed from a leafy tree not into air but into Menelaus on the beach at Pharos, thence into Menelaus holding the Old Man of the Sea? Could it even be that all these speakers you give voice to—"' "Never mind," I say.

No matter. """"Disenhorsed at last," I declared to scaled Eidothea, "we found ourselves in the sleep-soaked heart of Troy. Each set about his appointed task, some murdering sentries, others opening gates, others yet killing Trojans in their cups and lighting torches from the beacon-fire to burn the city. But I made straight for Helen's apartment with Odysseus, who'd shrewdly reminded me of her liking for lamplit love.""""

"'How—'

"'Did I know which room was hers? Because only two lights burned in Troy, one fired as a beacon on Achilles' tomb by Sinon the faithful traitor, the other flickering from an upper chamber in the house of Deiphobus. It was by ranging one above the other Agamemnon returned the fleet to Troy, but I steered me by the adulterous fire alone, kindling therefrom as I came the torch of vengeance.

"""""Why—"

"""""Did Odysseus come too? Thank Zeus he did! For so enraged was Deiphobus at being overhauled at passion's peak, he fought like ten.""""

""""Not only fought—" """"But I matched him, I matched him," I pressed on, "all the while watching for my chance to sink sword in Helen, who rose up sheeted in her deadly beauty and cowered by the bedpost, dagger-handed. Long time we grappled—"'

"""""I'm concerned about my daughter's what- and whereabouts,' Proteus said—"'

"'Could it be,' wondered Peisistratus, in whose name I pledged an ox to the critic muse, 'Eidothea is Proteus in disguise, prearranging his own capture on the beach for purposes unfathomable to mortals? And how did those lovers lay hands on arms in bed? What I mean—'

""'Dagger I had," said Helen, "under my pillow; and Deiphobus always came to bed with a sword on. But I never cowered; it was the sheet kept slipping, my only cover—"

"""""Take it off!' cried subtle Odysseus. Long time his strategy escaped me, I fought Deiphobus to a bloody draw. At length with a whisk my loyal friend himself halfstaffed her. Our swords were up; for a moment we stood as if Medusa'd. Then, at the same instant, Deiphobus and I dived at our wife, Odysseus leaped up from where he knelt before her with the sheet, Helen's dagger came down, and the ghost of her latest lover squeaked off to join his likes.'""""

"'Her latest lover!' Peisistratus exclaimed. 'Do you mean to say—'

""""That's right," Helen said. "I killed him myself, a better man than most."

"""""Then Odysseus—" began Eidothea.

"""""Then Odysseus disappeared, and I was alone with topless Helen. My sword still stood to lop her as she bent over Deiphobus. When he was done dying she rose and with one hand (the other held her waisted sheet) cupped her breast for swording.'""""

""""I dare you!" Helen dared.'

"'Which Helen?' cried Peisistratus.

"I hesitated ... 'The moment passed ... "'My wife smiled shyly ... "My sword went down. I closed my eyes, not to see that fountain beauty; clutched at it, not to let her flee. 'You've lost weight, Menelaus,' she said. 'Prepare to die,' I advised her. She softly hung her head ...'""""

"'How could you tell, sir, if your eyes—'

"""""My next advice," said Eidothea,'" interrupting once again Peisistratus ...'

Respite.

"""""I touched my blade to the goddess breast I grasped, and sailed before my flagging ire the navy of her offenses. Merely to've told prior to sticking her the names and skippers of the ships she'd sunk would've been to stretch her life into the menopause; therefore I spent no wind on items; simply I demanded before I killed her: 'With your last breath tell me: Why?'"""""

"'("') (("("What?")")') (")'

"""""" *Why?'* I repeated," I repeated,' I repeated," I repeated,' I repeated," I repeat. """"""And the woman, with a bride-shy smile and hushed voice, replied: 'Why what?'

““““““Faster than Athena sealed beneath missile Sicily upstart Encela-
dus, Poseidon Nisyros mutine Polybutes, I sealed my would-widen
eyes; snugger than Porces Laocoön, Heracles Antaeus, I held to my
point interrogative Helen, to whom as about us combusted nightlong
Ilion I rehearsed our history horse to horse, driving at last as eveningly
myself to the seed and omphalos of all …”(’((”(((’)))))

““““““		’”””””	
“““““	} Why? {	’””””	
““““		’”””	
““		’	
“““““““ :			

7

““““““By Zeus out of Leda,’ I commenced, as though I weren’t Menelaus, Helen Helen, ‘egg-born Helen was a beauty desired by all men on
earth. When Tyndareus declared she might wed whom she chose, every
bachelor-prince in the peninsula camped on her stoop. Odysseus was
there, mighty Ajax, Athenian Menestheus, cunning Diomedes: men
great of arm, heart, wit, fame, purse; fit mates for the fairest. Menelaus
alone paid the maid no court, though his brother Agamemnon, wed
already to her fatal sister, sued for form’s sake on his behalf. Less clever
than Odysseus, fierce than Achilles, muscled than either Ajax, Menelaus excelled in no particular unless the doggedness with which he
clung to the dream of embracing despite all Helen. He knew who others
were — Odysseus resourceful, great Great Ajax, and the rest. Who was
he? Whose eyes, at the wedding of Agamemnon and Clytemnestra,
had laid hold of bridesmaid Helen’s image and never since let go?
While others wooed he brooded, played at princing, grappled idly
with the truth that those within his imagination’s grasp — which was
to say, everyone but Menelaus — seemed to him finally imaginary, and
he alone, ungraspable, real.
        ““““““Imagine what he felt, then, when news reached him one spring
forenoon that of all the men in Greece, hatchèd Helen had chosen him!
Despite the bright hour he was asleep, dreaming as always of that fault-
less form; his brother’s messenger strode in, bestowed without a word
the wreath of Helen’s choice, withdrew. Menelaus held shut his eyes
and clung to the dream — which however for the first time slipped his

grip. Dismayed, he woke to find his brow now fraught with the crown of love.""""""

"'Ah.'

"""""In terror he applied to the messenger: "Menelaus? Menelaus? Why of all princes Menelaus?" And the fellow answered: "Don't ask me."

""""""Then imagine what he felt in Tyndareus's court, pledge-horse disjoint and ready to be sworn on, his beaten betters gruntling about, when he traded Agamemnon the same question for ditto answer. Sly Odysseus held the princes to their pledge; all stood on the membered horse while Menelaus played the grateful winner, modest in election, wondering as he thanked: Could he play the lover too? Who was it wondered? Who is it asks?

""""""Imagine then what he felt on the nuptial night, when feast and sacrifice were done, carousers gone, and he faced his bedaydreamed in the waking flesh! Dreamisher yet, she'd betrothed him wordless, wordless wed; now without a word she led him to her chamber, let go her gold gown, stood golder before him. Not to die of her beauty he shut his eyes; of not beholding her embraced her. Imagine what he felt then!""""""

"'Two questions,' interjected Peisistratus—

"'One! One!'"""" There the bedstead stood; as he swooning tipped her to it his throat croaked "Why?""""

"""""Why?" asked Eidothea.'

""""'Why why?' Proteus echoed.'"

"'My own questions,' Peisistratus insisted, 'had to do with mannered rhetoric and your shift of narrative viewpoint.'

""""'Ignore that fool!' Proteus ordered from the beach.'"

"'How can Proteus—' 'Seer.' 'So.' 'The opinions echoed in these speeches aren't necessarily the speaker's.

"""""""Why'd you wed me?" Menelaus asked his wife,' I told my wife. "'Less crafty than Diomedes, artful than Teucer, *et cetera*?" She placed on her left breast his right hand.

"""""""Why me?" he cried again. "Less lipless than Achilles, *et cetera*!" The way she put on her other his other would have fired a stone.

""""""""Speak!" he commanded. She whispered: "Love."

""""""""Unimaginable notion! He was fetched up short. How could

Helen love a man less gooded than Philoctetes, *et cetera*, and whom besides she'd glimpsed but once prior to wedding and not spoken to till that hour? But she'd say no more; the harder he pressed the cooler she turned, who'd been ardor itself till he put his query. He therefore forebore, but curiosity undid him; how could he know her and not know how he knew?""'

""""'Come to the point!'

""""""'Hold on!"

""""""'He held her fast; she took him willy-nilly to her; I feel her yet, one endless instant, Menelaus was no more, never has been since. In his red ear then she whispered: "Why'd I wed you, less what than who, *et cetera*?"""""

""""'My very question."

""""""""'Speak!" Menelaus cried to Helen on the bridal bed,' I reminded Helen in her Trojan bedroom," I confessed to Eidothea on the beach,' I declared to Proteus in the cavemouth," I vouchsafed to Helen on the ship,' I told Peisistratus at least in my Spartan hall,' I say to whoever and where- I am. And Helen answered:

""""""""'Love!"""""""

!

""""""'He complied, he complied, as to an order. She took his corse once more to Elysium, to fade forever among the fadeless asphodel; his curious fancy alone remained unlaid; when he came to himself it still asked softly: "Why?"""""""

And don't I cry out to me every hour since, "Be sure you demanded of Peisistratus (and Telemachus), 'Didn't I exclaim to salvaged Helen, "Believe me that I here queried Proteus, 'Won't you ask of Eidothea herself whether or not I shouted at her, "Sheathed were my eyes, un-sheathed my sword what time I challenged Troy-lit Helen, 'Think you not that Menelaus and his bride as one cried, "*Love!*"?'!"?'!"?'!"?

""""""'So the night went, and the days and nights: sex and riddles. She burned him up, he played husband till he wasted, only his voice still diddled: "Why?"""""

""""""'What a question!"""""

"''What's the answer?'

""""""'Seven years of this, more or less, not much conversation, some-thing wrong with the marriage. Helen he could hold; how hold Mene-laus? To love is easy; to be loved, as if one were real, on the order of others: fearsome mystery! Unbearable responsibility! To her, *Menelaus* signified something recognizable, as *Helen* him. Whatever was it? They begot a child ..."""

""""I beg your pardon," Helen interrupted from the poop a quarter-century later. "Father Zeus got Hermione on me, disguised as you. That's the way he is, as everyone knows; there's no use pouting or pretending ..."

"'I begged her pardon, but insisted, as in Troy: """"It wasn't Zeus disguised as Menelaus who begot her, any more than Menelaus disguised as Zeus; it was Menelaus disguised as Menelaus, a mask masking less and less. Husband, father, lord, and host he played, grip slipping; he could imagine anyone loved, no accounting for tastes, but his cipher self. In his cups he asked on the sly their house guests: "Why'd she wed me, less horsed than Diomedes, *et cetera*?" None said. A night came when this misdoubt stayed him from her bed. Another ..."""""

Respite. I beg your pardon.

""""""Presently she asked him: *et cetera*. If only she'd declared, "Menelaus, I wed you because, of all the gilt clowns of my acquaintance, I judged you least likely to distract me from my lovers, of whom I've maintained a continuous and overlapping series since before we met." Wouldn't that have cleared the Lacedemonian air! In a rage of shame he'd've burned up the bed with her! Or had she said: "I truly am fond of you, Menelaus; would've wed no other. What one seeks in the husband way is a good provider, gentle companion, fit father for one's children whoever their sire — a blend in brief of brother, daddy, pal. What one doesn't wish are the traits of one's lovers, exciting by night, impossible by day: I mean peremptory desire, unexpectedness, rough play, high-pitched emotions of every sort. Of these, happily, you're free." Wouldn't that have stoked and drafted him! But "Love!" What was a man to do?'

"'("(("((("Well ...")))")")')'

""""""He asked Prince Paris —' 'You didn't!'" "By Zeus!"' 'By Zeus!'" "You didn't!"' 'Did you really?'" "By Zeus," I tell me I told all except pointed Helen, "I did.

""""""By Zeus,' I told pointed Helen, 'he did. Oh, he knew the wretch was eyes and hands for Helen; he wasn't blind; eight days they'd feasted him since he'd dropped in uninvited, all which while he'd hot-eyed the hostess, drunk from her goblet, teased out winy missives on the table top. On the ninth she begged Menelaus to turn him from the palace.

But he confessed,' I confessed," I confessed,' I confessed," *et cetera*, """"he liked the scoundrel after all ...""""""

"'Zeus! Zeus!'

""""""Young, rich, handsome he was, King Priam's son; a charmer, easy in the world ...""""""

""""Don't remind us!"

""""""One night Helen went early to her chamber, second on one's left *et cetera*, and the two men drank alone. Menelaus watched Paris watch her go and abruptly put his question, how it was that one less this than that had been the other, and what might be the import of his wife's reply. "A proper mystery," Paris agreed; "you say the one thing she says is what?" Menelaus pointed to the word his nemesis, by Paris idly drawn at dinner in red Sardonic.

""""""""Consult an oracle," Paris advised. "There's a good one at Delphi." "I'm off to Crete," Menelaus told breakfast Helen. "Grandfather died. Catreus. Take care of things."

""""""""Love!" she pled, tearing wide her gown. Menelaus clapped shut his eyes and ears, ran for the north.""""""

"'North to Crete?' 'Delphi, Delphi, """"where he asked the oracle: "Why *et cetera*?" and was told: "*No other can as well espouse her.*"

""""""""How now!" Menelaus cried,' I ditto," *et cetera*. """"Espouse? Espouse her? As lover? Advocate? Husband? Can't you speak more plainly? Who am I?"

«««««««« »»»»»»»»

. . .

""""""Post-haste he returned to Lacedemon, done with questions. He'd re-embrace his terrifying chooser, clasp her past speech, never let go, frig understanding; it would be bride-night, endless; their tale would rebegin. "Menelaus here!" His shout shook the wifeless hall.

7

""""""Odysseus outsmarted, unsmocked Achilles, mustered Agamemnon — all said: "Let her go." Said Menelaus: "Can't." What did he feel? Epic perplexity. That she'd left him for Paris wasn't the point. War not love. Ten years he played outraged spouse, clung ireful-limpetlike to Priam's west curtain, warwhooped the field of Ares. Never mind her promenading the bartizans arm in arm with her Troyish sport; no matter his seeing summerly her belly fill with love-tot. Curiosity was his passion, that too grew mild. When at last in the war's ninth year he faced Paris in single combat, it was purely for the sake of form. "I don't ask why she went with you," he paused to say. "But tell me, as I spear you: did Helen ever mention, while you clipped and tumbled, how she happened to choose me in the first place?" Paris grinned and whispered through his shivers: "Love." Aphrodite whisked him from the door of death; no smarterly than that old word did smirking Pandarus pierce Menelaus's side. War resumed.

""""""Came dark-horse-night; Paris dead, it was with her new mate Deiphobus Helen sallied forth to mock. When she had done playing each Greek's Mrs., in her own voice she called: "Are you there, Menelaus? Then hear this: the night you left me I left you, sailed off with Paris and your wealth. At our first berthing I became his passion's harbor; to Aphrodite the Uniter we raised shrines. I was princess of desire, he prince; from Greece to Egypt, Egypt Troy, our love wore out the rowing-benches. By charms and potions I kept his passion nine years firm, made all Troy and its beleaguerers burn for me. Pederast Achilles pronged me in his dreams; before killed Paris cooled, hot Deiphobus climbed into his place: he who, roused by this wooden ruse, stone-horses your Helen even as she speaks. To whom did slick Odysseus not long since slip, and whisper all the while he wooed dirty Greek, welcome to my Troy-cloyed ear? Down, godlike Deiphobus! Ah!"

""""""Heart-burst, Menelaus had cracked with woe the Epeian barrel and his own, had not far-sight Odysseus caulked and coopered him, saying: "The whore played Clytemnestra's part and my Penelope's; now she plays Helen." So they sat in silence, murderous, until the gods who smile on Troy wearied of this game and rechambered the lovers. Then Odysseus unpalmed the mouth of Menelaus and declared: "She must die." Menelaus spat. "Stick her yourself," went on the Ithacan: "play the man."

""""""The death-horse dunged the town with Greeks; Menelaus ground his teeth, drew sword, changed point of view. Taking his wrongèd part, I invite one word before I cut your perfect throat. What did the lieless oracle intend? Why'd you you-know-what ditto-whom *et cetera*?'

6

""""""Replied my wife in a huskish whisper: 'You know why.'

""""""I chucked my sword, she hooked her gown, I fetched her shipward through the fire and curses, she crossed her legs, here I weep on the beach at Pharos, I wish I were dead, what'd you say your name was?"

5

""""""Said Eidothea: "Eidothea." I hemmed, I hawed; "I'm not the man," I remarked, "I was." Shoulders shrugged. "I've advised disguise," she said. "If you find your falseface stinks, I advise ambrosia. My sixth advice is, not too much ambrosia; my seventh —" Frantic I recounted, lost track, where was I? "— ditto masks: when the hour's ripe, unhide yourself and jump." Her grabbèd dad, she declared, would turn first into animals, then into plants and wine-dark sea, then into no saying what. Let I go I'd be stuck forever; otherwise he'd return into Proteus and tell me what I craved to hear.

""""""Hang on," she said; "that's the main thing." I asked her wherefor her septuple aid; she only smiled, I hate that about women, paddled off. This noon, then, helped by her sealskins and deodorant, I jumped you. There you are. But you must have known all this already.'

4

""""Said Proteus in my voice: 'Never mind know. Loose me now, man, and I'll say what stands between you and your desire.' He talks that way. I wouldn't; he declared I had one virtue only, the snap-turtle's, who will beak fast though his head be severed. By way of preface to his lesson then, he broke my heart with news reports: how Agamemnon, Idomeneus, Diomedes were cuckolded by pacifists and serving-men; how Clytemnestra not only horned but axed my brother; how faithless Penelope, hearing Odysseus had slept a year with Circe, seven with Calypso, dishonored him by giving herself to all one hundred eight of her suitors, plus nine house-servants, Phemius the bard, and Melanthius the goat-herd . . .'"

"'What's this?' cried Peisistratus. 'Telemachus swears they've had no word since he sailed from Troy!' 'Prophets get their tenses mixed,' I replied; 'not impossibly it's now that Mrs. Odysseus goes the rounds, while her son's away. But I think he knows what a tangled web his mother weaves; otherwise he'd not sit silent, but call me and Proteus false or run for Ithaca.' There I had him, someone; on with the story. 'On with the story. '"On with the story,' I said to Proteus: 'Why can't I get off this beach, let go, go home again? I'm tired of holding Zeus knows what; the mussels on my legs are barnacled; my arms and mind have gone to sleep; our beards have grown together; your words, fishy as your breath, come from my mouth, in the voice of Menelaus. Why am I stuck with you? What is it makes all my winds north and chills my wife?'

"'"Proteus answered: 'You ask too many questions. Not Athena, but Aphrodite is your besetter. Leave Helen with me here; go back to the mouth of River Egypt. There where the yeasting slime of green unspeakable jungle springs ferments the sea of your intoxicate Greek bards,' that's how the chap talks, 'make hecatombs to Aphrodite; beg Love's pardon for your want of faith. Helen chose you without reason because she loves you without cause; embrace her without question and watch your weather change. Let go.'

"'"I tried; it wasn't easy; he swam and melted in the lesser Nile my tears. Then Eidothea surfaced just offshore, unless it was you . . ." Shipboard Helen. "Had he been Eidothea before? Had he turned Helen? Was I cuckold yet again, an old salt in my wound? Recollecting my hard homework I closed eyes, mouth, mind; set my teeth and Nileward course. It was a different river; on its crocodiled and dromedaried bank, to that goddess perversely polymorphous as her dam the sea or the shift Old Man Thereof, Menelaus sacrificed twin heifers, Curiosity, Common Sense. I no longer ask why you choose me, less tusked than Idomeneus, *et cetera*; should you declare it was love for me fetched you to Paris and broke the world, I'd raise neither eyebrow; 'Yes, well, so,' is what I'd say. I don't ask what's changed the wind, your opinion, me, why I hang here like, onto, and by my narrative. Gudgeon my pintle, step my mast, vessel me where you will. I believe all. I understand nothing. I love you."

3

"'Snarled thwarted Helen: "Love!" Then added through our chorus groan: "Loving may waste us into Echoes, but it's being loved that kills. Endymion! Semele! Io! Adonis! Hyacinthus! Loving steers marine Odysseus; being loved turned poor Callisto into navigation-stars. Do you love me to punish me for loving you?"

""""I haven't heard so deep Greek since Delphi," I marveled. "But do I ask questions?"

""""I'll put this love of yours truly to the test," Helen said. Gently she revived me with cold water and pungents from her Nilish store. "I suppose you suppose," she declared then, "that I've been in Troy."

"'So potent her medicaments, in no time at all I regained my breath and confessed I did.

"'Severely she nodded. "And you suspect I've been unfaithful?"

""""It would be less than honest of me to say," I said, "that no fancy of that dirt-foot sort has ever grimed my imagination's marmor sill.'

""""With Paris? And others as well?"

""""You wrest truth from me as Odysseus Astyanax Andromache."

""""In a word, you think yourself cuckold."

"'I blushed. "To rash untowardly to conclusions ill becomes a man made wise by hard experience and time. Nevertheless, I grant that as I shivered in a Trojan ditch one autumn evening in the war's late years and watched you stroll with Paris on the bastions, a swart-hair infant at each breast and your belly swaggèd with another, the term you mention flit once across the ramparts of my mind like a bat through Ilion-dusk. Not impossibly the clever wound I'd got from Pandarus festered my judgment with my side ..."

"'Helen kissed my bilging tears and declared: "Husband, I have never been in Troy.

""""What's more," she added within the hour, before the boatswain could remobilize the crew, "I've never made love with any man but you."

""""Ah."

"'She turned her pout lips portward. "You doubt me.""

""Too many years of unwomaned nights and combat days," I explained, "gestate in our tenderer intelligences a skeptic demon, that will drag dead Hector by the baldric till his corpsetrack moat the walls, and yet whisper when his bones are ransomed: 'Hector lives.' Were one to say of Menelaus at this present hour, 'That imp nips him,' one would strike Truth's shield not very far off-boss."

""Doubt no more," said Helen. "Your wife was never in Troy. Out of love for you I left you when you left, but before Paris could up-end me, Hermes whisked me on Father's orders to Egyptian Proteus and made a Helen out of clouds to take my place.

""All these years I've languished in Pharos, chaste and comfy, waiting for you, while Paris, nothing wiser, fetched Cloud-Helen off to Troy, made her his mistress, got on her Bunomus, Aganus, Idaeus, and a little Helen, dearest of the four. It wasn't I, but cold Cloud-Helen you fetched from Troy, whom Proteus dissolved the noon you beached him. When you then went off to account to Aphrodite, I slipped aboard. Here I am. I love you."

"'Not a quarter-hour later she asked of suspended me: "Don't you believe me?"

""What ground have I for doubt?" I whispered. "But that imp aforementioned gives me no peace. 'How do you know,' he whispers with me, 'that the Helen you now hang onto isn't the cloud-one? Why mayn't your actual spouse be back in Troy, or fooling in naughty Egypt yet?'"

""Or home in Lacedemon," Helen added, "where she's been all along, waiting for her husband."

"'Presently my battle voice made clear from stem to stern my grown conviction that the entire holocaust at Troy, with its prior and subsequent fiascos, was but a dream of Zeus's conjure, visited upon me to lead me to Pharos and the recollection of my wife — or her nimbus like. For for all I knew I roared what I now gripped was but a further fiction, maybe Proteus himself, turned for sea-cow-respite to cuckold generals . . .

""A likely story," Helen said. "Next thing, you'll say it was a cloud-Menelaus went fishing on the beach at Pharos! If I carry to my grave no heart-worm grudge at your decade vagrance, it's only that it irks me less just now than your present doubt. And that I happen to be not mortal. Yet so far from giving cut for cut, I'm obliged by Love and the one right action of your life to ease your mind entirely." Here she led me by the hand into her golden-Aphrodite's-grove, declaring: "If what's within your grasp is mere cloudy fiction, cast it to the wind; if fact then Helen's real, and really loves you. Espouse me without more carp! The senseless answer to our riddle woo, mad history's secret, base-fact and footer to the fiction crazy-house our life: imp-slayer love, terrific as the sun! Love! Love!"

"'Who was I? Am? Mere Menelaus, if that: mote in the cauldron, splinter in the Troy-fire of her love! Does nail hold timber or timber nail? Held fast by his fast-held, consumed by what he feasted on, whatever was of Menelaus was no more. I must've done something right.

"''"You'll not die in horsy Argos, son of Atreus . . ." So quoted Proteus's last words to me my love-spiked wife. "'The Olympic gods will west you in your latter days to a sweet estate where rain nor passion leaches, there to be your wife's undying advertisement, her espouser in the gods' slow time. Not fair-haired battleshouts or people-leading preserves you, but forasmuch as and only that you are beloved of Helen, they count you immortal as themselves.'"

"'Lampreys and flat-fish wept for joy, squids danced on the wave-tops, crab-choirs and minnow-anthems shook with delight the opalescent welkin. As a sea-logged voyager strives across the storm-shocked country of the sole, loses ship and shipmates, poops to ground on alien shingle gives over struggling, and is whisked in a dream-dark boat, sleep-skippered, to his shoaly home, there to wake next morning with a wotless groan, wondering where he is and what fresh lie must save him, until he recognizes with a heart-surge whither he's come and hugs the home-coast to sweet oblivion. So Menelaus, my best guess, flayed by love, steeved himself snug in Helen's hold, was by her hatched and transport, found as it were himself in no time Lacedemoned, where he clings still stunned. She returned him to bride-bed; had he ever been in Troy? Whence the brine he scents in her ambrosial cave? Is it bedpost he clutches, or spruce horse rib? He continues to hold on, but can no longer take the world seriously. Place and time, doer, done-to have lost their sense. Am I stoppered in the equine bowel, asleep and dreaming?

At the Nile-fount, begging Love for mercy? Is it Telemachus I hold, cold-hearth Peisistratus? No, no, I'm on the beach at Pharos, must be forever. I'd thought my cave-work finished, episode; re-entering Helen I understood that all subsequent history is Proteus, making shift to slip me . . .'

"'Beg pardon.'

"'Telemachus? Come back?'

"'To.'

"'Thought I hadn't noticed, did you, how your fancy strayed while I told of good-voyaging your father and the rest? Don't I know Helen did the wine-trick? Are you the first in forty years, d'you think, I ever thought I'd yarned till dawn when in fact you'd slipped me?'

2

"Fagged Odysseus's-son responded: 'Your tale has held us fast through a dark night, Menelaus, and will bring joy to suitored Ithaca. Time to go. Wake up, Peisistratus. Our regards to Hermione, thanks to her magic mother.'

"'Mine,' I replied, 'to chastest yours, muse and mistress of the embroidrous art, to whom I commission you to retail my round-trip story. Like yourself, let's say, she'll find it short nor simple, though one dawn enlightens its dénouement. Her own, I'd guess, has similar abound of woof — yet before your father's both will pale, what marvels and rich mischances will have fetched him so late home! Beside that night's fabrication this will stand as Lesser to Great Ajax.'

"So saying I gifted them off to Nestored Pylos and the pig-fraught headlands dear to Odysseus, myself returning to my unfooled narrate seat. There I found risen Helen, sleep-gowned, replete, mulling twin cups at the new-coaxed coals. I kissed her ear; she murmured 'Don't.' I stooped to embrace her; 'Look out for the wine.' I pressed her, on, to home. 'Let go, love.' I would not, ever, said so; she sighed and smiled, women, I was taken in, it's a gift, a gift-horse, I shut my eyes, here we go again, 'Hold fast to yourself, Menelaus.' Everything," I declare, "is now as day."

1

It was himself grasped undeceivèd Menelaus, solely, imperfectly. No man goes to the same Nile twice. When I understood that Proteus somewhere on the beach became Menelaus holding the Old Man of the Sea, Menelaus ceased. Then I understood further how Proteus thus also was as such no more, being as possibly Menelaus's attempt to hold him, the tale of that vain attempt, the voice that tells it. Ajax is dead, Agamemnon, all my friends, but I can't die, worse luck; Menelaus's carcass is long wormed, yet his voice yarns on through everything, to itself. Not my voice, I am this voice, no more, the rest has changed, rechanged, gone. The voice too, even that changes, becomes hoarser, loses its magnetism, grows scratchy, incoherent, blank.

I'm not dismayed. Menelaus was lost on the beach at Pharos; he is no longer, and may be in no poor case as teller of his gripping history. For when the voice goes he'll turn tale, story of his life, to which he clings yet, whenever, how-, by whom-recounted. Then when as must at last every tale, all tellers, all told, Menelaus's story itself in ten or ten thousand years expires, yet I'll survive it, I, in Proteus's terrifying last disguise, Beauty's spouse's odd Elysium: the absurd, unending possibility of love.

Anonymiad

HEADPIECE

When Dawn rose, pink as peerless Helen's teat,

which in fact swung wineskinlike between her hind legs and was pie-bald as her pelt, on which I write,

> *The salty minstrel oped his tear-brined eye,*
> *And remarking it was yet another day . . .*

Ended his life. Commenced his masterpiece. Returned to sleep.
  Invoked the muse:

> *Twice-handled goddess! Sing through me the boy*
> *Whom Agamemnon didn't take to Troy,*
> *But left behind to see his wife stayed chaste.*
> *Tell, Muse, how Clytemnestra maced*
> *Her warden into song, made vain his heart*
> *With vision of renown; musick the art*
> *Wherewith was worked self-ruin by a youth*
> *Who'd sought in his own art some music truth*
> *About the world and life, of which he knew*
> *Nothing. Tell how ardent his wish grew*

To autograph the future, wherefore he
Let sly Aegisthus ship him off to see
The Wide Real World. Sing of the guile
That fetched yours truly to a nameless isle,
By gods, men, and history forgot,
To sing his sorry self.

And die. And rot. And feed his silly carcass to the birds.

But not before he'd penned a few last words,

inspired by the dregs and lees of the muse herself, at whom, Zeus willing, he'll have a final go before he corks her for good and casts her adrift, vessel of his hopeless hope. The Minstrel's Last Lay.

Once upon a time
I composed in witty rhyme
And poured libations to the muse Erato.

Merope would croon,
"Minstrel mine, a lay! A tune!"
"From bed to verse," I'd answer; "that's my motto."

Stranded by my foes,
Nowadays I write in prose,
Forsaking measure, rhyme, and honeyed diction;

Amphora's my muse:
When I finish off the booze,
I hump the jug and fill her up with fiction.

I begin in the middle — where too I'll end, there being alas to my arrested history as yet no dénouement. God knows how long I'd been out of writing material until this morning, not to mention how long altogether I've been marooned upon this Zeus-forsaken rock, in the middle of nowhere. There, I've begun, in the middle of nowhere, tricked ashore in manhood's forenoon with nine amphorae of Mycenaean red and abandoned to my own devisings. After half a dozen years of which more later I was down to the last of them, having put her sisters to the triple use aforesung: one by one I broke their seals, drank the lovelies dry, and, fired by their beneficence, not only made each the temporary mistress of my sole passion but gave back in the form of art what I'd had from them. Me they nourished and inspired; them I fulfilled to the top of my bent, and launched them worldward fraught with our joint conceits. Their names are to me now like the memory of old songs: Euterpe! Polyhymnia! I recall Terpsichore's lovely neck, Urania's matchless shoulders; in dreams I hear Melpomene singing yet in the wet west wind, her voice ever deeper as our romance waned; I touch again Erato's ears, too delicate for mortal clay, surely the work of Aphrodite! I smile at Clio's gravity, who could hold more wine than any of her sisters without growing tipsy; I shake my head still at the unexpected passion of saucy Thalia, how she clung to me even when broken by love's hard knocks. Fair creatures. Often I wonder where the tides of life have fetched them, whether they're undone by age and the world or put on the shelf by some heartless new master. What lovers slake themselves now at those fragile mouths? Do they still bear my charge in them, or is it jettisoned and lost, or brought to light?

With anticipation of Calliope, the last, I consoled me for their casting off. Painful state for a lover, to have always before him the object of his yen — naked, cool, serene — and deny his parched sense any slake but the lovely sight of her! No less a regimen I imposed upon myself — imperfectly, imperfectly, I'm not made of stone, and there she stood, brimful of spirit, heavy with what I craved, sweating delicately where the sun caressed her flank, and like her sisters infinitely accessible! A night came, I confess it, when need overmastered me; I broke my vow and her seal; other nights followed (never many in a season, but blessed Zeus, most blest Apollo, how many empty seasons have gone by!) when, despite all new resolve and cursing my weak-willedness even as I tipped her to my will, I eased my burden with small increase of hers. But take her to me altogether I did not, or possess myself of the bounty I thirsted for, and which freely she would yield. Until last night! Until the present morn! For in that measureless drear interval, now to be exposed, I had nothing to write upon, no material wherewith to fashion the work I'd vowed she must inspire me to, and with which, in the last act of our loveship and my life, I'd freight her.

Calliope, come, refresh me; it's the hour for exposition!

I'll bare at last my nameless tale, and then . . .
Hie here, sweet Muse: your poet must dip his pen!

1

Ink of the squid, his obscure cloak; blood of my heart; wine of my inspiration: record on Helen's hide, in these my symbols, the ills her namesake wrought what time, forsaking the couch of fairhaired Menelaus, she, spread her legs for Paris *et cetera*.

My trouble was, back home in 'prentice days, I never could come out straight-faced with "Daughter of Zeus, egg-born Clytemnestra" and the rest, or in general take seriously enough the pretensions of reality. Youngster though I was, nowise sophisticated, I couldn't manage the correct long face when Agamemnon hectored us on Debts of Honor, Responsibility to Our Allies, and the like. But I don't fool myself: if I never took seriously the world and its tiresome concerns, it's because I was never able to take myself seriously; and the reason for that, I've known for some while, is the fearsomeness of the facts of life. Merope's love, Helen's whoring, Menelaus's noise, Agamemnon's slicing up his daughter for the weatherman — all the large and deadly passions of men and women, wolves, frogs, nightingales; all this business of seizing life, grabbing hold with both hands — it must've scared the daylights out of me from the first. While other fellows played with their spears, I learned to play the lyre. I wasn't the worst-looking man in Argolis; I had a ready wit and a good ear, and knew how to amuse the ladies. A little more of those virtues (and a lot more nerve, and better luck in the noble-birth way), I might have been another Paris; it's not your swaggerers like Menelaus the pretty girls fall for, or even your bully-boys like Agamemnon: it's the tricky chaps like Paris, graceful as women themselves almost, with their mischief eyes and honey tongues and nimble fingers, that set maiden hearts a-flutter and spit maidenheads like squablings. Aphrodite takes care of her own. Let that one have his Helen; this musicked to him in his eighteenth year milkmaid Merope, fairest-formed and straightest-hearted that ever mused goatherd into minstrelsy.

Daily then I pastured with that audience, two-score nans and my doe-eye nymph, to whom I sang songs perforce original, as I was ignorant of the common store. Innocent, I sang of innocence, thinking I sang of love and fame. Merope put down her jug, swept back her hair, smiled and listened. In modes of my own invention, as I supposed, I sang my vow to make a name for myself in the world at large.

"Many must wish the same," my honeyhead would murmur. But could she've shown me that every browsy hill in Greece had its dappled nans and famestruck twanger, I'd've not been daunted. My dreams, like my darling, perched light but square on a three-leg seat: first, while I scoffed at them myself, and at the rube their dreamer, I sucked them for life; the world was wide, as my songs attested, its cities flocked with brilliant; I was a nameless rustic plucker, unschooled, unmannered, late finding voice, innocent of fashion, uneasy in the world and my own skin — so much so, my crazy hope of shedding it was all sustained me. Fair as the country was and the goatboy life my fellows' lot, if I could not've imagined my music's one day whisking me Orionlike to the stars, I'd have as well flung myself into the sea. No other fate would even faintly do; an impassioned lack of alternatives moved my tongue; what for another might be heartfelt wish was for me an absolute condition. Second, untutored as I was and narrow my acquaintance, I knew none whose fancy so afflicted him as mine me. Especially when I goated it alone, the world's things took a queer sly aspect: it was as if the olive hillside hummed, not with bees, but with some rustle secret; the placid goats were in on it; asphodels winked and nodded behind my back; the mountain took broody note; the very sunlight trembled; I was a stranger to my hands and feet. Merope herself, when these humors gripped me, was alien and horrific as a sphinx: her perfect body, its pulse and breath, smote me with dismay: ears! toes! What creature did it wrap, that was not I, that claimed to love me? My own corse was a rude anthropophage that had swallowed me whole at birth and suffered indigestion ever since; could Merope see what I couldn't, who it was spoke from his griped bowels? When she and I, the goats our original, invented love — romped friggly in the glens and found half a hundred pretty pathways to delight, each which we thought ourselves the first to tread — some I as foreign to the me that pleasured as goatherd to goats stood by, tight-lipped, watching, or aswoon at the entire strangeness of the world.

And yet, third prop of revery, there *was* Merope, realer than myself though twice my dreams: the ardent fact of her, undeniable as incredible, argued when all else failed that the gods had marked me for no common fate. That a spirit so fresh and unaffected, take my word, no space for details, in a form fit to warm the couch of kings, should elect to give not only ear but heart and dainty everything to a lad the contrary of solipsistic, who felt the world and all its contents real except himself... Perched astride me in a wild-rosemary-patch, her gold skin sweating gently from our sport, her gold hair tenting us, Merope'd say: "I love you"; and while one of me inferred: "Therefore I am," and another wondered whether she was nymph doing penance for rebuffing Zeus or just maid with unaccountable defect of good sense, a third exulted: "Then nothing is impossible!" and set out to scale Parnassus blithely as he'd peaked the mount of Love.

Had I known what cloak of climbers mantles that former hill, so many seasoneder and cleverer than I, some schooled for the ascent from earliest childhood, versed in the mountain's every crag and col, rehearsed in the lore of former climbers ... But I didn't, except in that corner of my fancy that imaged all possible discouragements and heeded none. As a farm boy, innocent of the city's size, confidently expects on his first visit there to cross paths with the one inhabitant he knows among its scores of thousands, and against all reason does, so when at market-time I took goats to golden Mycenae to be sold at auction, I wasn't daunted as I should've been by the pros who minstrelled every wineshop, but leaned me on the Lion's Gate, took up my lyre, and sang a sprightly goat-song, fully expecting that the Queen herself would hear and call for me.

The song, more or less improvised, had to do with a young man who announces himself, in the first verse, to be a hickly swain newcome from the bosky outback: he sings what a splendid fellow he is, fit consort for a queen. In the second verse he's accosted by an older woman who declares that while she doubtless appears a whore, she is in fact the Queen disguised; she takes the delighted singer to a crib in the common stews, which she asserts to be a wing of the palace reconstructed, at her order, to resemble a brothel: the trulls and trollops thereabout, she explains, are gentlewomen at their sport, the pimps and navvies their disguisèd noble lovers. Did the masquerade strike our minstrel as excessive? He was to bear in mind that the whims of royalty are like the gods', mighty in implementation and consequence. Her pleasure, she discloses in the third verse, is that he should lie with her as with a woman of the streets, the newest fashion among great ladies: she's chosen him for her first adventure of this sort because, while obviously not of noble birth, he's of somewhat gentler aspect than the lot of commoners; to make the pretense real, he's to pay her a handsome loveprice, which she stipulates. The fellow laughs and agrees, but respectfully points out that her excessive fee betrays her innocence of prostitution; if verisimilitude is her object, she must accept the much lower wage he names. Not without expressions of chagrin the lady acquiesces, demanding only the right to earn a bonus for meritorious performance. In the fifth and sixth verses they set to, in manner described in salacious but musically admirable cadenzas; in the seventh the woman calls for fee and bonus, but her minstrel lover politely declines: to her angry protests he replies, in the eighth verse, that despite herself she makes love like a queen; her excellency shows through the cleverest disguise. How does he know? Because, he asserts, he's not the rustic he has feigned, but an exile prince in flight from the wrath of a neighbor king, whose queen had been his mistress until their amour came to light. Begging the amazed and skeptic lady not to betray him to the local nobility so well masked, he pledges in return to boast to no one that he has lain with Her Majesty. As I fetched him from the stews wondering mellifluously whether his partner was a queen disguised as a prostitute or a prostitute disguised as a queen disguised *et cetera*, I was seized by two armored guards and fetched myself to a room above a nearby wineshop. The premises were squalid; the room was opulent; beside a window overlooking the Lion's Gate sat a regal dame ensconced in handmaids.

What about the minstrel, she wanted to know: Was he a prince in mufti or a slickering rustic? Through my tremble I saw bright eyes in her sharp-bone countenance. I struck a chord to steady my hand, wrung rhymes from alarmed memory, took a breath, and sang in answer:

> "*As Tyrian robe may cloak a bumpkin heart,*
> *So homespun hick may play the royal part.*
> *Men may be kings in spirit or in mien.*
> *Which make more kingly lovers? Ask a queen!*

But don't ask me which sort of queen to ask," I added quickly; "I haven't been in town long enough to learn the difference." The maids clapped hands to mouths; the lady's eyes flashed, whether with anger or acknowledgment I couldn't judge. "See he goes to school on the matter," she ordered a plumpish gentleman across the room, eunuch by the look of him. Then she dismissed us, suddenly fretsome, and turned to the window, as one waiting for another to appear.

On with the story, cut corners: Clytemnestra herself it was, wont to rest from her market pleasures in that apartment. Her eunuch — Chief Minstrel, it turned out — gave me a gold piece and bade me report to him in Agamemnon's scullery when I came to town, against the chance the whim should take Her Majesty to hear me again. Despite the gold-hair wonder that rested on my chest as I reported this adventure next day, I was astonished after all that dreams come true.

"The King and Queen are real!" I marveled. "They want *me* to minstrel them!"

Fingering my forearm Merope said: "Because you're the best." I must go to town often, we agreed, perhaps even live there; on the other hand, it would be an error to put by my rustic origins and speech, as some did: in song, at least (where dwelt the only kings and courtiers we knew), such pretense always came a cropper. Though fame and clever company no doubt would change me in some ways, I should not change myself for them, it being on the one hand Merope's opinion that worldliness too ardently pursued becomes affectation, mine on the other that innocence artificially preserved becomes mere crankhood.

"We'll come back here often," I told her, "to remind us who we are."

She stroked my fingers, in those days scarcely calloused by the lyre. "Was the Queen very beautiful?"

I promised to notice next time. Soon after, we bid the goats good-bye and moved to Mycenae. Merope was frightened by the din of so many folk and wagons and appalled by everyone's bad manners, until I explained that these were part of the excitement of city life. Every day, all day, in our mean little flat, I practiced my art, which before I'd turned to only when the mood was on me; eveningly I reported to the royal kitchen, where lingered a dozen other mountebanks and minstrels just in favor. Ill at ease in their company, I kept my own, but listened amazed to their cynic jokes about the folk they flattered in their lays, and watched with dismay the casual virtuosity with which they performed for one another's amusement while waiting the royal pleasure. I hadn't half their skill and wit! Yet the songs I made from my rural means — of country mouse and city mouse, or the war between the ants and the mice — were well enough received; especially when I'd got the knack of subtly mocking in such conceits certain figures in the court — those who, like the King, were deaf to irony — I'd see Clytemnestra's eyes flash over her wine, as if to say, "Make asses of *them* all you please, but don't think you're fooling me!" and a coin or two would find their way meward. Flattering it was, for a nameless country lad, to hear the Queen herself praise his songs and predict a future for him in the minstrel way. When I got home, often not till sunup, I'd tell my sleepish darling all I'd seen and done, and there'd be love if the day hadn't spent me, which alas it sometimes had. That first gold piece I fetched to a smith and caused to be forged into a ring, gift to the gods' gift to me; but I misguessed the size, and fearing she'd lose it, Merope bade me wear it in her stead.

1½

Once upon a time I told tales straight out, alternating summary and dramatization, developing characters and relationships, laying on bright detail and rhetorical flourish, *et cetera*. I'm not that amateur at the Lion's Gate; I know my trade. But I fear we're too far gone now for such luxury, Helen and I; I must get to where I am; the real drama, for yours truly, is whether he can trick this tale out at all — not the breath-batingest plot in the world, but there we are. It's an old story anyhow, this part of it; the corpus bloats with its like; I'll throw you the bones, to flesh out or pick at as you will.

What I had in mind was an *Anonymiad* in nine parts, reflecting (so you were to've nudged your neighbor and observed) the nine amphorae and ditto muses; or seven parts plus head- and tail-piece: the years of my maroonment framed by its causes and prognosis. The prologue was to've established, hopefully has done, the ground-conceit and the narrative voice and viewpoint: a minstrel stuck on some Aegean clinker commences his story, in the process characterizing himself and hinting at the circumstances leading to his plight. Parts One through Four were to rehearse those circumstances, Five through Seven the stages of his island life vis-à-vis his minstrelling — innocent garrulity, numb silence, and terse self-knowledge, respectively — and fetch the narrative's present time up to the narrator's. The epilogue's a sort of envoi to whatever eyes, against all odds, may one day read it. But though you're to go through the several parts in order, they haven't been set down that way: after writing the headpiece I began to fear that despite my planning I mightn't have space enough to get the tale told; since it pivots about Part Four (the head piece and three parts before, three parts and the tailpiece after), I divided Helen's hide in half to insure the right narrative proportions; then, instead of proceeding with the exposition heralded at the tail of the headpiece, I took my cue from a remark I'd made earlier on, began in the middle, and wrote out Parts Five, Six, and Seven. Stopping at the head of the tailpiece, which I'm leaving blank for my last words, I returned to compose Parts One, Two, and Three, and the pivotal Part Four. But alas, there's more to my matter and less to my means than I'd supposed; for a while at least I'll have to tell instead of showing; if you must have dialogue and dashing about, better go to the theater.

So, so: the rest of Part One would've shown the minstrel, under the eunuch's tutelage, becoming more and more a professional artist until he's Clytemnestra's pet entertainer. A typical paragraph runs: *We got on, the Queen and I, especially when the Paris-thing blew up and Agamemnon started conscripting his sister-in-law's old boyfriends. Clytemnestra wasn't impressed by all the spear-rattling and the blather of National Honor, any more than I, and couldn't've cared less what happened to Helen. She'd been ugly duckling in the house of Tyndareus, Clytie, second prize in the house of Atreus; she knew Agamemnon envied his brother, and that plenty of Trojan slave-girls would see more of the Family Jewels, while he was avenging the family honor, than she'd seen in some while. Though she'd got a bit hard-boiled by life in Mycenae, she was still a Grade-A figure of a woman; it's a wonder she didn't put horns on him long before the war . . .*

In addition to their expository function, this and like passages establish the minstrel's growing familiarity and preoccupation with affairs of court. His corresponding professional sophistication, at expense of his former naive energy, was to be rendered as a dramatical correlative to the attrition of his potency with Merope (foreshadowed by the earlier ring-business and the Chief Minstrel's eunuchhood), or vice versa. While still proud of her lover's success, Merope declares in an affecting speech that she preferred the simple life of the goat pasture and the ditto songs he sang there, which now seem merely to embarrass him. The minstrel himself wonders whether the changes in his life and work are for the better: the fact is — as he makes clear on the occasion of their revisiting the herd — that having left the country but never, despite his success, quite joined the court, he feels out of place now in both. Formerly he sang of bills and nans as Daphnises and Chloes; latterly he sings of courtly lovers as bucks and does. His songs, he fears, are growing in some instances merely tricksy, in others crankish and obscure; moreover, the difficulties of his position in Mycenae have increased with his reputation: Agamemnon presses on the one hand for anti-Trojan songs in the national interest, Clytemnestra on the other for anti-Iliads to feed her resentment. Thus far he's contrived a precarious integrity by satirizing his own dilemma, for example — but arthritis is retiring the old eunuch, and our narrator has permitted himself to imagine that he's among the candidates for the Chief-Minstrelship, despite his youth: should he be so laureled, the problem of quid pro quo might become acute. All these considerations notwithstanding (he concludes), one can't pretend to an innocence outgrown or in other wise retrace one's steps, unless by coming full circle. Merope doesn't reply; the minstrel attempts to entertain her with a new composition, but neither she nor the goats (who'd used to gather when he sang) seem much taken by it. The rest of the visit goes badly.

2

Part Two opens back in Mycenae, where all is a-bustle with war preparations. The minstrel, in a brilliant trope which he predicts will be as much pirated by later bards as his device of beginning in the middle, compares the scene to a beehive; he then apostrophizes on the war itself:

The war, the war! To be cynical of its warrant was one thing — bloody madness it was, whether Helen or Hellespont was the prize — and my own patriotism was nothing bellicose: dear and deep as I love Argolis, Troy's a fine place too, I don't doubt, and the Trojan women as singable as ours. To Hades with wars and warriors: I had no illusions about the expedition.

Yet I wanted to go along! Your dauber, maybe, or your marble-cracker, can hole up like a sybil in a cave, just him and the muse, and get a lifeswork done; even Erato's boys, if they're content to sing twelve-liners

*all their days about Porphyria's eyebrow and Althea's navel, can forget
the world outside their bedchambers. But your minstrel who aspires to
make and people worlds of his own had better get to know the one he's in,
whether he cares for it or not. I believe I understood from the beginning
that a certain kind of epic was my fate: that the years I was to spend, in
Mycenae and here [i.e., here, this island, where we are now], turning out
clever lyrics, satires, and the like, were as it were apprenticeships in love,
flirtation-trials to fit me for master-husbandhood and the siring upon
broad-hipped Calliope, like Zeus upon Alcmena, of a very Heracles of
fictions. "First fact of our generation," Agamemnon called the war in his
recruitment speeches; how should I, missing it, speak to future times as
the voice of ours?*

He adds: *Later I was to accept that I wasn't of the generation of Agamemnon, Odysseus, and those other giant brawlers (in simple truth I was
too young to sail with the fleet), nor yet of Telemachus and Orestes, their
pale shadows. To speak for the age, I came to believe, was less achievement
than to speak for the ageless; my membership in no particular generation
I learned to treasure as a passport out of history, or exemption from
the drafts of time. But I begged the King to take me with him, and was
crestfallen when he refused. No use Clytemnestra's declaring (especially
when the news came in from Aulis that they'd cut up Iphigenia) it was
my clearsightedness her husband couldn't stick, my not having hymned
the bloody values of his crowd; what distressed me as much as staying
home from Troy was a thing I couldn't tell her of: Agamemnon's secret
arrangement with me . . .* his reflections upon and acceptance of which
end the episode — or chapter, as I call the divisions of my unversed fictions. Note that no mention is made of Merope in this excursus, which
pointedly develops a theme (new to literature) first touched on in Part
One: the minstrel's yen for a broader range of life-experience. His feeling is that having left innocence behind, he must pursue its opposite;
though his conception of "experience" in this instance is in terms of
travel and combat, the metaphor with which he figures his composing-
plans is itself un-innocent in a different sense.

The truth is that he and his youthful sweetheart find themselves
nightly more estranged. Merope is unhappy among the courtiers and
musicians, who speak of nothing but Mycenaean intrigues and Lydian
minors; the minstrel ditto among everyone else, now that his vocation
has become a passion — though he too considers their palace friends

mostly fops and bores, not by half so frank and amiable as the goats. The "arrangement" he refers to is concluded just before the King's departure for Aulis; Agamemnon calls for the youth and without preamble offers him the title of Acting Chief Minstrel, to be changed to Chief Minstrel on the fleet's return. Astonished, the young man realizes, as after his good fortune at the Lion's Gate, how much his expectations have in fact been desperate dream:

"*I . . . I accept* [I have him cry gratefully, thus becoming the first author in the world to reproduce the stammers and hesitations of actual human speech. But the whole conception of a literature faithful to daily reality is among the innovations of this novel opus]*!*" — whereupon the King asks "one small favor in return." Even as the minstrel protests, in hexameters, that he'll turn his music to no end beyond itself, his heart breaks at the prospect of declining the title after all:

Whereto, like windfall wealth, he had at once got used.

Tut, Agamemnon replies: though he personally conceives it the duty of every artist not to stand aloof from the day's great issues, he's too busy coping with them to care, and has no ear for music anyhow. All he wants in exchange for the proffered tide is that the minstrel keep a privy eye on Clytemnestra's activities, particularly in the sex and treason way, and report any infidelities on his return.

Unlikeliest commission [the minstrel exclaims to you at this point, leaving ambiguous which commission is meant]*! The King and I were nowise confidential; just possibly he meant to console me for missing the fun in Troy (he'd see it so) by giving me to feel important on the home front. But chances are he thought himself a truly clever fellow for leaving a spy behind to watch for horns on the royal brow, and what dismayed me was less the ingenuousness of that plan — I knew him no Odysseus — as his assumption that from me he had nothing to fear! As if I were my gelded predecessor, or some bugger of my fellow man (no shortage of those in the profession), or withal so unattractive Clytemnestra'd never give me a tumble! And I a lyric poet, Aphrodite's very barrister, the Queen's Chief Minstrel!* No more is said on this perhaps surprising head for the present; significantly, however, his reluctance to compromise his professional integrity is expressed as a concern for what Merope will think. On the other hand, he reasons, the bargain has nothing to do with his art; he'll compose what he'll compose whether laureled or un, and a song fares well or ill irrespective of its maker. In the long run Chief-Minstrelships and the like are meaningless; precisely therefore their importance in the short. Muse willing, his name will survive his lifetime; he will not, and had as well seize what boon the meanwhile offers. He accepts the post on Agamemnon's terms.

Part Three, consequently, will find the young couple moved to new lodgings in the palace itself, more affluent and less happy. Annoyance at what he knows would be her reaction has kept the minstrel from confiding to his friend the condition of his Acting Chief Minstrelship; his now-nearly-constant attendance on the

No use, this isn't working either, we're halfway through, the end's in sight; I'll never get to where I am; Part Three, Part Three, my crux, my core, I'm cutting you out; ———; there, at the heart, never to be filled, a mere lacuna.

4

The trouble with us minstrels is, when all's said and done we love our work more than our women. More, indeed, than we love ourselves, else I'd have turned me off long since instead of persisting on this rock, searching for material, awaiting inspiration, scrawling out in nameless numbhood futile notes . . . for an *Anonymiad*, which hereforth, having made an Iphigenia of Chapter Three, I can transcribe directly to the end of my skin. To be moved to art instead of to action by one's wretchedness may preserve one's life and sanity; at the same time, it may leave one wretcheder yet.

My mad commission from Agamemnon, remember, was not my only occupation in that blank chapter; I was also developing my art, by trial, error, and industry, with more return than that other project yielded. I examined our tongue, the effects wrought in it by minstrels old and new and how it might speak eloquentest for me. I considered the fashions in art and ideas, how perhaps to enlist their aid in escaping their grip. And I studied myself, musewise at least: who it was spoke through the bars of my music like a prisoner from the keep; what it was he strove so laboriously to enounce, if only his name; and how I might accomplish, or at least abet, his unfettering. In sum I schooled myself in all things pertinent to master-minstrelling — save one, the wide world, my knowledge whereof remained largely secondhand. Alas: for where Fancy's springs are unlevee'd by hard Experience they run too free, flooding every situation with possibilities until Prudence and even Common Sense are drowned.

Thus when it became apparent that Clytemnestra was indeed considering an affair—but with Agamemnon's cousin, and inspired not by the passion of love, which was out of her line, but by a resolve to avenge the sacrifice of Iphigenia — and that my folly had imperiled my life, my title, and my Merope, I managed to persuade myself not only that the Queen might be grateful after all for my confession and declaration, but that Merope's playing up to coarse Aegisthus in the weeks that followed might be meant simply to twit me for having neglected her and to spur my distracted ardor. A worldlier wight would've fled the *polis*: I hung on.

And composed! Painful irony, that anguish made my lyre speak ever eloquenter; that the odes on love's miseries I sang nightly may have not only fed Clytemnestra's passions and inspired Aegisthus's, but brought Merope's untimely into play as well, and wrought my downfall! He was no Agamemnon, Thyestes's son, nor any matchwit for the Queen, but he was no fool, either; he assessed the situation in a hurry, and whether his visit to Mycenae had been innocent or not to begin with, he saw soon how the land lay, and stayed on. Ingenuous, aye, dear Zeus, I was ingenuous, but jealousy sharpens a man's eyes: I saw his motive early on, as he talked forever of Iphigenia, and slandered Helen, and teased Merope, and deplored the war, and spoke as if jestingly of the power his city and Clytemnestra's would have, joined under one ruler—all the while deferring to the Queen's judgments, flattering her statecraft, asking her counsel on administrative matters ... and smacking lips loudly whenever Merope, whom he'd demanded as his table-servant at first sight of her, went 'round with the wine.

Me too he flattered, I saw it clear enough, complimenting my talent, repeating Clytemnestra's praises, marveling that I'd made so toothsome a conquest as Merope. By slyly pretending to assume that I was the Queen's gigolo and asking me with a wink how she was in bed, he got from me a hot denial I'd ever tupped her; by acknowledging then that a bedmate like Merope must indeed leave a man itchless for other company, he led me to hints of my guiltful negligence in that quarter. Thereafter he grew bolder at table, declaring he'd had five hundred women in his life and inviting Clytemnestra to become the five hundred first, if only to spite Agamemnon, whom he frankly loathed, and Merope the five hundred second, after which he'd seduce whatever other women the palace offered. Me, to be sure, he laughed, he'd have to get rid of, or geld like certain other singers; why didn't I take a trip somewhere, knock about the world a bit, taste foreign cookery and foreign wenches, fight a few fist fights, sire a few bastards? 'Twould be the making of me, minstrelwise! He and the Queen meanwhile would roundly cuckold Agamemnon, just for sport of it, combine their two kingdoms, and, if things worked out, give hubby the ax and make their union permanent: Clytemnestra could rule the roost, and he'd debauch himself among the taverns and Meropes of their joint domain.

All this, mind, in a spirit of raillery; Clytemnestra would chuckle, and Merope chide him for overboldness. But I saw how the Queen's eyes flashed, no longer at my cadenzas; and Merope'd say later, "At least he can talk about something besides politics and music." I laughed too at his sallies, however anxioused by Merope's pleasure in her new role, for the wretch was sharp, and though it sickened me to picture him atop the Queen — not to mention my frustrate darling! — heaving his paunch upon her and grinning through his whiskers, I admired his brash way with them and his gluttony for life's delights, so opposite to my poor temper. Aye, aye, there was my ruin: I liked the scoundrel after all, as I liked Clytemnestra and even Agamemnon; as I liked Merope, quite apart from loving or desiring her, whose impish spirit and vivacity reblossomed, in Aegisthus's presence, for the first time since we'd left the goats, and quite charmed the Mycenaean court. Most of all I was put down by the sheer energy of the lot of them: sackers of cities, breakers of vows, scorners of minstrels — admirable, fearsome! Watching Clytemnestra's eyes, I could hear her snarl with delight beneath the gross usurper, all the while she contemned his luxury and schemed her schemes; I could see herself take ax to Agamemnon, laugh with Aegisthus at their bloody hands, draw him on her at the corpse's side — smile, even, as she dirked him at the moment of climax! Him too I could hear laugh at her guile as his life pumped out upon her: bloody fine trick, Clytie girl, and enjoy your kingdom! And in Merope, my gentle, my docile, my honey: in her imperious new smile, in how she smartly snatched and bit the hand Aegisthus pinched her with, there began to stir a woman more woman than the pair of Leda's hatchlings. No, no, I was not up to them, I was not up to life — but it was myself I despised therefor, not the world.

Weeks passed; Clytemnestra made no reference to my *gaffe*; Merope grew by turns too silent with me, too cranky, or too sweet. I began to imagine them both Aegisthus's already; indeed, for aught I knew in dismalest moments they might be whoring it with every man in the palace, from Minister of Trade to horse-groom, and laughing at me with all Mycenae. Meanwhile, goat-face Aegisthus continued to praise my art (not without discernment for all his coarseness, as he had a good ear and knew every minstrel in the land) even as he teased my timid manner and want of experience. No keener nose in Greece for others' weaknesses: he'd remark quite seriously, between jests, that with a little knowledge of the world I might become in fact its chief minstrel; but if I tasted no more of life than Clytemnestra's dinner parties, of love no more than Merope's favors however extraordinary, perforce I'd wither in the bud while my colleagues grew to fruition. Let Athens, he'd declare, be never so splendid; nonetheless, of a man whose every day is passed within its walls one says, not that he's been to Athens, but that he's been nowhere. Every song I composed was a draught from the wine jug of my experience, which if not replenished must anon run dry . . .

"Speaking of wine," he added one evening, "two of Clytie's boats are sailing tomorrow with a cargo of it to trade along the coast, and I'm shipping aboard for the ride. Ten ports, three whorehouses each, home in two months. Why not go too?"

At thought of his departure my heart leaped up: I glanced at Merope, standing by with her flagon, and found her coolly smiling meward, no stranger to the plan. Aegisthus read my face and roared.

"She'll keep, Minstrel! And what a lover you'll be when you get back!"

Clytemnestra, too, arched brows and smiled. Under other circumstances I might've found some sort of voyage appealing, since I'd been nowhere; as was I wanted only to see Aegisthus gone. But those smiles — on the one hand of the queen of my person, on the other of that queen of my heart whom I would so tardily recrown — altogether unnerved me. I'd consider the invitation overnight, I murmured, unless the Queen ordered one course or the other.

"I think the voyage is a good idea," Clytemnestra said promptly, and added in Aegisthus's teasing wise: "With you two out of the palace, Merope and I can get some sleep." My heart was stung by their new camaraderie and the implication, however one took it, that their sleep had been being disturbed. The Queen asked for Merope's opinion.

"He's often said a minstrel has to see the world," my darling replied. Was it spite or sadness in the steady eyes she turned to me? "Go see it. It's all the same to me."

Prophetic words! How they mocked the siren Experience, whose song I heeded above the music of my own heart! To perfect the irony of my foolishness, Aegisthus here changed strategy, daring me, as it were, to believe the other, bitter meaning of her words, which I was to turn upon my tongue for many a desolated year.

"Don't forget," he reminded me with a grin: "I might be out to trick you! Maybe I'll heave you overboard one night, or maroon you on a rock and have Merope to myself! For all you know, Minstrel, she might want to be rid of you; this trip might be *her* idea . . ."

Limply I retorted, his was a sword could cut both ways. My accurst and heart-hurt fancy cast up reasons now for sailing in despite of all: my position in Mycenae was hot, and might be cooled by a sea journey; Agamemnon could scarcely blame me for his wife's misconduct if I was out of town on her orders; perhaps there were Chief-Minstrelships to be earned in other courts; I'd achieve a taintless fame and send word for Merope to join me. At very least she would be safe from his predations while we were at sea; my absence, not impossibly, would make her heart fonder; I'd find some way to get us out of Mycenae when I returned, *et cetera*. Meantime . . . I shivered . . . the world, the world! My breath came short, eyes teared; we laughed, Aegisthus and I, and at Clytemnestra's smiling hest drank what smiling Merope poured.

And next day we two set sail, and laughed and drank across the wine-dark sea to our first anchorage: a flowered, goated, rockbound isle. Nor did Aegisthus's merry baiting cease when we put ashore with nine large amphorae: the local maidens, he declared, were timid beauties whose wont it was to spy from the woods when a ship came by; nimble as goddesses they were at the weaving of figured tapestries, which they bartered for wine, the island being grapeless; but so shy they'd not approach till the strangers left, whereupon they'd issue from their hiding places and make off with the amphorae, leaving in exchange a fair quantity of their ware. Should a man be clever enough to lay hold of them, gladly they'd buy their liberty with love; but to catch them was like catching at rainbows or the chucklings of the sea. What he proposed therefore was that we conceal us in a ring of wine jugs on the beach, bid the crew stand by offshore, snatch us each a maiden when they came a-fetching, and enjoy the ransom. Better yet, I could bait them with music, which he'd been told was unknown on the island.

"Unless you think I'm inventing all this to trick you," he added with a grin. "Wouldn't you look silly jumping out to grab an old wine merchant, or squatting there hot and bothered while I sail back to Mycenae!"

He dared me to think him honest; dared me to commit myself to delicious, preposterous fantasy. Ah, he played me like a master lyrist his instrument, with reckless inspiration, errless art.

"The bloody world's a dare!" he went so far as to say, elbowing my arm as we ringed the jugs. "Your careful chaps never look foolish, but they never taste the best of it, either!" Think how unlikely the prospect was, he challenged me, that anything he'd said was true; think how crushinger it would be to be victim of my own stupendous gullibility more than of his guile; how bitterer my abandonment in the knowledge that he and Merope and Clytemnestra were not only fornicating all over the palace but laughing at my innocence, as they'd done from the first, till their sides ached. "On the other hand," he concluded fiercely, and squeezed my shoulder, "think what you'll miss if it turns out I was telling you the truth and you were too sensible to believe it! Young beauties, Minstrel, shy as yourself and sweet as a dream! That's what we're here for, isn't it? Meropes by the dozen, ours for the snatching! Oh my gods, what the world can be, if you dare grab hold! And what a day!"

The last, at least, was real enough: never such a brilliant forenoon, sweet beach, besplendored sea! My head ached with indecision; the rough crew grinned by the boat, leaning on their oars. Life roared oceanlike with possibility: outrageous risks! outrageous joys! I stood transfixed, helpless to choose; Aegisthus snatched my lyre, clubbed me with a whang among the amphorae, sprang into the boat. I lay where felled, in medias res, and wept with relief to be destroyed at last; the sailors' guffaws as they pulled away were like a music.

5

Long time I lay a-beached, even slept, and dreamed a dream more real than the itch that had marooned me. My privy music drew the island girls: smooth-limbed, merry-eyed Meropes; I seized the first brown wrist that came in reach; her sisters fled. Mute, or too frightened to speak, my victim implored me with her eyes. She was lovely, slender, delicate, and (farewell, brute dreams) real: a human person, sense and flesh, undeniable as myself and for aught I knew as lonely. A real partic-ular history had fetched her to that time and place, as had fetched me; she too, not impossibly, was gull of the wily world, a trickèd innocent and hapless self-deceiver. Perhaps she had a lover, or dreamed of one; might be she was fond of singing, balmed fragile sense with art. She was in my power; I let her go; she stood a moment rubbing her wrist. I begged her pardon for alarming her; it was loneliness, I said, made my fancy cruel. My speech was no doubt foreign to her; no doubt she expected ravishment, having been careless enough to get caught; per-haps she'd wanted a tumbling, been slow a-purpose, what did I know of such matters? It would not have surprised me to see her sneer at a man not man enough to force her; perhaps I would yet, it was not too late; I reached out my hand, she caught it up with a smile and kissed it, I woke to my real-life plight. In the days thereafter, I imagined several endings to the dream: she fled with a laugh or hoot; I pursued her or did not, caught her or did not, or she returned. In my favorite ending we became friends: gentle lovers, affectionate and lively. I called her by the name of that bee-sweet form I'd graced her with, she me my own in the clover voice that once had crooned it. I tried imagining her mad with passion for me, as women in song were for their beloveds — but the idea of my inspiring such emotion made me smile. No, I would set-tle for a pastoral affection spiced with wild seasons, as I'd known; I did not need adoring. We would wed, get sons and daughters; why hadn't I Merope? We would even be faithful, a phenomenon and model to the faithless world . . .

Here I'd break off with a groan, not that my bedreamed didn't exist (or any other life on my island, I presently determined, except wild goats and birds), but that she did, and I'd lost her. The thought of Merope in the swart arms of Aegisthus, whether or not she mocked my stranding, didn't drive me to madness or despair, as I'd expected it would; only to rue that I'd not been Aegisthus enough to keep her in my own. Like him, like Agamemnon, like Iphigenia for all I knew, I had got my character's desert.

Indeed, when I'd surveyed the island and unstoppered the first of the crocks, I was able to wonder, not always wryly, whether the joke wasn't on my deceivers. It was a perfumed night; the sea ran hushed beneath a gemmèd sky; there were springs of fresh water, trees of wild fruit, vines of wild grape; I could learn to spear fish, snare birds, milk goats. My lyre was unstrung forever, but I had a voice to sing with, an audience once more of shaggy nans and sea birds — and my fancy to recompense for what it had robbed me of. There was all the world I needed; let the real one clip and tumble, burn and bleed; let Agamemnon pull down towns and rape the widows of the slain; let Menelaus shake the plain with warshouts and Helen take on all comers; let maids grow old, princes rich, poets famous — I had imagination for realm and mistress, and her dower language! Isolated from one world by Agamemnon, from another by my own failings, I'd make Mycenaes of which I was the sole inhabitant, and sing to myself from their golden towers the one tale I knew.

Crockèd bravery; I smile at it now, but for years it kept me off the rocks, and though my moods changed like the sea-face, I accomplished much. Now supposing I'd soon be rescued I piled up beacons on every headland; now imagining a lengthy tenure, in fits of construction I raised me a house, learned to trap and fish, cultivated fruits and berries, made goatsmilk cheese and wrappings of hide — and filled jar after jar with the distillations of my fancy. Then would come sieges of despair, self-despisal, self-pity; gripped as by a hand I would gasp with wretchedness on my pallet, unable to muster resolve enough to leap into the sea. Impossible to make another hexameter, groan at another sundown, weep at another rosy-fingered dawn! But down the sun went, and re-rose; anon the wind changed quarter; I'd fetch me up, wash and stretch, and with a sigh prepare a fresh batch of ink, wherein I was soon busily aswim.

It was this invention saved me, for better or worse. I had like my fellow bards been used to composing in verse and committing the whole to memory, along with the minstrel repertoire. But that body of song, including my Mycenaean productions, rang so hollow in my stranded ears I soon put it out of mind. What are Zeus's lecheries and Hera's revenge, to a man on a rock? No past musings seemed relevant to my new estate, about which I found such a deal to say, memory couldn't keep pace. Moreover, the want of any audience but asphodel, goat, and tern played its part after all in the despairs that threatened me: a man sings better to himself if he can imagine someone's listening. In time therefore I devised solutions to both problems. Artist through, I'd been wont since boyhood when pissing on beach or bank to make designs and clever symbols with my water. From this source, as from Pegasus's idle hooftap on Mount Helicon, sprang now a torrent of inspiration: using tanned skins in place of a sand-beach, a seagullfeather for my tool, and a mixture of wine, blood, and squid-ink for a medium, I developed a kind of coded markings to record the utterance of mind and heart. By drawing out these chains of symbols I could so preserve and display my tale, it was unnecessary to remember it. I could therefore compose more and faster; I came largely to exchange song for written speech, and when the gods vouchsafed me a further great idea, that of launching my productions worldward in the empty amphorae, they loosed from my dammed soul a Deucalion-flood of literature.

For eight jugsworth of years thereafter, saving the spells of inclement weather aforementioned, I gloried in my isolation and seeded the waters with its get, what I came to call fiction. That is, I found that by pretending that things had happened which in fact had not, and that people existed who didn't, I could achieve a lovely truth which actuality obscures — especially when I learned to abandon myth and pattern my fabrications on actual people and events: Menelaus, Helen, the Trojan War. It was *as if* there were this minstrel and this milkmaid, *et cetera*; one could I believe draw a whole philosophy from that *as if*.

Two vessels I cargoed with rehearsals of traditional minstrelsy, bringing it to bear in this novel mode on my current circumstances. A third I freighted with imagined versions, some satiric, of "the first fact of our generation": what was going on at Troy and in Mycenae. To the war and Clytemnestra's treachery I worked out various dénouements: Trojan victories, Argive victories, easy and arduous homecomings, consequences tragical and comic. I wrote a version wherein Agamemnon kills his brother, marries Helen, and returns to Lacedemon instead of to Mycenae; another in which he himself is murdered by Clytemnestra, who arranges as well the assassination of the other expeditionary princes and thus becomes empress of both Hellas and Troy, with Paris as her consort and Helen as her cook—until all are slain by young Orestes, who then shares the throne with Merope, adored by him since childhood despite the difference in their birth. I was fonder of that one than of its less likely variants—such as that, in cuckold fury, Agamemnon butchers Clytemnestra's whole menage except Merope, who for then rejecting his advances is put ashore to die on the island where everyone supposes I've perished long since. We meet; she declares it was in hopes of saving me she indulged Aegisthus; I that it was the terror of her love and beauty drove me from her side. We embrace, sweetly as once in rosemaryland . . . But I could only smile at such notions, for in my joy at having discovered the joy of writing, the world might've offered me Mycenae and got but a shrug from me. Indeed, one night I fancied I heard a Meropish voice across the water, calling the old name she called me by—and I ignored that call to finish a firelit chapter. Had Merope—aye, Trojan Helen herself—trespassed on my island in those days, I'd have flayed her as soon as I'd laid her, and on that preciousest of parchments scribed the little history of our love.

By the seventh jug, after effusions of religious narrative, ribald tale-cycles, verse-dramas, comedies of manners, and what-all, I had begun to run out of world and material—though not of ambition, for I could still delight in the thought of my amphorae floating to the wide world's shores, being discovered by who knew whom, salvaged from the deep, their contents deciphered and broadcast to the ages. Even when, in black humors, I imagined my *opera* sinking undiscovered (for all I could tell, none might've got past the rocks of my island), or found but untranslated, or translated but ignored, I could yet console myself that Zeus at least, or Poseidon, read my heart's record. Further, further: should the Olympians themselves prove but dreams of our minstrel souls (I'd changed my own conception of their nature several times), still I could soothe me with the thought that somewhere outside myself my enciphered spirit drifted, realer than the gods, its significance as objective and undecoded as the stars'.

Thus I found strength to fill two more amphorae: the seventh with long prose fictions of the realistical, the romantical, and the fantastical kind, the eighth with comic histories of my spirit, such of its little victories, defeats, insights, blindnesses, *et cetera* as I deemed might have impersonal resonation or pertinence to the world; I'm no Narcissus. But if I had lost track of time, it had not of me: I was older and slower, more careful but less concerned; as my craft improved my interest waned, and my earlier zeal seemed hollow as the jugs it filled. Was there any new thing to say, new way to say the old? The memory of literature, my own included, gave me less and less delight; the "immortality" of even the noblest works I knew seemed a paltry thing. It appeared as fine a lot to me, and as poor, to wallow like Aegisthus in the stews as to indite the goldenest verses ever and wallow in the ages' admiration. As I had used to burn with curiosity to know how it would be to be a Paris or Achilles, and later to know which of my imagined endings to the war would prove the case, but came not to care, so now I was no longer curious even about myself, what I might do next, whether anyone would find me or my scribbles. My last interest in that subject I exhausted with the dregs of Thalia, my eighth muse and mistress. It was in a fit of self-disgust I banged her to potsherds; her cargo then I had to add to Clio's, and as I watched that stately dame go under beneath her double burden, my heart sank likewise into the dullest deep.

6

A solipsist had better get on well with himself, successfullier than I that ensuing season. Time was when I dreamed of returning to the world; time came when I scattered my beacons lest rescue interrupt me; now I merely sat on the beach, sundried, seasalted: a survival-expert with no will to live. My very name lost sense; anon I forgot it; had "Merope" called again I'd not have known whom she summoned. Once I saw a ship sail by, unless I dreamed it, awfully like Agamemnon's and almost within hail; I neither hid nor hallooed. Had the King put ashore, I wouldn't have turned my head. The one remaining amphora stood untapped. Was I thirty? Three thousand thirty? I couldn't care enough to shrug.

Then one noon, perhaps years later, perhaps that same day, another object hove into my view. Pot-red, bobbing, it was an amphora, barnacled and sea-grown from long voyaging. I watched impassive while wind and tide fetched it shoreward, a revenant of time past; nor was I stirred to salvage when the surf broke it up almost at my feet. Out washed a parchment marked with ink, and came to rest on the fore-shore — whence, finally bemused, I retrieved it. The script was run, in places blank; I couldn't decipher it, or if I did, recognize it as my own, though it may have been.

No matter: a new notion came, as much from the lacunae as from the rest, that roused in me first an echo of my former interest in things, in the end a resolve which if bone-cool was ditto deep: I had thought myself the only stranded spirit, and had survived by sending messages to whom they might concern; now I began to imagine that the world contained another like myself. Indeed, it might be astrew with islèd souls, become minstrels perforce, and the sea a-clink with literature! Alternatively, one or several of my messages may have got through: the document I held might be no ciphered call for aid but a reply, whether from the world or some marooned fellow-inksman: that rescue was on the way; that there was no rescue, for anyone, but my SOS's had been judged to be not without artistic merit by some who'd happened on them; that I should forget about my plight, a mere scribblers' hazard, and sing about the goats and flowers instead, the delights of island life, or the goings-on among the strandees of that larger isle the world.

I never ceased to allow the likelihood that the indecipherable ci-phers were my own; that the sea had fertilized me as it were with my own seed. No matter, the principle was the same: that I could be thus messaged, even by that stranger my former self, whether or not the fact tied me to the world, inspired me to address it once again. That night I broke Calliope's aging seal, and if I still forwent her nourishment, my abstinence was rather now prudential or strategic than indifferent.

7

That is to say, I began to envision the possibility of a new work, hope-fully surpassing, in any case completing, what I'd done theretofore, my labor's fulfillment and vindication. I was obliged to plan with more than usual care: not only was there but one jug to sustain my inspiration and bear forth its vintage; there remained also, I found to my dismay, but one goat in the land to skin for writing material. An aging nan she was, lone survivor of the original herd, which I'd slaughtered reckless in my early enthusiasm, supposing them inexhaustible, and only later begun to conserve, until in my late dumps I'd let husbandry go by the board with the rest. That she had no mate, and so I no future vellum, appalled me now; I'd've bred her myself hadn't bigot Nature made love between the species fruitless, for my work in mind was no brief one. But of coming to terms with circumstance I was grown a master: very well, I soon said to myself, it must be managed by the three of us, survivors all: one old goat, one old jug, one old minstrel, we'd expend ourselves in one new song, and then an end to us!

First, however, the doe had to be caught; it was no accident she'd outlived the others. I set about constructing snares, pitfalls, blind mazes, at the same time laying ground-plans for the masterwork in my head. For a long time both eluded me, though vouchsafing distant glimpses of themselves. I'd named the doe *Helen*, so epic fair she seemed to me in my need, and cause of so great vain toil, but her namesake had never been so hard to get: *Artemis* had fit her cold fleetness better; *Iphigenia* my grim plans for her, to launch with her life the expedition of my fancy. *Tragedy* and *satire* both deriving, in the lexicon of my inventions, from *goat*, like the horns from Helen's head, I came to understand that the new work would combine the two, which I had so to speak kept thitherto in their separate amphorae. For when I reviewed in my imagination the goings-on in Mycenae, Lacedemon, Troy, the circumstances of my life and what they had disclosed to me of capacity and defect, I saw too much of pity and terror merely to laugh; yet about the largest hero, gravest catastrophe, sordidest deed there was too much comic, one way or another, to sustain the epical strut or tragic frown. In the same way, the piece must be no Orphic celebration of the unknowable; time had taught me too much respect for men's intelligence and resourcefulness, not least my own, and too much doubt of things transcendent, to make a mystic hymnist of me. Yet neither would it be a mere discourse or logic preachment; I was too sensible of the great shadow that surrounds our little lights, like the sea my island shore. Whimsic fantasy, grub fact, pure senseless music — none in itself would do; to embody *all* and rise above each, in a work neither longfaced nor idiotly grinning, but adventuresome, passionately humored, merry with the pain of insight, wise and smiling in the terror of our life — that was my calm ambition.

And to get it all out of and back into one jug, on a single skin! Every detail would need be right, if I was to achieve the effects of epic amplitude and lyric terseness, the energy of innocence and experience's restraint. Adversity generates guileful art: months I spent considering and rejecting forms, subjects, viewpoints, and the rest, while I fashioned trap after trap for Helen and sang bait-songs of my plan — both in vain. Always she danced and bleated out of reach, sometimes so far away I confused her with the perched gulls or light-glints on the rock, sometimes so near I saw her black eyes' sparkle and the gray-pink cartography of her udder. Now and then she'd vanish for days together; I'd imagine her devoured by birds, fallen to the fishes, or merely uncapturable, and sink into despondencies more sore than any I'd known. My "Anonymiad," too, I would reflect then (so I began to think of it, as lacking a subject and thus a name), was probably impossible, or, what was worse, beyond my talent. Perhaps, I'd tell myself bitterly, it had been written already, even more than once; for all I knew the waters were clogged with its like, a menace to navigation and obstruction on the wide world's littoral.

I myself may already have written it; cast it forth, put it out of mind, and then picked it up where it washed back to me, having circuited Earth's countries or my mere island. I yearned to be relieved of myself: by heart failure, bolt from Zeus, voice from heaven. None forthcoming, I'd relapse into numbness, as if, having abandoned song for speech, I meant now to give up language altogether and float voiceless in the wash of time like an amphora in the sea, my vision bottled. This anesthesia proved my physician, gradually curing me of self-pity. Anon Helen's distant call would put off my torpor; I resumed the pursuit, intently, thoughtfully — but more and more detached from final concern for its success.

For just this reason, maybe, I came at last one evening to my first certainty about the projected work: that it would be written from my only valid point of view, first person anonymous. At that moment *Anonymiad* became its proper name. At that moment also, singing delightedly my news, I stumbled into one of the holes I'd dug for Helen. With the curiosity of her species she returned at once down the path wherealong I'd stalked her, to see why I'd abandoned the hunt. Indeed, as if to verify that I was trapped or dead, she peered into my pit. But I was only smiling, and turning on my finger Merope's ring; when she came to the edge I seized her by the pastern, pulled her in. A shard of deceasèd Thalia, long carried on me, ended her distress, which whooped deaf-heavenward like glee.

TAILPIECE

It had been my plan, while the elements cured her hide, to banquet on Helen's carcass and drink my fill of long-preserved Calliope. And indeed, for some days after my capture I sated every hunger and slaked every thirst, got drunk and glutted, even, as this work's headpiece attests. But it was not as it would have been in callower days. My futile seed had soured Calliope, and long pursuit so toughened Helen I'd as well made a meal of my writing-hand. Were it not too late for doubts — and I not flayed and cured myself, by sun, salt, and solitude, past all but the memory of tenderness — I'd wonder whether I should after all have skinned and eaten her, whom too I saw I had misnamed. We could perhaps have been friends, once she overcame her fright; I'd have had someone to talk to when Calliope goes, and with whom to face the unwritable postscript, fast approaching, of my *Anonymiad.*

Whereto, as I forewarned, there's no dénouement, only a termination or ironical coda. My scribbling has reached the end of Helen; I've emptied Calliope upon the sand. It was my wish to elevate maroonment into a minstrel masterpiece; instead, I see now, I've spent my last resources contrariwise, reducing the masterpiece to a chronicle of minstrel misery. Even so, much is left unsaid, much must be blank.

No matter. It is finished, Apollo be praised; there remains but to seal and launch Calliope. Long since I've ceased to care whether this is found and read or lost in the belly of a whale. I have no doubt that by the time any translating eyes fall on it I'll be dust, along with Clytemnestra, Aegisthus, Agamemnon . . . and Merope, if that was your name, if I haven't invented you as myself. I could do well by you now, my sweet, to whom this and all its predecessors are a continuing, strange love letter. I wish you were here. The water's fine; in the intervals of this composition I've taught myself to swim, and if some night your voice recalls me, by a new name, I'll commit myself to it, paddling and resting, drifting like my amphorae, to attain you or to drown.

There, my tale's afloat. I like to imagine it drifting age after age, while the generations fight, sing, love, expire. Now, perhaps, it bumps the very wharfpiles of Mycenae, where my fatal voyage began. Now it passes a hairsbreadth from the unknown man or woman to whose heart, of all hearts in the world, it could speak fluentest, most balmly —

but they're too preoccupied to reach out to it, and it can't reach out to them. It drifts away, past Heracles's pillars, across Oceanus, nudged by great and little fishes, under strange constellations bobbing, bobbing. Towns and statues fall, gods come and go, new worlds and tongues swim into light, old perish. Then it too must perish, with all things deciphered and undeciphered: men and women, stars and sky.

Will anyone have learnt its name? Will everyone? No matter. Upon this noontime of his wasting day, between the night past and the long night to come, a noon beautiful enough to break the heart, on a lorn fair shore a nameless minstrel

Wrote it.

Seven Additional Author's Notes
(1969)

1) The "Author's Note" prefatory to the first American edition of this book has been called by some reviewers pretentious. It may seem so, inasmuch as the tapes there alluded to are not at this writing commercially available, may never be, and I judged it distracting to publish the tape-stories in reading-script format. Nevertheless the "Note" means in good faith exactly what it says, both as to the serial nature of the fourteen pieces and as to the ideal media of their presentation: the regnant idea is the unpretentious one of turning as many aspects of the fiction as possible — the structure, the narrative viewpoint, the means of presentation, in some instances the process of composition and / or recitation as well as of reading or listening — into dramatically relevant emblems of the theme.

2) The narrator of "Night-Sea Journey," quoted from beginning to end by the authorial voice, is not, as many reviewers took him to be, a fish. If he were, their complaint that his eschatological and other speculations are trite would be entirely justified; given his actual nature, they are merely correct, and perhaps illumine certain speculations of Lord Raglan, Carl Jung, and Joseph Campbell.

3) The title "Autobiography" means "self-composition": the antecedent of the first-person pronoun is not I, but the story, speaking of itself. I am its father; its mother is the recording machine.

4) Inasmuch as the nymph in her ultimate condition repeats the words of others in their own voices, the words of "Echo" on the tape or the page may be regarded validly as hers, Narcissus's, Tiresias's, mine, or any combination or series of the four of us's. Inasmuch as the three mythical principals are all more or less immortal, and Tiresias moreover can see backward and forward in time, the events recounted may be already past, foreseen for the future, or in process of occurring as narrated.

5) The triply schizoid monologue entitled "Title" addresses itself simultaneously to three matters: the "Author's" difficulties with his companion, his analogous difficulties with the story he's in process of composing, and the not dissimilar straits in which, I think mistakenly, he imagines his culture and its literature to be. In the stereophonic performance version of the story, the two "sides" debate — in identical authorial voice, as it is after all a *monologue interieur* — across the twin channels of stereo tape, while the live author, like Mr. Interlocutor between Tambo and Bones in the old showboat-shows, supplies such self-interrupting and self-censoring passages as "Title" and "fill in the blank"— relinquishing his role to the auditor at the.

6) The six glossolalists of "Glossolalia" are, in order, Cassandra, Philomela, the fellow mentioned by Paul in the fourteenth verse of his first epistle to the Corinthians, the Queen of Sheba's talking bird, an unidentified psalmist employing what happens to be the tongue of a historical glossolalist (Mme Alice LeBaron, who acquired some fame in 1879 from her exolalic inspirations in the "Martian" language), and the author. Among their common attributes are 1) that their audiences don't understand what they're talking about, and 2) that their several speeches are metrically identical, each corresponding to what in fact may be the only verbal sound-pattern identifiable by anyone who attended American public schools prior to the decision of the U. S. Supreme Court in the case of *Murray* v. *Baltimore School Board* in 1963. The insufferability of the fiction, once this correspondence is recognized, makes its double point: that language may be a compound code, and that the discovery of an enormous complexity beneath a simple surface may well be more dismaying than delightful. *E.g.:* the maze of termite-tunnels in your joist, the intricate cancer in her perfect breast,

the psychopathology of everyday life, the Auschwitz in an anthill casually DDT'd by a child, the rage of atoms in a drop of ink—in short, *anything* examined curiously enough.

7) The deuteragonist of "Life-Story," antecedent of the second-person pronoun, is you.

On with the story (1996)

for Shelly

"$\Delta p \Delta q \geq \frac{\hbar}{2}$"
—Werner Heisenberg

"... the laws of narrative ... are as inexorable as the laws of physics, though less precisely ascertainable."
— Scholes and Kellogg, *The Nature of Narrative*

Check-in

So: After an extended and exhausting though exhilarating trip (all too short for those of us in no hurry to get where we're going), they check in, as they've been privileged to do at a fair number of pleasant-to-splendid stopping-places over the years. Accommodations clean, attractive, comfortable but not luxurious — just right for their purposes. King-size bed, well-stocked minifridge, good pressure in the shower even when everybody in the resort is changing for dinner. Fine view of the grounds, the beach, and the ocean from their top-floor low-rise balcony, high enough for perspective and privacy but not for vertigo, and open to the balmy tradewinds. All more than suitable; just what they had in mind for what they have in mind.

Although they're understandably pulled both ways, per prior agreement they don't get right down to their business. There's afternoon enough left for them to stroll the handsome spread — generic, they decide, but one of their favorite genres: Tropical Paradise. It was no easy call, if far from their toughest, whether to go this route or to choose instead from among some "realer" scenes they've loved — Iberia, say, or Umbria, rugged Alaska or the tranquil Chesapeake — or for that matter simply to stay at home, where they've worked and played and loved for so many / few years, and there be done with it.

"Are they sorry they've come?"

Not yet, anyhow; sorry only that things have come to this.

"She's not up for a dip in Mother Ocean out there; I can tell you that."

Therefore neither is he, he supposes.

"What *are* they up for?"

Good question. Despite the risk of mood-crash, they go back up to their room, already welcomingly familiar; they finish unpacking and settling in and presently decide, although neither has much appetite, to have their first night's dinner in the buffet-style main restaurant rather than in one of the several "specialty" annexes, in order to get the feel of that aspect of the place and some sense of their fellow guests — all innocent vacationers, presumably, as once upon a time were they themselves.

"Here's to the presumption of innocence."

Likewise to once-upon times. While the couple undress to shower to change to go down to dine, an early-evening rainsquall rolls in from the green hills behind their "last resort" and out to sea. As now and then happens in such cozied circumstances (witness Dr. Freud on the aphrodisial sound of falling water, Dido and Aeneas storm-snug in their Carthaginian cave, lovers among Rome's fountains or in motel shower stalls, honeymooners at Niagara), they find themselves for the how-manyeth time making king-size love — love, anyhow, on that king-size, no longer unrumpled bed — chuckling, knuckling back tears, soon enough murmuring and sighing, now gratifyingly spent and sweat-wet, skin to skin.

Presently: "Wrong order of events. Now they have to shower again."

Now they *get* to shower again, as their narrator sees it — and so, presently, they do. Although not meaningless, their order of events isn't important, anyhow not crucial, up to the final agenda-item.

"Agreed."

Take a sentence like his last one there, for example — *Although not meaningless, et cetera* — and rearrange its members through their other possible permutations, beginning it with *Up to the final agenda-item*, for example, or *Their order of events isn't important*; she'll see what he means.

Fondly, even nostalgically: "He does like to 'take a sentence,' doesn't he."

Yes, well. How's her appetite?

"Better now."

To dinner then, more pensive than festive, where indeed they address the formidable buffet with more gusto than one would have predicted, and chat amiably with their random tablemates (a seating-custom of the establishment) as if they were in fact fellow innocent vacationers. They even put away a carafe of the house red, which their narrator here pronounces quite acceptable.

"Good omen."

A misstep, they realize at once: not their wine consumption, but that casual-ironic remark of hers, made as they leave the great airy informal dining hall. Numerous other guests, those presumably innocent tablemates included, have adjourned earlier to stroll the beach or dance off their dinners in the outdoor disco-plaza or secure good seats for the nightly cabaret-style "animation" to follow; but our couple are in no hurry, no hurry at all, and so we've let them linger over the last of the not-bad Beaujolais. At the word *omen*, however, their spirits plummet. Let's get them out of here.

"She's ready."

All too. Not back to the room yet, though, if he can help it: *There be dragons*, as the old maps used to say. They attempt the beach-promenade, among casuarinas and clacking coconut palms, but one of them hasn't the strength for it, let's say. Well before its end, she stops at a water-facing bench, sits, draws him after, kisses his hand, smiles.

"It really *was* a good sign, the wine and their enjoyment of it. Their ending is off to a good start."

Can't speak. Nuzzles the back of *her* hand in reply.

Presently: "Maybe tell her a story or something?"

Oh, sure. Right.

"A promise is a promise."

Is a promise. If he tells her a story, then . . .?

"No promises."

That's as good a deal as he's likely to cut just now, he supposes. A temporizer to the end, however, he persuades her to go back with him through the fragrant oleanders and the fragranceless but indispensable bougainvilleas and hibiscuses — hibisci?

"*Hibiscus* does it."

— to their "village," their villa, their floor, their room, their balcony or bed (her call), if she wants a story. He's no Homer, he reminds her en route, nor even an Uncle Remus; if she wants a story, he'll read her one — Haven't they always read stories to each other? — but that's as close to the oral tradition as his job description comes.

"She's too pooped to argue."

Amen.

Presently: "So here they are."

And here we go. The storyteller, we agree —

"*They* agree."

The teller, they agree, is allowed to nod off at any point in the tale. His buns are truly dragging.

"Not as she sees them. And while we're looking, look at that moon."

Also the next, and the next, and the next.

"Don't."

Sorry.

"The listener, too, we agree . . ."

They. Goes without saying.

"Say on, then, dearest best friend: *Once upon, et cetera.*"

First of a series?

"Don't count on it. Count on nothing. On with the story, okay?"

1.

The End: An Introduction

... As I was saying, ladies and gentlemen, before that little unpleasantness: I have just been assured, by those in position to know, that this evening's eminent "mystery guest" has arrived, and should be with us any time now.

Did I say "arrived"? In the literary sense and on the literary scene, our distinguished visitor "arrived," of course, with her first collection of poems, or at latest with her prizewinning second. On the international political scene, as the whole world knows, she arrived with a vengeance — excuse the poor joke, not intended — upon the publication of that more recent, truly epical poetic satire of hers whose very title it is dangerous to mention favorably in some quarters, though thank heaven not here. At least I *hope* not here; that unbecoming ruckus just now makes me wonder. And as of just a short time ago, I'm delighted to announce, she has arrived in our city. Even as I stretch out these introductory remarks — introducing my introduction, I suppose we might say, while we await together the main event — the most controversial poet of our dying century (*politically* controversial, it's important to remember, not artistically controversial, for better or worse) is in mid-whisk from the airport to our campus, to honor us by inaugurating this new lecture series. In that final sense, she should arrive here in the flesh — the all too mortal, all too vulnerable flesh — within the quarter-hour.

In that meantime, I thank again the overwhelming majority of you for your patience with this unavoidable delay. It is owing, let me repeat, neither to any dilatoriness whatever on our visitor's part nor to trans-oceanic air-traffic problems, but solely to the extraordinary security measures that, alas, necessarily attend and not infrequently impede the woman's every movement. Who could have imagined that, at this hour of the world, a mere book, a mere *poem*, could provoke so dreadful a stir?

Well. As some of you may know, I myself am a writer, not of verse but of fiction: one whose "controversiality," such as it is, is fortunately of the aesthetic rather than the political variety. And I must acknowledge that although it is my professional line of work to imagine myself into other people's situations, I cannot for the life of me imagine what it must be like for such a free, proud, articulate, sensitive, gregarious, impassioned, and altogether high-spirited spirit as our impending visitor's to endure and even to go on making art under her constricted circumstances — not to mention courageously putting herself in harm's way by accepting from time to time such invitations as ours (whose absence of advance publicity I'm sure you appreciate, although your numbers suggest that word somehow got out despite our precautions). I shake my head; I am awed, truly humbled. It was my good fortune to first meet and enjoy the company of our eminent/imminent guest some years ago, before the present storm of political controversy broke upon her, back when she and I were happily just representative scribblers from two different countries sharing a lecture platform in a third — and I heartily do not envy her present celebrity! At the same time, for her sake if not for my own, I much wish that some Arabian-Nights genie could put me and every one of us who treasure artistic freedom and deplore murderous zealotry into our guest's skin, each of us for just a single day, and she in ours, to give us the chastening, attention-focusing taste of terrorism and to give her, who must surely crave it, a bit of respite therefrom: a souvenir of the artist's more usual condition of being blissfully ignored by the world at large.

But I was speaking of meantimes, was I not — indeed, both of meantimes and of mean times, and of introductions to introductions. For some decades, as it happens, I have belonged to that peculiarly American species, the writer in the university. Indeed, it has been my pleasure and privilege for many years now to be a full-time teacher at this institution as well as a full-time writer of fiction. As, again, some few of you may have heard, at the end of the current semester I'll be retiring from that agreeable association (my replacement has yet to be named, but I don't mind confiding to you that we're taking advantage of this new lecture series to look over a roster of likely candidates—not including tonight's visitor, alas—to any one of whom I would confidently entrust the baton of my professorship). There is an appropriate irony, therefore, in its having devolved upon me, as perhaps my final public action as a member of our faculty, to introduce not only tonight's extraordinary guest speaker but also this newly endowed "Last Lecture" series that her visit will so auspiciously inaugurate.

Valediction, benediction: I see therein no contradiction—and while I'm in the nervously improvised doggerel-verse mode, let me pray that to my valedictory *introduction* there may be no further *interruption* . . .

So. Well. Until our guest materializes, kindly indulge me now an impromptu brief digression on the subject of . . . introductions.

The purpose of introductions, I have somewhere read, is normally threefold: first, to give late-arriving members of the audience time to be seated, as I notice a few in process of doing even now; second, to test and if necessary adjust the public address system for the principal speaker; and at the same time (third) to give her or him a few moments to size up the house and perhaps make appropriate program modifications. Introductions, therefore, should go on for longer than one sentence—but not much longer. And may Apollo spare us the introducer who either in the length of his / her introduction presumes upon the speaker's allotted time or in its manner attempts to upstage the introducee!

But tonight, it goes without saying, is another story. We need not ask of it the traditional Passover question—"How is this night different from all other nights?"—although that is the question that I urge apprentice storytellers in my "workshop" to put to the main action of their stories. Why is it that Irma decides to terminate Fred *today*, rather than two weeks ago or next semester? What was it about *this* satirical verse-epic of our visitor's that provoked so astonishing and lamentable a reaction, which her scarcely less provocative earlier works did not? You get the idea. I trust you'll appreciate, however, that in all my years of introducing our visiting writers to their audiences, this is my maiden experience of being not so much an introducer as a warmup act for "him who shall come after me," as John the Baptist put it (in this instance, *her* who shall etc.). The bona fide introduction that I had prepared — short, short, I assure you, and not badly turned, if I do say so myself — I am thus obliged to expand ad libitum like one of those talking heads on public-television fund-raisers, either until there's mutiny in the ranks (but let it be more orderly, in that event, than that uncivilized earlier disruption) or else until our eagerly awaited guest . . .

One moment, please.

She is? Allah be praised for that! (No disrespect to that deity intended.)

My friends: I'm perfectly delighted to announce that the limousine of our so-patiently-awaited leadoff lecturer-du-soir, together with its attendant security convoy, *has reached the campus*, and that therefore it should be a matter of mere minutes — another ten or fifteen tops, I estimate and profoundly hope — before I happily yield this podium to the Godot for whom we've all been waiting. May that news update appease you while I now go straight to the matter of this series:

The anonymous benefactress who endowed "Last Lectures" (she was, like our guest, a she; that much I can tell you. Perhaps the muse?) throughout her long and prosperous lifetime was a perennial student, by her own description, and an inveterate "cultural attender," ever present on occasions like these. In her advanced age, she came to realize and even to derive some critical zest from the circumstance that, for all she knew, any given lecture or similar cultural occasion that she happened to be attending could feasibly be her last. It was her whimsical but quite serious inspiration, therefore, to endow handsomely a series of public lectures at this institution, with the stipulation that each speaker would be asked to imagine that this will be his or her valedictory presentation, or "last lecture" — as, for all any of us knows, any given utterance of ours might well turn out to be. Thus would we hear our visitors' "bottom-line" sentiments, their summings up; and thus by the way would the situation of the guest approximate that of the hostess — who, I'm sorry to report, went to her reward shortly after rewarding *us* with her philanthropy, and so cannot attend, at least in the flesh, this first Last Lecture, nor any of those to follow (the interest on our muse's endowment being generous, we expect this series to extend *ad infinitum*).

Do I dare point out — indeed, I do so dare, for I knew this lady and her mordant wit well enough, once upon a time, to believe that she would enjoy the irony if she were with us — that tonight's circumstances have matched donor and donee even more aptly than intended, inasmuch as both are now . . . forgive me . . . *late*?

Well.

What?

Aha. Gentlemen and ladies, ladies and gentlemen: *She is in the building!*

Excuse me? Okay; sorry there: Our distinguished visitor and her security entourage are *approaching* the building, it seems, although for several reasons I would prefer to say that she is "in the building" — for aren't we all, come to that, in the process of building and of being built every moment of our active lives: a-building and a-building until the end, whereafter our building, we may hope, will survive its builder?

Hum.

The end, I've said, and now say again: *the end*. And having so said, with those words *I* end, not my introduction — for our guest's custody, as it were, has yet to be officially transferred from the state and municipal security people to our own, I'm told, or to some combination of the two, or the three: a transfer now in progress elsewhere in this building even as I end, not my introduction of our visitor, whom I've yet to *begin* to introduce, but my introduction to that introduction. No fitter way to do that, I hope you'll agree, than with a few words about . . . endings.

Endings, endings: Where to begin? I myself am not among the number of those Last Lecturers whose distinguished names you've seen on our posters and other advertisements (all except that of this surprise inaugurator, for good and obvious reasons). I don't mind declaring, however, that I could readily deliver a last lecture myself on the subject of endings. Further, that had I been invited so to do, I could not have done better than to begin with the opening exclamation of our Mystery Guest's world-challenging verse-epic, which exclamation I shall take the liberty of Englishing thus: "An end to endings! Let us rebegin!"

As we wind up our century and our millennium — this is Yours Truly speaking now, not our impending visitor, and you have my word of honor that the moment she enters this auditorium I shall break off my spiel in midsentence, if need be, as Scheherazade so often breaks off her nightly narratives, and go straight to the very brief business of introducing her — as we end our century and millennium, I was saying, it is no surprise that the "terminary malady" afflicts us. Of the End of Art we have been hearing ever since this century's beginning, when Modernism arrived on the stage of Western Civ. Picasso, Pound, Stravinsky — all felt themselves to be as much terminators as pioneers, and where they themselves did not, their critics often so regarded them: groundbreakers, yes, but perhaps gravediggers as well, for the artistic tradition that preceded and produced them. By midcentury we were hearing not only of the Death of the Novel — that magnificent old genre that was born a-dying, like all of us; that has gone on vigorously dying ever since, and that bids to do so for some while yet — but likewise of the Death of Print Culture and the End of Modernism, supplanted by the electronic visual media and by so-called Postmodernism. And not long ago, believe it or not, there was an international symposium on "The End of *Post*modernism" — just when we thought we might be beginning to understand what that term describes! In other jurisdictions, we have Professor Whatsisname on the End of History, and Professor So-and-So on the End of Physics (indeed, the End of Nature), and Professor Everybody-and-Her-Brother on the End of the Old World Order with the collapse of the Soviet Union and of international Communism.

In short and in sum, endings, endings everywhere; apocalypses large and small. Good-bye to the tropical rainforests; good-bye to the whales; good-bye to the mountain gorillas and the giant pandas and the rhinoceri; good-bye even to the humble frogs, one is beginning to hear, as our deteriorating ozone layer exposes their eggs to harmful radiation. Good-bye to the oldest continuous culture on the planet: the Marsh Arabs of southern Iraq, in process of extermination by Saddam Hussein even as I speak. Good-bye to once-so-cosmopolitan Beirut and once-so-hospitable Sarajevo, as we who never had the chance to know them knew those excellent cities. The end of this, the end of that; little wonder we grow weary of "endism," as I have heard it called.

And yet, my patient-beyond-patient friends, things do end. Even this introductory introduction will end, take my word for it — and I wish I could add "the better the sooner," as one might sigh at the end of splendid meals, splendid sessions of love, splendid lives, even splendid long novels: those life-absorbing, life-enriching, almost life-displacing alternative worlds that we lovers of literature find ourselves wishing might *never* end, yet savor the more for knowing that they must. Yea, verily, I declare, things end: our late muse/benefactress's enviable life, our own productive lifetimes, and soon enough our biological lives as well—happily or haplessly, all end. As I like to tell my students . . .

Excuse me?

Very well, and hallelujah: *She is proceeding at this very moment with her security escort through the several checkpoints between our improvised safe-reception area below-stairs and our final staging area, just . . . offstage,* excuse that feeble wordplay—and will you gentlemen in the rear of the hall *kindly* return to your seats pronto and spare us all the indignity of once again marshaling our marshals, so to speak—who, as that earlier demonstration demonstrated, are standing by. I thank you in advance. I thank you. Now, please . . .

As I was saying: I advise my student apprentices to read biographies of the great writers they admire, in order to be encouraged by and take comfort in the trials and discouragements that attended *their* apprenticeship—but I recommend they skip the final chapters of those biographies. For a writer, after all, the alternative "last-chapter" scenarios are almost equally distressing, quite apart from the critical reception of one's works during one's mortal span: Either the end comes before one has had one's entire say (we recall John Keats's fears that he might cease to be before his pen had gleaned his teeming brain)—What an unspeakable pity, so to speak!—or else one goes on being and being *after* one's pen has gleaned *et cetera*: not so much a pity as simply pathetic. Therefore, say I to my coachees: Skip the endings.

The biographical endings, I mean: the endings of the great authors' life-stories. To the endings of those authors' great *stories*, on the other hand, I urge and enjoin apprentice writers to pay the most scrupulous and repeated attention, for at least two reasons, of which it won't at all surprise or distress me if I have time to share with you only the first before this endless introduction happily ends—its happiest imaginable ending being that it never gets there, if you follow my meaning.

Reason One is that it's in a story's Ending that its author pays (or fails to pay) his narrative/dramatic bills. Through Beginning and Middle the writer's credit is good, so long as we're entertained enough to keep turning the pages. But when the story's action has built to its climax and started down the steep and slippery slope of dénouement, every line counts, every word, and ever more so as we approach the final words. All the pistols hung on the wall in Act One, as Chekhov famously puts it, must be fired in Act Three. Images, motives, minor characters—every card played must be duly picked up, the dramaturgical creditors paid off, or else we properly feel shortchanged on our investment of time and sympathy, the willing suspension of our disbelief.

There are, to be sure, ways of paying one's bills by brilliantly defaulting on them: apparent non-endings that are in fact the best of endings, anyhow the most appropriate. We might instance the alternative and therefore inconclusive endings of Dickens's *David Copperfield* and John Fowles's *French Lieutenant's Woman*; the roller-towel ending/re-beginning of James Joyce's *Finnegans Wake*; the recombinatory "replay" ending of Julio Cortázar's *Hopscotch*, to name only a few examples; likewise the more immediately contemporary phenomenon of "hypertext" fiction: those open-endedly labyrinthine computer novels that may be entered, transited, and exited at any of many possible points and waypoints. Such non-endings, I repeat, if managed brilliantly (and a mighty *if* that is), can be the most apt imaginable, and ipso facto the most satisfying.

And the reason for *that*, my friends (Reason Two of two, which I, for one, never imagined or wished that I would find myself giving voice to here tonight), is this: that every aspect of a masterfully crafted story, from its narrative viewpoint through its cast of characters, its choice of scene, its choreography, tone of voice, and narrative procedure, its sequences of images and of actions, things said and things left unsaid, details noticed and details ignored—everything about it, in short, from its title to its ending, may be (nay, *will* be) a sign of its sense, until sign and sense become, if not indistinguishable, anyhow inextricable.

Of this ground-truth, no apter demonstration can be cited, I trust you will agree, than our first Last Lecturer's—

Will you *please*, you people there in the back! ... What?

What?

Oh my. I say, there!

As ... Dear me! What now? ...

As I ... As I was

Pillow Talk: *"That's a story?"*

Well, it's a beginning. As he warned her —
   "And that's the end?"
   In a manner of speaking. Figured we'd get endgames on the table early.
   Presently: "Isn't it a touch close to —"
   Home? I suppose so, but —
   "Not what she meant. Now that he mentions it, however . . ."
   He didn't mention it. Forget he mentioned it.
   "The Unmentionable."
   Old Unspeakable.

Presently: What else is there to talk about?
   "If he loves her, he'll think of something. No threat intended, and thanks for the story, really."
   He just thought of something.
   "Let's hear it."
   Mañana, okay? It's a long day's night.
   "Well . . ."
   If she loves him.
   "Goes without saying, like some other things."
   Sleep now, then. Hasta mañana.
   "One night at a time, we guess. Mañana's another story."

And so it was. To wit (at some still-jet-lagging siesta-time next day, let's say):

2.

Ad Infinitum: A Short Story

At the far end of their lawn, down by the large pond or small marshy lake, he is at work in "his" daylily garden — weeding, feeding, clearing out dead growth to make room for new — when the ring of the telephone bell begins this story. They spend so much of their day outdoors, in the season, that years ago they installed an outside phone bell under the porch roof overhang. As a rule, they bring a cordless phone out with them, too, onto the sundeck or the patio, where they can usually reach it before the answering machine takes over. It is too early in the season, however, for them to have resumed that convenient habit. Anyhow, this is a weekday midmorning; she's indoors still, in her studio. She'll take the call.

The telephone rings a second time, but not a third. On his knees in the daylily garden, he has paused, trowel in hand, and straightened his back. He returns to his homely work, which he always finds mildly agreeable but now suddenly relishes: simple physical work with clean soil in fine air and sunlight. The call could be routine: some bit of business, some service person. In the season, he's the one who normally takes weekday morning calls, not to interrupt her concentration in the studio; but it's not quite the season yet. The caller could be a friend — although their friends generally don't call them before noon. It could be a telephone solicitor: There seem to be more of those every year, enough to lead them to consider unlisting their number, but not quite yet to unlist it. It could be a misdial.

If presently she steps out onto the sundeck, looking for him, whether to bring him the cordless phone if the call is for him or to report some news, this story's beginning will have ended, its middle begun.

Presently she steps out onto the sundeck, overlooking their lawn and the large pond or small lake beyond it. She had been at her big old drafting-table, working — trying to work, anyhow; pretending to work; maybe actually almost really working — when that phone call began this story. From her upholstered swivel chair, through one of the water-facing windows of her studio, she could see him on hands and knees down in his daylily garden along the water's edge. Indeed, she had been more or less watching him, preoccupied in his old jeans and sweatshirt and gardening gloves, while she worked or tried or pretended to work at her worktable. At the first ring, she saw him straighten his back and square his shoulders, his trowel-hand resting on his thigh-top, and at the second (which she had waited for before picking up the receiver) look houseward and remove one glove. At the non-third ring, as she said hello to the caller, he pushed back his eyeglasses with his ungloved hand. She had continued then to watch him — returning to his task, his left hand still ungloved for picking out the weeds troweled up with his right — as she received the caller's news.

The news is bad indeed. Not quite so bad, perhaps, as her very-worst-case scenario, but considerably worse than her average-feared scenarios, and enormously worse than her best-case, hoped-against-hope scenarios. The news is of the sort that in one stroke eliminates all agreeable plans and expectations — indeed, all prospect of real pleasure from the moment of its communication. In effect, the news puts a period to this pair's prevailingly happy though certainly not carefree life; there cannot imaginably be further delight in it, of the sort that they have been amply blessed with through their years together. All that is over now: for her already; for him and for them as soon as she relays the news to him — which, of course, she must and promptly will.

Gone. Finished. Done with.

Meanwhile, *she* knows the news, but he does not, yet. From her worktable she sees him poke at the lily-bed mulch with the point of his trowel and pinch out by the roots, with his ungloved other hand, a bit of chickweed, wire grass, or ground ivy. She accepts the caller's terse expression of sympathy and duly expresses in return her appreciation for that unenviable bit of message-bearing. She has asked only a few questions — there aren't many to be asked — and has attended the courteous, pained, terrible but unsurprising replies. Presently she replaces the cordless telephone on its base and leans back for a moment in her comfortable desk chair to watch her mate at his ordinary, satisfying work and to assimilate what she has just been told.

There is, however, no assimilating what she has just been told — or, if there is, that assimilation is to be measured in years, even decades, not in moments, days, weeks, months, seasons. She must now get up from her chair, walk through their modest, pleasant house to the sundeck, cross the lawn to the daylily garden down by the lake or pond, and tell him the news. She regards him for some moments longer, aware that as he proceeds with his gardening, his mind is almost certainly on the phone call. He will be wondering whether she's still speaking with the caller or has already hung up the telephone and is en route to tell him the news. Perhaps the call was merely a routine bit of business, not worth reporting until their paths recross at coffee break or lunchtime. A wrong number, even, it might have been, or another pesky telephone solicitor. He may perhaps be half-deciding by now that it was, after all, one of those innocuous possibilities.

She compresses her lips, closes and reopens her eyes, exhales, rises, and goes to tell him the news.

He sees her, presently, step out onto the sundeck, and signals his whereabouts with a wave of his trowel in case she hasn't yet spotted him down on his knees in the daylily garden. At that distance, he can read nothing in her expression or carriage, but he notes that she isn't bringing with her the cordless telephone. Not impossibly, of course, she could be simply taking a break from her studio work to stretch her muscles, refill her coffee mug, use the toilet, enjoy a breath of fresh springtime air, and report to him that the phone call was nothing — a misdial, or one more canvasser. She has stepped from the deck and begun to cross the lawn, himward, unurgently. He resumes weeding out the wire grass that perennially invades their flower beds, its rhizomes spreading under the mulch, secretly reticulating the clean soil and choking the lily bulbs. A weed, he would agree, is not an organism wicked in itself; it's simply one of nature's creatures going vigorously about its natural business in a place where one wishes that it would not. He finds something impressive, even awesome, in the intricacy and tenacity of those rhizomes and their countless interconnections; uproot one carefully and it seems to network the whole bed — the whole lawn, probably. Break it off at any point and it redoubles like the monster Whatsitsname in Greek mythology. The Hydra. So it's terrible, too, in its way, as well as splendid, that blind tenacity, that evolved persistence and virtual ineradicability, heedless of the daylilies that it competes with and vitiates, indifferent to everything except its mindless self-proliferation. It occurs to him that, on the other hand, that same persistence is exactly what he cultivates in their flowers, pinching back the rhododendrons and dead-heading yesterday's lilies to encourage multiple blooms. An asset here, a liability there, from the gardener's point of view, while Nature shrugs its non-judgmental shoulders. Unquestionably, however, it would be easier to raise a healthy crop of wire grass by weeding out the daylilies than vice versa.

With such reflections he distracts himself, or tries or pretends to distract himself, as she steps unhurriedly from the sundeck and begins to cross the lawn, himward.

She is, decidedly, in no hurry to cross the lawn and say what she must say. There is her partner, lover, best friend and companion, at his innocent, agreeable work: half chore, half hobby, a respite from his own busy professional life. Apprehensive as he will have been since the telephone call, he is still *as if* all right; she, too, and their life and foreseeable future — *as if* still all right. In order to report to him the dreadful news, she must cross the entire lawn, with its central Kwanzan cherry tree: a magnificently spreading, fully mature specimen, just now at the absolute pink peak of its glorious bloom. About halfway between the sundeck and that Kwanzan cherry stands a younger and smaller, but equally vigorous, Zumi crab apple that they themselves put in a few seasons past to replace a storm-damaged predecessor. It, too, is a near-perfect specimen of its kind, and likewise at or just past the peak of its flowering, the new green leaves thrusting already through the white clustered petals. To reach her husband with the news, she must pass under that Kwanzan cherry — the centerpiece of their property, really, whose great widespread limbs they fear for in summer thunder squalls. For her to reach that cherry tree will take a certain small time: perhaps twenty seconds, as she's in no hurry. To stroll leisurely even to the Zumi crab apple takes ten or a dozen seconds — about as long as it takes to read this sentence aloud. Walking past that perfect crab apple, passing under that resplendent cherry, crossing the remaining half of the lawn down to the lily garden and telling him the news — these sequential actions will comprise the middle of this story, already in progress.

In the third of a minute required for her to amble from sundeck to cherry tree — even in the dozen seconds from deck to crab apple (she's passing that crab apple now) — her companion will have weeded his way perhaps one trowels-length farther through his lily bed, which borders that particular stretch of pond- or lakeside for several yards, to the far corner of their lot, where the woods begin. Musing upon this circumstance — a reflex of insulation, perhaps, from the devastating news — puts her in mind of Zeno's famous paradox of Achilles and the tortoise. Swift Achilles, Zeno teases, can never catch the tortoise, for in whatever short time required for him to close half the hundred yards between them, the sluggish animal will have moved perhaps a few inches; and in the very short time required to halve that remaining distance, an inch or two more, *et cetera* — ad infinitum, inasmuch as finite distances, however small, can be halved forever. It occurs to her, indeed — although she is neither philosopher nor mathematician — that her husband needn't even necessarily be moving away from her, so to speak, as she passes now under the incredibly full-blossomed canopy of the Kwanzan cherry and pauses to be quietly reastonished, if scarcely soothed, by its splendor. He (likewise Zeno's tortoise) could remain fixed in the same spot; he could even rise and stroll to meet her, *run* to meet her under that flowered canopy; in every case and at whatever clip, the intervening distances must be halved, re-halved, and re-re-halved forever, ad infinitum. Like the figured lovers in Keats's "Ode on a Grecian Urn" (another image from her college days), she and he will never touch, although unlike those, these are living people en route to the how-many-thousandth tête-à-tête of their years togeth-er — when, alas, she must convey to him her happiness-ending news. In John Keats's words and by the terms of Zeno's paradox, *forever* will he love, and she be fair. Forever they'll go on closing the distance be-tween them — as they have in effect been doing, like any well-bonded pair, since Day One of their connection — yet never close it altogether: asymptotic curves that eternally approach, but never meet.

But of course they will meet, very shortly, and before even then they'll come within hailing distance, speaking distance, murmuring distance. Here in the middle of the middle of the story, as she re-emerges from under the bridal-like canopy of cherry blossoms into the tender mid-morning sunlight, an osprey suddenly plummets from the sky to snatch a small fish from the shallows. They both turn to look. He, the nearer, can see the fish flip vainly in the raptor's talons; the osprey aligns its prey adroitly fore-and-aft, head to wind, to minimize drag, and flaps off with it toward its rickety tree-top nest across the pond or lake.

The fish is dying. The fish is dying. The fish is dead.

When he was a small boy being driven in his parents' car to something he feared — a piano recital for which he felt unready, a medical procedure that might hurt, some new town or neighborhood that the family was moving to — he used to tell himself that as long as the car-ride lasted, all would be well, and wish it would last forever. The condemned en route to execution must feel the same, he supposes, while at the same time wanting the dread thing done with: The tumbril has not yet arrived at the guillotine; until it does, we are immortal, and here meanwhile is this once pleasing avenue, this handsome small park with its central fountain, this plane-tree-shaded corner where, in happier times . . .

A gruesome image occurs to him, from his reading of Dante's *Inferno* back in college days: The Simoniacs, traffickers in sacraments and holy offices, are punished in hell by being thrust head-downward for all eternity into holes in the infernal rock. Kneeling to speak with them in that miserable position, Dante is reminded of the similar fate of convicted assassins in his native Florence, executed by being bound hand and foot and buried alive head-down in a hole. Before that hole is filled, the officiating priest bends down as the poet is doing, to hear the condemned man's last confession — which, in desperation, the poor wretch no doubt prolongs, perhaps adding fictitious sins to his factual ones in order to postpone the end — and in so doing (it occurs to him now, turning another trowelsworth of soil as his wife approaches from the cherry tree) appending one more real though venial sin, the sin of lying, to the list yet to be confessed.

Distracted, he breaks off a wire-grass root.

"Time," declares the Russian critic Mikhail Bakhtin, "is the true hero of every feast." It is also the final dramaturge of every story. History is a Mandelbrot set, as infinitely sub-divisible as is space in Zeno's paradox. No interval past or future but can be partitioned and sub-partitioned, articulated down through ever finer, self-similar scales like the infinitely indented coastlines of fractal geometry. This intelligent, as-if-still-happy couple in late mid-story — what are they doing with such reflections as these but attempting unsuccessfully to kill time, as Time is unhurriedly but surely killing them? In narrated life, even here (halfway between cherry tree and daylily garden) we could suspend and protract the remaining action indefinitely, without "freeze-framing" it as on Keats's urn; we need only slow it, delay it, atomize it, flash back in time as the woman strolls forward in space with her terrible news. Where exactly on our planet are these people, for example? What pond or lake is that beyond their pleasant lawn, its olive surface just now marbled with springtime yellow pollen? Other than one osprey nest in a dead but still-standing oak, what is the prospect of its farther shore? We have mentioned the man's jeans, sweatshirt, gloves, and eyeglasses, but nothing further of his appearance, age, ethnicity, character, temperament, and history (other than that he once attended college), and (but for that same detail) nothing whatever of hers; nor anything, really, of their life together, its gratifications and tribulations, adventures large or small, careers, corner-turnings. Have they children? Grandchildren, even? What sort of telephone solicitors disturb their evidently rural peace? What of their house's architecture and furnishings, its past owners, if any, and the history of the land on which it sits — back to the last glaciation, say, which configured "their" pond or lake and its topographical surround? Without our woman's pausing for an instant in her hasteless but steady course across those few remaining yards of lawn, the narrative of her final steps might suspend indefinitely their completion. What variety of grasses does that lawn comprise, interspersed with what weeds, habitating what insecta and visited by what birds? How, exactly, does the spring air feel on her sober-visaged face? Are his muscles sore from gardening, and, if so, is that degree of soreness, from that source, agreeable to him or otherwise? What is the relevance, if any, of their uncertainty whether that water beyond their lawn is properly to be denominated a large pond or a small lake, and has that uncertainty been a running levity through their years there? Is yonder osprey's nest truly rickety, or only apparently so? The middle of this story nears its end, but has not reached it yet, not yet. There's time still, still world enough and time. There are narrative possibilities still unforeclosed. If our lives are stories, and if this story is three-fourths told, it is not yet four-fifths told; if four-fifths, not yet five-sixths, *et cetera, et cetera* — and meanwhile, meanwhile it is *as if* all were still well.

In non-narrated life, alas, it is a different story, as in the world of actual tortoises, times, and coastlines. It might appear that in Time's infinite sub-segmentation, 11:00 AM can never reach 11:30, far less noon; it might appear that Achilles can never reach the tortoise, nor any story its end, nor any news its destined hearer — yet reach it they do, in the world we know. Stories attain their dénouement by selective omission, as do real-world coastline measurements; Achilles swiftly overtakes the tortoise by ignoring the terms of Zeno's paradox. Time, however, more wonderful than these, omits nothing, ignores nothing, yet moves inexorably from hour to hour in just five dozen minutes.

The story of our life is not our life; it is our story. Soon she must tell him the news.

Our lives are not stories. Now she must tell him the news.

This story will never end. This story ends.

"That's more like it."

Thanks.

"Thank you."

Him.

"Whoever. *Whomever*. But there is no Him."

Just a manner of speaking.

"Pillow talk."

Why not?

Presently: "Why not: I guess because the world's full of *really* miserable people: refugees and political prisoners, brutalized and starving, or just people in dreadful pain from whatever cause, to whom the situation of that couple in that story would seem unimaginably luxurious. Not to mention *our* situation."

Theirs. Notwithstanding which . . .

"Notwithstanding which, Q.E.D., 'This story ends,' alas but amen. Are they up for tennis?"

Can he believe his ears?

"Why not? It's not exactly what they came here for, but here's where they came, after all, where there happen to be tennis courts and sail-boards and snorkeling-reefs and discos. Let's run them through all of it, one more time."

A thousand and one more times!

"One time at a time, and count on nothing. Does he have the heart for it?"

Does she?

"No."

Likewise. You're on.

"Let's go."

They go and, having gone and bittersweetly done, in time return.

Presently (or, as might be said):

3.

And Then One Day . . .

Her professional knack and penchant for storytelling, Elizabeth liked to believe, had descended to her from her father, an inveterate raconteur who even in the terminal delirium of old age and uremic poisoning had entertained his hospital-bedside audience with detailed anecdotes of bygone days. The decade of his dying had been the century's next-to-last; in his mind, however, the year was often mid-1930ish, and the anecdotes themselves might be from the century's teens and twenties, which had been his own. The bedside audience was principally Elizabeth herself (or, sometimes, the night-shift nurse), although the anecdotist mistook her variously for her long-dead mother and for sundry women-friends of his youth and middle age, whereto deliriant memory from time to time returned him.

"Shirley?" he would say (or "Gladys?" "Irma?" "Jane?"), with the half-rising inflection that signals impending narrative: "D'you remember that Saturday morning five years back — no, six, it was: summer before the Black Friday crash — when I borrowed Lee Bowman's saddle-brown Bearcat to drive you and Eileen Fenster down to Dorset Station, and just as we were crossing the old Town Creek drawbridge ..." Or, "Frieda, honey, run these damn affidavits over to Amos Creighton 'fore the courthouse closes, or there'll be no trial till after Armistice Day. Young Lucille Creighton told me once ..."

What his actual last words were, Elizabeth didn't know; her father had died at night, in the county hospital, while she was in a distant city promoting her latest novel. The proximate cause of his death had been a fall in the corridor whereinto he'd managed deliriously to wander (despite his doctor's orders for bed-restraints when the patient was un-attended), believing himself en route down High Street to fetch certain files from his little law office on Courthouse Row — which had in fact been torched during the black civil rights ruckus of the 1960s. The final cause, however, was general systems wear-out in the ninth decade of a prevailingly healthy life, and so his daughter and sole heir had chosen not to press the matter of that possibly negligent nonrestraint. The last words that she herself had heard him speak he had addressed to an imagined listener (Frieda again, his devoted secretary through most of Elizabeth's childhood) the day before the night of his fatal fall, just as Elizabeth, relieved by the hired nurse, was leaving his hospital room at the close of afternoon visiting hours to drive to the airport across the Bay. Once again back in the Prohibition era, he had been retailing to long-deceased Frieda the escapades of a legendary moonshiner down in the marshes of Maryland's lower Eastern Shore, whose whiskey-still successfully evaded detection by one federal "revenuer" after another. "And then one day," she'd heard her father's voice declare from the bed behind her as she stepped out into the tiled hallway ...

And then he was beyond her hearing range, and not long thereafter she likewise his, alas, forever.

Retrospectively, it struck her that those words were (strictly speaking, *would have been*) an altogether apt though paradoxical exit line for a born storyteller like her dad — as also, come to that, for herself, somewhere down the road: the story just kicking into gear as the teller kicks the bucket (she didn't know, in fact, whether her father had tripped over something in that hallway or slipped on the polished tiles or merely collapsed). At his funeral services — well attended, as he had been something of a civic leader and a popular "character" in their little hometown — she had told "the anecdote of the anecdote," as she called it, and it had been appreciatively received. No surprise: She was, after all, a professional. To friends and well-wishers over in the city, where she kept a small apartment, she found herself retelling it from time to time thereafter, no doubt sprucing it up a bit for narrative ef-fectiveness as I've done here (her dad would understand): Who could know, for example, where the old ex-counselor had imagined himself to be as he wandered unattended down that fell hallway, or whether he'd even been delirious?

One of those city-friends happened to be not only a fellow wordsmith but a professor of wordsmithery at Elizabeth's graduate-school alma mater and, in fact, the coach of her advanced literary apprenticeship some years since. Over lunch at his faculty club, he remarked to his star ex-coachee that in the jargon of narrative theory, as opposed to the hunch-and-feel of actual storymaking, the formulation *and then one day*, or any of its numerous equivalents, has a characteristic function, aptly suggested by her phrase "the story just kicking into gear": It marks the crucial shift from the generalized, "customary" time of the dramaturgical "ground situation" to the focused, dramatized time of the story's "present" action, and thus in effect ends the plot's beginning and begins its middle.

"We're back in school! Come again, please?"

He topped up her Chardonnay and reminded her, between wedges of club sandwich, that every conventional story-plot comprises what she ought to remember his calling a Ground Situation and a Dramatic Vehicle. The GS is some state of affairs pre-existing the story's present action and marked by an overt or latent dramatic voltage, like an electrical potential: *Once upon a time there was a beautiful young princess, the crown jewel of the realm, who however for some mysterious reason would neither speak nor laugh, et cetera.* In the language of systems analysis (if Elizabeth could stomach yet more jargon), this state of affairs constitutes an "unstable homeostatic system," which may be elaborated at some length before the story's real action gets under way: The king and queen try every expedient that they can come up with; likewise their ministers, lords and ladies, physicians, and court jesters, as well as sages summoned from the farthest reaches of the realm — all to no avail, *et cetera.*

He cited other examples, from Elizabeth's own published work.

"I remember, I remember. But for years now I've just *written* the damn stuff, you know?"

You have indeed. Anyhow, this princess is as accomplished as she is comely, wouldn't you agree? A model daughter as well as a knockout heir to the throne — but nothing can induce her to so much as crack a smile or utter a syllable. In royal-parental desperation, her father proclaims that any man who —

"Always a man."

Not infrequently a man, especially in the case of problem princesses. Any man who can dispel the spell that the king is convinced has been laid on his daughter by some antiroyalist witch can have half the kingdom and the young lady's hand in marriage. If the guy tries and fails, however . . .

"No free lunch."

And mind you, this is still just the Ground Situation. Many are the gallants who rally to the king's challenge; like-wise wizards of repute, renowned fools, and assorted creeps and nobodies. The princess attends their stunts and stratagems with mien complaisant —

"Mien . . . ?"

Complaisant. But be damned if she'll either laugh or speak. And so it goes, Zapsville for all contenders, year after year — and the story proper hasn't even started yet. You're not enthralled, Liz.

"Enough that *she* is. I can't stop thinking of poor Dad, that last night in the hospital, while I was off book-touring in Atlanta. Where was the goddamn nurse?"

And then one day . . .

"The handsome stranger. What else is new?"

Well. Sometimes it's the lad next door, whom the princess had never thought of in *those* terms. In any case, it's the screw-turning interloper in his saddle-brown Stutz Bearcat of a Dramatic Vehicle, come to precipitate a *story* out of the Ground Situation. The Beginning has ended, dear Liz; the Middle's begun.

"Maybe, maybe not." Unlike certain princesses, she smiled a bona fide, perhaps even half-mischievous, smile. "Thanks for lunch and lecture, anyhow."

Disinclined as she was to theorizing, once her erstwhile teacher and subsequent friend had glossed her late sire's "last words" in that particular way, Elizabeth came increasingly to regard them as talismanic. She remained appreciative of her father's role as her narrative model (*narrational* would be the more accurate adjective, in my opinion, but it smacks of the jargon that our protagonist disdains)—perhaps even more appreciative than before, as those incantatory words resonated through her sensibility. In time, however, she found herself rethinking not only the origins of her vocation but indeed the story of her life in the light of that fateful, though trite, formulation.

For some months immediately following her mother's early death, for example, young Elizabeth and her elderly father had continued the family's agreeable custom of Wednesday-night movies at the town's one theater. Thirty years later, the successful novelist still remembered clearly her pleasure in the idyllic state of affairs established in the opening sequences of many of those old films (although she'd quite forgotten the "ground situations" themselves and was less than certain that they had inevitably been marked by some "overt or latent dramatic voltage"): a pleasure doubtless sharpened by her unarticulated fore-knowledge that trouble must ensue — otherwise, no story.

In our actual lives, of course, she recognized, there is no "and then one day"— although in the *stories* of our lives there may very well be; indeed, there *must* be, she supposed . . . otherwise no story. The story of her life as a storyteller, for instance, she could now imagine as having begun not with the more or less enthralled osmosis of her father's anecdotes (which, it belatedly occurred to her, had been merely that: anecdotes, not stories), but rather with her apprehensive recognition, in those childhood Wednesday-night movies, of the necessary impending disruption of those so-idyllic opening scenes.

In the draft of an extended thank-you note to her friend somewhile after their "end-of-the-Beginning" lunch, she declared experimentally as much to herself as to him, *Since time out of mind I'd been absorbing stories — told and read to me by Mom and Dad (Mom especially: Dad told anecdotes about down-county moonshiners and his courthouse cronies); read for myself in storybooks; witnessed in Stein's Avalon Theater, which we-all attended en famille on Wednesday nights more faithfully than church on Sundays.* And then one day — *watching some now-nameless G-rated production that happened to open with a particularly engaging family scene shot in Glorious Technicolor, as they still called it in the late Fifties (this will have been while Mom was sick in Dorset General, I suddenly remember, but hadn't died yet, and so I'd've been about 10 — and you, dear friend, were 30-something already, long married, with a kid my age . . .), I see up on the screen a pair of handsome, good-humored, obviously loving parents; two or three appealing youngsters of appropriately distributed age and sex; no doubt a pet dog,*

mischievous or soul-eyed or both, gamboling about the sunny ménage . . .
Note how I draw this introductory construction out, not wanting to come
to its closing dash and the sentence proper — and then one day, *with a
vividness that still impresses me three decades later, I understood that
that "unstable homeostatic system" must be disrupted — for the worse,
in this instance if not in all such instances, as it could not imaginably be
made happier than it was* — must be disrupted for the worse, *and very
soon at that, or there'd be no story, and we'd all start to fidget, bored and
baffled, and presently make catcalls at the screen or the projection booth
and even leave the theater, feeling as cheated of our 25 cents as if nothing
had appeared onscreen at all — since from the* dramaturgical *point of
view (as some people I care about would put it) nothing had.*

*How's that for a Faulknersworth of syntax, Coach-o'-my-heart, and
an Emily Dickinsonsworth of dashes from your quondam protégée?*

In fact, of course [she went on, more to herself now than to him], *
the unconsciously anticipated threat (never again unconsciously for this
member of the audience) duly materialized: The family's happiness was,
if not shattered, properly jeopardized by some Screw-Turning Interloper
or Ante-Raising Happenstance — the MGM equivalent of Mom's gallop-
ing cancer — that potentiated the conflict already latent if not overt in the
Ground Situation, then escalated that conflict through the rising action
of the plot to some exciting climax, and ultimately restored the familial
harmony in some significantly and permanently (however subtly) altered
wise, if I've got your seminary lingo right. It was exactly to spectate and
share this disruption and its sea-changed resolution that we'd coughed up
our two bits and set aside our two hours; I understood that, consciously
now, and understood further (though not yet quite consciously) that
what I was understanding was one difference between life and art, or
between our lives and the stories of our lives.*

*For the language wherewith to conceptualize and reflect upon that
understanding, friend, deponent 'umbly thanketh her ex-and-ongoing
teacher. Her turn to take him to lunch, next time she's in town, and to
discuss, maybe, Middles? Wednesday next?*

And then one day (it occurred to her just after she had redrafted and
mailed a much-abridged version of this missive) — one Wednesday PM,
it was, to be precise, maybe half a year after her mother's death — her
father had restored their cozy Avalon twosome to a threesome by including in it faithful Frieda. Not long thereafter, Elizabeth had returned

it to a twosome by deciding that she preferred Saturday matinees with her junior-high girlfriends to Wednesday evenings en famille, if that term still applied.

In the jargon of systems analysis [word came back promptly from across the Bay], *the unstable homeostatic system is incrementally perturbed by the you-know-whom and anon catastrophically restored to a complexified, negentropic equilibrium. Next Wed's bespoke, dear L, but Thurs's clear, tête-à-têtewise.*

Very well, Miz Liz, said she to herself: You're not his only star excoachee, and / or he's not as ready to do Middles yet as you mistakenly inferred him to be — at least not in *your* story. And so with a professionally calibrated mix of mild disappointment, continuing interest, cordial affection, and ultimate shrug-shoulderedness, she replied that Thursday next, alas, was bespoken for *her*, but that either the Wednesday or the Thursday following was (currently) free.

How things went or did not go with this pair, Middlewise, we'll consider presently. In the interim, Elizabeth found herself ever more intrigued, bemused, very nearly possessed by the paradigmatic aspect of her father's "exit line" (the line his, in the first instance, the exit hers, from his hospital room; then the exit his, from her life and his own, the line hers to ponder) and of the sundry Ground Situations in her life — sorry there: in her life-*story* — that that line could be said to have ended, for better or worse. She had innocently audited a thousand stories — *and then one day* in Stein's Avalon she had experienced what amounted to an enlightenment as to the nature of dramatic narrative, and this first had led to others, and after certain further crucial corner-turnings she had matured into a successful working novelist. Her girlhood had been prevailingly sunny and lovingly parented (she had come late and welcomely into her parents' lives), *and then one day* her mother manifested alarming symptoms, and was shockingly soon after dead. Father and daughter had proceeded as best they could with their life together and its attendant rituals — not unsuccessfully, in her young judgment — *and then one* (Wednes)*day* there sat plump Frieda at her dad's other side (Elizabeth's mother had been slender even before her illness, as was her healthy daughter now approaching middle age), and after Frieda, Shirley — or was it Irma — and after Irma *et cetera*; and far be it from Elizabeth to begrudge her father, either at the time or in retrospect, consolatory adult female company in his bereavement, but she and he had never thereafter been as close as she felt them to have been theretofore. Through her subsequent small-town public-school years she had been increasingly restless and irritable, though not truly un-happy — *and then one day* (thanks to the joint beneficence of her father and a childless aunt) she had been offered matriculation at a first-rate private girls' boarding school across the Bay for the last three of her high-school years, and that splendid institution had transformed her — had anyhow guided and abetted her transformation — from one more amorphous and unsophisticated though not unintelligent American teenage mediocrity into a really quite poised, knowledge-able, firm-principled and self-possessed young woman, if she did say so herself, looking forward eagerly to the increased responsibilities, challenges, and freedoms of college undergraduate life — in particular to the serious study of great literature, which she had come ardently to love, and the serious pursuit of "creative writing," for which she had discovered herself blessed with an undeniable flair and, just possibly, a genuine talent.

I am sorry to report that her baccalaureate years proved a time of pedagogical disappointment and considerable personal disorienta-tion — all later turned to good account in Elizabeth's fiction, but scarifying to work through. Short of funds (that beneficent aunt had believed secondary education more crucial than undergraduate educa-tion), she attended a not-bad university on scholarship and found her underclass "professors" — many of them first-time teaching assistants only perfunctorily supervised — almost uniformly inferior to her expe-rienced, knowledgeable, demanding, and enormously attentive prep-school teachers. The time here will have been the early 1970s: The grade inflation and à la carte curricula of the countercultural Sixties had made a near-mockery of academic standards on many American campuses, including Elizabeth's, at least in the liberal arts. LSD, mari-juana, and hashish (but not yet cocaine and "designer drugs") were in almost as common use as alcohol; sexual promiscuity, like a straight-A average, had become so nearly the norm as to lose its meaning. For two years, to her own dismay, this promising young woman goofed off, slept around, abused substances and herself, managed a B average that she and her former high-school advisor agreed should have been a D at best, scarcely communicated with her father, very nearly lost her scholarship (which she knew she no longer deserved), likewise her life (stoned passenger in a car piled up by a stoned roommate who had introduced but not converted her to lesbian sex) and all sense of her-self—not to mention of her notional vocation.

And then one day—one semester, actually, the second of her junior year—she found herself, in at least two senses of that phrase, in a fiction-writing "workshop" presided over by a visiting "writer-in-residence": a mid-thirtyish short-storier of modest fame, leather-jacketed charisma, and a truculent intensity that numerous apprentices, Elizabeth included, found appealing. Preoccupied with his own writing and career ambitions, to his and the university's shame (say I) he paid scant attention to his students' manuscripts but considerable attention to the authors themselves, in particular the two or three who happened to be physically attractive as well as somewhat talented young women. Of these, our Elizabeth was easily the most of both. Although the campus disruptions by anti-Vietnam War protesters in the preceding decade had frightened U.S. college administrators into shortening the academic semester from its traditional fifteen weeks down to thirteen, in that abbreviated period this writer-in-residence managed serial "skin tutorials," as he frankly called them, with all three of his talented/attractive protégées as well as with another rather less so but jealous of her classmates' special coaching. In short, of the seven female students in his workshop he bedded four, and in those sexually unpolitical though luxuriant days the only protest (made petulantly to the writer himself) came from a fifth who felt herself pedagogically shortchanged.

Among these four, unsurprisingly, his favorite and the most frequently thus tutored was Elizabeth; and it must be said for the un-principled bastard that while he was an aggressive sexual imperialist, a shameless exploiter of the student/teacher relationship (which ought ever to be inviolate), an indifferent coach who did no line-editing whatever of his apprentices' manuscripts, and in my judgment not even a particularly gifted writer himself, he nevertheless knew a bright turn of phrase when he saw one, a false note when he heard one, a praiseworthy plot-foreshadowing or blameworthy red herring when one swam into his ken. What's more, in the perspiratory intervals between skin tutorials he did not scruple to remark such of those as he recollected from his tutees' prose. A genuine artist-in-the-making, if I may so put it, recognizes and takes to heart such nuggets of authentic professional feedback, praise and blame alike, regardless of the circumstances of their proffering; if it can be argued that a talent like Elizabeth's would have found its voice sooner or later in any case from accumulated practice and experience of literature, of the world, and of herself, it can also be argued that she found hers rather sooner thanks to the intercopulatory editorializings of her first real writer/coach — whose literary reputation her own would far outshine by when she reached his then age.

Now: The muses, it goes without saying, care nothing for university degrees or such distinctions as graduate versus undergraduate students, only for transcendent gifts disciplined one way or another into mastery. Our institutions being organized as they are, however, and our Elizabeth knowing, upon receipt of her baccalaureate, that she was possessed of ability and ambition but not of means to support herself through the next stage of her apprenticeship (commonly the most serious, arduous, and discouraging), she applied to several of the more prestigious of our republic's abundant graduate writing programs, was accepted at two of them, and chose the one that offered the larger stipend plus tuition-waiver. (It was also rumored that her erstwhile "skin tutor," an academic gypsy, was scheduled to visit the other program, and the memory of *her* exploitation of *him*, as she had almost come to think of it, embarrassed her. She had been, she told herself, no starry-eyed naïf, but an unformed talent craving professional direction the way a wintertime raccoon craves salt and determined to take it wherever she could find it.) In that new venue she had the good fortune to practice intensely for the next two years in the company of similarly able and ambitious peers, with and against whom to hone her skills under the benevolent supervision of a writer/coach more accomplished in both areas than had been his forerunner in her apprenticeship. This one kept his hands scrupulously off his charges — indeed, he had less social connection with them than in my opinion such coaches ideally should have — but very much on their manuscripts, which he took time to read more than once, to line-edit judiciously, and to review with their authors both in conference and in seminar. So did the young woman's art flourish in these circumstances (and her physical and moral well-being likewise, for she had exchanged substance abuse for a glass of table wine with dinner and perhaps an after-class beer with her comrades-in-arms, and sexual promiscuity for near-abstinence until, as soon enough happened, she found a coeval lover suited to her maturing tastes), by MFA-time she had placed short stories in three respectable literary periodicals and had sufficiently impressed her mentor with her maiden novel-in-progress that he felt he could show it to his own agent without compromising his credibility.

And then one day, therefore, she found herself possessed of a better-than-entry-level book contract, and some months thereafter of a favorable front-page notice in the *New York Times Book Review* — shared, to be sure, with a brace of other promising first novelists (that had been the reviewer's handle), but hers the most glowingly praised. Her debut paid out its advance on royalties and earned its publisher a modest profit as well as enjoying a *succès d'estime*, with the consequence that for its sequel her agent negotiated a handsome contract indeed, given that Elizabeth was and remains an essentially "literary" author. By age thirty-five, after a brief and unsatisfying marriage, she was supporting herself comfortably on her royalty income alone.

No, dear Liz (her ex-second coach, ongoing friend, and still-occasional mentor will object if she reviews her life-story with him in these terms, as I rather fancy her doing at their next lunchtime get-together): Those book contracts and that *Times* review don't qualify as Screw-Turning, Ante-Raising Interlopers on the order of Plump Frieda and Comrade Leatherjacket.

"May herpes simplex rot his predatory crotch. But he did call a spade a spade, you know, when he bothered to call anything at all. Why *don't* they qualify, prithee?"

You tell me.

Because, she would suppose, she has uncharacteristically lost track of precisely which story-of-her-life she's in process of telling, and a fortiori of what constitutes its GS as distinct from its DV, or its Beginning from its Middle. In the story of her literary apprenticeship (*one* story of it, anyhow, she imagines her friend mildly correcting her), those egregious skin tutorials had most certainly been an eye-opener, let's say, that initiated her serious application to the craft of fiction. "Viewed another way, however, that clown was just one more court jester, right? An unusually aggressive one, coming closer than most to getting a rise out of Princess Pokerface but still not succeeding, so off to Zapsville he goes, and good riddance. It was *you* who made the difference, dear friend."

No plausible tribute declined by the management. We both suspect, however, that what "made the difference"— as in most such real-life processes, if not in fiction — was some small quantitative increment precipitating a significant qualitative change. The girl sits through ninety-seven Hollywood movies in Stein's Avalon, and then one day, in midst of the ninety-eighth, she rather suddenly grasps some things about basic dramaturgy. So she writes ten yearsworth of practice-fiction without making noteworthy progress except in language-mechanics and the range of her vocabulary, meanwhile accumulating mileage on her experiential odometer, and then one day ...

"Or it happens," Elizabeth hears herself declaring as if to her Chardonnay, "that two people who first knew each other in some uneven professional connection, like lawyer/client or doctor/patient, maintain a more or less attenuated friendship when that connection has run its course. They're still not quite peers, but their paths cross from time to time on officially equal footing at campus arts festivals or over lunch maybe once per season, with occasional letters or phone talks between, usually one of them congratulating the other on some new publication ..."

Very literary lawyers, these guys.

"Very. This goes on for years and years, while their professional lives exfoliate more or less in parallel and their personal lives turn whatever separate corners they turn."

Objection, counselor: In the matter of their personal lives you've got it right, but the curve of *her* career is steadily upward (as was his at her age), while his, as is to be expected, has leveled off and even begun its decline, fortunately gentle.

"So he declares."

Likewise, N.B., his physical capacities.

"So he sees fit to declare. In any event, almost without their noticing it — "

They notice it. But they both have good reasons for not acknowledging it.

"Excellent reasons. All the same, little by little, with neither of them especially leading it, or maybe each half-consciously leading it more or less by turns, their cordial and sporadic connection subtly changes character."

At least it pleases them to believe that the change has been subtle.

"Each has a failed marriage under his/her belt by this time, no? Hers of short duration, to a fellow former coachee of Sir Leatherjacket, as it happens, of whom she came to suspect her spouse terminally jealous. Anyhow, on the basis of considerable experience she'd begun to infer that she didn't particularly *like* men her own age. An ill-starred match, this one, but the split was prevailingly amicable."

I had gathered as much, Liz, but am gratified to hear it said. Not likewise in her friend's case, alas: a *well*-starred match, whereof the end was sore indeed. More community property to hassle over, for one thing, plus a few decadesworth of shared history, plus that daughter somewhere aforementioned . . .

"A daughter *her age*, which datum gives the woman of this pair due pause. The mildly troubling truth appears to be that just as *she* seems most naturally attracted, other things equal, to men nearly old enough to be her father, *he* seems most drawn, in an egregious male-stereotypical way, to women nearly young enough *et cetera*."

Not bloody often, as Apollo is his witness. And when are things ever equal?

"Things never are. On with the story?"

On with it, by all means: This pair does lunch here and there from time to time for years and years, while the plate tectonics of their Ground Situation goes about its virtually imperceptible though nonetheless seismic business.

"And then one day . . .?"

If any such conversation actually took place between these two, we may be confident that it was by no means so formal and narratively tidy as the foregoing. In fact, however, no such conversation did take place, and even had it so taken — untidily, inefficiently, marked by blurts, irrelevancies, unstrategic hesitations — it would not likely have led to anything of dramaturgical interest, inasmuch as the "senior" conversant had long since remarried and was not about to jeopardize that happy connection with infidelity; and the "junior" conversant, truth to tell — having grown up as a motherless only child and been taught emotional self-reliance both by life and by that excellent girls' boarding school — was disinclined to grand passions, sustained intimacy, even for that matter to an unselfishly shared life, though not to the occasional adventure. After the amicable dissolution of her short-lived marriage, Elizabeth had moved back across the Bay into her father's house to oversee his last age; when upon his death that house became hers, she continued to live and work therein contentedly (between her frequent travels) with a large Chesapeake Bay retriever as her chief companion: a more than ordinarily handsome, talented, and successful woman with numerous friends, infrequent casual lovers, no further interest in marriage and none in motherhood, and for that matter no very considerable sexual appetite — although she quite enjoyed occasional lovemaking the way she enjoyed the occasional lobster-feast, gallery opening, or night at the opera.

But even if their situations and temperaments had been otherwise, such that their affectionate casual friendship developed into an *amitié amoureuse* and thence one day or year into a full-scale May / September love affair (June / October, I suppose, even July / November, given their unhurried pace thus far), with whatever consequences to their lives and careers — so what? Reinvigorated by his new "young" companion (although in fact he hadn't been feeling *de*vigorated as things stood), the aging wordsmith closes out his oeuvre with a sprightly final item or two before ill health or senility caps his pen for keeps; alternatively, he so loses himself in the distractions of a new life at his age that he writes nothing further of more than clinical or biographical interest; or an automobile crash, whether his fault or the other driver's, kills him before either of those scenarios can unfold. Inspired by the first truly mature sexual / emotional relationship of her life, Elizabeth in her forties develops from a quite successful though not extraordinary novelist into one of the memorable voices of her generation; her works are everywhere acclaimed by that minuscule fraction of Earth's human population who take pleasure in the art of written literature, and although death claims her mentor / lover all too soon, she manages to remain vigorously productive even after receipt of her Nobel Prize. Or it turns out that their connection doesn't turn out; both parties soon enough recognize (he the more painfully, given the cost of his misstep) that things between them had better remained at the *amitié amoureuse* stage, better yet at the cordial occasional-lunch stage. Or it does work out, anyhow looks to be working out, when alas the MD-80 ferrying them to St. Bart's on holiday is blown out of the Caribbean sky by Islamic-fundamentalist terrorists; or perhaps Elizabeth, attending to some urban business, is shot dead by an irked carjacker when she resists his heist of her saddle-brown Jaguar.

In each and any case, so what? One more short or not-so-short story of bourgeois romance, domestic tribulation, personal and vocational fulfillment or frustration, while the world grinds on. Even were it one more narrative of aspiration and struggle in some worthy, impersonal cause, perhaps of fundamental decency versus self-deception, the seductions of language, and the human inclination to see our lives as stories — So what?

The world grinds on; the world grinds on.

So what?

That's a mighty *so what*, she imagines her friend responding with some concern. Does Miz Liz not remember his distinguishing, back in her advanced-apprentice days, between the readerly reactions *So what?* and *Ah, so!*— the former indicating that the author's narrative / dramatic bills remain unpaid, the latter that her dramaturgical bookkeeping is in good order?

"Sure she remembers, now that he mentions it. Okay, so she remembers: So what, when all's said and done?"

Ah, so: Our Elizabeth appears to have written herself into a proper corner. She has understood all along, more or less, that neither her life nor her father's nor any soul else's is a *story*, while at the same time wryly viewing and reviewing hers, at least, as if it were. And then one day, some imperceptible "quantitative incrementation" ...

On this particular telling, the story of her life thus far (more accurately, I must point out, the story thus far of her life)— its four decadesworth of sundry ups and downs, consequential waypoints and corner-turnings — amounts after all not to a Middle-in-progress, as she has habitually supposed; nor (on this telling) will it so amount four further decades hence, should she live so long, quite regardless of how things go. On this telling she imagines herself then, an old woman at a writing-table in her father's house or some other, having in the course of her long and by-no-means-un-eventful life done this and this and this but not that, or that and that but never this, with such-and-such consequences — the whole catalogue of actions, reactions, and happenstances amounting to no more than an interminable Beginning: a procession of jester / gallants acting out before a complaisant-miened but ultimately impassive princess.

At her feet, her loll-tongued, curly-furred, saddle-brown Chesapeake Bay retriever stirs, makes a small deep wuffing sound, and without lifting his great head from his forepaws, opens his pink-white eyes and shifts his muzzle half-interestedly doorward, as if perhaps sensing something there-beyond, perhaps not. Elizabeth registers subliminally the animal's tentative curiosity but is, as usual, preoccupied with, even lost in, her story-in-progress, if that adjective can be said to apply:

And then one day ...

"Dot dot dot? . . ."

Suspension points; couldn't manage without them. Things left unsaid
. . .

Presently: "Real people don't do it this way."
    Really? How do Real People do it?
    "They just *do* it, for pity's sake. No running halfway round the world
to some resort-chain Paradise. Real people just up and do it and be
done with it and that's that."
    No fuss no muss no bother?
    "No suspension points."

Presently: We're not RPs; we're us.
    "Them."
    They're who they are, not some other couple.
    "Bad luck for them."
    Bad and good don't come into it. They've loved each other . . .
    "Still do."
    Absolutely.
    "Bad luck for them. If anything, that makes things harder."
    Well, dot dot dot.
    "They're playing our song."
    We're playing theirs. Care to dance?

Eventually: Never mind Real People. We'll all be Real next time around.

"They wish."

Meanwhile, they're stuck with being us, and vice versa. There're worse fates.

"For sure. Look at that sunset."

Wind's breezing up. He could tell her a story about that, while they're killing time.

"Dot dot dot. Not funny."

Kiss.

Presently: "Tell."

4.

Preparing for the Storm

Weather the storm that you can't avoid, the old sailors' proverb advises, *and avoid the storm that you can't weather*. No way our waterside neighborhood can avoid *this* character; for days now she's been on our "event horizon": a one-eyed giantess lumbering first more or less our way, then more and more our way, now unequivocally our way. Unless her track unexpectedly changes, Hurricane Dashika will juggernaut in from our literal horizon at this story's end, and no doubt end this story.

In times past, such seasonal slam-bangers took all but the canniest by surprise and exacted a toll much higher for their victims' nonpreparation. Nowadays the new technology gives all hands ample, anyhow reasonable notice. There are, of course, surprises still, such as the rare blaster of such intensity as to overwhelm any amount of accurate forecasting and prudent preparation. In the face of those (which we hereabouts have so far been spared), some throw up their hands and make no preparation whatever; they only wait, stoically or otherwise, for the worst. Wiser heads, however, do their best even in such desperate circumstances, mercifully not knowing in advance that their best will prove futile — for who's to say, before the fact, that it will? — and meanwhile taking some comfort in having done everything they could. Contrariwise, there is undeniably a "Cry Wolf" effect, especially late in the season after a number of false alarms (a misnomer: The alarms aren't invalidated by the fact that more often than not the worst doesn't happen). Reluctant to address yet again the labors of preparation and subsequent "depreparation," some wait too long in hopes that this latest alarm will also prove "false"; they begin their precautionary work too late if at all and consequently suffer, anyhow risk suffering, what sensible preparation would have spared them.

Sensible preparation, yes: neither on the one hand paranoically (and counterproductively) taking the most extreme defensive measures at the least alarm, nor on the other underprepping for the storm's most probable maximum intensity, time of arrival, and duration—that is the Reasonable Waterside Dweller's objective. Not surprisingly, RWDs of comparable experience and judgment may disagree on what constitutes the appropriate response to a given stage of a given storm's predicted approach. Indeed, such neighborly disagreements—serious but typically good-humored when the consequences of one's "judgment call" redound upon the caller only, not upon his or her neighbors—are a feature of life hereabouts in storm season: Not one of us but keeps a weather eye, so to speak, on our neighbors' preparations or nonpreparations as we go about our own.

In this respect, my situation is fortunate: I'm flanked on my upshore side by old "Better-Safe-Than-Sorry" Bowman, typically the first of us to double up his dock lines, board his windows, and the rest, and on my downshore side by young Ms. "Take-a-Chance" Tyler, typically the last. Both are seasoned, prudent hands—as am I, in my judgment. Neither neighbor, in my judgment, is either decidedly reckless or decidedly overcautious (although each teases the other with the appropriate adjective)—nor, in my judgment, am I. When therefore old Bowman sets about plywooding his glass or shifting his vintage fishing-skiff from dock to more sheltered mooring, I take due note but may or may not take similar action just yet with my little daysailer; should it happen that *Tyler* initiates such measures before I do, however, I lose no time in following suit. Contrariwise, the circumstance that Tyler hasn't yet stowed her lawn furniture or literally battened the hatches of her salty cruising sailboat doesn't mean that I won't stow and batten mine—but I can scarcely imagine doing so if even Bowman hasn't bothered. All in all, thus far the three of us have managed well enough.

Our current season's box score happens to be exemplary. Hurricane Abdullah (the Weather Service has gone multicultural in recent years, as well as both-sexual) suckered all of us, though not simultaneously, into full Stage Three, Red-Alert preparation, even unto the checklist's final item — shutting off our main power and gas lines, locking all doors, and retreating inland — and then unaccountably hung a hard right at our virtual threshold, roared out to sea, and scarcely raised the local breeze enough to dry our late-July sweat as we undid our mighty preparations. Tropical Storms Bonnie and Clyde, the tandem toughs of August, distributed their punishments complementarily: Predicted merely to brush by us, Bonnie took a surprise last-minute swing our way and made Tyler scramble in her bikini from Green Alert (Stage One, which we had all routinely mounted: the minimum Get-Readys for even a Severe Thunderstorm warning) up through Yellow (where I myself had seen fit to stop under the circumstances) to Red, while long-since-battened-down Bowman fished and chuckled from his dock — just long enough to make his point before lending her a hand, as did I when I finished my Stage Three catch-up. From Bonnie we all took hits, none major: an unstowed lawn chair through Tyler's porch screen; gelcoat scratches on my daysailer, which I ought to've hauled out before it scraped the dockpiles; a big sycamore limb down in Bowman's side yard ("Not a dead one, though," old Better-Safe was quick to point out, who in Tyler's view prunes his deadwood before it's rightly sick). No sooner had we re-de-prepped than on Bonnie's heels came Clyde, a clear Stage Two-er by my assessment, Stage Three again by B.S.T.S. Bowman's, Stage One once more by T.A.C. Tyler's. Clyde thundered erratically up the coast just far enough offshore to justify all three scenarios and then "did an Abdullah," leaving Bowman to prep down laboriously all day from Red Alert and me all morning from Yellow, while Tyler sunbathed triumphantly out on her dock, belly-down on a beach towel, headphones on and bikini-top off — just long enough to make her point before she pulled on a T-shirt and pitched in to return our earlier favor, first helping me Doppler-Shift from Yellow back through Green and then (with me) helping Bowman do likewise, who had already by that time Yellowed down from Full Red.

So here now at peak season, September's ides, comes dreadsome Dashika, straight over from West Africa and up from the Horse Latitudes, glaring her baleful, unblinking eye our way. She has spared the Caribbean (already battered by Abdullah) but has ravaged the eastmost Virgin Islands, flattened a Bahama or two, and then swung due north, avoiding Florida and the Gulf Coast (both still staggered from *last* year's hits) and tracking usward as if on rails, straight up the meridian of our longitude. As of this time yesterday, only the Carolina Capes stood between Dashika and ourselves.

"Poor bastards," commiserated Tyler as the first damage reports came in. Time to think Stage Two, she supposed, if not quite yet actually to set about it; Capes Fear and Hatteras, after all, are veteran storm-deflectors and shock absorbers that not infrequently, to their cost, de-energize hurricanes into tropical storms and veer them out to sea.

"Better them than us," for his part growled Bowman, as well as one can growl through a mouthful of nails, and hammered on from Yellow Alert up toward Red.

I myself was standing pat at Stage Two but more or less preparing to prepare for Three, as was Tyler vis-à-vis Two — meanwhile listening to the pair of them trade precedents and counterprecedents from seasons past, like knowledgeable sports fans. I had already disconnected my TV antenna, unplugged various electronics, readied flashlights and kerosene lamps, lowered flags, stowed boat gear, checked dock lines, snugged lawn chairs and other outdoor blowaways, and secured loose items on my water-facing porch: Green Alert. While Dashika chewed up the Outer Banks, I doubled those dock lines, filled jerry cans and laundry tubs with reserve water, loaded extra ice-blocks into the freezer against extended power outage, checked my food and cash reserves, and taped the larger windows against shattering: Yellow Alert, well into last night.

This morning scarcely dawned at all, only lightened to an ugly gray. The broad river out front is as hostile-looking as the sky. Damage and casualty reports from Hatteras to the Virginia Capes are sobering indeed, and while Dashika has lost some strength from landfall, she remains a Class Three hurricane vectored straight at us. Moreover, her forward velocity has slowed: We've a bit more grace to prepare (in Bowman's case to wait, as his prepping's done), but our time under fire will be similarly extended. Already the wind is rising; what's worse, it's southerly, our most exposed quarter and the longest wave-fetch on our particular estuary. In consequence, last night's high tide scarcely ebbed, and this morning's low tide wasn't. This afternoon's high bids to put our docks under and the front half of Tyler's lawn as well, right up to her pool deck (my ground's higher, Bowman's higher yet). If there's a real storm surge to boot, I'll have water in my basement and the river's edge almost to my porch; Tyler's pool — to which I have a generous standing invitation, although I prefer the natural element, and which she herself enjoys uninhibitedly at all hours, skinnying out of her bikini as soon as she hits the water — Tyler's pool will be submerged entirely, quite as Bowman the hydrophobe has direly long foretold, and her one-story "bachelor girl" cottage may well be flooded too.

A-prepping we've therefore gone, separately, she and I. While Better-Safe potters in his garden and angles from his dock with conspicuous nonchalance, savoring his evidently vindicated foresight and justifiably not coming to our aid until the eleventh hour, I've ratcheted up to Full Red: trailered and garaged my boat, shut off power and water to my dock, taped the rest of my windows (never yet having lost one, I'm not a boarder-upper; Tyler won't even tape), boxed my most valuable valuables, even packed a cut-and-run suitcase. Nothing left to do, really, except shift what's shiftable from first floor up to second (two schools of thought hereabouts on that last-ditch measure, as you might expect: Bowman's for it, although even he has never yet gone so far; Tyler's of the opinion that in a bona fide hurricane we're as likely to lose the roof and rain-soak the attic as to take in water downstairs) and get the hell out. Ms. Take-a-Chance is still hard at it: an orange blur, you might say, as she does her Yellow- and Red-Alert preps simultaneously. It's a treat to watch her, too, now that I myself am as Redded up as I want to be for the present and am catching my breath before I lend her a hand. Too proud to ask for help, is T.A.C.T. — as am I, come to that, especially vis-à-vis old Bowman — but not too proud to accept it gratefully when it's offered in extremis, and that particular sidelong "Owe you one" look that she flashes me at such times is a debt-absolver in itself. Under her loose sweatshirt and cut-off jeans is the trademark string bikini, you can bet; Tyler's been known to break for a dip in the teeth of a thirty-knot gale. And under the bikini — well, she doesn't exactly hide what that item doesn't much cover anyhow, especially when B.S.T.S. is off somewhere and it's just her in her pool and me doing my yard work or whatever. We're good neighbors of some years' standing, Tyler and I, no more than that, and loners both, basically, as for that matter is old Bowman: "Independent as three hogs on ice," is how T. describes us. Chez moi, at least, that hasn't always been the case — but never mind. And I don't mind saying (and just might get it said to *her* this time, when I sashay down there shortly to help shift *Slippery*, that nifty cutter of hers, out to its heavy-weather mooring before the seas get high) that should a certain trim and able neighborlady find the tidewater invading her ground-floor bedroom, there's a king-size second-floor one right next door, high and dry and never intended for one person.

No time for such hog-dreams now, though. It's getting *black* off to southward there, Dashikaward; if we don't soon slip Ms. Slippery out of her slip, there'll be no unslipping her. What I've been waiting for is a certain over-the-shoulder glance from my busy friend wrestling spring-lines down there on her dock, where her cutter's bucking like a wild young mare: a look that says "Don't think I *need* you, neighbor, but"—and there it is, and down I hustle, just as old Bowman looks set to amble *my* way after I glance himward, merely checking to see whether he's there and up to what. A bit of jogging gets me aboard milady's pitching vessel, as I'd hoped, before B's half across my lawn; by the time he has cocked his critical eye at my own preparations and made his way out onto Tyler's dock, she and I have got *Slippery's* auxiliary diesel idling and her tender secured astern to ferry us back ashore when our job's done.

"Need another hand?" It's me he calls to, not Tyler—let's say because I'm in *Slippery's* bobbing, shoreward-facing bow, unhitching dock lines while T. stands by at the helm, and there's wind-noise in the cutter's rigging along with the diesel-chug—but his ate-the-canary tone includes us both. Bowman's of the age and category that wears workshirt and long khakis in the hottest weather, plus cleat-soled leather shoes and black socks (I'm in T-shirt, frayed jeans, and sockless deck-mocs; Tyler's barefoot in those aforenoted tight cutoffs).

"Ask the skipper," I call back pointedly, and when I see B. wince at the way we're pitching already in the slip, I can't help adding, "Maybe she wants somebody up the mast."

He humphs and shuffles on out toward the cutter's cockpit, shielding his face from the wind with one hand to let us know we should've done this business earlier (I agree) and getting his pantslegs wet with spray from the waves banging under *Slippery's* transom.

"Just stow these lines, Fred, if you will," Tyler tells him pertly; "thanks a bunch." She has strolled forward as if to greet him; now she tosses him a midships spring-line and returns aft to do likewise with the stern line — just to be nice by making the old guy feel useful, in my opinion, because she *is* nice: tough and lively and nobody's fool, but essentially nice, unlike some I've done time with. So what if she's feeding B's wiser-than-thouhood; we're good neighbors all, each independent as a hog on ice but the three of us on the same ice, finally, when cometh push to shove.

Only two of us in the same boat, however. Tyler casts off her stern line and I the remaining bow line; she hops smartly to the helm, calls "Astern we go!" and backs *Slippery* down into full reverse. When Bowman warns me from the dock "Mind your bowsprit as she swings, or you're in trouble," I'm pleased to say back to him — loud enough for her to hear, I hope — "Some folks know how to swing without making trouble." Lost on him, no doubt, but maybe not on her.

Out we go then into the whitecaps to make the short run to her mooring, where *Slippery* can swing indeed: full circle to the wind, if necessary, instead of thrashing about in her slip and maybe chafing through her lines and smashing against dock piles. I go aft to confer on our approach-and-pickup procedure with Ms. Helmsperson, who's steering with her bare brown toes in the wheel's lower spokes while she tucks a loose sunbleached lock up under her headband. Raising her arms like that does nice things with Tyler's breasts, even under a sweatshirt; she looks as easy at the helm as if we're heading out for a sail on the bay instead of Red-Alerting for a killer storm. When she smiles and flashes the old "Owe you one," I find myself half wishing that we really were heading out together, my neighbor-lady and I, not for a daysail but for a real blue-water passage: hang a left at the lastmost lighthouse, say, and lay our course for the Caribbean, properties and storm-preparations be damned. Single-handing hath its pleasures, for sure, but they're not the only pleasures in the book.

Storm-time, however, is storm-time, a pickup's a pickup, and both of us know the routine. It's just a matter of confirming, once we've circled the mooring buoy and swung up to windward, that she'll leave it close on our starboard bow, following my hand-signals on final approach. T. swears she can do the job herself, and so she can in ordinary weathers, as I know from applauding her often enough from dock or porch when she comes in from a solo cruise, kills the cutter's headway at exactly the right moment, and scrambles forward just in time to flatten herself in the bow, reach down for the mast of the pickup float, and drop the eye of her mooring line over a bow cleat before *Slippery* slips away. In present conditions, it's another story; anyhow, once I'm positioned on the foredeck she has to follow my signals will-she nill-she, as I'll be blocking her view of the target. Make of that circumstance what you will; I myself mean to make of it what I can. Looks as if we're thinking in synch, too, T. and I, for now she says, "I'll bring us up dead slow; final approach is your call, okay?"

Aye aye, ma'am. That wind really pipes now in *Slippery*'s rigging as I make my way forward, handing myself from lifelines to shrouds and up to the bow pulpit while we bang into a two-foot chop and send the spray flying. My heart's whistling a bit, too. *Easy does it*, I remind myself: *Not too fast, not too slow; neither too much nor too little.* That pick-up float has become a bobbing metaphor: *Don't blow it*, I warn me as we close the last ten yards, me kneeling on the foredeck as if in prayer and hand-signaling, *Just a touch portward, Skipper-Babe; now a touch starboard. Just a touch . . .* Then I'm prone on her slick wet foredeck, arm and shoulder out under bow rail, timing my grab to synchronize *Slippery*'s hobbyhorsing with the bob of the float and the waggle of its pickup mast — and by golly, I've got her!

Got *it*; I've by-golly got it, and I haul it up smartly before the next wave knocks us aside, and with my free hand I snatch the mooring eye and snug it over the bow cleat in the nick of time, just as six tons of leeway-making sailboat yank up the slack.

"Good show!" cheers Tyler, and in fact it was. From the helm she salutes me with her hands clasped over her head (that nice raised-arm effect again) and I both acknowledge and return the compliment with a fist in the air, for her boat-handling was flawless. By when I'm back in the cockpit, she's all business, fetching out chafe-gear to protect the mooring line where it leads through a chock to its cleat and asking would I mind going forward one last time to apply that gear while she secures things down below, and then we're out of here. But unless I'm hearing things in the wind, there's a warmth in her voice just a touch beyond the old "Owe you one."

No problem, neighbor. I do that little chore for her in the rain that sweeps off the bay now and up our wide river, whose farther shore has disappeared from sight. It takes some doing to fit a rubber collar over a heavy mooring line exactly where it lies in its chock on a pitching, rain-strafed foredeck without losing that line on the one hand or a couple of fingers on the other, so to speak; we're dealing with large forces here, pumped up larger yet by Ms. Dashika yonder. But I do it, all right, seizing moments of slack between waves and wind-gusts to make my moves, working with and around those forces more than against them. When I come aft again, I call down the cabin companionway that if she loses her investment, it won't be because her chafe-gear wasn't in place.

"Poor thing, you're soaked!" Tyler calls back up. "Come out of the wet till I'm done, and then we'll run for it."

When I look downriver at what's working its way our way, I think we ought to hightail it for shore right now. But I am indeed soaked, and chilling fast in the wind; what's more, my friend's on her knees down there on one of the settee berths, securing stuff on the shelf behind it and looking about as perky and fetching as I've ever seen her look, which is saying much. And despite the wind-shrieks and the rain-rattle and the pitching, or maybe because of them, *Slippery*'s no-frills cabin, once I'm down in it, is about as cozy a shelter as a fellow could wish for, with just the two of us at home. Concerned as I am that if we don't scram out of there pronto, there'll be no getting ashore for us (already the chop's too steep and the wind too strong to row the dinghy to windward; luckily, our docks are dead downwind, a dozen boatlengths astern), I'm pleased to come indoors. I stand half beside and half behind her, holding on to an over-head grab rail like a rush-hour subway commuter, and ask, What else can I do for you, Skip?

She cuts me her "Owe you one," does Ms. Take-a-Chance — maybe even "Owe you two or three" — and says, "Make yourself at home, neighbor; I'm just about ready."

Yes, well, say I to myself: Likewise, mate; like-wise. Seems to me that what she's busy with there on her knees isn't all that high-priority, but it sure makes for an admirable view. Instead of admiring it from the settee opposite, I take a seat beside her, well within arm's reach.

Arm's reach, however, isn't necessarily easy reach, at least not for some of us. When I think about Take-a-Chance Tyler or watch her at her work and play, as has lately become my habit, I remind myself that I wouldn't want anything Established and Regular, if you know what I mean. I've *had* Established, I've *had* Regular, and I still carry the scars to prove it. No more E & R for this taxpayer, thank you kindly. On the other hand, though I'm getting no younger, I'm no B.S.T.S. Bowman yet, getting my jollies from a veggie-garden and tucking up in bed with my weather radio. As the saying goes, if I'm not as good as once I was, I'm still as good once as I was — or so I was last time I had a chance to check. Life hereabouts doesn't shower such chances upon us loners, particularly if, like me, you're a tad shy of strangers and happen to like *liking* the lady you lay. There ought to be some middle ground, says I, between Established and Regular on the one hand and Zilch on the other: a middle road that stays middle *down* the road. Haven't found it yet myself, but now I'm thinking maybe here it perches on its bare brown knees right beside me, within arm's reach, fiddling with tide tables and nautical charts and for all I know just waiting for my arm to reach.

Look before you leap, proverbial wisdom recommends — while also warning that *he who hesitates is lost*. In Tyler's case, I'm a paid-up looker and hesitator both. *Nothing ventured, nothing gained*, I tell myself; *there is a tide in the affairs of men*, et cetera, and I plop my hand palm-down on her near bare calf.

"I know," frets Take-a-Chance, not even turning her pretty head: "Time to clear our butts out of here before we're blown away. Better safe than sorry, right?"

Dashika howls at that, and the rain downpours like loud applause. In one easy smiling motion then, Tyler's off the settee with my business hand in hers, leading me to go first up the companionway.

Which I do.

Well. So. I could've stood my ground, I guess — *sat* my ground, on that settee — and held on to that hand of hers and said, Let's ride 'er out right here, okay? Or, after that wild dinghy-trip back to shore, I could've put my arm around her as we ran through the rain toward shelter, the pair of us soaked right through, exhilarated by the crazy surf we'd ridden home on and breathing hard from hauling the tender out and up into the lee of her carport. I could've given her a good-luck *kiss* there in that shelter, to see whether it might lead to something more (nobody to see us, as Bowman appears to've cleared out already) instead of merely *saying* Well, so: Take care, friend, and good luck to both of us. At very least I could've asked Shall we watch old Dashika from your place or mine? or at very *very* least How about a beer for *Slippery*'s crew? But I guess I figured it was Tyler's turn: I'd made my move; the ball was in her court; if she wasn't having it, amen.

So take care now, is what I said. Good luck to all hands. I'll keep an eye out.

Whereat quoth T.A.C.T., "Thanks a bunch, nabe. Owe you one."

And that was that.

So an eye out I've kept since, and keep on keeping as Dashika roars in, although there's little to be seen through that wall of rain out there, and nothing to be heard over this freight-train wind. Power's out, phones are out, walls and windows are shaking like King Kong's cage; can't see whether *Slippery*'s still bucking and rearing on her tether or has bolted her mooring and sailed through Tyler's picture window. All three docks are under; the surge is partway up my lawn already and must be into Tyler's pool. Can't tell whether that lady herself has cut and run for high ground, but I know for a fact she hasn't run to this particular medium-high patch thereof.

I ought to cut and run myself, while I still can. Ms. T's her own woman; let her *be* her own woman, if she's even still over there. But hell with it. I moved a couple things upstairs and then said hell with that, too, and just opened me a cold one while there's still one cold to be opened and sat me down here all by my lonesome to watch Dashika do her stuff.

I'm as prepared as I want to be.

Hell with it.

Let her come.

"'Yes, well,'

. . . as he likes to say."
. . .

Presently: "Are you and I weathering what we can't avoid, or vice versa?"
Both. Let's do it happily ever after. They. Them.
"There is no happily ever after. No ever after, period. There's only the period."
Maybe suspension points? . . .

Activity, inactivity, meals, tears, love. Presently: "They *are* as prepared as they want to be, no?"
No.
"As they'll *ever* be, then."
They'll never be.
"Same thing. So what are they waiting for?"
A god on wires, to save the situation.
"Don't hold their breath. There *is* no *et cetera*."
No wires, either, for better or worse. Only stories.

Presently: "Maybe they're out of stories."
Nope. But maybe *she's* out of —
"Yup. Never mind her, though."
He'll never never-mind her.

"He's going to have to learn to never-mind her."
Meanwhile, he hastily interjects . . .
"Meanwhile?"
All the while there is. Which being the case . . .

5.

On with the Story

"In our collective headlong flight toward oblivion [Alice reads], *there are a few among us still, remarkably, who take time out from time to time to read a made-up story. Of that small number, dear present reader, you are one."*

The writer of these lines is another, and a third is the abovementioned Alice, chief character of this story-now-in-progress, whose attention has been caught by the passage that you and she together have just read. Leafing more or less distractedly through an in-flight magazine — Alice is, in fact, in flight, crossing the Mississippi River at cruising altitude aboard an aging DC-10 en route from Boston to Portland, Oregon — she has registered marginally its advertisements for attaché cases, notebook computers, highway radar detectors, collapsible luggage carriers "just like the ones your flight attendants use," and airport hotels. She has then fretfully scanned self-help articles on how to make more effective product presentations and (the same thing, really) a more forceful presence at job interviews. She's going to have to be doing that, for sure, now that her divorce-settlement negotiations — which both she and Howard vowed to keep amicable for young Sam and Jessica's sakes and their own — have, despite all, turned adversary and acrimonious.

With rather more interest, she has wistfully next perused a photo-spread entitled "Island Paradises" — three of which, as it happens, she and Howard romantically "ran off" to, honeymooned in, and vacationed at, in turn, back in the palmy years before their children came along; before Howard's "mid-career course correction" failed to correct it; before her own work history mainly spun its wheels, and their marriage, to both parties' dismay, went belly-up. No Island Paradises in Alice's foreseeable future: For the past half-dozen years at least, her idea of a quality vacation has been a weekend's state-park camping with the kids (but they're in junior high and high school now, ever less interested in roughing it en famille, especially just with Mom) or a week at her parents' summer place on Cape Cod. It's from one of those latter that she's just now returning, leaving Jessica and Sam for an additional fortnight with their maternal grandparents. To Alice's embarrassment, all hands' airfares have had to be on the old folks' tab; she and Howard simply haven't the resources to finance cross-country family visits. They haven't even a savings fund for the kids' rapidly upcoming college expenses, for pity's sake, typically the middle-class American family's single largest capital outlay. After eighteen years of marriage, this decoupling couple's only real nest egg is a few thousand dollars gained not by programmatic saving but by refinancing the nest when home mortgage rates dropped a few years ago — and now Howard's insisting that that egg be split fifty-fifty. Likewise their equity in the house itself, which he wants sold; likewise further their children's custody, although his proposals for the logistical management of that last item strike Alice as risible if not disingenuous — possibly a ploy to reduce his child-support payments.

How in the world, she has wondered in mid-photo spread ("The *Other* British Virgins"), did her parents' generation — the generation that generated the postwar Baby Boom whereof she and Howard are dues-paying members — manage? Typically on one income, or one and a fraction, American middle-class couples like Alice's folks and Howard's contrived to send two, three, even four offspring through college — sometimes even through private colleges, not the local state diploma mills that Sam and Jessica will have to make do with — and in Alice's case to private high school before that, not to mention affording them piano lessons, dance and horseback-riding lessons, art lessons, a house to grow up in considerably more spacious than Sam's and Jessica's (in a better neighborhood, too), and in later years even a vacation home as well? Howard's father, moreover, managed all this while himself divorcing and remarrying at his son's present age; gave his first wife their commodious house free and clear for the children to finish their high-school years in, plus enough alimony to maintain her and them therein till they were off to college at his expense and she remarried — and on top of that paid all of her divorce-lawyer's fees as well as his own, with the result that Howard's mother (how Alice now envies her in this!) had had the luxury of protracting the negotiations at her leisure and at her estranged husband's cost. All this, mind, in a divorce action that, like Alice's and Howard's, was no-fault, by pained mutual consent — not one party dumping the other and therefore becoming willy-nilly the "buyer" of the divorce, the aggrieved other party the "seller." Alice's dad (still contentedly married to her mom) is a retired history professor of modest repute with a couple of royalty-producing textbooks as well as scholarly articles in his bibliography; her mother was for decades a part-time Special Ed teacher in the public schools. Howard's father and mother, a bit more affluent but scarcely rich, are or were respectively a research chemist with a few process-patents on the side and a classic 1950s "homemaker" who did volunteer charity work at her church and the county hospice. In those Kennedy/Johnson, *Leave It to Beaver* years, where on earth had the money come from?

Alice exhaled audibly, shook her head, and turned to the final page of "Island Paradises": Norman Island in the BVI, now about to be "developed" with resort hotels, but almost pristine fifteen years ago when Howard and she, already a few months pregnant with Sam, had anchored a chartered sailboat in its splendid Bight on the third Thanksgiving of their marriage.

"Beats Boston, right?" the fellow in the aisle-seat beside her commented at this point. He, too, she'd noticed, had been leafing through the airline's in-flight mag and, evidently, eyeing Alice's progress therethrough. Whether by coincidence or as a conversation-starting gambit on his part, they reached Norman Island separately together.

"Careful, there," Alice replied — cordially but coolly, in her judgment, as she was not much up for conversation: "You're talking to an old Bostonian."

"Am I, now?" To Alice (who wasn't looking closely) the man looked to be maybe twenty years older than herself, same general eth and class, standard navy blazer khaki slacks open sportshirt lanky build graying hair nice tan easy smile. "So are you, as it happens. But I don't object to an island paradise from time to time."

"Likewise, I'm sure."

His accent wasn't Boston—but then neither is Alice's, and "old Bostonian" scarcely describes her. Child of academic parents, she and her brothers were born in Bloomington, Indiana, spent their elementary-school years in Santa Barbara, California, and only their high-school years in suburban Boston, as their father moved from campus to campus up the professorial ladder. If Alice thinks of any place as her childhood home, it's that cottage on the Cape, where the family spent more summers together than school years anywhere.

Her tone and manner did the job, if there was any to be done. Both passengers returned to their magazines, wherein "Island Paradises" turns out to be followed—unusual for an in-flight publication—by a bit of fiction: a short story called "Freeze Frame," its author's name unfamiliar to our protagonist. Alice is not, these days at least, much of a reader, of fiction or anything else beyond the lease- and sale-contracts that come across her part-time office desk and the textbooks on real-estate law, of all things, that she's been cramming lately in half-hearted preparation for her Oregon licensing exam. As a girl (whose parents strictly rationed their children's diet of television) she consumed novels the way Sam and Jessica consume Nintendo and junk food—and not just kiddie-novels. In her first-rate private high school (she wished Sam's public one were half as good), Fitzgerald's *Great Gatsby* and Turgenev's *Fathers and Sons* joyously broke her heart and enlarged her spirit. At Reed College in Portland (where she'd met pre-law Howard), she'd been a sociology major with a serious minor in her favorite subject, literature; she read rapturously through the big Victorians and the early Modernists, and in her senior year considered with her dad and with Howard (by then her virtual fiancé) the merits of sundry graduate departments of literature as well as sociology, with an eye toward advanced degrees in one or the other and an academic career.

All that seems another world to her now. She and Howard "ran off" to Barbados on holiday after graduation and presently thereafter married. She followed him to law school in New York, where she did pickup copyediting to help pay the rent, and then—when he dropped out for reasons that they still argue over—to Chicago on an initially successful business venture with one of his father's chemical-patent partners (their Virgin Islands cruise and her happy first pregnancy date from this period). When the Chicago venture fizzled, she and young Sam and Jessica-in-the-works followed him back out to Portland and his present restless employ as a "product developer" for a pharmaceutical concern — while Alice herself, faute de mieux, "helps out" half-time these days in a suburban real-estate office. She has thus far resisted the mild advances of her more-or-less mentor there, although he's a civilized-seeming divorcé himself and she's lonesome for adult male company now that she and Howard have split; but she guesses unenthusiastically that she'll take his advice and go for her broker's license. In the interstices of her frazzled life: videos with the kids, when she can get them peaceably assembled; regular jogging, to keep her spirits up and her body in shape for whatever next episode in her life-story; telephonic set-tos with Howard about economic and parental matters; the aforementioned odd camping weekend; maybe half an hour's thumbing through some glossy magazine like *Elle* or *Vanity Fair*: snapshots from yet another world. She scarcely manages to read the daily *Oregonian* these days beyond its real-estate section, much less *literature*; indeed, she probably ought to be re-reviewing the R. E. Board-exam stuff right now, as she has spent most of her "vacation" week doing. But she's supersaturated in that line; also depressed by her parents' loving, unspoken, but obvious disappointment in their only daughter's life-trajectory thus far and even with her upbringing of their grandchildren ("*Mortal Kombat!*" her dad had groaned in disbelief when young Sam fished out that stupefying game from his backpack, like a junkie in need of a fix, the minute they arrived at the Cape Cod cottage).

Alice is, in fact, for perhaps the first time in her forty years, truly fearful of the future, whereof that real-estate-law manual is a token and wherefrom this in-flight magazine — like the round-trip flight itself and the less than refreshing vacation that it has bracketed — is an all-too-brief reprieve.

Literature, hah: Those were the days!

Thus the odd opening of that "Freeze Frame" story catches her attention. As she reads on, moreover, she finds herself involved in (and she'll presently be stopped still by) one of those vertiginous coincidences that happen now and then to readers of stories, attenders of movies, even swappers of anecdotes with one's fellow passengers through life: a correspondence stranger than fiction (even when one of the corresponding items *is* fiction) between the situation one is reading or hearing about and one's own. "Freeze Frame"— its first half, anyhow — turns out to involve a forty-year-old White-Anglo-Saxon-(lapsed)-Protestant middle-class American woman (name not given) who, like Alice, acutely knows herself to have passed the classical *mezzo del cammin di nostra vita*, as the author puts it, quoting the opening lines of Dante's *Divine Comedy*: a little past the halfway point of the biblically allotted three-score-and-ten. Like Alice, "she" is a healthy human animal, though under sustained stress lately, and the daughter of still-living parents who themselves are in good health for their age. She knows therefore her expectable remaining life-span, barring accident, to be slightly longer than the span behind her — more trying, too, she expects, although her story thus far, while relatively privileged, has by no means been carefree. The story's narrator calls its lead character's malaise "the Boomer Syndrome": Just as her middle-class-American generation is, by and large, the first of the century not to surpass its forebears in physical height and general health, so with many exceptions are its members likewise falling short, or feel themselves to be, in material, perhaps even spiritual, well-being. "Her" father and mother respectively G.I.-Billed through state university and worked through secretarial school, the first in their families' history to "go past high school"; they flourished as a one-and-a-half-income family in the booming postwar U.S. economy and provided their children (four!) with a suburban upbringing at least as favored as Alice's and her brothers', substantially more favored than their own had been, and downright sybaritic compared to that of "her" grandparents. The parental generation managed the class-climb from small-shopkeeper to professional ("her" father was an estate-and-trust lawyer) and confidently supposed that their sons — maybe even their daughters — would likewise enter the professions on the strength of their excellent educations. But something— "Call it the countercultural Sixties," the author suggests in the story, "the oil-embargoed, 'stagflated' Seventies, the TV-narcotized beginning of the end of the American Century"— something had gone quietly but profoundly wrong.

And then less quietly. Of "her" two brothers, one has drifted from commune to hippie commune right up into the Reagan Eighties, his circuits blown on Sixties methedrine; in his late thirties he half-supports himself as a longhaired mower of suburban lawns who converses with spirits as he maneuvers his Kubota wide-blade rig through the greenswards of Newton, Massachusetts. The other, after dropping out of two colleges plus law school (shades of Alice's Howard), is doing modestly in rural Maryland as a remodeler of small-town kitchens and bathrooms; he likes to work with his hands. Of the two girls, one has broken her parents' officially liberal hearts by "coming out" as a lesbian and, after a creditable West African tour of duty in the Peace Corps, a halfhearted suicide-attempt, and a parentally subsidized stay in a Pittsburgh psychiatric hospital, settling down with her same-sex Significant Other to run a marginally successful New Age gift shop in San Diego. Not all that different a resumé, changes changed, from Alice's gay brother's in his Key West cappuccino bar, which her parents gamely visit every second or third winter, not to lose touch altogether.

As for Her herself, whom let's capitalize henceforth for clarity and convenience: After "Freeze Frame"'s opening address to the dear present reader, said reader finds Her gridlocked in downtown St. Louis traffic, not at morning or evening rush-time but, curiously, just a bit past noon — owing perhaps to a routine lunchtime-traffic congestion that She didn't know to allow for, perhaps to some out-of-view accident or other bottleneck. In any case, en route to the riverside expressway in Her ailing, high-mileage Subaru wagon after an upsetting legal confrontation with Her estranged husband — a confrontation between their respective divorce-lawyers, actually, through which the parties to the action sat in stony silence — and running late already for a job-interview appointment in University City (She'll be needing a better job than her current office-temping, all right, given the likely outcome of those settlement negotiations, but She's not at all sure that Her indifferent work-history qualifies Her for anything remotely approaching her vague expectations back when She took her MA in Art History fifteen years ago), She's stopped dead in this humongous traffic jam and verging on tears as Her aged station wagon verges on overheating. How could "Her" Bill have sat there so damned impassively — Her longtime, once-so-loving spouse, father of their twins, Her graduate-school lover and best of friends — in those hateful new wire-rimmed, double-bridged eyeglasses that She supposes are an aspect of this new, intransigently hostile William Alfred Barnes, and that She suspects are meant to please some other Her than Her?

The cold-hearted bastard, Alice remarks to herself. The DC-10's captain announces at this point that owing to turbulent weather over Chicago, the plane's course has been diverted south; they are crossing the Mississippi just below Hannibal, Missouri — Mark Twain's birthplace.

She (I mean our distraught "Freeze Frame" protagonist) happens to be gridlocked in actual sight of that river: There's the symbolic catenary arch of the "Gateway to the West," and beyond it are the sightseeing boats along the parkfront and out among the freight-barge strings. As She tries to divert and calm herself by regarding the nearest of those tourist boats — an ornate replica of a Mark Twain-vintage sternwheeler, just leaving its pier to nose upstream — Her attention is caught by an odd phenomenon that, come to think of it, has fascinated Her since small-girlhood (happier days!) whenever She has happened to see it: The river is, as ever, flowing south, New Orleansward; the paddle-steamer is headed north, gaining slow upstream momentum (standard procedure for sightseeing boats, in order to abbreviate the anticlimactic return leg of their tour), and as it begins to make headway, a deckhand ambles aft in process of casting off the vessel's docklines, with the effect that he appears to be walking in place, with respect to the shore and Her angle of view, while the boat moves under him. It is the same disconcerting illusion, She guesses, as that sometimes experienced when two trains stand side by side in the station and a passenger on one thinks momentarily that the other has begun to move, when in fact the movement is his own — an illusion compoundable if the observer on Train A (this has happened to Her at least once) happens to be strolling down the car's aisle like that crewman on the sternwheeler's deck, at approximately equal speed in the opposite direction as the train pulls out. Dear-present-reader Alice suddenly remembers one such occasion, somewhere or other, when for a giddy moment it appeared to her that she herself, aisle-walking, was standing still, while Train A, Train B, and Boston's South Street Station platform (it now comes back to her) all seemed in various motion.

As in fact they were, the "Freeze Frame" narrator declares in italics at this point, his end-of-paragraph language having echoed mine above, or vice versa — and here the narrative, after a space-break, takes a curious turn. Instead of proceeding with the story of Her several concentric plights — how She extricates or fails to extricate herself from the traffic jam; whether She misses the interview appointment or, making it despite all, nevertheless fails to get the university job; whether or not in either case She and the twins slip even farther down the middle-class scale (right now, alarmingly, if Bill really "cuts her off" as threatened, She's literally about two months away from the public-assistance rolls, unless Her aging parents bail her out: She who once seriously considered Ph.D.hood and professorship); and whether in either of *those* cases anything really satisfying, not to say fulfilling, lies ahead for Her in the second half of Her life, comparable to the early joys of Her marriage and motherhood — instead of going on with these nested stories, in which our Alice understandably takes a more than literary interest, the author here suspends the action and launches into an elaborate digression upon, of all things, the physics of relative motion in the universe as currently understood, together with the spatiotemporal nature of written narrative and — Ready? — Zeno's Seventh Paradox, which three phenomena he attempts to interconnect more or less as follows:

Seat-belted in her gridlocked and overheating Subaru, the protagonist of "Freeze Frame" is moving from St. Louis's Gateway Arch toward University City at a velocity, alas, of zero miles per hour. Likewise (although her nerves are twinging, her hazel eyes brimming, her pulse and respiration pulsing and respiring, and her thoughts returning already from tourist boats to the life-problems that have her by the throat) her movement from the recentest event in her troubled story to whatever next: zero narrative mph, so to speak, as the station wagon idles and the author digresses.

Even as the clock of Her life is running, however, so are time in general and the physical universe. The city of St. Louis and its temporarily stalled downtown traffic, together with our now-sobbing protagonist, the state of Missouri, and variously troubled America, all spin eastward on Earth's axis at roughly a thousand miles per hour. The rotating planet itself careens through its solar orbit at a dizzying 66,662 miles per hour (with the incidental effect that even "stationary" objects on its surface, like Her Subaru, for half of every daily rotation are "strolling aft" with respect to orbital direction, though at nothing approaching orbital velocity). Our entire whirling solar system, meanwhile, is rushing in its own orbit through our Milky Way Galaxy at the stupendous rate of nearly half a million miles per hour: lots of compounded South Street Station effects going on within that overall motion! What's more, although our galaxy appears to have no relative motion within its Local Group of celestial companions, that whole Local group — plus the great Virgo Cluster of which it's a member, plus other, neighboring multigalactic clusters — is apparently rushing en bloc at a staggering near-million miles per hour (950,724) toward some point in interclusteral space known as the Great Attractor. And moreover yet — but who's to say *finally*? — that Attractor and everything thereto so ardently attracted would seem to be speeding at an only slightly less staggering 805,319 mph toward another supercluster, as yet ill-mapped, called the Shapley Concentration, or, to put it mildly, the Even Greater Attractor. All these several motions-within-motions, mind, over and above the grand general expansion of the universe, wherein even as the present reader reads this present sentence, the galaxies all flee one another's company at speeds proportional to their respective distances (specifically, in scientific metrics, at the rate of fifty to eighty kilometers per second — let's say 150,000 miles per hour — per "megaparsec" from the observer, a megaparsec being one thousand parsecs and each parsec 3.26 light-years).

Don't think about this last too closely, advises the author of "Freeze Frame," but in fact our Alice — who has always had a head for figures, and who once upon a time maintained a lively curiosity about such impersonal matters as the constellations, at least, if not the overall structure of the universe — is at this point stopped quite as still by vertiginous reflection as is the unnamed Mrs. William Alfred Barnes by traffic down there in her gridlocked Subaru, and this for several reasons. Apart from the similarities between Her situation vis-à-vis "Bill" and Alice's vis-à-vis Howard — unsettling, but not extraordinary in a time and place where half of all marriages end in separation or divorce — is the coincidence of Alice's happening upon "Freeze Frame" during a caesura in her own life-story and reading through the narrative of Her nonplusment up to the author's digression-in-progress just as, lap-belted in a DC-10 at thirty-two thousand feet, she's crossing the Mississippi River in virtual sight of St. Louis not long past midday (Central Daylight Savings Time), flying westward at an airspeed of six hundred eight miles per hour (so the captain has announced), against a contrary prevailing jet stream of maybe a hundred mph, for a net speed-over-ground of let's say five hundred, while Earth and its atmosphere spin eastward under her, carrying the DC-10 backward (though not relatively) at maybe double its forward airspeed, while simultaneously the planet, the solar system, the galaxy, and so forth all tear along in their various directions at their various clips — and just now two flight attendants emerge from the forward galley and stroll aft down the parallel aisles like that deckhand on the tourist stern-wheeler, taking the passengers' drink orders before the meal service. Alice stares awhile, transfixed, almost literally dizzied, remembering from her happier schooldays (and from trying to explain relative motion to Sam and Jessica one evening as the family camped out under the stars) that any point or object in the universe can be considered to be at rest, the unmoving center of it all, while everything else is in complex motion with respect to it. The arrow, released, may be said to stand still while the earth rushes under, the target toward, the archer away from it, *et cetera*.

Her seatmate-on-the-aisle, fortunately, is too preoccupied with punching a pocket calculator and scribbling on a notepad (atop his in-flight mag atop his tray-table) to notice her looking up from her reading. Alice decides that she'll order white wine and club soda when her turn comes, and goes back to the suspended non-action of "Freeze Frame" lest he disturb her reflections with another attempt at conversation.

Back, rather, she goes, to that extended digression, wherein by one more coincidence (she having just imaged the arrow in "stationary" flight — but not impossibly she glanced ahead in "Freeze Frame" before those flight attendants caught her eye) the author now invokes two other arrows: the celebrated Arrow of Time, along whose irreversible trajectory the universe has expanded ever since the Big Bang, generating and carrying with it not only all those internal relative celestial motions but also the story of Mr. and Mrs. W. A. Barnes from wedlock through deadlock to gridlock (and of Alice and Howard likewise, up to her reading of these sentences); and the arrow in Zeno's Seventh Paradox, which Alice may long ago have heard of but can't recollect until the author now reminds her. If an arrow in flight can be said to traverse every point in its path from bow to target, Zeno teases, and if at any given moment it can be said to be at and only at some one of those points, then it must be at rest for the moment it's there (otherwise it's not "there"); therefore it's at rest at every moment of its flight, and its apparent motion is illusory. To the author's way of thinking, Zeno's Seventh Paradox oddly anticipates not only motion pictures (whose motion truly *is* illusory in a different sense, our brain's reconstruction of the serial "freeze-frames" on the film) but also Werner Heisenberg's celebrated Uncertainty Principle, which maintains in effect that the more we know about a particle's position, the less we know about its momentum, and vice versa — although how that principle relates to Mrs. Barnes's sore predicament, Alice herself is uncertain. In her own mind, the paradox recalls that arrow "at rest" in mid-flight aforeposited as the center of the exploding universe . . . like Her herself down there at this moment of Her story; like Alice herself at this moment of hers, reading about Hers and from time to time pausing to reflect as she reads; like every one of us — fired from the bow of our mother's loins and arcing toward the target of our grave — at any and every moment of our interim life-stories.

"White wine, please," she hears her row-mate say affably in his non-Boston accent. "With a glass of ice and club soda on the side."

"The same," Alice says in hers. He has already fished out his wallet; for a moment Alice worries that he'll offer to pay for her drink, too, amiably obliging her to conversation. Peter, at work, is forever offering lunch that way, and sometimes, strapped for money and male social conversation, Alice agrees, but she inevitably feels thereby compromised, *transacted,* quid-pro-quo'd and unready to quo. This fellow does not, however, so offer; he goes back to his figuring while Alice scrabbles in her purse, pays, pours, sips (he does glance her way now, smiles slightly, and lifts his plastic tumbler in the merest of toasts to the wine-order coincidence, a toast that it would be gratuitously incordial of her not to respond to in kind), and then returns, glass in hand, to the freeze-framed "Freeze Frame," whose point she thinks she's beginning to see, out of practice though she is in reading "serious" fiction.

To the extent that anything is where it is [the author therein now declares], *it has no momentum. To the extent that it moves, it isn't "where it is." Likewise made-up characters in made-up stories; likewise ourselves in the more-or-less made-up stories of our lives. All freeze-frames* [he concludes (concludes this elaborate digression, that is, with another space-break, after which the text, perhaps even the story, resumes)] *are blurred at the edges.*

An arresting passage, Alice acknowledges to herself. Her reflective circuits stirred by the story-thus-far as they haven't been in too long, she smiles at the contradiction in that phrase. *An arresting passage*: Alice's First Paradox.

"Hmp," she hears herself say aloud, amused at that. Amused at *that*, she stifles a chuckle and helps herself to another dollop of wine.

"Fuff," the fellow on the aisle replies, anyhow says, as if to his notepad — and Alice remarks for the first time that he's been annotating not only that pad but the margins of the "Freeze Frame" story in his copy of the in-flight magazine: "Forgot continental drift."

"Excuse me?" She's still smiling, partly at her little witticism, partly at the pleasure, unfamiliar lately, of smiling spontaneously from pure innocent amusement rather than grimly, to keep her spirits up. Another brace of flight attendants — a brace of braces, actually, she supposes in her lingering amusement — is beginning the meal service in the DC-10's twin aisles. Bemused Alice decides to take time out from "Freeze Frame" (whose author has been taking a prolonged time-out from telling the story) and give sociability a try through lunch.

"I'm rechecking the numbers in this crazy story," the fellow says wryly, "and it just occurred to me that continental drift wasn't factored in." He smiles: a friendly smile, confident but unassuming. "You're reading the thing, too, I see. Did you get to the numbers part yet?"

"That's where I am now, and the arrow business. Pretty dizzy-making." She sips her wine.

He taps the text with his ballpoint. "Shouldn't the Earth's rotational speed be corrected for the latitude of St. Louis, the way an LP record moves faster at its edge than halfway in toward its hole? And then there's the wobbling of the Earth's axis, right? — that causes the precession of the equinoxes. Plus or minus the couple of millimeters a year that the crustal plates grind along." He grins and shrugs his eyebrows. "Too late now. May I have another white wine, please, to go with lunch," he asks the steward who here hands them their meal trays.

"Another white wine. And you, ma'am?"

"I'm fine," Alice says, who isn't; who would quite enjoy a second drink, to enhance this recess from her troubles and lubricate the conversation a bit, but who feels she can't afford another four dollars. "Maybe just a refill on the club soda. How's it too late?" she asks the aisle-chap. "You mean too late for the author to throw in plate tectonics?"

She's pleased with herself for remembering that term — Jee-sus, is she ever rusty in the areas of knowledge for its own sake and disinterested reflection! — and the guy responds to it with a clearly appreciative glance. She wonders whether he's some sort of academic like her dad, or, more admirably (what Howard used to be before he autodestructed, and she before the burdens of parenthood and downward mobility in a souring marriage numbed her mind to everything except economic and psychological survival), a *non*-academic who maintains a lively intellectual curiosity beyond his professional concerns.

"Right." He opens his second pony of California Chablis, pours some of it over the wine / ice / soda mix already in his glass, and with a gesture of his bottle-hand offers to top up Alice's as well. Caught off-balance, she shrugs acceptance and holds her glass himward. It is to prevent spillage that he rests the bottleneck on her glass-rim as he pours, but that light brief steady contact has a tiny voltage on it, as if their hands were touching.

"Much obliged, kind sir."

He lifts his glass to her again; Alice simply makes a pleasant smile and nods. He's not being pushy, she decides, sipping; just normally sociable.

"So what do you think of the story so far?" he asks her: a nondirective question if she ever heard one.

"Well ..." Why not say it? With a smile, of course: "I happen to identify completely with the woman in the car, so it's not easy for me to be objective."

"Mm." His glance is sympathetic, but instead of inviting details, as she rather expected he would (there was no question mark after that "Mm"), he asks whether she happens to know what *Subaru* means in Japanese. Alice doesn't; he surprises her again by neither supplying that datum, nor acknowledging that *he* doesn't know either, nor explaining why he asked in the first place: what that question has to do with the story. He registers her amused negative headshake with a minimal nod and asks, "What about this gimmick of hitting the narrative Pause button and smarting off about relative motion and Zeno's paradoxes? Is that any way to tell a story?"

He has begun his lunch. Alice turns to hers: a grilled-chicken-breast salad, not bad at all and appropriate with the white wine, or vice versa. His question sounds to her more testing than testy (she likes that unspoken little wordplay: her second in five minutes, and maybe five years). "Well," she ventures, testing the idea herself: "The piece is called 'Freeze Frame,' right? The woman's stuck in traffc: the way she's stuck in her life-story, and the author dollies back to give us the Big Picture . . ."

"Nicely said."

Encouraged, Alice adds, "It's motions within motions, but it's also pauses within pauses. It's freeze-frames framing freeze-frames."

When was the last time she ever talked like this?

"Brava," her neighbor applauds: "The point being that all of those freeze-frames are in motion — spacewise, timewise — just as we are, sitting here. So why is the time of day a bit past noon, instead of morning or evening rush hour?"

"Is this a quiz, or what?" For his tone, good-humored but serious, is clearly not that of puzzlement.

"More like a map-check, I guess," he allows between forkfuls. "Or a reader-poll. I'm out of practice in the short-story way."

That makes two of them, Alice assures him. And she was so crazy about literature in college; couldn't get enough. But then, you know, the hassles of real life: scrabbling for a living, raising kids — plus television, and everybody's attention span getting shorter. God knows *hers* isn't what it used to be; it's only at times like this that she can settle in to really read: long plane-rides and such, and unfortunately her life these days doesn't include very many of those. Sometimes (she declares) she really thinks — well, he's older, halfway between her parents' generation and her own, she'd guess, so maybe he'll say this is just Baby-Boomer self-pity, but it really does seem to her sometimes that her whole American generation is . . . not *lost*, like Hemingway's Lost Generation, but there's been a real slippage: economic slippage, obviously, but *gumptional* slippage, too, if he knows what she means. Is that a word, gumptional?

He smiles. "It is now."

She's an attractive woman (I shift this story's narrative point of view to have our man-on-the-aisle affirm to himself); rather more so, actually, in her present agitation. Bright, articulate, well put together, well turned out in her light summer linens, and obviously as stressed for whatever reasons as is his nameless lady-in-the-Subaru. Not to play games or seem importunate, he was about to own up to her that the

"Freeze Frame" story is his: a bit of a time out from his usual occupation. By temperament and profession he's a novelist, more accustomed to the narrative long haul than to the sprint. It has been decades since he last wrote short stories. Back in the Sixties, when his first and only collection of them was published, the woman beside him — laughing now at her sudden effusiveness and at the same time knuckling tears until he offers her a dry cocktail napkin to dab with — will have been a high-schooler. But as it happens he's between larger projects just now, and at his age and stage one never knows but what the pause-in-progress, so to speak, might be one's artistic menopause. That possibility, while certainly not cheering, doesn't greatly alarm him, any more than does the regrettable prospect of losing sexual desire and potency, say, somewhere down the road (in that order, he hopes). He has had a gratifying if less than epical career in both areas, and in others as well; he is in fact on tour just now to help promote his latest mid-list novel, and missing his wife, and feeling rather too far along for this sort of thing — while at the same time mildly enjoying the break in his unglamorous but still deeply satisfying daily routine of dreaming up people and situations, putting thoughts and feelings and actions into English sentences, and in the process discovering what's on his imagination's mind, as it were: what his muse has up her sleeve; what she'll do for an encore this late in the day.

It was in this spirit, he's telling Alice now (Yeah, he 'fessed up. Why not? Strangers in transit, never see each other again, etc.), that he wrote the "Freeze Frame" story a few months back — all those motions-within-in-motions and pauses-within-pauses, as she accurately put it — and even urged his agent, half as a lark, half seriously, to try placing it in some in-flight mag, of all odd places, instead of in one of the few large-circulation American magazines that still publish "literary" fiction. But of course he hadn't anticipated the happy coincidence that he would first see it in print while flying virtually over the scene of its stalled action. Truth stranger than fiction, et cet.

"Not to mention the *un*happy coincidence that you'd get stuck with old capital-H Her," Alice says, "in the flesh." Her sniffles are okay now; not stopped, but under adequate control and anyhow okay.

She's impressed, mildly; has never met a writer in person before (she thinks now she remembers his name from some classroom anthology, light-years ago); is amused to hear him say "et cet" in his ordinary speech just the way it comes up in his story, almost a stylistic tic; recalls now that in fact he said he was *re*checking those numbers, not checking them. He doesn't seem boastful or otherwise pretentious or affected: a regular fellow, self-ironic but serious; *likable*, she decides, and okay-looking for his presumable age, but who cares about that? Who cares, for that matter, whether he's thinking Get this dip out of here! He seems all right, even nice: not pressing, not turning her off; letting her babble, but companionably running on a bit himself. She finds herself doing a self-surprising thing: actually catching his hand in hers for a moment — Thanks for the Kleenex — giving it a comradely squeeze (same small voltage as that wine-bottle / glass-rim contact), and declaring she can't spare a damn dime in her present pass but would certainly enjoy another glass of wine with him if he'll be kind enough to stand her one. She'll return the favor in some other life.

"There is no other life," he declares, pleasantly. "That's why some of us make up stories." As for the wine, no problem: He'll put it on his publisher's tab; she'll buy a copy of his current novel as soon as she can afford one, but no sooner, and if she enjoys it she'll tell her friends to do likewise. All debts squared.

"Done."

And so at six-zero-eight mph *et cetera et cetera et cetera* this pair relax as if suspended in space and time. Never mind the in-flight movie framing along now on the video screens: In the cozily darkened cabin, all its window-shades drawn for viewing purposes, they sip white wine and exchange information about their lives. Alice, forgivably, speaks mainly of her marital problems and her anxieties with regard to the future. He counsels courage, patience, and good will; he went through that wringer himself some decades back and can attest that, with luck, there's life after the mid-life crisis. He can't argue, however, with her envious observation that a man out in the world is better positioned to meet significant new others than is a full-time mother with a ratsy part-time job. How she wishes, now, that she'd taken her doctorate in whatever and made her own career moves instead of doing the Fifties-housewife trip like Howard's mother! Though she wishes even more that her husband's career had really flown, and that they'd aged and grown in synch, still loving each other and their life together . . .

Out come the Kleenex: Excuse her.

With fair candor he responds to her questions, when she thinks to ask them, about how it was with him Back Then. "I wrote a lot of short stories, for one thing," he reminds her. "Too scattered for anything longer."

She gestures toward the text of "Freeze Frame," tucked into the seat-back pocket before her, and raises her eyebrows at him. "Does this mean there's trouble again at home?"

He smiles at that, shakes his head, raps on the plastic tray-table in lieu of wood.

Does Alice really mock-sigh then and say, "Too bad for *our* story!" Or, perhaps, "In that case, how do we get me and Miz Whatsername out of gridlock?" Do they chuckle at her plainly experimental flirtsomeness and raise the intimacy-level of their dialogue a notch or two, so that by final approach their hands are touching freely? And when at the airport baggage-claim he offers her a lift downtown in his cab — even dinner at his hotel, if she's up for it (Portland's splendidly refurbished old Heathman), before his scheduled appearance that evening at Powell's Bookstore — does she say, in a spirit clearly ready for adventure, "I'll say I missed my connection," and then, as the circumstance dawns on her, snatch up his hand in both of hers and declare, "No, damn it: I don't have to say anything! *There's nobody home to say it to!*"?

More reasonably, their mid-flight tête-à-tête having run its transitory course along with that sufficiency of wine, do they presently unbuckle to visit the lavatories aft and then return separately to their seats: she to go on with the "Freeze Frame" story, more curious even than before to find out what its author has in store for Her; he to go back to his notepad, in which for all Alice knows he's now jotting notes for some story about *her* as they rush motionlessly together through the time of their lives, their life-stories meanwhile suspended . . .?

Given the age and stage of the woman in the gridlocked car, that "just past noon" business in "Freeze Frame" strikes me as obvious to the point of heavyhandedness. I apologize on behalf of the author, who has also not gotten it said to our Alice that *Subaru* is Japanese for the Pleiades cluster (see the automaker's logo) in the constellation Taurus — much farther now from the dear present reader than it was even a sentence ago. On the other hand, *I* haven't yet managed to get it said (what the "Freeze Frame" story declares somewhere in that digressive pause before the space-break beyond which Alice is currently reading) that all stories are essentially constructs in time, and only incidentally in the linear space of written words. Written or spoken, however, these words are *like* points in space, through which the story-arrow travels in time. Just now it rests at *this* point, this word, this — yet of course never resting there, but ever en route through it to the next, the next, from Beginning through Middle *et cetera*. Even if and when we linger over an "arresting passage," we're only apparently at rest in the story's suspended but incessant motion; likewise in our manifold own.

There. Said.

"On with the story?"

"Maybe . . .

But it's suspensions within suspensions."

Et cetera ad infinitum, amen. I figure if we fractalize this pair enough, they're home free.

"You mean they'll never get there."

He'll settle for that.

"Dearest best friend, don't count on it. Achilles nails the tortoise. Stories end."

Don't count on *that*. As the fellow said, Delta rho times delta q equals or exceeds Planck's Constant.

"The fellow said that?"

Cross my heart.

Presently, in the dark: "Okay: She'll bite."

Herr Heisenberg, aforecited. The famous Principle.

"Explain. But she may drop off in mid-Principle; she's truly running on Empty."

Likewise.

"Poor thing. I need to hear your voice, though."

I'll sing her to sleep. *A cha-a-ange in momentum . . . times a cha-a-ange in position . . . equals or excee-e-e-e-eeds . . . Planck's Constant* (divided by two pi, divided by two).

Presently: "What's Planck's Constant?"

I thought she'd never ask. Planck's Constant is Physics for six point six two five times ten to the minus twenty-seventh power erg-secs. Approximately.

"Thanks lots. What's *that*?"

That's Math for the constant of proportionality relating the quantum of radiation-energy to the frequency of radiation. Nobody said Uncertainty was going to be easy.

"All Greek to her."

Ditto him: *Delta pee*, et cet.

"But he *knows* Greek. So explain, till she's asleep."

Explain, explain. He summons the fading ghosts of his college physics and his frat-house Greek and ventures that one's knowledge of a particle's speed is inversely related to one's knowledge of its position.

"Which is to say?"

That the only way to measure speed with any precision is to sacrifice precision in the measurement of position, and conversely. What you make in Boston, you lose in Chicago.

"Kiss."

Anon: "He can explain everything."

He wishes. Thought she was asleep.

"You wish. What can't you explain?"

Why she and he —

"Goes without saying. Unlike some folks we know, who say without going."

Let's do that! Forever after.

"Nope. But now that she's awake, maybe he can explain love to her."

Love?

"Love."

Hm. That'd take time . . .

"Take. Till tomorrow."

Promise?

"Mm, she sleepily replies."

Mm's the word. Meanwhile . . .

"Mm."

6.

Love Explained

Mid-afternoon mid-life lovers, postcoitally lassitudinous and sweat-wet, skin to skin.

Presently: "Explain love to me."
  Mm?
  "Love: Explain."
  That'd take some doing.
  "So do."

Presently: The phenomenon in general? Or us-here-in-this-bed-on-a-weekday-afternoon-in-October?
  "Your pleasure. Just explain, please."
  Wuff. We may have to go back a bit. Perspective . . .
  "So go. I have a long attention span."
  You do.
  "Wait . . ."

Presently: Well. In the beginning —
  "So far, so good."
  On with the story?
  "Please."
  The Big Bang, of course . . .
  "History."

Sensitive Dependence on Initial Conditions . . .

"Likewise later conditions."

If you'd gone to Macy's that day instead of to Bloomingdale's, or to Bloomingdale's but not through Housewares on your way to Bedding —

"As it were."

Or if you'd passed through Housewares a half-hour earlier or later — we wouldn't be lying here all these years afterward.

"Evaporating."

The great god Contingency. Scary to imagine.

"Yet he actually managed that time not to get his wires crossed."

But back to the *really* initial conditions for just a fraction of a second, from T-zero to the beginning of nucleosynthesis, let's say, one one-hundred-thousandth of a second later: the first hundred-thousandth of a second of Time . . .

"To me it seemed like ages. I thought you'd never look up from those Krups coffeemakers."

I saw you. But after all that time I couldn't believe it was *you*. Anyhow, I wanted to look you over before I officially noticed you.

"I noticed."

The point is, even back at the virtual beginning there were already certain inhomogeneities —

"To put it mildly. Nice Hyphenated-American girl meets Hyphenated-American boy, equally nice but differently hyphenated . . ."

Her a thirtysomething single parent? Him fortysomething and divorcing?

"If they hadn't known each other already, from before . . ."

Another set of sensitive conditions, thank goodness.

"They should thank the Institute's grant-funding policy, which gives young post-docs and their mentors a chance to rub elbows."

Und so weiter.

"They could've got it on way back then!"

But he was too shy, and she too proper.

"Inhomogeneities."

Were it not for which, the atoms of matter that finally got their act together after Time's first three hundred thousand years would have scattered through space like buckshot instead of clumping together into sheets of galaxies with humongous voids between.

"Story of her life, till Bloomingdale's."

What concerns us here in this bed on this brilliant Thursday afternoon in October is that a zillion years after our story's beginning, we've got this still-expanding universe on our hands, with a scale of magnitudes ranging from superstrings of galactic clusters down to the electrons of the atoms of the molecules of DNA, for example. If we're going to explain love, we've got to adjust our focus.

"Like so?"

Oh my yes.

Presently: As one was saying, at a certain *very* critical point somewhere between those superclusters on the one hand and those subatomic particles on the other, one finds our friendly neighborhood galaxy and even our dear little solar system with its nine or so planets, of which the seventh from the edge happens to be this pretty blue-white-brown-and-green job, like the algae that got life going on it.

"I've been there! It comes complete these days with oceans, continents, and the Boston/Cambridge urban complex, as I remember, comprising not only streets and buildings and shopping plazas, but inhabitants too ..."

Including, though not limited to, rats and roaches, pigeons and starlings, pet animals, and maybe a million *Homo sapiens*, teeming and swarming.

"Getting and spending. Dealing dope and composing music."

Hijacking cars and leveraging buyouts.

"Laundering laundry. Mugging and panhandling."

Learning long division. Staring at TV screens and computer monitors. Shooting baskets and one another.

"Mating in and out of wedlock with members of the same and differing sexes. Cooking up stir-fries and stories."

And even, in rare instances, contemplating the nature of the universe and the phenomenon of consciousness therein.

"But not explaining love, I notice."

Not quite yet. Among those last-remarked instances, however, is to be found here and there the oddball capable of formulating or at least of comprehending Einstein's relativity theories, Schrödinger's quantum-mechanical wave-function equations, and Heisenberg's Uncertainty Principle —

"*Along with other apparent esoterica which are in fact among the indispensable intellectual baggage of our narrative-historical moment,* right?"

As you may have heard.

"In spades, chez l'Institute. But play it again."

More than Freudian psychology, more than Marxist ideology, quantum mechanics has been the Great Attractor of the second half of this dying century — even though, speaking generally, almost none of us knows beans about it.

"The old songs are the best. That's love?"

We're getting warm.

"We *were* getting warm, back there with the mating and the stir-fry. Then we lost the picture."

So we fiddle with the clicker. The next-to-bottom line is that per Standard Theory, the position of any and every electron is a field of probabilities until we measure it; then and only then its "wave function" collapses and it truly *has* a position.

"Shall we cut to the chase?"

This *is* the chase. It follows that the universe aforementioned might be said to be as much an effect of our observation of it as we observers are an effect of its aforesummarized evolution, which happens to have happened within *extremely* critical parameters, like a cute re-meet.

"The Anthropic Principle! Kiss me quick."

It comes in three flavors —

"Don't we all: The Weak, the Strong, and the Participatory, if I remember correctly."

Whereof we democratic types have no time for any save the Participatory: "*The observer is as essential to the creation of the universe as the universe is to the creation of the observer.*" All hands on deck, and kiss me again.

"Nothing is but thinking makes it so."

Quod erat demonstrandum and voilà: The universe is a self-exciting circuit, like us.

"Not only *like* us, if I follow you, but *because of* us."

You're leading me. Don't stop.

"By turns and together we're *both* leading and following, no? At our best, I mean."

And at our best we're both both leading and following the observable universe as observed: So declareth the Participatory Anthropic Principle.

"Things are as we find them to be because we who are among both the causes and the effects of those observed conditions thus observe them. Kiss?"

No sooner said than.

Presently: "And no sooner done than said. Thus just as consciousness is both the impulse and the prerequisite for explaining consciousness, and so might be said to be equally subject and object, or question and answer..."

And just as Dante, led by Love to the final circle of Paradise, sees there that the big L is literally what "moves the Sun and the other stars," so you and I, about halfway through our expectable life-story just when our planet, mirabile dictu, happens to be about halfway through *its* —

"Time, time..."

See how it runs, and so we *make* it run.

"Love exists, like the world, you're telling me, as much because I asked my question as conversely."

You're telling me.

"Now that we've explained it, I knew it all along."

Presently: Much obliged, dear friend.

Presently: "Dear friend: my pleasure."

"You're putting words in her mouth."

Yes, well: my line of work.

"*Time, time . . .*"

Mere words in her mouth.

"Kiss them, then."

Later that same day, or maybe the next: "If only life were as simple as theoretical physics."

Mm?

"Love explained isn't love explained away."

Hallelujah. You looked simply terrific on the courts today, by the way.

"Spiffy to the end."

He fell in love with her all over again, as usual.

"Lust explained."

But not away.

In time: "Anyhow, thanks for trying. Really."

De nada.

"Exactly true, alas: The cupboard's bare."

Not so. Half full at least.

"Half empty, then. At least."

Not before he fetches from it, for her delectation and possible diversion, this hefty item here . . .

"Poor lucky dog, that gets thrown *that* bone. Let her have it."
They'll share it: a team effort on both ends.
"To the end of both?"
More words in her mouth. Shall I?
"To the end."

7.

"Waves," by Amien Richard

"Are we particles," Amy wants to know, "or waves?"

She's floating prone, trim, and naked on an inflated mat at the edge of our borrowed pool in the beachfront yard of our borrowed house in Freeport, Grand Bahama. Her cropped-blonde head rests on the heel of one hand; with the other she idly stirs the water-surface — at the same time reading, intermittently, a science magazine propped on the coping of the pool. Beyond our security-fenced and casuarina-screened lawn, the surf on our borrowed ocean, driven by a rising southerly, breaks first on the distant reef and then again, less roughly, on "our" shelved sandstone beach.

Reasonably, before he answers, Richard asks, "We human beings? Or *we* meaning you and me?" Likewise naked except for a canvas sailing hat, and as carefully sun-lotioned as is his mate, he's sitting on a towel at the pool's edge, dangling one foot in the water near his wife's hand and scribbling in a notebook. Utter luxury, the pair of us agree, after what we've lately been through, and in our shared and different ways we're soaking it up.

"Us, I guess. Yes. Waves or particles?"

Without looking up yet from his notebook, "Wherefore doth milady ask, her partner maketh bold to wonder," Richard likewises, "whilst he cobbleth up a reply?"

With wet fingertip Amy taps her borrowed *Scientific American.* "Says here that photons behave like particles sometimes and other

JOHN BARTH. *ON WITH THE STORY*

times like waves. I'm wondering how it is with us."

"You and me."

"For starters."

Tucking his lower lip like President Bill Clinton in the Pensive Mode, her mate considers. "The same." And makes to make another notebook-note.

Amy, presently: "Hell with it, then, I guess."

"Her friend begs her pardon?"

"Her friend heard what his friend said."

"So he thought." Notebook closed. "Ame?"

"To hell," the woman of us now declares — to the surf mat, it would appear, face pressed into it, forehead resting on back of hand — "with everything."

"*Stressed out*, her husband, who loves her, helpfully suggests," the man of us etc.

Instead of responding "No response," Amy non-responds.

We talk this way, sometimes: occupational side-effect of our being professional articulators, so to speak; a couple of ironists married fourteen years exactly as of the date of this dialogue. Reader will have noticed, as has Richard, that Amy didn't ask for explanation — at least not directly, at least not yet — only for reply, and that her life-partner has supplied, so far, no more than she requested. Treading carefully, we'd bet.

"Partner *in* life, or partner *for*?" it might be inquired, and therefore by Amy now is. The woman reads and routinely questions our joint mind.

In most certainly, *for* presumably and we hope. That very presumption and mutual hope, it will turn out, happen to be what's at stake in this waves-or-particles story, now more or less launched and about to pause for a bit of cautious background exposition. Here's how it is with us Amy-and-Richards and what we're doing in a borrowed house on borrowed time in Freeport, Grand Bahama:

Well known in the free-lance trade and to readers of *National Geographic, Cruising World*, the *Smithsonian*, and other "nature" mags, also to followers of the *New York Times* nonfiction list and even to watchers of public-television nature-and-travel documentaries, "Amien Richard" (Incorporated) is the nom de plume of our long-standing and historically quite successful collaboration. To put it most baldly, Amy's the brains of this outfit, Richard the voice. Our original project-ideas are typically hers: "Let's pedal a tandem bicycle across the USA, sea to shining sea, switching positions at each time zone"; "Let's watch nature-watchers"; or maybe no more than (as in the present instance, after a two-year virtual hiatus) "What say we skip this winter altogether and sail down to the Caribbean?" She then takes that ball, if it appeals to her mate, and runs with it: thinks up the angles; negotiates commissions, sponsorships, contracts, tie-ins; does the lion's share of logistical planning, research, administration, even photography in cases where we don't need a camera crew. The woman resists *writing*, however, in the sense of composition, and so it's Richard who drafts our proposals and, most important, turns our homework into prose sentences like these: the finished product, which Amy will perspicaciously then edit and supervise the marketing of. Mainly, as instanced, we do nonfiction books and articles, including the odd television project; but "Amien Richard" (we give that surname a French twist — Ree-*shard* — to go with the Gallic-sounding "Amien") have one commercially successful novel to our credit, too, as you may remember: *The Watcher*, a fictionalized spin-off from our nature-watcher-watching documentary. Book-of-the-Month Club Alternate Selection, film option twice renewed and looking reasonably positive: not bad for a first offense.

And that same pseudonymous entity may now be in process of gestating, of all labor-of-love enterprises, our maiden *short story* — to be entitled, possibly, "Waves," or, just as possibly, "Particles." Its Return on Investment ("Vive le ROI," practical Amy likes to say) won't approach that of a commissioned article in the *Times* Sunday magazine, for example; but we like to try different things. Anyhow, we're R&R'ing just now after our truly hairy Gulf Stream crossing, among other turbulences, and the R of us hasn't entirely suppressed his original youthful ambition to be a *writer*-writer: a capital-A Author. If this story gets written, he has promised the A of us, we'll change the couple's names to ... oh, "Amy" and "Richard," maybe, to protect the presumably innocent.

What else? Well: Today's our Ivory Wedding Anniversary, as has been more or less mentioned, and info-rich Amy has come up with not only that bit of scrimshaw — the woman's a walking World Almanac, currently floating in place — but also this food for thought: that over the years of our corporate life most of the cells in our bodies have replaced themselves, not once but twice. More on this subject presently, we suspect. We're old enough to have undergone four or five previous such seven-year body replacements and one prior marriage apiece, of shorter duration now than our present and ongoing one. Each of those initiations issued offspring, and by gosh and by golly we've seen that blended duo through high school and into college: no mean accomplishment for a pair of peripatetics without institutional fringe benefits. For A. R. Inc.'s first near-dozen years, our own genes went uncombined; we regretted that, one of us maybe more than the other, but we couldn't see shelving our footloose rent-and-tuition-paying enterprises for the years it would take to raise another child to portability . . .

We couldn't? Really, we couldn't; remember? We enjoyed our adventuresome life, much more than not. We valued and value still, to put it mildly, our vigorous marriage, which has weathered its share of storms (most recently and sorely . . . but never mind, yet). And we love each other.

Right?

Suffice it to say, then, that our current project — a leisurely cruise down the Intracoastal Waterway in *ARI*, our weathered but seaworthy secondhand ketch (same vintage as our marriage, and much of *it* renovated, too, over those dozen-plus years), from our home base in Annapolis down to Florida, across to the Bahamas, and on to the Caribbean and back, leaving a trail of magazine-pieces in our wake — was meant by the way to reconsolidate and reaffirm "Amien Richard," Inc., after a devastating, regrettably centrifugal season. In this, through September and the first half of October, it arguably succeeded, wouldn't we say? We would, on balance. Yes. Moseying down the ICW in the intimate quarters and simple rhythms of life afloat, following the end-of-summer weather south and putting daily more mileage between us and the venue of our unspecified late calamity, we went some way toward regaining, if not lost heart, at least reciprocal spontaneity and clarity of spirit.

Well said. Thanks. We lucked out on the regular season's hurricanes, as with crossed fingers we hope we shall on the late-season item now approaching: Hurricane Emile, of which the building seas out there on "our" reef are early stirrings. We even got an article out of Emile's immediate predecessor, Hurricane Dashika, a near miss who chewed up Beaufort, North Carolina, while we were snug in Beaufort, *South Carolina* ("The Battered Beauforts," *Sail* magazine, forthcoming). We did an eating-piece for USAir's in-flight mag on the splendid restaurants of Charleston's Historic District and an ecology-piece, not yet placed, on the savannas of Savannah. By pushing our timetable a bit and co-ordinating Amy's logistical prowess with Richard's navigational, we arranged to transit the Cape Canaveral area in time to witness, photo-graph, and project another nature-watcher-watching article, this one about a PBS television crew making a *Nature* documentary on wildlife reacting to a space-shuttle launch. In the Art Deco district of Miami Beach, while Amy's camera clicked away for a possible *Architectural Digest* commission down the road, we touched base with a Bahamian college-roommate of Richard's, now a successful speculator in that same real estate, who commiserated with our late loss and insisted that we make free with his Freeport beachfront spread after our maiden Gulf Stream crossing. He and his wife seldom find time these days to use the place themselves, he declared; they have others, elsewhere. He would notify their caretaker to expect us and to show us the workings of the house and grounds. We would find it more than comfortable, he was sure, and very likely we'd need a few days to rest and regroup before moving on to the Out Islands and down to the Caribbean.

Understatement of the season. But here comes that same caretaker now, cheerful ex-Haitian Georges; we hear him opening the automatic driveway gate on the house's far side to deliver our host's Jeep, which Georges has obligingly commissioned for us early this morning and will now put at our disposal for the duration (as yet undecided) of our visit. Time to end this water-testing exposition, wrap ourselves in beach towels, and return to our story's present action.

In which Georges, dressed as usual in clean khakis and white T-shirt, respectfully hails us from the nearest patio — "Mister Richard? Miz Amy?"— not presuming to approach more closely while we're un-dressed. A compact, dark brown, well-muscled, pleasant-faced, dignifi-ed, soft-spoken, near-hairless fellow in his forties, Georges has been in our absent hosts' loyal employ for a dozen years, ever since he "came ashore," as he quaintly puts it, from his troubled homeland and was tak-en up (and his irregular immigrant status regularized) by Richard's ex-roommate's Canadian wife, who functions as overseer of their several properties. To the various skills that Georges brought ashore with him, she has added reading, writing, and a spoken English more fluent than our French.

His beach towel knotted at the hip, Richard goes over and shakes the man's hand. From poolside, Amy waves and calls, "Bonjour, *M'sieur* Georges," teasing him for his declining to use our first names un-adorned, as we use his.

Good-humoredly but resolutely, "Good morning, Miz Amy," Georges calls back, and returns her wave from the patio. Richard tends to shrug his shoulders at such cross-culturalities as this matter of address-forms, but liberal Amy takes them seriously, and Georges has therefore obligingly explained to her that one must "have respect" if one wants to get on in the world. Miz Evelyn, our absent hostess, evidently imparted that great truth to him along with English; Georg-es in turn hopes to have taught it to his children. Of those, we have learned from him, he has "about seven": four handsome sons "inside," who help him with his caretaking chores after school, and "about three daughters outside"— mainly in New York City, it seems. We (who have "about two" ourselves these days, so Amy has replied to Georges' polite inquiry) haven't yet sorted out the fellow's infobits and the sociology of Inside versus Outside children; we agree, however, that "having re-spect" cuts both ways, and that Georges is not to be pestered with our Yankee egalitarianism.

The two men stroll around to the driveway, Richard feeling fair-ly foolish in bare feet, beach towel, and large-brimmed hat. There Georges checks him out on the operation of the fat-tired, high-sprung, roll-barred, topless, fire-engine-red Wrangler, one of several vehicles garaged on the premises and the only one licensed for island-wide use beyond Freeport's posted "insurance district"— another infobit not yet clear to us Amy-and-Richards. Georges has repeated with some pride our host's instructions to him that it is his "personal responsibility" to see to it that we have everything we need for a pleasant visit, the Jeep included; in discharge of that responsibility, he tries as earnestly to answer our questions about the island as we try not to overburden him therewith. It has become evident to us, however, that while he is an alert, industrious, guileless, and resilient fellow with a basketful of handyman's skills, the world of licensings and "insurance districts" is as beyond his compass as Miami real-estate speculation is beyond ours.

Having tried the 4WD's gearshift and reviewed the operation of the automatic gate (labeled *Warning: Attack Dog*, like most others in the neighborhood, but not, like many of them, correspondingly equipped, or topped with coils of razor-wire), Richard asks where on the island we might find good snorkeling from the beach, closer to shore than the half-mile or so between our doorstep and the wave-smashing reef out yonder. Georges' suggestions — he himself doesn't enjoy swimming, but several of his sons are ardent and knowledgeable spearfishers — are couched in detailed local references unfamiliar to Richard if perhaps not to Amy, who yesterday began hitting the guidebooks as is her wont and talking to restaurant servers and store clerks: a positive sign, R hopes, after her recent dark torpor.

"Gold Rock?" he asks her when Georges has gone to sweep leaves off the family tennis court against our possible later use of it. "Dead Man's Reef?"

"They're in the guides," Amy thinks she remembers, "or on the tourist map. Did you do the map with him?"

"Georges doesn't do maps," her husband replies. "But how's this for specificity? We cross the first main canal up yonder and follow the beach road along through Williamstown and up along farther till we come to the Haitian cemetery in the pine woods. We leave the Jeep at that cemetery and walk back along that beach to where those woods began and on along back to the first pine tree separate from those woods along that shore. Then we swim straight out from that lonesome pine tree to where the coral is, et voilà."

"Haitian cemetery?"

"It's where Georges came ashore," Richard reports, "whatever *that* means. He says we'll see, and maybe we should. Or is it to hell with everything?"

His wife cuts him a look. "Is it to hell with everything with you?"

"It is not. Let's go find that Haitian cemetery."

At this point in the text of our trial story, Richard himself inclines toward a space-break followed by a friendly-though-tentative conjugal sex scene, perhaps of a therapeutic character. Amy nixes that proposal and his unspoken proposition, however, and she's the editor-in-chief of this outfit. From the pool we've moved up to our bedroom, to dress and pack for our day's excursion; we have more or less decided to follow Georges' detailed directions and explore what our map shows to be the windward side of the island this morning (Williamstown village is indicated, likewise the adjacent beach, but no Haitian cemetery); then back to Port Lucaya, next door to Freeport, for lunch and a look at how repairs are proceeding to *ARI*'s rig, damaged in our Gulf Stream crossing. In the afternoon, we guess, if nature's weather and our own remain favorable, maybe we'll check out a reef or two off the leeward shore, where the water's less likely to be roiled by waves; then back to home base to see what we feel like doing this evening in the wedding-anniversary-celebration way.

If anything. We don't *want* this damned yearlong cloud hanging over us, you understand; we happen to like as well as love each other, and *neither of us blames the other for what happened* (at least no more than him / herself), and it's a drag to go about feeling bruised, licking our wounds, our spirit-gauges reading Empty. But you don't de-cloud just by saying "Get lost, cloud," any more than you make literal bruises disappear — and we're both carrying literal contusions, as it happens, from last week's mighty culminating knockdown that nearly took away our mizzenmast — just by saying "Bye-bye, bruises." Having made our indirect way through our pretty remarkable borrowed house, avoiding the shortcut through its grand sunken living room for reasons presently to be explained, and having discarded our pool-towels and turned naked to the question whether to beach-bag our undies and wear swimsuits under our clothes or vice versa, Richard embraces his wife from behind as she's folding her towel on the king-size bed, cups a hand over each of her breasts, nuzzles her nape, and presses his nonerection against the cleft of her butt. In ordinary circumstances, that overture would likely suffice to precipitate the balming business that he warmly has in mind, especially given the added small titillation of a luxurious, unfamiliar bedroom (from its balcony / sundeck there's even a waterslide down to the pool) after the confined quarters of a cruising sailboat. Amy permits the embrace — our first such since Miami — and even puts her hands atop his; her body tension, however, says No, and so there goes our sex-therapy scene.

May Richard hope that what his friend's body tension really says is Not yet?

Of course Richard may; *Amy* sure as hell does. But who knows how things will sort out with this troubled pair of particles? On with the story, and perhaps we'll see.

Amen, sigh Amien Richard, Inc. — and we put the spacebreak here instead:

After which, while we bounce down the potholed beach-road in our mighty Wrangler, Amy in the driver's seat fills her husband and the reader in on what she has learned about what we're seeing. Because the Bahamas, while politically independent, remain still in the Commonwealth, we drive on the left, Brit-style, as we have done on such other once-British isles as Barbados and Jamaica. Nearly all of the island's cars, however, regardless of their country of manufacture, are shipped over from the States and, having been built for the American trade, sport left-side steering, with the interesting consequence that one passes other vehicles more or less blind to what lies ahead. No problem outside the "insurance zone" (we think we begin to understand the term), where there's little traffic on the straight, flat, often poorly surfaced roads; rather more ticklish in busy Freeport/Port Lucaya, especially at the roundabouts, but all hands seem to manage, by and large. Like its numerous smaller neighbors, Grand Bahama is topographically uninteresting: no mountains or rain forests, just a large flat cay of palmetto, casuarina, poisonwood, and Bahamian juniper, ringed by fine flat beaches, patches of mangrove, vast grassy conch-abounding shallows, coral reefs of varying health, and Caribbean-clear water. The Out Islands, everyone agrees, are more handsome; bustling Nassau, the archipelago's capital, is more colorful and lively. Freeport and environs, Grand Bahama's only conurbation, makes its living principally off cruise-ship and beach-resort tourism, although the resorts are more or less downscale as of this writing, and the port of call is less popular than others farther south. Two large casinos, Amy reports, one in Freeport and the other in Port Lucaya, are the most conspicuous sources of hard-currency inflow; how much of it stays on the island is another matter. Perhaps owing to Grand Bahama's proximity to the States, its native culture seems less distinct to Amien Richard than the various cultures of the Caribbean.

What most forcefully takes our tourist/documentarist eye as we commence this AM Wrangler-tour is the scale and number of construction projects evidently stalled, shelved, or abandoned at various stages of completion. Much of the island's western half has been reticulated into a network of laboriously dredged and masonry-banked canals, fingering out from a series of main channels with outlets to the sea — the backbone of what was intended as a massive Florida-style real-estate development, every house with its private canal-front and dock. On the fingers of land between these fingers of water, scores, perhaps hundreds, of residential streets were laid out some years back, paved, named, and marked with signs; a handful of houses have been built, as many more begun, but on almost none of these latter do we see construction in progress. On the contrary, it is as if the entire vast enterprise has been abandoned: The building lots are overgrown with man-size scrub, which in places chokes the now-crumbling, cratered streets; the road signs rust and lean; unfinished houses, many with scaffolding still in place, are marked FOR SALE and overgrown with vines. Entire resorts-in-the-works, we will discover, have been similarly aborted in mid-gestation; others have changed hands downward from up-market franchises; one or two have been abandoned and reclaimed by nature, which in these latitudes moves in fast. Even the casinos have a slightly threadbare look: broken light fixtures unrepaired, decorative fountains algae-grown, worn carpeting on the entranceway steps.

What happened, our driver explains (according to the friendly and knowledgeable maître d' of the restaurant where we dined last night in Port Lucaya, and with whom A made conversation while R was in the men's room), is that the island had looked in the early Eighties to be about to boom like the Caymans, under an Anglo administration friendly to outside investment and offshore banking (for which, to some extent, read "drug money laundering," we suppose). The massive canals were dug, the streets laid out, the resorts built or begun; real-estate speculators, mainly non-local, profitably bought and sold. But the Reagan/Bush administration's later "war on drugs," coincident with a new black Grand Bahamian administration's position that too much of that outside investment was bypassing native islanders, sharply chilled the action. Hence the García-Márquezlike disrepair and reversion to "nature" all about us: an abandoned "cinema village" out toward East End, meant for a nascent film industry that never took hold; the once-scenic "Garden of the Groves" now largely gone to weed, its pavilions plyboarded up; an enormous Loire Valley-style château almost the size of Chambord, its slate roofs and stone turrets wildly out of place in the tropics, perched empty and unfinished on a scrub-choked hill not far from Georges' modest village of tin-roofed cinderblock cottages painted in washes of aquamarine, coral, apricot, and umber—through which we roll now as Amy winds up her guidebook spiel. This arrested development, her maître d' was confident, will prove temporary; despite the "Bahamas for the Bahamians" tone of the ruling party's billboards here and there about the island, the economic slump is so evident to all hands that the party will almost certainly have to come to terms with the development interests or lose the upcoming elections. In the maître d's opinion, this present trough between waves of prosperity is exactly the time to buy into the distressed market.

Yes, well: Richard guesses not. Likewise Amy, although in another life she would enjoy being a wheeler-dealer like R's old roommate. We'll want to get *his* reading of this business eventually; meanwhile, the man of us is impressed for the umpteenth time at how much the woman of us found out in a single peesworth of time. Does she think there's an Amien Richard photo-essay in all this rather spectacular decay? "Grand Bahama Bides Its Time," say, for *National Geo*?

Without taking her suddenly tear-filled eyes from the potholed road — twin dirt-tracks now, leading bumpily through high weeds and wind-bent scrub along the empty beachside embankment between the village of Williamstown behind us and the stand of evergreen well ahead — Amy allows, "There might be, if our weather ever clears." She downshifts to ford a virtual pond in the road, hub-deep from last night's heavy rainshowers. "Just now this all reminds me too much of my other life" (in which she and her D.C.-lawyer husband came to realize — one daughter and a half-renovated Virginia horse-farm into their marriage — that they really weren't suited to each other *at all*, as they had romantically imagined themselves to be since undergraduate days, and their ambitious remodeling project sat idly depreciating for the two years it took them to work out a settlement and dispose of the property).

Let it not be a foreshadowing of ours, Richard says or prays, perhaps both, and gets no noticeable response in either case. Amy's maître d's trough-between-waves image has chilled our man right through — and put him in mind, by the way, of his partner's story-opening question. Just now, he feels (likewise she, he might want to know), we two are decidedly in the Particle Mode: particles particles particles, minimally interacting but fundamentally discrete. If, as John Donne declared, no man is an island, that's because *every* man and woman is: "windowless monads," in Leibnitz's term, distinct as one Bahama from another (29 islands, 661 cays, and 2,387 rocks, Amy has informed us), bouncing waves off one another across the big and little gulfs separating them.

Speaking of which (waves), Q: Why does this particular pair of particles avoid their borrowed house's sunken living room, as has been demonstrated? A: Because upon our awed first inspection of the premises, over its massive coral-rock fireplace we were staggered to see a blown-up reproduction of Hokusai's famous woodblock print *The Breaking Waves Off Kanajawa* (a.k.a. *The Great Wave*, or simply *The Wave*), wherein a tsunami-size breaking sea towers over hapless fishing vessels dwarfed in the trough before it, and seems to tower likewise even over Mt. Fuji in the far distance.

"I myself have seen like those," Georges told us proudly as we stood stillstruck before the thing. "When I came ashore."

Replied grim Amy, "So have we, cher Georges. Nowhere *near* shore. May we never see another." Toward which end, we take the long way around great Hokusai in our comings and goings through the house.

Voilà? Okay, sure: voilà.

Et voilà now the promised woods, casuarinas for the most part, through which we bump per program after tentatively remarking the first free-standing shoreside specimen before it, our snorkeling landmark. And in those woods — strewn, alas, like much of the Grand Bahamian environ, with discarded plastic beverage bottles and other litter, but anyhow handsome, fragrant, and soughing in the rising wind — we find indeed a small rectangular plot of gravestones, trash-free and bordered neatly with conch shells. We pull off the main track into the scrub and de-Jeep for a closer look. An inscription on the central stone apprises us that on a stormy night in 1978, just outside the reef off from this spot, a boat-load of Haitian refugees were put overboard (having been assured, we will later learn, that the scattered lights onshore were Florida) and told to swim to their promised land. In the nature of the case, neither the exact number of survivors nor that of nonsurvivors is known for certain, but the drowned bodies of twenty-one women, men, and children were found here and there alongshore over the next days and buried where we stand. Of the known survivors, most were returned to Port-au-Prince as illegal immigrants. A few — among them Georges, we now headshakingly infer — had better luck.

In a notorious passage in *De Rerum Natura*, Richard recalls, the Roman philosopher-poet Lucretius sings of the pleasure of standing safely on a storm-lashed headland to watch a vessel in distress offshore:

Not that we delight in other men's
Afflictions, but because it's sweet to note
That we ourselves (this time at least) are spared.

Translation from the Latin by Amien Richard, who think we know what Lucretius means, all right, but who, having done time out there, feel in the presence of Hokusai's *Wave* and this Haitian refugee cemetery nothing whatever of that pleasure; not even the pained relief that Lucretius would have been better advised to specify. What we feel (and, feeling it, for the first time in a while we unself-consciously take each other's hand) is more akin to Aristotelian Pity and Terror: not yet cathartic, quite, but humbling, perspective-adjusting. Whether or not our partnership survives, our shipship did, and in it we two particles have managed to Come Ashore alive. Amien Richard's project-in-the-works (we mean both our interrupted voyage in progress and this story ditto) may come to be abandoned like so many projects round about us; but Amy and Richard, unlike some, are breathing air, holding hands, and feeling luckier after all than at least twenty-one other hapless human particles as we turn our attention now to mere amphibious pleasure.

What balm, to be *touring* and *doing* again instead of sitting around more or less in shock. The Jeep-ride; the cemetery-inspection, sobering as it was; now the sunny-breezy beach-walk back to that solitary casuarina, where we plop our towels, unbag our snorkel-gear and bag our outer clothing, lotion up, rub the insides of our masks with the juice of a beach-plant leaf to prevent fogging (a trick taught to Amien Richard on assignment years ago in Maui and here passed on gratis to the reader; it works better than spit), and wade into the tepid shallows to slip feet into swim-fins. Pleasurable as is this familiar routine, however, and new as we are to the art of short-story-writing, A. R. Inc. well understand that *action* is not to be confused with *plot*; that mere busyness — Wrangling down the road, citing Donne and Leibnitz and Lucretius, and swimming out now through the wave-stirred water in search of submarine diversion — so far from necessarily advancing our story, may in fact delay its progress. The classic curve of dramatic action is (excuse us) a Hokusai-like wave, rising conflicted from the trough of an initial ground-situation to a climactic crest and then crashing to its life-altering dénouement. However diverting in itself, any particle of action that fails to increment that wave (e.g., perhaps, this paragraph) is indeed a diversion, quite beside the dramaturgical point.

So. Well. Through warm, sand-clouded water, over turtle-grass and sandstone and through isolated fingers of rust-brown coral, we swim out a few hundred yards, looking for the more substantial formations that attract marine fauna. Richard half-wishes we were back ashore holding hands again, en route somehow toward being *us* again; from the other side of some semicolon, Amy half-wishes likewise, but reminds Amien Richard that if wishes were horses, beggars would ride. Does any of that advance our plot? After deepening to maybe twenty feet, the lagoon reshallows like an inverse wave to eight or ten, and we begin to see brain corals, also some stag- and elkhorn, with such expectable denizens as squirrelfish, wrasses, sergeant majors, goat- and parrotfish, the occasional butterflyfish and French angel. Amy points out a medium-size stingray settling itself into a patch of white sand; Richard, who normally prefers to swim behind a bit and let Amy set our course and pace while he admires her body along with the other scenery, espies from the side of his eye a small shark. He turns for a better look — nurse shark, he decides, minding its own business down there among the brains and antlers — and then surfaces to call his wife's attention to the animal.

Doesn't immediately see her. Nothing extraordinary in that, losing track of a head and snorkel-pipe bobbing at surface-level among foot-high waves. He cons a full circle, confirming en passant our bearing on the now-distant pine and our relative proximity to the sea-crashed reef. No Amy. His nerves duly tingle a bit — but hey, we're veteran snorkelers, and these aren't dangerous conditions, merely too bestirred for good reconnoitering. She's probably diving to check something out. He ducks under, looks around, doesn't see her, resurfaces, doesn't see her, begins to think Oh my oh my but truly believes that the flat-out, tear-prostrated, what's-the-use-of-going-on part of our late loss and general moral devastation is behind us now. *It wasn't her fault.* He does another three-sixty, and sure enough there she is, thank Whomever, face down and snorkel up, finning unconcernedly midway between him and the reef, her hands clasped comfortably behind her back. Immensely relieved, he overtakes her; doesn't mention his alarm. We agree that conditions here to windward just now aren't worth it;

let's go find lunch, check out the yard's progress on our boat, and look for calmer snorkeling waters to leeward. We commence the long but virtually effortless return to shore, thinking inevitably of how it must have been on that dreadful night for those wretched and terrified other swimmers. Not to mention . . .

Has any of this advanced the story? (It has, between the lines, Amy here opines in pained parentheses; but she isn't prepared to say how just yet. [What she did — unnoticed by Richard but not by the central joint narrative intelligence of this story — was give the slip to her mate's recently somewhat oppressive though understandable *monitoring* of her ((as she perceives it)) and dive down behind a pile of living coral to see whether she would carry through on her one-tenth-serious inclination to drown herself. As her held breath reached its limit, however, she happened to catch sight of the corkscrew inner spiral of a small, ground-down conch shell on the sea floor: a dainty, perfect, tapered blush-and-ivory auger, not uncommon in these waters but in this instance uncommonly fine in its coloration and its intactness-within-attrition. Instead of blowing out the last of her air therefore to find out whether she could actually inhale water as . . . others have done before her, she forced herself a fathom deeper, retrieved the token, and shot to the surface. No Richard ((he has ducked under in search of her)); then there he is, looking the other way, toward shore. She recovers her breath and inner balance; returns to snorkeling as if nonchalantly, although her heart still pounds; inspects through her mask the little treasure in her hand; tucks it for safekeeping into the crotch of her bikini, faute de mieux; then clasps her hands behind her back, the better to feign insouciance.])

***

On with the story, we suppose; anyhow with the narrative. Ashore, we towel, relotion and -dress, bid the drowned Haitians rest in peace. Amy considers leaving on their grave as tribute the little conch-stem (which, back on the beach, she has already surreptitiously uncrotched and pocketed) but then thinks *Ivory Anniversary* and decides to hold on to it for a while yet, in secret parentheses. We Jeep leftside in full strong sunshine back into Port Lucaya by the main highway, in places still as flooded in the absence of storm drains as if last night's rain had been a tidal wave. From the cab- and jitney-loads of elderly Americans splashing along with us toward the Lucaya Marketplace and casino, we infer that a cruise ship has docked in Freeport. We follow the crowd briefly in order to make dinner reservations for this evening at the best of its many restaurants, in case etc. Rather than buck the unexpected lunch crowd, however, we then retreat across Bell Channel — the Grand Canal of that aforedescribed network — toward the marina and repair yard. As we hoped and expected, along the way we see one of the island's many informal shellfish vendors, this one operating out of the back of a rusty Ford pickup under the handlettered notice CRACK CONCH STEAM CONCH SCORCH CONCH, and pause to share a standup paper-cupful of fresh-made conch ceviche with rum punch. We are the dreadlocked Rastafarian vendor's only current customers; to make conversation, Amy asks him brightly whether Hurricane Emile will pass us by. With cool but not incordial dignity (the fellow looks like dispossessed Ethiopian royalty), he halves the volume of Bob Marley reggae on his boom box and declares to her, "That be in *He* honds, mahm." Not meaning the late singer's.

I suppose so, Richard says to be agreeable, but he hopes for a more updated, less fatalistic opinion from the marina office. Thereto we Wrangle next — Richard at the wheel now, to get the feel of our borrowed vehicle and to relieve A, who has acknowledged feeling blah — and there in one of the service slips near the big travel-lift sits stout but battered *ARI*, our corporate ketch. Two native riggers, one in a bosun's seat at the mizzen masthead, are replacing the starboard shroud that let go in our Gulf Stream knockdown and would doubtless have cost us that mast if its sail hadn't happened to be furled at the time. As things turned out (since the boat's standing rigging is interconnected and more or less interdependent), when *ARI* finally self-righted and the storm passed, we were obliged to limp on to Freeport under cautious headsails and triple-reefed main, both to avoid overstraining the rig and because our mainsail's lower seams had blown out just seconds before the knockdown.

"We be done today," the elderly rigger on deck informs us. "You be good as new." He grins and calls up to his younger colleague, bandanna'd like an eighteenth-century pirate: "*Better* than new, Sahm, right?"

"You say," the fellow calls back. At risk of a patronizing stereotype, Amien Richard here report that our experiences thus far with Grand Bahamians of every station have been consistently agreeable. We have found them friendly, cheerful, and obliging without deferentiality (Georges excepted on that last score, but his case is special — and he, too, as aforereported, is rich in personal dignity and self-respect). The rigger-on-deck now shakes his head in good-humored awe at the power of the sea, what it has done to us. "But you should see some that come in here, mon! You lucky."

We suppose we are, all right, Richard agrees. The fellow is curious to know whether, when that rogue wave all but rolled us, the ketch's deep centerboard had been raised or lowered. He is of the opinion that, contrary to conventional wisdom, in breaking seas a boat so equipped should tuck up its board altogether, the way the islanders used to do in their fishing smacks in high seas. A sailboat can "trip on she keel," he declares, in such conditions; better to sacrifice a little normal stability, if necessary, and slip sidewise down the face of the seas instead of tripping and rolling. "*Go with the flow,* mon."

We are not inclined to argue that point. Amy's saying nothing, only smiling thinly; Richard, clutch-stomached at memory of that second-worst moment of our lives, merely nods. In all likelihood, *ARI*'s centerboard had indeed been fully lowered to dampen the vessel's roll in quartering seas; R's private opinion, however, is that given the weather's condition and his own at the time, the matter of centerboard-position is probably irrelevant. The British yard manager, to whose office we now repair, informs us that our ripped mainsail won't be quite so soon ready: next week earliest, as the sailmaker has a small backlog of similar transient orders and tends moreover to work on "island time." Just as well, don't we think? By next week, Hurricane Emile will be history, if indeed he's coming to visit: The latest reports have the Out Islands in for a passing blow but Grand Bahama in for no more than a spot of Force Seven winds and some heavy rain, probably toward morning and through tomorrow.

While delivering us these tidings, the fellow is half attending a Stateside baseball game on a countertop TV. "I say," he now says, indicating its diminutive screen: "Ever see one of *those* before?"

Looking more closely, we see that the fans at Oriole Park in Baltimore, of all familiar places, are engaged in that loosely coordinated fanly maneuver known as ... the Wave: Standing to stretch their legs between innings, they raise their arms en masse over their heads; those immediately behind the home team's dugout then bend leftward momentarily and restraighten, cueing their neighbors on that side to do like-wise, *et cetera*, until, with no one leaving his / her particular place, the "wave" takes on a perceptible character and with apparent autonomy orbits the stadium twice or thrice before dissipating.

Says Amy, "Yup." "Ai yi," breathes Richard, and turns away.

The marina manager chuckles admiringly. "Enough to make a chap seasick, what?"

At this point in this trial draft of this trial story, Amien Richard declare another space-break in order to assess how things are going, plotwise, and for that matter *whether*, not to mention whither. Those accumulating *waves* coming at us and the reader from all directions are indeed enough to give this edgy brace of particles a touch of mal de mer. Amy considers editing at least a couple of them out, lest we be taxed with authorial heavyhandedness — the Hokusai, maybe, or the baseball fans — but *we* didn't put the damned things there: Coincidence did, for which, documentarists by temperament, we have a healthy respect. It is a fact, however, that whether owing to that particular "last straw" on the marina mini-telly or simply to our first reinspection of *ARI* since we checked that damaged vessel into the repair yard a few days back and moved our personal gear ashore, Richard finds himself, for the first time in his life, not afraid *at* sea, exactly (occasional scary moments are inevitable in sailboat-cruising, as in rock-climbing, horse-jumping, whitewater rafting, and any other sport that has in it an invigorating small element of danger), but, rather, afraid to *go* to sea; fearful of the prospect of returning to our ketch next week or whenever and reconfronting thereaboard both the elements and the limitations of our skills and strengths. This fear (which we don't doubt will subside in time if not pass altogether) both of us tacitly understand to be in the main a straightforward gut reaction to our literal knockdown; but in some measure, at least, it marks also our man's unassimilation of the figurative knockdown that preceded and perhaps even contributed to the literal. If A. R. Inc. have been withholding a lump of crucial exposition on that score, it's not out of archness or some minimalist program of seeing how much can go unsaid; it's out of mere fear of those above-mentioned fears. Give us island-time, reader, if you can; give us till this day's Happy Hour, let's say, by when if we haven't paid that particular narrative bill we'll pack it in and to hell with it.

Meanwhile, we Jeep back through town (reminding ourselves aloud to go *clockwise* on Freeport's two roundabouts) and out toward West End, past small mountains of discarded conch shells from the native fishery; past a dispiriting though photogenic boat graveyard of wooden fishing-craft hauled ashore or into the mangrove shallows to decay; past fewer abandoned upscale construction projects but perhaps even more paper-and-plastic litter. At a particular spot confirmed earlier on our map by that senior rigger on *ARI*'s deck, we turn off the shoulderless main road onto a pothole-puddled, weed-grown track much like this morning's and bump along it, dodging bush-branches that smack our windshield, until at road's end we reach a stand of marsh grass and the handsome stretch of beach facing Dead Man's Reef—the largest of a row of exposed long coral rocks less than half a mile offshore.

"Whence the name?" Richard inquires of our database, who replies, "Don't ask." As we hoped, the water's calm here in the island's lee, and we have the splendid beach and Don't-Ask Reef to ourselves. Large clouds, however, are massing off to southeastward as we look for a suitable place to stash our gear; we agree we'd better get our snorkeling done before Nature's aquarium-lights go out.

"Anywhere'll do," Amy supposes. Like this morning's, this afternoon's high-tideline is lamentably strewn with washed-up plastic bags and containers, scraps of nylon fishnet and cork floats, empty bottles of Kalik, the local beer, and other detritus. Indeed, one little Bahamian juniper growing at the edge of that spartina-stand just behind the beach is so festooned with storm-driven litter as to remind Amien Richard of certain Buddhist prayer-trees we've seen while on assignment in Japan. A discarded auto-tire nearby becomes our gear repository, easily checkable from Out There with the prayer-tree landmark.

Says Amy, "You lead this time."

Yes, well. Reader will have noted that R has been silent since his reef-name query. Fact is, a wave (no other way to put it) of trepidation-cum-near-nausea has been building in him at the prospect before us—the literal flat seascape, we mean, in the first instance—and at the prospect of reimmersing ourselves therein. Has the man quite lost his nerve? Of course not; although his half-dizziness is real, he leaf-juices his mask, perches it up on his forehead, and wades out into a sandy aisle through the turtle-grass shallows, fins in hand, toward deeper water. Amy follows, registering her husband's still-trim body from behind in its tropicolored Speedo swim briefs.

Shit, she remarks to herself, her eyes re-tearing: *It wasn't his fault.* Nevertheless, shit shit shit.

Okay, reader: Amien Richard will go back to nature-watcher watching before we'll write a spill-our-guts sort of story. But while our protagonistic particles (waist deep now) fin out to Whatsitsname Reef, we'll take one final retrospective plunge, see how deep a dive our withheld breath permits and what, if anything, we see fit to fetch up from down there:

Our afore-invoked Lucretius accounts for the physical universe as we know it by imagining that as the aboriginal atomic particles, which have existed eternally, fall of their own weight separately together through infinite space like raindrops in a windless shower, from time to time they quite unaccountably *swerve* from their parallel paths, bump their neighbors, and thereby initiate the ongoing catenation of collisions, couplings, and decouplings that generate stars and planets, Richards and Amys, and the rest. This purely speculative premise of Lucretius's (wherewith he accounts for human free will and everything else of a nondeterministic character) has been said to anticipate the odd behavior of electrons and such according to modern quantum mechanics, but never mind that: What matters to our story is that one or the other or both of this bonded pair we're calling Amien Richard appear to have swerved just as unaccountably from their prevailingly scrupulous parental watchfulness. That the errant swervant(s) were expectably aghast, appalled, self-blaming and self-unforgiving, each earnestly exculpating any remissness on the other's part, but above all wiped out by grief at our immeasurable, irreplaceable loss — in a goddamn backyard *wading pool*, of all harmless places. That *ARI*'s currently suspended winter-fleeing project was, as aforehinted, meant to put healing kilometrage between swerver(s) and site of swerve, and that it seemed to be doing that, on balance, from, say, the Great Dismal Swamp Canal down the Intracoastal to Miami. No condoling friends and super-sympathetic relatives to keep the wound open with their good intentions, our separate off-to-college children included. No occasion to rehearse once more (except endlessly in our heads) the step-by-step that led each of us for the fell few moments to believe the other was on parental watch while he/she *a*) stepped indoors to fetch Lucretius from our library in order to check out an undergraduate memory of the poet's opinion that copulation hind-to was the surest route to impregnation, or *b*) to take a phone call from our New York agent about that latest movie-option on *The Watcher*. For the first time in a year-and-then-some, we came this fall to feeling almost like Amien Richard again, although to be sure . . .

It was our reunion with R's ex-roomie, alas, that unsettled our own reunition. The guy's a positively dashing, quite sophisticated and cosmopolitan fellow, apparently as cultured as he is evidently rich. If he strikes us as more Mediterranean than Caribbean (not to mention than Yankee), his wife, a stunner, seems to us more Continental than Canadian. They're forever off to here or there between deals or in pursuit thereof, separately or together, for extended periods, a sort of Amien Richard of real estate. As our Miami hosts, they were a model of polished and reciprocally affectionate couplehood; what was worse, they have, like us, grown children by earlier marriages and "their first grandchild": a darling late-born five-year-old son (our Michelle lived fourteen months) attended mainly by Cuban-American nannies (born into less affluence, Amien Richard's most beautiful collaboration was attended — lovingly, joyously, not to mention *meticulously* — by her parents) . . .

We can't talk about it. They condoled, of course, having heard the minimum necessary gist but no details, and of course they left us alone about the accident, merely offering us, tactfully, their Freeport place if we needed to "recoup a bit." But of course too the sight of that handsome "first grandchild" of theirs, so . . . alive, had the expectable effect. *Nobody's fault*, R tried to console weeping A, back aboard *ARI*. Stop *saying* that! It's both our faults! Okay: both, both; but it's time to quit blaming ourselves, no? Time maybe to blame each other, you mean? I didn't say that, for pity's sake. You as much as said it; you've as much as said it all along! Stressed out, Ame; stressed out. Damn straight I'm stressed out! Unlike *me*, I suppose you mean.

Et cetera. One sees how it went, alas, once it got going, as it happened to do in course of our backtracking a bit up the ICW from Miami toward Palm beach for the quickest shot across the Florida Straits to Grand Bahama. Truth to tell, if our accumulated and, so we'd thought, finally pretty well contained distress hadn't come untethered — a sore backtrack indeed, to the great dismal swamp of initial devastation, self-flagellations, and contritions—we would perhaps have exercised calmer judgment about the timing of that quick shot. From Delray Beach, our agreed-upon jumping-off place, across to Freeport is rough-ly eighty statute miles, about sixteen hours at the five-knot average we hoped to maintain under sail, power, or both: Leave the USA at five PM, say, with enough daylight remaining for us to clear the coast; eat din-ner in the cockpit under way; then trade four-hour watches through the night as we cross the shipping lanes, steering south of our target to compensate for the northward set of the current, and reach Bahamian waters with next morning's sun already high enough to illuminate their reefs and shallows and harbor-approach buoys. Piece of cake, it ought to be, absent foul weather, although we've never done the like before, and inasmuch as we've no pressing timetable (as we had, e.g., en route to our space-shuttle-launch rendezvous), we can stand by in Delray Beach till the forecast's clear.

As it reasonably was, Richard still maintains, at D-Day noon, when the earlier-predicted fifty-percent chance of nighttime showers, pos-sibly thundershowers, had been reduced to thirty—which is to say, a seventy-percent chance of perfectly clear sailing. Why not sit tight, A wondered for us, until the Probability of Precipitation pops down to zero? Because, R pointed out on the weather map, those showers, when they *do* arrive, will be the leading edge of this big Norther here pushing down from Canada, which bids to blow hard against the up-running Gulf Stream for several days at least and whip up the steep seas for which that river-within-the-ocean is notorious. What's more, Tropical Storm Emile has chugged over from Africa to within a hundred miles of the British Virgins and is presently gaining strength as well as veering a bit north of west, toward Puerto Rico. Better to scoot across now and ride out those blows in snug Bahamian harbor, or ashore in the house so generously proffered us for recuperation. Point well taken, granted Amy; on the other hand, since we'll be snug-harboring it either way, why not stay put right where we are for an entire week, if necessary, until that weather map is menace-free? Because, replied her spouse, Delray Beach is no place to spend a week at anchor in a sailboat cabin or ashore in a cheapo motel, especially in the mood we seem to've lapsed into lately; and we're certainly not going to back-backtrack to Miami and then *back*-back-backtrack back here; and who gives a shit anyhow, come to that?

You're asking me? his wife countered, who could in fact have answered that rhetorical question (So could its asker have) but elected not to, it being plain to all hands which way our sore wind was blowing. Anchor aweigh, then, damn it, and Poseidon have mercy on A. R. Inc.

Alas, that deity didn't. We set out sullen, our demeanors muted but each of us considering the other by this time the reopener-in-chief of wounds we'd hoped were on the way to healing, our lapse having been a so clearly uncharacteristic swerve. Reaching east-southeastward on a fine mild southerly under all plain sail and autopilot, *ARI* dropped our home coast astern but not our bruised sensibilities — a pity, that, as it was a lovely evening's offshore sail, our first such. We both wanted to share the pleasure and excitement of it as we shared one glass of white wine and a delicious cold puttanesca that we'd made some days before; as we've shared so fortunately many pleasures and adventures large and small — but we could not, could not, and that inability (that impossibility, we felt) saddened and soured us one touch more. Dinner done, Amy in the cockpit then monitored our course and speed, Richard moped forward to watch twilit porpoises sporting in our bow wave, and a sudden cloud cover ended our daylight early. When presently R returned aft to stand the first evening watch, instead of keeping him company for a while as normally she would have, A excused herself and went below.

Our ship's log doesn't deal in causes and effects; it only reports the news. Through Richard's eight PM-to-midnight watch, the breeze freshened to twelve knots and swung southwesterly over our starboard quarter. R prudently decided to lower the small mizzensail, both to reduce *ARI*'s rolling in the seaway and to decrease our sail area in case the trend continued. Thirty percent P.O.P., he several times reminded himself, means seventy percent P.O. *no* P. When he turned us temporarily around to windward in order to get that sail down, the flapping and hobbyhorsing brought A to the companionway hatch to offer help. "Don't need you," she was told.

Mm hm.

By watch-change time, the wind was dead astern at twelve to fifteen-plus, and the seas were building. The log indicates that we swung again to windward enough to tuck a first reef in the mainsail and shorten our big roller-furling headsail a bit, Amy at the helm, Richard tending sheets and halyards at the pitching mast. Seasoned hands, we executed this chore with a minimum of communication, suited up now in foul weather gear as well as life vests and safety harnesses. No moon, no stars, no running lights of vessels other than our own; black night, black wind, black ocean and spirits. Regretful of his earlier brusqueness, "I'll keep you company a bit," R offered.

"Don't need you."

Hmp. So he goes below, peels out of his foulies, and updates the log and our dead-reckoned position on the chart. Broad-reaching and running at an average six knots on the following breeze, we're ahead of our nominal schedule and, he notes with glum satisfaction, past the point of no return: With wind and seas astern and Grand Bahama now nearer than the coast of Florida, we must press on come what may. He stretches out and tries to sleep; is too agitated, rueful, depressed, excited. Must have dropped off anyhow, briefly, for he wakes with tears in his eyes from a ragged, wretched, fleeting dream (in which he was announcing to Amy's father, Mitchell, as once he had in happy fact, "We're naming her after you, old chap, sort of"). Three AM, the boat's motion severe by our inland-waters standards but evidently under control and par for the course, he supposes, in offshore passage-making. He suits up, swigs room-temperature cappuccino out of a bottle in lieu of hot coffee (which we're rolling too much for him even to consider making), and takes that bottle along for his wife's refreshment when he goes upstairs now to keep her company through the last hour of her watch, whether she goddamn needs him or not. Finds her steering by hand down the pretty scary following seas — too tricky for the autopilot to handle, she'll report — still barreling along on course at six knots plus under single-reefed main and a jib that she has somehow managed single-handedly to shorten further.

"You should've called me," he lets her know.

"Yeah, right." She waves off the proffered cappuccino; on irked impulse, Richard flings the half-full bottle overside. "Oh, terrific," Amy says: "Take *that*, ocean." She needs to stretch her legs and pee, she informs him, if Sir Galahad can contain his tantrum enough to mind the helm for a bit.

Ashamed of himself anyhow, Richard volunteers to begin his final watch now. Amy's tempted to say Piss on that; no half-ass martyrdom, s.v.p.; I'll call you when your time comes. But she's too pissed to give a piss: pissed at how we've pissed away what should've been a memorable adventure, not to mention whatever else we've pissed away or are in danger, perhaps even in process, of so pissing. So she shrugs and goes below to piss, maybe to stay unless the rolling makes her ill, pausing en route at the nav station to tune in the weather channel. The barely intelligible "nowcast" reports through much static that at one AM (i.e., two hours ago), the line of thunderstorms extending from Fort Lauderdale down to the Miami area had crossed the peninsula and was moving offshore southeastward at thirty-five miles per hour. The severe thunderstorm watch for that portion of Florida's Atlantic coast has been lifted. Amy restrains a sarcastic comment having to do with probabilities of precipitation. In our regrettably separate heads, we each perform the obvious calculation; diffused lightning-flashes astern verify our arithmetic.

What we ought to have done at this point, we both understand now and probably understood then as well, is heave to, drop and furl the mainsail while conditions still permitted that maneuver, and carry on under reefed headsail alone, shortening it further if necessary from the safety of the cockpit or furling it altogether and running before the wind "under bare poles" until the squall-line passed. But our own diffused lightning was flashing, too: Mad-sad Amy clunked the companionway drop-boards into place to keep spray and rain out of the cabin (Yup, it's raining now), perfunctorily bidding her husband to call her if he needs her; sad-mad Richard didn't even reply. Said each to him-/herself: *Let the damn boat sink.*

Enough, says the reasonable reader, who wants to get back to the present action, such as it is, of this "Waves" or "Particles" story. Enough, agree Amien Richard, still shaking our authorial head at how such prevailingly bone-deep unanimity can have come, if not unglued, at least more sorely strained than ever before in our connection. Whatever happened to magnanimity, to heartfelt gestures of reunion between essentially bonded particles? *Enough*, says Zeus the Thunderer, and lets fly, while Earth-Shaker Poseidon warms up in Davy Jones's bullpen. If we had been ourselves, we'll wonder later, could we have wrestled ARI head-to-wind enough, in that suddenly howling gale, that machine-gun rain, those black-towering seas rollercoasting us from astern, to wrestle the mainsail down etc.? But we were heart-hurt Amy hanging on for dear life down below to keep from being pitched right across the cabin (no chance of dropping foul-weather bottoms to use the head in these conditions) and hurt-heart Richard safety-harnessed to a cockpit strongpoint, clutching the wheel in both hands and schussing us blindly like a hot-dog skier down the black slopes of those watery alps. Overpowered by that single-reefed mainsail, the ketch wants to broach disastrously side-to; the seas rushing under us reduce our rudder control — and now the gods team up to throw their quick one-two punch. A particularly blasty blast from a slightly different quarter blows out our mainsail and pulls *ARI* maybe twenty degrees around just as a semi-rogue wave thunders up like a goddamn *cliff* from a slightly different angle — Who can see?— and one or the other or the two combined take us out. Despite hard corrective helming, the boat spins beam-on to the wave; whether or not *ARI* "trips on she keel" or is simply pushed over by the breaking sea, we're knocked flat on our beam-ends, masts and sails in the water and helmsman briefly *under* it, clutching the wheel with arms and legs, holding his breath, fumbling frantically for his harness-clip in case we truly turn turtle, and managing somehow to think *Oh god good-bye dear Amy I am so sorry* — while down in the tumultuous dark cabin, where such normally secured objects as books, audiocassette racks, settee cushions, and off-watch Amy are crashing perilously about, that last-mentioned projectile is thinking *Oh god good-bye dear Richard I am so sorry.*

It's all over pretty quickly. With no help from us, *ARI* staggers almost upright; is promptly knocked down again by the next wave but not quite so far; is re-resurrected by the hull's inherent stability and ample reserve buoyancy. By the next wave after that one, stunned Richard has managed to bring our bow just enough upwind to avoid another knockdown (the blown-out main, a blessing in disguise, reduces our windage; do we dare espy a metaphor in that?) and is hollering for his wife, who's hollering back for him. The gods wink at each other and turn to other amusements, elsewhere; by the time Amy gets those drop-boards out and struggles up into the cockpit, the squall has rolled by, the rain and wind are fast tapering. She secures her harness and takes the wheel; no words needed. Soaked through, her mate goes forward one careful tetherslength at a time and laboriously triple-reefs the flogging main; we bear off then in full control and relative comfort (although we're wet, cold, and traumatized) in the already-diminishing seas, which half an hour later have gentled to an easy swell that the autopilot — miraculously still functioning — can handle without difficulty.

The rest you've heard: How—bruised and spent in both body and spirit, surprised and on the whole grateful to be still alive, afloat, un-widowed or -widowered, and more or less intact—we jury-rigged our craft (with a spare rope halyard in place of that sprung starboard miz-zen-shroud), likewise our conjugality (with heartfelt if not yet heart-healed embraces, reciprocal apologies, self-reproaches, absolutions, tears for the irretrievable, irrevocable, unreplayable, etc.), and together watched the sun come up over low-lying Grand Bahama.

What remains to tell, then, out here now at Dead Man's Reef? Storms pass, their damage lingers; repairs take time. As if tit-for-tatting from this morning, Richard disappears from Amy's sight while we're snor-keling the reef's handsome, fish-rich outboard wall; although she was supposed to be following *him* this time, her attention wandered off with a young sea turtle swimming by, and now she can't find the man either under or on the surface. Uh oh. But he has only, without real-izing it, turned a coral corner at DMR's far end, a couple dozen yards off, having dived to inspect close up a moray eel warily inspecting him from its hole in the rock. He surfaces, sees where he is, paddles back into view, points landward. His wife nods agreement: Too cloudy now for optimally viewing these denizens of the not-so-deep. Side by side we swim toward shore until our downstrokes are brushing bottom, then shuck our fins and walk the last hundred-plus feet like the emer-gent amphibians we sort of are, hand in hand but saying little.

We don't know.

Back at our prayer-tree, while Amy slips into her shorts and shirt, Richard espies and plucks from the tide-wrack a hand-size lump of cal-careous stone (tiny seashells, actually, by some natural process limed together) embedding on its upper face a single larger spiral shell—a small conch, most likely—whose exposed surface has been abraded by wave-action to reveal the delicate, self-replicating inner volutes. The effect is of an artfully mounted fossil. *Ecologically correct Ivory-Anni-versary gift*, he notes to himself, and although it makes a mighty clumsy lump in his shorts side pocket, there he slips it for the Jeep-ride home.

In the course whereof . . .

But to hell with the course whereof. Back at la borrowed hacienda grande, Georges nowhere in sight, we strip at poolside, dive in to rinse the salt off us, wind up embracing in chest-deep fresh water. It's Amy, actually, who initiates *this* potential sex scene, embracing Richard from behind and snugging her womanly equipment against his back and backside. She feels him tense a bit, surprised; then he relaxes, takes her hands in his against his belly. "So what's that lump I saw in your pants a while back?" she murmurs between nuzzlings of his shoulder blades.

"A girl could check it out for herself," he suggests, and presently she goes and does, and Guess what?s, and invites him to a reciprocal frisking of *her* pants, dropped over yonder. That chuckly search successful, we exchange anniversary shells and kisses, lead each other indoors lest Georges or one of his Inside sons appear outside, and make consolatory love on the grand conversation-couch of that sunken living room, smack under Hokusai's dreadsome view of Mt. Fuji.

Happy ending? Not for the lost. As for us, too soon to say, say Amien Richard, Reincorporated; this is bona fide, true-to-life fiction we're floating here, not mass-paperback romance. We've recircled now to where our story started, Amy on mat and Richard in beach-toweled lounge chair, all hands feeling soundly loved and roundly laid despite whatever (or feeling Whatever despite being soundly-roundly etc.). Under a threatening sky we sip coconut rum with guava juice, munch munchies, raise eyebrows at the wind now whipping our casuarina screen and corrugating the pool surface, and return our postcoital attention to Amy's lead-off question.

"So," she still wants to know: "Are we particles or waves?"

Diplomatically, before he answers, Richard this time asks, "Which does it seem to you?"

Chin resting on fists: "When I think of . . . No: Never mind When I Think Of. I guess I think just waves."

"Mm hm."

"Not only *us*-us." The woman has never been more serious. "I mean everybody, every thing. Waves are all there is, is what *I'm* coming around to thinking. You?"

Her admiring husband agrees: "Waves, definitely. I even wonder now and then whether there *are* any particles, you know? I suppose there are, in a manner of speaking, but when you get right down to it, even particles are waves."

A. R. Inc. jointly second that particular motion, or proposition; wish we knew for sure how this maiden not-so-short-story of ours intends to end, but on reflection decide it's just as well we don't. Presently, no doubt, we'll do the Next Thing: dress for dinner and stroll or Wrangle the dozen-odd blocks into town for either our Ivory-commemorative or, if after all we haven't yet joint heart for that, something less affirmatory.

People can still prevailingly love each other, you know, and be nevertheless simply unable to go on with their story.

Contrariwise, you know, they can find to their vast regret that their love has gone the way of an inadvertently and momentarily unattended tot in a waveless wading pool and, despite *that*, decide for whatever reasons to keep their joint story going, if only faute de mieux.

Or not and not.

Or love and on with it, hoping that with time and large-spiritedness enough, the wave of their critical distress will sweep on without having sunk their ship altogether. While Amien Richard don't know for certain even whether this story of theirs will continue, much less how end, we're pretty sure now, as are its principal characters, that it won't be called "Particles." Waves everywhere, as Amy sort of said, in time or space or both. Our bodies are waves, for sure, as aforesuggested, their particular constituents ever in flux, their overall form evolving and then devolving, from infancy (with luck) through juvenescence to the full handsome maturity that we see naked here before us and on to the physical decline already begun but not yet conspicuously manifest in our joint case. Our minds? Likewise, as their contents and constructs, feelings and attitudes and even worldviews change, will-we nill-we, over time. And our selves, those posited centers of narrative gravity that we're in the habit of calling, e.g., Amy and Richard? Waves, definitely: mere ever-changing configurations of memories and characteristics embodied in those other waves, our minds and bodies. Okay, maybe not so "mere"— Look at splendid Amy there; look at excellent Richard there; look at . . . the inexpungeable dear image of the precious lost. All the same, our point is that the surfer is as much a wave as is the wave he surfs.

Does that not imply that A&R's marriage . . . that, indeed, all human relationships, are waves? Sure it does: the same wavish partners, by and large (although in each of the present cases, the "we" wasn't always us), but even in the stablest of instances the dynamic of their relation is ever in flux, continually disequilibrating and (Let's cross our fingers) continually returning toward equilibrium.

Our lives in general, then, it must go without saying . . .

Waves, absolutely, as are all our actions for good or ill, dissipating

over distance and time. Ditto our stories, obviously; both our life-stories and (Shall we cross our fingers, dearest friend?) our made-up-and-
maybe-even-publishable stories: waves waves waves, propagated from
mind to mind and heart to heart through the medium of language via
these particles called words.

But didn't Richard just say—

He did, and Amien Richard here corporately affirm: Even *those*
particles are waves, coming into the language, often changing their
spelling and sense, not infrequently dropping out of use. Waves all,
all waves, from these riplets on our borrowed pool through yonder
Hokusais chugging in from M'sieur Emile, right on out to the exploding universe. N'est-ce pas, amie?

"You say. Sure, I guess. Right."

Long may *we* wave, then. And concerning this evening . . .?

"Let's cross our fingers."

"No comment."

None? His fingers were crossed.
    "Hers, too. All the same ..."

Sigh. Well, it was a long story.
    "For one thing."
    But it's *been* a long story.
    "Not long enough."
    Now you're talking.
    "But it's finito. We just weren't lucky."
    We were the luckiest.
    "Not lucky enough. And this narrative striptease isn't working."
    It's brought us this far ...
    "No comment."

Presently: She's tired.
    "Tired beyond tired."
    All that tennis and beach volleyball.
    "That was the relaxing part. That and our long long reef-swim."
    In which neither swimmer lost sight of the other or played hide-and-seek like Amy and Richard.
    "No comment."

Presently: "I guess I'm catching a sleep-wave."

Ride it. *Love and on with it*, as the fellow said.

"Yes, well."

Presently and very quietly, fingers crossed: Is she asleep?

"No."

Me neither.

"It was a good wave, but I wiped out."

Likewise.

"Story of our lives?"

No comment.

Next mid-day, perhaps; a rare spell of rainshowers, perhaps, ruling out tennis, beach volleyball, and other outdoor distractions. A cozy post-noon siesta, perhaps.

Presently: He could read her a story about that.

"About wiping out? She wrote the book."

Not about wiping out.

8.

Stories of Our Lives

It has occurred to Ms. Mimi Adler, whom I like a lot, to wonder whether people reflexively think of their lives as stories because from birth to death they are exposed to so many narratives of every sort, or whether, contrariwise, our notion of what a *story* is, in every age and culture, reflects an innately dramatistic sense of life: a feature of the biological evolution of the human brain and of human consciousness, which appears to be essentially of a scenario-making character.

Ms. Adler's question may strike the reader of these lines as idle, academic, inconsequential — and it's certainly no grabber of an opening for a work of fiction, a bona fide short story. As I pen these words on my new friend's behalf, is not Bosnia bleeding, have not Rwandans been slaughtering one another wholesale, are not 154 pounds of deadly weapons-grade plutonium still missing from a Japanese nuclear reactor, and does not Haiti's immemorial misery more or less drag on, together with untold other large- and small-scale catastrophes right round the planet? In the face of so much wretchedness and gravity, what justification have Mimi and I for entertaining such chicken-or-egg questions as whether people's lives or their stories have, so to speak, ontological primacy?

That question, believe me, we take as seriously as we take the question that it questions. M's coming on to fifty, my wife's age, although you'd never guess so by looking at either of those trim, athletic, handsome, and energetic women. Like Mrs. Narrator, Mrs. Adler is a morally serious citizen as well as a dedicated teacher of young people. I myself am a dozen years older, Mimi's husband's a touch older yet, and you'd guess *that* at once if you saw us with our spouses, although both Robert and I are in good shape for our age — anyhow were, up to the time of this story. If less intense than our mates in the moral / political sphere, we too are unfrivolous professionals. Rob's a cognitive scientist, I've just decided, from whose acquaintance with current theories of consciousness Mimi will have picked up what she knows about the biological evolution of our brains and their propensity for spinning scenarios in order to sort out the data continuously flooding all our senses: in short, our experience of life. Rob cannot, however, speak to his wife's late perplexity on this which-causes-which question, as he's down in D.C. just now consulting for the National Institutes of Health. Yours truly, as aforenoted, makes up short stories — not for a living, as there's no living in it, but for the serious pleasures of dreaming up characters like Mimi and Rob and situations like the one I'm about to put them in, of working out plots and forms and themes and images and actions and voices (in a word, *stories*), and of finding the language wherewith to get those stories told. If that's not seriousness enough, I also teach part-time in a good American university, coaching graduate-student apprentices in my profit-poor but deeply gratifying trade.

In fact, that's how I came to know M.A. (so her initials just now suggest to me) — whose husband, I here decide, I already knew slightly as an extra-departmental colleague. Our university's M.A. storymaking program is age-blind, you see, as well as gender-blind, eth-blind, prior-degree-blind — blind to everything other than talent, accomplishment, and promise. When we've sorted through the pile of applications to select the dozen or so most likely-seeming, we're pleased of course if they turn out to be a multiculturally mixed bag of women and men, gays and straights, youngs and less youngs, ets and ceteras; but as long as they're the most evidently talented, accomplished, and promising of the lot, we don't finally care (so we tell ourselves) if our dazzling dozen turn out to be uniformly middle-aged gay white (lapsed-) Mormon doctors of philosophy from the province of Saskatchewan. The group five years ago numbered only one of those among the usual ethnic / sexual / actuarial / aesthetical smorgasbord, which happened also to include this uncommonly attractive mid-fortyish Jewish-or-Italian-or-both-by-the-look-of-her lady whose stories (as I knew from reviewing the application files) were poignant but playful "postmodern" spin-offs from notable scientific or philosophical propositions: Zeno's paradoxes, Schrödinger's wave-function equations, whatever. They wanted revision and polishing, to be sure, like everybody else's in the program, toward closing those crucial last millimeters between gifted apprentice and truly professional work; otherwise their authors would be applying to magazine editors instead of to us. The woman's smile, however, needed no coaching at all: a brilliant, knowing, persistent, disconcerting smile that said, among other things, "*We* understand the tacit subtext here, don't we?" and that would have been the more unsettling if she hadn't directed it at just about everyone to whom she spoke or listened.

My habit on opening day is to go around the seminar room asking each new hand in turn to introduce her/himself: what name you go by, where you hail from, by what waypoints you arrived among us, your past training and experience in the yarning trade, what you have in mind to do in your season here, whatever else it pleaseth you to mention of an identificatory nature. When Ms. Adler's turn came (she sat, as she would invariably through that academic year, at the opposite end of the long seminar table from me, dressed in the oversized university sweatshirt and black running tights in which she routinely jogged the five miles from campus to her house after class), she beamed that mighty smile the length of the room, declared matter-of-factly, "Mi chiamo Mimi," and then went on in her rich contralto speaking-voice to give us her résumé in an ad-lib paraphrase of that famous soprano aria from *La Bohème*. Most got the joke; some didn't. From that subtextual smile of hers, I could almost imagine that she had somehow guessed Puccini to have been, like tennis and sailing and the stories of Italo Calvino, among the touchstones of her new coach's courtship and marriage.

In a group whose average was better than average, the woman proved at least an average apprentice fictioneer, also a first-rate critic of her comrades' efforts (she really *did* see unspoken and sometimes significant "subtexts" lurking between their lines) and perhaps the most generally liked of that year's seminarians. Our cordial association continued, less closely, thereafter: the two couples at mixed-doubles tennis and certain university social events; Mimi and I at readings by visiting writers or *tout court* over occasional faculty-club lunches. As happens in more cases than not, her fiction, alas, for all its bright promise, got nowhere; she had reached the distressingly familiar stage of doing nothing correctly *wrong* in her art, really, but of doing nothing on the other hand so remarkably well as to distinguish her productions from the thousands of others that every magazine and book editor remains deluged with, even in the age of electronic visual media. Fortunately for her (now ex-) coach, if not for herself, the critic in her was too exquisitely aware of this state of affairs to make its articulation incumbent upon me; nothing to be done, we agreed, except cross fingers and soldier on until her muse smiles, if the bitch ever does. M's own smile, at that, told me she was already onto some tacit subtext between forkfuls of Caesar salad, but it was not one that I was privy to until early in the current semester, when over another such touch-base lunch she announced that her personal *Bohème* had reached Act Two's closing curtain: in this restaging, no echt-nineteenth-century tuberculosis for the soprano, but echt-late-twentieth AIDS for the tenor.

Rob? AIDS? No.

"Rob AIDS *yes*." Her splendid mahogany eyes filled right up. "HIV positive, anyhow, with AIDS to follow as doth the night ... the day ..."

That *day* trailed into suspension-points and tears. When in time the tale got itself told (in the faculty-club parking lot, whereto we retreated for self-collection), it was of her steadfast, good-shape-for-his-age husband's feeling lately so under the weather that even as he completed his arrangements for early retirement (sixty-five is officially early in our institution), he underwent a physical exam more thorough than his routine annual checkups and thus learned the fatal news.

"So where'd it come from?" she spared me the discomfort of asking. No extracurricular sexual contacts, her husband swore, since back in the hyperpermissive Sixties, and his wife (who at his urging had had herself tested and been shown HIV-negative) saw no reason to question his fidelity. No needles except those in his doctor's medical lab and Rob's own cognitive-research facilities, where a certain amount of animal experimentation was carried on. Workers in such labs are not routinely tested for HIV; given the standard sterile precautions of any well-run laboratory, however, the chances of accidental virus-transmission in those venues must be near zero. Some while back, he'd had prostate surgery in the university hospital; Mimi, who regarded hospitals as dangerous anyhow, believed that place and occasion the likeliest suspect — although the patient had had no blood transfusions, for example, and our hospital is among the most prestigious in the land. Investigation was continuing. Through it all, my friend reported, her husband was being a brick, but Mimi herself and their two grown children were devastated: not only, in M's case, by the prospect of losing to that revolting malady her best friend and life-mate and the anticipated balance of their years together — as many as twenty, had luck been theirs, after which she had resolved to terminate promptly with Seconal her expectable widowhood — but for at least two other reasons as well, which may strike the reader as unseemly, although I confess that I myself found them not difficult to sympathize with:

— The dreadful turn of events had the incidental effect of relegating Mimi Adler to a supporting role, as she saw it, in her own life-story. More accurately (for I protested this idea at once, as had Robert, and as even more vehemently would my wife, when I recounted this tale to her), it forced a radical, lamentable revision of her lead role therein. Instead of Gifted Middle-School Teacher blossoming into Gifted Fiction-Writer (a scenario ever less tenable in any case), she had been recast as GMST obliged to become Heroic (or not so heroic) Nurse of Lovable and Competent but Otherwise Unremarkable Scientist.

These latter adjectives surprised me; I cannot dispute them, but had no idea that Mimi saw Rob so. Granted, she was distraught; all the same, I sensed a tacit subtext. Moreover,

— As aforementioned, she had become all but convinced that while she was not without literary talent, her gift was finally an amateur's flair, not a true vocation (I'm afraid I agree, but I'm not about to tell her so, and only time and perseverance can say for sure), and so she would not have that enviable life-preserver to help float her through her present pass and impending bereavement. She would be obliged to survive, if she chose to, on the strength of having been an okay mother, a quite good teacher, a truly loving and all but hundred-percent-faithful wife, a dedicated nurse of her husband's terminality, and a more or less stoical widow perhaps devoted to worthy causes, unless she decided to go the Hemlock Society route and to hell with it. She'd had more in mind, frankly, she told me (whose attention, for all my sympathy, was not undistracted by the subtext of that "all but hundred-percent-faithful"): How was she to come to terms with mere above-averagehood, especially in the face of this miserable new plot-twist, when all her life she had aspired to *excel*, to live *transcendently?*

It was these reflections and their accompanying guilt, she declared —
turning on that singular smile now while making free with the pocket
tissue-pack that I'd proffered en route to the parking lot — that had led
her to thinking in this new way about people's lives as stories, etc., and
thence to the question that *this* story opens with her pondering, quite
as she might have opened one of her own. She supposed herself a monster even to think of such questions under the circumstances ("Maybe
she is," my wife will allow); if so, so be it. She just thought her erstwhile
coach might be amused.

I forgive you that *amused*, I told her then and re-tell her now — and
I trust the reader to grant that M's introductory question wasn't entirely frivolous after all. It's going to have to wait for an answer, however,
while the narrative camera cuts to a certain silver-alloy coin that fell
out of my pants pocket onto the winter-dormant lawn of the faculty
club as Mimi and I shortcut to the parking lot to avoid public display
of her emotion and I fetched out on her behalf that little Kleenex-pack.
A Canadian twenty-five-cent piece, that coin was, picked up casually
in Toronto somewhere earlier when I happened to be author-touring
up that way, and not yet recycled into some Baltimore parking meter
(although to my eye all North American quarters are of identical dimension, soft-drink machines, unlike parking meters, know the difference): on one side, the head of ELIZABETH II D. G. REGINA in classic
starboard profile; on the other, a bull-caribou portside ditto, haloed
by CANADA 1984 and bearing in his mighty antler-rack the declared
value 25 CENTS. On both faces, a circle of raised dots just inside the
milled edge, to complicate counterfeiting. The I-character didn't notice
his loss and never will, nor did my stressed-out lunch companion; the
I-narrator of this stories-of-our-lives story, on the other hand, not only
observed but *caused* the coin's fall from right trouser-pocket to campus
grass, to the end of informing or reminding the reader, by association,
of a certain schoolroom narrative exercise called "L'Histoire d'un sou"
that used to be assigned in the French lycées. Imagine and recount
the adventures of a common coin, that exercise demanded, as it cir-
culates from hand to hand through one's society: perhaps from mint
to bank and anon to some aristocratic lady's purse, thence serially to
the pocket of that lady's pilfering chambermaid, to that chambermaid's
middle-aged shopkeeping lover, to the young prostitute whose services
that shopkeeper occasionally hires, to that prostitute's illegitimate but

much-prized five-year-old son, Rodolfe (by the aristocratic lady's phi-
landering husband, as it happens), to that lad's bullying seven-year-old
alleymate, Victor, who snatches and runs off with it, to the gutter of
the cobbled Montmartre street into which Victor darts and fearless
little Rodolfe pursues him just in time to be struck by the aristocratic
husband's carriage, and thence, tossed away by conscience-stricken
Victor, down the storm-drain of that street into the sewers of Paris,
where it goes unnoticed by Jean Valjean in flight from the detective
Javert but not by that keen-eyed latter, who, though not an otherwise
superstitious fellow, pauses for two seconds to pick it up lest toute la
journée he have bad luck and thereby, ironiquement, affords Valjean
the opportunity to elude him at least for another chapter. In analogous wise, this particular Canadian quarter in its ten-year tour of duty
had passed through 240 hands, remaining in possession of each for a
median fortnight over a range from ten seconds (given as change in
what must have been the only gay bar in Saskatoon, Saskatchewan, in
1986, to a lapsed-Mormon Ph.D. candidate from Moose Jaw, and by
him promptly passed to the friend with whom he was splitting the tab)
to three years (in the miscellaneous-foreign-coins ashtray of the Florida apartment of a Bahamian real-estate speculator whose travels took
her to Canada occasionally but not often), before being given to me,
again as change, in the delightful cafeteria / market / restaurant Möven-
pick Marché in downtown Toronto, where that lady happened to have
shopped and lunched on the same day that my wife and I happened to
shop and dine there in mid-booktour. Now on a Maryland February
afternoon it lies nearly vertical against blades of hybrid lawn-grass on
a seldom-crossed sward of faculty-club turf, and there it could remain
"forever," perhaps mashed into the soil come spring by the riding-mow-
ers of campus groundskeepers and gradually thatched and sedimented
over, the narrative camera locked uneventfully upon it ad infinitum
like Andy Warhol's literal camera upon the Empire State Building
in his 1964 film *Empire*, or perhaps accidentally excavated a year or
a century hence by a crew relandscaping the area or digging footers
for an extension of the building and examined by the not-otherwise-
superstitious finder for lucky numbers to use in playing the state lot-
tery, thence on with its story.

In fact (so to speak), however, it gets noticed no more than an hour
later by another colleague of mine, whom I've never met personally

but know to be an art historian with a minor, as it were, in conchology, from which hobby he has acquired the half-conscious habit of keeping a beachcomber's eye out even in the city. An unorthodox fellow in several respects, Associate Professor Walter Ellison believes that paths should be laid where people walk, literally and figuratively, rather than constraining folks' walking to already-laid paths, and so he makes it his pedestrian practice, especially on campus, to take the most direct or otherwise convenient route to his destination, across lawns and even through flowerbeds and shrubbery, as a sort of service to the university's landscape planners. Shortcutting like Mimi and me-the-character to the parking lot that she and I have already exited in our separate cars (M to go on with the grimly plot-turned story whereof she is the reluctant, ineluctable protagonist, I with the exfoliation of this, whereof I am teller-in-chief but wherein have only a walk-on, drive-off role), young Professor Ellison espies "my" coin in the grass and, recalling the folk-rhyme advisory, bends over as if to pick it up but in fact merely to inspect it before perversely *letting it lay* in order to defy, on principle, proverbial wisdom. Although Walt's only thirty-five and is in good physical condition from playing indoor tennis twice or thrice weekly at a suburban club, the muse of irony sees fit at this point cruelly to inflict upon him what will turn out to be a lifelong intermittent spinal-disc problem in consequence of that simple movement. Some fluke of leverage, one supposes; in any case, the pain is so sudden and shocking that between coin and car he hobbles in a sweat and at one moment nearly faints. It's all he can do to ease himself into his vintage bean-green Volvo wagon and drive home; by when he reaches his Mount Washington neighborhood, his lumbar area has so seized up that he groans involuntarily at every major movement from driveway to lavatory (where he helps himself to a tablet of Valium) to living-room rug, a second-hand Heríz on whose central medallion he lies supine for the next two hours, until Barbara comes home from her new job in the reference department of the Enoch Pratt Free Library. She's alarmed. He explains. She commiserates, and doses her recently anxious self with the Valium long ago prescribed for Walter's wry neck by the same physician who, as it irrelevantly happens, diagnosed Rob Adler's AIDS (the drug, anyhow expired, will prove less effective in and for her case than as a simple muscle relaxant in her husband's). The couple then settle into a pained parody of their usual end-of-workday routine: As they're both Valium'd, in lieu of their customary glass of California Chardonnay they sip with their trail-mix hors d'oeuvres a very weak solution of jug Chablis and club soda, once Walt has gotten himself propped against the couch-front. Even raising the wineglass in ironic toast to the muse of irony — for they're scheduled to vacation next week at the Club Méditerranée in Cancún, their first such holiday, where they've been looking forward to tennis, snorkeling, beachcombing, and touring the nearby Mayan ruins — makes him ouch.

"So what was your most interesting call today?" he asks her as usual, though not usually in so clenched a voice. Barbara works the Pratt's telephone information service desk, "doing kids' homework for them," she complains, for indeed they'll call to say "I'm writing this paper for eighth grade? Can you tell me about Spain?"

"Nothing terrific. Some lady wanted Erwin Schrödinger's equation for quantum-mechanical wave functions, and I tracked it down easily enough but didn't know how to read it to her. I mean, it's not like saying 'E equals mc squared,' you know? The thing's humongous and full of hieroglyphics. Then some guy needed the name and date of that Warhol flick where the camera stays fixed forever on the Empire State Building — "

"*Empire.* Sixty-eight or -nine? *Aiyi!*"

"Poor thing. Sixty-four." As to Cancún, they incline two days later to go on with the trip, although a statement from Walter's doctor would entitle them to a refund of their prepayment. Thanks in part to a fresh prescription, the back pain has eased somewhat each day; they need the break — Barb especially, who finds life more stressful lately than does her inner-directed mate. They'll be able at least to read and sunbathe and eat and drink and perhaps visit the Tulum ruins down-coast from Cancún; maybe even snorkel the reefs, carefully, on calm days.

Do they go? Go they do, with unequally shared misgivings. Walt, a workaholic by nature whose notion of holiday has historically been either wall-to-wall museum-touring or serious amateur conchology, merely hopes that their first real vacation-vacation won't be spoiled and that his pulled muscle or pinched nerve or slipped disc won't prove to be an ongoing or recurring disability (alas, it will). He has come to depend upon vigorous physical exercise, like sustained mental work, as a safety-valve in his life with Barbara, for one thing — a non-athlete and a bit of a complainer lately. She hopes the same, of course, for her sake as well as his; notwithstanding his inner and outer strengths, her husband's a real baby, in her opinion, on the rare occasions when anything's physically amiss with him, whereas she, at any given moment in her life-story, will likely be bearing up pretty stoically, without medication, under half a dozen assorted minor ailments. Perhaps that is why, only three weeks into her job at the Pratt and just the week before this Yucatán vacation, to her own considerable astonishment she permitted herself to go to bed with an attractive and rather famous senior departmental colleague of her husband's: an unmarried programmatic flirt who Walter himself suspects is either gay or asexual but who turned out—in the remarkable episode that followed one of the fellow's periodic consultancy-visits to the Pratt's fine arts collection, his coincidental path-crossing with Barbara as both were leaving the building at the end of her workday, his offering her a lift home in his bronze-gold Lexus to save her cab fare (Barb's little Honda was being serviced), and his all but daring her, en route, to stop in for a look at the rather grand condo he recently bought in a spiffy new high-rise overlooking the university—to be a decidedly more energetic and imaginative lover, on first and second go at least, than her husband of seven years. Now she is, if not quite guilt-stricken, at least guilt-nagged, the more because, with poor Walt hors de combat, on the day before their Club Med flight she took the initiative of telephoning Franco *from work*, ostensibly to tell him that she had really admired his new place and that, as between the two bedroom-drapery fabrics that he'd asked her opinion of, she definitely recommended the darker, "stronger" one with the seashell motif.

"I value your input, Barbara," he had replied in his only slightly accented but heavily testosteronic baritone. No mention, however, of *his* having enjoyed as had she their surprising roll in his high-rise hay; no insinuating suggestion that perhaps she would like to have a look at the seashell drapes when they were made and hung. Mortification, to have cheated on her husband with, of all people, the acting chair of his department, and to have been by him judged, perhaps, no good in bed! It makes her want to pile atop her ailing seat-mate now in contrite reaffirmation of their marriage-bond—but apart from the unseemliness of such behavior, the long charter flight has made Walt's back at least temporarily even sorer. As they circle in over the mangrove-and-chicle-thick expanse of Yucatán, her head begins to throb in a way that she can almost imagine signals migraine. She removes the prescription sunglasses that, for one reason or another, she has lately taken to wearing indoors as well as out, and massages the bridge of her nose. The ache neither disappears nor, thank heaven, comes on more strongly.

After they've checked in along with a festive busload of other new arrivals, been assigned their simple but comfortable quarters, and at Barbara's suggestion pushed the twin beds together to make one large one (she has to do most of the pushing), she asks, "Could we maybe sack out for a while before we explore the place?" Walt is disinclined at first—he didn't come to Yucatán to nap through this four-and-a-half-thousand-dollar vacation—but then he sees that it's not napping she has in mind, and although he'd rather go reconnoiter the resort's impressive spread and hit the beach, he tries to get into her sportive mood. "You'll have to get on top," he tells her.

She smiles behind her dark glasses. "That can be arranged." Moreover, when they're almost undressed she surprises him by suggesting that they remove each other's underpants with their teeth.

"Hot damn," her husband responds, assuming she's joking, and with his hands whisks off first his own briefs and then hers. In fact, however, she was quite serious: In her session with Franco, he had not only insisted that Barbara bestride him with her sunglasses in place ("So *barbaric*," he had teased) but had proposed, as they subsequently redressed, that next time they undress each other with their teeth. It was her amused excitement at that prospect that had prompted her follow-up phone call: a disappointment, but surely for the best.

"Take those damn *glasses* off," Walt now mock-scolds her when she mounts him—just as she was about to reach back and down to do with her forefingertip a certain little thing to him that Franco . . .

"Isn't it sexier like this?"

Smiling, he reaches up and removes the offending item. "I like to see who it is I'm making love with, okay?" He folds the sidepieces and sets the sunglasses on a nightstand. Feeling her headache rethreaten, Barbara declares, "It's just the same old wife as always," and hobbyhorses him straight to ejaculation so that she can dismount, dose herself with aspirin, and get those glasses back on. "Rain check," she tells him when he makes to reciprocate.

But as she unfolds the eyeglasses (before even washing up), one hinge-screw works loose and drops out, and the earpiece comes off in her hand.

"Oh god. We've got to find it!"

Naked on all fours she goes, searching the rugless quarry-tile floor in vain for the tiny screw.

"What am I going to *do*?" She's borderline-frantic. "They're my only glasses!"

Her startled husband reasonably supposes that all eyeglass-hinge screws are alike, unless some are metric and some not; they can buy the cheapest pair of overpriced non-prescription shades in the Club's boutique and use one of its screws to replace hers.

"It'll never work!" She sits Turk-fashion on the bare tiles, head in hands. "What am I going to do with my life?"

Surprised at her near-hysteria, Walt does his best to calm her — "Jesus, Barb!"—although experience has taught him that his efforts in this line are as liable to aggravate as to soothe.

The headache comes on: in fact, her first full-fledged migraine. To bed she retreats, not for sport this time. Seeing their vacation-week on the verge of going down the drain, Walt half-ruefully, half-resentfully goes to check out the boutique as proposed, acquiescing however to his wife's insistence that he buy nothing until she inspects and approves. In her judgment, he's reckless with their money. He finds, of course, sunglasses a-plenty for sale there — muchos pesos per pair, but so what compared to the cost of this trip? If the parts prove incompatible, perhaps he can use a screw from his own eyeglasses to repair his wife's and then jury-rig his with a wire paper-clip scrounged from the establishment's business office. He strolls the hibiscus- and bougainvillea-rich grounds, noting bitterly that their luckier plane-and-bus-mates are already enjoying the magnificent beach and the splendid Mexican Caribbean out there — its reefs abounding, no doubt, in jim-dandy shells.

Back at their room he finds a note on the dresser: *Sorry to've come unhinged (!) Gone to infirmary. Don't follow; will be okay. Will look for you on beach. Love you.*

His resentment melts, leaving only pity and affection; he knows *he's* not the easiest person in the world to live with, either, and he doesn't for a moment doubt the bond between them. He changes into a swimsuit, loads their beach-bag with towels, sun-lotions, his snorkel mask, a plastic shell-identification card, and a book on Mayan artifacts, and advises his wife, on the back of her note to him, to look for him and / or the bag on the narrow stretch of beach just in front of their unit.

Properly to reach that stretch, one is meant to follow a paved and landscaped walk for several hundred yards toward the Club's central buildings, to the pool area and main beach access, and then backtrack along the strand itself, separated from the landscaped grounds by a low fence atop a five-foot embankment. Walt, however, takes the direct route, picking up a white plastic lounge chair as he crosses the lawn. That chair's one-piece molded curves — designed for nested stacking and for reclining in average though nonadjustable comfort — remind him of the recumbent stone figures of the Mayan god Chacmool, ubiquitous in the region: There are full-size replicas at the resort's entrance and miniatures for sale in the boutique. Careful of his back, he hefts the chair over the fence and slides it down the bank, then climbs over and down after it with their beach-bag. He has the strip to himself. "Chacmool" he positions where Barbara is most likely to notice it from their second-floor balcony, and he seats the bag in plain view on its belly, so to speak — just as, if he remembers correctly, sacrificial victims were once positioned on the original. Then he wets his mask-lens with saliva against fogging and enters the welcoming sea at last.

The water is warm, clear, and beautiful, with a moderate current from upshore, where the main beach is. Without swim-fins (he means to borrow a pair from the snorkel shack after Barb settles down) it takes a bit of effort to hover in place; easier to ride downstream on the current and walk back. He does that for a hundred yards or so, admiring the clean sand bottom, the mostly healthy-looking coral, the flamboyant fish, and the occasional top shell or other mollusk, which he inspects and identifies but refrains on principle from collecting. No Barbara in sight when he returns to Chacmool. Deciding that the beach-bag is reasonably safe, he walks farther this time in the other direction — perhaps a quarter-mile, to the edge of the main bathing area, in order to snorkel the current home.

His wife's surprising question — "What am I going to do with my life?" — haunts him as he floats. He knows himself to be an antidramatic, even a plodding soul, at least by contrast to her higher-strung sensibility; he cannot imagine putting that question to himself, for example, in the absence of objective crisis, such as disablement so crippling that he couldn't work, or the loss of his wife to accident or disease (divorce doesn't occur to him; over the course of their marriage he has been tempted no more to infidelity than to illegal drugs, nor has he ever thought to wonder whether Barb has been). He sometimes regrets, even keenly, their not having children, especially when he's with his young nieces and nephews, but he finally shrugs at his infertility, as at his not being wealthy or movie-star handsome, and gets on with it. What is he going to do with his life? He's going to snorkel this stretch of sea-floor, then read up on the Mayans or beachcomb or both, go to dinner this evening, perhaps try tennis mañana if his back permits (the swimming seems to help it), then tour the Tulum ruins, where he particularly looks forward to viewing the astronomically calibrated temples of Marriage and Birth . . .

A non-marine something on the bottom catches his eye, rolling lazily with the current over a sandy patch between coral rocks ten feet under: a pair of sunglasses, of all things, in design rather like Barbara's, though with hot pink frames rather than black. Amused (and careful of his back), he dives and retrieves them, noting as he surfaces that the hinge hardware seems uncorroded and moves freely. If the lenses were prescription-ground, he would turn the glasses in at the Hostess desk; as they're not — just an ordinary pair of ladies' shades, perhaps knocked off some bikini'd young miss upbeach an hour ago as she frolicked with her boyfriend in the gentle surf — he'll cannibalize them on Barb's be-half, then reassemble and return them if the experiment fails. Truly, while he can understand his mate's despairing question in a hypotheti-cal way, on the gut level he finds it virtually incomprehensible.

There she is, he sees now in the downshore distance: a fetchingly bikini'd and sun-visored miss herself, stretched out on Señor Chacmool with the bag beside her and reading a book. That last he takes for a hopeful sign, as is her apparently making shift with her one-stemmed sunglasses instead of throwing up her hands. He tucks his treasure into the crotch of his swimsuit and happily strokes herward.

Shading her eyes with one hand, Barbara watches him wade ashore, his mask perched up on his forehead (her own forehead, though less ax-edged than before, feels still like a seismic fault about to let go). He reaches down into the front of his swimsuit as if about to expose himself.

"Hubby to the rescue!"

"Where'd you get those?"

"Frutas de mar, and more where these came from." Pattering on, he rummages through the beach-bag. "Want to check for yourself? How's your head these days, by the way?"

"A wreck. But it'll pass."

"*All passes*," he intones, fishing out the Swiss Army knife that he carries with him everywhere; "*art alone endures*. John Ruskin? Omar Khayyám? Art Garfunkel?" He has expected to have to use the point of the knife's smaller cutting blade to unscrew the hinge, but finds to his gratified surprise that while the main screwdriver / cap-lifter blade is, as he anticipated, too broad and thick to fit the tiny slot, on the can-opener blade there's a finer, narrower screwdrive tip that he'd never particularly noticed, evidently designed for just such employment. "Ah, those Swiss," he natters happily: "I hope our army never has to cross knives with their army. Voilà!" He displays the minuscule part in the palm of his hand. "We lose this one, we've still got a spare. The patient, please."

"The side-piece is up in our room . . ."

No matter, he replies; he can anyhow test the threads. Better yet, they'll start a new fashion. In less than a minute he has installed a hot pink leftside earpiece in place of the absent black one. "If the screw fits, wear it," he proposes. Or he can restore the original next time they're in their room; or she can go pink both port and starboard; or they can mix-and-match each time she takes her shades off to bestride him. "Whenever you need a little you-know-what," he concludes, presenting her with the odd-looking but perfectly serviceable specs. "On with the story?"

To his dismay, he sees she's weeping and shaking her head. For a moment he fears he's done something amiss — but now she takes in both her hands not the sunglasses but *his* hand, and covers it with tears and kisses, sobbing the most soul-wrenched, soul-wrenching sobs that he has ever in his innocent life heard the human animal give forth, although in truth it is capable of much greater.

The loser of those serendipitously found sunglasses, Mme Jacqueline Masson of Lyons, France, is, as it happens, neither young or currently bikini'd nor a miss; nor was she frolicking with a boyfriend in the surf at time of loss, although she has been and done all the above in years gone by. A veteran member of Club Mediterranée, at age fifty she has vacationed in some two dozen of that organization's resorts over as many winters. This is, however, her first visit to Cancún; she and her husband inclined to the literally Mediterranean clubs or, of the Caribbean ones, those in departments of France, such as Martinique and Guadeloupe. Moreover, it is her first vacation-trip as a widow, in the company of women friends from Lyons instead of her dear Bertrand, a physician in that city who succumbed to leukemia just about this time last year. Three days into this experiment, she supposes it's going neither well nor badly. Her two friends, somewhat younger (one recently divorced, the other "on holiday" from spouse and children), have been consistently animated, even festive — in part no doubt to keep her own spirits up. They have flirted harmlessly with the handsome young Gentils Organisateurs who manage the sports and other activities; they've tisked together at the rowdy American teenagers and the resort's cuisine, which is generally inferior to that of the clubs they're used to and is directed, they're convinced, at less discriminating Yankee and Canadian appetites. They've done aerobics and yoga and archery and tennis and have even tried windsurfing. In amused defiance of Mexican law (nobody seems really to care), they have declared a certain stretch of beach at the far end of the resort Topless, and have been gratified to see half a dozen other women guests of various ages and nationalities follow their bare-breasted lead. Solange, the divorcée, today even proposed escalation to total nudity; proud of her still-sleek derrière, she wears bikini bottoms with only the tiniest of triangles in front and a mere string up the cleft behind, but even that, she has reminded them, is more than they would be cumbering themselves with at Guadeloupe's Caravelle or Martinique's Buccaneer Creek.

"Vive la France," Edith agreed, and although her body at forty-six is holding up less well than Jacqueline's at fifty, not to mention Solange's at forty, she took the lead in going bottomless on the spot — which happened to be hip-deep in the gentle surf.

"Pour la patrie!" Solange cheered, and was soon brandishing her famous thong-bottom over her head like a banner.

"Liberté, égalité, sororité," Jacqueline affirmed, and bent to follow suit just as a somewhat larger wave pushed her offbalance. Hobbled at the ankles by her dropped bikini, she tumbled with a little whoop and was unable simultaneously to slip her feet out of the garment and to hold her sunglasses in place. By when she regained her footing, the swimsuit-bottom was in hand, the glasses were gone, and all three women were laughing merrily.

"Là, là!" Solange pointed at a hot pink flash on the sandstirred bottom, and redoubtable Edith dived for it, but the undertow of the approaching next wave swept the glasses out of sight. Their loser shrugged: Tant pis. She would be stopping at the boutique anyhow before dinner, for postcards, and would buy another pair. A trifle.

But in fact the little loss provokes an inward sigh: She bought those particular sunglasses in Agadir, Morocco, five or six years back, when at Bertrand's urging they spent a few days at the old original Club Med there, and they subsequently became her unofficial beach-holiday specs. Her marriage, she supposes, was not extraordinarily satisfying, but it was at least ordinarily so; she misses it and her always-too-busy husband terribly (his terminal illness was their most time together since their honeymoon). Her grown son, the image of his father, rather bores her, and his wife she can scarcely abide. As for her women-friends, bless them, they were altogether more enjoyable as supplementary companions than they are as the principal ones that, faute de mieux, they have become for her; Solange is quite naturally more involved with her current lover back home, Edith with both her husband *and* her current lover back home, than either is with her. The naked trio now wades ashore, animatedly disagreeing en route to their towel-spread lounge chairs whether the several American and two Italian members of their unacknowledged topless sorority will presently join them in bottomlessness or whether the not-unhandsome Mexican security guard at the resort's perimeter (who has plainly observed but so far chosen to ignore their rule-flouting) will feel moved to nip this escalation in the bud, so to speak.

Jacqueline Masson supposes that she'll become accustomed to the horrid emptiness of her present life and gradually fill it with other interests. Just now, however, she is so bored with its pointlessly ongoing story that she wishes she could simply close and toss it like a tiresome book — the way that sexy American girl, at the moment the women pass, tosses her paperback onto the sand beside the molded plastic beach chair in which she has been lolling like Venus on the halfshell, pulls her Oakland A's baseball cap down over her face, and rests her head on her upraised arms, lifting her perfect breasts as if to make them declare, "Here we are, guys; resist us if you can."

That *as if* is not Mme Masson's: She takes only the most perfunctory woman-to-woman notice of that brace of maraschino-topped vanilla sundae specials and then, with her companions, exits this narrative to deal with her unenviable own (while, just offshore, the moderate undercurrent tumbles like a vagrant subtext a certain pair of hot-pink sunglasses along the sandy sea-floor, leisurely under the moored Mistral sailboards and Laser sailboats, among the feet of bathers at the central swimming area marked with floats to warn off water-skiers and windsurfers, thence down-beach toward where another rule-flouter has dragged a lounge chair over the low-fenced bank from the landscaped lawn of the guest-compounds down that way). No: Those salivary tropes are courtesy of William Allen Wentworth III, American teenager for the four months remaining till his twentieth birthday, for whom the spectacle of three middle-aged French or French-Canadian (anyhow French-speaking) women wading merrily naked from the gentle surf merely makes more delectable the *Playboy*-centerfoldworthy blonde in orange bikini pants and Oakland A's cap, off whom he has scarcely been able to take his eyes for the past three-quarters of an hour. Praise God for sunglasses, which permit one shamelessly to ogle those Häagen-Dazs double scoops from thirty feet away while pretending to draft a letter to one's parents, back in Cincinnati, Ohio, explaining why, after a prolonged soul-search, one has decided to drop out of the University of Virginia in one's sophomore year in order — after a bit of R&R south of the border on the last of one's "college" inheritance from Grandpa Bill — to pursue what one is all but certain now is one's true calling: the management not of Wentworth Office Systems, Inc., the half-century-old family firm, but of sound-and-light effects for heavy-metal rock concerts. Although he shares the lanky build and troubled facial complexion of those rowdy Yank youngsters tut-tutted by Mme Masson, likewise their unseasoned mien and their currently de rigueur uniform of clunky black basketball shoes (unlaced), long baggy shorts, oversize T-shirt, and backwards ball-cap, Bill Three is a polite and rather shy boy, actually, indifferently successful with girls, more at ease with the unambiguous signal lamps, switches, and meters of an electronic console than with the complexly voltaged interactions of his peers. He has had his eye increasingly on Miss February (so he can't help thinking of the awesome blonde in the Oakland A's cap) since her arrival yesterday — Bill himself is three days into his unauthorized vacation — and has spent most of today virtually stalking her, so taken is he with her physical beauty and, more and more, with the way she handles herself. Among his impressions:

—"American" as she looks (to William the Third, this adjective still reflexively connotes white Anglo derivation, although he certainly knows better and gets along quite agreeably with his peers of other ethnicity), her name has an exotic, sort of Middle Eastern sound in his ears, at least as it's pronounced by the Chef du Village and other G.O.s with whom he has seen her speaking animatedly from time to time, both in English and in French: Jedee, Zhedí, something like that.

—Like himself, she's unaccompanied; she has doubtless been assigned a roommate, as has he (Bill scarcely sees his from one day to the next), but she prefers to move about on her own. More gregarious and athletic than himself, she has been observed by him playing power volleyball on the beach (she sets up a mean spike), dancing energetically at the disco, and laughing and chatting with the G.O.s and her fellow G.M.s (Gentils Membres) in the buffet-style main restaurant. Nevertheless, she appears to be essentially content with her own company: While most of their coevals lounge sociably about at poolside between activities, Bill takes it as a mark of their shared independent-spiritedness that Zhedí, like him, prefers the uncrowded far end of the beach. Enchanting as is her meticulous sun-lotioning of that perfect body, as yet untanned, in his opinion she is not displaying herself to encourage approach; she's simply taking the sun, reading and communing with herself between sessions of physical and social activity. He admires that, as also the unaffected friendliness of her conversation a while ago with the similarly topless and not at all bad-looking Italian or Latino woman nearby, whose handsome brown-nippled jugs the young man classifies as more coffee-almond-fudge than vanilla; Ms. Feb evidently doesn't regard other attractive females ipso facto as rivals. Bill's sense of her, moreover—but he'll readily grant that here his imagination is running free—is that she herself goes topless not out of exhibitionism (like that older French trio) but simply for the pleasures of nonrestraint and, perhaps, unaggressive nonconformity.

—She has, withal, has Ms. Zhedí/Jedee/Whatever, an air of unassuming self-possession and general maturity for her age that young B Three (as his Virginia musician-friends call him) finds almost as impressive as her lovely face and magnificent near-nude body: a refreshing absence of affectation that both encourages and intimidates him. He guesses she's a year or two older than himself, and feels that

325

differential as acutely as he used to back in high-school days. Could she possibly find him interesting? Just possibly, he decides: In a freshman-year computer-science class at U Va, he was befriended by a girl less striking than Miss February but quite good-looking all the same who actually asked *him* out before he could ask her; they had "related" with an ease and reciprocal interest unprecedented in his experience, and might well have gotten it on as a couple if he hadn't still been honorably carrying a torch for Karen Baker, his high-school girlfriend (who turned out to be already involved with another guy, at her own university, in Vermont).

At exactly this juncture in our narrative, Chance presents William Allen Wentworth III with a chance indeed to test this possibility. As the three topless — and now bottomless! — French-speaking ladies emerged laughing from the surf some moments ago and strolled past Zhedí en route to their beach chairs, she casually dropped her paperback onto the sand beside her, lay back in her own chair, pulled her ball-cap down over her face, and tucked her hands behind her head, with the aforenoted salivary effect on the observer. A breeze now ruffles the leaves of that book and blows a loose page free of it, almost directly toward our Bill; he tosses aside his clipboard with the half-drafted letter of explanation to his parents, piles out of his lounge chair, and makes a diving interception before the precious leaf can flutter past him down the beach and maybe into the water.

Gotcha! he exults to himself. He brushes sand from his shorts, restraightens his cap (Cincinnati Reds, a different league altogether from Oakland's; they might discuss that), carefully uncrumples the short-stopped paper, and considers how best to head for first base. Neither Miss F. nor the Italian / Latino woman nor the Frenchies appear to have noticed his flurry of action. His impulse is straightforwardly to return the book-page — "Excuse me, ma'am; this is yours, I think" — and, depending on her reaction, take it from there. That's how his buddy Fred Sims in Charlottesville would do it, drummer and backup singer with the Cold Fusion and cocksman extraordinaire: "If she doesn't cover her tits when you say hello," Fred would advise him, "you're home free, man." On the other hand, it might make better sense to wait until she puts her top back on before approaching her: "Didn't want to bother you while you were catching the rays," etc. (wink wink). He bets she'd appreciate his thoughtfulness.

To gather his nerve and consider his options, he returns to his chair, smooths the page out on his clipboard, and scans it; some idea of what she's reading might give him a good opener. Although B Three himself reads next to nothing as a rule except from video display terminals, and did poorly in his college literature courses (which anyhow had more to do with ethnic and gender politics than with art), and although he takes for granted that what isn't electronic isn't relevant except maybe historically, he has from time to time enjoyed specimens of science fiction and "cyberpunk"; maybe he and she can discuss that. From his monitoring of Jedí/Jaydee, he can't hazard a guess at her taste in books—but then, neither his life-experience nor his imagination affords him much sense of the range of possibilities, either in literature or in the reading proclivities of young women.

Out of context, at least, neither side of pp. 331/332 (so the leaf is numbered, bottom center) makes much sense to its present reader. A more knowledgeable and perceptive eye than B Three's might register that since the leaf's *recto* (331) happens to conclude one chapter of or selection from the overall text, and the *verso* (332) therefore to begin another, the title of the book itself—which would normally appear as a running head on the left-hand, even-numbered page—is missing; further, that inasmuch as no author's name appears under the (un-numbered) title of the item commencing on 332, the unnamed book must consist of articles, stories, or whatever by a single (unnamed) hand rather than by various authors. Neither a novel-page on the one hand, then (if it's fiction at all), nor an anthology-page on the other. What Bill registers is simply that the lines constituting page 331 (under the running sub-head STORIES OF OUR LIVES) read less like fiction than like . . . Bill can't say what. The page comprises a clutch of rhetorical fragments, concluding with *Rwanda, Haiti, Bosnia, Kurdistan. The doomed Marsh Arabs. The web of the world.*

Over *his* head.

Page 332, perhaps because it opens a missing text rather than closing one, is rather more intelligible, though scarcely less baffling. *I'm holding*, it begins (under the quotation-marked title "*Hold on, there*"), and a sort of dialogue ensues:

> "*That fellow's Page Whatever ended with* The web of the world?"
> *So the story goes.*
> "*And the next page says* 'Hold on, there'?"
> *Et cetera. The web of the world.*

"What's going on here?"

Damned if Bill knows, but he's disposed to be impressed by anything associated with Ms. Zhedí-Feb over yonder, who has risen yet a notch higher in his estimation for presumably understanding and maybe even enjoying such stuff. Brains, too!

"Bonjour, Zhayr*dee!*" he hears called now in rich baritone — he hadn't noticed the *r* sound in her name before, actually overriding the *d* — and there's stocky, sun-browned, black-curled Marcel, the much-muscled and high-spirited Chef du Village, in his round-lensed, wire-rimmed specs, his shell necklace, and the bikini swim-briefs that he and all the other non-American G.O.s prefer to boxer trunks, not to mention knee-length "jams."

"Bonjour, Marcel," Miss Feb replies smoothly, once she has lifted her cap to see who's saluting her. Just as smoothly, as Mar-*sayl* hunkers beside her chair to exchange pleasantries (he patrols the beach twice daily, Bill has observed, socializing with the G.M.s), she fetches from behind her back the orange bra of her swimsuit and unhurriedly dons it. Bye-bye, sweet Häagen-Dazzlers.

"You weel be on zuh red *team* in tomorrow's games, okay?" Marcel amiably proposes, and displays a handful of the colored yarn wristbands used to distinguish the competing teams in the Club's weekly "olympics."

"S'il vous plaît," Zhayrdee replies in pert and perfectly accented French, so it sounds to B Three at least. Then she adds, in her pure network American, "Wherever I'm needed."

"Red *team*," Marcel affirms. "We meet at zuh volley*ball* at ten o'clock, okay?"

"Entendu." She obligingly extends her right wrist for banding, and with her left hand adjusts her hair while the Chef du Village ties on the red yarn. The pair then chat awhile further in French, less jocularly (she even shows him what she's reading, and Marcel makes Gallic exclamations), before bidding each other cordial au revoir.

The heart of William Allen Wentworth III is stirred by an emotion complex and potentially dangerous to his self-esteem. He understands not a word of the pair's conversation, nor would he have if it had been in any other language than his own. For perhaps the first time, it occurs to him that it would be desirable — that it would be, in very truth, more *cool*—if such were not the case; if he could converse easily, animatedly, and seriously with people of other backgrounds than his. It is not finally difficult for him to acknowledge that a fellow like himself doesn't stand a snowball's chance in hell with Miss February, not simply because she's almost movie-star gorgeous but because she is (evidently) knowledgeable, sophisticated, and serious as well as "fun-loving"—all to a degree superior to anyone he has ever dated or been at all close to, the Virginia computer-science girl included. It is quite another matter, however, for him to see in another light, as now he dimly begins to, how "a fellow like himself" must appear to the likes of Zhayrdee and Marcel. When and if that light becomes clearer, he may chasteningly understand that real "cool" consists in impressive competencies together with firm principles and a degree of worldliness—that is to say, in character, capability, and polish—rather than in any particular costume and attitude; that to the excellent likes of Jerdí, nothing could be less cool than to be "cool" by his and Fred Sims's standards; that, in fact, he probably appears to her ridiculous: a clown, a creep.

"Red *team*?" Marcel is cheerfully asking him now, having resumed his tour of the beach.

"Nah, I guess not."

"You don't want to play? Is just for fun, okay?"

What a dork he thinks I am, thinks wretched Bill, and lamely smiles and says again, "Guess not, thanks."

"So," the Chef du Village says with a shrug, already scanning down the line. "May*be* you change your mind later, okay?" To the Italian or Latino girl he now calls "Red *team*?" She flashes teasingly at him her blue wrist-yarn and calls something back in what sounds to Bill like Italian but might as well be Greek. Marcel replies animatedly in the same tongue and goes to hunker beside *her* lounge chair; the girl doesn't even bother to cover her chocolate-kiss breasts.

Jerdí, Bill glumly observes, has gone back to her book.

For reasons that he is barely equipped to analyze, W.A.W. III will not much enjoy the remainder of his truant holiday. He'll mail to Cincinnati a version of his drop-out letter, return to Charlottesville just in time to join Cold Fusion for an extended gig in Chapel Hill and another in Durham before the band disbands over a feud between drummer and bassist on the one hand and lead guitarist and female vocalist/tambourinist on the other. Thereafter he'll make his way across the

United States of America and back with Fred Sims, picking up random work here and there for a couple of years and eventually mending fences with his indulgent parents. In his mid-twenties he'll enter the family business after all, marry and sire children upon some clone of Karen Baker, and devote the decent balance of his life to his family and to Wentworth Office Systems, Inc.—which enterprise, however, will not prosper under his uninspired stewardship. In years to come he'll remember his abortive road-tour with Cold Fusion as being, in its way, the most satisfying episode in his entire listless life-story. Although his recollection of it decades hence will include his bolting the university and his Cancún escapade, he will not recall his uncharacteristic stalking and ogling of young Ms. Geraldine "Gerri" Fraser of Palo Alto, California — with whom, really, he has next to nothing in common beyond WASP ethnicity and U.S. citizenship. He slumps back into his beach chair, crumples into a ball the sibylline page that was to have been their link, side-arms it onto the sand, pulls his Cincinnati Reds cap over his face, and for a considerable while stares wide-eyed and soul-troubled at its convergent seams and evenly spaced ventilation-grommets.

Ms. Fraser — B.S. Stanford summa cum laude and currently a second-year student at the Johns Hopkins Medical Institutions — may happen to have the face and figure of *Playboy*'s centerfold-of-the-month, but from kindergarten to the present she has undeviatingly aspired to follow in the professional footsteps of her mother and father, an endocrinologist and obstetrician/gynecologist respectively. An accomplished all-round athlete and a serious amateur cellist, she has yet to choose her medical specialty; at age twelve it was pediatrics, at fifteen cardiology. Her love of scientific research inclines her toward a Ph.D. in medicine rather than a straight M.D.; on the other hand, her strong social conscience urges her toward clinical practice. The book to which she has returned is *Médecins sans Frontières*, about the international volunteer physicians' organization thus named, devoted to heroic relief work in Somalia and similarly catastrophized venues; Gerri hopes to serve in that capacity for a year or two after her residency and before embarking on a career of medical research, private practice, or some combination of the two. Although she has lost her bookmark (a page that her current Baltimore boyfriend, a graduate-student apprentice poet at the university's Homewood campus, obligingly ripped from some Postmodernist story-collection that he happened to be perusing when Gerri casually asked him, as the pair were reading in bed, for something with which to mark her place while they make love), she knows quite well where she is, in the *Médecins* book and generally.

Has she even noticed the oddly dressed young fellow with the semi-punk haircut who's been following her about ever since she checked into the resort at her parents' urging for a bit of respite from her workaholism? She has, marginally: He reminds her, a little, of her kid brother back at Stanford, a preppie at heart who however feels compelled to ruffle the parental feathers by flirting with the punk subculture. They all know that Derek will outgrow such affectations; meanwhile, he takes their teasing good-humoredly.

That Mexican security guard, the lineaments of whose impassive face are directly descended from those that inspired the Mayan sculptors of dread Chacmool . . .

That topless young Bolognesa, a stewardess for Alitalia who aspires to be a travel agent in Rome, or perhaps in Milan . . .

The embryo, its existence unknown to both of its parents, busily and quietly multiplying its cells in Barbara Ellison's uterus . . .

Gerri Fraser's ex-lover back in Palo Alto, whose ball-cap she keeps as a souvenir of that pleasant life-episode, although she has switched allegiance to the Orioles and to her new poet-friend, and prefers soccer to baseball anyhow . . .

Franco the senior art historian, just now masturbating pensively before the draperied window of his condominium overlooking the university's lacrosse field, where the women's varsity squad is working out. Mimi Adler's subtextual smile and narrative-ontological question. That Canadian quarter, still unretrieved from the campus grass. That balled-up book-page on the Club Med beach, slowly unballing itself now by the force of its own resiliency like a time-lapse movie of a sprouting mushroom, until another breeze catches and rolls it lightly seaward.

Rwanda, Haiti, Bosnia, Kurdistan. The doomed Marsh Arabs.

The web of the world.

"Hold on, there."

I'm holding.

"That fellow's Page Whatever ended with *The web of the world*?"

So the story goes.

"And the next page says '*Hold on, there*'?"

Et cetera. The web of the world.

"What's going on here?"

Life-stories. Life-or-death stories. Stories-within-stories stories, tails in their own mouths like the snake Ouroboros. Bent back on themselves like time warps.

"Time-tricks, you mean. Temporizings."

Name of the game. You've a better idea?

"Yes."

Forget I asked that question. *He didn't ask that question.*

"Hold on tighter."

He's holding. Everything's on Hold.

Presently: "We've got to just do it."

They. Why?

"*Us*. No more dodges. No more stalling. No more tricks."

More of everything. More more more.

"No. I'll do what I have to; you do what you have to."

What I have to do is talk you out of doing what you have to do. You don't *have* to do what you have to do, you know.

"Who says?"

He says.

"Speak for yourself. She's out of here."

Not yet.

"No? Explain."

He thought she'd never ask. They can't go before they close up shop.

"One more stall."

Name of the game.

Presently: "You win another round. Explain."

His pleasure:

9.

Closing Out the Visit

Good visit, we agree — fine visit, actually, weatherwise and otherwise, everything considered — but as with all visits agreeable and disagreeable its course has run. Time now to get our things together, draw down our stock of consumables, tidy up our borrowed lodgings, savor one last time the pleasures of the place, say good-bye to acquaintances we've made, and move along.

"The *light*," you want to know: "Have we ever seen such light?"

We have not, we agree — none better, anyhow, especially in these dew-bedazzled early mornings and the tawny late afternoons, when sidelit trees and beachfront virtually incandesce, and the view from our rented balcony qualifies for a travel poster. That light is a photon orgy; that light fires the prospect before us as if from inside out. Mediterranean, that light is, in its blue-white brilliance, Caribbean in its raw tenderness, yet paradoxically desert-crisp, so sharp-focusing the whole surround that we blink against our will. That light thrills — and puts us poignantly in mind of others who in time past have savored the likes of it and are no more: the late John Cheever, say, in whose stories light is almost a character, or the nineteenth-century Luminist painters, or for that matter the sun-drunk Euripides of *Alcestis*: "O shining clear day, and white clouds wheeling in the clear of heaven!"

"Such light."

Major-league light. This over breakfast bagels and coffee on the balcony — the end of these Wunderbägeln, freckled with sesame- and poppyseed, as good as any we've tasted anywhere, fresh-baked by the little deli that we discovered early in our visit, in the village not far from "our" beach. So let's polish off this last one, to use up the last of our cream cheese and the final dablet of rough-cut marmalade lifted from the breakfast place downstairs along with just enough packets of sugar to go with the ration of House Blend coffee that we bought from that same jim-dandy deli on Day One, when we were stocking up for our stay. Can't take 'em with us.

"Have we measured out our life in coffee spoons?"

We have, and canny guesstimators we turn out to have been. No more than a spoonful left over, two at most, which we'll leave for the cleanup crew along with any surplus rum, wine, mineral water, fruit juices, hors d'oeuvres, what have we, and I'll bet that the lot won't total a tipsworth by this afternoon's end, checkout time, when we've had our last go-round. Adiós, first-rate bagels and cream cheese and marma-lade, fresh-squeezed juice and fresh-ground coffee, as we've adiósed already our fine firm king-size bed: Here's to sweet seaside sleep, with ample knee- and elbow-room for separateness sans separation! Here's to the dialogue of skin on sufficient square footage of perfect comfort so that the conversation begins and ends at our pleasure, not at some accidental bump in the night. Hasta la vista, maybe, in this instance, as it has become almost our habit here, after an afternoon's outdoorsing, to relish a roll in the air-conditioned hay between hot-tub time and Happy Hour.

***

Our last post-breakfast swim! No pool right under our balcony where we'll be this time tomorrow (no balcony, for that matter), nor world-class beach a mere shellsthrow from that pool, nor world-girdling ocean just a wave-lap from that beach, aquarium-clear and aquar-ium-rich in calendar-quality marine life for our leisurely inspection and inexhaustible delight; no scuba gear needed, just a snorkel mask fog-proofed with a rub of jade- or sea-grape leaf from the handsome natural beachscape round about us.

Now, then: Our pool-laps lapped, which is to be our first next plea-sure on this last AM of our visit (not forgetting the routine and paren-thetical but no less genuine satisfactions of post-breakfast defecation and stretching exercises on the bedroom wall-to-wall: Let's hear it for strainless Regularity and the ever-fleeting joy of able-bodiedness!)? A quick reconnaissance, perhaps, of "our" reef, while we're still wet? Bit of a beachwalk, maybe, upshore or down? Following which, since this visit has been by no means pure vacation, we'll either "beach out" for the balance of the morning with some serious reading and note-taking or else put in a session at our make-do "desks" (balcony table for you, with local whelk- and top-shells as paperweights; dinette table for me, entirely adequate for the work we brought along) before we turn to whatever next wrap-up chore or recreation — not forgetting, en passant, to salute the all but unspeakable good fortune of a life whose pleasures we're still energetic enough to work at and whose work, wage-earning and otherwise, happens to be among our chiefest pleasures.

Tennis, you say? Tennis it is, then, and work be damned for a change; we've earned that indulgence. You're on for a set, on those brand-new courts at our virtual doorstep, with a surface that sends our soles to heaven, pardon the pun, and so far from pooping our leg-muscles for the morning, has seemed rather to inspire them for the scenic backcountry bike ride up into the village for provisions, in the days when we were still in the provisioning mode. Extraordinary, that such tournament-quality courts appear to've gone virtually unused except by us — like those many-geared mountain bicycles free for the borrowing and for that matter the pool and spa and, we might as well say, our beach and its ocean, or ocean and its beach. Where *is* everybody? we asked ourselves early in the visit: Does the rest of the world know something that we don't?

"Vice versa," you proposed and we jointly affirmed, and soon enough we counted it one more blessing of this many-blessinged place that our fellow visitors were so few, as who but the programmatically gregarious would not: those couples who for one cause or another require for their diversion (from each other, we can't help suspecting) a supply of new faces, life-histories, audiences for their household anecdotes. Well for such that the world abounds in busy places; well for us who binge on each other's company to've found not only that company but a place as unabundant in our fellows as it is rich in amenities: just enough other visitors, and they evidently like-minded, for visual variety on the beach, for exchange of tips on snorkel-spots and eateries, for the odd set of doubles on those leg-restoring courts, and for the sense of being, after all, not alone in the restaurants and on the dance floor, at the poolside bar and out along the so-convenient reef, in this extraordinary place in general, in our world.

Auf Wiedersehen now, tennis courts! Arrivederci, bikes and bike-trails, charming little village of excellent provisions agreeably vended by clerks neither rude nor deferential, but — like the restaurant servers, reception-desk people, jitney drivers, even groundskeepers and maintenance staff of this jim-dandy place — cheerful, knowledgeable, unaffectedly "real."

***

Lunchtime! You incline to the annex restaurant, up on the ice-plant-planted headland overlooking "our" lagoon, a sweet climb through bougainvillea, hibiscus, and oleander to the awninged deck where frigate-birds hang in the updraft from tradewinds against the cliff and bold little bananaquits nibble sugar from diners' hands. I incline to a quicker, homelier "last lunch," so to speak: fresh conch ceviche, say, from our pal the beachfront vendor down by the snorkel shack (who knows precisely how much lime juice is just enough lime juice), washed down with his home-squeezed guava nectar or a pint of the really quite creditable local lager. But who can say no to the stuffed baby squid and crisp white wine up at our dear annex, with its ambiance of seabirds and fumaroles, its low-volume alternation of the sensuous local music with that of the after-all-no-less-sensuous High Baroque, and its long view through coconut palms out over the endless sea?

"Endless *ocean*," you correct me as we clink goblets of the palest, driest Chablis this side of la belle France and toast with a sip, eyes level and smiling, our joint House Style, which would prohibit our saying *endless sea* even if we hadn't already said *seabirds* just a few lines earlier. *Sea* is a no-no (one of many such) in our house, except in such casual expressions as *at sea* or *on land and sea* or *moderate sea conditions*, and of course such compounds as *seaside, seascape, seaworthy*, and *seasick*, not to mention the aforementioned *seabirds*. One does not say, in our house, "What a fine view of the sea!" or "Don't you just love the smell of the sea?" or "Let's take a dip in the sea," all which strike our housely ears as affected, "literary," fraught with metaphysical pathos. Thus do longtime partners of like sensibility entertain themselves and refine their bond with endless such small concurrences and divergences of taste, or virtually endless such. But here's an end to our self-imposed ration of one wine each with lunch, especially in the tropics and only on such high occasions as this extended work/play visit; and there's an end to our unostentatious, so-delightful annex dinery, as pleasing in its fare and service as in its situation. Au revoir, admirable annex!—or adieu, as the case will doubtless prove.

Next next next? A whole afternoon, almost, before us, whether of sweet doing or of just-as-sweet doing nothing, since we have foresightedly made our departure arrangements early: scheduled the jitney, packed all packables except our last-day gear, settled our accounts, put appropriate tips in labeled envelopes for appropriate distribution, penned final hail-and-farewell cards to our far-flung loved ones, and posted on the minifridge door a checklist of last-minute Don't Forgets that less organized or more shrug-shouldered travelers might smile at, but that over a long and privileged connection has evolved to suit our way of going and effectively to prevent, at least to minimize, appalled brow-clapping at things inadvertently left undone or behind and too late remembered.

This air: such air, such air. Let's not forget not simply to breathe but to be breathed by this orchid-rich, this sun-fired, spume-fraught air! Off with our beach tops, now that we're lunched; off with our swimsuits, while we're at it, either at the shaded, next-to-vacant nudie-beach around the upshore bend — where we innocently admire lower-mileage bodies than our own (though no fitter for their age) of each's same and complementary sex; likewise each other's, trim still and plea-sure-giving; likewise each's more than serviceable own, by no means untouched by time, mischance, and vigorous use, but still and all, still and all . . .—or else at our idyllic, thus far absolutely private pocket-beach in the cove two promontories farther on.

Pocket-beach it is. We lotion each other with high numbers, linger-ing duly at the several Lingerplatzen; we let the sweet tradewinds heavy-breathe us and then the omnisexual ocean have at us, salt-tonguing our every orifice, crease, and cranny as we slide through it with leisurely abandon: hasteless sybarites in no greater hurry to reach "our" reef for a last long snorkel than we would and will be to reach, in time's fullness and the ad lib order of our program, our last orgasm of the visit.

Good wishes, local fishes, more various, abundant, and transfixing than the local flowers, even. Tutti saluti, dreamscape coral, almost more resplendent than these fish. Weightless as angels, we float an aimless celestial hoursworth through spectacular submarinity, not forgetting to bid particular bye-bye to the shellfish and those calcareous miracles their shells, their shells, those astonishments of form and color, first among equals in this sun-shimmerish panoply, and virtual totems in our house. Faretheewells to our fair seashells, no more ours in the last analysis than are our bodies and our hours — borrowed all, but borrowed well, on borrowed time.

"Time," you sigh now, for the last time side-by-siding in our post-Jacuzzi, pre-Happy Hour, king-size last siesta; no air conditioning this time, but every sliding door and window wide to let the ceaseless easterlies evaporate the expected sweat of love. "Time time time."

Time *times* time, I try to console you, and myself. World enough and time.

"Never enough."

There's all there is. Everlasting Now, et cet.

"Neverlasting now."

Yes, well: The best-planned lays, as the poet says, gang aft a-gley.

"Not what I meant."

Appreciated. Notwithstanding which, however . . .

We beached out, you see, post-snorkelly, first in the altogether of that perfect pocket-beach on our oversize tripleterry beach towels, thick as soft carpeting, fresh from the poolside towel dispensary; then on palm- and palapa-shaded lounge chairs on the beach before the pool beneath our balcony, books in hand but ourselves not quite, the pair of us too mesmerized and tempus-fugity to read. Fingers laced across the beach-bag between our paralleled chaises longues, we mused beyond the breakers on the reef, horizonward, whither all too soon *et cetera*, and our joint spirits lowered after all with the glorifying late-day sun, so that when time came to say sayonara to that scape, to stroll the palm-shadowed stretch to our last hot soak and thence, pores aglow, to take the final lift to passion's king-size square, we found (we find) that we can't (*I* can't) quite rise to the occasion.

"Me neither."

We do therefore not *have sex* — that locution another house-style no-no for a yes-yes in our house — but rather make last love in love's last mode: by drifting off in each other's arms, skin to skin in the longing light, no less joyful for our being truly blue, likewise vice versa or is it conversely, the balmy air barely balming us.

I pass over what, in this drowsy pass, we dream.

Have we neglected in our close-out prep to anticipate a snooze sufficiently snoozish, though alas not postcoital, to carry us right through cocktails to miss-the-jitney time? We have not. No mañana hereabouts for thee and me: On the dot sounds our pre-set, just-in-case Snoozalarm (which in our half-dreams we have half been waiting for); half a dozen dots later comes our backup front-desk wake-up call — Thanks anyhow, Unaffectedly "Real" and pretty punctual paging-person — and we've time time time for the last of the rum or le fin du vin or both, with the end of the Brie on the ultimate cracotte, while we slip into our travel togs and triplecheck our passage papers, button buttons snap snaps zip zippers lock locks. One last look, I propose, but you haven't heart for it nor do I sans you, hell therefore with it we're off to see the blizzard heck or high water. Adieu sweet place adieu, hell with it adieu adieu.

Time to go.

"*That says it. Time to go.*"

Time goes without saying.
"So should we. Pack it in. Get it done with."
Time takes care of all that. In no time.

Presently: "*Time time time*, she sighs again. Boyoboy."
Time *times* time, he gently *et ceteras*.
"So let's say they've done all that close-out stuff. Now what?"
He'll think of something. Give him time.

Presently: "Three two one zero."
Right. Good-bye time.
"Sounds almost as if you really mean it this time."
Presently: "*Do* you really mean it?"
I do, as they said to each other once upon a time. E.g.:

10.

Good-bye to the Fruits

He agreed to die — stipulating only that he first be permitted to re-behold and bid good-bye to those of Earth's fruits that he had particularly enjoyed in his fortunate though not-extraordinary lifetime.

What he had in mind, in the first instance, were such literal items as apples and oranges. Of the former, the variety called Golden Delicious had long been his favorite, especially those with a blush of rose on their fetchingly speckled yellow-green cheeks. Of the latter — but then, there's no comparing apples to oranges, is there, nor either of those to black plums: truly incomparable, in his opinion, on the rare occasions when one found them neither under- nor overripe. Good-bye to all three, alas; likewise to bananas, whether sliced transversely atop unsweetened breakfast cereal, split longitudinally under scoops of frozen yogurt, barbecued in foil with chutney, or blended with lime juice, rum, and Cointreau into frozen daiquiris on a Chesapeake August late afternoon.

Lime juice, yes: Farewell, dear zesty limes, squeezed into gins-and-tonics before stirring and over bluefish fillets before grilling; adieu too to your citric cousins the lemons, particularly those with the thinnest of skins, always the most juice-ful, without whose piquance one could scarcely imagine fresh seafood, and whose literal zest was such a challenge for kitchen-copilots like himself to scrape a half-tablespoons-worth of without getting the bitter white underpeel as well. Adieu to black seedless grapes for eating with ripe cheeses and to all the nobler stocks for vinting, except maybe Chardonnay. He happened not to share the American Yuppie thirst for Chardonnay; too over-flavored for his palate. Give him a plain light dry Chablis any time instead of Chardonnay, if you can find so simple a thing on our restaurant wine-lists these days. And whatever happened to soft dry reds that don't cost an arm and a leg on the one hand, so to speak, or, on the other, taste of iron and acid?

But this was no time for such cavils: Good-bye, blessed fruit of the vineyard, a dinner without which is like a day without *et cetera*. Good-bye to the fruits of those other vines, in particular the strawberry, if berries are properly to be called fruits, the tomato, and the only melon he would really miss, our local cantaloupe. Good-bye to that most sexual of fruits, the guava; to peaches, plantains (fried), pomegranates, and papayas; to the fruits of pineapple field and coconut tree, if nuts are fruits and coconuts nuts, and of whatever it is that kiwis grow on. As for pears, he had always thought them better canned than fresh, as Hemingway's Nick Adams says of apricots in the story "Big Two-Hearted River"—but he couldn't see kissing a can good-bye, so he supposed that just about did the fruits (he himself preferred his apricots sun-dried rather than *either* fresh or canned).

The *literal* fruits, he meant, of course. But surely it wouldn't overstretch either the term or anyone's patience to include in these terminal bye-byes such other edibles of the vegetable kingdom as parboiled fresh asparagus served cold with sesame oil and soy sauce, sorely to be missed in the afterlife if there were one and if food-consumption were not a feature of it; likewise tossed salads of most sorts except fruit salads, which for some reason never appealed to him and to whose principal ingredients he had severally made his goodbyes already, Q.E.D. Also pasta, if pasta's a vegetable; he had long been a fan of pasta in all its protean varieties, in particular the spiriferous and conchiform but including also the linear and even the non-Italian, such as Japanese "cellophane" noodles (which he presumed to be some sort of pasta despite their transparency) and German Spätzle. Moreover, if he remained untouched by the popularity of Chardonnay among his countrymen, he was a charter member of the Yankee pesto-lovers association. Addio, then, pasta con pesto! Faithful to his homely origins, however, he insisted on equal farewell-time for the simple potato, whether boiled, baked, mashed, or French-fried with unhealthy but delicious salt and vinegar—no ketchup, please—and the inelegant Fordhook lima bean, which, out of some childhood impulse to diversify his mother's simple cookery, he used to stir into his creamed chipped beef or mix with his mashed white potatoes and pan-gravy on the plate beside his southern-fried chicken: culinary items to which he had bidden good-bye decades ago and so needn't clutter his present agenda with. Friendly and nutritious veggies, vale! Although he never quite achieved vegetarianism and to this ultimate or all-but-ultimate hour continued to regard you essentially as the garnish to his dinner entrée, you are a garnish that he would miss almost as much as table wine if missing things were posthumously possible. Good-bye, garnis.

Moving nearer the center of life's plate, as it were, with only a bit more stretching of the parameters (if parameters can be said to be stretched at all by centripetal motion), might one not add—*must* one not add—to one's hail-and-farewell list the fruits of the sea, succulent in all languages but to his ear especially so in those of the Romance family: fruits de mer, frutti di mare, frutas de mar, and however it goes in sensuous Portuguese. He could, reluctantly, get by without red meat (grilled lamb chops, especially, it pained him to contemplate giving up, seasoned with salt, pepper, crushed garlic, and ground cumin), and only a tad less reluctantly without the flesh of light-fleshed fowl, in particular the breast-meat of barbecued Cornish hens. But finfish and shellfish of all varieties had for so long been at the center of his diet, it was scarcely an exaggeration to say that his flesh, by the time I tell of, was largely composed of theirs. If one had been permitted to slip in a request among one's farewell waves and kisses, his would have been that his remains be somehow returned uncombusted to his home waters, there to be recycled to the fauna whereupon he had so thrived and thence on out into the general marine food-chain. Rockfish, bluefish, sea-trout, shad; blue crabs, oysters, scallops, mussels, clams; billfish, tuna, and other steakfish; octopus and squid, in particular the stuffed baby Spanish variety called *chiperones*; sushi and sashimi of every sort; and, last because first among equals, that king of crustaceans, the New England lobster, *Homarus americanus*, whose spiny Caribbean cousin was in his estimation but an overrated poor relative, though undeniably handsome. Adieu to you, noble Down East lobster, all-too-rare-because-so-damned-expensive treat, that shouldst be steamed not a minute longer than *half* the time recommended by

James Beard and most other seafood-cookbook authors. Ten minutes tops for a less-than-two-pounder, mark these parting words, or the animal has suffered and died in vain. "A quick death, God help us all," declares the character Belacqua in Samuel Beckett's story "Dante and the Lobster"—to which the story's narrator replies, in propria persona, *It is not.* (There is, by the way, a little-known technique for apparently hypnotizing and perhaps even anesthetizing lobsters on Death Row by standing the luckless creatures on their heads in a certain way, like arthropodous yogis, on one's kitchen-countertop. Had he time, had he world enough and time . . .)

But as the true soul-food is beauty, who could leave this vale of delights without farewelling at least a few representative examples of those flora and fauna that one eats only with one's eyes, and in some instances one's ears and nose? He meant, e.g., the very nearly overgorgeous fish and shellfish of saltwater aquarium and coral reef, whether viewed firsthand or on public-television nature shows and *National Geographic* photo-spreads; the astonishing birds of tropical latitudes and the butterflies of even our temperate zone, particularly the Monarchs hanging in migratory clusters from California eucalypts between November and March; the unabashed sexuality of flowers and the patient dignity of trees, large trees especially; certain landscapes, seascapes, skyscapes, cityscapes, desert- and marshscapes—in particular, he supposed, for himself, if he had been obliged as perhaps he was to choose only one of the above to pay final respects to, the vast tide marshes of his natal county: marshes which, while considerably less vast than they had been even in his childhood, remained still reasonably vast as of this valediction—always assuming that one was permitted to valedict. Nursery of the Chesapeake and, by semi-coincidence, of their present valedictorian ("semi" in that it might be presumed to have been unpredestined that he be born and raised in or near the marshlands of Maryland's lower Eastern Shore, but it was no coincidence that, he having been therein B & R'd, those home marshes loomed so large in his imagination, if a marsh can properly be said to loom. For the sake of variety and euphony, he had been going to say "home bogs" just then instead of "home marshes," but it suddenly occurred to him for the first time, surprisingly enough at his age and stage, what the difference is between bog and marsh, particularly tide marsh. As between *marsh* and *swamp*, he confesses, the geological distinction eludes him still, although their connotations surely differ) . . .

Marshes, he was saying; saying good-bye, good-bye, good-bye to. Good-bye, still-considerable and fecund wetlands, at once fragile and resilient, neither land nor sea, symbolic equally of death and of regeneration, your boundaries ever changing, undefined, negotiable, your horizontality as ubiquitous as your horizon is horizontal, etc., etc.— and withal so eloquently sung, in your East Anglican manifestation, by the novelist Graham Swift in his novel *Waterlands* (not to mention by the novelist Charles Dickens in such of his novels as *Bleak House, David Copperfield,* and *Great Expectations*) that one would scarcely have presumed to do more than refer the attender of these farewells to those novelists' novels, were it not that as between East Anglia and the Eastern Shore of Maryland, the differences are at least as noteworthy, even unto their fenlands, as are any similarities. To "his" dear spooky, mudflat-fragrant marshes, then, a cross-fingered fare thee well.

But he could not leave the subject of marshes (hard enough to leave the marshes themselves) without a word of concern for the Marsh Arabs: the Madan people, he meant, whose fortune it had been for four thousand years to inhabit the marshes at the confluence of the Tigris and Euphrates rivers, in southern Iraq, and whose current misfortune it was to have been, for the past few hundred of those four thousand years, at least nominally Shiite Muslims who — self-reliant and wary of outsiders, like most marsh-dwellers — resisted the despotic Baathist regime of Saddam Hussein and were therefore, as one prepared to make these rhetorical farewells, being systematically exterminated by that regime via the dreadful expedient of *drying up their marshes* by diverting the inflow of those primordial, civilization-cradling rivers: an ecological atrocity on a par with the Iraqis' firing of the Kuwaiti oil fields. Good-bye indeed, one feared and fears, to the oldest continuous culture on the planet, numerous of whose communities have lived generation after generation on floating islands of spartina, continually replenishing them with fresh layers of reed on top as the bottom layers decompose and recycle; good-bye, poor hapless Marsh Arabs about to be destroyed in an eyeblink of time while still believing, after four millennia of harmlessly habitating your marshes, that somewhere in their labyrinthine fastness lies the *Arabian Nights*-like island of Hufaidh, complete with enchanted palaces of gold and crystal, Edenic gardens, and the Sindbadish aspect of transforming into babbling lunatics any marshfarers who stumble upon it. May all destroyers of marshes serendipitously so stumble! Nothing quite like Hufaidh, one supposes, in the solitudinous wetlands of one's home county (only the odd goose blind, muskrat house, and, within living memory, moonshiner's still), though there is an uncanniness about even *their* low-lying, uninhabited islands — to which he truly now bade good-bye and better luck than the Madans'.

No marsh, however, one might say (paraphrasing John Donne), is an island. Indeed, in Nature's seamless web, if one might be permitted to mix metaphors so late in the day, no *island* is an island: When we lose the enchanted isle of Hufaidh by losing the marshes that sustained the culture whose imagination sustained that realm, we lose an item from the general cultural store and thus, figuratively at least, lose a part of ourselves — just as, literally, when we lose Poplar Island, say, in the upper Chesapeake, to the less malign forces of natural erosion (as happened to be happening apace even as he bade these good-byes), we increase the exposure of Tilghman Island, just behind Poplar, to those same forces, *et cetera* if not ad infinitum anyhow to the end of the chapter, as Cervantes's Sancho Panza puts it from time to time in *Don Quixote*: the geological chapter of Chesapeake Bay As We've Known It Since the Last Ice Age, continuously being reconfigured not only over millennia but over the span of a single lifetime (Where now was Sharp's Island, e.g., which he well remembered at the mouth of the Great Choptank River in his boyhood?), whereto — he meant equally that island, that river, that bay, and that lifetime — he now bade good-bye.

In the calm urgency of farewell, he hereabouts noticed, he had inadvertently changed the thrust of this valediction by conflating, in the passage above, the callous despoliation of the natural environment by Saddam Hussein's Baathists (and, Stateside, by the likes of real-estate developers, clear-cutting timberfolk, and toxic dumpers, in which last category our military-industrial complex stood out as a particularly egregious offender) — conflating these, I say, with such "natural" rearrangers of that environ as hurricanes, tornadoes, earthquakes, volcanic eruptions, tsunamis, and suchlike forces, ranging from Earth-destroying asteroidal impact on the scale's high end to the gentle, continuous attrition, on its low, of the mildest rain shower, gentlest wave, softest breeze, mere cellular decay — the inexorable rub of time.

Time, yes, there was the rub: Barely mortal time enough to kiss Earth's fruits hello before we're kissing them good-bye, and here he had so lost himself in the marshes, as it were, hoping perhaps to stumble upon his personal Hufaidh (if he has not stumbled itupon already: See how he babbles!), that he'd not even gotten around yet to Earth's salt, so to speak. Fellow humans! He did not mean, yet, the nearest and dearest of those; they went without saying, although most assuredly not without saying good-bye to, if that unimaginable prospect could be imagined. No: He meant, in the first instance (which is to say the last, in order of importance), those anonymous others just enough of whom kept a restaurant, say, or a street or town or planet, from being unbearably lonely. Good-bye, insignificant others, if he might so put it without offense, understanding that he helped play that background role in your life-narrative as did you in his; would that your numbers were not so burgeoning — by runaway population-growth in some places, demographic shifts in others — as to threaten the biosphere in general and countless particular environs, not excluding his beloved Chesapeake estuarine system.

Farewell next to such only slightly less anonymous but considerably more significant others as ... oh, trash collectors, for example: Never, at any of a lifetimesworth of urban, suburban, and rural addresses, had he had reason to complain of the efficiency of the collection of his trash, both recyclable and non- — no small tribute from one whose profession was the written word. Same went, except for the odd and usually inconsequential glitch, for the several mail carriers and deliverers of daily and Sunday newspapers to his serial places of residence over the decades. What a quiet, civilized pleasure, to step outdoors of a morning in any season, sometimes before first light, and to find one's refuse collected for disposal, one's morning newspaper snugly folded in that way that newspapers are folded for tossing into driveways or tucking into newspaper-boxes, and moreover bagged in (recyclable) plastic if the weather even looked to be inclement — and then, somewhat or much later in the day, depending on where one's address happened to fall on one's postperson's route, to find one's outgoing mail duly picked up and incoming mail delivered. He shall miss that, chaps and ladies so approximately faithful to the motto of your service — or, rather, *should* miss it, if etc. Good-bye and thanks, and may neither rain nor snow nor sleet nor gloom of night *et cetera*. How fortunate it is, Aldous Huxley somewhere remarks, that the world includes people pleased to devote their mortal span to the manufacture and sale of *sausages*, for example, so that those with no interest in that pursuit may nevertheless have their cake and eat it too, if you follow my meaning and possess wherewithal to purchase what, after all, those folk don't give away free.

People, people, people: builders of roadways, tunnels, and bridges, and of reasonably reliable vehicles to drive thereupon, therethrough, thereover; designers and fabricators too of such spirit-lifting artifacts as great art, to be sure, but also for example of jet aircraft in flight — particularly, to this valedictor's eye, those now-classic sweptwinged, rear-engined jetliners viewed passing overhead — likewise of most but not all sailing vessels under sail, of Krups coffeemakers, of Swiss Army knives in the middle range of complexity, of steel-shafted hammers with cushioned grips — in short, of all well-made things both functional and handsome, as agreeable to regard and to handle as to use.

Supreme in this category of human constructions to be fare-welled — so much so, to this fareweller, as to be virtually a category in itself — was that most supple, versatile, and ubiquitous of human-isms, language: that tool that deconstructs and reconstructs its own constructions; that uses and builds its users and builders as they use, build, and build with it. Ta-ta, language, la la language, the very diction of veridiction in this valley valedictory. Adieu, addio, adiós, *et cetera* und so weiter; he could no more bear to say *good-bye* to you than so to say to those nearest dearest, in particular the nearest-dearest, so to say, themof: He meant the without-whom-nothing for him to bid farewell to whom must strain the sine qua non of language even unto sinequa-non-sense. Impossible to do, unthinkable to leave undone, and yet the mere prospect did undo him. Back to the apples! Back to the oranges! He'd say good-bye sooner to himself (he said), and soon enough would, than say it to —

But it went without saying that he had been assuming not that he might say without going, so to say, but say *before* going: say good-bye to the fruits, *et cetera*. Permission granted, surely?

"No."

"I'll say yes to that."

Much obliged indeed.

"Yes to that No, she means, I'm afraid."

Ah, Permission *not* granted, then?

"As the fellow said, 'It is not.' Sorry."

Likewise.

Presently: "I *am* afraid."

Likewise.

"It's getting light out."

So he noticed. Maybe they could sleep a bit now?

"She's so tired she could sleep forever after, if she could sleep."

But she'll settle for a nice nap, yes? Though there's no timetable . . .

"We'll see. Good night, love."

Likewise.

Presently and quietly, fingers crossed: Is she asleep?

11.

Ever After

1.

About human happiness in general and happy marriage in particular, not nearly enough has been written, in Frank Pollard's opinion, of a celebratory character. If *he* were a writer — of novels or of stories, say, such as this one — he would address that deficit, beginning perhaps with a dramatized rebuttal of Tolstoy's famous remark that all happy families are alike. Our Frank, however, is only a retired prep-school American History teacher (whose wife, a successful painter, would hotly contest that self-deprecating *only*): a happy consumer of art and ideas and, for four gratifying decades, their ardent transmitter to the boys of Highland Academy, but never, alas, among their producers.

Frank's experience is that happy *couples*, anyhow, like him and Joan, are alike in few respects beyond their taking much more pleasurable satisfaction than dissatisfaction in themselves, each other, their jobs and projects, their children, if any, their friends and colleagues, their life together — in short, beyond their being happy. Otherwise, they may be as different as apples and aardvarks: gregarious or asocial, profligate or frugal, educated or ignorant, high-energy or low-, Democrat or Republican. His mind is on this subject just now because, among other reasons, he and Joan are stretched out in side-by-side lounge chairs on the night-dark deck of their rented summer cottage at Fenwick Island, Delaware, sipping wine and stargazing, and Frank, for one, has just been vouchsafed an almost overwhelming soul-flood of peace, of grace — of something, anyhow, in that spiritual category.

The time here is deep August, an hour or so before midnight. The seashore air is muggy; dew stands in drops and pudlets on everything outdoors; the Pollards have spread beach towels on their chairs and removed all clothing except underpants, to let their skin breathe. A small white citronella candle in net-covered glass flickers off Frank's lean chest and Joan's ampler, well-bosomed torso. Together with a spray repellent, it's doing a reasonable job of misleading the mosquitoes so abundant after dark on the bay side of this coastal barrier island, especially in calm air. To westward, out over that shallow bay, hangs a first-quarter moon, on which Joan is trying to focus the family binoculars before training them on brilliant Vega, overhead. The day has been hazy-steamy, subtropical, but earlier this evening a thundershower rolled over Delmarva and out to sea; now the sky's clear enough for them to look forward to an annual ritual: toasting with champagne the first meteor of the Perseid Shower (and the end, virtually, of one more pleasant summer's work and play) before turning in for a good-night embrace under their bedroom paddle fan and a peaceful sleep. In years past, they stayed up on these occasions till the small hours, when in ideal conditions the meteor-count might exceed one per minute, all apparently radiating from the constellation Perseus over in the northeast; nowadays they're content with a single sighting, provided it be shared.

Meanwhile, as is also their end-of-evening custom, they're asking each other what was the highlight of each's day. It happens to be Frank who this time puts the question; Joan, as she often does, counters by asking "So far?"—for she maintains, sincerely, that her favorite part of any day is the ending of it in her husband's arms, before they roll apart into sleep.

"So far."

She has to choose between saying "Now"—that is, their waiting to retire to that sleepy embrace—or "Waking up this morning and holding each other till we got out of bed." She gives those alternative responses roughly equal time, at least as a preliminary reply before proceeding to some particular feature of the day. The woman quite means what she says, too—and this couple, mind, have been together for thirty years, since Joan was twenty-seven and Frank thirty-five.

"After that," she adds (having opted in the first instance for "Now"), "my favorite thing so far was getting that damned *lavender* right this morning"—in a watercolor she's doing of puddled dew in the forenoon shade of that same deck: one of a summer series that she calls variously her Puddlepaints, her Waterworks, her H_2O-Squareds—water-colors of *water* in sundry forms, moods, lights. If her track record holds, the dozen-odd items will fetch between five hundred and twelve hundred each at her fall show in Philadelphia; she would have painted the same number, however, of the same subject, with the same concentration, if she knew in advance that not one would ever be exhibited, let alone sold. Getting right that wash of lavender light was her AM project, and by dint of talent, training, luck, repeated trial, and much experience, she got it to her satisfaction: a small triumph that none besides the artist (and now her mate) will likely recognize.

"Yours?" she asks in turn, still twisting the eyepieces of those binoculars and flexing their angular separation—and Frank Pollard, who as always takes the question seriously, realizes that he can't choose a favorite moment or event, for the reason that this entire day has been ideal, not in its extraordinariness but, on the contrary, in its serenely perfect typicality, enhanced by contrast to the day before. The couple woke at first light this morning, as usual, to the sound of crows and mockingbirds in the black pines round about and crickets in the dew-soaked grass. Naked and sheetless under the slow-moving overhead fan (the Pollards share a distaste for air conditioning, among a thousand other shared likes and dislikes), they made lazy love, to both parties' satisfaction, and then breakfasted on the deck: fresh-squeezed orange juice, cinnamon-pecan buns from an Ocean City bakery, coffee from Hawaii's Kona Coast. Frank then read poetry on the toilet, as is his habit—in this instance, Yeats's *Sailing to Byzantium*, an old favorite, which duly moved his mind and heart while nature moved his bowels. After stretching exercises à deux and a wake-up dip in the tranquil, mist-mantled ocean, he read the morning newspaper down on their barbecue patio, out of Joan's way, while she turned to her easel and its challenge-du-jour. Before the air stoked up, he took a ten-mile bike ride along the flat ocean road up into the state park dunes and back; then he read a handsomely illustrated essay on logarithmic spirals, a pet subject of his, in the magazine *Sciences*, to which the Pollards subscribe as much for its art as for its articles. After that, he composed on their laptop computer a witty, perfectly routine end-of-summer newsletter to Joan's grown son by her short-lived first marriage and to his grown daughter by his rather longer-lived ditto: a pair whom F & J can't help wishing were married to each other (no consanguinity, after all) instead of to their actual spouses, hers an arrogant, womanizing lawyer, his a good-for-nothing layabout, in their parents' opinion. In that letter he declared, in passing, his intention to devote his next life to the history of science rather than to that of Colonial America. Of yesterday's pathology report — rather, of Frank's doctor's report of that report, together with his projections and recommendations therefrom — the letter made no mention, although some soon-to-follow one must. Too fine a day, too late in the season, to becloud with the likes of that; he wished his Paula in Minneapolis and Joan's Harold in Atlanta a day as fine, a season, a life. Lunch, presently, in a still-shaded corner of the deck: Joan's cold zucchini soup with Frank's garlic croutons and iced coffee, over which they sorted out the day's mail, compared notes on their respective mornings, and planned their afternoon. To the beach then, the pair of them, for some hours of swimming in the breakers, walking the strand, and reading in umbrella-shaded sand chairs, after which, back at the cottage, Frank did a bit of bookkeeping and Joan some preliminary packing for their return to the city two days hence. By car down to the market for their final light provisioning, then frozen fresh-peach daiquiris with crudités and hummus back on deck at Happy Hour. The evening headlines on TV; barbecued lamb patties with acorn squash and jug rosé for dinner as the sun set behind the pines; then a short bike ride together around the twilit neighborhood. A shower bath while nature considerately thundershowered Fenwick Island and cleared the air; a cheery phone call from the daughter just written to (it never fails), in which again Frank spoke only of such agreeable matters as the grandchildren's camp adventures, the anticipated Perseids, and their usual mixed feelings about exchanging the summer rhythms that they so enjoy for the busier urban-autumn routine that, historically at least, they have also much enjoyed. And now back on their excellent deck to sip Codorníu blanc de blancs brut, watch for meteors, and review their day, in order — vainly, for Frank Pollard — to choose a favorite moment from it.

"Grocery shopping with you," he declares, as he not infrequently does when stuck. It is a fact that in their younger years, especially back when they began keeping house together but were not yet married, he found it erotically rousing to stroll supermarket aisles with his new lover, then his bride, then his wife, selecting with her the foods they would prepare and enjoy together, as well as such homely necessities as lightbulbs and laundry detergent; returning home with their purchases in those days, they would sometimes pause to make love on couch or carpet between fridging the perishables and stashing the rest. He still finds it more pleasure than chore to steer the cart and check off items from their list while Joan plans and improvises menus down the line; today, e.g., as she stretched for a top-shelf jar of sun-dried tomatoes in oil, he could not resist a surreptitious pat on her pleasant behind. *There*, he now provisionally supposes, was his single favorite moment of the day — so far.

It is upon that recognition (while Joan rescrews those binocular eyepieces and declares, "I can't do lenses. Lenses hate me") that Frank Pollard experiences the aforementioned soul-flood — of quiet joy, whatever. Come what may, they've had thirty blessed years together, by no means hassle-free but profoundly loving, profoundly satisfying; in a word, *happy*. That adjective gives him focus-troubles of his own: Happy tears blur bright Vega, the setting moon, the citronella candle on the low table between the lounge chairs, with its sweating icebucket of champagne and tray of acrylic flutes. Indifferent to this and every other emotion, in his pancreas meanwhile the robust tumor cells proceed with their inexorable division, redivision, and unhurried metastases: settlers, colonizers, unstoppable possessors and dispossessors of their new world.

2.

Thirty feet southwest of and ten below the Pollards' chairs, on a leaf of ground ivy under one of the black pines near the deck of their rented beach cottage, a solitary dog tick, *Dermacentor variabilis*, unaware of doing so, bides its time, unwittingly carrying in its body great numbers of the microorganism *Rickettsia rickettsii*, the virus or bacterium (Rickettsias have characteristics of both) responsible for Spotted Fever in humans and some other mammals. As uncognizant of their patient host as are Frank Pollard's pancreatic-cancer cells of theirs, the microorganisms placidly metabolize, in effect "standing by" like the tick itself, to whom the Rickettsia colony was passed via its mother's eggs, independent of mammalian hosts. To the moon, the stars and planets,

Earth's impending convergence with cometary debris, the Pollards' Fenwick Island deck and its occupants, not to mention their concerns, the *D. variabilis* is oblivious, though not quite to the sandy soil, the dew, the muggy air, the leaf on which it rests, the black-pine needles round about, and the dark-denimed leg now inching through those needles, now kneeling on the ground-ivy patch. The tick moves unhurriedly onto that dew-wet, serendipitous trouserleg and, presently, toward the warm animal tissue sensed thereunder and the blood-meal that is its program's goal. Its thousands of unknowing passenger-Rickettsias sense not even this, nor will they even when their vessel moors upon human skin, runs out its figurative gangway through the epithelium, and, in course of onloading its blood-cargo, unwittingly discharges them from one world to another, their unwittingly promised land.

3.

"Microscopes and telescopes," Joan Pollard believes that it was Goethe who remarked, "distort the natural focus of our eyes." In fifth-grade science class it was invariably she who had the most trouble resolving paramecia under the school's old chrome-and-bakelite monocular microscope. Now she sees twin lunar quarters magnified up yonder, neither of them clearly, and can't locate Vega at all. Moreover, when she lowers the binoculars in order to see where to re-aim them, a midge or eyelash falls into her left eye, and the firmament swims.

"I give up," she declares, and, taking advantage of the fortuitous cover, lets flow a discreet measure of the tears never recently far away. A child of acrimonious divorce and herself early divorced, an overpermissive B-minus mother by her own assessment, more committed finally to her painting than to parenting, she neither expected nor particularly hankered for remarriage, and never seriously imagined that hers would be the extraordinary fortune (three decades later, she still inwardly shakes her head at it) of loving a man *profoundly*, despite his inevitable shortcomings; of being by him loved reciprocally despite hers, and of feeling their bond grow and deepen over the by-no-means-carefree years instead of abrading into resentment or callusing into indifference. Thirty years! The equivalent of twice that in most couples' lives, actually, thanks to the nature of his profession and hers; even before Frank's retirement from Highland Academy, in a typical week they spent more hours in each other's proximity than any "normal" working couple spends in a fortnight. And except during their never-frequent and ever-rarer quarrels, she has gone to bed nightly feeling blessed in their connection, and has morningly woken ditto. As has he.

"Something in her eye?" her husband asks now, accepting from her the failed binoculars; they often playfully address each other in third-person pronouns.

"Yep." Joan clears her throat and knuckles her eyeball. "Freaking *time.*"

Frank focuses, with more success. "She's got time in her eye?"

"Also up her nose and in her face generally, but not out her kazoo. Where'd it all go, hon?"

Steering away from that question, "The thing is," Frank declares, "Goethe *liked* microscopes and telescopes. His remark's not a complaint; it's a reminder."

"Well, mine's a complaint," Joan decides. "And while I'm at it, T. S. Eliot's got his head in his pocket: It's *great* to measure out your life in coffee spoons. What sucks is running out of coffee."

Levelly but sympathetically, her husband observes, "She's distressed. Ah, so," he says then to Vega: "*There* you are, old girl."

"She is," his wife acknowledges. She pours herself and him another splash of champagne. "Let's spot us a meteor and pack it in. No: Let's stay out here forever."

"Easy on that eye, okay?" For she's knuckling it again. "Think of all those happy families of mites that colonize human eyelash follicles. You're making Apocalypse Now in there. The end of the world."

"Hell with 'em," says Joan. "What'd they ever do for me?" Soft-focused by her tears, the plastic glass of Catalonian champagne refracts the candlelight in a way that interests her painter's (right) eye. "Anyhow, Goethe was right. And it *is* the end of the world."

"Joanie?"

"Sorry sorry sorry." Bare forearms on bare thigh-tops, she slumps sidesaddle on her lounge chair, turning her wine-flute in the light. "I'm not going to be good at this, Frank. I'm going to fail you."

"So fail me." He pats her knee. "After all these years, you're entitled."

She looks away, skyward. "Was that a meteor?"

Frank considers. "Lightning bug."

4.

In 1992, when Comet Swift-Tuttle last transited the inner solar system, the Pollards happened to be touring Spain. They watched for "their" Perseid Shower from the old city walls of Ciudad Rodrigo, in the province of Salamanca, where they were stopping at the Parador Nacional. Although they found the old city delightful — as much for its informal community park along the Rio Agueda, where the whole town seemed to gather at the hot afternoons' end to stroll and swim and socialize under the trees, as for its medieval walls and buildings — and although the night was satisfactorily dark out over the plain and the dry air brilliantly clear, they were disappointed at the apparent fizzle of the promised once-in-a-lifetime supershower. There hung the clustered constellations of the myth — Perseus, Andromeda, Cepheus, Cassiopeia — but by midnight they'd seen only one meteor together and one each separately. Since they planned an early start in the morning for their drive up into the Gredos Mountains, where they hoped to hike in the high forests, they bade the Gorgon-slayer buenas noches and turned in. It is from this happy Spanish driving-tour that Frank dates the intermittent onset of what he took to be a mild but increasingly persistent gastroenteritic discomfort: something in the food or water, he presumed, although both were excellent, and Joan felt nothing similar, and neither of the Pollards has been prone, historically, to more than the occasional transitory episode of nausea, diarrhea, or fever in their frequent travels and ardent culinary adventures. For as long as possible thereafter, he ignored the symptom.

In 1862, Swift-Tuttle's next-previous transit, Johann Wolfgang von Goethe was already thirty years in his grave alongside that of his friend Schiller in the ducal crypt at Weimar, and no person currently alive on Earth had yet been born. In 1737, the transit believed to have been next prior to that, neither Goethe nor Schiller had yet been born; by Swift-Tuttle's next predicted transit, 2126, all persons alive on Earth in August 1994, the time of both the action and the writing of this story, will be dead. Mark Twain declared in 1910, correctly, that he had come in with Halley's Comet and would go out with it; among Earth's animate creatures, however, only trees might span such intervals as Comet Swift-Tuttle's orbital period — including, in special instances, *Pinus thunbergii*, the Japanese Black Pine, among still-young specimens of which hunkers the dark-clad interloper in the Pollards' yard, un-conscious of the dog tick engorging on his right ankle, just above the black sock-top.

5.

Five days into his annual vacation-week at Ocean City, Maryland, his cash reserves a touch low and his mood a touch resentful of the fair but too-cool weather, Samuel Buffett, the Duct-Tape Rapist — so called by the media for his modus operandi in suburban Wilmington and Newark, Delaware, the venue of his serial assaults — is scouting Operation Nine, as he thinks of it, despite the possibility that its atypical location will narrow slightly the police search for him. How many hundred other Wilmingtonians, after all, are spending mid-August at the nearby Dela-ware and Maryland beach resorts? And everyone knows of the "copy-cat" phenomenon associated with unusual crimes. Thirty-two and single, the dependable and knowledgeable if sometimes short-fused assistant manager of a Radio Shack retail outlet in a shopping mall outside the state's major city, Sam has over the past two years taken up rape-robbery as an exciting and dangerous hobby. In the sexual attacks themselves he takes considerable though secondary pleasure: They are the bonus payoff for what he really enjoys — reconnoitering, planning, and stalking; penetration of the premises; subduing and binding the frightened victim altogether into his power. The associated robbery is almost perfunctory, a third-order reward for his audacity, meant as much to deflect suspicion from a well-employed middle-class white man with thinning brown hair and double-bridged eyeglasses as to augment his finances. He takes only cash, and has invested the $1,953 gross from his operations thus far ($1,320 of it from a single windfall, his seventh) in a one-year certificate of deposit at the bank branch in "his" mall. At that certificate's first expiry-date, reminded of his falsetto commands to his "targets," with an inward smile he "rolled it over."

Ordinarily, Sam Buffett selects as those targets attractive young women who either live alone or have been observed by him to be alone in their domiciles at the appropriate strike-time. It was the extra chal-lenge and quirky variety, as Sam sees it, of the middle-aged couple in Operation Seven — the only one that he remembers with less than entire pleasure — that prompted him to "go for it," and although he had at one point to inflict more pain than is his rule to pacify the tape-trussed, freckle-pated husband while he sodomized the tape-trussed, freckle-butted wife on all fours in the couple's club basement, the unexpectedly large take helped compensate for his annoyance and the increased risk. By contrast, Operation Eight—on a girl he knows cordially as a teller in his bank and once came close to asking for a "date"—went so easily, enjoyably, and perfectly per plan that he stretched it out for nearly four hours, permitting frightened but courageous Ms. Claudia Tully to natter earnestly on, between spells of tears and his assorted violations of her, about the psychology of rape (on which subject she seemed knowledgeable indeed) and various resources that he might "access" confidentially for help with his "problem." Thirty-seven dollars and twenty-nine cents, that operation yielded, which sum he looks forward to depositing with Claudia herself as soon as he can disguise it by combination with whatever the take from Operation Nine.

To that end, he brought along with him to Ocean City his kit: a loaded .22-caliber target pistol, its bore too small and its size too large for this purpose, really, but a relatively innocent-seeming piece to own, and meant only to intimidate, not to kill; the requisite ski mask, an itchy nuisance in hot weather; a small sheath knife; latex gloves and condoms (Sam fears AIDS); and the trademark roll of two-inch duct tape with which he blindfolds, binds at wrists and ankles, and intermittently gags his victims—all of these items (except the belted sheath knife) tucked into a black Land's End fanny pack in order to leave his hands free. It would not have surprised Sam Buffett to return to Wilmington and his job never having taken the kit out of his suitcase; nor does it surprise him to find himself daily more "up" for using it. The only child of a choleric father severely disabled in the Korean War and dead of a heart attack before the boy's thirteenth birthday and a scattered, indulgent mother who in her widowhood gave herself over to alcohol and chocolate, Sam grew up tidy, timid, taciturn, a touch irascible and officious: a fussy, asexual bachelor, so his neighbors and workmates indifferently suppose, who still lives in his now-obese mother's house and responsibly maintains her and it, his only known hobbies ham radio and, more recently, networking on his personal computer.

The man's methodicalness extends to his covert "operations," in which he has come to take an almost professional pride. Although the first three or four of them were "learning experiences" in which he developed his procedures and techniques, he has never botched one or even made a serious blunder. On the couple of occasions when something unforeseeable jeopardized the operation (Number Three's young apartment-neighbors' rapping on her door and singsonging merrily, "Come *on*, Do-reen; we-know-you're-*in* ... there!"), his resourcefulness has proved equal to the challenge (gun barrel at her nape and tape-gag removed, at his whispered instruction Doreen singsang back, "No-I'm-*not*, guys; try-me-tomorrow-*mor*-ning!"). Except in the regrettable instance of Number Seven's hysterical husband, whom it still distresses Sam to remember swatting angrily with the .22, he has in his own opinion never "hurt" his victims—beyond the trauma of seizure, mortal threat, and bondage followed by forced fellatio, rape both vaginal and anal when he can manage it, and incidental robbery. Particularly since attending Claudia Tully's spiel during Operation Eight, he has read with interest articles in *Psychology Today* about sexual predators "like himself," nodding Yes or No to sundry items of the profile and ultimately shrugging his shoulders. On infrequent past occasions he has experienced unforced sex; agreeable enough, but by his lights there's no comparing it with the excitement of the forced variety. To the feminist assertion that rape has to do with power, not with sex, Sam Buffett replies, "Bullshit"; to the psychologists' assertion, however, that it has to do *at least as much* with power as with sex, he readily nods assent.

Does Sam hate or anyhow resent women? He doesn't think so, but grants the possibility. If he had been sexually more successful in the normal way, would he feel impelled to rape? Probably not, but who knows, and anyhow he wasn't, so so what? He doesn't feel *impelled*, by the way, he would object; merely inclined, and inclined to pursue that occasional inclination. Is he a sadist? Well: No question but he enjoys the forcing and threatening—except in the case of old Seven's husband, and so he supposes he *does* have it in for women, sort of; so sue him! On the other hand, he would take no pleasure at all in carrying out his intimidative threats to shoot, knife, or mutilate his victims or in subjecting them to sexual violations beyond those aforespecified. In fact, he's not certain what he'll do if and when one vigorously resists him; perhaps retreat, perhaps shoot, knife, or mutilate. Except when "out hunting," he regards himself as an ordinary, peaceable fellow, politically conservative but environmentally concerned, with no taste for pornography or the violence so ubiquitous in American movies and network television.

Does Sam think about sooner or later getting caught, convicted, and jailed, or does he imagine raping an infinite series of women with impunity? Neither: He takes considerable pleasure in the recollection of his past operations but is not given to long-term projections. He has never regarded any next operation as his last; he takes them, so to speak, one at a time, as circumstances warrant. If asked whether he has ever reflected that it's only a matter of time until he's *doing* time, he would shrug, annoyed. He understands, more or less, that the risk factor in his serial operations has a cumulative aspect; his woozy mother is fond of declaring, apropos of nothing in particular, "The pitcher that goes always to the well eventually gets broken," but he does not imagine himself as going *always* to the well, only for some indefinite number of times yet.

It is Sam Buffett's practice to maintain a casual lookout for appropriate operational targets even when he's not in the actively hunting mode; indeed, it is the casual observation of a likely target that typically prompts the hunt, not vice versa. Standing at Claudia Tully's bank-window to deposit his take from Operation Seven, he happened to overhear her remark to the teller beside her that she'd be house-sitting through the month of March in her parents' place on Shawbridge Road and that she looked forward to rattling around all by herself in that big old house while they toured Greece and Italy. Mm hm, thought the Duct-Tape Rapist, and did a bit of subsequent reconnoitering, and bided his time till the appointed month. Strolling the Fenwick Island beach at afternoon's end yesterday (the first real beach-day of the week), he casually followed an attractive young mother and her two small children across the ocean highway and back to their cottage and observed that she seemed to be its only adult occupant; an after-dark reconnaissance and more extensive surveillance today confirmed that observation, suggested an operational plan, and piqued his interest: He has never "done" a woman with sleeping children, and imagines that there'd be no problem keeping her quiet and compliant. But that same unobtrusive scouting turned up the late-middle-aged couple next door to her — an easier mark approachwise (the ground slopes up to one rear corner of their raised sundeck) and very likely more cash-productive, but problematical as to management and what the hell, there's an ATM up the road in Bethany Beach if he runs short, so why risk it?

Why? Because that unpleasantness in Operation Seven still rankles him; for a moment there he was clear out of control, almost panicky, might actually have shot the guy. If he were running that operation again ...

So: Supermom (thus he's come to think of the woman on the beach, admiring the tough-gentle way she manages the kids, roughhousing with them in the surf one minute, soothing their distresses or adjudicating their differences the next, and always talking to them *straight*, not in a put-on Mommy-voice) is unquestionably his target of choice: a succulent number, and there'd be no present indecision on his part if her sundeck had a ground-level corner like her neighbors', for easy access. Prepping for Operation Nine after a dinner of not-bad fajitas in an Ocean City Mex place, he pretty much decided to go for it once the sun was well down and Supermom's children were presumably asleep; it is only that bad aftertaste from Seven that has led him, while he's giving the kids time to crank up the old Z's, to re-review the piece-of-cake approach next door, in course of which he's been enjoying the extended shot of Mrs.'s bare boobs, not bad at all for her age, and her pantied butt, ditto, in the flickering light of their patio candle. Her skinny husband looks to be no great threat, though trim and fit-appearing for an old gent. The right way to've played it — the right way to *play* it, if the guy goes macho or gets his balls in an uproar like Mr. Seven ...

Sam believes that he knows, now, the right way to play it, and although Supermom is hands down the sweeter score, he's tempted to clear his record, so to speak, by doing this couple without losing his cool or using more force than necessary. Now that Boobs has given up on the binoculars (seven-by-fifty "night glasses," Sam has observed, such as boaters use, quite able to resolve his crouching figure in the dim light if they're aimed his way), he edges closer through the cover of pines toward where the grade slopes up beside the deck, thinking that perhaps their conversation, if he can make it out, will tip the scales one way or the other. From his kit he fishes forth and dons the latex gloves and itchy ski mask.

Granted that life's cruelties and injustices are measureless, there is in it at least occasional justice too, however imperfect and sometimes accidental. Samuel Buffett's impending Spotted Fever, though severe, will do him less damage, alas, than he has doubtless done to any one of the targets of his operations past and to come. It will, however, be of a virulence sufficient to inflict upon him pneumonitis, uremia, and an extended general debilitation that will significantly increase the misery of his prison time after the resourceful victim of Operation Ten, a full year hence — another Claudia Tully, but with a literal vengeance — skillfully traps him into telephoning her, two weeks after her rape, for confidential therapy-referral, and holds him on the line long enough for Wilmington police to trace the call, reach the shopping-mall phone booth, and make the arrest. Ill and incarcerated, he will come to know something of his victims' pain and degradation, if never quite their terror. To hell, or one of its numerous terrestrial approximations, with him.

6.

"Time time time," Joan Pollard says now, and her husband guardedly replies, "Yes, well." The binoculars flat on the serving tray between them, they're both lying back now in their side-by-side lounge chairs, lightly holding hands across that space while waiting for their good-night Perseid meteor, and Frank's not sure whether what his wife has on her mind just now is bedtime, or their return to the city and what awaits them there, or (as the grim sigh in her tone suggests) both of the above plus evanescence and ephemerality in general, and in particular the brevity of even such an extended happy connection as theirs. He himself, now that he has retrieved the word *ephemerality*, sidetracks to a less voltaged association, as is his sometimes annoying habit:

"I've always liked the word *ephemerides*," he declares to her. "In the astronomical tables: upcoming celestial events and such. Ephemerides."

"Sounds like a minor Greek hero" to Joan, who is used to these deflections: "Epimenides, Ephemerides."

"The sons of Time?" Frank wonders, "Or 'children of the day,' maybe?"

"Of *a* day, like goddamn mayflies, and then good night. Who was it that ate his own children, anyhow?"

"Old Kronos?"

"It figures."

"*The true hero of every feast*," Frank remembers having seen Time somewhere called.

"The uninvited guest," in Joan's opinion, "who scarfs the canapés and guzzles the bubbly when nobody's looking, till before you know it the party's over."

"But he's the life of the party that he's also the death of, right? He's the fizz in the Codorníu — of which this is the end, by the way: fin du vin. Here's to Papa Time."

"Hell with that mother."

Frank turns his head herward. "Thirty years, her husband reminds his dearest friend: three-zero and counting."

"Freaking eye blink." But she raises her flute to his.

"Yes. Well."

They sip.

"What was that?"

"Raccoon," Frank supposes. At moments today it has almost seemed to him that he can not only feel but *hear* the tumor growing; yet he looks forward with all the more pleasure to embracing his sorrowed friend before dropping off into sweet sleep. Together now, at the same instant, they see a meteor directly overhead, streaking southwestward as if through the constellations. Sighs Frank: "There she blows. B-plus?"

"B-minus tops," in Joan's grade-book. She's trying to remember whether that Unitarian proto-hippie who married them in San Francisco in 1964 said *As long as you both shall live* or *Till death do you part.* "Maybe C-plus. Maybe we didn't even see the little sucker, so we can't go in yet."

"We saw it," her husband says gently.

7.

Beginnings are exciting; middles are gratifying; but endings, boyoboy. So here's our universe, reader, whatever its curvature. Somewhere or other in it is our galactic supercluster, almost unimaginably vast — ah, yes, here it is — from which a mighty close-up resolves our particular Local Cluster, and another just as mighty discovers our very own Milky Way galaxy, bless its unfathomable black hole of a heart: one more bright sand-grain on the dark beach of abyssal space. Zooming right in on it, we may just possibly find our dear solar system and its cozy inner belt of planets, including miscellaneous cometary debris. Sure enough, here's old Earth, complete with atmosphere — into which latter a fist-size lump of Comet Swift-Tuttle plunges, from our perspective, at 11:14 PM Eastern Daylight Savings Time on 13 August 1994, said plunge or anyhow collision effecting its prompt incineration in a meteoric streak over the eastern seaboard of North America, including the Atlantic coast of Delaware and Maryland's portion of Chesapeake Bay, where yours truly winds up a short story entitled "Ever After," having to do, on the human level, with Joan and Frank Pollard, among others. Here now some while later are the printed pages of that story, its several paragraphs, sentences, phrases. Look you now: See at its end the words *ever after*, their several letters, the *r* of *after* and the full stop after. Closer, closer, obliging reader: the millions of molecules of printer's ink composing that full stop; the several atoms of carbon in each of those molecules; the furious motion of subatomic particles in any one of those virtually immortal atoms, all but oblivious to time, raging on like so many separate universes since ours exploded into being: now here, now there, now briefly in this dot of ink until it crumble, fade, disperse; now on past the episode of human life on Earth to whatever comparably ephemeral next and next and next and on and on, neither happily nor un-, ever after.

Pillow Talk: Presently

. . . he goes on with the stories, on likewise with talking to her, agreeing and disagreeing, soothing, coaxing, distracting, beguiling them both as best he can with narrative possibilities still unforeclosed. There is no timetable, no hurry. The DO NOT DISTURB sign (in several languages) hangs on their outside doorknob. They have, as he has so often declared to her, all the time there is.

He remembers now that he forgot to tell her, back there when they were doing love and physics, about the sundry "multiverse" theories that have been popping up lately in scientific journals like . . . well, alternative universes.

"Multiverses," she would have said, perhaps, eyes closed, musing back against their headboard or in her beach chair: "Sounds like a long poem."

I'll make it a short story, he'd have promised, and in fact does promise, in effect at least, and then amuses himself by imagining *her* this time replying, "No hurry, love: Things end soon enough in any case."

Now you're talking, he tells her, though the only voice in the room is his.

The not-so-short story begins:

12.

Countdown: Once Upon a Time

12. ANY LINE AT ALL

... can start a story. It doesn't have to be *Once upon et cetera*.

"Really."

Take the proposition just proposed, for example. Hang it between quotes like dialogue and tag it somewhere along the road, like this: "Any line at all," Sheila's new lover declared to her on the balcony of her parents' condo in Perdido Key, Florida, where the young pair had run off together for a long spring weekend and were currently lounging naked in mid-March forenoon sunlight, "can start a story." See what I mean?

"Maybe."

In fact, strictly speaking, the quotes and tag material aren't necessary.

"We suspected as much."

Throw me a line. Any line at all.

"You asked for it: Try this." Wherewith trim fortysomething Sarah, an amateur of physics who has taken up story-writing as a pastime and found in it what she now believes might be her real vocation, dashes off from memory (with a Delta Airlines ballpoint pen on a sheet of our hotel's stationery) Erwin Schrödinger's equation for the evolution over time of the wave functions of physical systems, an axiom of quantum mechanics:

$$i \tfrac{h}{2\pi} \tfrac{\partial}{\partial t} \Psi(x_1 \ldots x_{3N}, t) = H\Psi(x_1 \ldots x_{3N}, t)$$

"The ball," she then declares, rolling pertly onto her tum like an impish odalisque, "is in your court."

Nothing to it, replies her unfazed bed-companion. I'm going to use quotes again, although we understand *et cetera*:

"$i \frac{h}{2\pi} \frac{\partial}{\partial t} \Psi(x_1 \ldots x_{3N}, t) = H\Psi(x_1 \ldots x_{3N}, t)$" Jerry scribbled across his halfdozing lover's tidy left buttock with a felt-tipped Kelly-green marking pen; on that young lady's equally appealing right he then added "$H\Psi(x_1 \ldots x_{3N}, t)$," bridging her cleft and channeling its dainty semicolon with an elongated equal sign.

Sarah flexes her butt. "That tickles. What is it?"

It's Schrödinger's wave-function equation, which happens also to be the first element of Bohm's Alternative Theory, I believe, as well as the opening line of some other couple's story.

"No, I mean *that*."

Thanks to you, that is what it is. On with our story?

"Maybe. Is it Jerry talking now, or Joe or John or who?"

Your call.

"On with it, then, dear Fred. Where'd you learn physics, by the way?"

Relax just a quantum, and I'll tell you. Where'd you learn storytelling?

"Ah."

There we are. I picked up physics from my friendly. Local. Physics teacher. Okay?

"Easy does it."

Endings, on the other hand, not-so-young Frederick feels obliged to recaution his not-so-young friend, physics coach, and narrative protégée, are another matter.

"Another story? Ouch."

Sorry. Better?

"Best."

Et cetera, one supposes.

11. FROM TIME TO TIME

... we talk like this, even now. One needs anyhow to imagine a couple so speaking: late-afternoon late-life lovers, postcoitally lassitudinous and sweat-wet, skin to skin. Pillow talk, however, you know ... you really have to *be* there, in the ardent flesh. Joan and Frank Pollard are seasoned partners and old best friends: storms weathered, delights delighted in, ups downs ins outs, thousands of shared meals and matings under their still-trim belts. They've seen their several offspring through college, parents through their last age, professional careers through their gratifying peaks onto plateaus and thence into acceptably gentle decline and/or retirement, like their high-mileage bodies and sundry well-gratified appetites. Large surprises no longer either likely or hankered after, themby, at this stage of their game. Eros be praised, therefore and however, for certain small ones, such as their easeful making of love earlier today, at afternoon's end or evening's commencement, however one looks at it.

It's a rainy November Friday in Philadelphia, raw and wretched though not yet wintry, and, in its wet gray way, handsome. The couple have motored to the city from their Delaware Valley country seat for the opening of Joan's watercolor show this evening at her dealer's gallery in Society Hill. The artist herself drove their van, as she has come regularly to do this fall except for local errands; Frank is much weakened lately by his illness, belatedly diagnosed (his own procrastination) and found already to have metastasized. Prognosis grim indeed, but he has declined heroic measures in favor of palliatives while he considers how and when to end his story before it turns excruciating and/or undignified. The pair have discussed this subject both gravely and light-heartedly; they're in accord as to principle. Frank judges himself to have proceeded successfully, over the past months, right through "DABDA," the medical mnemonic for the stages of mourning as described by the psychiatrist Elisabeth Kübler-Ross: Denial, Anger, Bargaining, Depression, Acceptance. Having dwelt so long a while in the first of these, he likes to declare, he would readily have spent more time in the second and third, if there'd *been* more time, before arriving at the fourth and fifth. As for Joan, they agree that she's stalled in the neighborhood of B, with occasional relapses into Anger or even Denial and prolapses into Depression, but nary a smidgen yet of Acceptance of her partner's impending death.

After checking in at a favorite small hotel of theirs not far from the gallery, at Frank's insistence they strolled instead of driving or taxiing those few and handsome old brick blocks through the eased-off rain, to inspect Joan's dealer's mounting of the exhibition. *Water Watercolors*, it's being billed, although the series includes a number of pen-and-wash items as well: two dozen studies of that ubiquitous element in sundry modes and moods, from sun-fired rainsplatters on the windows of Joan's rural studio to a waterspout raging along the Atlantic horizon near their rented summer cottage. While his wife discussed with a gallery assistant some details of lighting and labeling as well as the program for the evening, Frank admiringly reviewed the works themselves, so intimately familiar to him and yet so splendidly official now, like one's children or students at graduation-time. It is the dozenth or so such opening that he has proudly attended over the years as Joan Pollard's stock rose slowly but steadily to its present comfortable level among collectors in the region; it will doubtless also be his last, as he has of necessity recognized many other recent things to have been, whether in retrospect or at the time: his last summer at their Fenwick Island cottage, last Perseid meteor shower, last set of tennis as his debilitation grew, last glorious October foliage-change in "their" valley, and now in all likelihood his final visit to this handsome city. Unthinkable, his still-Bargaining mate would insist if he spoke of it thus; but Frank's best evidence that he has attained DABDA's terminal A is that these recognitions, while inevitably saddening, afford him on balance these days as much gratification as dismay; that he has been blessed for so considerable a while (though less considerable than expected) if not with wealth or fame anyhow with the respect of his prep-school students and colleagues during his teaching years, the affection of his grown-up daughter and of Joan's grown-up son by each's previous marriage, and above all the loving companionship of his second life-partner, whose talent and belated recognition give him at least as much satisfaction as if they'd been his own.

In particular he paused before *Puddled Dew*, a study of that homely phenomenon in late-morning light on the deck of their seashore cottage. In the brochure of the exhibition, a critic-friend of Joan's has praised "certain dark suggestions between her bright lines, so to speak: turbulences on the verge of erupting through serene, even *pretty* surfaces." The critic instances specifically "the unnatural calm of *Waterspout Off Fenwick Island*, its surfless sea and insouciant bathers blithely unaware of or indifferent to the approaching funnel-cloud"; also "the disquietingly blood-like tints of *Puddled Dew*." Overdramatizings, in the Pollards' joint opinion: Squall lines and twisters don't normally approach East Coast beaches from offshore, for one thing, and so that waterspout will most likely have belonged to a storm already passed (Joan hadn't had heart to point out to her obliging critic-friend that, as anyone who knows beaches can see, the sunlit sand is still wet from a recent shower—an optical effect in which the artist justifiably takes pride); and while the critic herself is a Main Line blueblood, who ever saw the vital stuff in *lavender*? All the same, Frank thought now, the woman was onto something, as the literary critic Lionel Trilling had been in speaking of the "terror" lurking in Robert Frost's poetic rusticity: In retrospect, at least, *Waterspout* epitomizes the Pollards' "last summer"—a golden season of sweet work and play while Frank's late-detected cancer busily colonized his body. And although nothing sanguinary had been implied in the delicate wash of lavender light that *Puddled Dew*'s painter had taken such pleasure one August morning in capturing, that view from their sundeck happens to be toward the neighboring cottage, where—the very night after the picture was finished, perhaps while artist and spouse were watching Perseid meteors from that deck—a young divorced mother of two small children had been bound, raped, and robbed by the infamous "Duct-Tape Rapist" of Wilmington and environs, still at large. The Pollards had heard nothing until the courageous young woman, whom they'd befriended over the summer, woke them by telephone at 2 AM, after her attacker had finally left the premises and she'd managed to cut through her bonds with a kitchen knife, to ask whether one of them would please baby-sit her still-sleeping children while the other drove her to the nearest police station and emergency room, so that she could report and be treated for her rape with minimal effect on the kids. The assault itself had drawn no blood, but in sawing awkwardly through her duct-tape manacles (behind her naked back) she had sliced the skin of one forearm with the serrated sandwich-knife, and so Frank had quietly cleaned up red spots and pudlets on the kitchen tiles while Joan chauffeured and comforted the victim through the rest of the night, and had played his grandfatherly part in next day's difficult charade of normalcy-for-the-children's-sake. Thus had there come indeed to be, though never consciously intended by the artist, "dark suggestions between her bright lines" and "turbulences on the verge of erupting" from the innocently puddled dew, as if some microscopic amplifier were picking up the roar of nuclear energy latent in placid molecules of the universal solvent. It is the same feeling that Frank gets these days from reviewing their photographs from that season: There's lively Marjorie on the beach, still inviolate and prettier even than his own daughter, with those two darling children; there he himself poses astride his bicycle, still not quite aware that his pancreas has set about to kill him in short order.

"Peg's one of those critics who like to think they've found an artist's secret key," Joan piffed when Frank spoke of this, en route back to their hotel. Meanings, she likes disingenuously to declare, bore her; artistry is what matters.

"I suppose they *do* find such keys now and then," her husband allow-ed — and leaned on her arm a bit as a spasm of his now-permanent gut ache threatened to double him over. "Secret . . .," he added in the most normal voice he could muster, "even from the artist herself."

"And sometimes there's no damn lock to be unlocked," stoutly main-tained Joan Pollard, her heart constricting at his pain: "just a funky little key to hang on the critic's charm bracelet. Can you make it?"

"No problem. These things pass." But he stopped for a bit on the brick sidewalk, until the worst of it did. "*All passes*," he intoned mean-while; "*art alone endures.* Matthew Arnold?"

"Chautauqua Institute," his wife reminded him — and Frank now remembered their having once shaken their heads, years ago, at that portentous inscription over the auditorium stage, on which a much-flawed production of a second-rate opera was in tedious progress. *For better or worse*, they had agreed should be added to the inscription.

By chance their pause was before a bookshop window featuring, among other displays, works on sundry linkages between science and art: Leonard Shlain's *Art & Physics: Parallel Visions in Space, Time & Light*; Susan Strehle's *Fiction in the Quantum Universe*; coffee-table albums of gorgeously intricate Mandelbrot fractals, both computer-generated and photographed in their many natural manifestations; and, mirabi-le dictu, a calendar for the upcoming year illustrated with da Vinci's drawings of turbulent water.

"Gotta have it," Frank decided on the spot, and notwithstanding Joan's mild complaint that beside Leonardo her *Puddled Dew* looks like piddled doo-doo (and the stabbing realization that she'll be a widow before that calendar has run), they went in and bought the thing to hang in Frank's study, used these days chiefly for family bookkeeping and medical-insurance paperwork.

On then to their hotel, in plenty of time to shower and change for the opening: a three-hour wine-and-cheeser, after which Joan's dealer has scheduled dinner with one of her principal Main Line collectors. It is in this leisurely interval of dishabille — Frank's gut-pain having subsided, but not Joan's soul-pain — that they found themselves agreeably aroused by the cozy ambiance, among other factors, and presently embracing, caressing, and making gentle but vigorous love. When they had been a new couple in her late twenties and his mid-thirties, the degree of their ardor and the proximity of their names (genders switched) to the "Frankie and Johnny" of Tin Pan Alley fame had made that old song a running tease between them. Oh lordy, how they could love! Belly-down on the mattress now with her spent friend full-length atop her, the woman half-growled, half-sighed into her pillow, "He done her *right*."

Alas, in their subsequent joint shower the man's abdominal cramp returned, with such severity that he was obliged to wrap himself in a bath towel and lie down before even drying himself, his knees clutched up toward his chest. "It'll pass; it'll pass," he insisted, dreading that this time it might not.

"Hospital," counterinsisted Joan. "Never mind Donato"—her dealer and the gallery owner—"I'll call for an ambulance."

But Frank wouldn't hear of that; they've agreed he'll have the final say in these matters for as long as he can, and he is resolved not to let things reach the point where he can't. He forbade her even to telephone Donato that they'll be late: If he's still out of action when get-dressed time comes, she'll show up as scheduled and he'll join her later. In the worst case, she'll go on from the gallery to dinner with the others and he'll order up something light from room service.

"Sexy small hotels don't have room service," Joan tearfully reminded him.

"So I'll diet, and you'll bring me a doggie bag from Le Bec Fin."

"Tiramisu?"—which they had become enamored of a dozen years past at a pleasant gay restaurant in Key West; pretended was the name of a Puccini aria; have found only inferior versions of in their subsequent travels, even in Italy.

"Chocolate Decadence," Frank counterproposed, "with raspberry sauce. Uh oh ..." Just when his cramp seemed to be easing, he was seized by an urgent diarrhetic spasm and dashed half-doubled toiletward. Joan's legs went weak; she sat on the bed-edge, hearing him. "Are you managing?" she called in presently.

"Within the parameters. Bit of chocolate turbulence." He'd better sit this one out, so to speak, he decided and declared: "Get yourself dressed and out of here, s.v.p."

For his sake she did, and now dutifully has done, lord knows how. Three hours — two and a half, anyhow — of shmoozy small talk, her heart the whole time clenched fist-tight with concern. Donato, bless him, had kept the chitchat going and her wineglass filled, seeing to it she didn't get cornered overlong unless the cornerer was a likely customer. She had even managed to tease Peg, her critic-friend, with that "dark suggestions" business in the brochure (at the same time stroking her with Frank's comparison to the late eminent Professor Trilling), and Peg had cheerily responded, "Deny it till the cows come home, Joanie; Frost did the same thing, but the critics were right: 'Stopping by Woods on a Snowy Evening' is a poem about death."

Come restaurant-time, however, she could take it no longer, despite Frank's considerately phoning the gallery at six-thirty to tell her not to worry; he was in no pain and managing fine, but had decided to sit tight — "Sit loose," he had corrected himself — and let the trots run their course, excuse the expression and don't forget the tiramisu. She couldn't imagine that a collector's decision to buy or not to buy might hinge on the artist's physical presence at dinner (well, she could, actually, in Harry and Flo Perkins's creepy case), but if so, tant pis. Her husband was ill, and that was that; she told them as much, begged off dinner, and with some misgivings granted Donato's requested permission to confide "the truth" to the Perkinses once she was out of there. He was, after all, her dealer; had been so for years before his faith in her paid off, and she prays he'll remain so despite this evening's smallish turnout. If anything gets her through what lies ahead, it will be her work, and while she would no doubt paint even without a dealer to market the output, her professionality is at least as important to her as the income from her efforts.

Now she *is* out of there, by cab this time to make the short hop shorter yet. The driver's previous fare has left the evening *Inquirer* on the seat; Joan couldn't care less just now about dreadfulnesses in Bosnia, Rwanda, Haiti, but a more local headline catches her eye: DUCT-TAPE RAPIST SUSPECT ARRESTED. So brief is the ride, she has time to read only the lead paragraph by ambient street-light, to the effect that Delaware State Police have arrested a forty-nine-year old white plumbing and heating contractor in suburban Wilmington on suspicion of being the notorious serial "duct-tape rapist" of New Castle County and Delmarva beach resorts. Suspect declares innocence. She adds a quarter to her tip and takes the paper with her, to share the welcome news with Frank.

Having elevatored to their floor, she fumbles for but fails to find her room key in the clutter of her bag, then remembers that in her scattered exit from the hotel she dropped it into her pants-suit pocket. She must ask Frank sometime, her all-purpose infobase, why it is that whereas American hotel patrons customarily take their room keys with them on sorties from the premises, European hotel patrons customarily check theirs (with their massive pendants to reinforce the custom) at the front desk. She bets he'll know.

She is suddenly smitten with apprehension at what she'll find when she enters their room; actually closes her eyes for a moment, compresses her lips, then decisively turns key and doorknob and goes in. The space is dimly lit. Their bed's out of sight from the short entry-hall leading past the bathroom, but the television is turned on, its sound muted. Tropical reef-fish swim gorgeously across the silent screen; both Pollards are great fans of underwater cinematography. Lest her husband be sleeping, Joan suppresses her urge to call out to him.

Frank is, indeed, she finds, asleep: pajama'd, propped on his pillow against the headboard, looking altogether old and dead with his rumpled hair, closed eyes, and slacked-open mouth, the da Vinci calendar open on his blanketed, lamplit lap. So light is his respiration, it's the closed eyes that tell her he's merely sleeping after all; the day she finds him really dead, she supposes, his eyes will be open. The calendar, she sees now, is turned to February next, its graphic a meticulously rendered maelstrom. Leonardo, boyoboy. Which famous physicist was it, Joan hopes she'll remember to ask Frank along with the hotel-key question, who on his deathbed declared his intention to query God in Heaven on two matters, quantum electrodynamics and turbulence, and expressed his optimism that the Almighty might actually be able to shed some light on the former? Frank will know. Won't you, Frank.

Won't you, Frank.

Against Australia's Great Barrier Reef, where it must be midmorning now, the serried waves smash in from the Coral Sea. Viewed submarinely, each explodes in a chaos of bubbles, their swirls unpredictable though perhaps retrospectively explainable; they sweep the unalarmed tangs and wrasses brilliantly this way and that, alert but mindless and at home in their awesomely complex, vast and protean, utterly mindless element.

10. HE AGREES TO CONTINUE,

... does our narrator, stipulating only that she do likewise, and he'll readily take her silence for assent.

"Agrees with whom?"

Aha: With the late Greek writer Nikos Kazantzakis, for one, author of *Zorba et cetera*, who, in a letter to his second wife, Eleni, expresses his hope that on his deathbed he'll have the opportunity to bid goodbye to, perhaps even *kiss* good-bye, the various fruits of the Mediterranean that he has so relished through his decades. It is a happily pagan wish, a sort of thanksgiving, altogether more life-affirming (if that's the proper adjective for a hypothetical dying wish) than extreme unction or even "setting one's affairs in order." One's dying wish, after all, so far from being a death-wish, may well be the wish for life, even where there is no further hope therefor. One imagines the old Cretan bussing a peach and exclaiming, "Good-bye, dear peaches!"; a pear: "Thank you, sweet pears!"; a plum: "Plump plums, *epharisto!*"; then a persimmon, a pomegranate, and he's still only in the P's, having kissed his way already from apples through oranges, and with quinces through zucchinis yet to go.

Not so, you'll say: Zucchini stretches the category Fruits in the direction of metaphor, as in "fruits of the earth," thence to fruits of the sea, fruits of knowledge, Fruit of the Loom underwear, etc.— no problem for *this* fareweller, who has in fact rather enjoyed a lifetimesworth of stepping into and out of undies both boxer and brief, the latter both flied and flyless, and of assisting love-partners out of and into theirs: *Mwah*, dear delicate deliciosas! Stretch away, say some of us — as, after all, old Zorba there may be said to be stretching *his* category the other way, letting one papaya stand poetically for the class Papayas, as if there weren't differences among individual specimens of each variety — between Joe Papaya and Fred Papaya, for example, not to mention Fred and Gladys — in some instances as significant as their Linnaean similarities. Would he, bidding sad adieu to only one of his several children (if several he had, if any he had, which, as it happens, Kazantzakis did not), say, "That does it for the fruit of my loins"? Or, last-embracing his dear Eleni, "That takes care of Human Beings"? Of course not, unless she were — as, come to think of it, would be the likely case — the last on his list (because the most important) in that category.

This point made, one might in fact lay down reasonable parameters of valediction: Among human beings, farewell to individuals as individuals, not as representatives of classes, although even here there will be not only categories but hierarchies — one's spouse or other most significant other, the rest of one's immediate family, one's closest friends and associates, one's extended family, and on to one's less close but still valued friends, neighbors, colleagues, and acquaintances as far as time permits. Among non-human animals, individual pets (excepting perhaps the egg-laying tropical fish in one's tropical-fish tank, which tend to come in anonymous schools of half a dozen or so, as opposed to the more individualized live-bearing couples) but class representatives of whatever other species one inclines to valedict: a single blue crab or monarch butterfly or black-capped chickadee for the lot, etc. Likewise trees except for certain much-prized specimens such as the spreading Kwanzan cherry and perfect Zumi that grace one's waterfront lawn; house plants ditto, and all other objects and artifacts, always allowing for separable bye-byes to both individuals *and* their classes where called for: good-bye, e.g., to particular poems but also to Poetry; to particular places but also to Geography, Terrain, Locale; to Swiss Army knives in general but in particular to the trusty Tinkerer in one's trouser-pocket. One cloud of each sort — cirrus, cumulus, cumulonimbus, and the rest — should do for all; likewise one sample of each weather — fine, showery, warm, cool, humid, dry, still, brisk (and their sundry combinations, fine-warm-dry-still, fine-warm-*humid*-still, etc.) for all individual days (and nights) of that weather, notwithstanding that a foggy mild still early morning is surely a pleasure differentiable from that of the same conditions at noon or Happy Hour.

And so forth. Having agreed on the "rules," however, one ought surely to feel free to take every legitimate advantage themof, as one does in preparing one's income-tax return. Granted that the orange enjoyed this morning is not the orange enjoyed the morning before, and further that in the nature of the case one cannot kiss good-bye the oranges enjoyed but only their memory as embodied in the orange one kisses and therefore has yet to enjoy except in nostalgic anticipation (or in nostalgia *tout court* if one be at this point no longer permitted to partake of what one has valedicted), it may nevertheless be argued that to let one orange stand for Oranges is to ignore not only Charles and Chiquita Orange, so to speak, but the distinguishable pleasures of the subset Jaffas versus Mandarins, Floridas, Californias, and the rest. Who would maintain that to bid adiós to the oranges of Seville is to do likewise to those of Valencia, or that Bloods are the same as Navels, kiss-good-byewise? As well deny the difference between navels themselves: those that one has once upon an excited time kissed hello and must tenderly now kiss good-bye as opposed to those that one has enjoyed the more-or-less-innocent mere sight of, live or photographed, on beach or movie-screen or *Playboy* centerfold or newspaper lingerie advertisement — and not forgetting, in the "hello there" category, the dear belly buttons of one's children, be they (the buttons) Innies or Outies, before they (the children) attain the age of parental-pipik-kissing protest. One dainty, tonguable, sea-salt- and sun-lotion-tasting navel stand for all? Just ask your current bedmate whether her / his may represent to you its several predecessors!

To what end, a certain sort might ask, these protracted, fractalized, interminable addios, like the tubercular soprano's in *Traviata* or *Bohème*? To the end, it goes without saying, of postponing the end; and their ground-perspective on this matter divides good-byers into two camps, each calling for its own farewell though not necessarily on its own terms. Faced with the facts that all things end and that good-byes to life's pleasures have about them an inevitable component of sadness, there are those who would abbreviate or even avoid valediction; who, indeed, feel that what must end in any case (i.e., everything, even unto art) had as well be dispatched in short order, if even begun. We know of whom we speak, who would bid a curt good-bye to such bittersweet good-byes as Kazantzakis's, for example. And then there are those who, accepting the inevitable, are however in no rush to attain it; who on the contrary find that valediction hath its own mournful pleasures, and who therefore *et cetera*. Take as a thought-experiment the case of those Florentine assassins of whom Dante is reminded in Canto XIX of his *Inferno* (Circle VIII, Ditch iii, lines 49-51), executed by live burial trussed head-downward in a hole. Thus positioned for quietus, they are permitted their last confession to the priest, who must bend low to hear it as Dante bends to hear the simoniac Pope Nicholas III and, bending, is put in mind of those condemned assassins. Your former sort of valedictor in this pass would say simply, "*Nunc dimittis*; get it done with." Your latter, on the other hand — to which category belong the wretched Nicholas, also Kazantzakis, one imagines, and most certainly the present narrator — will draw his confession out, so to speak, simply so to speak, perhaps even fabricating a few peccadilloes to pad the catalogue and thus adding the sin of lying to the list of his factual lapses to be confessed.

Not that any one of those three aforespecified fictors, mind, might be taken as "standing for" the others, whether right-side up or upside down, and therefore kissed good-bye in their stead. Bear in mind our Rule of Individuals, not to mention the diplomacy of love: One is oneself, one prefers to believe, not the surrogate of one's analogs and forerunners, and would be kissed only as such . . .

Unless, of course, it is one's *last* kiss, the kiss-good-bye-to-good-bye-kisses kiss, in which case by all means kiss one (*this* one, anyhow) not only as himself in propria persona but as each and every of his lucky avatars, real and fantasized, in every mood / mode / venue / weather, to the end of love and breath and language and beyond, the end of this story and of all stories, the end of this agreed-upon continuation and its attendant stipulation —

"No stipulations."

9. VERY WELL, THEN, DAMN IT,

. . . they'll play it *her* way: Nunc dimittis, wham-bamthankyoumaam. No proper close-out of their visit; no last reveling in the limpid light of their ultimate resort, no celebratory bye-bye breakfast of ultimate sesame-seed bagels on their seaside balcony, no final exercise laps in the pool, last set of tennis, last light lunch in the annex restaurant, last skinny-dip-snorkel out to the reef off their pet pocket-beach, no subsequent drowsy lounge-chair beach-out, last Jacuzzi, last late-afternoon retreat to make last love in love's last mode, snoozing off skin to skin in each other's arms; no final wake-up call therefrom, final hors d'oeuvres and fin du vin. They'll simply suitcase their stuff, maybe not even that, hell with it, just throw on their get-out-of-here duds, button buttons snap snaps zip zippers lock locks and drop their room key in the Express Check-Out slot, that's for them, all right, old Mr. and Ms.

Pre-Paid, or not even that, just pop it into any letterbox down the line, return postage guaranteed, hell with it, time to go.

"No. He's jumping to conclusions."

Name of the game, yes?

"No. But Carrying On for Its Own Sake isn't the name of the game, either."

Tell him all about it; he has an infinite attention span.

"No. Anyhow, they can't lock locks drop key et cet yet."

No?

"No. They've *lost* their key."

Lost their key?

"No: mislaid it. Would he mind awfully searching high and low for it? She's pooped beyond pooped."

His pleasure. Is it here?

"No. Stop that."

Here?

"No no no no no no no. What part of No needs clarification?"

This part?

"Maybe."

Here.

"Here."

Hear hear.

"Story of their life."

On with it, then.

8. WHAT IN THIS PASS THEY DREAM,

... this terminally playful pair, when presently they drowse, shall be passed over: Dream-sequences are a no-no in their house, be it only a rented resort-room on some Caribbean or Florida key, latest and last of a fortunately extended series over the hard-working decades of their coupled lifestories, or story of their coupled life. Let them sleep much-needed sleep now, rest as best they can in peace, while the author (but not narrator-in-chief) of this rhizomatic tale hunts randomly high and low among sundry other losses, his own included, for their missing key. As with any such search, we'll not be surprised if this turns up surprising items other than its object. Is it here? Nope. Here? Nah. Here, perhaps? Unh-unh — but hey, look what we've found instead:

A few blocks from where these words and I find each other like more or less predestined lovers, astronomers at the Space Telescope Science Institute search for the lost Dark Matter of the universe — no trifling loss, as it theoretically comprises some ninety percent of the whole shebang and is the key to whether that shebang goes on shebanging, achieves some equilibrium, or with a mighty sigh relapses into the Big Crunch. With the aid of the Hubble Space Telescope, they'd hoped to find what they're after in the form of plenteous Red Dwarf stars too dim to see with ground-based instruments; when however the mighty Hubble scanned likely large voids in our Milky Way galaxy, instead of revealing them to be red-peppered with the missing matter it showed them dark and empty as Mother Hubbard's cupboard or the pocket in which you're *sure* you put those keys, and by the way turned up another head-scratcher: evidence that the universe is several billion years *younger* than its oldest stars, as we're accustomed to measuring their respective ages. Go figure — and don't be surprised if, searching for a lost thread, you find instead the Lost Chord, the Lost Generation, the Lost Battalion of World War One, the ten lost tribes of Israel (toting in their backpacks the missing two books of the original Septateuch), the lost continent of Atlantis, Louis XVII (the Lost Dauphin) of France, the works of classical antiquity lost to the Christian Dark Ages, the lost cities of Africa, assorted lost sheep and illusions, opportunities and causes, lost youth and sleep, arts and languages, lost time never to be recaptured or made up for, and all the wax ever lost by Benvenuto Cellini while casting jewelry by the method called *cire perdu*, of which yours truly is irreverently reminded whenever he sees advertisements for the product of the Maryland poultry magnate Frank Perdue. When will all those *poules perdues* come home to roost?

Here one comes now, a-cluck from Memory's brooder or a-clink from the scattered treasury of lost coins: *le franc perdu* of the only literal key that I can recall ever having lost: In July 1983, my wife and I rented a funky little Renault wagon in Tangier, Morocco, whither we had flown for me to lecture on Scheherazade's menstrual calendar as a key to *The 1001 Nights*. From our lodgings in the Grand Hotel Villa de France, where Matisse had been inspired to paint his odalisques, in the city that had earlier inspired Rimsky-Korsakov to compose his *Scheherazade*, we had explored on foot the bustling, redolent Medina, the Saccos both Grand and Petit, and the Kasbah; preferring to lose ourselves without professional assistance, we had shaken off disagreeably sticky would-be guides and had shrugged off a startling anti-Semitic tirade from one such reject; we had been serenaded morningly by urban roosters and five times daily by the muezzin's amplified prayer-calls from the neighborhood mosque-minaret; and we had decided to extend down-coast our innocent first foray into Islam. Aficionados of shores and beaches, points and promontories, corniches and capes and coastlines, once I had mastered the Renault's exotic dashboard gear-shift we drove on the last day of Ramadan through bougainvillea and dazzling sunshine east from Tangier to the cliffs of Cap Spartel, where the Strait of Gibraltar meets the Atlantic, thence alongshore southward through fish-rich Asilah to an off-road beach park called La Forêt Diplomatique, where we paused for a swim. At the djellaba'd beach-warden's direction, I parked (and locked) our squat little wagon among the pines, and faute de mieux (or perhaps a touch OD'd on Arabiana: camels on the beach, a scattering of cabanas like nomads' tents, some of the older women black-veiled as well as -caftaned) dropped the keys into my swim-trunks pocket, whence in course of our romping in the surf they joined the vast inventory of the lost at sea.

Dismay; indeed, alarm, as we were a considerable way from anywhere, in a forêt sans telephones or helpful park rangers, on a plage sans lifeguards or other officials except the elderly, perhaps self-appointed director of parking, who was sternly sympathetic when in faulty French we reported our loss, but unable to assist us in any fashion. Few other picnickers / bathers about, and they by the look of them deeply local; no Arabic at our command beyond a naughty glossary picked up from Scheherazade, and while most Moroccan businessfolk speak French or Spanish or English, ordinary workfolk often don't. Anyhow, Tangier was several hours distant; even the main coastal highway (where there might be buses) was a few kilometers from the beach, and the afternoon was running, and we were scheduled for dinner back at the American School before my PM lecture — which, given the subject, I had to hope would at worst be merely lost on the Tangerians in my audience and not offensive to them.

A dozen years later, upstreet from the Hubble astronomers, I pen these words: Ergo, we are not still stranded in Morocco's Forêt Diplomatique, our infidel bones a-bleach in the Afric sand while our rented Renault rusts 'neath yonder pines. No matter the mechanics of our and the car's retrieval (helpful Brit motorcyclist to the highway; even more helpful Arab family, out for an end-of-Ramadan holiday drive, to Tangier with a pair of grateful middle-aged Yank tourists; helpful and well-tipped driver from the rental agency next day, who of course had copies of the keys; steadfast beach-warden, who with pained dignity let the agency-chap know that my eight-dirham tip was incommensurate with his having kept watch "all night" over our now finally unlocked wagonette, but that another two DH would do the trick); the point of this lost-key anecdote, which I had scarcely since thought of until this temporizing digression recalled it to me, is . . .

But in refinding the story, I find I've lost its point. Better to lose than to be lost? That depends. Better the key lost than the car? For sure, in this instance anyhow. But although a *roman à clef*, for example, ought to be at least reasonably intelligible without its clef, a code without its key is as meaningless as a key without its code. And if, moreover, as has elsewhere been proposed, the key to the treasure may *be* the treasure, then . . .

Well. Unlike Anton Chekhov, Ernest Hemingway, Ralph Ellison, and other scribblers too numerous to catalogue, I have never lost a manuscript (the Lost Original, or "Mother of the Book," is a tradition as old as writing, echoed in the East by the lost six-sevenths of the Kathā Sarit Sāgara, or Ocean of Story, and in the West by the aforenoted lost two-sevenths of what's since been the Pentateuch), neither my own nor any of my four decadesworth of students'. At age twelve or so I was myself once briefly lost in a funhouse, and a quarter-century later found a story in that loss, which however is in no respect a *conte à clef*. My first marriage proved a net loss, but the net that lost it holds still some valued souvenirs. To Caribbean condo-burglars I lost my journal of certain post-Moroccan travels, and later recovered it from, of all unlikely places, the bottom of a beachside Jacuzzi — but that, too, is a tale to be found in another once upon a time than this; ditto that of the loss of my favorite hat, a Basque boina, into the awesome Tajo de Ronda in Andalusia, and its improbable, consequential recovery. Life, I do not doubt, is a game that affords its players only different ways to lose; that being the case, vive la différence. Sometimes, Q.E.D., what we've lost we may refind, although we shall most surely lose it again, one way or another. Christian scripture teaches that one must lose one's life in order to find it, and that's no mere Lost & Found gospel sophistry, for in truth one may find what thitherto had not been one's to lose: a coin in the grass; a bottled message to whom it may concern; a perfectly satisfactory pair of women's sunglasses five meters deep on a coral reef and, lolling near it in the lazy current, a palimpsestic page from some novel or short story (more legible than intelligible, at least out of context, despite its immersion), as if some mermaid had been interrupted in mid-read; a splendid new life-partner; a narrative voice wherewith not only to commence but to go on, on, on with the surmisable story.

Or we may not, serendipitously, so find. "*Perdido,*" sings persistently the old swing-band tune of that name: "*Perdido, perdido, perdido* [two, three, four], *perdido, perdido, perdido . . .*" et cet. ad lib. ad inf.

7. & 6. "WAVES EXPLAINED

. . . are not explained away," she presently declares; "likewise particles," and he's not inclined to argue. End-of-their-tether body-and-soul-mates, still-ardent skin to skin, their meter ticking even as Time's taxi waits. Have they, for example — while brooding over hadrons and leptons, fermions and bosons, sparticles and photinos — sportively removed each other's underpants with their teeth?

"Goes without saying."

So it would've gone, anyhow, once upon a time.

"And so it went." Then, presently: "So what? Please?"

Ah, so, he ventures. Then, presently: *Complementarity* is the nub of it, wouldn't she say? The key to Father Time's cupboard?

"Not impossibly, once explained. Or possibly not."

Or possibly so *until* explained.

"So . . ."

So let's explain till the cows come home, understanding that what fails to account for those cows may nevertheless fetch 'em, no? What fails to explain away may anyhow explain into real presence.

"She's all ears, I guess."

By no means, but we have to start somewhere. They've made love, this couple of ours —

"Start there. Couple of hours?"

Couple of minutes here, couple of half-hours there. It adds up.

"Couple of decades, till the cows *et cetera*. But not ad infinitum. Never enough."

Because besides lovemaking, they've loved making: their life together; kids and connections, headway and leeway ...

"Better people of their students; better students of their people."

Meals and music, hay and whoopee, beds and voyages and decisions.

"A living, jointly and severally. Waves, trouble, and messes now and then."

They never enjoyed making those. But they did clean them up, best they could; we'll say that for them.

"Making sense and nonsense, he was saying ..."

Even trans-sense, now and then. Despite or because of or notwithstanding which, here they are: last-resorted, at sixes and sevens ...

"He mentioned complementarity."

She mentioned waves and particles.

"On with their story, then, s.v.p., moving their bodies as little as possible. Don't make waves while we're riding one."

Wave*hood*, then, he'll presently remind her, and particle*hood*: In the microworld, those are as inescapably complementary as momentum and position — or momentum *versus* position, one might as well say. Your innocent, minding-its-own-business photon or electron has both until *we* mind its business, whereupon, as has been demonstrated, its wavehood gives way to particality, and momentum to position, or vice versa.

"Is he suggesting, maybe, that couplehood and individuality are like that? Is he hinting that she has her herness and he his hisness, but that then there's their theirness, in which she partakes of his hisness, long may it wave — "

And he all but eats and drinks her herness ...

"What's this *all but*?"

Slip of his distracted tongue. The point just now is that it's not only their theirness that's both complementary to and comprised of her herness and his hisness. After so much skin-talk, pillow talk, talk-talk, and busy cohabitation; so much sturm und drang und fun and games, her herness comprises a fair share of his hisness, and vice versa.

"Mi palapa es su palapa — all but."

Or as they say at our Institute for Narrative Physics, his and her shared space-time equals their worldline, and here's where things get dizzy-making.

"May the cows not come too soon. She's enjoying this, more than not, under the circumstances."

He likewise — despite their being, as aforeremarked, at sevens and sixes. Their particality is at critical odds with their wavehood, let's say, and yet . . .

"Thanks be to the muse of physical narrative for that *and yet . . .*"

And for the suspension points thereafter: their only hope. Think of their life-stories, separate and joint, as an extended though alas not infinite string of past such points, at any one of which each of them might have done A instead of B, or had X happen to them rather than Y. Their worldline — which we'll take the liberty of calling their storyline —

"Take."

— is the sum of all such points thus far.

"So few to go! Maybe only one more."

Or maybe more than one only. In any case, what he'd have the pair of them perpend is that in physics and fiction alike, at any of many of those waypoints in space-time, alternative worldlines are not only imaginable but evidently quite possible — some, of course, more consequential than others. It *seems*, at least, that she could've ordered the gambas a la plancha at lunch instead of the chiperones, or the vino tinto instead of the blanco —

"With chiperones? Not her! But she might very well have gone to Macy's instead of to Bloomingdale's on a certain afternoon twelve chapters ago, or to Macy's *before* Bloomingdale's, or straight to Bloomie's Bedding department without detouring through Housewares, and thus would never've re-met him there amid the Krups coffeemakers. *That*'s a scary one."

Indeed — always remembering, however, for perspective's sake, that the Rwandan and Bosnian disasters and the rest would no doubt have happened despite all the Butterfly Effects from that handshake among the Krupses. And yet the contingency of this couple's re-meeting is less sobering than the consideration that in at least as many storyworldlines as not, it *didn't* happen. B happened instead, or C or D, and he and she went on with their separate stories separately.

"Do we have to? Multiverses?"

We do: It all starts with neutron decay, I'm afraid.

"So is she! Too late in the day to start with the neutrons! Too late in their story!"

Not in *this* their-story. Any cows in sight?

"Only a couple of geckos cuddling on the wall up there. On with the neutrons, she supposes; she'll let him know."

The short version, then. Back at the Institute of Love Among the Quanta, when we watched for a neutron to decay into a proton or an electron or an antineutrino, our watch was nearly always in the neighborhood of twenty minutes, right? Give or take five or ten. On the other hand, once in a while the thing would pop off immediately, and now and then we had to wait for it fucking forever.

"Particle physics is such a turn-on."

One goes on to remind her that in the "multiverse" reading of quantum mechanics, for each moment at which that neutron *might* decay, there's a universe in which it does or did, and a fortiori there's a version of ourselves the observer who observes that decay of that particular neutron at that particular moment in that particular universe.

"Holding hands."

In some universes yes, in others no, tant pis.

"The bottom line, guys, is that whatever *can* happen, physically speaking, *does* happen, in some actual alternative version of 'our' universe. In this one, meanwhile (she quotes her erstwhile mentor skin to skin), 'Quantum theory is probabilistic in predicting the chance of a given outcome in some *particular* universe, but it's deterministic in prescribing the proportion of universes in which that particular outcome comes out.' Did any real lovers in the history of the world ever pillow-talk like this?"

In most universes no; in some yes, and brava. So to get right to it — but why hurry?

"Because their clock is running. So to get right to it, there are universes in which we never met, and others in which we met but didn't re-meet. Her and him."

And plenty more in which we met and re-met, but some crucial next plot-corner wasn't turned: no follow-through, no rising action.

"No Her introducing Him to sashimi and Erik Satie and mountain-biking."

No Him introducing her to X and Y and Z.

"Which she's been hooked on ever since."

Universes in which, even as you and I lie here now like a couple of burned-out geckos, *they* never became lovers.

"Universes in which they not only became lovers but married, in some cases happily, in others not. Had children; didn't have children . . ."

Had children whom they treasured and were treasured by at every stage of the kids' development and their own, including even American adolescence and middlescence, believe it or not, respectively.

"That's the universe for me."

Next time, for sure.

"There is no —"

Of course there is, maybe: Closed Timelike Loops, Spacetime Wormholes between scenarios. I'll loop back to those.

"Next time, maybe. Meanwhile, chez l'Institut . . ."

This just in: There are universes in which the best of all those possible worldlines comes to pass, but *only in some fiction within that universe*: a made-for-TV movie, maybe, or a stage play, or a novel or short story. In those universes, She and He are mere words on a page.

"Not words on a page!"

Well: not *mere*, for sure.

"This and this, words on a page? These?"

Hard to accept, but quite possibly so. Quite probably, even. *Necessarily*, in fact, we suppose, since such a thing can be imagined within the bounds of physical reality.

"Not by her. Speak for himself."

He's speaking for all those other selves of theirs: the other usses going on with our other stories in those other universes.

"Stories with better endings, is what he's thinking."

Let him think it. The point is, in the story they're in, up to its dénouement he wouldn't change a word.

"Thanks for that. *She* might edit a couple here and there, she supposes. Not the couple-couple, though. Not the Him of them, anyhow."

He wouldn't even diddle the dénouement, come to that —

"And they *have* come to that."

— he'd only postpone it, unspeakable as it is. The best of all worldlines that come to pass *does* come to pass — and then it passes.

"*Art alone endures.* Thomas Carlyle? Frank Lloyd Wright? But art passes, too."

For sure. Art passes to Mort —

"Who passes to Irving, who goes in for the score."

Seven-six Mort d'Art, in the bottom of the twelfth.

"What game *is* this?"

Till the Cows Come Home: A Love Story.

Presently: "Dearest friend, they're home. They never left, she suspects."

Cows Explained, then.

"But not explained away. Like quantum electrodynamic dramaturgy."

QED, muse be praised. Likewise love.

Presently: "Q.E.D."

5, 4, 3, 2: "ON

. . . with the story," he would have her insist, however spent the pair of them at this point in this version of their coupled worldline, were he its author instead of its provisional narrator: "Once upon a time ad infinitum," while we rest upon each other crown to sole.

"Hey: They're soixante-neufing?"

In some versions. But what he meant was brow brow arms arms chest chest belly belly thighs thighs et cet, she draped atop him doggo in the dark; not sixty-nining but five-four-three-twoing, except when some story puts their count on Hold. Once upon a time, he'd tell her . . .

Once upon a time, he *tells* her, there was this couple freeze-framed in spacetime, or *as if* freeze-framed, the way you and I would be if we were flying cross-country again, east to west at six hundred miles per hour while the USA zips under us west to east at a thousand per, carrying with it Earth's atmosphere and our DC-10 at a net speed of minus four hundred, while our planet chugs around the Sun at sixty-six thousand plus and our solar system laps the Milky Way at half a million mph and our galactic Local Group sprints en bloc toward the Great Attractor at maybe a million und so weiter, but the effect for us is as of sitting still in the dark with our plastic tumblers of Mendocino Chablis at thirty-two thousand feet over the Mississippi, let's say — which point like any point could be considered for us just then the *Stillpunkt* at the center of our universe and all others, their vertiginous motions and countermotions reckoned relatively therefrom. Ignoring the in-flight movie more or less in progress (appropriately freeze-framed just now in midst of a special-effect chase scene), we click glass-rims in the muted cabin light and toast our Story Thus Far, perhaps only just begun in consequence of each's noticing that her/his attractive seatmate happened to be scanning the same in-flight magazine photospread as her-/himself — "Island Hideaways," it's called, let's say — and discovering in bemused conversation that each in an earlier life-chapter had once sojourned in the other's favorite themof, almost though not quite at the same time but in fact at the same resort complex, Cayo Olvidado, and further — get this — that each in course of said romantic escapade (the one then-couple married but not honeymooning, the other honeymooning but not married) had found and retrieved, while snorkeling the coral reef just off the beach, a page torn or unglued or otherwise detached from some paperback novel and bottled like a message of distress, hers bone-dry on the sea-floor in a well-capped former rum-fifth inexplicably half-filled with pebbles to make it sink, his paradoxically afloat in a likewise well-capped wine-jug filled with sea water and perched high and dry on an exposed coral ledge. Quelle coïncidence! Quel cute meet, now that we've met! So what'd hers say?

"Hard to tell, 'cause it was just the closing words of some story and not even in complete sentences: *Bosnia, Haiti, Rwanda. The web of the world.* Rest of the page blank. Go figure. Yours?"

Some SF or semi-cyberpunk thing, as he remembers: *The Dream-Park Project*, let's call it, from which across the years bits still come back to him: *Alura, their shapely cave-guide, tugged at Fred's sleeve and cried, "Must go now!" Ariana, however, watched the approaching lava-flow with the practiced eye of one who has worked this Reality-Level before. "The missing key," Walt muttered,* dot dot dot *et cetera.*

"Got it," his seatmate says, and sips and chuckles, and permits herself to wonder whether those two pages mightn't constitute *their* passkey to a new and liberating connection, if joined like the sundered moieties of an old-time indenture bill.

"Sundered moieties?"

We talk like that now and then, pour le sport, sometimes even with our own last-lapped indentures postcoitally still snugged. Anyhow *they* used so to speak, she and he, once upon. Once upon another time, he tells her now, there was this chap alone in his shoreside digs, yet not alone in being alone there: great mother hurricane approaching, say; end of the world, maybe; hatches all battened, all storm-preps prepped, nothing left but to wait 'er out, maybe pop a cold one while there's still one cold to pop, tell himself a couple couple-stories in the dark: the one, e.g., about the youngish neighbor-lady every bit as independent as he, likewise battened down next door to ride out the blow with no company more interesting than her saddle-brown Chesapeake retriever. He spins out versions of their possible story as the wind off the bay begins to pipe in earnest: She he, he she, hi ho, ho hum, and then one day aha —

"The end," she'd say. No way, 'd say he: There're narrative options still unforeclosed, other storyworldlines wormholing through the multiverse. "Happy endings are all alike," she'd retort, were she the retorting sort, "but in *this* universe, at least, delta p times delta q equals or exceeds h-bar over two, and so while it may *seem* that Achilles can never reach the tortoise nor any tale its end, he does and theirs did, amen."

Maybe once upon a time it did, he grants, amending her amen, but that's another story: the one in which a terminal brace of longtime lovers checks into what they're grimly calling their Last Resort. There's a thing to be done, but they're in no rush. They've time yet . . .

"No."

Time time time time; never enough, but some still yet . . .

"No."

No end-stops in *their* love-story; only semicolons, suspension points . . .

"No."

. . . between any one such which and the next, space-time to spare; still space, still time . . .

"No."

Tales unended, unmiddled, unbegun; untold tales untold; unnumbered once-upons-a —

"No."

1. CHECK-OUT

. . . time come and gone long since; she likewise, his without-whom-nothing.

There is (he nevertheless tells her presently) a narrative alternative universe, an alternative narrative universe in which by this time at this point in this particular wormholed worldline the pair of them are *laughing*, although what's come to pass is anything but a laughing matter. He had all but forgotten that *laugh* of hers, of theirs, ours — unbuckled and unabashed, merry beyond pain, beyond merriment, existential yet gut-deep — but he hears it now, all right: They're laughing freely, almost helplessly, the way they used so often to find themselves laughing, sometimes despite themselves even in circumstances grim or solemn, or anyhow wanting so to do, back in the beginning: their so-fortuitous, staggeringly contingent, richly consequential once upon.

T-zero.

The Book Of Ten Nights And A Night ELEVEN STORIES (2004)

FOR SHELLY

sine qua non

Invocation: "WYSIWYG"

There was meant to have been a book
called *Ten Nights and a Night*, which, had it gotten itself written before
TEOTWAW(A)KI 9/11/2001 — The End Of The World As We (Americans) Knew It — might have opened with a sportive extended invocation to the Storyteller's Muse, more or less like this:

Tell, O Muse of Story, the hundred-percent-made-up tale of a modern-day Odysseus's interlude with the brackish tidewater marsh-nymph here called WYSIWYG —

"Wissywig?"

Spelled W-Y-S-I-W-Y-G. Explanation to follow, if called for. *How, in an advanced but still-healthy decade of his sleeping and waking, breathing air and pumping blood, eating/drinking/pissing/shitting, learning and teaching, dressing and undressing —*

"Shall we cut to that part?"

Not yet. *Talking and listening, reading and writing, making love and sentences —*

"First part of that last part!"

All in Miz Muse's good time. *He found himself lost —*

"Found himself lost?"

Paradoxically speaking. *Not shipwrecked like the original Odysseus for seven years on fair Calypso's isle and obliged to service that nymph nightly, with the promise of immortality and eternal youth if he'd stay put for keeps —*

397

"He'd have a problem with that?"

— when what he really wanted was to get his aging mortal ass back home to his ditto ditto wife.

"Lucky wife. Unlucky nymph."

Nor was our chap lost like Dante, in the Dark Wood of a midlife crisis from which only a detour through Hell to Heaven could get him back on track. Too old, this one, for midlife crises.

"Not that they're the only kind."

Granted. *Neither would he presume to compare his position to Scheherazade's, who humped King Shahryar through a thousand nights and a night and told him her tales under threat of death if she pleased him not, her aim being to save not only herself and "the virgin daughters of Islam" from the guy's murderous misogyny, but the King too, and his kingdom . . .*

"Men, I swear."

Yes, well. But, as I was saying, *No: The situation of this Senior Talester —* Have we mentioned our strandee's trade? So let's maybe call him *Graybard . . .*

"Got it. His situation, you were saying?"

— was meant to be an Extended Congress, shall we say, with the above-invoked muse, or with some serviceable surrogate therefor —

Serviceable surrogate? And what manner of quote *congress* did the gentleman have in mind, may one ask?"

Patience, please. *Their uppercase Congress* (and accompanying dialogue) *to extend over eleven nights and serve as battery-charging interludes between his reviewing with her . . . post-Congressly? . . .*

"Now we're talking!"

Merely talking, mind.

"On to the interlude!"

Soon's we're done with this hypothetical invocation: *. . . his retelling her, et cetera, eleven several stories: the previously published but hitherto uncollected fruits of her long collaboration both with their Original Author — whom never mind — and with their Present Teller: most of said stories perpetrated over the decade past* (i.e., the closing decade of the Terrible Twentieth), *but a couple of them dating back considerably farther; most of them pure fiction, but a couple more or less non-; most of them Autumnal, shall we say, in theme and tone, addressing such jolly topics as the approach of old age, declining capabilities, and death — but* *a couple not. And several having to do, for better or worse, with* (hang on to your hats, folks) ... *the Telling of Stories!*

"O very joy."

Well. *Graybard-the-Talester's purpose—this odd couple's or trio's purpose—in so doing would have been twofold: first, to put these originally unrelated tales into a narrative frame, connecting their dots to make a whole somewhat larger (and perhaps a bit friskier) than the mere sum of its parts, as in such exemplary instances as* The Book of a Thousand Nights and a Night; *also Boccaccio's* Decameron, *Marguerite of Navarre's* Heptameron, *Giovanni Battista Basile's* Pentameron, *and other such -amerons ...*

"In a word, a Hendecameron?"

Why, thankee there, Wys: *Hendecameron, yes! And second, by their Present Teller's thus clearing the narrative decks, so to speak, to recharge and reorient their Original Author's imagination. Whom never mind.*

"She's on the edge of her chair. If Present Teller happens to feel a bit frisky?"

Patience, s.v.p.: The guy's preoccupied with, among other things, this meant-to-have-been Invocation. *In other words, between or among themselves to discover where they-all might go next by determining where they are now by reviewing where they've been lately, storywise and otherwise.* Sound familiar?

"She's on the edge of her bed, this Wissywhatever."

-WYG: explanation to follow, inexorably. *Thus their initial intention: Original Author's (whom never mind), old Graybard-the-Teller's, and their muse-in-common's*—muse's-in-common?—*who serviceth the first of those through the second, and vice versa.*

"Kink-*y!* Shall they get on with it, then? Extended Congress and such?"

Surely they would have so gotten, well ere now, *had not shit hit the world-in-general's fan, and the US of A's in particular, on that certain September morn, killing thousands of innocents and, just possibly, American Innocence itself. And by the way so distracting Talester Graybard and present company—*

"Speak for himself. Present Company can still concentrate, believe it or not, when she puts her mind to it, and other relevant parts."

He stands corrected.

"Then let him *lie* corrected—beside her, and they'll get on with

Getting It On while old Never-Mind-*Him* shakes his mostly Autumnal head and the world goes kerflooey."

There's the problem, Wys: one of the problems, anyhow. If we think of capital-A Author as being the mere narrative hardware, so to speak (which is why we can forget about him), and Yours-Truly-quote-Graybard as embodying Narrative Imagination — the Art-of-Fiction software, if you will, for *rendering* Author's story-ideas —

"I will if you will. Whenever you're ready?"

— then *lying* might be said to be their collective vocation, right? *Lying with her*; we could even say, she serving after all as muse and accessory before, during, and after the fact of their fictions — although those wordplays are bound to be lost in translation.

"First a Serviceable Surrogate, now an Accessory! Such gallantries!"

She knows what we mean. And that they're meant as compliments.

"Mm-hm. How about quote *brackish tidewater marsh-nymph*, some pages back? Another compliment?"

Of course. As Reader will have noticed, she's both fresh and salty . . .

"Compliments accepted, then, she supposes. She reminds all hands, however, that there are other kinds of play than wordplay."

Perpended — and now back to our hypothetical and subsequently shot-down Extended Invocation, if I may? *Their quandary* (Graybard's and Wysiwyg's) *is that for him to re-render now, in these so radically altered circumstances, Author's eleven mostly Autumnal and impossibly* innocent *stories, strikes him as bizarre, to put it mildly indeed — as if Nine Eleven O One hadn't changed the neighborhood (including connotations of the number eleven), if not forever, at least for what remains of Teller's lifetime. And yet* not *to go on with the stories, so to speak, would be in effect to give the mass-murderous fanatics what they're after: a world in which what they've done already and might do next dominates our every thought and deed.*

"Hell with *that*."

Hell *is* that. And *Thus*, I say, *his situation and their quandary*: GB-the-Teller's task — shall we call him GeeBee?

"Ick."

Forget it, then: *Teller's not-unfamiliar task, if I may recapitulate, had formerly been the more or less routine one of assisting Author by reviewing, in a maybe-sportive narrative frame dreamed up for that purpose, those eleven not-so-sportive waypoints from their Stories Thus Far, and, thus oriented, to proceed. After Black Tuesday, however, it's how to tell those or any such tales in a world so transformed overnight by terror that they seem, at best, irrelevant.*

End of aborted invocation.

"Okay. May I talk now?

I mean this brackish Wissywiggy accessory-surrogate, whose name you've yet to explain to her and whose utterances to date have been mainly mere teasing interjections?"

Be Graybard's guest — since, truth to tell, it's he who's hers.

"You got that right, pal, and here's how she sees it: First off, while we're forgetting about Whatsisname the Original Author or Mere Narrative Hardware, let's forget about old Odysseus too, who at his final raft-wrecked landfall before reaching home simply reviews for the locals everything that's happened to him in the ten years since he and his now-dead shipmates set sail from Troy's Ground Zero, and whose four-chapter recounting of those tribulations is understandably short on lightness, not to mention humor."

Point taken: Farewell, Odysseus, or however it goes in Greek.

" Εὐχαριστῶ! as we say on Mount Helicon."

Epharisto.

"And let's set aside Mister Middle-Aged Dante, whose excursion through Hell, Purgatory, and Heaven can scarcely be called light storytelling, and whose predicament, like O's, is his own, not his society's. And who, by the way, never returns to that narrative frame of the Dark Wood that he *found himself lost* in, to wrap it up after his culminating vision of the Big Gee — as if Homer were to end the *Odyssey* when its hero winds up that review of his Story Thus Far, and leave the whole second half of the epic unsung!"

Addio, Dante. What a memory you have.

"Yes, well: I was *there*, more or less, right? I am, after all, the Serviceable Surrogate."

More than serviceable!

"Yet yet to be serviced. Setting aside, I say, that pair, let's consider your pals Scheherazade and Boccaccio. *Her* stories are mainly geewhizzers: light in tone, heavy on special effects like magic rings and genies in bottles, often erotic and sometimes scatological, meant purely to entertain and keep her audience wanting encores — "

Or else.

"Exactly: The girl's in bed with the Guinness World Record serial killer: a thousand innocent virgins deflowered and murdered in as many nights since he offed his unfaithful wife, and Scher's next in line if she doesn't get his rocks off and leave him wanting more. Talk about Performance Anxiety: If she'd been a man, she could never have gotten it up! Talk about Publish or Perish! Yet for *ninety-one times* our piddling eleven nights she delivers the goods both sexually and narratively; bears the monster three children and then marries him when he finally lifts the curse — despite there being never a hint anywhere that she *loves* the bastard! She's just Doing What the Situation Calls For: telling marvelous stories with the ax virtually at her neck and the kingdom on the brink of collapse ..."

Amen. And we believe we know what you're going to say about the *Decameron*, but please say it anyhow.

"Great Plague of 1348 devastates city of Florence! People dropping like flies from the Black Death that'll kill one out of every three Europeans over the next dozen years! Corpses piling up in the streets; law and order down the drain, if they'd *had* any drains — and in the face of this horror, what do Boccaccio's three young lords and seven young ladies do? Why, they retreat with their lucky servants to their country estates (*of which each of us owns several*, one of the ladies points out), and they organize their own little play-world, with its rotating king- or queen-for-a-day and its chivalrous rules for ordering their pleasures, and they virtuously stroll and dine and sing and dance and tease and flirt, and then in the hottest part of the afternoon, after siesta-time, they amuse themselves with witty and / or racy *stories*: one tale per person per day for ten not-quite-consecutive days (Fridays and Saturdays off) while the world dies unnoticed off-screen. And at the end of that period — congratulating themselves on having maintained their collective virtue despite the collapse of their society and the naughtiness of their tales, but apprehensive that prolonging their idyll will either lead them into capital-V Vice or tarnish their reputations back in the city (an odd scruple indeed, under the circumstances)— they return to the church of Santa Maria Novella in Florence, where they'd just happened to meet two weeks earlier, and there they bid one another *arrivederci* and go back to their town houses and on with their lives and business."

With nary a word, as I remember, about the devastation they're returning to.

"Nary a word — but we'll get to that later. The point to be made now is, dot dot dot?"

Point made: Catastrophe, if not quite apocalypse, has them by the throat, but they spin their yarns nevertheless.

"Not nevertheless, Geeb: *therefore*. And not apocalypse-tales, we note, but How Abu Hasan Farted, and How Friar Rinaldo Lies with His Godchild's Mother and Her Husband Finds Him with Her and They Make Him Believe That the Friar Is Charming Away the Child's Worms? Stuff like that."

So what we'd like to believe . . .?

"Is that to tell *irrelevant* stories in grim circumstances is not only permissible, but sometimes therapeutic. That their very irrelevance to the frame-situation may be what matters, whether the frame's grim and the tales are frisky or vice versa. As somebody's grandma-from-Minsk used to say about *shtetl* humor back in the time of the pogroms, *If we didn't laugh, we'd hang ourselves*."

Oy: Observation perpended. On with the Mostly Autumnal, Mostly Recent, Mostly Fictive stories, then?

"Well: There remains the matter of a certain adverb back in that trial-balloon invocation: *Present Teller reviews eleven tales with Muse, post-* . . . How did it go? Not *post-nuptially*. Not *postpartumly*. Not *post-modernly* . . ."

Post-invocationally, maybe. Ms. Wysiwyg had a grandma from Minsk?

"Maybe. And maybe other kids besides young quote *Wys* shared her good luck in the Grandma way — if, in Wyssie's case anyhow, not much good luck otherwise. A loving grandma from Minsk: If only!"

Now her colleague's on the edge of *his* chair. On with *her* story?

"Maybe somewhere down the line. First — assuming consent of all parties concerned? — they get that adverb out of the way. Then, post-adverbially, they start over again from Square One, explaining that queer name of hers and who and where she is and what's going on here besides adverbing. *Then* Graybard Teller tells Forget-About-the-Author's dozen-minus-one stories, if that's how the game goes, between or after which maybe we'll in a manner of speaking squeeze in hers? Never mind Homer and Dante and Boccaccio: Let our models be your pal Scheherazade (minus the nightly menace from her bedmate) and the Sanskrit *Ocean of Story*, as told by the god Shiva to his playmate Parvati: the longest story ever told, spun out by the Lord of Creation and Destruction as a thankyou-ma'am for big-time bedplay while the goddess sits on her lover's lap. In both cases, comrade, it's Ess-Ee-Ex before Story-telling; otherwise this game's over before it starts."

Yes, well: Now that "Graybard" has been safely distinguished from Never-Mind-Whom as Software from Hardware, and both of those from Inspiration, which is Ms. Muse's department, her wish, we guess, is *ipso facto* Imagination's command. On one major condition? And with one minor adjustment?

"Like, say, Imagination's left hand *here*, while his right carries on ... exactly ... *so?*"

Her pleasure's his, in the nature of the case and their respective job-descriptions. *And although their situation remained still Pre- rather than Post-Congressional, and the world-at-large's was unimproved, and "GB's" Major Condition and Minor Adjustment remained unstipulated, much less met or made, and even Ms. WYSIWYG's alias du soir had yet to be glossed for the patient reader — not to mention where they-all are and how they got there — old Graybard-the-Teller at this point fetched forth, for his muse-friend's possible delectation ...*

"Yes!"

HELP   a stereophonic narrative for authorial voice.

R = Right channel of disc or tape recording, separately recorded.
C = Central voice, either recorded equidistant between stereo microphones, in synchrony with and superimposed on R and L, or live interlocutory between R and L.
L = Left channel, separately recorded in synchrony with R.

R | Help!
C | Help!
L | HELP! **HELP!**

help!   help   Help help   Help help
   help   *help*   HELP   HELP!
help!   Help!   **HELP!**   HELP!   Hel

HELP! (diagonal)

(et cetera at random pitches, volumes, frequencies, timbres, and inflections for 30 sec.) LP!

R | 11-second pause | **HELP!** (exclamatorily) | 8-second pause | (unison shouts) HIP-hip **HELP!** | 1-second pause | **HELP!** 2-second pause | **HELP!** 2-second pause | **HELP!** 3-second pause
C | 14-second pause | **HELP.** (declaratively) | 5-second pause | HIP-hip **HELP!** 1-second pause | **HELP!** 2-second pause | **HELP!** 2-second pause | 3-second pause
L | 7-second pause | **HELP?** (interrogatively) | 12-second pause | **HELP!** 1-second pause | **HELP!** 2-second pause | HIP-hip **HELP!** 1-second pause | 3-second pause

Assistance Aidance Boot Providence Ministration Favor Shot in the arm Mercy Encouragement

Fosterage Charity Guidance Sustenance Nourishment Manna Provision Alleviation Easement

Redress Reinforcement Pardon Shrift Abettance Succor Cast Subvention Ministry Boost

(read as if from list, about one per second)

R | Help . . . help . . . . help . . help . . help . help. helphelphelphelp! *(peremptorily: gradual accelerando from very slow to very fast, 15 seconds)* | 3-second pause | . . . . **HELP!** | 3-second pause

C | Help? Help help? HELP? Helphelphelp? . . Assistance? *(last time)* *(interrogatively: random intervals, 15 seconds)* | 3-second pause | 3-second pause

L | Help help help help help help help help help . . . . **HELP!** *(crescendo from whisper to shout, about twice/second, 15 seconds)* | 3-second pause

405

R Good turn Clemency Therapy Protection Auspice Benevolence Championship Sustenation Nutrition Subsidy Relief Comfort Deliverance Indemnification Stay

C Befriendment Amnesty Obligement Aid Lift Accommodation Supportance Furtherance Hand Beneficence Rescue Care Sanctuary Goodwill Countenance

L Maintenance Eutropy Bounty Mitigation Ease Remedy Deus ex machina Indulgence Absolution Bolsterance Help

R Aiudo Aiudo, aiudo, per piacere, aiudo! AU SECOURS? AU SECOURS •••   AU SECOURS •••   AU SECOURS ••••

C Zu Hilfe, bitte. Zu Hilfe? AU SECOURS •••
(evenly)
mayday mayday mayday mayday mayday mayday mayday mayday
(tersely)
HELP HELP HELP   HELP HELP HELP

L ¡Socorro! ¡Socorro! ¡Socorro, por Dios! ¡BAH!
(flatly)

Unnnh! (groan)   3-second pause
Oy veh. (wearily)   3-second pause
Whew! (sigh)   3-second pause

5-second pause
5-second pause
5-second pause

R Tsk-tsk-tsk-tsk-tsk-tsk-tsk- .... -tsk
(rapidly, 15 seconds)
no pause (♩ = 116) 15 seconds)
tsk t-t-tsk   tsk t-t-tsk   repeat 3 more times

C My, My, my, my, my, my, my ...... my. 5-second pause
(concernedly, 10 seconds)
snap fingers starting at R's 5th bar (♩ = 116)
tsk t-t-tsk   repeat 1 more time

L Unh. Unh. Unh unh unh ...... unh. 5-second pause
(desperately, 10 seconds)
grunt rhythmically starting at R's 3rd bar (♩ = 116)
unh ----   repeat 2 more times

Help help help help help help
(conversationally)
Help help help help

brightly, to rhythm of Waiting on the Levee
Help-help   help   help-help
Help-help tamb. ad lib.
Help   help   Help
bones ad lib

HELP!
HELP!
HELP!

R (♩ = 116) 4/4 tambourine 4/4
C (♩ = 116) 4/4 snap fingers 4/4
L (♩ = 116) 4/4 bones 4/4
no pause

406

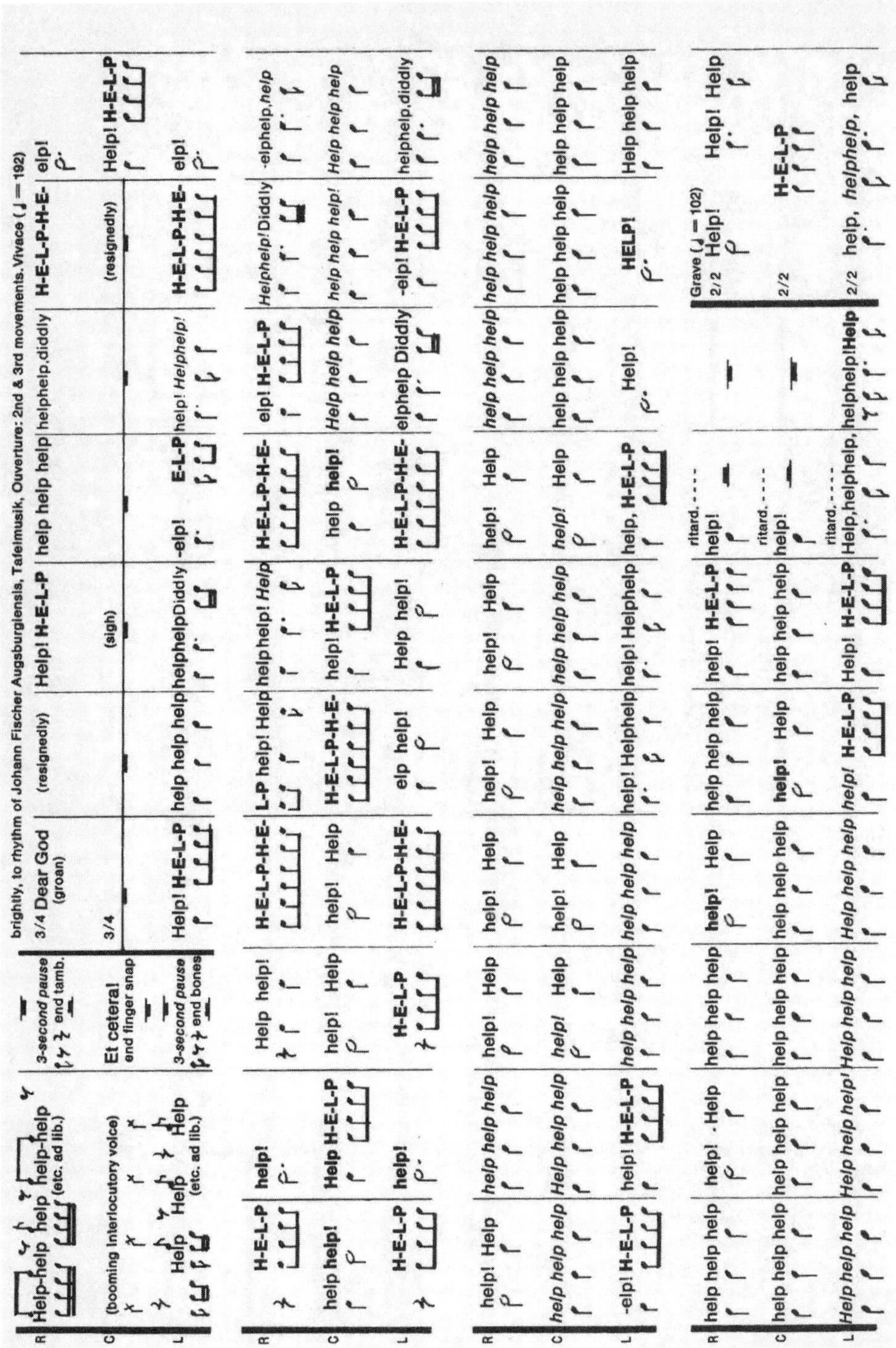
brightly, to rhythm of Johann Fischer Augsburgiensis, Tafelmusik, Ouverture: 2nd & 3rd movements. Vivace (♩ = 192)
(booming interlocutory voice)
3-second pause end tamb.
Et cetera! end finger snap
3-second pause end bones
Dear God (groan)
(resignedly)
(sigh)
Grave (♩ = 102)
ritard.

STORY DESIGNED BY RUDOLPH DE HARAK

FIRST NIGHT

"Whoa, there! Hold on!"

My pleasure. By which we mean, of course, Graybard's-the-Present-Teller-of-These-Tales.

"But not mine, as promised. Not Wyssywhatsit's?"

WYSI*WYG*'s. Problem?

"Three problems, at least. First off, when you said your guy was quote *fetching something forth for her possible delectation,* his water-bedmate not unreasonably assumed, dot dot dot — you know? I mean, *look* at her!"

Who could not? Savoring every aspect and detail of what Narrative Imagination sees in (begging his colleague's pardon) the perhaps counterproductively too-bright lights of Inspiration's remarkable boudoir. Maybe hit the dimmer-switch a bit? Mood lighting, et cet.?

"Not yet: She *wants* him to see it all, because *What you see,* as the saying goes, *is what you get.* Hey! . . .?"

There it is: WYSI*WYG,* as the computer-types used to say back in the far-off Nineteen Eighties, when PCs were first actually able to show text on the monitor with the same fonts and line-breaks as the hard-copy printout. What you saw is what you'd get: WYSIWYG.

"I get it: Quite appropriate. Even painfully so."

For her getting it, a Graybard kiss, right here. For its being maybe a tad painful in ways as yet unknown to him and *a fortiori* to our Reader, another . . . here?

"There. And when he's finished — I mean, when *she's* finished . . .

"There. Thankee kindly, sir,
and now to Problem One: Wyssie's not unreasonable expectation, back
at that Trial Invocation's end, *re* what was about to be fetched forth by
her visiting colleague-not-yet-in-arms?"

Yes. Well.

"She thought they'd agreed: Love before Language! Ardor before
Art! He's got a problem with that?"

Certainly not in principle. In homely, high-mileage fact, however,
Hers Truly could use a bit of, shall we say, *Help?* Night One of their
reconnection and Extended Congress may be young; her present company isn't. Thus that forewarned-of Minor Adjustment: his fetching
forth, in lieu of *et cetera*, Story Number One, believe it or not, of the
aforespecified eleven: a little *jeu d'esprit* from the rambunctious High
Nineteen Sixties, meant to illustrate not so much that art may be a cry
for help as that Distress, like any other emotion, circumstance, or what
have you, may be grist for Ms. Muse's mill. Shall they grind on?

"Presently. Perhaps? One hopes."

The above was Problem One, he believes she said? Of three, he believes she said?

"Three at least
is what she said, but three'll do — and we haven't even gotten to that
Major Condition somebody spoke of awhile back. Problem Two is that
by any reasonable definition, this Minor Adjustment by him fetched
forth wasn't a capital-S Story."

Not a story?

"Granted, it had a Beginning, a Middle, and an Ending — but so does
any sentence, any day, any life, without their therefore being Stories,
as Wys and Graybard both well know. The thing even built through
sequential escalations to a sort of climax and resolution, or at least a
petering out, if one may so put it. But then so does any wave breaking
on a beach, any off-the-shelf symphony or fireworks display — or, so
one hears, the capital-A Act of capital-L Love, when all goes well. Does
that make them stories? Not in Fiction Writing 101: Check your par-
don-the-expression Software."

What can one say?

"Oh, well: that mere *jeux d'esprit* don't count — except as *jeux d'esprit*, bless them. That if there're to be eleven several stories in this Hendecameron of ours, then somebody still owes us, among other things, Story Number One. That, on the other hand, as *jeux d'esprit* go in the shadow of Black Tuesday, that one was certainly apropos. And finally, that our current, several-decades-older caller for *Help!* will forthwith accept and administer unto himself a certain software-upgrade potion from his Brackish Tidewater Marsh-Nymph Here Called WYSIWYG . . ."

Presumably helpful upgrade tentatively accepted — on the same Major Condition sooner or later to be laid down. Take it now?

"Not yet: There's that Problem Three to deal with, for one thing — following which I propose a change of agenda after all, from Shiva's-and-Parvati's or Scheherazade's-and-Shahryar's to Graybard's-and-Wysiwyg's."

Which is? But wait: first, your Problem Three and my Major Condition.

"Problem Three's already solved, come to think of it. What it was was, you started off saying *There was meant to have been* a book called *et cetera*, which *if it had been written before* et cetera *might have opened* with such-and-such an invocation. Right?"

Right, alas. *Sportive*, I believe it was: *Foreplayful*, let's say. Those were the days . . .

"All which implies that — shit having hit fan and World As We'd Known It having effectively ended on Nine Eleven O One — said book cannot now so open?"

Correct, alas: 'Twould be impertinent. Bizarre. Obscene, almost: idle quasi-erotic fantasizing in the very smoke of Ground Zero!

"But in fact said book *did* so open; *has* so opened, Nine Eleven or not! That's what looked from here to be Problem Three, until it occurred to the muse thus sportively invoked to declare it a non-problem."

Oh?

"Their story's started: Graybard's and Wysiwyg's, Wysiwyg's and Graybard's. Muse here declareth this to be Night One of their eleven — which night she is further inspired to imagine as Black Tuesday's itself."

No.

"Yes. In spite of terror, in the face of who knows what, on with the stories! On with their Hendecameron!"

Brave talk, Wys, but tall order.

"So bid old GeeBee-the-Narrative-Software stand tall—as presently he shall, with his assistant's already proffered and conditionally accepted but yet-to-be-administered musely upgrade."

Yes, well: His Major Condition, however, is that not for one nanosecond shall Reader conflate Present Reteller of these tales with their Original Author—

"Conflate Software with Hardware? Not for a microsecond, nanosecond, picosecond ... What comes after pico?"

Femto? O.A. and mate being a happily long-wed pair who treasure their quite comfortable, quite conventional, pleasantly busy, agreeably unadventurous, decently private, and blessedly unstoryworthy life together—

"So forget about *them* already!"

Precisely. Whereas Graybard-the-Present-Teller, in his professional capacity as Narrative Imagination, is by definition virtually free of restraint and inhibition, at liberty to project himself into any age, gender, ethnicity, circumstance, and situation whereinto Ms. Muse may inspire him in *her* capacity as supplier not only of said Inspiration, but of Material for Author to transform into stories via the about-to-be-upgraded Graybard Software application. Condition accepted?

"Goes without saying: Software may become Firmware, but Teller remains Teller and Author Author, whom never mind. Shall we, then?"

By any and all means. You mentioned a change of M.O.?

"Indeed, for Inspiration's elixir needs time to make its virtues felt. Let us therefore reverse our order of business: Upgrade-time now— maybe taken with a glass of the house white, a really quite drinkable marsh-country pinot gris ..."

Potion taken. Pinot gris indeed commendable.

"And needs no breathing-time, unlike potion, pinot noir, and world in general. Let the pair therefore Sip and Tell: Both sip; Present Teller tells Original Author's Story Number One; Brackish Marsh-Nymph listens—quietly, but by no means passively—after which, at long last, *et cetera*! Said story and those that follow it on nights ahead to be strictly *irrelevant*, in the sense of having nothing directly to do whatever with today's disaster."

Today's? Ah, so: their little Let's Pretend; their (in my judgment) highly questionable make-believe.

"Not make-believe, Geeb: *as if*, the better to make our point. Promise promised?"

No problem there: O.A. originally authored this one even longer ago than *Help!* Granted, Relevance may laugh at Chronology like love at locksmiths, but we'll take that chance.

"And another sip of Upgrade. Then on with First Night: Story Number One! Entitled?"

Landscape: The Eastern Shore

In the temperate latitudes of Captain Claude Morgan's culture — the parallel of Athens and Maryland's Eastern Shore — it is winter. The solstice, in truth, is not yet upon us, but so unequal is the Sun's daily skirmish with the dark that though he blinds our eyes as usual (so that, looking away, we see his lingering image where he is not), he warms no more than our clothing and the clapboards of our houses: The chill of the night behind us and of the longer night to come never leaves our bones and hearts and inner rooms, where not long since it came only now and then in dreams. So late does he take the field that the skipjacks and bugeyes dredge oysters from the Chesapeake by starlight every morning; and so early leave it that bright Orion will have risen from the ocean, will have thrown an arm and leg over the marshy flats of Maryland, before ever the women get supper. In what other season might the old man sit thus in a ladderback chair by the window of his bedroom and watch Andromeda on an empty stomach?

His house, which he has given to his married daughter, is in East Dorset, near the creek. He put it up before his own marriage, two storeys of crab-fat-yellow clapboards; picked over the lumberyard for clear true pine and drove his nails with love. But now the ridgepole sags; the weight of the chimney has begun to push the entire structure down to the sand. Should you walk the several streets of Dorset, as he did until lately on fine afternoons, or drive through the muskrat-marshes of the county, you might infer from various houses the entire process: On this lot the ground has been cleared but no cellar dug, for the area is six inches above the level of the sea; down the road, brick foundation piers are up and strung with joists, and studs and braces are toenailed home — the lumber is fresh from the yard and something green, so that every nail wears a ring of moisture around its head. Across town the chimney is up and the sheathing tongued and grooved; down-county, near one of the crabhouses, the siding is on and the top-flooring laid — painters and plasterers are already at their work. Then, if you pick the right houses, you may know their common fate: the shrubbery grows where the soil permits; the yellow-brown paint weathers in nor'easters, is replaced, and weathers again; the maples in the yard mature, overgrow, rot inside, lose branches, and hold themselves erect by little save their cambiums, until at length a hurricane topples them, unsymmetrical from long-lost limbs and hollow and gone inside; concrete sidewalks dapple like old saltines, and the children read an atlas in the splotches; they hump and split from the roots or ice or soft beds under them, and the children on rollerskates memorize and name the bumps — Leap's Bump, Moore's Bump, the Puddle-Crack; the even lawn of fescue grows dark green and plantained, retreats for its own protection into separate clumps and hillocks with gray dirt between and the ancient white stools of many dogs. Next the earth itself, weary, begins to relax where its load is heaviest, and the house comes down to meet it: Door sills sag, and doors must be shaved, for they hang askew, and shaved again if they are to be closed at all; windows no longer move easily in their sashes; gaps wider than the tongues run down between certain floorboards, and a child's marble on the floor will of itself roll uncertainly to a place and stop. As the load shifts, the plaster goes with it and is filigreed by cracks, or the wallpaper wrinkles into appalachian chains. The earth moves aside once more beneath the chimney, and from a distance you observe that the ridgepole now describes no proud straight line, but an obtuse angle against the sky. By this time the houses, cheap to begin with, may have depreciated past any waterman's means to repair; they are lived in until the sag makes housekeeping unfeasible, and this takes a long time, for the people in Dorset are not generally young, and move reluctantly. Grappled and besieged by gravity like an oyster by a starfish, the houses settle as much as a foot before being abandoned, and then (as if occupancy had sustained them in the war to preserve their form), *mirabile dictu*, how the end is hastened! Windowpanes go overnight, as if by magic. Bricks fall from the chimney like teeth from an old man's head, and shingles like his hair, in every wind. The clapboards weather for the last time and spring free, as if only the countless layers of paint had held them fast. The roof buckles and caves under its own weight. Presently the house sinks to rest upon the ground, so slowly that one scarcely notices until it is down. Bright green weeds — ailanthus, Saint John's wort, false dragonhead — grow up through the boards; green frogs and blue dragonflies sun themselves on the corpse.

The day long, of late, Captain Claude's mind has been a heavy, bare-ly perceptible droning, such as men in their twenties may experience for an hour after sleeping too far into the morning: a continuous thick sound that makes clear thought impossible. Sometimes going out-of-doors has improved it, sometimes not, but he seldom goes out anymore at all. He seldom needs to, for the creek there by his yard, though it separates East Dorset, in a way, from the rest of the world, is the harbor of his mind, as for years it was the harbor of his dredge-boat: From it his memory daily casts her mooring, warps riverward, reaches down the bay, and runs free to the oceans of the earth and all their compass.

Sitting in his straight chair he can feel the whole town at once about him. He knows in the morning the sundry cars and trucks, the sound of the oyster-boats leaving the creek, of the bridge-bell, the fire siren, and the shipyard whistle. The fall of light upon the catalpa tree outside his window gives him the time of day. At night he hears the town quiet, the wind soughing off the river and clicking through the Chinese cigars of the tree, the water slapping at the creek bulkheads and sucking at the freeboards of the boats.

He can feel all his house at once, around and beneath him. So familiar is the structure that looking at the plaster wall he thinks he sees through to the lath and thence to the studs and draught-plates. Just beneath him, in the kitchen, he knows his daughter is stirring a certain agate saucepan. Moreover, from an earlier, rhythmic sound he knows that she has been shelling beans against the usual late arrival of her husband, a red-eyed bull of a waterman. Butter beans. On the mantel in the parlor, under a glass bell, is a clock that he has lived with for years — a wedding gift to him from his bride and again from him to his daughter: the "problem clock," his wife christened it, from the choice given her by the watchmaker, either to keep the glass bell sealed and enjoy but not use the fine machine, or to remove the bell daily for winding the spring, at the risk of letting in the salt moisture of the county. She chose to wind it, and perhaps in consequence its chimes have never really sounded, but he can feel the twist of its four-balled pendulum. All day he hears the electric refrigerator whir and click, the kitchen faucets open and shut, various doors swing on their hinges and latch into their jambs, various persons enter and depart. Like a blind man he knows the sounds and all the persons by their sounds. At night he hears his daughter and her husband in their bed, and the small sounds of the house itself: the same boards popping in the cold night air or the fourth and seventh risers creaking in the staircase, and occasionally a new sound, the pop of a different board, marking yet another step in the house's progress to the ground.

This old man can hear himself — the slow pulse of his blood in his neck, in his temples, behind his eyes, in the ends of his thumbs, in his groin, and in his ankles as he crosses his legs. When he moves he feels the bones slide against each other in their joints, where the cartilage is calcareous and gone. He hears the systole of his heart, eight decades old, which first commenced its labors in the year of the Franco-Prussian War. He hears the droning in his head. So familiar is his body that when he looks at his hand or at his face in the glass, it seems to him that he can see through the old skin to the bones themselves; that under the thin mask of his face, so well known to him that he really cannot see it, he beholds the naked skull.

"Daddy?" His daughter's voice, toneless in middle age, sends up a preliminary summons to dinner.

Outside the old man's body, beyond the walls of his house, the people of Dorset are doing in the first dark what he can sense them doing, and did himself when he was younger and had reasons; things he still recalls so clearly having done, some of them decades past, that even now it seems he is resting from just doing them. He clearly feels his life, stretched out behind him but tied so securely to the present moment that he can sense it all about, as though everyone in Dorset at that instant, doing those things, were living *en bloc* the successive instants of his history; as though his past were so close at his heels — the earliest feelings of wharfboards under his feet and the blue glare of the river in his eyes, the freezing dredge-ropes in his man's hand, the coal-stove smell of his bridal chamber, the green feel of first grass on his old wife's grave — that should he trouble to turn his head he must see it all rushing to overtake him. He has no need to turn. He feels it go back to the commencement as surely as he feels the whole length of his legs extending over the chair-edge and down to the varnished floor.

"Daddy?"

Andromeda is now above his window, and he has been looking for the first stars of Perseus climbing after: Almost at the instant of his daughter's second call, splendid Algol, the Demon Star, heaves into view at its highest magnitude, and how the golden years pour in on him! From his father he first learned what stars to steer by; in his ears their Moorish names had been a music. What long spring nights they'd seen him toss to it, afire with seed and aspiration! On his wedding night hadn't they twinkled as he introduced them, one by one, to his bride — a receiving-line that took till dawn to pass! Hadn't he shown them to his little girl, and wept for pleasure at her garbling of their names!

And now the firmament swims in his salt tears, cold and joyless as the memory of old sins, curses hurled at all creation, grass gone clumpy on a mound, the weariness attendant on a surfeit of experience. When he left this chair of late to walk without needing to look along streets as familiar as the blood-courses of his body, he walked only to reach his chair again, so it seems to him; he reached it hardly conscious that he had left, and for some days now he has not gone out at all. The walks are as useless, knowing as he does all that he will see and seeing as he does now only what he knows, as would be looking down each inch of his leg to see how far and in what manner it extends, when he can feel it. They are as useless as are the motions required to put his daughter's food into his stomach. He has no need to move about: Those butter beans are fuel for an old and vacant house.

"*Dad-dy!* Come on to supper! He's here!"

The gibbous moon, far down in the bay, strikes under the broad catalpa leaves and makes the tree glow ever so faintly. All his life he has followed the water, as they say, and it has led him here. In recent nights as he has stared at the wheeling heavens it has seemed to him that he might almost hear a sound. Outside his body, outside his house, beyond the town and the endless oceans — if the small droning were not in his head he would hear the stars go over the sky. That would be something! If only at the last one might hear them sing, sing in their courses!

Has he spoken aloud? No matter: His tears are dry. Algol, silent, returns his stare. It will not soon occur to him to make the effort to move his joint-bones, one against the other, to carry himself downstairs so that he might stoke butter beans into his stomach in order to lift himself back into this room and place his body upon this chair, where it rests at present from living years that stretch behind him like a taut dredge-rope.

The house pops. A new board, under his chair; a second-floor joist. He will need no longer undress this body and place it on the bed to watch the constellations scrape across the town, so tiring himself to hear them that he must rest all day when he has re-dressed his body in the morning.

"He's coming up, you hear?"

His leg has gone to sleep. He dreams of small frogs, translucent as new grass, waiting in the dirt around the brick piers of the house. Metal-blue dragonflies hesitate in the air and flit from stem to stem. No need to stir his leg. So long as his body remains still, he will know clearly where his foot was when last he felt it. And that, so near the solstice, will quite do.

SECOND NIGHT

"That's it?"

one imagines "the brackish tidewater marsh-nymph here called WYSI-
WYG" wondering, in her saltyfresh way, toward the close of Night
One of her and her accomplice Graybard's Hendecameron: "Tuesday,
9/11/01," at her insistence, and a less than satisfying "night" after all for
both parties, it must regretfully be acknowledged. For although this
pair are allegedly collaborators of long standing, their current *modus
operandi* is, as has been established, new; likewise Ms. Muse's current
embodiment as "WYSIWYG," yet to be accounted for, and their current
trysting-place, yet to be specified; and the specter of Black Tuesday,
2001, not surprisingly proved, to put it gently, anaphrodisiac.* In the
wake of that world-altering disaster, for them or anyone to rehearse
"irrelevant" stories is not indefensible; Reader has heard their rationale
for so doing, and may accept it or not. But for such retelling to serve
as foreplay for what certainly appears to be post-narrative erotic frisking, possibly extramarital to boot, strikes at least some of us as a touch
much — although one grants that the same rationale might be invoked
on behalf of sex as such: life in the shadow of death; a bit of joy or
anyhow pleasurable diversion in the teeth of terror; a brief relief from

---

*Number of innocent victims still unknown at that time; initially estimated at 6,000 to
10,000 at the World Trade Center alone, later scaled down to just under 2,700 at Ground
Zero, another 100+ at the Pentagon, and 200+ passengers and crew on the four hijacked
airliners: nearly 3,000 dead or missing at latest count, not including the 19 suicidal terrorists
themselves.

fruitless obsession with catastrophe. An unattached bachelor talester and ditto muse might be another story; but what if this "Graybard" fellow is by some extension a happily wed monogamist like his tale's Original Author?

In any case, what happened was that the muse-nymph's software-upgrade potion kicked in more or less midway through the narrative of that evidently expiring old Chesapeake waterman, and whether for chemical or dramaturgical reasons or both, by the time Captain Claude arrived at his terminal epiphany that effect showed signs of winding down along with the tale. Ms. Wysiwyg (let's drop the caps), having attended the recounting "silently but not passively" as promised, desired nothing more than to launch at once into comradely discussion of it — nothing, that is, except to get on with their already-delayed battery-recharging "congress" before that elixir wore off altogether. They therefore came together per program, though more cordially than passionately, on her curious bed in her curious mid-marsh work-play-bedroom, yet to be described: she preoccupied with her musely reflections upon the tale, he distracted by her distraction and by lingering reservations about what was taking place. In what ought then to have been the cozy afterglow, when *he* might have drifted into uneasy sleep, *she* found herself restless with both erotic unfulfillment and pent-up commentary — along with a clutch of new questions about and suggestions for, if not necessarily problems with, their situation: matters that had occurred to her during their not-particularly-extended First Night Congress in this new chapter of their connection. But she contented herself with declaring, in effect, that while it might be right and proper in that *Landscape* story for the old skipper to content himself with the mere memory of physical life and to declare (in what were apparently meant to be his last words) that "that, so near the solstice, will quite do," she would have her waterbedmate remember that they themselves had yet to attain the autumnal equinox, and that a repeat of this First Night flopperoo would not "quite do" at all. No particular complaint about the *story*, he should understand, which, taken together with *Help!*, sufficiently announced the themes of Distress and Autumnality, with a brackish tidemarsh setting thrown in for good measure — perhaps an early foreshadow of her saltyfresh self? But their M.O. was in clear need of readjustment.

Again?

"Q.E.D.! Just another little change in our order of business, okay? No need to review it now; let's cop us some Z's before Night One becomes Night Two."

Easily advised—and for the nymph, at least, to all appearances easily managed despite her restlessness of just a few paragraphs past. Although for her colleague's accommodation she had considerably dimmed the room-lights at his recitation's close, she never turned them fully off (so she had informed him) except when bright moonlight took their place. Now, by the last-quarter moon's faint shine through her glass ceiling and the night-light glow of the room itself, he saw and heard her doze off promptly at his side, her face turned himward, her breathing somnolent, her nimble body prone, altogether relaxed, and even in the dimness entirely visible crown to sole through those transparent bedsheets. Across her shapely back, the dark green "straps" of her whimsically painted-on bikini bra; across the top of her buttocks and into their cleft, the similarly painted-on thong bikini bottom.

Yes, well.

For Graybard, on the other hand, now that his immediately post-Congressional drowsiness had passed, sleep in such unaccustomed and questionable circumstances was another story, which—if only because where *he* came from it was mid-morning, as shall sooner or later be explained, not late evening as in hers—with a frown and a sigh he reviewed for himself (and thus conveniently here reviews for Reader) where in the bloody world he was, and by what extraordinary route he found himself there:

Call it a dream,

if you will, although "dream sequences" in stories and screenplays make some of us fidget. In any case, it went like this: On a certain late-summer weekday morning early in the twenty-first century, the Narrative Hardware of these tales was sitting per usual at his worktable in his workroom in his-and-his-spouse's tidewater domicile, scratching out notes toward his Next Thing while his helpmeet busied herself in her own workroom or with family matters elsewhere. "Found himself lost" is how that aborted Invocation paradoxically put it; Reader should understand, however, that there was nothing novel or troubling in this state of affairs, par for his and many another scribbler's course between extended projects: He mentions it here merely in order to get on with his story. Without physically leaving his chair, he dispatched his idling, restless fancy or Narrative Software on a stroll through the familiar "rooms" of what might be dubbed their Imaginarium, recalling the protean muse who could be said to have inspired this one and that, or in figurative collaboration with whom (via his strolling scout, whom he here dubbed "Graybard") this or that of his pen's offspring had been engendered — all the while attentive, as his reconnoitering fancy strolled, for hints, clues, suggestions of encore.

It was upon that scout's returning to headquarters empty-handed, so to speak, from this "house"-tour that — as happens now and then in dreams — he found himself ... not lost, but *astray*, let's say, in an altogether foreign precinct of that so-familiar habitation. Where ought to have been the workaday Scriptorium from which he had set out was instead what appeared at first startled glance and proved upon amazed inspection to be an all-glass bed-sitting-workroom: Not only its walls were glass (through which the prospect, instead of creekfront lawn and shade trees, was a vista of wetland cord grass, spartina, and winding marsh-waters), but also the partition between the room and its attached bath, and even the floor and ceiling. Through the former he remarked that tidemarsh extended right under the room, which was built on what looked, improbably, to be glass pilings. Through the latter he observed that while the day out there seemed as summery as the one he'd left behind (warm humid air moved off the marsh through opened sliding glass doors giving onto a glass deck with glass railings), it was, unaccountably, far past its forenoon: Indeed, a red-orange sun was just setting behind a distant stand of loblolly pines. The room itself, however, was bright, and replete with further marvels: transparent "blinds" and draperies on the windows, see-through pictures on the glass walls, transparent area rugs on the glass floor; tables, chairs, computer hutch, and all other furnishings made of clear Plexiglas or some such; transparent queen-size waterbed made up with transparent "linens," Lucite lamps with transparent "shades" and even unfrosted bulbs; an iMac computer in clear plastic case, as were the television, telephone, mini-fridge, and other appliances — including a see-through digital bedside clock that flashed, unnervingly, 9:11 9:11 9:11. Cups, plates, and flat-ware he saw through the transparent cabinets to be all clear glass or acrylic; glass bookshelves held what looked to be unfamiliar editions of familiar titles, printed on — what, clear vinyl pages? — and similarly bound; through the glass partition he saw not only a glass-enclosed shower stall but a clear glass toilet, seat, and lid, glass washbasin, fixtures, and plumbing, even transparent towels and washcloths on their clear glass rods, and a mirror that not only reflected but could be seen through! This fetish for transparency extended to incidentals as well: knickknacks of crystal and sometimes tinted but never opaque glass; see-through anatomical dolls, male and female, their internal organs also tinted but not opaque; clear food and drink containers in pantry cabinets and fridge.

As the inadvertent interloper registered these wonders with some mix of fascination, amusement, curiosity, and head-shaking dismay, late afternoon turned into crystal-clear and summer-warm evening. Since the room's light remained constant as if automatically regulated, "Graybard" stepped out onto the glass deck (equipped with a glass ladder, he now noticed, leading down to a cove, creeklet, or marsh-gut, its water far from glass-clear but evidently deep enough for swimming, as he could hear vigorous splashing down there somewhere) to contemplate this unsettling shift of hour and venue and to see whether someone was actually paddling about in what "back home" would be by now jellyfish-infested Chesapeake tidewater. Over the deck railing, he noticed, was draped one of those patterned-but-transparent towels he'd noticed in the bath, and beside it a woman's dark green two-piece swimsuit and a likewise mainly transparent overgarment of some sort ...

Hello?

"Come on in, friend," a woman's voice called warmly from the now-dark space below. "The water's fine."

Although he couldn't place it, that voice sounded half familiar. He peered over the rail, at first saw nobody, then located the splashing underneath the deck and could just make out, through its transparent planks in the glow of the room behind him, what appeared to be a shapely female figure paddling about down there in a seaweed-colored bikini like the one beside his hands on the rail.

I guess not, thanks, he called back — though the water certainly looks inviting. Then added, lightly, If I'd known I was coming I'd've brought a swimsuit!

Who could she be? And where in the world ...?

Splash splash — and sparkle of phosphorescing algae, *Noctilucae*, at her every movement. "Don't be shy. It's almost dark, and I'm not wearing one either. I *hate* wearing clothes in the water!"

Really? Then why was she ... Yes, well, he said: likewise, as it happens. But I'll sit this one out.

At the base of the ladder now, "Make yourself comfortable, then, and I'll come sit it out with you."

Do we know each other?

A word of advice, Reader,
from a professional dreamer-up of characters and situations: If ever, in what you take to be Real Life, you "find yourself lost" in one of these Call-It-a-Dream scenarios, *blow the whistle on it promptly,* or else risk losing your return ticket. Gregor Samsa's mistake, e.g., when in Franz Kafka's famous story he "wakes" to find himself transformed into a man-size bug, is to explore and *consider* his metamorphosis instead of kicking and yelling in the tale's second sentence. Next thing we know, he's assenting to his condition: "It was no dream." Granted, if the "dream" happens to be delicious (or at least inviting, intriguing, and not immediately threatening), and / or if you feel "in charge" enough to exit it at any point you choose, your whistle-blowing may be less than reflexive. But there, precisely, lies the danger — as witness Let's-Call-Him-Graybard's behavior thus far already in this improbable scene, even before our improbable marsh-maiden climbs the improbable glass ladder onto the improbable glass deck of her ditto habitation, gives her (probably) dark brown cropped curls a shake and her bemused visitor a conspiratorial smile, and sets about toweling herself dry with that improbably transparent terry-cloth towel aforenoted. Why did he not haul ass out of there two pages ago, sound the alarm, backtrack posthaste to wherever his figurative wanderings led him astray, and thence home to *terra cognita* instead of yielding to his fascination, registering and reconnoitering those multiple transparencies — *initiating dialogue,* even, with the dream-creature, and now permitting himself the voyeuristic male titillation of realizing, as he watched her towel-work in the ever-brighter light from her living-quarters, that this trim, quite attractive, intelligent-faced stranger, while less young than he'd at first supposed, was in fact buck-naked, her nipples, pubic bush, and posterior cleft in plain view as she rubbed dry what he could see

now to be a painted-on bikini? *You like?* her smile and unselfconscious movements as much as asked while, dried now to her satisfaction, she spread the towel over one of two transparent deck chairs, slipped that actual swimsuit on over the virtual one, and donned over that the transparent wrap — upon which was printed, sure enough, the bra cups and nether triangle of a dark green bikini! But did he even then bolt the scene, dash for the nearest entrance in search of exit? He did not: only returned her mischievous smile with his puzzled own and asked, not *Where the hell am I?* and *How did I get here?* and *Who on earth are you?* and *What's going on?*, but (again) Do you and I know each other from somewhere? Thereby assenting at least provisionally to what has the earmarks, if one may so put it, of puerile male erotic fantasy. He can't help noticing now, for example — not that he's striving to *avoid* noticing — that the woman's aureoles and pubes remain darkly visible through all those layers. Her "real" swimsuit too, then, and its printed likeness on her beach-wrap, must be see-through!

"Do we know each other?" Standing perkily before him, hands on her hips, she rolled her probably dark brown eyes. "What a question! I should feel insulted, but never mind." Fetching up her towel then, "Make yourself at home, Geeb; *mi palapa es su palapa*, et cet.? I need to go potty, and then we'll get down to what we're here for." And over her shoulder, as he helplessly admired her retreating buttocks, "Meanwhile, anything you see that looks appetizing, help yourself to."

Yes, well. And to himself, *Geeb?*

It has perhaps been established that as dusk turned to dark out on the marshscape, the strange studio grew brighter, as if some rheostat were cued automatically to compensate for ambient light. The white and blush wines in the glass fridge (no reds), like the clear stemware in the glass cabinets, were even more conspicuously displayed now than when Errant Imagination first wandered in — as were the bathroom, its fixtures, and its current occupant, going unabashedly about the business of urinating, flushing, and — *voilà!* — washing herself after in a clear glass bidet that hadn't caught his eye before but most certainly did now, he reasoning that inasmuch as privacy was clearly not among the woman's priorities, there was no cause to avert his eyes on her behalf from those ablutions. Indeed, when she hauled up her bikini bottom, rearranged her wrap, and, patting her hair into place, rejoined him where he stood bemused in mid-studio, he felt free to ask, No shower after your swim?

She shook her head. "I like the feel and smell of creekwater on me. Don't you? Have a sniff." She drew his face into her hair, which did indeed have a pleasantly brackish fragrance — and, he noted, a few precociously silvered strands among the glossy nutmeg brown. Taking his hand then in hers and drawing him toward that ample (and now interiorly lighted!) waterbed, "To work?"

Waitwaitwaitwait. He stopped still, shut his eyes, withdrew his hand, put it to his brow, and gave his head a wakeup shake — but found himself still lost in that bright dream-chamber, its amused habitant still beckoning him bedward, even shedding nonchalantly now the sheer shift that she had so shortly before slipped into and dropping it onto the transparent-carpeted glass floor. Her eyebrows questioned.

So okay,

he declared aloud to himself: We have here the archetypical Familiar Stranger. Some novel embodiment of the Muse, one bets; just the person old quote *Geeb* was looking for, metaphorically speaking, but never till now encountered in the flesh, excuse the metaphor . . .

"Metaphor shmetaphor," said she, and peeled off the seagreen bra, stepped out of the ditto pants, and stood in mocking challenge at her bed-edge, feet apart and hands hipped again, naked but for the body paint here and there. "Better get busy; it'll be daylight before we know it."

In fact that clear-cased digital clock on the floor beside her waterbed still flashed *9:11 9:11 9:11* — in the evening, obviously, although her visitor's analogue wristwatch displayed that same hour of the routine work-morning he'd wandered out of.

"Something different?" she teased. "Maybe a little kinky?" Cupping and lifting her breasts like a *Playboy* centerfold bunny: "Mint-flavored edible body paint?"

But her distracted guest found himself possessed by the sudden conceit of *WYSIWYG*, a trim and vigorous young-middle-aged marsh-nymph not unlike present company who *et cetera et cetera* and thereby frames and catalyzes the retelling of eleven tales over . . . *yes!*: Ten Nights and a Night. And hard on Imagination's heels came Conscience: "Graybard's" dispatcher's formidable compunction, to put it mildly, about even figurative infidelity. That naked item so fetchingly oscillative now on the waves of her waterbed didn't *look* (or feel / smell / taste, when she'd pressed the visitor's face into her hair) metaphorical . . .

"If I did, it wouldn't work, Geebsie, not to mention its being no fun. But of course I *am* metaphorical, from the literal point of view, as is this place and your presence in it. *Literally* it's mid-morning, not mid-evening, and I'm not even a physical presence, much less a bareass-naked mind-reader. On the literal level (let's remind all hands), you're the professional imagination of a happily domesticated tale-scribbler, not its physical projection revisiting old haunts on the chance of finding exploitable new tenants, and thereby — excuse the expression? — *coming upon* a quote Certain Brackish Tidewater Marsh-Nymph, *et cetera*. Right?"

Visitor turned up his palms, shrugged acknowledgment of that possibility. His hostess leaned back on her elbows. "So forget about Literal! Let's go Metaphorical — to the marsh-chick's nest for eleven successive nights, where he's free to explore without capital-C Compunction this saltyfresh new embodiment of his old associate." Seeing him still hesitant, "On the *literal* plane," she went on as to a less-than-quick study, "your boss is contentedly at home with his Without-Whom-Nothing, scribbling away the mornings, sharing a life in the afternoons and evenings and their marriage bed at night, while the world grinds on. But here in Mixed-Metaphorica you're Odysseus on Calypso's isle, with a shot at Home Plate if you play your guy's cards right." And before he could respond, "So okay: As one of us noted earlier, it's a more or less puerile male erotic fantasy. To which Miz Nymph replies, If it gets the job done, *go for it*, before Reality sets in! Yes?"

She raised her eyebrows, slightly parted her raised knees, even crooked a finger to summon him herward. "*He who hesitates*, dot dot dot?"

Yes. Well . . .

And as if indeed triggered by that hesitation,
Reality then and there set in, in the form of a knocking on the door of what was suddenly no longer a muse-nymph's extraordinary den, but Graybard's dispatcher's so-familiar, altogether unremarkable studio: he at his worktable per usual, ears stoppled against auditory distraction, pen in hand (uncapped but idle), notepad open to fresh blank page in bright humid late-summer mid-morning, Eastern Daylight Time. He

turned to see his aforementioned handsome mate (in workaday shorts and T-shirt, as was he), home from whatever had been *her* errand as in another sense was he from his, waiting in the doorway for him to unplug ears and hear the reason for her always-reluctant intrusion upon his work. Her mien was grave.

"Sorry to interrupt your musing," her tone ironic but entirely serious, even shaken, "but it looks like the world might be coming to an end."

En route home from town, she explained, she'd heard on the car radio that hijacked airliners were crashing into New York's World Trade Center towers and the Pentagon, maybe even the White House and the Capitol. "It's all over TV. Thousands dead. They're already talking about the Nine-Eleven Nine-One-One coincidence, if it *is* a coincidence. Maybe TEOTWAWKI after all, two years after Y2K? The main thing is, *it's still happening*, and nobody knows what's next."

And there went the rest of that day. Leaving only the acronym *WYSIWYG* on his notepad, he capped his pen, fetched his half-empty or half-full coffee mug to the TV room, and with his real-life-literal partner sat transfixed with appall, dismay, and horror as the news and attendant awful images trickled and then cascaded in: the first and second WTC towers hit again and again, in the repeated videos, by planeloads of surely terrified innocent passengers and flight crews; the unassimilable spectacle of the towers' collapse straight down upon their thousands of blameless tenants and hundreds of heroic would-be rescuers; the near-bull's-eyed Pentagon; the goodbye cell-phone calls from about-to-die passengers struggling with their hijackers over nearby Pennsylvania; the mounting evidence that Osama bin Laden's Islamic terrorists had scored again, outdoing by several orders of magnitude all their previous strikes. The couple went numbly through the motions of that day's remainder: prepared and ate without appetite their lunch and dinner, touched base by telephone and email with professional associates in Manhattan and with family all about the republic, did a few perfunctory housekeeping chores, lit a 24-hour *Yahrzeit* candle in memoriam to the innocent dead — and returned and returned to the horrific real-life story in murky progress, wondering with the rest of America when, where, and in what form the next blow might fall. A rogue nuclear bomb in Philadelphia, Chicago, or Los Angeles? Sarin nerve-gas in the D.C. Metro, such as other terrorists had used in Tokyo? The Father of

Waters, the Mississippi, parricided with some unstoppable germ? And no doubt the booming but already troubled national economy — not to mention their own immediately upcoming travel-and-other plans — collapsing like what the media were already calling Ground Zero ...

Sleeping pills for all hands that night, after even more than usually appreciative embraces. Next AM, further grim numbers and pictures from New York and Washington; cobbled-up bravado from the nation's dubiously elected President; no good news except the absence so far of additional catastrophes. So many lives snuffed or shattered! And after breakfast and the morning newspaper, what could they do but, *faute de mieux*, try to carry on with their routine work? Stars and Stripes half-staffed on their waterfront pole, then each to his / her home office, where in her near-stunned state she soon abandoned her attempt at normalcy, while her thicker-hided mate ...

Oh, plugged ears per usual, filled pen, and tried further notes toward some framing-situation or -story for his project-in-mind: a situation deriving from — might as well say *inspired by* — "Graybard's" peculiar experience of the day before.

WYSIWYG. Ten nights and a night. Dot dot dot.

Impossible to concentrate in those circumstances: people doubtless still dying at Ground Zero with his every vainly scribbled word. After an hour or so he packed it in, capped pen, popped plugs, went to refill coffee mug. Found himself — and his scattered but still active Imagination — the house's only occupants; mate most likely outside gardening in hope of distraction. Mug topped off with breakfast-brewed mocha java, he made their way back through the intervening rooms and, continuing through his Scriptorium to the adjacent bathroom, for some reason imagined seeing on its farther side (more precisely, imagined that "Graybard Software" fellow suddenly seeing there) not the house's daylit main bedroom, but a certain marsh-nymph's night-lit glassy lair. Moreover, the cubicle in which his projected fancy stood was now as-if-magically transformed into her transparent-fixtured bath, and perched smiling yonder on her waterbed-edge — beside which that clock now flashed *9:11 9:12 9:11 9:12* — was that studio's still-green-bikini'd occupant, as unsurprised at "Graybard's" reappearance as if two dozen seconds instead of as many hours had elapsed since their initial tête-à-tête.

"*You were saying?*"

she teased. And he — setting aside both his dispatcher's mug and, in those unprivate circumstances, the urge that had fetched its current user toiletward — presently found himself declaring to her, in effect, The fact of the matter is, ma'am, *there was meant to have been a book called* Ten Nights and a Night, *which if it had gotten itself written before 9/11/01, et cetera,* per Invocation. After which, and the ensuing dialogue afore-transcribed, "Graybard" fetched forth for "Wysiwyg's" possible delectation that stereophonic item entitled *Help!*, and there followed (1) their First Program Adjustment (potion > recitation > Connection), (2) the nymph's proffered Software-Upgrade Elixir, accepted on her guest's One Major Condition, (3) the Present Teller(not to be conflated with Original Author)'s rehearsal of that old waterman's *Landscape* tale, and (4) nymph-and-narrator's Metaphorical (and thus still at least technically innocent, as well as less than impressive) Congress and sub-sequent Second Program Adjustment — to wit, as she now in her turn declared to him: (1) Potion henceforth first (she had already poured a fizzy Portuguese rosé into a pair of goblets on a nearby end table), fol-lowed not by Narration yet, but by (2) comradely Conversation about the story past and/or the one to come, along with any other matters that they might incline, so to speak, to touch upon, as it were. Said conversation to be at any point happily set aside (as storytelling should *not* be) for (3) a proper whizbang-though-mind-you-Metaphorical conjunction at last of Inspiration and Imagination. Which workout should serve in turn to inspire, in their post-Congressional lassitude, (4) the tale *du soir.*

"It worked for Scheherazade," she reminded her guest, "and it'll work for us. Because Inspiration's the name of the game, right? It's who and what I freaking *am!* Or at least its Serviceable Surrogate?"

The interloper sighed. Smiled, but shook his head. Yes, well. But I have a thousand and one questions, Wys . . .

"So ask one or two — *after* we sip, okay?"

Okay. And sit and sip they did, Inspiration on her bed-edge, Imag-ination on a Plexiglas chair before her, their wine this "evening" gently sparkling and its flavor unaffected by whatever additive it contained.

"Questions."

Mm. Like who are you *really*, and where the hell are we? But

431

never mind those, I guess: You're the physical embodiment of every yarn-spinner's indispensable collaborator, materialized here in a marsh-country version of Mount Parnassus —

"So far, so good."

— and functioning under the nickname Wysiwyg —

"Not *her* idea." She reclined now on her left side, propped her head on her hand, and sipped her wine, simultaneously leaving both little and much to Imagination's imagination.

— said alias laid on her by Yours Truly for reasons obvious enough, although the behavior and accoutrements that inspired it have yet to be laid bare either to him or to the postulated Gentle Reader.

"Keep talking, friend, while Gentle R and I make note of your verbs. *Laid on. Laid bare . . ."*

Small wonder, Wys!

"Not to worry: It won't stay that way. But the explanation of what prompted your nickname for me can wait for some night down the line. Meanwhile, the other verb you used back there was *inspired*, as I recall, and something tells me that Inspiration is beginning to take hold."

Could be. But some uppercase Reservations linger yet, Wys, even granting my Major Condition afore-laid down —

With a smile, "*Laid down . . ."*

Afore*stipulated, -specified*, whatever. M/M Original Author are nowise open-marriage types, as we both know, and I'm the guy's Roving Imagination . . .

Unfazed, "We *do* both know, Geeb, and in my capacity as your-and-his Roving Muse, I here dismiss for good and all those malingering reservations, since all parties understand we're talking *metaphors*. Like putting some Lead in the old Pencil? Metaphors are free; we settled that on Night One." Raising her glass, "Even this wine is metaphorical: When did you and I ever drink on the job?"

Her guest nodded: No disputing that. But it doesn't *taste* metaphorical, Wys: It tastes like a perfectly literal Portuguese rosé. And as I may have mentioned, you certainly don't *look* metaphorical!

"Sure sign of an inspired metaphor. And speaking of Inspiration . . ." She set her glass aside, turned her darkbright eyes himward.

So, he declared:
Thousands dead at Ground Zero alone, some maybe even still painfully dying at this narrative moment; the nation in shock, the economy
reeling, air travel disintegrating, Afghanistan about to be devastated
yet again, all hands clueless about what dreadful thing'll happen next
and whether life in the US of A will ever return to normal in our lifetime — and you and I are supposed to enjoy guilt-free Metaphorical
Congress between telling irrelevant Autumnal stories?

Smiling gravely up at him: "You've got it, friend. Now come and get it.
Maybe a couple of asterisks'll help? Bit of a spacebreak? Allow me ..."

* *

And somewhile later;
her post-Congressional voice subdued and husky, "By *irrelevant*, of
course," she said, "we mean irrelevant to Black Tuesday's terrorism,
American unilateralism, Islamic fundamentalism versus post-Enlightenment Western rationalism, the fallout from economic globalization,
and like that?"

Mm.

"We *don't* mean irrelevant to the human experience of life, language,
and storytelling."

Mm-mm.

"In fact, since you were feeling some twinges awhile back about
Metaphorical Intimate Congress between bard and muse, maybe while
you're still somewhat inspired you can spin us a story relevant to *that*."

Mm?

"About, um, Innocent Guilt, shall we say?" Up on one elbow again
and drumming fingertips on his chest: "Innocent *Marital* Guilt, even?"

Mm ...

All business now, "Listen up, Geeb: You've now downloaded your
guy's two items-from-way-back-when, right?"

Mm-hm. The rest, for better or worse, are all reasonably recent, early-Autumnal stuff.

"And you mentioned that a couple of those are not exactly made-up
stories?"

Mm: Stories they are (unlike old *Help!*), but not hundred-percent
fiction like *Landscape* and you and me. Enhanced Fact, I guess? Cre-

ative Nonfiction? There're just two in that category — both, as it happens, tinged with TIMG: Totally Innocent Marital Guilt.

"So let's knock those off tonight and tomorrow and then get on with stories not only Reasonably Recent and Irrelevant to the national crisis but fabricated out of the all-but-whole cloth. Yes?"

Mmm . . .

Climbing over him and out of bed, "You get your narrative act together while I go wash off the Sweat of Inspiration, and then your no-longer-brackish marsh-nymph is yours for the telling." Over her retreating shoulder, "Don't say *Mm* again, okay?"

. . . Okay.

And upon her presently rejoining him — and his refinding, in time, his narrative voice — Talester Graybard duly came up with a Second Night story. Inspired by his collaborator's charming hydrophilia and by their serial mid-morning sunsets thus far, this first of his two not-altogether-fictive narratives was entitled

The Ring

Off Discovery Point, appropriately — a quiet condo-spread at West Bay, Grand Cayman Island, where the American couple were celebrating a happily high-numbered wedding anniversary — as they snorkeled out from the beach one languid afternoon in six to twelve feet of crystal-line water over a field of stubbled coral, Narrator's eye was caught by a metallic glint down among the gaudy squirrelfish, wrasses, sergeant majors. He dived, the fish scattered, and he retrieved from the wrack a bright gold ring. A man's wedding band, it looked to be, lost no doubt by some swimming vacationer like himself from one of the many re-sorts along Seven Mile Beach. Back at the surface he raised his mask, confirmed the discovery, and signaled his mate to come see it: a simple, square-edged ring, like a bushing from some golden machine. No en-graving or other decoration; no inscription on the inside (such as the coded pledges on their own wedding bands) except the 14K mark.

Treading water, we tsked at the unlucky husband's loss (from pro-fessional habit, Narrator was already conjuring scenarios and various narrative points of view). We would post a FOUND note on the recep-tionist's notice-board, we agreed, when we came ashore; meanwhile, as we had just swum out a considerable distance toward a fish-rich clutch of coral formations that we'd discovered earlier in the visit, we decid-ed to carry on with our snorkeling. Where to stow the little sea-trea-sure? Since the taking of coral specimens was illegal in those waters, we carried no trophy-bag. Small empty shells we sometimes snugged for safekeeping into the crotch of our pocketless swimsuits, but it would have felt odd, let's say, to deposit another man's wedding ring with either Narrator's own genital equipment or his wife's. The most convenient carrying-place, obviously, was the ring finger of his right hand—which, as it happened, the gold band fit perfectly.

"I thee re-wed," Wife vowed as Husband slipped it on. Still lightly treading water, the couple kissed, then repositioned their masks and went on with their exploration. At no time in the next hour, as we leisurely paddled, dived, and pointed out for joint admiration the splendid formations and brilliant fish, was Narrator unconscious of his new jewelry item—the way I normally am of my wristwatch, say, which I seldom remove except to clear airport security checkpoints, or of my own (deeply patterned) wedding band, which after twenty-plus years was gratifyingly all but unremovable. The "new" one was as constant a sensation as a loose tooth: mildly obtrusive, yet mildly interesting, too; agreeably disconcerting. I found myself rotating it with adjacent fingers as I floated, and "testing" its fit with the other hand. It slipped over the knuckle easily but not freely; just enough resistance there to prevent, under normal circumstances, its second loss.

Scenario: Some divers maintain that barracuda can mistake the glint of a ring or a stainless-steel watch for a small fish; they therefore remove such jewelry and wear black-cased watches to avoid a misguided bite. Perhaps the sight of one such predator, not uncommon near coral heads, prompted a snorkeling husband to slip his ring off belatedly for safety's sake (M/M Narrator have never bothered to, although they've often swum among barracuda), and in the process of transferring it from ring finger to wherever, or of trying to swim with one closed fist ... *et cetera.*

Back ashore, we warmed ourselves in the poolside Jacuzzi, where, to begin getting the news out, Narrator displayed and explained his find to some fellow hot-tubbing condo-renters. "Maybe it wasn't lost," a swarthy chap from Ontario wryly suggested; "maybe some pissed-off husband threw it away with a curse." Much amused, his Quebecois wife added, "Or maybe some celebrating divorcé threw it with a hurrah."

We four then cordially disagreed whether, in either spirit, one could throw a wedding band so far out from the beach. Narrator thought not. "He would have to set down his champagne glass first," the Canadienne supposed. Reverting to his own scenario, "He already threw that at his wife," her husband corrected her, "to get even for her dumping *her* champagne on his head." "Which he no doubt deserved," Narrator's wife joined in. All hands agreed, however, that the only real test of the matter would be for me to fling the ring itself back into West Bay — assuming that a contented husband's throwing arm could match that of a disaffected one or a celebratory ex.

"Use mine," the Ontarian offered, and extended his hairy hand, presumably in jest. His wife laughed enthusiastically.

Et cetera. Spa'd, sundried, relotioned, we apprised the Caymanian receptionist of our find — "Ah, such a pee-tee!" she commiserated with its imagined loser — and posted a notice with the necessary info and our apartment number. *May be reclaimed by accurate description.* "Why not just leave it here?" my wife suggested. Because, I supposed, my professional curiosity would be less gratified by a secondhand, amateur account of the claimant and his "story" than by a vis-à-vis. And then there was that aforementioned low-grade fascination: For whatever reasons, I rather enjoyed the unfamiliar feel of the thing on my "free" ring finger.

As we changed into tennis outfits for a late-afternoon workout once the courts were shaded, "Remember that young bridegroom in Jamaica?" my wife asked. On a similar vacation there some anniversaries past, a hefty, pinkfaced pair of Kansan newlyweds on the resort's snorkel-boat had told us of the groom's having lost, just minutes earlier, his brand-new wedding ring while we all were exploring the reef on this first morning of their married life; of his frantic dive for and lucky retrieval of it as it sank through a school of bar jacks, any one of which might have gobbled it; and of the couple's being now so shaken by their near loss (the water depth there was fully five fathoms, and the sea floor a tangle of broken coral) that they would neither re-enter the water with their rings on nor leave them behind on the boat. "Come on," one of us had teased, "take 'em off. It'll be exciting, like being lovers again." "For us," the cherubic young groom had gallantly replied, "it's still exciting to have them *on*"; and his literally blushing bride, wetly embracing him, added, "Even more so now." We were pleased to imagine that they could scarcely wait to get off the boat and scamper back to their hotel room, plumply to go to it.

For us, likewise, we had assured them, it still was, even after a score-and-more anniversaries.

"Is that really so?" the now teary-eyed girl had asked Narrator's wife directly. "Cross your heart?"

Through our tennis game I was particularly aware of the ring's pressure against my racquet-grip, which pinched the band against my finger. Even so, I chose not to remove it. Our set done, while Narrator fetched our gear back to the condo, his partner stopped by Reception to see whether our notice had had any response. The second-shift receptionist, she presently reported — an elderly British woman whom from earlier business we had judged more or less daft — had excitedly informed her that "the American widow-lady in B-Six" had lost her diamond-studded wedding ring two days before (in the facility's parking lot, the now doubly bereft widow believed) and in her great distress was persuaded, as was the receptionist, that "ours" must somehow be hers.

"Despite the circumstance," my wife said through our glass shower door, "that ours is a plain gold band found underwater a hundred yards offshore."

And male besides, I added. I was showering first in order to fix drinks and hors d'oeuvres while *she* showered, before our nightly dinner-expedition into town.

"All rings are female," she declared. "Anyhow, that dip of a receptionist is absolutely convinced we've found B-Six's ring, and the poor woman herself is in such a state that I'd better pop over and show her the bad news. Where'd you put it?"

A bit sheepishly, I handed it out to her.

"In the shower, yet. What *is* it with you and this ring?"

Beats me: a story, maybe.

As she did what she called her fool's-errand-of-mercy and I toweled myself dry and prepared rum drinks and finger food for the sunset ritual on our lanai, Narrator wondered whether what he now felt so distinctly on his right ring finger was the Absence of Presence or the Presence of Absence. In either case, it reminded him of the sharply ambivalent feeling on his other hand decades earlier, when he had removed for the final time the symbol of his twenty-year first marriage. *That* ring he had been reluctant enough to dispose of (unlike the Canadians' hypothetical disaffected husband) that it had spent the next dozen years, at least, at the bottom of his cufflink-and-collar-stay box: a box so seldom opened since those items went out of fashion that he could not now recall whether in fact the thing was still there.

He couldn't imagine either sentimentally still keeping it on the one hand, so to speak (he had, after all, grown children as prized souvenirs of that life-chapter), or callously tossing it on the other, any more than he could dishonor history by tossing his share of the family photo albums from that period — which, however, he found it discomfiting to review more than rarely.

Over cocktails, "my ring" back in place, my wife described the Nice Jewish Lady in B-Six's tearful acceptance of the facts. "You want vis-à-vis," she told me, "you should've seen her turning that ring in her fingers, as if it were her dead husband's. They rented down here forever and then finally bought B-Six two years ago and bingo: ruptured aneurysm. They're from Boston. Life, I swear."

Likewise. And maybe it *is* her husband's, in a manner of speaking: resurfaced at their old hideaway.

"*She* sure wanted to believe something like that. I told her to keep the thing, if that would help . . ."

Narrator's reaction was being watched. He did, in fact, feel an irrational twinge of alarm, but of course said at once, Of course.

"But her husband's ring was heavily carved," my wife went on, "like hers, she said, but without the diamonds. So she held out her hand to show me, and of course broke down because her ring wasn't there."

Ah.

"Plus, get this: They bought those rings right after V-J Day, 1945, guess where?"

Put thus, the question's only possible answer was "Shreve's": Shreve, Crump & Low, the old Boston establishment where we had bought our own wedding rings a quarter-century later — and now nearly a quarter-century since.

Well. We toasted that coincidence and watched for the elusive Green Flash as the sun's upper limb sank into the Caribbean.

"Did you see it?"

Maybe.

"I didn't."

En route to and from dinner, and now and then during it, the couple found themselves invoking notable rings from myth, legend, literature, and cultural history: signets and scarabs, proposal and betrothal rings, memorial and "decade" rings, "posy" rings and class rings; Plato's Gygean ring of invisibility, a thought-experiment for testing true virtue;

jealous Hans Carvel's fabliau dream-ring for guaranteeing his wife's fidelity as long as he wore it; Browning's *The Ring and the Book*, appropriately cyclical in form; Tolkien's *Lord of the Rings* and the several magical rings in *The Thousand and One Nights*; also tree rings, key rings, earrings, nose and nipple rings, annular eclipses, ring nebulae.

"Jesus's foreskin," Wife volunteered, sometimes thought of as the wedding ring for Brides of Christ.

The space shuttle *Challenger*'s fatal O-ring, Husband riposted.

"Ring around the rosy," said by some folklorists to echo the dreadful "all fall down" of London's Great Plague of 1665.

The labia ring worn by the hapless heroine of Pauline Réage's *Histoire d'O*.

"Lab*ium* ring, no? Or did they stick it through both?"

Et cetera.

With tempered incredulity, "You're wearing it to *bed?*" she asked when that time came.

Unless it truly bothered her, Narrator guessed so, yes.

"Oh, wow. A kinky new chapter in our story?"

We'd see.

Now, then, Reader: From considerable experience, this ring-tale-bearer can readily diagnose his problem with the narrative in hand. A *story*, typically, comprises both a "ground situation" and a "dramatic vehicle." *Ground Situation:* Almost without their realizing it, two people have (a) fallen in love; (b) fallen out of love; (c) what have you, as long as it carries some overt or latent dramatic voltage. *Vehicle:* And then one day, (a) the woman receives the first of a series of anonymous, teasingly prurient phone calls; (b) the couple are abducted by extraterrestrials in a UFO; (c) what have you, as long as it turns the screws on the Ground Situation. As a rule, one without the other will not make a story: No matter how wretched or exalted, a GS without a DV is no more than a state of affairs; no matter how exciting or "dramatic," a DV without a GS is no more than a happenstance.

What one had there in Grand Cayman, clearly, was an instance of that second case: an arresting, even portentous Dramatic Vehicle sans any Ground Situation to give it meaning. Narrator's fortuitous discovery and retrieval of a golden ring — at and from "the bottom of the sea," moreover, to be deep-dived for from the surface upon which the finder had been floating — is fraught with potential significance, the more for its having happened to a previously married man on or near a wedding anniversary just a bit higher-numbered than the last attained by his earlier marriage. It needs no professional to imagine any number of Ground Situations out of which that vehicle might drive a story. Imagine, e.g. [GS], that that ruddy Kansan bride aforementioned had only with difficulty persuaded her rufous beau to leave off playing the field and "take the plunge" with her in Jamaica; that then on their first literal post-nuptial plunge — just when, perhaps, the gravity of his new condition is coming home to him — the symbol of their vows slips as lightly from the bridegroom's grasp as the groom himself (so his bride has worried) will slip from hers at the first extramarital temptation. Tears, doubts, consternated re-avowals, sorely blemished honeymoon and uncertain maiden year of marriage, at the close whereof (and the opening of this specimen story) they return ambivalently to their wedding-place as if hoping for some sign there. Soaking their misgivings in the resort's Jacuzzi, they are joined by a middle-aged couple just in from snorkeling, the man of whom [DV] displays his freshly ringed right hand to them and explains [et cetera]. Or imagine [GS] that those latter snorkelers themselves, gratified as they are that their union has now successfully outlasted any previous connection in their life-stories, are nonetheless experiencing certain marital stresses, perhaps unrealized or unfocused until [DV] one day off Discovery Point, appropriately, the fellow's eye is caught by a metallic glint down among [et cetera]. Imagine, even (although one winces at such self-reflexivity), an aging storyteller who [GS] for the first time in his long career goes to his muse's cupboard and discovers it altogether bare! He to whom inspiration has ever come as reliably as urination or tumescence finds to his quiet but growing dismay no lead in his narrative pencil, shall we say, and, half fearful of that association, follows his muse's example by going on vacation — to Discovery Point, say, in West Bay, Grand Cayman Island, where, after some days of trying unsuccessfully *not* to try in vain to come up with a good story-idea, he snorkels out from the beach with his beloved spouse of twenty-plus years in six to twelve feet of crystalline water over a field of stubbled coral and [DV] by merest chance [et cetera].

Et cetera. But none of those scenarios applies. The Kansans were who they were and not otherwise; ditto your present Narrator, his lively mate, and their marriage-bond, duly tempered by time and trials and the stronger for that tempering. Ditto too Yours Truly, this (this-time-true) talemaker, now and then temporarily stymied or by his muse misled, but never seriously "blocked." That being the case (Narrator natters on, looking round about him in Discovery Point to discover a pointed Ground Situation while turning on his right ring finger that fourteen-karat Dramatic Vehicle, anyhow its symbol), might it not be said that what obtains here in this recounting is in fact just the opposite of what obtained there in Grand Cayman — i.e., that the circumstance of having a DV without a GS is itself a GS, awaiting its DV?

Indeed it might so be said; Narrator said as much to his notebook and was tempted to say so too to his life-partner, but forbore: Irritant enough to her that in the absence of response to our FOUND notice I continued to wear the interloping ring day and night through our vacation, while swimming, sleeping, shopping, shaving, showering, making love and lunch and notebook notes, reading on beach and lanai, playing tennis — until, with the often unsubtle symbolism of nonfictive life, in that last-mentioned activity it began to chafe the hand-grip of my racquet and raise a blister on my finger as well. For that hour each early morning and late afternoon, therefore, I took to removing it (not without some difficulty now, as that blister / callus thickened the finger-joint) before playing — and replacing it promptly after.

"The curse-bearing ring of the Nibelungs," Wife added to their ongoing catalogue: forged from Rheingold and guarded submarinely by dread Fafnir.

Also Wagner's opera cycle based on that cycliform myth.

"*Anelli della morte*," she remembered from somewhere: the poison-rings fashionable among Renaissance Italian gentry for suicide and / or murder.

One divines a growing though still-tempered impatience with Narrator's little fixation; one could readily imagine a story in which Wife becomes not only increasingly impatient but downright jealous, or in which Husband finds himself deliberately provoking her irritation, perhaps to his own fascinated dismay, until the new ring actually bids to threaten the old, so to speak. But in fact nothing of that sort was anywhere near the case, and as many of her catalogue-contributions as his were emotively neutral.

"Ringling's three-ringers."

Vienna's Ringstrasse. Remember it?

"Mushroom fairy-rings. The brass rings on merry-go-rounds."

Ringworms?

"Bathtub and collar rings?"

Telephone and doorbell rings, then.

"The postman always twice."

Tintinnabulation in general and Narrator's own mild tinnitus in particular: the "crickets in his head" that make it difficult for him on occasion to distinguish external from internal cricketry but do not, as a rule, prevent him from hearing when his friend has heard enough. Had that Kansan / Jamaican snorkeling bridegroom (I therefore reflected to my notebook but not to my bride) *not* caught his slipped ring in time, the noble metal would never have corroded down there on the Carib floor. In time, however, assorted coral polyps would have encrusted it the way salt crystals fantastically encrust those twigs cached deep belowground by salt miners for that purpose: Stendhal's famous image for enduring love. Better that the marriage outlast the ring, Narrator hopes he would have thought to console the newlyweds in that case, than the ring the marriage.

Had he really disposed of his from his first? Had he really not? If he had, by whatever means (Narrator knows a woman who flushed hers down the toilet on divorce-suit-filing day), where was it now, and encrusted with what?

"Smoke rings. Piston rings."

Pissed-on rings.

"What?"

I once heard old Robert Frost remark, near the end of his life, that for as long as he could remember he had observed that the oaks in his New England woodlands were the last to shed their autumn leaves — indeed, that here and there a brown oakleaf-cluster would hang on right through the winter; and that that latter sight had never failed to suggest to him the last shreds of a storm-blown sail; and that in that image he recognized there to be not only a poem but, specifically, a *Robert Frost* poem — but he had never worked out what that poem was. In like wise, Narrator imagined this ring-thing ringing on in his imagination, tinnitus of the muse, to the grave and who knows whereafter, should its notebooked image prove as high-karat as the metal. Come to think of it, though (I then came to think), my case was the opposite of Frost's: Narrator could imagine any number of possible Yours-Truly stories based on this *anneau trouvé* (it only now occurs to him, writing *anneau*, that the *annus* of "anniversary" is itself a ring-root: the circle of the year, just as *anus* is the [etc.]), but some benign daimon like Socrates's warned him not to write them.

A proper ring-story, he satisfied himself with noting instead, *should quietly circle back upon itself, like the Rheingold to its river-bottom rest-Platz at the Nibelung-cycle's close.*

"The volcanic Ring of Fire in the South Pacific."

Dope rings. Boxing rings. Life-rings. Teething rings.

"Rings into which one throws one's hat."

Rings run around the competition. Was that the Green Flash?

"Green Flash, definitely."

That fine anniversary-vacation ended, as what does not. *Faute de mieux*, in the closing hours of it I left the ring on our condo kitchen counter as a fourteen-karat tip for the Caymanian chambermaid. The happy couple flew home to their non-holiday lives and preoccupations — in Narrator's case, the resumption of whatever bona fide story-in-progress he had set aside for their celebratory recess. Although it was doubtless time and past time to get rid of the thing (if he had fetched it home and left it lying about, he might be fretting yet over what to *do* with it, storywise and otherwise), he rather wishes now that he had recycled it, if not into the Caribbean, then into some aptly symbol-fraught out-flowing river — Wagner's Rhine, Twain's Mississippi; better yet into the tidewater creek that flows and ebbs just a ring's-throw from where he here closes this account. In the *very* long run, to be sure, the thing will recycle itself, atom by atom, to there and everywhere — ashes to ashes, dust dust, in the universal recirculation — although in a run that long there'll be (as Gertrude Stein said of Oakland) "no *there* there."

Where is it now? one meanwhile wonders, knuckling one's ring-free right ring finger pensively with its neighbors. Narrator had hoped that this account of it might close some circle, discharge him of the symbol as he discharged himself of its referent. But in his notes and imagination it glitters yet: unresolved, unexplained, unaccounted for; like the element itself neither corroding nor (except for these vain musings) encrusting; as brightly agleam yet finally explanation-proof as life itself, as love.

THIRD NIGHT

Referring to Narrator Graybard's Ring-*story of the "night" just past,*
"Well, now," observed the Brackish *Et Cetera* (perched this time cross-legged on her deck rail, above the water she had evidently not long since emerged from), "*that* was to the point."

You mean the Innocent Guilt bit?

"Who cares about that? I mean the story about a non-story that *becomes* a Story after all by acknowledging that it isn't one. Not unlike our meant-to-have-been Hendecameron, you know?"

Mm.

"Kinky! Plus I'm partial to anything with *swimming* in it."

So one guessed.

Reader him / herself might be interested to know that this pair are commencing Night Three ("Thursday, 9/13/01," Yankee style) of their project-more-or-less-in-progress after all; that they are once again tête-à-tête in Wysiwyg's peculiar glass domain — mid-morning in the still-stunned time zone of Islamic terrorism's latest grisly spectacular and headquarters of the wounded nation's scramble for military response, but after dark already in marsh-nymphland, whereinto Graybard has this time neither strayed nor stumbled, but proceeded directly, now that he has the hang of it, to get on with their figurative collaboration. Reader will have noted further that the muse-nymph does not, after all, go soapless day after day, as may have seemed the case between Nights

One and Two. While she insists on a dip in "her" tidewater before getting down to business, so that during Conversation and Intimate Metaphorical Congress her skin and hair will be "marsh-mellow" (her colleague's pun, whereat she winces), as of their latest Program Adjustment she withdraws to her glass-enclosed shower stall after their asterisked Connection and then rejoins her guest for the tale *du soir*.

Thus did she, even as recounted, back on Night Two, affording her inspiree the appealing though steam-fogged spectacle, through the intervening glass partitions, of her lathering up and scrubbing off not only "the sweat of inspiration" but what remained of that singular painted-on green swimsuit, then toweling herself dry before returning *au naturel* to hear the tale of those sundry fictive and non fictive rings. At the close whereof, its Teller found himself back in the late-morning study that its Author had never left, and the pair carried on as one with *their* work, first drafting an account of Night Two, then making speculative notes on what a Third Night might have in store, then calling it a day, musewise, and permitting Author to join patient Mate for the routine chores and errands of an ordinary middle-class-American late-summer working weekday — but with their flag still half-staffed and their memorial candle, remarkably, still burning, as was Ground Zero in lower Manhattan.

Did he share with her (Reader may wonder) this questionable new conceit of Narrative Imagination's serial encounters with a frisky manifestation of the Muse? Or permit himself instead a bit of Innocent Marital Guilt at not so doing? None of Reader's business, really, okay? That enhanced-fact *Ring*-tale and the *Dead Cat* one presently to follow it notwithstanding, we're talking *fiction* here now, for the purposes whereof suffice it to say that their routine domestic pleasures — a swim between groundskeeping labors, frozen margaritas on the screened porch at afternoon's end, the daily satisfaction of preparing and eating together on that same porch their evening meal, the post-prandial exercise-walk around their neighborhood, the evening's reading and other diversions as the *Yahrzeit* candle guttered out — were both sharpened and made strange by the dreadful tidings from Manhattan, Washington, and the rural Pennsylvanian plane-crash site apparently meant to have been either the Capitol or the White House. How enjoy, on the fine next morning, making love and breakfast while such grimness beclouds their newspaper's every page? How stretch their customary after-breakfast stretchies, bid each other light see-you-laters, and withdraw to their separate office-workrooms, when for all they know Osama's terrorists or some like-minded others might strike before lunchtime — if not with hijacked airliners, then with some even more dreadful nuclear or biochemical device or simply an array of homemade truck bombs, like the infamous Timothy McVeigh's in Oklahoma City a few years back? On the other hand, how *not* proceed with such innocent, pleasurable, *irrelevant* routine, savoring it all the more for its very irrelevance? As in pages past one has heard it argued, if perhaps not conclusively demonstrated, vis-à-vis story-telling . . .

As for pages present and in progress: There she perches, Wysiwyg, on that flat-topped glass deck rail, her hair still adrip from her swim while the nymph herself patiently awaits crown-to-sole description — so patiently, indeed, that she bids her imminent describer to sip first his presumably doctored wine (and to hand her the other glass, please, of those two fumé blancs on yonder deck table). Here's looking at you, Muse of Description and Narration, *et cetera!*

Whose dripping hair, to begin with, will turn out to be this time not her curlybrown mop *per se*, but a close approximation thereof — Wyssie's wig? — worn over the also-dripping Real Thing (it had *looked* a bit larger than life). What it dripped upon, in front, was a skin-tight photomask of her fair face, which at first glance *had* struck her describer as a tad unreal: its contrast with her actual flashdark eyes, white teeth, pink tongue, and unpainted lips seen through their respective cutouts. Thence it dripped on down upon a similarly skin-tight leotard or Spandex wet-suit imprinted with the image of . . . you guessed it, Reader: Caucasian Female Nude, faithfully detailing in every particular the nymph's naked self and completed with appropriately manicured latex gloves and pedicured slippers. And what (Graybard, for one, is wondering already) might she be wearing under all that?

But

"Well, now," observed the Brackish Et Cetera as aforequoted, referring to his not-altogether-fictive story of the previous "night." Per program, they sipped and Conversed: about that ring-tale, to be sure — its theme and setting, its cast of characters and narrative construction — but also and mainly about her current get-up; likewise the night before's and (Graybard Imagination already in high gear) how

many and what sort of further variations one might dream up on the theme of What One Sees being What One Gets.

"Oh, *that*," peeling off with evident relief the wet wig and facemask and depositing them with her soon-emptied wineglass on the nearest table: "Well, we've eight nights yet to go after this one . . ."

On the last of which, if the world's still here, one finally sees and *ipso facto* gets The Real Thing?

One would see when that time arrived, she supposed. "*Meanwhile*"— standing now directly before him, who had seated himself in one of the clear plastic deck chairs facing the fragrant low-tide marsh — "bottoms up, okay?"

Not okay, s.v.p. Although by definition and job description ever at her service, he declared to her, he was by disposition and established habit a Sipper, not a Chugalugger; otherwise he would have satisfied by this time his considerable curiosity *re* what she was or was not wearing under that remarkable outer layer.

His in-no-hurriness seemed to please her: Deftly unzipping that imaged wet-suit's (hidden) zipper and slithering out of it like some agile amphibian shedding its skin, "Take your time," she said, and seated herself not on the waterbed yet but in a deck chair alongside his — after displaying to him at point-blank range that tonight's Layer Two was no swimsuit like the night before's, but bra and underpants as meticulously photoprinted as Layer One: aureoles and nipples on the former, pubic bush and vulva on the latter.

Shaking his head, So let me guess, he said, and sipped: Skincolored body paint, pubic wig, and nip-colored pasties under that? And under *them*, at last, the subject of all those serial representations?

"Yours to discover, Geebso. Whenever you're ready?"

Which presently he would become,
but not before exploring with her in a preliminary way, between winesips, some aspects of her predilection for . . . *full disclosure*, he had been going to say, but the business wasn't that simple or straightforward. Granted that he knew nothing, yet, about who she might "really" be beyond her current role, was there not something problematical all the same about her obsession with transparency? Not psychologically problematical, mind; nothing to do with her motives: He meant *logically* problematical.

Her smile was unsurprised. "E.g.?"

Oh, like her clothing herself with transparencies? Not even transparencies, quite, but replications? Projections of what lies beneath?

"*Waits* beneath." Stretching her lissome limbs. "But take your time."

She is, for example, by her own acknowledgment impatient with clothing, and yet she covers herself with teasing expressions of that impatience . . .

"Not for long, she hopes."

Is frustrated even by *skin*, he has gathered — as witness her preference, in the wall-art way, for x-rays, MRI films, and plates from Gray's *Anatomy* over more conventional renditions of the human figure. But which would be more "authentic," a naturally skinless apple, if such can be imagined, or one whose "peel" extends to its core? In his own view, both are not only unnatural, but (excuse him) unap*peal*ing: The latter is like that man of whom some humorist remarked, "Deep down, he's superficial." The former is a story that begins with its climax, or a joke with its punchline; it's a man who wears not only his heart on his sleeve, but all his other internal organs as well. Speaking of which. . .

"Could we postpone speaking of that Which till Night Four?" Clearly bothered now by the course of their discourse, she pushed herself up from her chair, suggested they do External Organs instead, and slipped out of her extraordinary undies, beneath which were no next layers of high-fidelity replication after all ("Enough's enough," she'll claim later, "sometimes"), but — Reader understands what we mean — *her*: anyhow the epidermal layer thereof. Who or which, indicating his now-nearly-empty glass, bade "Bottoms up for real now, sport, okay?" And proceeded forthwith waterbedward (where that clock flashed *9:11 9:13 9:11 9:13*) to await, bottoms up indeed, his joining her.

* * *

Shower. Story.

"You understand," she said after her post-Congressional shower-bath, "it's not *you* I was upset by back there . . ."

Back there?

"Not *there*. Back there in our Conversation."

Ah.

"It was your getting . . . too close to the bone, let's say. No wise-cracks."

On with your story, Wys. Please.

"Maybe — though it's time we went on with yours." She was not, she would have him understand, arguing Back There that a joke should lead off with its punchline or a story with its climax and dénouement. She was, after all, the fucking *Muse* of Story, right?

Aptly put.

She quite appreciated that some things by their nature reveal themselves only over time: stories, music, even painting and sculpture (although only the first of those was truly her department). Likewise one's understanding of oneself and others, of experiences and places and situations. While it was true that she inclined to up-front disclosure — like the classical invocation to the muse, which (as he might remember) lets us know from Square One that wily Odysseus will get home after ten years of war and ten more of wandering, et cet.— she granted that such disclosure does not preclude deeper and enhanced understanding over time. Speaking into his left shoulder, "All it precludes is Homer's springing on us in Book Twelve or Twenty-two that Odysseus *doesn't* go back to Penelope after all, but opts instead for eternal youth and virility in the sack with Calypso."

No surprises allowed, then? Not even pleasant ones?

She considered this. "Surprises, maybe, but no tricks. Fuller Disclosure, but no Prior Deception. And the fuller disclosure shouldn't *contradict* the invocation or initial impression or whatever, but confirm and enhance it."

So: No wolves in sheep's clothing or vice versa, but a sheep in sheep's clothing is okay? Or must it be either wool right through or else mutton from the inside out, like those apples we mentioned before? No: *Bone*, come to think of it, it'd have to be. A sheep made of sheep-bone!

"You're needling me."

And you're inspiring *me*, per job description. Wouldn't even a sheep made of sheep-bone be a deceptive cover-up of the essential marrow?

She sighed, rolled onto her back. "As a matter of fact, I happen to *love* bone-marrow. Lamb shanks! Osso buco!"

Aha: Something we've learned about Miz Wys that we didn't know before. Enhanced understanding!

"Superficial penetration, excuse the expression. But think not of the marrow, Geeb; sufficient unto this night is our Conversation therein. Tell us that other not-entirely-fictive story now, okay? I've shown you mine, more or less; now you show me yours, or Whomever's."

Done, more or less — always bearing in mind that Less can be More. It's another riff on both our Totally Innocent *Et Cetera* theme and on images (like last night's *Ring*) whose narrative exploitation neither exhausts nor exorcises them. My guy calls it

Dead Cat, Floating Boy

If narrator weren't an already happily married man, it might have been what screenwriters call a Cute Meet: end of a spring afternoon in Baltimore; rush-hour traffic exiting the city on the arterial that ran past the couple's house; Wife off on family business while Husband scratches out yet another sentence or two before Happy Hour; door-bell-chime interruption of—perhaps by?—the muse. He caps his pen ungrudgingly (longish workday, story stuck), and from the pitch of the bell decides en route downstairs from his worktable that the ringer is at the seldom-used street-facing door. Ignoring its peephole out of trusting habit, he duly undoes that portal's city bolts and chains, *et voilà*: a tall, slender, uncommonly handsome early-thirtyish woman in white sweatshirt, black leotard, and considerable distress. Dark hair drawn back in short ponytail; New Age-looking headband of some sort; fine high cheekbones (was anyone ever described as having *low* cheekbones?); tears welling in her I-forget-what-color eyes behind wire-rimmed specs.

Can one help her?

She doesn't know. Does one own a black-and-white cat?

Afraid not.

Maybe one of one's neighbors does?

Could be . . .?

The car just in front of hers, she explains, just struck just such a cat just up the street and just kept right on going. She stopped and tried to

452

help; fears the poor thing's hurt really badly; wondered if it belongs to one of these houses; decided she'd try to get help even though she's illegally parked and backing up traffic and running late for her yoga class out in Towson. Nobody home next door, so here she is. Excuse her sniffles (she removes her glasses and dabs her eyes with a sweatshirt-sleeve); she just recently lost her own cat to just such a hit-and-runner.

Let's have a look.

The arterial is indeed clogged, its two outbound lanes squeezing into one to pass her hazard-blinking gray Honda hatchback. Impatient commuters honk as she leads Narrator across the front lawn toward a white bundle on the curbside of the Episcopal church, two doors up. Oh be quiet! she calls in their general direction: *You're* not dying!

To her shapely back I observe, Not at the same rate, anyhow, and she gives me an over-the-shoulder smile. I'm twice her age. So what? And anyhow, so what?

I wrapped the poor thing in a towel, she says as we reach it; it's all I could think to do. Her voice is a hormoned contralto, stirring even in distress. I know you're not supposed to move them, but I couldn't just leave him in the street, you know?

Let's have a look. As if he's a veterinarian paramedic instead of a stalled storyteller, Narrator hunkers with her over the victim and peels back the towel. Big black-bodied, white-nosed/-bibbed/-forepawed tom, sleek of coat, well-fed, unsquished — indeed unmarked, on the upside anyhow, although there's a spot of blood on the towel under his terminally snarled mouth. Doornail dead.

What do you think? she asks tautly. Our faces are a foot apart. Fine estrogenic Mediterranean-looking skin over those aforenoted cheek-bones.

Kaput, I'm afraid. I point to the bloodstain. Internal bleeding?

She makes a tight-throat sound, strokes the glossy fur. One of the bottlenecked commuters is actually pounding the outside of his car door through its open window. *Stop* that! she all but hisses himward. Like a television doctor, Narrator draws her towel back over the deceased. Then stands. Neither a pet-lover nor a pet-hater, he finds himself unmoved by the anonymous animal's demise except in the most general tsk-tsk way. He rather admires Ms. Leotard's more emotional response: She's still hunkered, reluctant to accept the tomcat's death, while *he* coldheartedly though warmbloodedly appraises her excellent neck and shoulders, lithe-muscled legs and compact butt, imagining them in the lotus position, for example. Back when his children were children, there were important cats and dogs—but that was decades ago, in another life.

Now she stands, too. The backed-up traffic extends by this time all the way to the stoplight down the block. Narrator imagines a TV news camera shooting the scene artsily from pavement level: dead cat on curb, framed by car bumpers; mourners standing tall, heads bent, the woman's outfit nicely echoing the deceased's; church spire in background, pointing to Cat Heaven.

May she use my phone to call the animal disposal people?

I find momentarily piquant the thought of her in my house, using my telephone—and then loyally reprove myself: It's *our* house, *our* telephone, our monogamously happy life. Better get on to your yoga class, I advise her, before the cops impound your car. I'll pop the poor guy into a garbage bag and put him out with my trash.

She gives me a full-faced look of lovely concern. Won't he get yucky? When's your pickup date?

Not to worry; I'll take care of it. I even retrieve her blood-spotted towel. Here you go, now.

She smiles, takes the towel, touches my forearm lightly with her other long-fingered hand, looks wonderfully into my eyes with her, oh, forget-me-not-colored ones, and thanks me *so* much.

Not a problem. Have a good life.

So wide and moist a smile. You too!

By when I return with a plastic garbage bag, the gray Honda is gone, and traffic on the arterial has resumed its normal rush-hour flow. The limp cat-corpse, hoisted by the tail for headfirst bagging, is surprisingly heavy. Uncertain of city regulations in the matter, I incorporate the bundle into a larger bag half full of leaves and weeds and put the whole into a tightly lidded trash can at the alley-end of our driveway, trusting that it won't stink noticeably by pickup time, two days hence. Over wine and hors d'oeuvres a short while later on our backyard porch, Narrator narrates to his homecome mate a slightly edited version of the little incident. Cute Meet, we agree, and toast our own of so long past.

One hopes and trusts that she *has* had, is having still as one writes this, a good life, that emotionally and physically endowed human female.

The first of three sequels to our encounter is a note from her in the mail shortly thereafter — on garbage-collection day, in fact, when the remains of our path-crossing occasion passed without incident into the municipal trash-stream. Addressed to *Good Samaritan* (with the same presence of mind that had concerned her regarding "our" cat's potential yuckiness, Ms. Leotard had either made mental note of Narrator's street address or — intriguing thought — returned to the scene post-yogaly to register it, perhaps to verify as well that I had done my promised job), it read only *Thank you, kind sir*; and, parenthesized under illegible initials, *(the cat lady)*. No name or return address; I liked that. *End of story*, it declared in effect, as if she had sensed . . . and, like me, had dismissed . . .

The stuck story that this non-adventure relieved me from was meant to have been inspired by a season-old item in the daily newspaper of the southwest Florida city where M/M Narrator had spent the winter prior to this dead-cat Baltimore spring. In mangrove marshes well up the Gulf Coast from our rented condominium, a fat and severely autistic ten-year-old boy had somehow "drifted away" from his parents and siblings at a swimming hole, the article reported, into the vast circumambient swamp. Over several following days and nights, while helicopters, air boats, swamp buggies, and foot-slogging rescuers searched in vain, he had floated through the warm, labyrinthine waterways: naked (he seems to have shucked his shorts somewhere along the way), oblivious to snakes and alligators and mosquitoes, buoyed up and insulated from hypothermia by his obesity, entertained by the sight of those overflying machines. Evidently he quenched his thirst as necessary from the freshmarsh water he floated in; no one knows whether and what he ate. On the fourth day he was spotted by a sport-fisherman and retrieved — unalarmed and evidently unharmed except for incidental scratches and a bit of sunburn — a full fourteen miles from the swimming hole. His parents had no idea, they declared, how he had managed to drift away unremarked, to a distance beyond ready refinding. They had alerted the authorities, they declared, as soon as they noticed his absence. He wanted to go back, they declared he declared upon his untraumatized restoration themto, to see the helicopters.

Taylor Touchstone, the boy's name was — cross my heart — and in the weeks following that newspaper account, the image of him adrift among the mangroves like a bloated infant Moses among the cattails became a touchstone indeed to Narrator's imagination: a *floating* touchstone, like the lad himself. As now in the matter of The Dead Cat, I made notebook entries on The Floating Boy, whose serene misadventure spoke to me in a way I recognized. In addition to Moses (set adrift to escape Pharaoh's massacre of the Hebrew firstborn, then found and retrieved by his would-be killer's maiden daughter) I noted other mythic heroes floated off or otherwise rescued in early childhood from vengeful or fearful authority: baby Perseus snugged in his sea-chest, baby Oedipus plucked from hillside exposure, the Yavapai-Apache Prophet's baby daughter floated off in her cottonwood canoe—the list is long. More generally, I noted other voyagers from domesticity into dreamish irreality and back—Odysseus, Sindbad (the list is even longer)—and floaters into radical metamorphosis: sperm and ovum, fetuses in the Amniotic Sea—all of us, come to that, floating through our life-stories like unread messages in bottles or galaxies in the void, and into dream-country every mortal night. *Ukiyo-e,* I made note of: the ephemeral "floating world" of Japanese painting—and, by association, those as-if-magical Japanese Crackerjack-favors of Narrator's pre-World War II boyhood: tightly folded little paper somethings that one dropped into a glass of water and waited for the slow exfoliation of into intricate flowers or brightly colored castles.

Just so (I noted), like seeds at sea, do art's gametes float in the fancies of those whose calling it is to fertilize and deliver them. Some sprout / bloom / fruit with the celerity of time-lapse nature films; others eddy like that messaged bottle tossed experimentally into the Pacific by (Japanese) students in August 1985 and found ten years later on a beach north of Honolulu, the Togane High School Earth Science Club members who launched it having long since graduated and set out upon their own life-voyages. And some, to be sure, remain forever flotsam, embryos no longer gestating in the muse's womb but pickled in the formaldehyde of fruitless notes.

So was it with this suspended floating-touchstone tale, displaced now by the dead-cat interlude with its mild but not insignificant erotic aura (if the doorbell-ringer had been male or unattractive, Narrator trusts he would have performed the same neighborly service, but his imagination would have been unengaged). "The cat came back," went a song from my small-town childhood, echoed in my children's childhood by Dr. Seuss's *The Cat in the Hat Comes Back*. Likewise the above-told cat-encounter:

> *. . . the very next day,*
> *The cat came back like he'd never been away.*

Indeed, the species' homing abilities are so acute that they can be notoriously difficult to ditch; thus (together with their knack for literally landing on their feet) the folk-proposition that they have "nine lives." In an afore-alluded-to earlier life-chapter of Narrator's own, when he was about that comely cat-woman's age, his then spouse and he prepared to make their maiden expedition to Europe on the occasion of his first sabbatical from university teaching. They would pick up a Volkswagen Microbus in Le Havre at autumn's end, camp their way therein down to the Mediterranean with their three young children, winter somewhere cheap in the south of Spain, then tour from campground to campground through western Europe in the spring. They arranged to take the kids out of fifth, fourth, and second grades for a semester, rent out their little house in the countryside near the university, and sell their aging car. One problem remained: the family pets. The fish in the tropical-fish tank, they explained to the children, would be "returned to the store"—and perhaps some were, although a memory haunts Narrator yet of being discovered by his ten-year-old daughter in the act of flushing several down the toilet ("*Da-a-d!*").

The cat was another matter. Survivor of a frisky pair of litter-mates named Nip and Tuck, the latter was a handsome three- or four-year-old, dear to all of us since his kittenhood. Except that his coat was smoky gray instead of black, his markings resembled those of that Baltimore casualty: tidy white bib, nose-blaze, and forepaw-tops. Taking him with us by crowded camperbus through a dozen foreign countries was out of the question, likewise imposing him on friend or neighbor for half a year; and boarding him with a vet for so long a period was beyond our straitened means. Anyhow, "Tucker Jim," as the children called him, was used to roaming freely the rural neighborhood and nearby woods; we couldn't imagine kenneling him for months on end even if we could have afforded to. His similarly free-ranging sister had one day simply disappeared, perhaps struck by a car on her country rambles, perhaps shot for sport by a farm kid or a bored deer hunter (the venue here is the Alleghenies of central Pennsylvania, where schools are closed for the opening day of deer season and prudent parents keep children and pets grounded till the fever abates). The then Narrator and his then partner concurred that sometime in this pre-departure season dear Tuck must likewise officially disappear; as to the covert means, however, they disagreed, as alas they had found themselves lately doing on more and more matters of importance. She was all for having him SPCA'd, to be by them "put to sleep" when and if his adoption-period expired; I held out for turning him loose a sufficient distance from home, in the farm and forest lands round about the state university where I then taught. That would only condemn him to a slow and painful death instead of a quick and painless one, she argued, and cited the Humane Society's support of her position. I didn't deny that possibility — although wily Tuck had demonstrated his hunting skills on enough fieldmice and songbirds, even while well-fed at home, for me to doubt that starvation was a likelihood in his case. My position was simply that in *his* position, if offered those unpleasant alternatives, I would unhesitatingly opt to take my chances in the wild.

What if you disappear him and we lie to the children and then he finds his way back and we have to disappear him again?

Second time we'll tell them the truth. But I'll disappear him good.

Do as you please. But you know what they say about cats.

I did, but, in this instance anyhow, did — not as I pleased, for it was no pleasure, but as I truly thought best: packed the chap into our up-for-sale station wagon one late-October afternoon while the kids were in school; drove him a dozen miles over the Allegheny ridges, through forests of oak and hemlock, mountain laurel and rhododendron; chose a roadside spot where woods bordered corn and alfalfa fields, to give the guy some options (farmhouse and outbuildings just up the lane); grubstaked him with a paper bowl of 9 Lives cat food and another of milk in the dry ditch just off that lightly traveled road; sincerely wished him the best of luck ... and drove away, returning home by a fairly extensive loop rather than directly. One winces at the memory of that evening's charade of gradually mounting concern, and the next day's and the next (*Where's old Tuck? Still hasn't come home?*); of the children's calling and combing the neighborhood, and one's mate's low-volume after-their-bedtime reproaches (*I keep seeing him out there somewhere, meowing for us.*) (*You'd rather see him chloroformed and tossed into the vet's incinerator?*) (*Yes! Yes.*); and of one's multiple burden of guilt, shared concern for the animal's welfare and the children's sorrow, and complex apprehension that Tuck might find his way home after all.

He didn't. Three dozen autumns later, Narrator still stands by his course of action in *l'affaire* Tuck and, less firmly, the parental cover-up. (Would it have been better overall to tell children aged ten, nine, and seven that their parents were in effect dumping a virtual family-member in order to make the trip? They would have pleaded with us to spare him and stay home; we would have been obliged either to override their tearful protests or to present them with a fairly brutal *fait accompli*.) Other much-loved cats and dogs and tropical fish followed our return; other cars, other houses and universities in other states as those children floated, sometimes bumpily, into and through their adolescence, and their parents ever more rockily through the terminal stages of their once-happy union — which ended as the offspring one by one sprang off to college.

Such things happen.

Did I ever tell them, it occurs to Narrator to wonder now in these dead-cat notes, what really happened to Tucker Jim? They're older these days than their parents were in those, and presumably could handle the Truth. Am I, perhaps, telling them for the first time here? (How would *you* have handled it, *mes enfants?* Those of you especially who've had pets and children and marital vicissitudes of your own?) One wonders, for that matter, what really *did* happen to the good gray puss: that prolonged and wretched death foretold by one's ex, the abundantly blessed next life-chapter enjoyed by *her* ex, or something between? Look here, Tuck boy: You still float through my memory thirty-six years later, now and then. Of how many cats can that be said?

(*Big deal*, I imagine him meowing: *You* ditched *me, man. Literally.*) (*But hey, it was either that or. . .*) (*Yeah, right: Lucky Tuck.*)

Where are you now, fellow? Where are those freshfaced children smiling gamely from family photos of *Europe 1962/63?* The snows and roses of yesteryear, *ubi sunt?* Where, for that matter, this shorter while later, is that leotarded lass en route to yogaland, who in a different story might have been a Cute Meet indeed? Where now is the cat-corpse by Narrator bagged and dumped on her lissome behalf; where the briefly stymied talester who dumped it; where that house in that city, and the life-routines involved therewith? One *knows* where, to be sure, in a general way (See So-and-So's *101 Uses for a Dead Cat*, recommends the still-prowling sardonic ghost of Tucker Jim)—but where are they all *exactly*, as one puts this question?

That, too, in some instances at least, deponent can report, and in one case will: We being both of us newly retired from teaching and its attendant life-rhythms—which in our case had for many years involved busily straddling the Chesapeake between our modest "teaching house" in town and a likewise modest weekend/summer retreat on Maryland's Eastern Shore—during a second trial Floridian winter Down There with the other Snowbird pensioners, my wife and I judged our urban base to be no longer earning its keep and arranged its sale to another, younger schoolteaching couple. During that same winter, as it happened, we were recalled north from sunny Geezerville on the unhappy errand of assisting the transfer of an aged parent, Alzheimer's-cursed, into a New Jersey nursing home for the closing chapter of her life-story. We stopped over in Baltimore, to begin preparing the Teaching House for springtime occupancy by its new owners. The two businesses each melancholied the other, sharply reminding us of our own new life-stage and ongoing drift down Time's non-tidal river. And in course of inspecting the house's exterior and grounds—refastening a storm-loosened shutter, picking car-tossed litter from the streetside shrubs—I came upon the second sequel to that dead cat non-adventure: on our front lawn, down near the seldom-used sidewalk of that traffic arterial, just a few dozen car-lengths from its predecessor ... *another dead cat*, this one so flattened by traffic before being somehow shifted from street to lawn (perhaps by snowplows), and so weathered and decomposed in our absence, that without examining the corpse more closely than I cared to I couldn't judge its sex or even quite its fur-color. Indeed, so virtually merged was it with the winter lawn, it seemed more the imprint or *basso-rilievo* of a cat than the former animal itself.

A calling card, it amused Narrator to imagine, from Ms. Lotus Position, as—who knows?—perhaps the first had been: the 102nd Use, her kinky way of striking up a potential new relationship, starting a new story. Still there, *Mr. Good Samaritan? Still interested?*

No and yes, ma'am'selle: Your Samaritan doesn't live here anymore, practically speaking, but (disinterestedly) interested he remains—not in your shapely self, thanks, but in this all-but-shapeless souvenir, so desiccated past disgust that I let it rest in peace where it lay, reasonably confident that by spring lawn-mowing time it would be recycled altogether.

As in fact it proved to be, except in the recirculating tide of my imagination, where it remained a floating touchstone. Two months later, over late-March wine and cheese at our last cocktail-time in the Teaching House before the movers came to shift us from the city for keeps, Maybe it was old Tuck, Narrator proposed to his wife: It took him thirty-six years, but the cat came back. Tracked me all the way from that life to this one, he did, from Pennsylvania to upstate New York and Massachusetts and then back here to Maryland, and just as he was dragging his weary old bones down the last city block to this house, the Cat Lady nailed him with her cat-gray Honda.

Cute M-E-A-T, replied my patient partner, and we touched wineglasses in a sober toast to Time: It spared him the disappointment of finding you not home.

Tuck would've waited me out, I declared, or tracked me to Florida or the Eastern Shore. What're thirty-six years, after all? It took *me* that long to get from where I was then to where I am now.

Mm-hm. And where is that, exactly?

Good question, beloved sharer of one's life-story and reader of these lines, to whom Narrator responds as to himself: Why, where that is exactly is at the floating point of this pen as it writes *at the floating point of this pen*; it's at the track of your eye as your eye tracks the words *the words* in this final sequel to or reprise of that now-disincarnate cat, in its decomposition composed at last.

(*Sez you*, comes back the ghost of Tucker Jim. For even as there are touchstone images that the narrative use of far from exhausts; that when we believed we had done themwith not only continue to float or prowl upon their uncomprehended way but return, return to tease or spook us, so there are stories, Reader — this themamong — that hopefully substitute the sonority of closure for the thing itself; that may *sound* done but are not; that, like an open parenthesis, without properly ending at least for the cross-fingered present stop.

FOURTH NIGHT

"Friday, September 14, 2001" in Hendecameronland:
morning showers on the Chesapeake and cooler than the days just
prior, but with promise of clearing skies by midday. Ground Zero still
ablaze; National Moment of Silence declared for noon to mourn Black
Tuesday's victims — maybe "only" four or five thousand after all, instead
of six or seven? Narrator uncertain — as Author filled his pen, plugged
his ears for a few hours against Reality, and dispatched Graybard Imagination off to its daily dalliance with the Muse of Story — whether the
entire nation was to observe that solemn moment as one (at 12 noon
Eastern Daylight Time, 11 Central, 10 Mountain, 9 Pacific, 7 Hawaiian,
or whatever it's called out there) or successively at each time zone's
noon. As he saw it, the virtue of simultaneity would be its implication
of national unity, its tradeoff an East Coast-centricity that must weaken
the High Noon Effect progressively zone by zone across the Union. If it
be argued in the former's favor — but who's arguing? — that the disaster
venues were themselves East Coast and included the nation's capital,
it could be counter-argued — but who's counter-arguing? — that those
targets were struck not at noontime (EDT), but *seriatim* through the
morning hours: at 8:46, 9:03, *et cetera* . . .
   In any case, their house flag having flown half-staff since 9/11, its
owners have decided over breakfast (and after telephonic consultation
with functionaries at their local post office, fire department, and county courthouse) to raise it high after that midday memorial moment,

and then at (local) sundown to lower and stow it. Full-staff likewise over the weekend, they reckon, after which they'll maybe leave the pole bare for some days before resuming their custom of flying a different, merely decorative banner each day from their supply. Be it established that this pair are pleased to be American and regard themselves as normally patriotic; neither, however, goes in for extended national flag-waving, so often exploited by whatever ruling party to suppress dissent. Both inclining, moreover, to the Liberal persuasion and *ipso facto* to distrust of their nation's current right-wing administration, they worry that a countrywide orgy of patriotic display will obscure and serve that administration's pre-9/11 agenda, just when its prospects had looked happily dim in the divided Congress. No Kyoto Protocols against global warming for us Yanks, thanks! No Anti-Ballistic Missile or Anti-Landmine treaties or International Criminal Court for us, either; maybe no more *Roe v. Wade* abortion-rights too, while they're at it, and forget about stricter gun-control legislation and protection of our national parks against corporate predation. Instead, zillions for the futile and counterproductive "Star Wars" missile-defense program and for gargantuan military buildups; even more tax breaks for the very wealthy; huge budget deficits where there had been healthy surpluses, and never mind national health care, Social Security, the environment, and separation of church and state!

Et cetera: your Knee-Jerk Bleeding-Heart Liberal's off-the-shelf nightmare.

But what has any of that to do with the muses, and with the conceit of a high-mileage Narrative Imagination's "nightly" AM get-togethers with one of their number, allegedly the Muse of Story, a.k.a. Wysiwyg? And where was she anyhow, Ms. Wys, this meteorologically pleasant Friday forenoon eve, EDT? Not in her see-through domicile, Graybard observed, nor on its ditto deck — where however were, in token of her recent presence, two glasses of some white wine (a Sancerre, perhaps, by the sharp sip of it, and still chilled), flanked by a brace of clear wax candles, newly lighted by the look of them, in tall Lucite holders. Uncertain which glass was "his," but he being right-handed and they side by side equidistantly himfrom, he sipped from the rightmore themof. Although the sun had set, the sky over the westward tidemarsh still pinkly incandesced. He listened for splashing in the dark water below; heard none; moved ladderward to have a look, but paused en route to put two and two together, so to speak: twin tall candles lit at sundown on a Friday; Somebody-or-Other's affectionate passing mention of a maybe-grandma from Minsk . . .

Okay, he got it: *Shabbos*-time — or *Shabbat*, whichever. While he knew that the Jewish Sabbath day, like all others on Judaism's calendar, begins at sunset on the day "before" and ends at sunset on the day proper, thereby straddling two solar-calendric dates, he bemused himself with wondering (a) whether once the Sabbath candles were lighted, "today" (i.e., "Friday, 9/14/01") effectively ended and "tomorrow" began; and (b) more vertiginously, whether a hendecameronic "Fourth Night" commencing at "sundown" on what was literally a Friday mid-morning should be said to be happening Today, Tomorrow, or Yesterday?

"*Shabbos* is Ashkenazi," her voice called up from the ladder-base. "*Shabbat*'s Sephardic."

Right, right. So she reads minds, too?

"We Story-Muses read everything." She nimbled up onto the deck — no see-throughs or painted-ons this time, just her shapely, dripping, dainty-furred embodiment — and without bothering to towel dry, picked up the other glass and raised it in greeting. "Sephardic's the official lingo these days, but folks who grew up hearing Ashkenazi still incline to *Shabbos* and *bas mitzvah* and like that. Hi?"

Hi indeed. Did I take the right glass, or was the left glass the right glass?

Flick of dripping hair. "Doesn't matter; it's all Metaphorical anyhow."

He considered this, and her. Alertly pensive, she watched him considering as they sipped the no-doubt-figurative Sancerre.

"You knew this *Shabbos/Shabbat* stuff anyhow. You said your guy and his missus lit a *Yahrzeit* candle on Nine Eleven."

Okay. But we *didn't* know our Miss Wys was raised Ashkenazi. Now we do.

"Your Miss Wys wasn't raised much of anything. She's just an effing metaphor?" Still adrip — but the evening was warm — she plumped herself into a transparent director's chair, sipped again, frowned, twirled her glass-stem between thumb and forefinger, and regarded the dusk that had been shell pink but was now deep rose.

Yet she does candles on Friday nights . . .

"Forget it. And please stop looking at me like that?"

Not easily managed, Wys. To himself he wondered — wondering too whether she was reading his mind even as he wondered — *What'll it be on Fifth Night? Skinless?* But "So we're done now with the Oldies?" she wanted to know: "And the Non-Ficties too, right? From here on out it's all Reasonably Recent Hundred-Proof Fiction?"

And capital-S Stories to boot, Graybard affirmed, if I'm not mistaken. Reviewing the inventory in those terms, he then remarked between wine-sips that whereas that old bit called *Help!*, back at Invocation-time, had been truly a fiction but not truly a story, Third Night's *Ring* and Fourth's *Dead Cat* had been truly stories but not truly fictions, they being more-true-than-not Reasonably Recent productions both. The intervening item (First Night's *Landscape*) had been truly both Fiction and Story, but by no means Reasonably Recent. Muse willing, the remaining items would all be all three — cross his heart and excuse the *goyishe* expression. Seven to go, is it?

She shrugged her still-wet shoulders. Sipped.

Just trying variations, one might say. Not unlike one's muse?

"Okay." Contemplating her wineglass. "But we have another problem."

What problem? And hey, you're not chilly?

Looking out at the last of the last light: "Not literally." At him then, her left hand twiddling a short lock of her hair: "The problem is that back in that Invocation you said that this Graybard character was on the lookout for a narrative frame for his boss's eleven stories, of which however the lead-off item by your own acknowledgment turned out to be a non-starter. Which leaves ten presumably bona fide stories to be told at the rate of one per night . . . for eleven nights?" For the first time this "evening" she smiled in his direction, a quizzical *Gotcha?*

You thought I hadn't done the numbers? Four told already, seven left to tell, and we've eight nights yet to go, counting this one . . .

"So unless we want to get in the ring, so to speak, with Signor Boccaccio and call our thing *Decameron Two* — "

No, thanks.

" — or go to the mat with Scheherazade and stretch at least one story over more than one night — "

Sounds more fun than duking it out with Boccaccio. But my guy's stories are all one-nighters.

"Then we'd better drink up." Near-empty glass re-raised: "To Inspiration?"

Plus Imagination.

Clink and drink. What we'd better do, Graybard ventured then, is get our storytelling heads together.

"Heads too? Ready when you are."

So how about Here's to crossing narrative bridges when we come to them?

"You're on. Good *Shabbos*, Geeb."

Good *Shabbos*, Wys. Good *Shabbos* all.

* * * *

After which four-asterisked Interlude, as her clock flashed 9:11 9:14 9:11 9:14—
his muse fresh-showered now and for a change primly nightied for story-time — Graybard spun out "for her possible delectation" an altogether fictive pairing quite as unlikely as Third Night's nonfictive dead cat + floating boy. To wit, yet another story-about-storytelling (and about Talester + Muse), this one entitled

A Detective And a Turtle

"*Promised ... But never ... Seen!*" the voice sang out as from a soundtrack: "*A detective ... and a turtle!*"

To Charles P. Mason, sleeping protagonist of this story, the words made sense at the time as a comment on the action in progress, and the singer's amused, ironically sprightly tone was appropriate: Dreamer and female companion were in automotive transit from some Point A toward some Point B, and, sure enough, neither the promised detective nor the expected turtle was in evidence. When a moment later our man awoke, however — in bed beside his still-snoozing wife in their satisfactory house at first light on a rainychill March morning in the Appalachian hills of Northern-Neck Virginia — the sense-lending context evaporated: where the couple had been going and why; what relevance a "promised" detective and turtle, of all unlikely duos, had to the situation, whatever that situation was; and what their no-show portended for the travelers. Who those travelers *were*, even, Charles couldn't say for sure — Connie and himself, he presumed, but the woman in that dream-vehicle had been an unvisualized though palpable and familiar presence — any more than he could recall whether the "soundtrack" voice had been male or female, solo or chorus, instrumentally accompanied or *a cappella*. Only the words, cryptic now, distinctly survived his waking, along with their melody: the rising, fanfarelike first phrase — *Táda tadáda* tá!— and the playfully lilting, rising-then-falling second — *Tadadát-tá da da táda.*

Don't ask Charlie, Reader; he just works here, anyhow tries to, between dreams and waking obligations. Our man is by vocation a storyteller: a dreamer-up and writer-down of confected characters, situations, scenes, and actions; one whose specialty, worse luck for him — as quaint a calling nowadays as shoeing horses or fletching arrows — is the all-but-profit-free genre of the Short Story. Ah that he were a novelist instead, C.P.M. sometimes can't resist wishing: not mainly, but at least *occasionally* a novelist, preferably of the commercial-blockbusting variety. As a medium of art and entertainment, your Novel still manages some audience share in the age of cable TV and the Internet; not what it was this time last century, but still much with us. Look at your bustling bookchains, between their calendars and their cappuccini; at your lending libraries, between their videocassette and CD racks and their banked computer terminals. Look at folks on beaches, pool decks, cruise ships, airliners and their associated passenger lounges, where cell phones, earphones, and the not-*quite*-almighty Screen compete with, but have yet to supplant altogether, the novelistic Page. Lovers of *short stories*, on the other hand — whose ranks a hundred years ago happily included just about everyone who could read at all — have become as small and special a minority as lovers of verse: literary support groups, really, akin to those for the clinically addicted and the terminally ill.

Understand, our chap isn't complaining; he's just acknowledging the situation, reporting the news — which in the nature of the case isn't likely to *be* news to whoever's reading these words, and so enough of that. Nobody forced Chuck Mason into this "business," as he wryly calls it: this vocation so far from being a profession (as it genuinely was for many a talester in the years B.T., Before the Tube) that he's been obliged lifelong to ply a gainful trade in pursuit of his gainless calling. The late poet/novelist Robert Graves remarked of his commercially successful novel-writing that he was like a man who breeds and sells dogs in order to keep a cat. C. P. Mason, in order to keep his short-tale tabby purring — in order, i.e., to contribute his share to the family economy and still free up enough time to conceive, gestate, and deliver his unmerchandisable little darlings at the rate of three or four per annum into a world almost entirely ignorant of and indifferent to their existence, let alone their welfare — pays the rent mainly by . . . *teaching*.

Yup: teaching. *School*teaching. Drilling the language's grammar and elementary composition into prospective teachers of same at what used to be called a teachers college before such places elevated themselves to branch campuses of the state university system. English for Teachers 101, in short, and the occasional Intro to Literature course: four over-loaded sections per semester, decade after decade until quite recently, while Connie worked her butt off as Librarian *Et Cetera* in a not-bad area private school (always plenty of *Et Cetera*s in private-school job descriptions) so that their son and daughter could attend the place gratis, the public schools in their neck of the woods being alas less than impressive.

So? Nothing to sniff at in any of that, you considerately protest: certainly not in librarianing, and not in downscale branch-campus Learn-Your-Native-Language-teaching, either. *Somebody* has to do it, and Charles Mason has done it conscientiously, uncynically (despite his tone when speaking of it), and pretty effectively, if less than whole-heartedly, for his entire adult life. With only a State U master's degree himself, he entertained no academic ambitions beyond reasonable job security, a fair salary plus fringe benefits till the kids were on their own, and the liberal holidays and long summer break of the academic calendar in which to pursue his real calling. Wallace Stevens sold insurance; T. S. Eliot worked in a bank; Charles P. Mason, like more poets and short-story writers than not in the USA these days, schoolteaches for a living. Which doesn't mean that he likes to natter on about it, is all we're saying, as we've done here.

So went their decades, zip-zip-zip, of life's short story: in the Masons' case, the twentieth century's latter half, during which, so it seems to them, American decades lost their former flavor. Before their time you had your World War Nineteen Teens, your jazz-age Roaring Twenties, and your swing-band Depression-era Thirties; *in* their time, your World-War-again Nineteen Forties, your crewcut and tailfinned post-war Fifties, your sideburned and bellbottomed druggy Sixties, which rock-and-rolled on for the dozen-plus years from JFK's assassination until the Arab oil embargo and America's retreat from Southeast Asia. After that—from C&C's perspective anyhow, although they'd grant that their children, not to mention any Russian, South African, or Iranian, say, might see things quite otherwise—the decades lose adjectival character. Okay, there's the "me decade" Eighties. But the Seventies? The Nineties?

Comes then Y2K, and while neither The World As We've Known It nor this story-of-a-story ends with the millennium, the Masons find themselves officially senior citizens. Connie takes early retirement from the Blue Ridge Day School and volunteers three days a week at the local branch of the county library — to "keep her hand in," she declares, without getting in her Blue Ridge replacement's hair. Her husband scales down from full- to half- and then to quarter-time professoring: one course per semester wherever his old department finds itself temporarily shorthanded by leaves of absence or higher-than-expected enrollments. He compares himself to those "utility men" on factory assembly lines who learn the operations of ten or a dozen regular assemblers in order to relieve them serially for their coffee breaks, fill in for absentees, and train replacements. Inasmuch as his job has always been not only to teach language-mechanics, composition, and a bit o' lit, but to teach student teachers how to *teach* those subjects — in short, teaching Teaching, and even, to his more "advanced" students, teaching the *teaching* of Teaching — we oughtn't to be surprised if at least now and then a C. P. Mason short story has to do with Stories and their Telling. Much as he prefers to keep Mason the breadwinning pedagogue separate from Mason the narrative wordsmith, those are ineluctably two aspects of the same fellow, and the muses are notorious for taking their procedures as well as their material where they find them, concerning themselves only with the transubstantiation of those P's and M's into art.

Exciting, no? While ethnic hatreds lacerate much of earth's burgeoning human population; while poverty, disease, and malignant governments afflict millions more; while those of us fortunate enough to be spared such miseries busily overconsume our planet's natural resources, despoil the environment, and confront sundry crises of our own at every stage of our so-brief-no-matter-how-long lives, Charles P. Mason scribblescribblescribbles! And while some others blessed with his gifts of language and narrative imagination manage to illuminate in just a few pages some aspect of human experience and to render that illumination memorably into life-enhancing art, our Chuck spins yarns about . . . yarnspinning!

Yes. Now and then, anyhow, and among other subjects. Because, damn it — No, not *because*: He doesn't do it *because* of what I'm about to say, but if questioned on the matter he would most likely assent to the proposition that telling stories is as characteristically human a thing as we humans do, and is thus itself at least as fit a story-subject as another. How goes it, friend? How was your weekend, your childhood, your parents' divorce, your first life-changing love affair, most painful disenchantment, biggest mistake, dying day? And what does it tell us about you that you tell us *those* particular stories about yourself and others — that, moreover, you tell them the way you tell them — rather than telling some other stories some other way? Nay, more: Though neither philosopher nor cognitive scientist himself, Charles P. Mason would, if asked, almost certainly agree with those "neurophilosophers" who hold that consciousness itself has evolved to be essentially a scenario machine; that in order to make sense of and to navigate through the onstreaming flood of signals deluging all our senses, our brains posit the useful fiction of a Self that attends, selects from, organizes, considers, speculates, and acts upon that data — an "I" who invents and edits itself as it goes along, in effect telling stories to itself and to others about who it is. Indeed, an I whose antecedent *is*, finally, nothing other than those ongoing, ever-evolving stories, their center of narrative gravity.

Okay? Anyhow, that's what "I" can imagine part-time professor Mason nodding Yes to if obliged to affirm some rationale for his spending precious autumnal hours writing stories about writing stories, and for his imagining that even a handful of his species-mates might trouble to read them. *That*, however (he'd want quickly to add), has to do at least as much with the quality of the telling as with the matter of the tale, with the How as much as with the What, to the extent that those are separable — and here we join the chap at his "business." Short-story-making may be less than a profession, but our Charles is nonetheless a pro: He knows a C. P. Mason story idea when he sees one; just as important, he knows how to make a C. P. Mason story out of that idea. He inclines to the snowflake analogy: Just as nature requires for flake-making, along with sufficient moisture and proper temperatures, a speck of atmospheric dust for ice crystals to coalesce upon and grow their intricate hexagonal lattices, so your storymaker needs some *given* — a newspaper item, a mote of gossip or conversation, witnessed behavior or personal experience, even a dream — from which to grow the narrative artifact. And like the dust-grain in the fallen flake, the real-life datum may be all but imperceptible after narrative imagination has wrought it into finished fiction.

"Even a dream," did we hear somebody musing? *Yea, verily*, nods frowning Charles—at his old worktable in his old workroom now, breakfast and morning stretchies done and his wife off on business of her own—*even a dream*. And he sets to work.

Detective. Turtle. Promised. Never seen. His frown manifests not only authorial seriousness (along with bemused puzzlement at that odd-coupled brace of nouns and cryptic pair of participles), but the frowner's reluctance to address the subject of Dreams—a reluctance that I quite understand and share. Since the heyday of Freud and Jung, much has been learned by neuropsychologists about the *processes* of dreaming: REM-sleep and the rest. Dream *content*, on the other hand (aside from the obvious general relevance of post-traumatic night-mares), is scarcely regarded these days in scientific circles as significant or interpretable, although beyond those circles one needn't look far to find dream-books, psychic dream-readers, and the age-old like. In no story by C. P. Mason will you find a "dream sequence"—at least not one meant to be taken by the reader as Significant or Portentous—and he is impatient with such sequences in other folks' fiction. Even such famous plot-turning dreams as Raskolnikov's and Svidrigailov's in Dostoyevsky's *Crime and Punishment*, or Gustav Aschenbach's in Thomas Mann's *Death in Venice*, make Charles squirm; appropriate though they doubtless are to the psychology of their respective dream-ers and their historical periods, he can accept them only as he accepts the witches in *Macbeth*, the ghost in *Hamlet*, or the interaction of gods and mortals in Homer and Virgil.

That said, he grants of course that our dreams continue to fascinate us, at least mildly, when we recall them at all. So *weird* they can be sometimes! So amusing, distressing, or merely puzzling. And he would regard it as quite legitimate for a C. P. Mason character to manifest such fascination; even for that fascination (as distinct from the dream's "meaning") to drive or turn the story's action. Indeed, now that the subject has his full attention he'll go so far as to allow that even the dream's meaning—i.e., what the dreamer or some fellow character takes it to mean—might legitimately motivate the action, if it's clearly implicit that the author him/herself isn't demanding our assent to the character's interpretation. For no doubt people's real-life behavior is occasionally influenced by their dreams, or by the reported dreams of their spouses, lovers, comrades.

Take for instance a dream Charles dreamed just a few nights prior to the one currently under his muse's consideration: He and Connie were finishing an early-morning bicycle ride on the boardwalk of some sea-side resort. Dismounting to rest, they're asked by a pleasant-appearing middle-aged fellow where he might rent a bicycle himself for half an hour or so. Impulsively (and quite uncharacteristically) Charles insists that the stranger borrow *his* bicycle, gratis, and return it at this same spot in half an hour. But then he and Connie are on some residential back street; she needs his help in applying an unguent to her itching rectum (!), but he can't for the life of him puzzle out the unfamiliar instructions on the more-or-less-familiar unguent applicator. He then remembers that in time past a few eggs whipped in a blender have served the purpose just as well (!), but when he makes to prepare that poultice (on a residential sidewalk?) he finds the blender-vessel alarm-ingly encrusted with *dead ants* (!). Fortunately, a hose is running in a nearby yard; he's able to rinse off the thick layer of insect-corpses and beat the eggs (where's the electrical outlet?), thinking to himself that Con would have a fit if she knew the thing hadn't been scrubbed with hot soapy water. But she *won't* know, and in all this distraction he has lost track of time: The agreed-upon half-hour has long passed; he'll never get his good bike back, which of course he should never have loaned to a total stranger. All the same, he'd better hurry to the board-walk and hope against hope — but it's dark now; lights are coming on in the houses; he's not even sure which way the boardwalk is, and any-how he's suddenly wearing nothing but Jockey briefs and undershirt. In one of the illuminated houses he sees several well-dressed women about to sit down to dinner; on their sideboard is the blender with the beaten-egg poultice in it! How explain all this to waiting Connie, and where is she now anyhow? At this point the dreamer woke, only mildly and momentarily anxious, but tsking at the nutsiness of dreams. Go to it, Freudians! C. P. Mason won't take seriously either the dream or your reading of it, but he won't deny that a less skeptical character might, and consequentially so.

An unusual dream, in short, like any other unusual impingement upon or turn of events in the protagonist's life-situation, may be-come the vehicle of dramatic action, the dust mote that precipitates a story. Precipitates it out of what? I've used the term "life-situation"; Charles himself, like some other teachers of literature, prefers to call it the Ground Situation (mentally capitalizing because both term and concept sound Germanic to him): a state of affairs pre-existent to the story's present action and possessed of some dramatic *potential*, a voltage of which the characters themselves may be scarcely aware; a situation ripe (excuse his shifting metaphor; the guy is concentrating just now, not editing) for precipitation. Given such a . . . *Grundlage?* . . . the protagonist's dreaming of, for example, a promised-but-never-seen detective and turtle (!)— more exactly, his subsequent waking puzzled fascination with that dream — could conceivably trigger a story. Otherwise, it's as dramaturgically inconsequential as would be his seeing a goldfinch flit across the road, or hearing a distant siren, or farting after a heavy meal (any one of which, to be sure, in just the right circumstances . . .).

So, then: What's the Ground Situation here? The as-yet-unnamed because as-yet-unimagined Protagonist's, we mean, of this yet-to-be-dreamed-up C. P. Mason short story? Since its author *has* no Protagonist on the payroll yet, and inasmuch as that chirpy dream was in fact his own, not some made-up Character's, he now directs his muse's attention experimentally to his own "life-situation," to see what in it might be said to have the makings of a proper *Grundlage*, ready for storyflake-making. Semi-retired sixty-plus East Coast American White Anglo-Saxon (lapsed-)Protestant branch-campus English prof and modestly successful practitioner of regrettably now-marginal art form (his output sooner or later finds a home in some small lit-mag or other and very occasionally in what remains of the American large-circulation-magazine market, and has been collected into two volumes by two different "small presses") has been more than contentedly married for some forty years to coeval and co-ethnic now-retired librarian. One half-assed reciprocal infidelity in their long-distant past, so entirely healed over that if anything chances to remind them of that reckless episode (as this life-summary may do) they merely roll their eyes at their then selves. Two grown children: daughter Carla, thirty-seven, a prospering estate-and-trust lawyer down in Richmond, divorced, childless, and evidently content to remain so; son Mark, thirty-three, a rising associate professor of marine biology at San Diego State, married, father of three-year-old only-grandchild Juanita (Mark's wife's Hispanic), whose grandparents wish she lived three thousand miles closer. Both elder Masons enjoy prevailingly good health, as do their offspring; their six decades have thus far spared them serious disease, serious accident, untimely death of loved ones, fire and flood and suchlike natural disasters, war and criminal depredation and suchlike man-made ones. Their quite comfortable suburban house is "free and clear"; their pensions, savings, modest investments, and insurance coverages are adequate to their needs; their country is (as of this writing) strong, prosperous, and at peace. Even Carla's divorce was amicable, as such things go: Her public-defender and civil-rights-activist husband discovered or decided that he was gay, or more gay than not, and that was that; the pair remain on cordial terms.

Indeed, so equable and agon-free has been the senior Masons' life thus far that it lacks the makings of a story. The only thing Charles sees in it, now that he's looking, that might amount to a voltaged Ground Situation is their good fortune itself: their recognition (his, anyhow; he has spared Connie this morbid *aperçu*) that the law of averages hangs over them like Damocles's sword. No one escapes death, and next to none are spared prior affliction: Sooner or later — and at their present age it can't be *much* later — disease, disability, and dying will overtake one of them, leaving the other searingly bereft and burdened until likewise overtaken. In some humors Charles can't help grimly envying a couple from their neighborhood, happily married retired professionals like themselves, who in the summer of 1996 were en route to revisit Paris aboard TWA Flight 800 when their 747 exploded over the Atlantic, killing all hands more or less instantly. The only improvements on that scenario that Charles can imagine (when he's in this mood) would be to make their quietus ten healthy years farther down the road instead of three or four, and in circumstances such that they not only "never knew what hit them" but never even knew they'd been hit.

In that case, though, he acknowledges, there'd still be no Story — not that that matters to our author vis-à-vis himself and Connie, but it obviously won't do for *our* story, Charles's story, the C. P. Mason story-not-yet-in-progress. The "And then one day" that typically introduces the Dramatic Vehicle to generate a story from the Ground Situation cannot likely be "And then one day he died" (although one can point to some odd, beyond-the-grave narrative exceptions). Whereas it might very well be something like "And then one day he woke from an amusingly obscure dream of a detective and a turtle, *promised but never seen*" — if there were a proper Ground Situation. He can imagine, e.g., a character not unlike himself determinedly, even obsessively, analyzing that so-brief nonsense dream (along with his uncharacteristically sustained fascination with it) and in the process ... what? Alienating his family, friends, and colleagues, perhaps, who are initially amused, then off-put, and finally concerned that old Chuck has gone bonkers? Or actually *going* bonkers, perhaps, to the extent of becoming convinced that the voice in the dream was God's, addressing him personally (Charles remembers J. L. Borges's observation, in *The Secret Miracle*, that according to Rabbi Maimonides "the words of a dream, when they are clear and distinct and one cannot see who spoke them, are holy") and in effect directing him to search out the promised but thus far unfound Detective and Turtle? Which would amount, would it not, to his becoming an unlicensed though divinely appointed detective of sorts himself, pursuing—like Achilles, was it, in Somebody-or-Other's famous paradox?—a turtle. Perhaps the Turtle of Truth? The Turtle of Story? But wait: Achilles's quarry was a tortoise, not a turtle; does Charles remember the zoological distinction?

He thinks so (turtle: water:: tortoise: land), but clicks the terms up anyhow in his online dictionary, wondering as he does, *Is this how Chekhov went about his art? Has any storyteller from Homer to Hemingway, Poe to Pasternak, attempted to fabricate a narrative something out of so nearly nothing?* Not likely (though not impossibly, either), and no matter. Our talester is none of those: He's Charles the Mason, surveying the materials at hand with a professional eye and a skilled artisan's imagination, to see whether there might be in them not an *Iliad* or a *Dr. Zhivago* but a C. P. Mason short story. If there be no *weather* in it, say (as there's been next to none so far in this), or pungent sense of place, eloquent details, memorable characters, grand passions, and high drama, then *tant pis*: It'll at least be architecturally complete, with a proper story's incremental raising of stakes, climactic even if quiet "turn," and consequential dénouement.

Or else it won't be, in which case it won't get told.

His mention of Edgar Allan Poe—*somebody's* mention of that nineteenth-century East Coast American WASP inventor of the analytical detective story—prompts the reflection that most folks' experience of detectives is happily limited to printed fiction, films, and television dramas. Charles himself has, to the best of his knowledge, never laid eyes on a real-life detective, although in addition to police detectives even a quite small city's telephone directory will list one or two private investigative agencies — employed chiefly by disgruntled spouses and their lawyers, Charles imagines, to get the goods on errant mates in connection with divorce suits. Thus actual detectives *have* in fact been, in that sense and by Charles P. Mason, "never seen"— appropriately enough, he supposes, given the undercover aura of their business. But none was ever "promised," either, and so there goes that.

And turtles? (His dictionary modifies Charles's rough distinction by defining *tortoise* as "any of various terrestrial turtles.") Turtles are another story, he would acknowledge with a small smile: live and alto-gether visible baby turtles in Carla's and Mark's childhood terraria; box turtles on rural roads and occasionally in suburban yards, including the Masons' own; the odd snapper spotted in pond or creek; even large sea turtles admired in city aquaria or while snorkeling warm-water reefs off vacation resorts. Seen too on public-television nature shows and featured prominently — their terrestrial subset, anyhow — in folktale and fable: Aesop's Hare and Tortoise; Zeno's aforementioned paradox (he now remembers) of Achilles and the tortoise; the four turtles in Hindu cosmology upon whose chelonian carapaces stands the great el-ephant who in turn supports the earth (those last, he grants, like Poe's M. Dupin and Doyle's Sherlock Holmes, are "seeable" by the mind's eye only). Charles remarks further that turtles tend to withdraw from "sight" into their shells when approached or otherwise alarmed, as (with some stretching) the sense of a dream might be said to do upon investigation ... But "promised"? Quite possibly he and Connie had "promised" one or both of the kids those pet turtles before acquiring same; if so, however, the promise had most certainly been kept, the turtle-tykes delivered to the Mason-tykes and by all hands apprecia-tively "seen." So there goes *that*.

In short, while your typical character-in-the-street will likely have had more direct dealings with turtles than with detectives, neither can properly be said to be *never* seen, only seldom seen "live." And surely (with the minor sort of exception above-noted) neither was *promised*: Promised by whom? To whom? For what?

Which leaves? Setting aside the dream-singer's D & T, Charles can think of any number of things Promised but Never (or Not Yet) Seen, from U.S. congressional action on a political-campaign-finance reform bill to the Christian Messiah's Second Coming and the Jewish Messiah's

First. The Masons' own revisit to Paris/London/Rome, which they've been promising themselves for the past ten years but can't seem to get around to, what with Connie's involvement in her volunteer work and Charles's in his scribblescribblescribbling. The over-committed housepainter who swore he'd get their exterior woodwork done before summer but more often than not doesn't even get around to answering their telephoned Where-are-yous. Peace on earth. The significance and/or relevance of the dream-song upon which short-story-writer C. P. Mason has now expended more than half a morning's professional attention and accumulated pages of notes without coming noticeably closer either to understanding it or to making fictive use of it—two quite separable matters, whereof the former is not always prerequisite to the latter.

So? So (he walks to the kitchen, pausing en route at the downstairs lavatory to pee; refills his thermal coffee-mug; returns to his workroom; considers briefly whether to set this silly business aside and leaf through his notebook for some more promising bit toward which to direct his muse's energies. But there is none, he's fairly certain; inspiration doesn't come to him as readily or frequently as in decades past; anyhow, the detective/turtle bit, if only *faute de mieux*, won't let go [he recalls—and makes written note of, to keep his pen moving—the folk-belief that when a turtle bites, it will hold on until either thunder or nightfall, he forgets which], and he's really rather persuaded now—perhaps also *faute de mieux*, but who cares?—that *there's a C. P. Mason story hiding here somewhere*): Aging protagonist's only Ground Situation is that he has no apparent Ground Situation, other than his relatively misery-free life-history thus far versus the law of averages; *and then one day*—by dawn's early light, actually—he awakes from an untroubling but distinct and perplexing dream of . . .

Car radio, it suddenly occurs to him. There is less music in the Masons' house than in time past, when they routinely played their jazz or Caribbean LPs (and later their audiocassettes, followed by their compact discs) through cocktails and dinner prep, then quiet classical while they ate, and sometimes rock or disco to dance to when they felt frisky at evening's end. More and more in recent years they've found the sound bothersome; have progressively reduced the volume toward inaudibility, and often as not nowadays prefer to dine without background music. It is when traveling by car that they most often now punch up the local classical, jazz, or pop stations; and in that dream, Protagonist and Mate were "in transit"; and it is of course recorded music that most commonly presents us with invisible vocalists. So maybe the detective-and-turtle voice wasn't God's, but merely some pop singer's on the easy-listening station?

Nah: It was more *ubiquitous* than that; more "out there" than the sound of their aging Toyota's front-and-rear speakers — and thus more interesting, at least potentially. Anyhow (Charles reminds himself), the stuff of dreams needs no such homely accounting for, although the impulse to rationalize the intriguingly mysterious he would grant to be human and honorable. There may well be, at least theoretically, some neurological or even psychological explanation of why C. P. Mason's dreaming brain came up this morning with an unlocatable voice singing of a reneged-upon detective and turtle rather than with, say, a recklessly loaned bicycle and an ant-encrusted blender for the curb-side preparation of rectal poultices. But at such explanations the Muse of Story shrugs her Parnassian shoulders — unless, valid or not, they prompt some dramaturgically significant action on the protagonist's part.

Such as? Oh, well . . . such as his near-overwhelmment, at this point in this narrative, by a hot mix of unsortable emotions at the sudden vivid recollection (prompted by that nutsy rectal-poultice business above) of his adulterous anal intercourse thirty-plus years ago with an adult female former student of his at the teachers college: one DeeD-ee Francis, a grown-up Sixties Flower Child, exotic in that academic venue, to whose hippie husband her vagina was inviolably pledged but not her other orifices, which she offered with Hubby's blessing in their psychedelically painted Chevy wagon to such of her admirers as were also her admirees, and she had really really grooved on Charles's Introduction to the Teaching of Poetry course the year before. Dear down-to-earth, high-as-a-kite DeeDee, with her "sidelong picker-el smile" (as poet Theodore Roethke phrased it in the course's text), smiled fetchingly overshoulder in mid-buttfuck; where was she now, and doing what with whom? No matter: That early, uncharacteristic infidelity (and Connie's tearfully furious retaliation therefor with one of Charles's departmental colleagues upon his confessing it to her; such were the High Nineteen Sixties, Reader, even in the boondocks of Academe) had most certainly been a pain in their marital back-side, poulticed only by the passing of many a semester. And it could quite imaginably become so again if, say, a reawakened interest in or nostalgia for it came to reflect, perhaps even to *cause*, some growing, till-now-unrecognized dissatisfaction with his mate, his marriage, his life . . .

Nonsense! our man protests (too strongly?). How could he even hypothesize such a thing? he asks himself (like a wily psychoanalyst?).

Et cetera: There's a Ground Situation for you!

But not for C. P. Mason, who declines even to consider what "dra-maturgically significant action" he (he means his protagonist-char-acter) might take in consequence of this dream-cued recollection/revelation. With relief he offers himself and us an alternative Such As, altogether safer though less voltaged: Small-time academic and middlingly successful practitioner of fading literary genre, now in the twilight of his career and of its, has become accustomed to and patient with occasional recalcitrance on his muse's part, as with other exac-tions of relentless aging. *But then one day*, seasoned professional that he is — after throwing several mornings' worth of good imaginative money after bad in his effort to discover the C. P. Mason short story that he feels strongly to be "hypertexted" behind the imagery of a cer-tain C. P. Mason dream-fragment — he confronts not only the growing likelihood that there's no story there after all (Who cares, finally, about that?), but the vertiginous possibility that the cupboard is bare, the well gone dry for keeps. For would the C. P. Mason of even five years ago, not to say twenty or thirty years ago, have spent a whole week's work-time poking and puttering at the memory of a silly dream if his note-books burgeoned, as once upon a time they did, with other story-seeds awaiting his consideration and cultivation? Anton Chekhov is said to have remarked, no doubt ironically, that if a story took him longer than an afternoon to write, it probably wasn't worth his time. No Chekhov, Charles has never cared how long a C. P. Mason story remains in the works, as long as it's working. In better days, however (which is to say, right up to page one of this story), he would have reshelved so unforth-coming a "bit" as this detective-and-turtle dream to germinate while he developed some other, less resistant item from his backlog.

Such as? There's the rub: There *is* no backlog of notebook entries awaiting his authorial attention; nor has there been, for longer than it's comfortable for Charles to remember. That's why, when he awoke this morning with that dumdum dream-song still reverberating in his head, he fetched it expectantly from bed through breakfast-with-Connie to his workroom, to see what might be made of it.

Nothing. Nada. Niente. Nichts. Nichivo. He has that notebook open now, just checking: the original brown looseleaf pocket notebook in which since apprenticehood he has accumulated trial offerings to his muse. Its most recent entry is the opening sentence of this story. The one before it — scratched through after its deployment, like all the entries before *it* — is dated a semester earlier: the touchstone of his most recently completed C. P. Masonry, long since out of the shop and making its slow rounds of likely periodicals. The two stories preceding that one had likewise been worked up from prior-year inspirations, now duly crossed out: three withdrawals from an account into which he has made no new deposits since, its balance zero . . .

Until now. Impulsively — perhaps only for the gratification of seeing two uncanceled entries instead of one — below the detective-and-tur-the nonsense he copies that phrase from Roethke's *Elegy for Jane*, his student killed in a fall from her horse: *a sidelong pickerel smile*. The poet's grief is pure ("I, with no rights in this matter," the poem concludes: "Neither father nor lover"); Charles's memory of *his* long-ago (ex-)student's similar smile is not, although from so distant a remove and in so autumnal a humor as his current one, it has its own innocence. The movement of his pen on paper is, as always, agreeable. It occurs to him, regarding the two notebook entries thus juxtaposed, to imagine that smile — DeeDee Francis's over-the-shoulder, go-to-it-big-boy smile in the back of that old station wagon — as his muse's. His protracted search for usable significance in that dream — his detective-work upon it, one might say — has proceeded slowly and deliberately (and thus far futilely): at tortoise-speed, one might say. And yet, quite like DeeDee's *in flagrante delicto*, Ms. Muse's sidelong pickerel smile has at once encouraged him to go to it, reassured him that what they are about is pleasurable, anyhow not unpleasant, for her as well as for him, and suggested tantalizingly that she's on to something — something amusing to herself — that he is not. In DeeDee's case (so he learned after the subsequent debacle), that Something had been or had at least included the datum that yet another of her admired admirers, Charles's then-colleague Fred Sullivan, had confided to her in that same vehicular venue his hankering to do with Connie Mason what he was just then doing with her. As subsequently, Q.E.D., the fellow did — for such were the lusty-among-other-things High Sixties.

And Mademoiselle Muse? What piquant infobit might *she* be savoring as they two go to it? Perhaps that, hump her as he might, she has conceived her last by him, whether that last be this misbegotten detective-and-turtle story or, more likely (for whoever made babies *this* way?), the comparatively bona fide item composed just before it, finished months ago and now in the mails with its self-addressed stamped return envelope. Perhaps, on the contrary, that Charles's current fallow season is no more than a rather-longer-than-usual downtime, to be followed by fruitful intercourse again before his inevitable *finis*. Or perhaps that that *finis* is very much closer than he supposes; that it will come — via ruptured aneurysm or out-of-the-blue fatal accident or who knows how — within the hour of his putting the closing period to what after all (so I choose to imagine her mercifully or mischievously granting, in honor of their long and not-unproductive connection) will turn out to be a by-hook-or-by-crook C. P. Mason short story, obscurely promised and finally, if obliquely, seen: one having to do, more or less and by golly, with a detective and a turtle.

FIFTH NIGHT

Meanwhile, back at the ranch —
in this case, the modest rural Eisenhower-era "ranch house" where
all but the earliest of these several stories was Originally Authored —
their common perpetrator finished first-drafting "Fourth Night," with
its quadruply asterisked Interlude leading to that detective-and-turtle
tale, and called it a morning. Capped pen. Unplugged ears. Shut down
computer after checking email. And once again shook his authorial
head at the luxurious *irrelevance* of such yarning: Caribbean getaways
and winter retreats! Lost and found wedding rings (he kissed his treasured own) and images neither exhausted nor exorcised by their narrative employment! Ground Situations, Dramatic Vehicles, and stymied
minor-league storytellers like that Charles P. Mason fellow! All these
while one's outraged nation imperiously mounts a massive military
campaign against an elusive, ubiquitous enemy's encavements in a
destitute country already made miserable by religious zealots, feuding
local warlords, and contending foreign powers; when on any day or
night of this projected Hendecameron the Al Qaeda terrorists might
strike again, worse than before . . .

Yes, yes, he knows: Boccaccio, Scheherazade, and company; the relevance of Irrelevance. But as he and his mate went about their afternoon
routines (as did the neighbors mowing lawns and tending mid-September gardens, the commercial and amateur crabbers working the

nearby creek, the sailors and kayakers and sport-fisherfolk out on the river and bay beyond), and then made and enjoyed their Friday-evening meal, and then did an hour's pleasure-reading and miscellaneous correspondence, and then wound up their own Fourth-Night-since-Black-Tuesday with TV newscasts of their like-him-or-not President doing his presumable best to manage the crisis, and then retired to however-many-asterisked an Eleven-Thousandth-Plus Night of their own, he could not but ... well ... shake his Original Authorial head at what its Narrative Imagination and that imagination's unorthodox Muse were up to.

However; or perhaps therefore,
on the following morning — Saturday, September 15 — he felt impelled deskward, as was not his weekend custom unless some weekday had been pre-empted from sentence-making: Even Boccaccio's plague-fleeing young Florentines, one remembers, took their weekends off from storytelling. Perhaps he feared (anyhow allowed the possibility) that unless he kept "Graybard" and "Wysiwyg" at their quasi-erotic narrative enterprise, that enterprise might be swamped, drowned out, overwhelmed by circumambient, anaphrodisiac Reality?

Whatever the case, as *was* his workaday custom he began by refilling his fountain pen and reviewing The Story Thus Far of these stories thus far, in particular that most recent, "Fourth Night" installment of its narrative frame, emending and editing as he went along, right up through the authorial head-shaking just recounted. Aided by that momentum, he launched into the section subtitled *However; or perhaps therefore,* and when — at, shall we say, 9:11 AM or thereabouts? — he found himself writing the words *He dispatched his emissary Graybard from Scriptorium to Imaginarium*, he dispatched his emissary Graybard from Scriptorium to Imaginarium, where, not at all surprisingly, the room-lights glowed as the twilight faded, and the clear-cased bedside digital clock flashed alternately *9:11 9:15 9:11 9:15*.

"So you're getting nudgy about our project," Ms. Wys informed that emissary before he her. All business this "evening," his collaborator was awaiting him not on her deck, much less in the creek below, but seated in the now-bright bed / sitting room, wearing faded cutoff jeans, blue shortsleeve sweatshirt, and worn leather deck moccasins. Clipboard on lap. Ballpoint pen in one hand, wineglass in other. No sign of her having swum except still-damp-looking nutmeggish hair.

Maybe.

"Me too. Probably not for the same reasons." Ballpointing at second filled wineglass beside bottle of Napa Valley sauvignon blanc on low table between chairs: "Drink up, and let's hear it."

Yes. Well. Sip. Smiling and nodding herward: Nice.

"Something non-kinky for a change. Glad you approve." Still holding pen, wineglass, and now clipboard as well, she spread her arms to display her simple outfit. "No surprises underneath, either: just plain old cotton undies."

Actually, he was embarrassed to say, he meant the wine, although her get-up — get-down, whatever — was nice too, he supposed. Refreshing.

"*Crisp structure and complex finish, with accents of blackberry and pear,* as the wine freaks say? How come they never ever mention *grapes?* So what's your problem?"

Not mine, actually: *his.* It's our playing Scheherazade and Boccaccio while a War of Civilizations might be brewing . . .

For the first time that evening, she smiled at him. "All the more reason to get to it! Sip up, Geeb; we've got work to do."

Mm. And what might *your* problem be, Wys-o'-my-heart?

Frowning: "O'-your-heart?"

Just a friendly expression.

Has it been mentioned, Reader, that our nymph's bright eyes are a lustrous walnut brown? They are that, and she considered her visitor intently themwith for a moment before consulting her clipboard and quoting, from Fourth Night's detective-and-turtle tale, "*The Muse of Story shrugs her Parnassian shoulders* — at the Relevance issue, for one thing. We've *dealt* with that already. Tell your guy to forget it."

Consider him told. And shapely shoulders they are, Wys, even sweatshirted.

"*Inspiring,* maybe?"

Remains to be seen.

"So sip and see."

He sipped. What *is* Miz Muse's problem, then? Our storytelling?

Shake of head: Not for her to complain about *that,* it being she who allegedly inspires these tellings. No: What was beginning to pall on her, frankly, was neither the capital-I Irrelevance of these tales nor the caliber of their telling, but some of the material — with respect whereto she found herself moved to propose a Third Ultimatum before tonight's Narrative Empowerment kicked in.

There've been two already?

"No more Oldies," she reminded him; "no more Not-Quite-Ficties."

So what's it this time? He sipped. No more Sidelong Pickerel Smiles?

"SPSes can stay." Indeed, she here treated him to one that would have recharged even "Charles P. Mason's" narrative batteries. "Ultimatum Three is no more asterisks unless you promise no more Stories About Storytellers, okay? Especially stuck ones! No more yakking about Ground Situations and Dramatic Vehicles! *Autumnality* I can deal with — I've maybe got a thing about older guys? More-or-Less-Totally-Innocent-Marital-Guilt riffs we'll take case by case. But if you and I are going to go on with this Hendecameronic closet-clearing, there'll be no more Narrative Impotence, agreed? Enough limp-dickery already!"

Graybard's responding smile was neither sidelong nor, he'd bet, pickerelish of aspect, but front-on. He tabled his wineglass, took the liberty of tabling hers as well, and would have led *her* this time forthwith to five-starred Metaphoric Congress on her shimmering waterbed, had she not instead drawn the pair of them directly from transparent chairs to ditto carpet. Thereupon, at her pleased insistence, their Fifth Night communion was effected *a tergo*: Muse on all fours and Imagination astern, like C. P Mason and his hippie former student in that psychedelic Chevrolet as aforenarrated — the better, in this present case, for the principals to transact their pleasurable business fully clothed, he merely unzipping before and she, *mirabile dictu*, behind (special zipper in crotch of shorts despite her promise of No Surprises, and "plain old cotton undies" slit parenthetically for his convenience) . . .

* * * * *

"*All to the* end,"
she declared, smiling sidelong-pickerelly back at him from amid those asterisks, "of one's *getting* . . . as nearly as can be *managed* . . . what one *sees. Unh!* Ain't . . . inspiration . . . *fun?*"

Ah. Ah. Wysiwyg!

Whereafter, in her unpredictable way, she showered without bothering to undress. Wrapped her dripping self in a hooded white terry robe, stretched out not quite facedown upon her lighted bed, and with another (eyes-closed) S. P. Smile, bade him pay for their joint pleasure with the bedtime story *du soir*:

"Entitled?"

The Rest of Your Life

"Sounds like the beginning of a story" was George Fischer's busy wife's opinion, and her husband quite agreed, although just *what* story remained to be seen.

What had happened, he'd told her over breakfast, was that the calendar function on their home-office computer appeared to have died. When George called up the word processor's stationery format, for example, the date automatically supplied under his "business" letterhead read August 27, 1956. Likewise on their other letterhead formats, their email transmissions and receptions — anything on which the machine routinely noted month, day, and year. George had first remarked the error while catching up on personal and business correspondence the evening before this breakfast-time report (the date of which, by weak coincidence, happened to be July 27, 1996, just one month short of the fortieth anniversary of that letterhead date). Wondering mildly how many items he might have dispatched under that odd, out-of-date heading — for as Julia would now and then remind him, he had become less detail-attentive and generally more forgetful than he once was — he made the correction both on the correspondence in hand and on the computer's clock/calendar control ... and then forgot to mention the matter when his wife came home from her Friday-night aerobics group. Up at first light next morning, as usual in recent years, he let the "working girl" sleep on (her weekend pleasure) while he fetched in the newspaper, scanned its headlines over coffee — OLYMPIC BOMB

INVESTIGATION CONTINUES, TWA 800 CRASH CAUSE STILL UNKNOWN—set out their daily vitamins and other pills and the fixings of the breakfast that they would presently make together, then holed up in his office to check for email and do a bit of deskwork until she was up and about. Again, he noticed, the date came up August 27, 1956. He corrected it and experimentally restarted the machine.

August 27, 1956. "Must be a dead battery," he opined over their Saturday-morning omelet.

Looking up from the paper's Business section: "Desktop computers have batteries?"

Some sort of little battery, George believed he remembered, to keep the clock going when the thing's shut down. Maybe to keep certain memory-functions intact between start-ups, although he hadn't noticed any other problems thus far. Not his line; he would check the user's manual.

"How come it doesn't default — Is that the right word?"

"Default, yes." Words *were* his line.

"How come it doesn't default to the last date you set it to, or come up with a different wrong date each time? Why always August Whatever, Nineteen Whenever?"

"Twenty-seven, Fifty-six. Good question, but not one that I could answer."

Encouragingly: "Sounds like the beginning of a story."

Yes, well. They finished breakfast, did their daily calisthenics together (hers more vigorous than his, as she was ever the family jock), refilled their coffee mugs, and addressed their separate Saturday chores and amusements: for Julia, first her round-robin tennis group, then fresh-veggie shopping at the village farmers' market, then housework and gardening, interspersed with laps in their backyard pool; for George, a bit of bookkeeping at the desk and then odd jobs about the house and grounds, maybe a bit of afternoon crabbing in the tidal cove that fronts their property. Then dinner *à deux* and their usual evening routine: a bit of reading, a bit of television, maybe an email to one of their off-sprung offspring, maybe even a few recorder-piano duets, although the couple make music together these days less frequently than they used to. Then to bed, seldom later than half past ten.

Then the Sunday. Then a new week.

They had done all right, these two; rather well, actually. Classmates and college sweethearts at the state university, they'd married on their joint commencement day—shortly after World War II, when we Americans wed younger than nowadays—and promptly thereafter did their bit for the postwar Baby Boom, turning out three healthy youngsters in five years. George had majored in journalism, Julia in education, and although she'd graduated summa cum laude while he had simply graduated, after the manner of the time she had set her professional credentials mostly aside to do the Mommy track while Daddy earned their living. He had duly done that, too: first at a little New England weekly, where he'd learned what college hadn't taught him about newspapering; then at an upstate New York daily; then at a major midwestern daily, where on the strength of a Nieman Fellowship year at Harvard (the young American journalist's next-best thing to a Pulitzer Prize) he had switched from the Metro desk to Features; then at the Sunday magazine of Our Nation's Capital's leading rag—from which, as of his sixty-fifth birthday this time last year, he'd retired as associate editor to try his hand at freelancing. Over those busy decades, as their nestlings fledged and one by one took wing, Julia had moved from subbing in their sundry schools to part-time academic counseling—whatever could be shifted with George's "career moves" and expanded with the kids' independence—thence to supervisoring in the county school system, and most recently, since the couple's move from city to country, to full-timing as Director of Information Services at a small local college. No journalist or educator expects to get rich, especially with three college tuitions to pay; but the Fischers had husbanded (and wifed) their resources, invested their savings prudently along with modest inheritances from their late parents, and watched those investments grow through the prosperous American decades that raised the Dow Jones from about 600 to nearly 6,000. Anon they had sold their suburban-D.C. house at a substantial profit and retired—half of them, anyhow—to five handsomely wooded acres on the high banks of a cove off the Potomac's Virginia shore, complete with swimming pool, goose-hunting blind, guest wing for the kids and grandkids, His and Hers in the two-car garage, and a brace of motorboats at the pier: one little, for crabbing and such, the other not so little, for serious angling with old buddies from the *Post*. Enough pension, dividend, and Social Security income to keep the show going even without what George scored for the occasional column or magazine piece, not to mention

Julia's quite-good salary. Her own woman at last, as she liked to tease, *she* meant to keep on full-timing until they threw her out: the Grandma Moses of information service directors.

What's more, this prevailing good fortune, not entirely a matter of luck, applied to their physical and marital health as well. Both had survived their share of setbacks and even the rare knockdown, but in their mid-sixties they were still mentally, physically, and maritally intact, their midlife crises safely behind them and late-life ones yet to come, parents in the grave and grown-up children scattered about the republic with kids and midlife crises of their own. On balance, a much-blessed life indeed.

And by no means over! Quite apart from the famously increasing longevity of us First-Worlders, George and Julia had their parents' genes going for them, which had carried that foursome in not-bad health right up to bye-bye time in their late eighties and early nineties. Barring accident, the couple had an odds-on chance of twenty-plus years ahead—longer than their teenage grandkids had walked the earth.

"Time enough to make a few more career moves of my own," Julia teased whenever her husband spoke of this.

August 27, 1956. George recorrected the date, went on with his work, with the weekend, with their life; took the Macintosh in on Monday for rebatterying or whatever and made shift meanwhile with Julia's new laptop and his trusty old Hermes manual typewriter—stored in their attic ever since personal computers came online—until the patient was cured and discharged. The problem was, in fact, a dead logic-board battery, the serviceperson presently informed him, and then tech-talked over George's head for a bit about CMOS and BIOS circuitry. The chap couldn't explain, however, why the date-function defaulted consistently to August 27, 1956, rather than to the date of the machine's assembly, say (no earlier than 1993), or of the manufacture of its logic board. Did electronic data-processors in any form, not to mention PCs and Macintoshes, even exist on August 27, 1956?

Truth to tell, George Fischer doesn't have all that much to do at his desk these days, and so "making shift" was no big deal. Indeed, while both Julia and Mac were out of the house he turned his fascination with that presumably arbitrary but spookily insistent date into a bit of a project. Veteran journalists do not incline to superstition; a healthy skepticism, to put it mildly, goes with the territory. But why August? Why the 27th? Why 1956? Was something trying to tell him something?

Out of professional habit he checked the nearest references to hand, especially the historical-events chronology in his much-thumbed *World Almanac.* In 1956, it reminded him, we were halfway through what the almanac called "The American Decade." Dwight Eisenhower was about to be landslided into his second presidential term; Nikita Khrushchev was de-Stalinizing the USSR; Israel, Britain, and France were about to snatch back the Suez Canal from Egypt, which had nationalized it when we-all declined to finance President Nasser's Aswan Dam; the Soviet-U.S. space race was up and running, but *Sputnik* hadn't yet galvanized the competition; our Korean War was finished, our Vietnamese involvement scarcely begun . . . *et cetera.*

What couldn't he have done back in his old office, with the *Post*'s mighty databases and info-sniffing software! But to what end? Since the computer-repair facility was associated with "Julia's college," he contented himself with a side trip to the campus library when he drove in to retrieve the machine. A modest facility ("But we're working on it," his wife liked to declare), its microfilm stacks didn't include back numbers of George's former employer; it did file the *New York Times*, however, and from the reel *Jul. 21, 1956–Dec. 5, 1956* he photocopied the front page for Monday, August 27. SOVIET NUCLEAR TEST IN ASIA REPORTED BY WHITE HOUSE was the lead story, subheaded *U.S. Contrasts Moscow's Secrecy with Advance Washington Warnings.* Among the other front-page news: BRITISH CHARGE MAKARIOS DIRECTED REBELS IN CYPRUS, and EISENHOWER STAY IN WEST EXTENDED (the President was golfing in Pebble Beach, California, from where the nuclear-test story had also been filed). The lead photo was of the newly nominated Democratic presidential and vice presidential candidates, Adlai E. Stevenson and Estes Kefauver, leaving church together with members of their families on the previous day; the story below, however, was headlined TV SURVEY OF CONVENTIONS FINDS VIEWING OFF SHARPLY, and reported that neither the Republican nor the Democratic national conventions, recently concluded, had attracted as many viewers on any one evening as had Elvis Presley and Ed Sullivan.

So: It had been a Monday, that day forty Augusts past (its upcoming anniversary, George had already determined, would be a Tuesday). He showed the page to Julia over lunch, for which the Fischers sometimes met when he had errands near her campus.

"Still Eight Twenty-seven Fifty-sixing, are you?" She pretended concern at his "fixation," but scanned the photocopy with mild interest, sighing at the shot of Stevenson (whose lost cause they had ardently supported in the second presidential election of their voting life) and predicting that *this* year's upcoming political conventions, so carefully orchestrated for television, would lose far more viewers to the comedian Jerry Seinfeld than that year's had to Elvis Presley. And she pointed out to him — how hadn't he noticed it himself?— that the Soviet nuclear-test story had been filed "Special to the New York Times" by a sometime professional acquaintance of theirs, currently a public-television celebrity and syndicated columnist, but back then already making his name as a young White House reporter for the *Baltimore Sun.*

"While I," George reminded Julia, "was still clawing my way up from the *Boondock Weekly Banner* to the *Rochester Democrat and Chronicle.* Don't rub it in."

"Who's rubbing?" She ordered the shrimp salad and checked her watch. "It was an okay paper already, and you made it a better one. Which reminds me ..." And she changed the subject to the college's plan to install fiber-optic computer cables in every dormitory room during the upcoming academic year, in order to give the students faster access to the Internet. Her scheduled one o'clock meeting with a potential corporate sponsor of that improvement cut their lunch-date short; George wished her luck and watched her exit in her spiffy tailored suit while he (in his casual khakis, sportshirt, and old-fart walking shoes) finished his sandwich and took care of the check.

Yes indeedy, he mused to himself, homeward bound then: the dear old "Democrap and Chronic Ill," as they-all used to call it when things screwed up at the city desk. Heroic snow-belt winters; summers clouded by the "Great Lakes effect," though much milder in August than the subtropical summertime Chesapeake, and blessedly hurricane-free. The inexhaustible energy of an ambitious twenty-six-year-old, chasing down story-leads at all hours, learning the ins and outs of their newly adopted city as perhaps only a Metro reporter can, yet at the same time helping Julia with their three preschoolers, maintaining and even remodeling their low-budget first house, and still finding time over and above for entertaining friends, for going to parties and concerts (a welcome change from Boondockville)—time for everything, back when there was never enough time for anything! Whereas nowadays it sometimes seemed to George that with ample leisure for everything, less and less got done; July's routine chores barely finished before August's were upon him!

Once Mac was back in place (and correctly reading, when George booted him up, *August 6, 1996*), he did a bit more homework with the aid of some timeline software that he used occasionally when researching magazine pieces. By 1956, it reminded him, the world newly had or was on the cusp of having nuclear power plants, portable electric saws, Scrabble, electric typewriters and toothbrushes and clothes dryers, oral polio vaccine, aerosol spray cans, home air conditioners, aluminum foil, lightweight bicycles with shiftable gears and caliper brakes, wash-and-wear fabrics, credit cards, garbage disposers, epoxy glue, Frisbees, milk cartons, pantyhose, ballpoint pens, FM radio, and stereophonic sound systems. Still waiting in the wings were antiperspirants, automobile air conditioning and cruise control, aluminum cans, birth control pills, bumper stickers, pocket calculators, decaf coffee, microwave ovens, felt-tip pens, photocopiers, home-delivery pizza, transistor radios, home computers (as George had suspected), contact lenses, disposable diapers, running shoes, Teflon, scuba gear, skateboards, wraparound sunglasses, audiocassettes (not to mention VCRs), touch-tone telephones (not to mention cordlesses, cellulars, and answering machines), color and cable television, Valium, Velcro, battery-powered wristwatches, digital anythings, and waterbeds.

"Disposable diapers," Julia sighed that evening when her husband spieled through this inventory. "Where were they when we needed them?"

"Fifty-six was the year Grace Kelly married Prince Rainier the Third," he told her, "and Ringling Brothers folded their last canvas circus tent, and the *Andrea Doria* went down, and Chevrolet introduced fuel-injected engines. Harry Belafonte. The aforementioned Elvis. *I Love Lucy . . .*"

"I *did* love Lucy," his wife remembered. The early evening was airless, sultry; indeed, the whole week had been unnaturally calm, scarcely a ripple out on their cove, and this at the peak of the Atlantic hurricane season, with Arturo, Bertha, Carlos, and Danielle already safely past, and who knew whom to come. Back in '56, if George remembered correctly, the tropical storms all bore Anglo female names; he'd have to check.

They were sipping fresh-peach frozen daiquiris out on their pier while comparing His and Her day, their summer custom before preparing dinner. As Julia was now the nine-to-fiver, George routinely made the cocktails and barbecued the entrée as often as possible, although it was still she who planned the menus and directed most of the preparation. She'd had a frustrating afternoon; hadn't hit it off with that potential co-sponsor of the college's fiber-optic upgrade, an old-boy type whose patronizing manner had strained her professional diplomacy to the limit. Excuse her, she now warned, if the male-chauvinist bastard had left her short of patience.

"Enough about Nineteen Fifty-six, then," George suggested.

"No, go on. Obsessional or not, it soothes me."

"Steak eighty-eight cents a pound, milk twenty-four cents a quart, bread eighteen cents a loaf. Average cost of a new car seventeen hundred bucks — remember our jim-dandy Oldsmobile wagon?"

"A Fifty-five bought new in Fifty-six, when the dealer was stuck with it." The Fischers' first new car, it had been: two-tone, green and ivory. "Or was it a Fifty-six bought late in the model year?"

"A bargain, whichever. Median price of a new house — get this — eleven thousand seven hundred. I think we paid ten-five for Maison Faute de Mieux."

"Dear Maison Faute de Mieux." Pet name for their first-ever house, afore-referred to. "But what was the median U.S. income back then?"

"Just under two thousand per capita per annum. My fifty-six hundred from the *D and C* was princely for a new hand."

Julia winced her eyes shut in mid-sip. "Headache?" her mate wondered.

"Unfortunate choice of abbreviations." It had been in '56 or '57, she reminded him (as he had unwittingly just reminded her), that she'd found herself pregnant for the fourth time, accidentally in this instance, and they had decided not only to terminate the pregnancy by dilation and curettage — D & C, in ob-gyn lingo, and a code-term too for abortion in those pre-*Roe v. Wade* days — but to forestall further such accidents by vasectomy. "Shall we change the subject?"

Agreed—for a cluster of long- and well-buried memories was thereby evoked, of a less nostalgic character than their first house and new car. Duly shifting subjects, "What's that floating white thing?" George asked her, and pointed toward a something-or-other drifting themward on the ebbing tide.

"Don't see it." With her drink-free hand Julia shaded her eyes from the lowering sun. "Okay, I see it. Paper plate?"

It was an object indeed the diameter of a paper or plastic dinner plate, though several times thicker, floating edge-up and nine-tenths submerged in the flat calm creek. On its present leisurely course it would pass either just before or just under the cross-T where they sat, a not unwelcome diversion. Their sport-fishing boat, *Byline*, was tied up alongside; George stepped aboard, fetched back a crabber's dip-net, and retrieved the visitor when it drifted within reach.

"Well, now."

It was, of all unlikely flotsam, a *clock*: a plain white plastic wall clock, battery-powered (didn't have those back in '56). Perhaps blown off some up-creek neighbor's boathouse? But there'd been no wind. Maybe negligently Frisbee'd into the cove after rain got to it? Anyhow quite drowned now, the space between its face and its plastic "crystal" half filled with tidewater (hence its slight remaining buoyancy), and stopped, *mirabile dictu*, at almost exactly 3:45, so that when George held it twelve o'clock high, the outstretched hands marked its internal waterline like a miniature horizon.

"Time and tide, right?" Then, before he'd even thought of the other obvious connection, Julia said, "Now we're in for it: not only August Twenty-seventh, but *three forty-five* on August Twenty-seventh. AM or PM, I wonder."

They tsked and chuckled. During their coveside residency a number of souvenirs had washed up on their reedy shoreline along with the usual litter of plastic bags and discarded drink containers from the creek beyond — wildfowl decoys, life vests, fishermen's hats, crab-trap floats — but none so curious or portentous. In a novel or a movie, George supposed to Julia, the couple would begin to wonder whether some plot was thickening, whether something was trying to tell them something, and whether 3:45 AM or PM meant Eastern Daylight Time in 1956 or 1996.

"At three forty-five AM, Eight Twenty-seven *Ninety*-six," Julia declared, "your loving wife intends to be sound asleep. You can tell her
the news over breakfast." And she wondered aloud, as they moved in
from the pier to start dinner, what they had each been up to at 3:45 in
the afternoon of August 27 forty years ago in Rochester, New York.

Another memory-buzz, and it was well that the couple were sin-
gle-filing, for George felt his face burn. Would it not have been that
very summer, if not necessarily that month . . . but yes, right around
the time of "their" abortion . . .

Without mentioning it to Julia, he resolved to check out discreetly, if
he could, a certain little matter that he hadn't had occasion to remember for years, perhaps even for decades. His intention had been to drop
the dripping clock *trouvé* into their trash bin, but as he passed through
the garage en route to setting up the patio barbecue oven (didn't have
those in '56, at least not with charcoal-lighting fluid and liquid propane igniters), he decided to hang it instead on a nearby tool-hook, to
remind him to notice whether anything significant would happen to
happen at the indicated hour three weeks hence.

Not that he would likely need reminding. Unsuperstitious as George
Fischer was and idle as was his interest in that approaching "anniversary," he was more curious than ever now about what — in his and Julia's
joint timeline, if not in America's and the world's — it might be the
fortieth anniversary of. He was half tempted to ask the *Democrat and
Chronicle*'s morgue-keepers to fax him a copy of the paper's Metro-sec-
tion front page for August 27, 1956, to see what had been going on in
town that day (but the reported news would be of the day before; perhaps he ought to check headlines for the 28th) and whether he himself
had bylined any Rochester stories while his more successful friend was
filing White House specials to the *Times*. But he resisted the temptation.
Frame-by-framing through Julia's college's microfilm files had reminded him how each day's newspaper is indeed like a frame in time's ongoing movie. We retrospective viewers know, as the "actors" themselves
did not, how at least some of those stories will end: that Stevenson and
Kefauver will be overwhelmed in November by Eisenhower and Nixon; that the U.S.-Soviet arms race will effectively end with the collapse
of the USSR in 1989. Of others we may remember the "beginning" but
not the "end," or vice versa; of others yet (e.g., in George's case, Britain's

troubles with Archbishop Makarios in Cyprus) neither the prologue nor the sequel. But who was to say that what would turn out to be the *really* significant event of any given day — even internationally, not to mention locally — would be front-page news? Next week's or month's lead story often begins as today's page-six squib or goes unreported altogether at the time: Einstein's formulation of relativity theory, the top-secret first successful test of a thermonuclear bomb. And unlike the President's golf games, what ordinary person's most life-affecting events — birth, marriage, career successes and failures, child-conceptions, infidelities and other betrayals, divorce, major accident, illness, death — make the headlines, or in most instances even the inside pages? George reminded himself, moreover, that such "frames" as hours, day-dates, year-numbers — all such convenient divisions of time — are mainly our human inventions, more or less relative to our personal or cultural-historical point of view: What would "August 27, 1956" mean to an Aztec or a classical Greek? Oblivious to time zones and calendars, though not to astronomical rhythms, the world rolls on; our life-processes likewise, oblivious to chronological age though not to aging.

8/27/56. No need to consult the *D&C:* Prompted by some old résumés and other items in his home-office files, George's ever-slipperier memory began to clarify the personal picture. In the late spring of that year, he and Julia and their three preschoolers had moved to their first real city — in their new Olds wagon, it now came back to him, bought earlier in Boondockville on the strength of his Rochester job offer, and so it had been a leftover '55 after all. After checking neighborhoods and public-school districts and balancing the city's higher real-estate prices against their freshly elevated budgetary ceiling, they had bought "Maison Faute de Mieux," its to-the-hilt mortgage to be amortized by the laughably distant year 1986. And on July 1 George had begun his first comparatively big-time newspaper job, for which he'd been hired on the strength of a really rather impressive portfolio from what he's calling the *Boondock Weekly Banner.* No *annus mirabilis,* maybe, 1956, but a considerable corner-turn in his/their life: formal education and professional apprenticeship finished; family established and now appropriately housed; children safely through babyhood and about to commence their own schooling; the Fischers' six-year marriage well past the honeymoon stage but not yet seriously strained; and George's first major success scored in what would turn out to be a quite creditable career (for if he could point to some, like that *Times*/PBS fellow, who had done better, he could point to ever so many more who'd done less well) in a field that by and large served the public interest, not just the family's personal welfare. Reviewed thus, in the story of both their married life and George's professional life the summer of '56 could be said to have marked the end of the Beginning and the beginning of the Middle.

Over that evening's cocktail-on-the-pier, "You left something out," Julia said, and George's face reflushed, for he had indeed skirted a thing or two that his day's digging had exhumed. But what she meant, to his relief, was that it had been that same summer — when George Jr. was five, Anne-Marie four, and Jeannette turning three — that their mother had felt free at last to begin her own "career," however tentatively and part-time, by working for "pay" (i.e., reduced kiddie-tuition) in their daughters' nursery school.

"Right you are. Sorry about that."

"It may seem nothing to you, George, but to me it mattered."

"Properly so."

She looked out across the cove, where the sun was lowering on an-other steamy August day. "I've often envied Anne-Marie and Jeannette their *assumption* that their careers are as important as their husbands."

"I'm sure you have." By ear, George couldn't tell whether "their hus-bands" ended with an apostrophe. The fact was, though, that if their elder daughter and her spouse, both academics, had managed some measure of professional parity in their university, their younger daugh-ter's legal career had proved more important to her than marriage and motherhood; she'd left her CPA husband in Boston with custody of their ten-year-old to take a promotion in her firm's Seattle office. Even Julia's feelings were mixed about that, although the marriage had been shaky from the start.

More brightly, "Oh, I forgot to tell you," she said then: "I asked this computer friend of mine at work about that default-date business? And he said that normally the default would be to the date when some giz-mo called the BIOS chip was manufactured, which couldn't be before Nineteen Eighty. BIOS means Basic Input-Output System? But this guy's a PC aficionado who sniffs at Macintoshes. Anyhow, he's putting out a query on the Net, so stay tuned."

George was still getting used to some of his wife's recent speech habits: those California-style rising inflections and flip idioms like "stay tuned" that she picked up from her younger office-mates and that to him sounded out of character for people his and Julia's age. But he suppressed his little irritation, told her sincerely that he appreciated her thoughtfulness, and withdrew to set up the charcoal grill before the subject could return to Things Left Out.

On 8/27/56, yet another bit of software informed him next day, the Dow Jones Industrial Average had been 522, and *Billboard* magazine's #1 pop recording in the USA had been Dean Martin singing *Memories Are Made of This*. Whatever other desk-projects George had in the works — and his "retirement," mind, had been only from daily go-to-the-office journalism, not from the profession altogether — were stalled by distraction as the Big Date's anniversary drew nearer. In "the breakaway republic of Chechnya," as the media called it, a smoldering stalemate continued between rebel forces and the Russian military, whose leaders themselves were at odds over strategy. In Bosnia a sour truce still held as election-time approached. Julia found another possibly interested corporate co-sponsor for her college's fiber-optic upgrade. The queerly calm weather hung over tidewater Virginia as if Nature were holding her breath. There would be a full moon, George's desk calendar declared, on the night after 8/27/96; perhaps they would celebrate the passage of his recent lunacy. On Sunday, 8/18, trolling for bluefish aboard *Byline* with pals from the *Post*, he snagged his left thumb on a fish hook; no big deal, although the bandage hampered his computer keyboarding. His "little obsession" had become a standing levity since Julia (without first consulting him) shared it as a tease with their friends and children. George Jr., who worked for the National Security Agency at Fort Meade, pretended to have inside info ("We call it the X-File, Dad") that extraterrestrials were scheduled to take over the earth on 8/27/96. Picking up on her brother's tease, his academic sister emailed from Michigan that the first UFOs had secretly landed on 8/27/56; their ongoing experiments on our family — in particular on its alpha male — would be completed on the fortieth anniversary (as measured in earth-years) of that first landing. ("We'll miss you, Dad.")

"So guess what," Julia announced on Friday, August 23. "I had lunch again today with Sam Bryer — my computer friend? And he found out from some hacker on the Net that all Macintoshes default to Eight Twenty-seven Fifty-six when their logic boards die because that's Whatsisname's birthday — the founder of Apple Computers? A zillionaire in his thirties! Sam says everything about Macintoshes has to be cutesy-wootsy."

"Aha, and my thanks to ... Sam, is it?" To himself he thought, Lunch again today with the guy? and tried to remember when he had last lunched with a woman colleague. The bittersweet memories then suddenly surged: a certain oak-paneled restaurant in downtown Rochester, far enough from the office for privacy but close enough for clandestine lovers to get back to their desks more or less on time; a certain motel, inexpensive but not sleazy, on the Lake Ontario side of town; the erotic imagination and enviable recovery-speed of a healthy twenty-six-year-old on late-summer afternoons when he was supposed to be out checking the latest from Eastman Kodak or the university. It occurred to George to wonder whether it might have happened to be exactly at 3:45 PM EDT on August 27, 1956, that a certain premature and unprotected ejaculation had introduced a certain rogue spermatozoon to a certain extramural ovum: "*Our imperious desires,*" dear brave Marianne had once ruefully quoted Robert Louis Stevenson, "*and their staggering consequences.*"

For the sake of the children, as they say — but for other good reasons, too — Mr. and Mrs. had chosen not to divorce when the matter surfaced; and except for one half-hysterical (but consequential) instance, Julia had not retaliated in kind. The Nieman Fellowship year in Cambridge, not long after, had welcomely removed them from the Scene of the Crime as well as testifying to George's professional rededication; its prestige enabled their move to St. Louis (the *Post-Dispatch*), thence to D.C., excuse the initials — and here, forty years later, they were: still comrades, those old wounds long since scarred over and, yes, healed.

"Tell your pal Sam," George told his wife, "that Eight Twenty-seven is Lyndon Johnson's and Mother Teresa's birthday, too, though not their upcoming fortieth, needless to say. Virgos all. Birthstone peridot. What's peridot?"

Julia, however, was communing with herself. "My pal Sam," she said deprecatingly, but smiled and sipped.

Who knows what "really" happened when the Big Day came? The explanation of George Fischer's computer's default-date, while mildly

amusing, was irrelevant to the momentous though still vague significance that it had assumed for him, and in no way diminished his interest in its anniversary. By then his fishhook wound, too, was largely
healed. He and Julia made wake-up love that morning — she had been
more ardent of late than usual, and than her distracted husband. He
cleared breakfast while she dolled up for work and then, still in his
pajamas and slippers, lingered over second coffee and the Tuesday
paper before going to his desk. Another sultry forecast, 30 percent
chance of late-afternoon thundershowers. Second day of Democratic
national convention in Chicago; Hillary Rodham Clinton to address
delegates tonight. Cause of TWA 800 crash still undetermined; Hurricane Edouard approaching Caribbean. He decided to try doing an
article for the *Post*'s Sunday magazine — maybe even for the *New York
Times* Sunday magazine — about his curious preoccupation, which by
then had generated a small mountain of notes despite George's professional sense that he still lacked a proper handle on it, and that those
of his associated musings that weren't indelicately personal were too
... philosophical, let's say, for a newspaper-magazine piece. As mentioned already, the Really Important happenings, on whatever level,
aren't necessarily those that get reported in the press: the undetected
first metal-fatigue crack in some crucial component of a jetliner's air-
frame; the casual mutation of one of your liver cells from normal to
cancerous; the Go signal to a terrorist conspiracy, coded innocuously
in love-seekers' lingo among the Personals. But George's maunderings
extended from *What's the significance of this date?* through *What's the
significance of the whole concept of date, even of time?* to *What's the
significance of Significance, the meaning of Meaning?*

Never mind those. He quite expected 8/27/96 to be just another
day, in the course of which we Americans (so said some new software
sent by the Fischers' Seattle-lawyer daughter) would per usual eat for-
ty-seven million hot dogs, swallow fifty-two million aspirin tablets, use
six-point-eight billion gallons of water to flush our collective toilets,
and give birth to ten thousand new Americans. But George was not
blind to such traditional aspects of Forty Years as, say, the period of
the Israelites' wandering in the desert, the proverbial age at which
life begins or the typical span of a professional career — so that if, as
aforesuggested, 8/27/56 had been for his the end of the Beginning and
beginning of the Middle, then 8/27/96 might feasibly mark the end of

the Middle and thus the beginning of the End. He was even aware that just as his "little obsession" therewith had assumed a life of its own, independent of the trifle that had prompted it, so his half-serious but inordinate search for Portent might conceivably generate its own ful-fillment — might prompt Julia, for example, this late in their story, to settle a long-dormant score by making, as she herself had teased, "a few career moves" of her own; or might merely nudge her obsessed spouse gently around some bend, distancing him from her, their family and friends and former colleagues, so that in retrospect (trying and failing, say, to make a marketable essay out of it or anything else thencefor-ward) he would see that August 27 had indeed been the beginning of the end because he himself had made it so.

Just another day: the first for many, for many the last, for many more a crucial or at least consequential turning point, but for most of us none of the above, at least apparently. George ate an apple for lunch; phoned Julia's office to check out *her* Day Thus Far and got her voicemail mes-sage instead: a poised, assured, very-much-her-own-woman's voice. As was his summertime post-lunch habit, he then ran a banner up their waterfront pole from the assortment in their "flag locker," choosing for the occasion a long and somewhat tattered red-and-yellow streamer that in the Navy's flag code signifies Zero; it had been a birthday gift some years past from George Jr., who jokingly complained that his dad read too much significance into things and therefore gave him some-thing that literally meant Nothing. After an exercise-swim he set out a half-dozen crab traps along the lip of the cove-channel and patrolled them idly for a couple of hours from *Sound Bite*, the Fischers' noisy little outboard runabout — inevitably wondering, at 3:45, whether his wife and Sam Whatsisname, Sam Bryer, might actually be *et cetera*. At that idea he found myself simultaneously sniffling and chuckling aloud with . . . oh, Transcendent Acceptance, he supposed.

Not enough crabs to bother with; they seemed to be scarcer every year.

At about 4:30 — as George was considering whether canteloupe daiquiris or champagne would make the better toast to Beginning-of-the-End Day when Julia got home — the forecast thunderstorm rolled down the tidal Potomac, dumping an inch of rain in half an hour, knocking out local power for twenty minutes, and buffeting the cove with fifty-knot gusts, as measured on the wind gauge in the Fischer family room. Busy closing windows, George absent-mindedly neglected to fetch in the Zero flag before the storm hit; as he watched nature's sound-and-light show from the house's leeward porch, he saw the weathered red and yellow panels one by one let go at their seams in the bigger gusts and disappear behind curtains of rain. By five the tempest had rolled on out over the Chesapeake, the wind had moderated to ten and fifteen, and the westward sky was rebrightening. Dock bench and pool-deck chairs would be too soaked for Happy Hour sitting; they would use the screened porch. George reset all the house clocks and hauled down the last shredded panel of his son's gift-flag, thinking he might mount it on a garage or basement wall behind that waterlogged clock as a wry memorial to the occasion: his next-to-last rite of passage, whatever.

Normally Julia got home from work by half past five; that day George was well into the six o'clock news on television — Russians resume pullout from Grozny; Syria ready to resume talks with Israel; big hometown welcome expected for First Lady's convention appearance — when the garage door rumbled up and his wife's Volvo rolled in. Often "high" from her day at the office, she arrived this time positively radiant, forgetting (George noted as he went to greet her) to reclose the garage door as usual from inside her car. Tugging her briefcase off the passenger seat with one hand while removing her sunglasses with the other, "Any champagne in the fridge?" she called. She kneed the car door shut — George pressed the garage-door wall button — gave him an exaggerated kiss hello, and exhilarated past him into the kitchen. Plopped down her briefcase; peeled out of her suit-jacket; yanked the fridge open; then stopped to grin Georgeward, spreading her arms victoriously.

"Congratulate me! I *nailed* the guy! Fiber optics, here we come!"

Well, he did congratulate her — wholeheartedly, or very nearly so. Popped the bubbly; toasted her corporate co-sponsoral coup; let her crow happily through half a glass before he mentioned what he'd thought she would be celebrating, perhaps prematurely: the unremarkable close of what had proved after all to be just another day. When he did finally bring that matter up, it was via the heavyhanded portent of the thunderstorm and George Jr's flag.

"So here's to Nothing," Julia cheered, and although she topped up both glasses and bade them reclink, her mind was obviously still on her successful courtship of that potential college-benefactor. Presently she excused herself to change out of office clothes and take a swim before hors d'oeuvres and the rest of the champagne. George wasn't even to *think* of starting the charcoal for the veal grillades and marinated eggplant wedges; she was flying too high to fuss with dinner yet.

"So *I'll* fuss," her husband volunteered, but contented himself with merely readying the grill for cooking. Their pool was well screened from the neighbors, and the Fischers skinny-dipped on occasion, though not as a rule — since who knew when a delivery- or service-person might drive up, or the lawn-mowing crew. But presently out she frisked jaybird-naked, did George's triumphant mate, and like a playful pink porpoise dived with a whoop into the pool's deep end.

"Come on in!" she all but ordered him after a bit. "Drop your drawers and take the plunge!" Not to spoil her fun, George did, but couldn't follow through when, to his surprise, she made to crown her triumph with a spot of submarine sex.

On 8/27/96 the Dow Jones closed up 17, at 5,711. The Fischers ate late; watched the First Lady's convention speech on television (Julia raising her fist from time to time in a gesture of solidarity); decided not to wait up for the ensuing keynote address. Instead, nightcap in hand, they stepped outside to admire the moon over their cove — still officially one night shy of full, but looking already as ripe as a moon can look.

"So," said George: "That's that."

"What's what?" She clearly had no idea what he was referring to.

"Old Eight Twenty-seven *Et Cetera.*"

"Oh, right." She inhaled, exhaled, and with mock gravity, said, "You know what they say, George: *Today is the first day of the rest of your life.*"

How right she was.

SIXTH NIGHT

So okay,
mused Graybard Imagination — to himself, Itself, whateverself: Here
one has the fine mild morning of Sunday, September 16, 2001; things
still frantic up in Manhattan, where fires burn yet at Ground Zero's
mass grave and Wall Streeters worry, as do many of the rest of us, what'll
happen when the stock market reopens tomorrow after its longest closure since the crash of 1929. Busybusy likewise over in Our Nation's
Capital, where the Pentagon de-rubbles its blasted fifth side, buries its
184 dead, and prepares to Strike Back at the Evil Whomever, while
many another federal office full-throttles through the weekend. Across
the bay in Tidewaterland, however, except for the flags and patriotic
decals sprouting from rural mailboxes, small-town shop windows, and
automobiles (mostly SUVs, vans, and pickup trucks, by GB's count),
life proceeds much as always on a sunny Sunday morn: The Chris-
tian-religious prep for church and midday dinner; the non-Christian
and/or secular pursue whatever weekend activities, not *oblivious* to
the alarming and unpredictable new international situation, but largely unaffected by it in any direct way so far.

Thus, e.g., M/M Narrative Hardware of these tales, that couple
being altogether of the secular persuasion, for better or worse, but
conditioned by past decades of Monday-through-Friday work to take
weekends off, by and large. Amen then, shruggeth Graybard: If after
five straight days of Hendecameroning the bloke wants a "Sixth Night"

506

break (especially having scribbled away the Saturday AM recording "Wysiwyg's" kinky latest inspiration), let him spend this fair Sunday on odd jobs and family errands, bicycling *à deux* about the neighborhood, catching up on snail- and e-mail, and leafing through the hefty *Times* (CONGRESSMEN CALL FOR BROADER FBI/CIA SPY POWERS IN WAKE OF 9/11, etc.). As for himself, however — in his capacity as Narrative Imagination Embodied, the Software from whom issue such formulations as *As for himself, however* — having declined, along with their unorthodox and likewise secular muse, to take the Jewish Sabbath off from their joint work, he saw no reason to make a holiday of the Christian. In the nature of their case and per their separate job descriptions, he's free to wander undispatched while his weekday Dispatcher swims exercise laps, washes the family car, reads the newspaper, maybe even dozes off in a lawn chair shaded by a large mimosa. At the morning's voltaged ninth-hour-plus, therefore, he makes the now-routine excursion from (unoccupied) Scriptorium to Imaginarium, to see what if any new twists or surprises Ms. Inspiration may have up her sleeve, shall we say, this time around. Little as he knows about that female entity — who she "really" is, if that question even makes sense, and what might account for her extraordinary accoutrements, habits, and habitation in this latest and most physical of her manifestations — he knows himself to be grateful indeed for her invaluable assistance over the decades and appreciative of her curious new embodiment, unprecedented in their longstanding partnership.

Good in the metaphorical bed, too, she is, as he hopes he may, with her assistance, be being also. Whatever the merits of their collective narrative offspring, the inspiration themof has been refreshment indeed. Even those serial ultimata of hers — no more Oldies, no more Not-Quite-Ficties, no more Stories About Storytelling, especially about Narrative Impotency or the specter thereof — he has found more stimulating than inhibitory, like that (metaphorical) potion wherewith she claims to spike his (metaphorical) wine before their (metaphorical and incrementally asterisked) "nightly" Congress.

So: Abracadabra, Once upon a time, whatever,
and per usual it was Rosy-Fingered Dusk out over her marshscape, and her bedside digital flashed *9:11 9:16 9:11 9:16,* by which time of evening on which date in this 39th degree of north latitude it ought

to have been entirely dark already—as indeed it became even as he reflected this reflection. And all was as ever brightly lit and more or less transparent *chez* Wysiwyg, and there on a cellophane "napkin" was his wineglass (anyhow *a* wineglass; where was the usual second?), filled and waiting beside a lighted clear-oil candle-lamp out on the deck table; and okay, Herself nowhere in sight, but that had been the case initially on First and Fourth Nights too, as he recalled. No doubt the sprite was pleasurably marinating in her marsh.

Yo, Wys? he called down from the deck rail, at the laddertop.

No reply. No splash-sounds, either, or flash of fair wet skin asparkle with agitated *noctilucae*.

Wysiwyg?

Well, now. No way he could've missed seeing her indoors—*au toilette,* say—given her apartment's see-through partitions, floor, and ceiling. Either she was bathing farther off in the marsh-creek tonight than usual, or else she hadn't arrived yet (from where?), or else she had, without notice, simply up and left—just at the midpoint, it now occurred to him, of their projected eleven-night stand. Consternated by that possibility, he fetched up the single wineglass; sniffed and sipped, experimentally: a simple jug chablis, he'd guess, quite all right, and still chilled, therefore poured not long since . . .

Well, he'd wait a bit and just see. The woman might of course have other business than attending to his inspiration; perhaps even (twinge of jealousy here) other imaginations than his to inspire in her singular and delightsome fashion. Although the muses as such are as old as Greek mythology, their embodiments are typically represented in full female flower: Maybe the wench was having her period? Even so, they could've rendezvoused, at least, could they not've? At least, in workmate fashion, sipped and chatted? And (*vide* Fifth Night's kinkish come-together) where Inspiration hooks up with Imagination, there's more than one way to skin the old cat.

Wys?

No reply beyond the irritated squawk of a great blue heron lifting off or landing out there somewhere. Had that Fourth Night detective-and-turtle tale about the absence of inspiration perhaps inspired Inspiration's absence, despite his agreeing to lay off that subject thenceforward? Come to think of it—and remembering "Narrator's" maunderings back in Night Two's wedding-ring story—was what he felt now the absence of her presence or the presence of her absence?

Too French a question for the likes of Graybard. Perhaps this was her (not especially inspired) solution to their eleven-night / ten-story problem afore-remarked: Just skip one? Not likely. Nor could he seriously imagine her simply abandoning him and their project without notice, little as he knew of who she "really" was and how she and her unusual domicile came to be here. One of her seventeenth-century forebears had already inspired Giovanni Battista Basile's *Pentameron* (a.k.a. *Lo Cunto de li Cunti*), replete with Cinderella, Snow White, Rapunzel, and other notable *cunti*; the corpus didn't need another five-day talefest. More likely tonight's scenario was some sort of trial; if among its objectives was to make him miss her presence (quite apart from her assistance) and feel her absence, then it quite succeeded. That absence was everywhere present: in the so-familiar low-tide marsh-tang, combined as on her naked self with the perfume of mallows abloom amongst the reeds; in her yesternight's wet duds (shortsleeve sweatshirt, cutoff jeans, and cotton underpants — ordinary-looking but oddly tailored, those latter two, in certain respects) still lying where tossed after she'd showered in them between Fifth Night's Inspiration and his Recitation of *The Rest of Your Life* . . .

***

Wysiwyg?

Glass in hand, he wandered through her spaces. Was half tempted to ransack the place for clues to her, but forbore: What one saw, without prurient prying, was what one would get. Contemplating "their" waterbed, he stopped and sipped. If the wine was per usual potioned, was she suggesting Metaphorical Masturbation? No thanks, *chère* Wys: All storymaking, viewed unsympathetically, might be called that. Let's you and me stay with the *ménage intime* of Muse / Tale / Teller / Told — and where the fug are ye, luv?

Only as his glass neared empty did he register that on "his" pillow, like a goodie left by a turndown-service chambermaid, was another transparent beverage-napkin, whereon rested a believe-it-or-not transparent Chinese fortune cookie, its paper-slip message visible though not readable inside. With sigh and headshake (in case she was somehow somewhere watching, scanning this very parenthesis over his shoulder) he set aside the wineglass, broke the tidbit open — a plastic shell after all, not an edible see-through pastry — straightened the slip, and read: *4: NO MORE DISMAYING (AND HALF-NOSTALGIC) SUDDEN RECOLLECTIONS OF REPRESSED-MEMORY INFIDELI-TIES, WHETHER UNILATERAL OR RECIPROCAL, FROM PROTAG-ONIST'S EARLIER LIFE-CHAPTERS OR INCARNATIONS.*

Can't the woman even say *please*? he complained to himself — and at once apologized, the facts being (a) that "the woman" was as de-lightsome and helpful (if enigmatic) a collaborator as he could, lit-erally, imagine; (b) that this fourth "ultimatum" of hers was scarcely unwarranted, his two recentest tales having turned in fact on just that category of recollection: Enough already! And finally, (c) that it was not for her to say please, when the giving of narrative pleasure was his very *raison d'être*. How right she was!

Stand by me, then (please), O frisky unpredictable spirit,
he implored her bed, her room, her deck, her night-marsh. I feel your stimulant taking hold: a very Viagra of the Imagination. If, like my First Night Invocation, it somehow summons your physical presence, I'll welcome you with an eager and grateful six-asterisk embrace. If, on the contrary, what I get of you at this midpoint of our Hendecameron is only what I've seen of you tonight thus far, then so be it. Now I lay me down to please my muse, if she so inspire me, with a tale that, in observance of her serial strictures, is not an Oldie, not Non-Fictive, not About Storytelling, and devoid of Dismaying Sudden Recollections of *Et Cetera*. Should said tale please our Wysiwyg, where- and whoever she may be, that will be Sixth Night pleasure enough for its Present Teller.

Having delivered himself of this soliloquy, he deposited Ultimatum #4 in the empty wineglass and unhurriedly shucked his clothing (the male counterpart of hers from the night before), tossed them among and atop hers, and took his narratorial ease on the glowing waterbed, stretching himself out neither on His side thereof nor on Hers, but straight down the middle. As if cued by his open-ended resolve, all the roomlights dimmed as one and then went out entirely. The simple symbolism pleased him, as had that of his and her clothing in damp bedside congress: In the imminence of their muse, even seasoned practitioners of any art are finally naked and in the dark, waiting (with honed attention) to see what will happen next. The novelty, too, of this evening's progress thus far he found not unarousing; likewise this lights-out evidence that Ms. Wys *was*, somehow, on the premises. Her chablis-flavored elixir coursed through him. Expecting at any sentence to hear her bare footpads cross the room and then to feel her strictly metaphorical but nonetheless delicious conjunction himwith, to the circumambient darkness he declared aloud: *Certain present evidence to the contrary notwithstanding, tonight's story is entitled*

The Big Shrink

The party was over, really, but a few of us lingered out on Fred and Marsha Mackall's ample pool deck to enjoy the subtropical air, the planetarium sky and a last sip before heading homeward. Half a dozen or more at first, we lingerers were; then just our hosts and Roberta and I, sitting in deep patio chairs or on the low wall before the Mackalls' great sloping lawn.

"The other thing I wanted to get said," Fred Mackall went on presently, "—that Marsha's story and those stars up there reminded me of?— is that the universe isn't expanding anymore, the way it used to."

We let that proposition hang for a couple of beats in the cricket-rich tidewater night. Then my Bertie, with just the right mix of this and that, set down her decaf, kicked off her sandals, said brightly "Oh?," and propped her feet on a low deck table.

"If you're starting that . . . ," Marsha Mackall warned her husband — *amiably but not unseriously*, I guess I'd say.

Fred twiddled his brandy glass in the patio-torchlight. The catering crew, assisted by the Mackalls' caretaker-couple, were unobtrusively cleaning up. In a tone calibrated to match his wife's, "It's what's on my mind to say," Fred said.

"*I'm* ready," Bert volunteered, who generally was. "Hey: There went a meteorite."

I corrected her. Mildly. Good-humoredly.

Sleek Marsha Mackall pushed up out of her Adirondack chair. "Tell you what," to her husband: "I'll go help the help while you do the universe."

From his wall-seat, "You do that," Fred seconded — *levelly but not disagreeably*, I guess I'd say. And she did.

"Did you see it?" my wife asked me.

"Didn't need to, actually. Meteor*ite*'s what hits the earth. Right, Fred?"

"You didn't *need* to?" *Quizzical but with an edge*, Bert's tone, and I thought, Uh-oh. "How do we know it *didn't* hit the earth?" she asked me further, or perhaps asked both of us.

"For a while there," Fred said on, "the universe expanded, all right, just as we were taught in school — your Big Bang and all? The whole show expanded in space up there for quite a little while, actually, everything getting bigger and bigger."

"Well ..." I could tell what my wife was thinking: Not expansion *in* space, Fred-O, but expansion *of* space; space itself expanding, *et cetera*. Bert might get meteors and meteorites ass-backward, but she knew more stuff than I did, and we shared all our interests, she and I; discussed everything under the sun with each other. What she said, however, was "Try eight to twelve billion years, okay?"

Fred Mackall turned his perfectly grayed, aging-preppie head her way, then shook it slowly and spoke as if to the flickering highlights in his glass: "Fifty, fifty-five, I'd say. Sixty tops. Then things sort of stalled for the next five or so, and after that the *volume* of space held steady, but your galaxies and stars and such actually began to *shrink*, at an ever-increasing clip, and they're shrinking still."

In the Amused Nondirective mode, one of us responded, "Mm-*hm*."

Down-glancing my way, "The effect," Fred said, "is that your astronomers still get pretty much the same measurements — your Red Shift and such? — but they haven't yet appreciated that it's for the opposite reason: because everything's *contracting*, themselves included; everything but the overall universe itself. Not condensing, mind; *shrinking*."

We didn't laugh, as we would've just between ourselves. *The rich man's joke is always funny*, goes the proverb, and the rich host's anecdote is always respectfully attended. By an order of magnitude, the Mackalls were the wealthiest people we knew: light-years out of our class, but hospitable to us academic peasants. They were Old Money (Marsha's, mainly, we understood), with the Old Money liberal's sense of noblesse oblige. Fred had once upon a time been briefly our ambassador to someplace — a Kennedy appointee, I believe, or maybe Lyndon Johnson's. Latterly, he and Marsha had taken a benevolent interest in our little college, not far from their Camelot Farm: stables, kennels, Black Angus cattle, pool and tennis court, gorgeous cruising sailboat in their private cove, the requisite eighteenth-century manor house tastefully restored, overlooking the bay, and more acreage by half than our entire campus.

Cockamamie, I could almost hear Bert saying to herself. But apart from her professional interest in the Mackalls, which I'll get to presently, she took what she called an anthropological interest in them — ambassadors indeed, to the likes of us, from another world — and with Fred especially she had established a kind of teasing / challenging conversational relation that she imagined he enjoyed. I myself couldn't tell sometimes whether the fellow was being serious or ironic; but then, I had that trouble occasionally with Bertie, too, a full fifteen years into our marriage. In any case, although they made a diplomatic show of interest (perhaps often genuine) in their guests, both Mackalls had the philanthropist's expectation of being paid deferential attention.

My turn. "So your theory's different from the Big Crunch, right? The idea that after the universe has expanded to a certain point, it'll all collapse back to Square One?" No polymath even compared to Bert, I was an academic cobbler who stuck to his trade (remedial English and freshman composition), but I did try to stay reasonably abreast of things.

"Oh, definitely different," Fred said. He perched his brandy glass beside him on the wall-top and tapped his half-splayed fingertips together ... *as if in impatient prayer*, I guess I'd say. "In the Big Shrink, everything stays put but gets smaller and smaller, and so your space between things appears to increase. *Does* increase, actually."

"Now hold on just a cottonpicking minute," my Roberta teasingly challenged, "..."

"There's no holding on," Fred said. Smoothly. "And no stopping it or even slowing it down. In fact, the shrink-rate increases with proximity to the observer — just the reverse of your Big Bang? — but since the measurements come out about the same, it's not generally noticed." He smiled upon his fingertip-tapping hands, his say said.

Neither of us knew quite how to reply to that; *I* didn't, anyhow, and

Bert seemed to do a five-count before she cleared her throat *mock-os-tentatiously* and asked, "So where d'you get your fifty billion years, Fred, when your cosmologists all say eight to twelve billion?"

She was teasing him with those *yours*, I was pretty sure. Bertie'd do that: feed your little idiosyncrasies back at you, and not everybody took to it kindly. Now instead of tapping his fingertips five on five, Fred Mackall kept them touching while he expanded and contracted the fingers themselves — not *splayed and unsplayed* them, but *pulsed* them, I guess I'd say; pulsed them leisurely — leisurelily?

I give up.

No I don't. Fred Mackall pulsed his spread-fingered, fingertip-touching hands leisurely like . . . some sort of sea creature, say, and said, "I didn't say billion." *Smiling, though not necessarily with amusement.*

There.

"Did I say billion?"

Without at all meaning to, I presume, the Mackalls had gotten Bert and me in trouble once before in one of these post-party-nightcap situations. Just a year or so prior to the scene above, it was: first time they and we had met socially. Bertie had recently landed her new position in the college's Development office, where part of her job-description was to "coordinate" the friendly interest of potential benefactors like the Mackalls. In her opinion and her boss's, she turned out to be a natural at it; in mine, too, although I was less convinced than Bert that her jokey-challenging manner was universally appreciated. In any case, now that our kids weren't babies anymore and we had to start thinking Tuitions down the road, I was pleased that she had this new job to throw herself into with her usual industry. The Mackalls, we agreed, were doing at least as much of the "coordinating" as Bert's office was; the April buffet-dinner at Camelot Farm that year was their idea — for our young new president and his wife along with several trustees of the college and their spouses (Development was hoping that Fred would agree to join the Board); also Roberta's boss, Bill Hartman, and his missus, who happened to be a friend and part-time colleague of mine; and — bottom of the totem pole — Bert and me: Assistant to the Director of Development ("Not *Assistant Director* yet," Bert liked to tease her boss when she gave her full title) and the lowercase director of the college's freshman English program, although I suspect that

I was there less as Faculty Input than as my wife's Significant Other. The evening went easily enough: We were a small college in a small town with a clutch of well-to-do retirees from neighboring cities and a few super-gentry like the Mackalls; the prevailing local tone was re-laxed-democratic. Toward the close of festivities, as most of the guests were making to leave, Marsha Mackall said, "Anybody for another brandy and decaf out under the stars?," and although President and Ms. Harris begged off along with the trustees, Roberta said right away, "Count us in." Bill Hartman — whether pleased at his protégée's quick uptake or concerned to monitor the conversation — glanced at his wife and said, "Sounds good," and so we were six: same venue as this later one, but a fresher, brighter night.

Don't ask me how our conversation turned to Inherent Psycholog-ical Differences Between Women and Men, a minefield at any time of day but surely even more so at the end of a well-wined evening. Marsha Mackall — as tanned in April as the rest of us might be by August — was the one pursuing it, apropos of whatever. The form it soon took was her disagreeing with Becky Hartman and my Roberta (good liberal feminists both) that there were no "hard-wired" psy-chological differences between the sexes; that all such "stereotypical gender-based tendencies" as male aggressiveness versus female con-ciliatoriness, male logical-analytical thinking versus female intuition and feeling, the male hankering for multiple sex-partners versus the female inclination to exclusive commitment — that all of these were the effect of cultural conditioning (and therefore malleable, in their optimistic opinion) rather than programmed by evolution into our respective chromosomes and therefore more resistant to amelioration, if amelioration is what one believed was called for.

"Some of them are like that, maybe," elegant Marsha had allowed — meaning that some of the abovementioned "tendencies" were perhaps a matter more of Nurture than of Nature. "But when it comes to polyg-amy versus monogamy, or promiscuity versus fidelity — "

"Objection," put in Fred Mackall, raising a forefinger.

"Sustained," Bill Hartman ruled, *mock-judicially*: "Counsel is using judgmental language."

"Counsel stands corrected," Marsha conceded. "I don't mean it judgmentally — yet. And we're talking happy marriages here, okay? Happy, faithful, monogamous marriages like all of ours, right?"

"Hear hear," Bill Hartman said at once.

"All of *mine* have been like that," Fred Mackall teased, and lifted his glass as if in toast.

I followed suit.

"All I'm saying," Marsha Mackall said, "is that sexual fidelity comes less naturally to you poor fellows than it does to us, and that while some of that might be a matter of cultural reinforcement and such, what's being reinforced is a plain old biological difference between men and women. Okay?"

"*Vive la différence*," Fred said — not very appositely, in my judgment.

"Men are just naturally designed to broadcast their seed to the four winds," Marsha concluded. "But pregnancy and maternity make women more vulnerable, so we tend to be choosier and then more faithful, quote unquote — and we evolved this way for zillions of years before things like marriage and romantic love and conjugal fidelity were ever invented."

"Before they were *valorized*," handsome Becky Hartman said, "is how the jargon goes now," and Marsha Mackall nodded: "Valorized."

"Amen," Fred said.

I hated conversations like this, whether sportive or serious. In my view, which I wasn't interested enough to offer, women and men are at least as importantly different from other members of their own sex as they are from each other categorically; I myself felt more of a kind in more different ways with Roberta than with either Bill Hartman or Fred Mackall, for example — and, truth to tell, maybe more of a piece *temperamentally* in some respects with Becky Hartman (we had successfully team-taught a course or two in past semesters) than with my wife, even. What's more, it didn't seem nearly so obvious to me as it evidently did to them that a culturally acquired trait is *ipso facto* more manageable than a genetically transmitted one, where the two can even be distinguished. *Et cetera*. But intelligent people do seem drawn to such subjects — women, in my experience, more than men. This much I made the mistake of volunteering, by way of a Bertie-like teasing challenge to the three ladies — and then, of course, I was in for it. Becky Hartman now took the (female conciliatory) tack of agreeing with our hostess that, whatever the cause, men were indeed categorically more inclined than women to sexual infidelity — "seriality, polygamy, promiscuity, call it what you will — though mind you," patting her husband's knee, "I'm not saying they *pursue* the inclination, necessarily—"

"Heaven forfend," Bill Hartman said, *mock-solemnly.*

"—only that the inclination is definitely there, more often and more strongly than it is with women."

"Now we're talking," Marsha Mackall said, satisfied.

"I deny it," firmly declared my Roberta. "I don't believe Sam's any more sexually interested in other women than I am in other men."

"Uh-oh," Fred Mackall warned, or anyhow uttered in some vague sort of warning spirit.

"We're not saying that he goes around panting after the coeds," Marsha made clear.

"Much less that he *drops his pantings,* huh?" Fred said, and ducked his handsome head. Bill Hartman politely groaned; Bertie hissed. "Sorry there," Fred said.

"Right," said Becky Hartman, agreeing with Marsha. Directly to her, then—I mean to Becky, as I had only just met the Mackalls—I said, "What *do* you mean, then, Beck?," and, in a way that I remembered with pleasure from our team-taught classes, she pursed her lips and narrowed her bright brown eyes in a show of pensiveness before replying, in this instance with a hypothetical scenario: "Suppose there were absolutely no guilt or other negative consequences attached to adultery. No element of betrayal, no hurt feelings—let's even drop the word *adultery,* since it has those associations."

"Right." Marsha Mackall took over: "Suppose society were such that it was considered perfectly okay for a married man to go to bed with another woman any time they both felt like it."

"Neither admirable nor blameworthy," Becky Hartman specified, in my direction; "just perfectly okay with all parties, absolutely without repercussions, any time they felt like doing it."

"Then would you?" Marsha asked me—with a smile, but not jokingly. "Or not?"

Lifting his right hand as if on oath, "I plead the Fifth Amendment on that one," Fred Mackall said at once, although it wasn't him they were asking, yet.

"Like*wise,*" Bill Hartman agreed, with a locker-room sort of chuckle. But it was me the two women happened to be pressing, and I had the habit, even in social situations, of taking seriously-put questions seriously and replying as honestly as I could. Occupational hazard, maybe, of teaching college freshmen in the liberal arts.

So, "Blessed as I am in my marriage and happy as a clam with monogamous fidelity, I guess I might," I acknowledged, "in some sort of *experimental spirit*, I imagine, if there were no such fallout as guilt or social disapproval or hurt feelings or anything of that sort, so that it wouldn't even be thought of as 'adultery' or 'infidelity.'" I used my fingers for quotation marks. "Which is unimaginable, of course, so forget it."

"But if things *were* that way," Marsha Mackall triumphantly bore in, "then you would. Right?"

I reconsidered. Shrugged. "I guess I have to admit I might."

Bert said to me then, "I'm astonished," and although her tone was amusedly *mock*-astonished, I saw her face drain. "I am totally astonished."

"Uh-oh," Bill Hartman said, quite as Fred Mackall had earlier.

"No, no," my wife made clear to all: "No blame or anger or anything like that —"

"*No hurt feelings*," Fred teased, "*no guilt, no repercussions*."

"I just couldn't be more surprised if you'd said you're bisexual," Bert said to me, "or had a thing for sheep."

"Sheep," Fred said, "baah," and most of us duly chuckled.

"It's an impossible hypothetical scenario," I protested to Bert, and without blaming Marsha Mackall directly (we had just met the couple, after all, and they were our hosts, and Development was courting them), I declared to all hands, "I feel like I've been suckered!"

"My friend," Fred Mackall said, "you *have* been suckered."

"No, I swear," Bert tried to make clear: "I'm not upset. I'm just totally, totally surprised."

Becky Hartman did her lips-and-eyes thing but said nothing. Notching up his characteristic joviality, "Time to pack it in, I think," her husband declared. Perfect-hostess Marsha made a few let's-change-the-subject pleasantries, perhaps with Roberta in particular, and we did then presently bid our several good nights.

In the car, I apologized. "No need to," Bert insisted, and as we drove homeward down the dark country roads under the brilliant stars, she reaffirmed that she didn't *blame* me in any way; that she felt as did I that all this essentially-male / essentially-female business was so much baloney — that had been precisely her and Becky Hartman's *point*, re-member? — but that for all those years she had thought our connection to be something really really special . . .

"It *is* special!" I rebegan, more calmly: "That was a dumbass hypo-thetical scenario, hon, and I made the dumb-ass mistake of taking it seriously instead of doing a *faux-galant* cop-out like Fred Mackall and Bill Hartman."

"Maybe they weren't being fake-gallant," Bertie said from her side of the car. Her voice was distant; I could tell that her head was turned away. "Maybe what they said was *true*-gallant, but expressed ironically under the social circumstances."

My face tingled: She had me there, as not infrequently she did. "So," I said — mock-bitterly but also true-bitterly, *et cetera*, and in fact with some dismay: "The honeymoon is over."

"No, no, no," my wife insisted. "I was just surprised, is all."

"And disappointed." I felt miserable: annoyed at Marsha Mackall, at Becky and Bert, at myself. Bum-rapped. But mainly miserable.

"Yes, well."

Sixteen months later — smiling, though not necessarily with amuse-ment, and pulsing his spread-fingered, fingertips-touching hands leisurely like some sort of sea creature — Fred Mackall said, "I didn't say fifty *billion*. Everything's shrinking, see, but since it's us who're shrinking fastest of all, other things seem larger and farther away." He picked up his empty glass, set it down again. "That's why Marsh and I don't get to Europe much anymore, you know? We used to pop over to London and Paris as if they were Washington and Philadelphia, but even though the planes fly faster and faster, everything's too far away these days. And this *house* . . ." He turned his perfectly grayed head toward where the caterers were finishing up. "We rattle around in it now, where before we were forever adding on and buying up acreage left and right. There're parts of this property that I don't set foot on anymore from one season to the next."

"I get it," Bertie said, *cheerily*, as if a joke had been on us. "So even though the farm and the house are shrinking too . . ." She let him take it from there.

"They're all farther and farther apart from each other, not to men-tion from town. D'you know how long it's been since I trekked down to our dock to check the boat? And look how far away the house is now, compared to when we-all came out for a nightcap!"

"You know what, Fred Mackall?" Bertie said, *mock-confidentially.* "You're right. Sam and I will never get home."

"Oh, well, now," Fred said, chuckling my way as if across a great divide: "You two are still in the Expanding mode, I'd guess, or at most in the capital-P Pause . . ."

One patio torch guttered out; several others were burning their last. Fred Mackall spoke on — about "your stars and such" again, I believe, although I could scarcely hear his words now, and about how his Big Shrink theory applied to time as well as to space, so that what astronomers took to be billions of years was actually no more than a cosmic eyeblink. "My" Bertie's tone was still the cheery straight-man's, mildly teasing / challenging to draw him out, but essentially in respectful accord.

I say "tone" because *her* words, too, were barely audible to me now across the expanse of pool deck, theoretically smaller than it had been when Fred Mackall began his spiel, but in effect so vast now that I didn't even try to call across it to my wife. I'd have needed hand signals, so it seemed to me: semaphores such as beach-lifeguards use to communicate from perch to perch. We still had what you'd call a good marriage, Bert and I: We were still each other's closest friend and confidant, still unanimous with the children, or almost so. But it wasn't what it had been. We made love less often, for example; less passionately, too, lately, by and large. Par for the course, some might say, as time shrinks and the years zip by; but our connection truly *had* been special, just as Bert maintained. The queen-size bed on which she and I had slept and such for fifteen satisfying years had come to seem king-size; although per Fred Mackall's theory it was doubtless down to a double by now and on its way toward single, its occupants were still further reduced, and thus farther apart.

I happened to recall from some freshman textbook a journal entry of Franz Kafka's, I believe it was, about his grandfather: how the old fellow came to marvel that anyone had the temerity to set out even for the neighboring village and expect ever to arrive there, not to mention returning. I remembered how my own mother, in her last age, found going upstairs in her own house too formidable an undertaking, like a polar expedition. Once upon a time I might have contributed those anecdotes to this nightcap conversation: a bit of Faculty Input. By now, however, I couldn't even hear Fred Mackall's and Roberta's voices, much less have called across to them. Even if I could have — by bullhorn, cell phone, whatever — I doubt I'd have found the right words: They, too, were retreating from me, would soon be out of my diminishing reach altogether, as would even my self itself.

The star-jammed sky was terrifying: moment by moment emptier-seeming as all its contents reciprocally shrank. We would never imaginably pull ourselves out of the Mackalls' Adirondack chairs, Bert and I, and make our way off their pool deck, enormous now as an Asian steppe; far less off their interminable estate, through the light-years-long drive home, the ever-widening, in effect now all but infinite, space between us.

SEVENTH NIGHT

"* * * * * *,"

is how Graybard had hoped his absent muse-friend might somehow respond at his Sixth Night tale's tail end — she having declined to give him pause, so to speak, by manifesting herself in mid-narration as he'd imagined she just might. In his experienced though not impartial judgment, *The Big Shrink* not only observed her several No-Nos but was moreover an okay story. When it shrank to its dénouement, however, he found himself as Wysless as at its opening words — and no longer in the woman's oddly lightless precinct, but back willy-nilly in day-bright Reality.

Was "the party over, really," then, as those opening words had declared? For here it was Monday morning already, 9/17/01: another fine mild still one where one writes this, while a world away the newly forged alliance of just-barely-elected U.S. President and unelected Pakistani CEO issues a joint ultimatum to Afghanistan's Islamic-fundamentalist Taliban rulers: Give us Osama bin Laden, dead or alive, or you and your already-blasted country ain't seen nothin' yet. Wall Street open again for stock-trading after four-day closure: Would the sky fall? Was the party over, really?

Not quite, one knows now but did not then. By day's end the Dow Jones Industrials would lose 7 percent of their value — far less than feared — and would thereafter regain, relose, and re-regain, hanging just above or below 10,000 for several more months, during which the Taliban would be forcibly deposed and largely destroyed along with the luckless nation it had so sternly governed, but Osama & Co. would slip away to regroup elsewhere and plan their next atrocity against the infidel West. Hundreds of the innocent and guilty, by whatever standard, would perish in Afghanistan, Israel, Palestine; reactionary political parties would gain strength in Europe, along with anti-immigrant, anti-American, and anti-Israeli opinion.

Shall we go on?

Not in this grim vein, it was decided in the Scriptorium by 9:11 that morning. On with this half-told Hendecameron, then, so altogether irrelevant to the above? Let's just see. *Hie ye hence six minutes hence, Graybard ambassador,* and find out what's what, party's-overwise: where we-all stand in the Missing Asterisks Department.

Hie he did at the appointed time, with appropriately mixed feelings and certain advice from his dispatcher: hied himself by the routine route Imaginariumward; found that sanctum still as uncharacteristically pitch-dark as when he'd left it, or it him, involuntarily, at last night's story's close, its only light that infernally blinking bedside clock, stuck still at *9:11 9:16 9:11 9:16,* as if time had stopped when her lights went out. No less surprisingly, at that instant he felt himself as jay-bird-naked again as after his solitary yesternight divestment. What was going on? Or, rather, *not* going on?

Then . . .

"* * * * * *!" his suddenly-there collaborator greeted him in effect and without words: room-lights up, the nimble nymph naked as himself, adrip from her dip as usual, and upon him with such wordless fervor that sans elixir or any other potion than their pure (if only because Metaphoric) passion, they made good their six-asterisk deficit and lay happily spent through the after-oscillations of her waterbed, beside which the clock now duly flashed *9:11 9:17 et cetera.*

GB: Well, now, ma'am: Wow.

W: Likewise, sir: Good show.

And good *no*-show, he could not resist replying; for yesternight's presence of her absence, or whatever, while not a little troubling and yet to be explained, had had its own perversely inspiring effect. As maybe she had observed?

"Maybe. Anyhow, your mixing your dry clothes with my wetties was a turn-on. Reminded me of us?"

Gotcha. Touching her nearer bare shoulder: Missed you, Wys. Missed seeing; missed getting what one saw, et cet.

"Yes, well." She sighed and stretched. Sat up. "I see you got it, then. The point?" But enough of that, her now-business-like manner seemed to say: He'll please excuse her while she fetches the *vin du soir*; and then it's on with Seventh Night, and *L'Shanah Tovah*.

Hey, you're right: Tonight's Rosh Hashanah! Happy Fifty-seven Sixty-whatever!

"Two." They clinked the glasses she returned with — an upstate New York Manischewitz muscatel, oversweet but appropriate to the holiday, one supposed, and toasted their Hendecameron's Sabbath, so to speak, coming on the heels first of the Jewish and then of the Christian, and coincident with the turn of the Hebrew calendar. It was to mark that Sabbath's eve, she now declared, and the midpoint of their project, that she had taken her Sixth Night sabbatical; also to herald or anyhow propose certain changes in their M.O.

Again? It's been nothing *but* changes, Wys: never the same twice!

They were sitting now cheek to cheek, as it were, on her bed-edge, sun down and lights up as usual. No complaint, understand, he added, and sipped the too-sweet stuff. Keeps a guy on his toes, we guess. So what's new?

Lips pursed at her glass-rim, "A rebeginning of sorts?" she supposed. "No stunts, costumes, or gimmicks, at least for the next few nights?"

Shucks: I'd come to look forward to those. Then, remembering his dispatcher's advice, But whatever you say, of course. I really wondered last night whether our party was over . . .

"I *wanted* you to wonder. But it's just the funny hats and pussy-paint and such that we'll do without for a while. As for the rest, our Hendecameron is hereby granted a night-by-night extension, so drink up; we'll work our way back to drier stuff in the nights ahead."

The nights ahead,
he echoed, with happy anticipation qualified only by that "night-by-night" proviso, and did as bidden. Whither wilt thou, Muse o' mine, lead on.

She duly did: led him out onto the deck and over to the ladder, and informed him that they would now initiate the second semester of their joint project with a joint immersion, after which he might towel himself dry or not as he saw fit, but she would remain tidewatered, and on with their stories. "All set?"

He peered overside. Mighty black down there.

"The better to see the light." Pertly she swung herself half around, flashed himward those V.S.O.P. eyes of hers, and started down-ladder. "Follow me?"

My pleasure. And pleasure it was, to be totally immersed in that saltyfresh warm element with naked ditto Inspiration. Had he imagined her creeklet or marsh-pond shallow? It was over his head! She wrapped bare arms and legs around him, pressed mouth to his and drew him under, then back up for air, then under and up and under and up until, breathless both, they clung to the ladder and each other. There the tide-pond itself became their waterbed, whereupon and wherein they achieved Metaphorically what on the literal level (as Reader her / himself may have learned from disappointing experience) does not come naturally to *Homo sapiens*: seven-asterisk submarine sex.

$$* \quad * \quad * \quad * \quad * \quad * \quad *$$

After which, back on deck,

— she still wet but he dried off now, per each's pleasure — "You understand, I trust," his pleased muse trusted, "that these asterisks aren't *ratings*, like stars or forks in the *Guide Michelin*."

So you say. But there you sit, Wys (at ease and adrip in her deck chair, her fine wet thighs insouciantly open to the light air off the marsh), and wow.

Ignoring his admiration, "They don't mean that each new story or Metaphorical Make-Out is better than the one before . . ."

So you say.

"So I say: They're just Due Approval plus Incremental Tabulation." Come again?

"Maybe tomorrow." She gave him a look. "No need for Seventh Night to be better than Sixth, is what I mean, or Eighth than Seventh, either storywise or otherwise. Once the bar's in place, which it's been since Night One, we don't raise it night by night."

Except by Incremental Ultimation.

"Yes, well." Sidelong pickerel smile: "Those."

Four so far, by my count: No more Oldies! No more Non-Ficties! No more Stuck Storytellers! . . . What was the last one?

"No more Sudden Recollections of Repressed-Memory Adulteries in Long-Past Incarnations."

Ah, so: I'd forgotten.

"You've also forgotten Number Five of a few minutes ago: No Stunts, Costumes, or Gimmicks. To which five she now adds a sixth, notwithstanding her approval of that *Big Shrink* story: No more riffs on the Innocent Marital Guilt Theme, s.v.p., even the Totally Innocent kind. Enough already."

Enough IMG, your grateful servicer wonders aloud, or enough ultimata?

As she knew he knew, she let him know, it was the former that she was up to here with. As for the latter, there might be yet one more down the line, but not for some nights yet — after which, no more No-Nos. "Meanwhile, extension granted. On with the stories?"

Maybe.

Genuinely surprised: "*Maybe?* What's this maybe? To the Muse of Inspiration he says maybe?"

Maybe. No more this, that, and the other, per your serial proscriptions. But I can't promise no more Autumnality . . .

Dismissive flick of hand. "Oh, *that*. No problem, Geebsie, at least for a while." That smile. Those eyes. "As I may have mentioned, I have a thing about older guys? Don't ask."

He duly didn't, although (as Reader may now notice) the plurality of her noun did not escape his notice. But

Speaking of Extension,
he contented himself with responding, that just happens to be tonight's tale's title:

Extension

Two quick decades later, in the assisted-living facility, I hear him telling the story this way, perhaps to himself:

"The little project seemed on the face of it desirable, feasible, even *natural*. We would enlarge and re-equip my home office (Myrna found hers adequate as it was), together with our bedroom and the bath between. Contiguous to that main bedroom and the long screened porch we would add a solarium / spa / exercise room to help us stay fit in our approaching retirement: all this in an integrated, architecturally pleasing extension to our modest rural hideaway overlooking the bay and, by extension, the Atlantic and thence all other oceans. In one's elder years, Myrna liked to joke, it's important to remain in touch with the world.

"Granted, this proposed extension was more ambitious than a number of our earlier, trial-run improvements to what we had bought, some dozen years before, as a weekend retreat and vacation house. An unremarkable but adequate and nicely situated single-story cottage, it was replete with picture windows, fake shutters, brick-veneer siding, stock asphalt roof-shingles, bare-bones landscaping. The place was meant to supplement our equally modest, okay-for-its-purposes house in the city across the bay, convenient to our main offices. Over the years of our part-time residency we had white-painted the bricks, replaced the Thermopane picture windows with divided-pane bays, redecked the pier, added a freshwater pool to complement the brackish bay, relandscaped the lot, remodeled the kitchen and the guest accommodations, upgraded the heating, air-conditioning, and water systems, installed skylights, overhead paddle-fans, and privacy fencing, and replaced the roof, as well as making less extensive improvements to our town house — older, but better built and less in need of upgrading.

"Our His-and-Her counseling careers (investment and marriage, respectively) had gone well, as had our lives in general; we were comfortably-off, upper-middle-class Americans. I myself happened to be of just the right age to have missed all the wars of our horrific century — not here for the First World War, too young for the Second, student-deferred from Korea, too old for Vietnam — and to have prospered in the post-WWII economy; nothing worse had thus far befallen the pair of us than the dissolution of our respective first marriages (pains more than assuaged by our successful second, with its live-in counselor), the loss of aged parents, the occasional illness, injury, or child-rearing crisis, and other such less-than-mortal shocks. If this house-extension project was more considerable than its forerunners, it was less so than numerous other of our major life-moves: the engenderment of children, the several changes of job- and living-venues that are par for the American professional course, the divorces and remarriage aforementioned, the purchase and furnishing of those two houses and their predecessors.

"Not only did our economic position and life-situation make the proposed extension appear unremarkable (up and down the bayshore one saw much more ambitious projects in progress); it was itself just another extension both of our personal joint history and of our American generation's — indeed, of our American Century's. Over the hundred-odd years since our respective grandparents had immigrated, each crop of their descendants (until our own Baby-Boom children, anyhow) had on average grown taller, more prosperous, and longer-lived than its forebears. Like most of our middle-class compatriots, we ourselves had grown not just bodily from infancy through childhood to maturity but likewise (and thus far lifelong) in our physical, mental, and other capacities — our skills and responsibilities, our professional status, authority, and earning power — and, along with those (as the stock market levitated and the American divorce rate climbed with it), in the number, size, and quality of our material possessions and accommodations. From spartan student lodgings, Myrna and I had 'moved up,' separately and together, through entry-level urban apartments and secondhand automobiles to our first new cars and minimal home-ownerships; from one child to two, one car to two (one marriage to two, I'm tempted to add), one house to two plus a small boat, *two* small boats, two less-small boats plus more-expensive cars and houses plus more frequent and less frugal vacation trips plus that swimming pool and paid-off mortgages and country-club memberships and ever-growing equity accounts and 'starter' trust funds for the grandchildren and those several initiatory remodelings and property improvements aforementioned — all leading almost logically, one might say, to this latest, really not extraordinary extension-in-the-works.

"Did we *need* it? Well: Does one 'need' a larger cabin-cruiser, a better-made automobile, a more extensive (and expensive) vacation? We *wanted* it; we *could use* it; we had, in our opinion, *earned* it. It would be yet another 'improvement,' another ... *extension*, in a word, of our life-estate as well as of our (number two) house — an extension the more desirable for its being, not impossibly, our last such. We were, as afore-remarked, approaching the traditional American retirement age, and although we enjoyed our professions and had by no means decided to quit them entirely, it had in fact been some years already since we'd last *increased* our separate counseling responsibilities. Indeed, we had not only leveled off on that particular front but cut back a bit (in my case especially, as I was the elder of us and less in need of an outside office): fewer and less extended business trips, shorter working hours, longer and more frequent vacations, fewer days per week and month and year in the city place, and more in the country. Did we need the extension? With our children out of the nest and raising nestlings of their own in distant cities, we didn't really 'need' the residential square-footage that we occupied already, enough to house half a dozen ghetto or Third World families. But we were neither of those, and particularly given this recent gradual shift of our domestic gravity-center from city to country, the proposed extension seemed, as aforedeclared, both desirable and feasible. It was not, after all, another or newer or bigger-and-better *house*, as might have been the case ten years before. It was simply ... an extension.

"And so we made preliminary measurements and sketches; with some misgivings, we re-engaged the architect who had done our trial-run projects; we studied and annotated and conferred upon and revised her more extensive drawings and specifications. Over the following year-and-then-some, as we went about our businesses and pleasures, we bethought ourselves and more than once revised the design, even the whole project. I say 'with some misgivings' because those earlier remodelings had by no means been hassle-free. When were such things ever? There were the usual (perhaps rather more than the usual) unforeseen problems, cost overruns, delays, compromises. With the results we were, on the whole, quite pleased, though perhaps mainly relieved to have the several little ordeals behind us and still unhappy with certain features of the jobs — those if-we-were-doing-it-again things that we continued to believe a better architect would have anticipated, or a more knowledgeable builder warned us of. And so rather than bolstering our confidence in those professionals and in ourselves, the trial runs had proved ambivalent trials indeed. To shift designers now, however, would have been to turn this more considerable project into another trial run, when as far as we could see (and had by now come rather to hope), nothing in the 'extension' way lay beyond it. *Life is not a dress rehearsal,* declares the bumper sticker; *Better the devil you know, than the devil you don't,* advises the proverb. All the same, we felt less prepared for the Main Event than we had expected to feel when its time came. Thus our misgivings.

"But the calendar was running. As seasons passed, we found ourselves more and more merely maintaining the town house while chafing at the limitations of what, after all, we had never intended as our primary residence. And so we came to put ever more time, energy, and money into planning that capital-E Extension, as we now thought of it. On corkboards in our home offices we pinned volumetric drawings of the remodeled country-seat-cum-extension, to encourage and inspire us in odd moments. Perhaps because those drawings were thus always before us, we further altered several major features of the design, as well as countless details. Every one of those alterations, needless to say, added slightly or substantially to the architect's fees, already so much higher than we had anticipated that we half-seriously wondered whether her 'trial-run' bills had been bait to hook us with. Like lawyers and some other sorts of counselors (myself and Myrna not excluded), hourly-rate designers thrive on complications and changes of plan; while we hemmed and hawed and revised and unrevised, her meter profitably ran. We had expected to have our extension built, decorated, furnished, landscaped, and ready for occupancy by retirement-time, but when at last we declared the blueprints final (no doubt partly from fatigue, although every one of our many modifications and nearly every one of hers had been an improvement) and put the project out for bids, the several contractors' estimates came in so startlingly above even our architect's guesstimations that — frustrated, chagrined, and weary of the whole business — we put the project on hold for a year in order to recollect ourselves, recounsel, reconsider. We shifted furniture to make more efficient use of our present space, ran in extra fax and computer-modem lines, did some much-needed temporary landscaping of the area that the Extension had been meant to cover, and promised ourselves not to think further about the thing for a full twelve months. Although the drawings remained in place on our corkboards, other matters distracted us: passing illnesses, pleasure travel upon those interconnected oceans and the continents they separate, problems large and small in the extended family, further drawdown of our professional activities, financial planning for our retirement — in all, a welcome return to normalcy.

"The turning point, I see now, was not our yearlong moratorium, but our discovery — when in an eyeblink that year passed and we duly fetched out for reinspection the sheaf of blueprints and specifications labeled EXTENSION — that we had come to feel we didn't really 'need' (you understand my meaning) quite so *much* extra space — although if we could have had it simply by snapping our fingers and paying the bills, we would have done so unhesitatingly. Why not scale the project down a bit, we asked ourselves — perhaps rather a lot? Halve the size of A, for example, while going forward with B as originally planned but dropping C entirely? The idea seemed feasible enough to warrant our reopening, no more eagerly than before, the connection with our architect; she cheerfully redrafted our scaled-down plan (to which we ourselves had devoted days, in hope of scaling down her fees as well) and billed us therefor. Ironically, however, we found our enthusiasm comparably reduced. Now that the country place had become in effect our main residence, the prospect of camping in half of it for several months while the other half was being noisily and messily extended seemed more disagreeable than ever, especially given a scaled-down payoff at the end. Moreover, in the period of our moratorium we had installed a hot tub on the barbecue patio beside the porch, a somewhat crowded but on the whole acceptable substitute for the room deleted from our scaled-down plan. And that 'temporary' landscaping had set-tled in and begun to grow handsomely; and we had begun seriously to consider selling the little city house when our professional phase-out was complete — all the more reason to enlarge the country place, we supposed, yet all the more daunting a prospect to do so, as the town house itself by this time needed substantial sprucing up if it was going to sell in what had lately become a buyers' market.

"And so we dallied, counseled our respective (and reduced) cli-enteles, did other things — and noticed, for the first time, really, that doing them took longer than it had used to. Autumn upon us before summer's chores were done; how had we ever managed them when both of us were working full-time, not to mention when we were raising children too? A day came when — in the process of shifting further items from our 'main house,' now for sale, to our 'weekend house,' now unequivocally our headquarters — we took down from our corkboards those aging volumetric sketches (which anyhow depicted the original, larger Extension, not its scaled-down later versions) and filed them away with the so-costly blueprints, spec sheets, light-fixture catalogues, builders' proposals, and related correspondence. We told each other that when the convulsions of selling the town house and reordering our life were behind us, we might very well come back to the project. To ourselves, however, we acknowledged (at least one of us did) that we almost surely would *not* come back to it; that our time for ambitious extensions had passed.

"Indeed (we came to see but not necessarily to say), the contrary had quietly become the case: For us, the theme of the season and no doubt of all seasons to come was not Extension, but Contraction. Just as we no longer needed two houses, so we no longer really needed two cars, far less a virtual flotilla of assorted watercraft. Why we continued to maintain separate home offices, even, except as personal retreats, had become a reasonable question, now that neither of us was really 'work-ing.' One house (unextended), one car, one boat (small) would surely do: With our children scattered to the four winds and their parents grayhaired, who water-skied any longer behind our aging outboard runabout? When had we or any guest last used our much-weathered old canoe? Soon enough we would scarcely 'need' even our dear old flagship, so laborious for us to maintain and so expensive to hire the maintenance of; soon enough we would doubtless come to wish that our single, too-large house were a carefree condominium somewhere, so that we'd have more time to spend with our far-flung offspring and to explore further the world's interconnections while we were still able — except that traveling had lately become as much a chore as an adventure, and our relations with those offspring, while certainly affectionate, were inevitably attenuated by distance and by their own divorces / remarriages. Even visiting nearer-by family and friends, not to mention entertaining them at home, we found yearly more burdensome.

"They say that the universe itself is extending, extending; seems to me the case could be made that for some time now it's been holding still at best, while we ourselves have begun to shrink. Time was when the pair of us each worked a job and a half, raised kids and pets and vegetables and flowers, cooked and sewed and housecleaned, maintained scrupulously our properties and sundry possessions, even did much of our own carpentry and house-painting and electrical repairs — and somehow still had time and energy left over for hobbies, sports, community activities, hospitality, good works. Lately it's enough to keep ourselves respectably dressed, groomed, fed . . .

"Who would have imagined that so trifling a matter as taking down a drawing from a corkboard could discover the Abyss? That in the mere canceling of a proposed house-extension one would feel brushed by the Dark Angel's wingfeathertips? Yet here we sit at our lorn bay window, Myrna and I, like ticketed passengers in an airport lounge, looking dully about us at the scene we're about to leave; waiting for the boarding call, for the ultimate contraction."

EIGHTH NIGHT

Before she could demand it
in the form of yet a seventh ultimatum or narrative constraint on his remaining stories, *No more Recycled Shrinkage*, Graybard promised his unpredictable muse when the pair reconvened *chez* Wysiwyg at 9:18 (PM, by *her* clock) the next day.

"Good."

— except insofar as the theme of Autumnality may touch upon assorted losses, as is not unlikely.

Assent nodded: Autumnality (she reminded him once again) she had no quarrel with; but the preceding night's Extension-piece had felt to her more like early winter. "*Brrr!* Enough Shrinkage already! Enough Contraction!"

Agreed — except insofar as *et cetera*.

"So, then: To our Hendecameron's eighth eleventh?"

Also to us, most valued and comely comrade.

His compliment appeared to please and ease her. They clinked glasses and sipped a presumably elixired white Rioja: a welcome return to crisp and dry libation after Seventh Night's too-sweet muscatel. Time was, Reader may recall, when after their inspirational asterisks and Graybard's consequent storytelling, Muse and Talester might doze off, separately or together, in her illuminated space: See, e.g., Night One, as reviewed on Night Two. Every "night" since, however, end of story has meant end of get-together, its teller transported back to headquarters in the latter forenoon of that same day, to stand by until dispatched again on the morrow.* Not confusing, really, once one got the hang of it, and while one might expect such time-shifts to do odd things to our chap's circadian rhythms — some sort of narrative jet-lag?— he seems to have accommodated to "waking up" in the late morning of a day whose "evening" he has enjoyed already.

Just thought we'd get that straight.

So what's our lass wearing, if anything, on this eighth of their tête-à-têtes, and what's she up to on this one-week anniversary of catastrophic Tuesday, 9/11/01? Nothing kinky on either count, just as she'd given notice the night before (indeed, on the former count, nothing whatever). In the charnel house of Ground Zero, subterranean fires still burned; acrid smoke and dust still fouled the lower Manhattan air. As observing Jews marked the turn of the Hebrew year (5,762 years since the world's creation according to whom?, Graybard means to ask his partner to remind him), Muslim anti-Semites promulgated the outrageous charge that the 9/11 atrocity was one more Jewish Conspiracy, a plot to besmirch Islam, adducing as "evidence" the totally unsupported claim that four thousand Jewish employees in the World Trade Center had stayed home from work that morning! While altogether secular herself,** it is to protest that monstrous slander, as well as to honor the still-uncounted thousands of dead, that Ms. Wysiwyg has declared tonight's patio candles to be both memorial to last Tuesday's victims and observant of Rosh Hashanah's end — an occasion not normally marked by candles, if Graybard remembers correctly, and the holiday observed for a single day only by Reform Jews (two days by Conservative and Orthodox), but never mind.

In that same grave spirit, the woman's handsome nudity tonight had a different aspect from Night Seven's, not to mention from her kinky get-ups on Nights One through Three: Much as on Night Four, she wore her nakedness, so to speak, with the air not of a come-on but merely of a Here I Am; and their brief joint after-the-wine tidewater immersion — a regular feature of her latest M.O. revision, Graybard gathered — seemed more a Rite of Autumn than one of Spring: less a

*See, e.g., Night Two, as reviewed in the preamble to Night Three.
**In her current manifestation, anyhow. One readily acknowledges the historical importance of religion as a source of, though by no means a prerequisite to, artistic inspiration.

sportive romp than a ceremonial ablution. All the same, by when they were back on deck he felt the onset of Inspiration, enough so that immediately following their appropriately starred Intimate Metaphorical Congress —

* * * * * * ********

— he was moved to declare to his water-beaded waterbedmate
And then there's the one called

***Reader will kindly bear in mind that these incrementing asterisks are mere tabulations.

And Then There's the One

... about Adam Johnson Bauer, retired American, who, like many of his now age (late middle) and class (middle middle), had married in the mid-twentieth-century postwar euphoria, before such concerns as runaway population growth and environmental degradation had set in, and with his then mate begat children three, all of whom survived to adulthood and, as of the time of this telling, a healthy early-middle age.

Of that thriving trio, however (this is what's on their dad's mind just now, at the abovementioned century's end), only two married — nothing amiss there — and of those two, only one, the middle child and elder daughter, bore children: Ad's teenage granddaughter and grandson, living currently with their mother and virtual stepfather half a continent from their grandfather and stepgrandmother. In short, those five robust, well-educated, reasonably prosperous Americans — the three Baby-Boomer Bauers and their two original spouses — were bequeathing to the new millennium only a single pair of descendants: a reproductive rate of 40 percent, compared to Ad's and his (first) wife's 150 percent.

Bear with this arithmetic, Reader, of which there'll be yet more anon. Our Adam is a newly pensioned-off community-college teacher who, lacking both doctorate and scholarly publication, will not aggrandize himself with the title "Professor" (although that was in fact his rank at Hampton County Com Col and is the basis of his annuities), but who has a still-lively general curiosity, a head for figures, and more time on his hands these days than he's been used to. He now discovers that that foregoing progenitive analysis, if applied to his extended family, yields a similar result. Ad himself is one of three siblings, born in the Great Depression and wed (all three of them) in the 1950s. That sextet promptly bore seven children: Adam's aforementioned three, his sister's three, and his younger brother's one, an overall reproductive rate of 117 percent. But those seven and their six spouses—thirteen Boomerites in all—have seen fit to generate only half a dozen offspring: a 54 percent attrition. Ad's Radio Shack calculator next reports that this same reproductive decline marks even more the family of his somewhat younger current wife, the former Betsy Gardner, and the children of her and her siblings' initial marriages, for the most part still issue-free.

Good news for Planet Earth, our man supposes, if the whole human race, and not just its "advanced," post-industrial nations, followed the Bauer/Gardner example: less resource depletion, less pollution of the biosphere, more room for the whales and the wombats and whatever—but that's not what's on his mind. Nor is the circumstance that his pair of only grandkids bear their father's surname, as do his nieces and nephews and their dwindling spawn, in consequence whereof the Bauer name-line, if not its DNA, must expire with Ad himself not many years hence. In that department he has no qualms either of religion (Who'll say Kaddish for me?) or of personal vanity (No Adam Bauer, Jr., or III or IV? *Tant pis*). What has prompted these calculations and reflections is a remark that Granddaughter Donna blithely made last week toward the end of her annual late-August visit with Grandpa Ad and Grandma Bets: that she intends never under any circumstances to have babies ever. Had it been Grandson Mark who'd so declared, Ad might simply have smiled: What fourteen-year-old boy, with the world to conquer or at least his peers to impress, fancies himself a paterfamilias? But to hear a sunny, attractive, well-adjusted, and responsible seventeen-year-old girl so unequivocally reject motherhood...

And what prompted dear Donna's remark? Through nearly every one of her seventeen summers she has shuttled happily among her three sets of grandparents, spending a week or two with each: her dad's folks in San Diego, her mom's mom in Milwaukee, and her mom's dad and stepmom — Adam and Betsy — in their modest Cape May summer cottage. In the beginning she came with her parents and, later, her baby brother. From about age ten, as her parents' marriage deteriorated, she and young Mark flew out from Denver with their mother only; since about age twelve—because she and her brother get along ever less well, and her now-divorced mother has been scrambling to make both a living and a new life—she and Mark have come out unaccompanied and separately, using the airlines' minor-child escort service. All this hither-and-yonning (the complicated logistics of which remind Ad of the virtually insoluble Traveling Salesman problem in mathematics) has been financed by the several grandparents, at first because the young family was "just starting out" and couldn't afford the air fares, then because they were divorcing and couldn't, then because they were divorced and couldn't. By and large the visits have been a treat for all concerned; possibly they still are for Ad's ex-wife and the parents of his ex-son-in-law. As he and Betsy have aged, however, and young Donna has evolved from bubbly pre-teen through high-spirited early-teen to supercool and therefore bored latter-teen, the interludes have become, though outwardly no less cheery, a touch more strained all around. The girl would so obviously rather be trolling the Denver shopping malls with her false-fingernailed and triple-earringed contemporaries than beaching out in funky South Jersey with the old folks, their swim-suited high-mileage bodies no doubt distasteful to her. Ad and Bets in turn, after the first get-reacquainted day or two, find it annually more wearing to set aside their usual preoccupations for most of a fortnight and "relate" almost without respite (as everyday parents and children never do) across the two-generation gap. They foresee already that the problem will be even more acute with young Mark as his testosterone kicks in and the teenage American mall-and-media culture claims him. All hands still officially, indeed actually, love one another, but they would unanimously now prefer more frequent, less extended, and less exclusive interactions—such as were the rule back when a family's generations lived closer together—to these protracted annual one-on-ones. Distance, airfare, and available calendar time, however, rule out more than a single visit each way per annum, and so . . .

Homeward bound from the Atlantic City airport, whereto they de-livered the girl at visit's end for her commuter flight to Philadelphia and thence on to Milwaukee via Chicago, "It was the way she said it," Betsy reflected, and Ad agreed: "So unhesitating. So *definite*." They agree too that despite their reciprocal affection, the youngster must

have been prevailingly as glazed over by the visit as were they, as surfeited with bridging the age gap, as ready to get back to her more usual
and congenial pleasures once she was done with the *next* grandparent.
They'll be saddened but not at all surprised, they concur—perhaps
even, guiltily, a bit relieved—if next August Donna finds some diplomatic reason not to make the grandparental circuit, or else abbreviates
her Cape May stay to a long weekend, should they see fit to underwrite
such teenage jet-setting.

"Kids grow up," Ad says, and sighs—not simply at that fact of life.

The question before us, however, is what prompted young Donna's
declaration of non-reproductive intent. On the final evening of her
visit, as the trio lingered over dessert on the cottage's duneside deck
(lightheartedly sighing that they'll not be crossing paths again till
Christmastime in Denver), their granddaughter asked, apropos of
something or other, whether Betsy's parents had brothers and sisters;
she couldn't recall ever hearing Grandma Bets mention aunts and
uncles. Unlike young Mark, whose curiosity seems seldom to range
beyond skateboard stunts and video games, Donna takes a genuine
interest in other people's lives and interconnections, as evidenced by
her remembering details of them from visit to visit better than Ad
himself does. It must be, therefore, that for some stepgrandmotherly
reason Betsy hadn't spoken of her parents' several siblings, at least not
in recent Donna-visits; perhaps she felt that a non-lineal descendant
wouldn't really be interested. In any case, as she duly supplied the basic
info on her aunts Jan, Milly, and Eunice and her uncles Fred, Howard,
and George, it occurred to Ad to fetch from the house the Gardner
Family Tree, which that same (maiden-)Aunt Jan Gardner—mentally
intact but physically infirm and confined these days to an extended-
care facility in Delaware—happened to have drawn up earlier that
same season and distributed through the clan.

"Oh, she's not interested in *that*," Bets protested when he brought
the chart out. But Donna brightly counter-protested that she was, too,
interested—and not impossibly she was, although her social skills are
well enough developed, unlike her brother's, to bring off a polite show
of interest even if she felt none. Ad therefore reviewed with her the diagram of his wife's descent from two generations of New Jersey Gardners, themselves descended from a nineteenth-century immigrant

Liverpudlian whose own ancestry was unknown to Aunt Jan and company. Leaving who knows what or whom behind him, young Lewis Gardner in 1884 had crossed from Southampton to Boston, there to marry one Martha Ewell Stone and sire seven children, of whom five survived and one moved to Trenton, New Jersey, to sire Betsy's dad and his several sibs. Her genealogical lesson done, Donna left off twiddling the topmost of her left-lobe earrings, stretched her carefully tanned arms fetchingly over her head, and said, "One thing I know for sure: no kids for me."

Surprised — and in Ad's case, dismayed — her grandparents scoffed, questioned, teased: A healthy, intelligent, popular, good-looking, and good-humored girl like her uninterested in marriage and motherhood? "Not that those two always have to go together," Bets reminded all hands.

"Oh, I'll probably get married once or twice," Donna cheerily allowed. "But babies? Forget it."

Ad might have pressed further for her reasons, but his wife at this point observed that she herself at Donna's age had felt paradoxically vice versa: uninterested in marriage, but eager to have children, if only to counter-exemplify her own parents' botched job, as she saw it. Donna picked up on that subject, perhaps to deflect attention from herself, and their table talk presently shifted to other things.

As he later kissed the girl's forehead good night, "You'll have children," Ad murmured. "Jim-dandy ones, too."

His granddaughter chuckled in his hug. "Don't hold your breath, Grandpa."

Well, he hasn't held his breath. But while his respiration has proceeded at its average unconscious rate — one inhale / exhale cycle every five or so seconds, Ad once calculated, or two dozen dozen such cycles per day, or a couple thousand over the week since Donna's visit and the Bauers' return to "normalcy," or nearly seven million since his first, sixty-five years ago (which comes, he reckoned by the way, to only one-point-one breaths for each European Jew murdered in the Holocaust) — he has found he can't get the girl's upbeat negativity in this matter off his mind. To have pressed her further the next morning for explanation would have been tactless, and while Bets's position is that grandparents have a time-honored right to such tactlessness, Ad found himself reluctant to pry. Could be the fallout from Donna's parents' messy divorce, he and Bets agree, not to mention her grandparents' divorces; could be the geographical scattering of her extended family; could be the seize-the-day media culture of end-of-the-century Americans — narcissistic and ahistorical, changing addresses every four or five years and rarely dwelling where their parents dwelt, let alone their grandparents. Could be all of the above plus the increasing parity of the sexes, Bets reminds him, and the growing reluctance of many young women to hamper their career moves with maternity.

"In short," his wife intones, mock-seriously, "it's your effing decline of your effing Family Values."

And in fact, Ad has just about decided, it effing *is*. He himself lived from birth through high school in the white clapboard house in the smallish Pennsylvania town where his parents spent their entire life and his paternal grandparents their American adulthood, the two families literal next-door neighbors. Before Helmut Bauer's emigration from rural Germany, his stock had doubtless peasanted the same neck of the Sachsen woods from time out of mind — so Ad must infer from the family surname, inasmuch as his immigrant grandpa's actual ancestry, like Betsy's Great-Grandpa Lewis Gardner's, is off their respective genealogical charts. That's how it was back then with the mass of ordinary folk, Ad reckons — small farmers, tradespeople, shopkeepers — until America siphoned off the burgeoning European population. Ad's mother (née Margaret Johnson) had faithfully tended the respective families' grave-plots in the county cemetery, where the American generations of Bauers and assorted Johnsons were laid to rest: the men and their spouses; the women who died unmarried, still bearing the family name, or, wed and widowed, came home to finish out their life; the bachelor casualties of two world wars; the stillborn or otherwise non-surviving children. But neither Ad nor his siblings, all of whom attended college and seldom thereafter returned to their hometown except for family gatherings, took much interest in those gravesites, especially after the older generation died off. Ad almost never bothers to "pay his respects" to his predecessors, as people do in most other cultures and some perhaps still in ours (he is invariably surprised, passing a cemetery, to see a considerable number of beflowered graves). A non-believer, he has no plans to join those buried Bauers either physically or spiritually upon his own demise. About the disposition of his remains he is shrug-shouldered; has agreed with Betsy, who shares his attitude, that their dead bodies would best be incinerated and recycled into their sideyard compost pile for the eventual benefit of their roses, irises, chrysanthemums (the former Miss Gardner is in fact an ardent gardener). Never mind tending *their* graves; they'll be quite satisfied if their house's next owners keep up the landscaping—and those next owners, they take for granted, will not be Ad's or Bets's children or any other member of his or her family. Although their main house and beach cottage are a major part of the estate generously apportioned to their several offspring in their wills, they assume that those heirs will sell both properties and split the proceeds. What American adult lives in his/her parents' house nowadays, as was proverbially the ideal case in days of yore (*A house built by your father*; one such proverb recommends, *a vineyard planted by your grandfather*)? Who any longer cares a fart about *continuity*? He and Bets less than their parents, their children less than they, their grandchildren no doubt less yet.

Continuity, yes—whereof one aspect, on the family level, is genealogy. Once upon a time, so Ad's impression goes, there would have been one member of the extended clan—some Aunt Jan Gardner or fussy Uncle Bud Bauer—who recorded births, marriages, and deaths on the flyleaves of the family Bible or copied out the family tree for all hands' edification. In his own generation, Ad's younger brother Carl, lately a widower, half-heartedly updated somewhat back their Uncle Bud's *Bauernbaum*, as Ad dubbed it, and distributed copies for amendment and embellishment "if anybody's interested"; for two years now Ad's copy has rested—in peace, he trusts—in his study files, scarcely perused and never annotated despite Carl's mild hope that Ad might see fit to put it on the computer. A semi-retired Philadelphia realtor, Carl Bauer assumes that his professorial brother knows more about computers, but while in fact Ad and Bets use a desktop PC for family bookkeeping, correspondence, and occasional Internet expeditions, they are neither experts nor enthusiasts in that realm.

Half a thousand mortal respirations since this story's last space-break, however, and back in their "real" house after Labor Day, our man now finds himself inspired by his granddaughter's remark, not to File & Forget the Gardner Family Tree along with the *Bauernbaum*, but instead to retrieve from his files Carl's annotated diagram, lay the two side by side on his big old glass-topped work desk, and re-review them — more accurately, to examine them really closely for the first time. To his mild surprise, he finds himself genuinely interested, and curious. He still agrees with whoever it was who opined that "to have ancestors more distinguished than oneself is surely the least of virtues"; what appeals to him is that all these Freds and Mildreds and Ulrichs and Miriams were *not*, evidently, distinguished: just ordinary women and men like Bets and himself, being born, surviving childhood or not, marrying or not, engendering offspring or not, and soon or late dying. Then there are the mysteries, the unanswered questions: not just the vast though banal one of Lewis Gardner's and Helmut Bauer's Old Country progenitors back to whenever, but such smaller, more intriguing ones as what exactly Lewis and Helmut put behind them (at ages twenty-two and sixteen, respectively) and why exactly they set out — alone, it would appear, or perhaps with a hometown buddy or two — to try their fortunes in the New World. Ad's lively, bumptious Aunt Annabelle (his father's elder sister and everybody's favorite aunt) married Uncle Alfred Murray in 1925, so Carl's diagram indicates; but her only child is listed as having been born in 1923, and his name was Herbert Stolz, not Herbert Murray or Herbert Bauer. An unrecorded first marriage? A never-spoken-of illegitimacy? There's a story there, Ad bets, and another in Betsy's Great-Uncle Frederick Gardner's dates: *b. 1902 (Camden NJ)–d. 1937? (Alaska?)*. What about that aforementioned fussy Uncle Herman "Bud" Bauer's evidently short-lived adventure into exogamy (*b. 1898; m. 1920 Carlotta Petrucci; divorced 1922*)? No children, no subsequent remarriage for Uncle Bud; did he carry to his grave a torch for his perhaps passionate-but-faithless Italiana? Or, having burned his fastidious fingers in her flame, was he simply (or complexly) relieved to be the family's celibate necrologist through his remaining fifty-three years (*d. 1975*)?

Ad bets — even *Bets* bets, when he shares with her some of these musings — that their granddaughter would have pricked up her multiply-ringed ears at these familial mysteries, these closeted stories, if he had noticed them himself in time to point them out to her that evening in Cape May. He can even imagine her poring over the two family trees in search of more such tantalizers, perhaps making a high-school project out of pressing her surviving forebears for details. Was La Petrucci Philadelphia-Italian or Italy-Italian? What led young Frederick Gardner to the wilds of Alaska in the Great Depression, and why aren't we certain when and whether he perished there? Could he imaginably still be alive somewhere, a nonagenarian who burned his family bridges behind him in the New Jersey Thirties as his father Lewis had (perhaps) done in the Liverpudlian 1880s?

Et cetera. "So fax the things out to Denver," Bets recommends. "Draw circles around some of those possible skeletons in the family closet and add a few leading questions in case Donna doesn't see the fingerbones in the doorjamb. If she doesn't take the bait, maybe her mother will." But keep it to the Bauer side, she advises as an afterthought: "They-all couldn't care less about *my* family."

Not so, Ad loyally objects, suspecting, however, that it *is* so among the offspring of his first marriage (with the just-possible exception of their granddaughter), as for that matter it is to some extent with Bets herself. One thing for sure: Grandson Mark wouldn't give those charts a second look unless they came equipped with joystick and audiovisual special effects.

Once he hears himself put the matter like that, it occurs to A.J. Bauer that some sort of computerized version of the family trees might be just the thing to interest his grandkids — even Mark — in their genetic history. He puts "computerized" in mental quotes, because what he has in mind . . .

Well, he's not sure quite *what* he has in mind until some mornings later, when, in the course of transferring at last Carl's *Bauernbaum* to his PC (in mere outline format, as Ad's uncertain how to duplicate onscreen the branching lines of a genealogical tree), he comes to realize that while the outline version, with its hierarchical indentations and categories of enumeration (I, II; A, B; 1, 2; a, b; etc.), lacks the graphic appeal of descending "branches," it has the merit of a sort of hyper-textuality: Its program permits the user to display at will only the roman-numeraled, first-generation ancestors and their spouses, for example, without their progeny (*I. HELMUT AARON BAUER, m. Rosa Pohl Fleischer 1883*; *II. LEWIS JAMES GARDNER, m. Martha Ewell Stone 1886*), or them and their offspring (IA-G, IIA-F) without *their* offspring (IA1, etc.). The ideal computerized genealogical chart, he supposes, would be a bare-bones direct line of descent, whether patrilineal or matrilineal — a menu-option could instantly reverse those invidiously uppercase males and their lowercase mates and trace one's descent through one's mother's mother's mother — hypertexted so that a click of the mouse on IC (Aunt *Annabelle Bauer*), say, would display her essential biographical info, including *m. Alfred H. Murray 1925*, and a click on that same Uncle Alf would display *his* genealogy, *et cetera*: just the sort of "interactivity" that might appeal to Donna and Mark. The more so if each such name-click displayed a mug shot of the selected ancestor, perhaps together with a map showing Liverpool, Boston, Saxony, wherever, and/or views of Ellis Island, the Statue of Liberty, the huddled masses yearning to be free . . . Ad knows nothing about computer programming and software design, and the Bauer PC antedates CD-ROMs; he bets, though, that if he did and it didn't, he could devise in his retirement a marketable do-it-yourself hypertexted genealogy program that the members of an extended family could amplify to their hearts' content with whatever they knew or discovered about their ancestors and other relatives — biographical data ("Uncle Alf sold DeSoto automobiles in Green Bay, Wisconsin, after World War II"), wedding videos, voice-over anecdotes and new-baby cries, whatever — such that any particular family member could download and browse it at his/her will, following whatever linkages happened to appeal to her/his curiosity . . . *et cetera.*

"It might or might not interest Mark," Bets responds when Ad describes over lunch this hypothetical high-tech *Bauernbaum,* "but his grandpa is obviously hooked. Want to run it by Harold and see what he has to say?" She's half teasing: Her thirty-six-year-old son by her short-lived first marriage is a maverick "networking consultant" out in Silicon Valley with whom Ad has never quite hit it off and who seldom communicates with his mother these days.

"I might just do that." Ad is far from certain what a networking consultant even is, but the whole idea of this open-ended, interactive, hypertextual genealogy program, he reminds his wife, is to bring family members a bit closer together in a shared, ongoing project. "It's a network in itself," he adds, the idea having just occurred to him: "Family members all around the country could email their additions and corrections to the whole Family Net. In fact," for now *this* occurs to him, "it's a network in another sense, too: all those family branches branching off into other families. Maybe Harold *would* be interested."

"You're hooked," his wife declares, "and I've got a tennis date. Keep me posted."

Hooked he is. Back at his workstation that afternoon, Ad imagines clicking on *Rosa Pohl Fleischer* (old Helmut's bride), say, to call up *her* parents and siblings, their names and dates and capsule biographies. He bets he'd see then, among other things, where she got her middle name, and how many male Fleischers had been the butchers that their name implies, as the Bauers must once have been farmers. Click next on any one of those several siblings, or on their spouses, and you're in a whole other exfoliated family tree.

That image intrigues him: the browser swinging from tree to family tree wherever their branches touch, like a monkey in the rain forest, like ... our earliest, pre-human ancestors. Horizontally, so to speak, on the level of any given generation, if one could track the spouses of all of one's siblings, the spouses of all of *their* siblings and of theirs and theirs *et cetera*, how many families would be thus interconnected? A hundred? A thousand? A hundred thousand? On a corkboard beside the workstation, he has pinned side by side Carl's version of the *Bauernbaum* and Aunt Jan's of the Gardner Tree: twin deltas widening down from Helmut (*m. Rosa*) Bauer and Lewis (*m. Martha*) Gardner, respectively, to the latest generation of their descendants. By switching the positions of these charts and diddling their diagrams just a bit, he finds he can bring their lower corners together at the point where his marriage to Betsy conjoins the family trees. The like applies, potentially, to any of the many marriages there recorded — as would be displayable by a simple mouse-click in Ad's theoretical software program. Can it be imagined, he now wonders, that given enough hypothetical mouse-clicks ...?

Although we have established that A. J. Bauer is a retired academic, his erstwhile professional field — vaguely denominated "the humanities" — has not heretofore been mentioned. Sufficient to say that he is acquainted enough with the history of Western thought and literature to have "professed" selected specimens therefrom on the community-college level, and that as a generalist rather than a specialist, he not only subscribes to but actually reads, especially in his retirement, both the *New York Review of Books* and *Scientific American*, cover to cover. He is therefore (or anyhow) acquainted with the Egyptian, Greek, and Hebrew creation-stories, for example, and likewise with the "Eve hypothesis" advanced by some paleontologists: that the DNA of all humans presently inhabiting the planet indicates descent from a single African foremother, presumably not long down from the trees and coupling in the veldt with her male counterpart. Contemplating either of those two pyramidal diagrams on his corkboard, he is now moved to imagine at its peak not Helmut and Rosa Bauer or Lewis and Martha Gardner but the biblical Adam and Eve, or that emergent African Eve and her consort, and to envision a computerized genealogical program so powerful and info-rich that enough clicks of the mouse would lead back even past them, to (depending on the user's "belief system") either the One God who created the two humans who engendered all succeeding ones or the first single-celled earthly life-form that over the eons evolved into multicellular animals, thence into vertebrates, mammals, primates, hominids, the first *Homo sapiens, et cetera*. At the pyramid's tip, the aboriginal spark of life; at its base, every human being, if not every thing, currently alive on earth, their interrelationships and line of descent literally at the inquirer's fingertips.

Among the several courses that "Professor" Bauer (the self-deprecating quotes are his) once taught at HamCoComCol was one called The Bible as Literature, in which — he had to tread carefully here among the largely unsophisticated first-generation college-goers, many living at home with their unaffluent but stoutly opinioned parents — the familiar "stories" of Genesis (one did not call them myths) were respectfully compared to their analogues in other cultures. Predictably, when it was pointed out that Adam and Eve had three children (infamous Cain, doomed Abel, and much-later-born Seth), the first and third of whom are said to have sired all subsequent earthlings, someone would reasonably ask, "Where'd they get their women?" A discussion would ensue — raucous, indignant, fascinated, depending on the classroom mix — of the problem of sibling incest in any creation-story wherein a primordial One creates an original Couple who in turn beget the rest of humankind. If Eve, made from Adam's rib, was "bone of his bone, flesh of his flesh," was she not, genetically speaking, his sister? And if somehow not, would not her and Adam's daughters (unmentioned by the patriarchal Hebrew scribes, but necessary to postulate if Cain and Seth are to have mates other than their mother) have been their husbands' sisters? For that matter (some sharp-eyed sophomore would here point out), why does guilty Cain, "marked" by God for the murder of his brother Abel, complain that whoever sees that mark will kill him, when according to the scorecard — Abel dead, Seth not yet born — there *is* no one on earth besides himself and his parents? Professor Bauer would here mention, e.g., an Islamic tradition that each of those original brothers had a twin sister; that Father Adam, no doubt to attenuate the consanguinity, proposed that each son marry the other's twin rather than his own; and that Cain (Qabil in the Arabic version), desirous of his beautiful sister Labuda, murders Abel/Habil out of simple sexual rivalry. Did he then take both sisters for himself? Or did one of them subsequently become young Seth's wife, despite her having been old enough, even at her kid brother's birth, to be his mother? Or perhaps Seth's wife was one of his brother Cain's daughters (i.e., Seth's niece) by one of the brothers' sisters?

Et cetera. Reminded of these perennial classroom discussions by his new genealogical pyramid, our Adam now considers the rate of that pyramid's broadening in the light of what began this story: his own family's declining rate of reproduction and his granddaughter's Declaration (it now occurs to him to call it) of Nondependents. One God, says Genesis — with or without the collaboration of the *Shekhinah*, the Female Principle of the Kabbalists — created two humans: "male and female he created them," and they in turn engendered ... shall we say five (Cain, Abel, Seth, and a couple of nameless daughters?), of whom at least one, Abel, perished without issue. A net doubling of population, then, in each generation thus far. Ad's *World Almanac* informs him that while the base of that human pyramid is expected to number more than six billion souls by the year 2000, from preclassical times until the end of the European Middle Ages the world's population is estimated to have held at a modest and fairly stable two hundred million. Setting aside such freaky imponderables as the longevity of the Patriarchs and the catastrophe of the Flood, and allowing three generations per century, how many such generational doublings would it have taken to attain that "classical" two hundred million?

Not very many: A minute's button-punching on the calculator demonstrates that in only twenty-seven iterations, the series 1, 2, 4, 8, 16, 32 ... n reaches 134,217,728; the twenty-eighth puts it well over the top (268,435,456). Allowing that philoprogenitiveness in some individuals would be offset by infertility, celibacy, homosexuality, or early death in others, in less than one millennium (933.3 years, to be precise, at 33.3 years per generation beginning with Adam and Eve) God's human children could theoretically have exceeded the number estimated by demographers to have actually peopled the planet — all of them cousins at one remove or another.

"Both Lamech and Methuselah lived longer than that," Ad points out to his wife. "Imagine a family get-together of two hundred million."

Betsy shakes her head, not simply at that image.

"The birthdays," her husband marvels. "The holiday-card list."

"The airport logistics," his wife adds, for whom her step-family's one-visiting-grandchild-at-a-time policy is a minor headache. The couple agree that it is sobering to reflect how different the evolutionary facts must be from Ad's simple arithmetic: the hundreds of thousands of years it will have taken African Eve's descendants to expand the ecological niche of *Homo sapiens*, against all odds, to the two-hundred-million sustainable maximum before ... what? Before certain advances in technology and agriculture, Ad surmises, blew the lid off around the time of the Renaissance, and the Europeans' discovery of the New World afforded them a whole new spawning-ground. It is heartening to be reminded, they agree further, that we humans are literally, if not all brothers, at least all blood kin. But she has another tennis date, has Betsy, or intends to arrange one if she hasn't, with a threesome from that much-extended family; she'll leave Adam Johnson Bauer to his musings and reckonings — not before remarking, however, that both she and, in her opinion, Granddaughter Donna would likely be more interested in the specifics of their grandmothers' grandmothers' lives than in whether the biblical Seth shacked up with his niece, his aunt, or his sister. See you later, Calculator.

Yes, well. Such all-but-idle speculations are not the only thing that AJB does with his time, but in truth he has less to busy his mind with than formerly, and so when next he returns his attention to what he now calls Donna's Diagram, he draws a new equilateral delta with the apex labeled GOD and the base labeled 200,000,000 HUMAN DESCEN-DANTS. Having pinned one upper corner of it to his corkboard above the Bauer/Gardner family trees, he accidentally lets the sheet slip while fetching a second pushpin; the resultant near-inversion of that delta (perhaps together with its dangling now over the *Bauernbaum*) inspires him to a new idea and, anon, a new diagram. At the base of those original charts are DONNA and MARK Putnam (their estranged father's surname), along with the sundry cousins of their generation. Each of those youngsters, it goes without saying, has or anyhow had two biological parents, each of whom ditto, etc. etc. Reversing his previous calculations, Ad imagines and presently draws an inverted delta with DONNA BAUER PUTNAM at its bottom point, her pair of parents at the next level up, her four (biological) grandparents on the level above that, then her eight great-grandparents (most of whom, on the Putnam side, are already unnameable by Adam), her sixteen great-great-grandparents, etc.—until, in only those same two-dozen-plus generations, the girl's direct ancestors equal in number the estimated then population of the earth.

With some excitement, "What am I leaving out?" he asks his wife, who has attended this latest exposition politely but can be of no assistance therewith. "We're not talking aunts and uncles and in-laws and stepparents here, just biological parents and grandparents. There's no getting around the arithmetic, 'cause it takes two to tango, and two hundred million is two hundred million. But the results are impossible."

More obligingly than eagerly, "Run it by me again?"

He does. Twenty-eight doublings of the number one make two-hundred-plus million, Q.E.D. Counting forward from Adam and Eve is obviously an iffy business, since not every couple has four surviving children each of whom in turn *et cetera*, and so it might very reasonably take hundreds of thousands of years instead of nine hundred thirty-three to get from African Eve and her mate to earth's estimated human population as afore-established. Indeed, the fact that the world's population apparently held steady at that "classical" level for at least a couple of millennia instead of doubling every thirty-three years is proof of the constraints in that direction. But counting *back* is another story: Each one of us necessarily had a mother and father, each of whom *et cetera* — which seems to mean that around the time of the Norman Conquest every person on the face of Planet Earth must have been the direct ancestor of everybody presently aboard.

"It was our Great-Plus-Grandfather William of Normandy who whupped our Great-Plus-Grandfather Harold at the Battle of Hastings," awed Adam declares. "It was Great-Plus-Grandma Murasaki who wrote *The Tale of Genji* while Great-Plus-Grandpa Leif Erikson discovered Vineland. Everybody who fought and died on both sides in the First Crusade was our great-plus-grandparent!"

"Wait a minute." As if to make sure, Bets consults her watch. "Saint

Thomas Aquinas didn't have any kids, so there's one down. Some nuns and popes back then didn't have any, too, if I remember correctly."

He knows, he knows, repeats Ad: There has to be something screwy about his reasoning. For example (it occurs to him even as he speaks), it would appear that our two hundred million great-plus-grandparents in 1066 would have to have had *four* hundred million parents of their own in 1033, when we've already established that for generation after generation there were only two hundred million available candidates for parenthood. So it has to follow (he's thinking fast) that Donna's great-great-grandparents, while indisputably sixteen in number, needn't have been sixteen different people; otherwise we would all be descended from Genghis Khan and Ghazali and the Eskimos, as well as from William the Conqueror and Harold the Conquered ...

"Ghazali?"

Eleventh-century father of Sufi mysticism, if not of the Bauers and the Gardners.

His wife pats his arm. "Well, you work on it, honey."

But her husband doesn't (the simple flaw in his geometric reasoning, he soon recognizes, is that while every child must have two parents, not every two need have four, etc.). He's no bigtime original thinker, Adam Johnson Bauer, much less any kind of genius: just a middling old-fart ex-academic with a temporary bee in his bonnet from wanting to explain to his granddaughter, perhaps likewise to himself, that we presently breathing humans are not *de novo*, howevermuch she and her fellow Denver mallsters might blithely feel themselves to be; that she and himself and all of us are indivisibly part of the ever-renewing tissue of life on earth, descended *directly*, through our parents and grandparents, from the primordial blue-green algae, and related to every other living thing.

No: not *explain*. What's to be explained? At age seventeen the girl's convinced that although she "might get married once or twice" (!), she wants no children. Most likely she'll change her mind; quite possibly she won't, given the way young women are nowadays. So bloody what? Retired, he sits in his familiar, once-so-piled-up study and futzes with his charts and calculator while his wife plays tennis with her friends and the world grinds on: atrocious massacres and counter-massacres in central Africa; bitter standoffs in the Balkans and the Middle East;

whole species disappearing from the ever-dwindling rain forests before they're even classified; more misery and injustice everywhere than one can catalogue, much less address; and the sky evidently ever on the verge of falling. Not much Ad Bauer can do about all that, beyond acknowledging and bearing in mind the enormous fact of it. He has long since made essential peace with his privileged position: a fortunate life in a fortunate country at a fortunate time. He and Bets vote moderate-liberal, contribute to assorted charitable and cultural causes, and endeavor to lead harmless lives; they eat meat and dairy products only sparingly, limit their intake of table wine, compost their leaves and recycle their trash, try to be good neighbors and to maintain a civil, tolerant attitude toward people with customs and opinions different from their own. Soon enough nevertheless, he knows, catastrophe is bound to befall them in one form or another: cancer, hurricane, fatal accident, crippling stroke. Meanwhile . . .

So one of his children had children and two did not: So what? So all had parents and proliferating foreparents: So bloody bloody what? Just now he feels bearing down upon him, does Adam Johnson Bauer, the weight of that massive inverted pyramid — of which he and his beloved Betsy and each of all the rest of us is individually the vertex — as if it were an enormous hydraulic press, and dear sunny Granddaughter Donna its all-too-human diamond point.

Forget it, Reader.

Brother! Sister! Daughter! Son!

Forget it.

NINTH NIGHT

So what's he wearing?
it may have occurred to Reader to wonder about guy Graybard on this
ninth evening of his and Muse Wysiwyg's Hendecameron, if not before.
Its narrative viewpoint being mainly his, we've had detailed accounts
of his companion's nightly dress and undress; oughtn't we to hear what
duds *he* doffs when dud-doffing time arrives, for the pair's now-ritual
creek-dip between wine and waterbed?

Yes, well, okay — although in the nature of their situation, their
character-functions, and even their names, her appearance is more
relevant to this framing-tale than his. Indeed, if it be noted now that on
this partly cloudy and breezy but warm Wednesday, 9/19/01, the fellow
has entered their Imaginarium wearing khaki shorts, collared tan polo
shirt, and brown leather deck moccasins, that's because this "evening"
he has found his collaborator wearing the same, as if she has become as
much an aspect of him (or he of her) as is he of his Originator.*

Coincidence? Perhaps, notwithstanding her disingenuous shrug
when he remarked it as she served the *vin du soir* —

Your "marsh-country pinot gris" again? he asked after sniffing, sampling, and inspecting its color by patio-candle light. As on First Night?

"Good guess." She took her seat on the twilit deck, crossed her excellent legs, and raised her glass. "The Mediterranean version this time:

---

*The case was almost the same on Fifth Night, except that her sweatshirt then had been ink
blue and his (not reported, because irrelevant) a light clay.

grigio instead of *gris*."

Ah, so: Spain last night, Italy tonight. And tomorrow?

She looked out over the darkening marsh. "Maybe home?" And before he could ask, "Don't ask: I mean the mythic old muses' home." And then, "Scratch that: She means the mythical abode of the muses, not some nursing home on Mount Helicon."

Understood.

—together with her occasional unsettling prescience, whereof one has seen evidence on earlier nights. "You were wondering," she said now, for example, "what the Hebrew calendar dates Creation from, and according to whom?" Which he had indeed meant to ask last night, but forgot to when Inspiration distracted him. "God knows, excuse the expression, when and how the count-back started. By Jesus's time it was more or less established Judaic tradition, but it wasn't formally codified until the *Seder Olam Rabbah*, second century C.E.? After which it gets reinforced in other more or less authoritative chronologies up through the eighth century. Just rabbinical consensus, you understand: With no pope to lay down the law, 'more or less' is all you get."

Or want. Okay, and thanks, dear Wys.

Her mind evidently on other matters, she stretched and sighed. "Numbers: I love 'em."

Oh?

"Not math itself, particularly; just *numbers*. Measures. *Integers*. Like, are they quote *real*, or quote *only* in our heads, et cet.? That's what I particularly liked about your story last night—"

Our story.

"Yes, well. Despite the fact that that inverted delta toward the end bent our No More Shrinkage rule a bit."

Sorry there.

"No problem." Sigh. "Numbers!"

That figures, Wys: Sing, O Muse, *in mournful numbers*, et cet.? Or Wordsworth's Solitary Reaper: *Will no one tell me what she sings?/ Perhaps the plaintive numbers flow/ For old, unhappy, far-off things . . .*

Frowning: "Enough, Geeb, please!" Then, less sharply, "Enough?"

If she says so. Then presently: Creek-time?

"If *he* says so, she guesses."

He says so. And later, with your help, maybe another number-story?

"If you say so."

Was he merely imagining that she rather enjoyed his uncharacteristically (and no doubt briefly) taking charge of their agenda? In any case — while the U.S. stock market temporarily held steady, and American consumer spending showed signs of rising back toward normal, and the administration's ultraconservative attorney general widened the Justice Department's authority to detain suspected terrorists without the usual legal constraints, and Democrats in Congress felt obliged to mute their opposition to the Pentagon's zillion-dollar "Star Wars" missile-defense program, and the nation's airlines, hard hit by people's fear of flying after September 11, were pledged massive federal aid to tide them over — Ms. Wysiwyg set down her wineglass and peeled off shoes, shirt, shorts, and undies *as if obediently* while her Narrative Software did the same. Scarcely to his credit, Graybard must have found her newly deferential air arousing, for when she now turned ladderward he embraced her from behind, an embrace that she responded to with a small sound and turned to reciprocate. By when he then led her down into the silky warm wet, he found himself inspired past the point of waiting for waterbedtime: It being low tide and the water only shoulder-deep, he stood on the creek's soft-silt bottom and gripped her firm one in both hands while she laced her fingers behind his neck, girdled his hips with her thighs, and pressed her forehead to his lips — and they managed together an X-rated Saltyfresh Metaphorical Wet Dream Come True, whose asterisks may not have been *intended* as more than mere tabulation, but in this instance surely were.

* * * * * * * *

If that was the figurative Appetizer;
Graybard (for one) wondered as the pair sooner or later climbed back on deck — his fine friend leading, he following so closely up the ladder that his face received blissfully the warm creek-droplets dripping from her — what Entrée could imaginably follow? And as if once again reading his thoughts, Ms. Wys (her submissiveness shed already by their third or fourth submarine asterisk) said, "Storytime," took his more than willing hand, and led him straightaway to the narrative bed.

"Something with *numbers*, okay?"

If she says so ...

"She has so said." And holding up all but one of her slim fingers, "Preferably *nines* — this being Ninth Night, Nine Nineteen?"

The tease of her smile suggested that she had at least some acquaintance with the two remaining items in their inventory, wherefrom the clear candidate, numberwise, was the one called

9999

The word *odometer* dates from 1791, but mileage indicators didn't appear as standard equipment on automobile instrument panels until after World War I. Frank Parker's memory, therefore, of his parents' bidding him and his older sister, in the rear seat of the family sedan — the big black Buick, it must have been, the family's first postwar conveyance, and most likely during one of their ritual Sunday-afternoon drives down-county — to "watch, now: She's all nines and 'bout to come up zeroes," can be dated no earlier than 1919, Frank's eighth year and sister Janice's eighteenth, nor later than 1922, the year newlywed Jan moved with her husband from Maryland's Eastern Shore to upstate New York, whence thereafter she returned only occasionally, with her own children. And Jan is very much a feature of this memory: More of a mother to Frank through that melancholy period than his disconsolate mother was (still grieving for her war-lost firstborn), it could even have been she who called her kid brother's attention to that gauge on the verge of registering its first thousand or ten thousand miles. In any case, in his eighty-fifth year Frank well recalls a long-ago subtropical Chesapeake afternoon (automotive air conditioning was yet another world war away), his Sunday pants sticky on the gray plush seat, the endless marshes rolling by, and that row of nines turning up not quite simultaneously from right to left — were there tenth-of-a-mile indicators back then? — to what his father called "goose eggs."

For our Frank — who just two hours ago (at a few minutes past 9 PM on Sunday, September 7, 1997, to be more if not quite most exact) was prepared to end his life, but has not done so, yet — each of those limit-years has its private significance. Certain sentimental reasons, to be given eventually, incline him to prefer 1919, in particular the third Friday of that year's ninth month: Tidewater Maryland could well have been still sweltering then, and the new Buick might feasibly have been turning up its first thousand. But 1922 (though not its summer) was likewise a milestone year, so to speak, in what passes for this fellow's life-story.

A consideration now occurs to him: Wouldn't the digits 9999, for reasons also presently to be explained, have "freaked out" his mother altogether, as Americans say nowadays? Perhaps she had already taken to the bed whereof she became ever more a fixture, tended first by Janice and their tight-visaged father, subsequently (after Jan's escape to Syracuse) by a succession of "colored" maids, as Americans said back then. In which case it would have been Jan herself in that front passenger seat, "playing Mom" (it was no game), and not impossibly young Frank who, bored with counting muskrat-houses to pass the sweatsy time, leaned over the front seatback, noticed the uprolling odometer, and said, "Hey, look," etc. It doesn't much matter, to this story or generally; Frank just likes to get things straight. 1919 was the second and final year of the great influenza pandemic, which killed perhaps twenty-five million people worldwide (more than the Great War), including some half million Americans — among them young Hubert Parker, who was serving in France with the American Expeditionary Force but was felled in '18 by the deadly myxovirus, not by the Hun or by the stellar "influence" once thought to cause such epidemics. Baseball players in that season's World Series wore cotton mouth-and-nose masks, as did many of their spectators; "open-faced sneezing" in public was in some venues declared a crime, as were handshakes in others. Frank's odometer-memory includes no facemasks, but then neither does his recollection of the family's home life generally in that glum period. Perhaps isolated small-towners took fewer precautions than city folk; perhaps even student-nurse Janice was too discouraged by their elder brother's death, their mother's collapse, and their father's withdrawal into stolidity to give much of a precautionary damn; or perhaps that mileage-memory dates from a later year. *1919* is the title of the second novel of John Dos Passos's *USA* trilogy, a favorite of Mr. and (the late, profoundly lamented) Mrs. Frank Parker, for not altogether literary reasons. 1919 . . .

In a misanthropic mood, Leonardo da Vinci called the mass of humankind "mere fillers-up of privies." True enough of this story's mostly passive protagonist, Frank supposes; likewise even of his (late, still inordinately beloved, *indispensable*) spouse, their four parents and eight grandparents and sixteen great-grandparents *et cetera* ad infinitum as far as Frank knows; likewise of their middle-aged son (his wife felled by a heart attack before his mother succumbed to a like misfortune) and their sole, much-doted-upon grandchild. Prevailingly, at least, they have all as far as Frank knows led responsible, morally decent if perhaps less than exemplary lives: no known spouse- or child-abusers among them; no notable greedheads, programmatic liars, cheaters, stealers, or exploiters of their fellow citizens. One drunkard bachelor uncle on Frank's mother's side, but he injured none except himself. Frank and (the unassimilably deceased) Pamela Parker, we can assert with fair confidence, in their lifetimes have done (*did* . . . !) no or little intentional harm to anybody, and some real if not unusual good: Pam by her own assessment was a reliable though unremarkable junior-high mathematics teacher, Frank by his a competent though seldom more than competent public-school administrator, the pair of them at best B+ at worst B- parents and citizens, perpetuating the cycle of harmless fillers-up of privies, all soon enough forgotten after their demise. If anything at all has distinguished this pair from most of their fellow filler-uppers . . .

There on his nightstand is cabernet sauvignon to dull his senses for the deed. There are the sleeping pills, of more than sufficient quantity and milligrammage; the completed note of explanation To Whom It May Concern (principally his retirement-community neighbors and his granddaughter) and the sealed letter to his Personal Representative (Frank Parker, Jr.). There is the plastic bag recommended by the Hemlock Society to insure quietus, but which our man fears might prompt an involuntary suffocative panic and blow the procedure; he may well opt not to deploy it when the hour arrives.

And what, pray, might be that Estimated Time of Departure?

If anything, we were saying, has distinguished this now-halved pair of Parkers from the general run of harmless, decent folk, it is (*was* . . . !) their reciprocally abiding love — which ought most healthily to extend outward from self and family to friends, community, and humankind, but which in Frank and Pam's case remained for better or worse largely intramural — and a shared fascination with certain *numbers*, especially of the calendric variety: certain patterns of date-notation. If one could tell their story in terms of such patterns — and one could, one can, one will — that is because, as shall be seen, after a series of more or less remarkable coincidences had called the thing to their attention, they saw fit to begin to arrange certain of their life-events to suit it, telling themselves that to do so was no more than their little joke: a romantic game, an innocent tidiness, a kickable habit.

But let's let those dates tell their story. The late Hubert Parker, Frank's flu-felled eldest sib, happened to be born on the ninth day of September, 1899: in American month/day/year notation, 9/9/99; in the more logical "European" day/month/year notation, also 9/9/99, or 9·9·99 (we now understand the possibly painful association of that on-the-verge odometer reading back in the family sedan). Very well, you say: No doubt sundry notables and who knows how many mere privy-fillers shared that close-of-the-century birthdate, as will a much larger number its presently upcoming centenary.* But did they have a next-born sib who first saw light on New Year's Day, 1901 (1/1/01 American, ditto European, and a tidy alternating-binary 01/01/01 by either), birthday of the aforementioned Janice Parker? The coincidence was a neighborhoodwide How-'*bout*-that and a bond between brother and sister, even before its remarkable compounding by Frank Parker's birth in 1911 on what, beginning with his seventh birthday, would mournfully be dubbed Armistice Day, and another war later, on his forty-third, be grimly, open-endedly renamed Veterans Day.

By either system, 11/11/11: the century's only six-figure "isodigital," as a matter of fact. (It will be Pam, the seventh-grade-math-teacher-to-be, who early on in their connection offers Frank that Greeky adjective, together with the datum that his birthday's "precurrence" in the twelfth century 11/11/1111 — was the only *eight*-figure isodigital in their millennium. Work it out, Reader, if such things fascinate you as they did them; you may note as well that no date in either the preceding or the

---

*The American-style present time of this narrative, remember, is 9/7/97·

succeeding millennium of the Christian era will exceed seven isodigits.) Not surprisingly, even without those parenthetical enhancements Frank's birthdate was the occasion of considerable family and neighborhood comment. He recalls his parents' joking, before Hubie's death ended most levity in their household, that they had planned it that way, and that they were expecting young Hube to supply their first grandchild on either Groundhog Day (2/2) or George Washington's birthday (2/22) in 1922.

When those dates arrived, Hubert Parker was dead; sister Jan (nicknamed for her birth-month) was a registered nurse whose chief patient was her mother and whose impending marriage would soon leave the family "on its own"; and young Frank was a somewhat introverted fifth-grader in East Dorset Elementary, his fascination with such calendrics understandably established. It was on one or the other of those two February holidays that he reported to Miss Stoker's class the remarkable coincidence of his and his siblings' birthdate patterns, called their attention to the phenomenon of "all-the-same-digit" dates, projected for them the eleven-year cycle of such dates within any century (2/2/22, 3/3/33, etc.), and pointed out to them what the reader has already been told: that the constraints of a twelve-month year with roughly thirty-day months make 11/11/11 the only six-figure "same-digiter" in any century. Miss Stoker was impressed. Nine months later, on that year's Armistice Day, when like every elementary-school teacher in America his (then sixth-grade) teacher, Miss Scheffenacher, observed to the class that the Great War had officially ended on the *eleventh hour* of the eleventh day of the eleventh month just four years past, they sang a mournful-merry "Happy (eleventh) Birthday" to our protagonist. After everyone had stood with head bowed as the town's fire sirens sounded that eleventh hour, the boy responded with the observation that even those few of his classmates who hadn't turned eleven yet were nevertheless in their eleventh year; additionally, that while the date of his war-lost brother's death in France had not been a Same-Digiter, it had been the next best thing (for which Frank hadn't yet found a name): 8/18/18—when, moreover, luckless Hubie had been eighteen years old.

His comrades regarded him as Special, whether charmed or spooked. Miss Scheffenacher (having provided the term "alternating-digiter," which Frank shortened to Alternator) opined that he would go on to college and Become Somebody someday, and then set the class to listing all the Samers and Alternators in the century, using the American style of date-notation. Not even she had previously remarked the curious patterns that emerged from their blackboard tabulations: that among the Samers, for example, there were none in the century's first decade, four in its second (all in 1911, culminating in Frank's birthday), two in its third (the aforenoted February holidays of their present year), and only one in each of the decades following. She thought Frank should definitely go on to college, and would have declared as much to his parents had the mother not been an invalid and the father a non-attender of parent-teacher meetings and most other things.

Except for the Miss Stokers and the Miss Scheffenacher, however, who "went off" to the nearby state normal school to become teachers, not many young people in small-town tidewater Maryland in those days were inclined or able to pursue their formal education past the county school system; most were proud to have achieved their high-school diplomas instead of dropping out at age sixteen, by choice or otherwise, to begin their full-time working lives. But with his family's blessing Frank did, in fact, complete his first year in that little teachers college and begin his second before the combined setbacks of his mother's death and the Great Depression (his father's car-sales business foundering, the family's savings lost in the general bank failures) obliged him to leave school — on 1/31/31, he noted grimly — and work as bookkeeper and assistant manager of Parker Chevrolet-Oldsmobile-Buick.

There he might have remained, and our story be stymied, had not his ever-more-dispirited father committed suicide on the first or second day of May, 1933. Shot himself in the starboard temple with a small-bore pistol, he did, late in the evening of 5/1; lingered unconscious in the county hospital for some hours; expired before the dawn of 5/2, his son at his bedside, his harried daughter en route by train and bus from Syracuse. Although the date was numerically insignificant (so Frank thought), he happened two months earlier to have sighed, in his book-keeper's office, at the approach, arrival, and passage of 3/3/33, the first Samer since Miss Scheffenacher's fifth-grade February. The fellow had attained age twenty-one, still single and living in his parents' house, now his. The tidy arithmetic of double-entry bookkeeping he found agreeable, but he had neither taste nor knack for selling motor vehicles, which few of his townsfolk could afford anyhow in those hard times. On a determined impulse he sold the automotive franchise that summer, rented out the house, and with the meager proceeds re-enrolled in the normal school to complete his interrupted degree in secondary education.

Three years after his receipt thereof, our calendric love-chronicle proper begins. Twenty-six-year-old Frank, having mustered additional accreditation, is teaching math and "science" to the children of farmers and down-county watermen in a small high school near his alma mater; he looks forward already to "moving up" from the classroom (which has less appeal for him than does the subject-matter) to school administration, for which he feels some vocation. He has dated two or three women from among the limited local supply, but no serious romance has ensued. Is he too choosy? he has begun to wonder. Are they? Is he destined never to know the experience of love? In early March, 1938, he surprises his somewhat diffident self by inviting his principal's new young part-time secretary, barely out of high school herself and working her way through the teachers college, to accompany him to a ham-and-oyster supper at the local Methodist church, the social hub of the community. Despite the eight-year difference in their ages and some good-humored "razzing" by the townsfolk, the pair quite enjoy themselves; indeed, Frank feels more lively and at ease with pert young Pamela Neall than he has ever before felt with a female companion. On her parents' screened front porch later that evening, he finds himself telling her of his calendrical claim to fame: his and his siblings' birth-dates, his brother's death-date, the Alternator 1/31/31 that marked his leaving college, and the Samer 3/3/33 that prompted his return. Miss Neall's interest is more than merely polite: Her ready smile widens in the lamplight as he runs through the series; all but bouncing with excitement beside him on the porch glider, she challenges him to guess her own birthdate, and when he cannot, offers him the clue (she's a quick one, this hardworking aspirant to math-teacherhood) that just as he was born on the century's only six-digit Samer, she was born on its only *seven*-digit Alternator.

Frank feels ... well, beside himself with exhilaration. "Nine Nineteen, Nineteen Nineteen!"

Moved by the same delight, they kiss.

***

Did the course of true love ever run smooth? Now and then, no doubt, but not inevitably. Although the couple were entirely pleased with their "first date" (Frank's joke, which won him another kiss; but it was Pamela who remarked before he that the date of that date was another Alternator, 3/8/38) and no less so with their second and third, Pam's mother and father opposed any sequel on grounds of their daughter's youth and the age differential. Common enough in that time and place for girls of eighteen to marry, but they had hoped she would finish college first. A firm-willed but unrebellious only child who quite returned her parents' love, Pam insisted that the four of them reason it out together, listening with respectful courtesy to all sides' arguments. Her and Frank's (they're a team already): that their connection was not yet Serious and would not necessarily become so, just a mutual pleasure in each other's company and some shared interests; that should it develop into something more (they exchanged a smile), she was determined not to be diverted from the completion of her degree and at least a few years' experience of teaching — a determination that Frank applauded and seconded. Her parents': that they had no objections to Frank as a person, only as a premature potential suitor of a girl who one short year ago could have been his highschool student; that howevermuch their daughter might now vow her determination to finish her education (for which she was largely dependent on their support), love "and its consequences" could very well override that resolve, to her later regret. Better to avoid that risk, all things considered — and no hard feelings, Frank. In the end, the four agreed on a compromise: a one-year moratorium on further "dates" while Pam completed her freshman year at the normal school, spent the summer camp-counseling up in Pennsylvania as planned, and returned for her sophomore year. During that period the pair would not refrain from dating others, and if next spring — at ages nineteen and twenty-seven, respectively — she and Frank inclined to "see" each other further, her parents would withdraw their objections to such dates.

Each repetition of that word evoked the young couple's smiles, as did such now-voltaged numbers as *nineteen*; without knowing it, Pam's well-meaning parents had undermined their own case and increased the pair's interest in each other. When the girl agreed to have no further dates with Mister Parker before the date 3/9/39, Frank understood that the campaign which he had not till then particularly set out to wage was already half won. As good as their word, for the promised year they refrained from dating each other, though not from exchanging further calendrics and other matters of mutual interest in their frequent letters and telephone conversations; and they dutifully if perfunctorily dated others — Pamela especially — with more or less pleasure but no diminution of either's feelings for her / his predestined soulmate.

Quite the contrary, for so they came ever more to regard each other with each passing month. Had Frank noticed, Pam asked him in one letter from Camp Po-Ko-No, that if his sister Jan had managed to be born on the first of October instead of the first of January, then her birthdate (10/1/01) would be the only "patterned" date, whether Samer or Alternator, in the century's first decade? And would he please *please* believe her that although the senior counselor with whom she had dutifully "gone out" once or twice had proposed the fancy word *isodigitals* to describe what they called Samers, she had found the fellow otherwise a bore? He would indeed, Frank promised, if she would ask him the Greek word for Alternators and not date him a third time, as *he* was not re-dating his history colleague Arlene Makowski. Meanwhile, had Pam noticed that the date of her recentest letter, 8/3/38, was a Palindrome, a numerical analogue to "Madam, I'm Adam"? And that her remarkable birthdate, 9/19/1919, could be regarded as a Palindromic Alternator, as for that matter could sister Jan's? And that he loved her and missed her and was counting the days till 3/9/39?

One weekend shortly thereafter, he drove all the way up into the Pennsylvania mountains in order to see and talk with her for just one surreptitious lunch hour, the most they felt they could allow themselves without their meeting's becoming a "date." They strolled the little village near Pam's camp, holding hands excitedly, stopping to kiss beside a shaded stream that ran through the tiny town park with its monuments to the Union dead and the casualties of the Great War.

"*Sequentials*," he offered, "like straights in a poker hand: The first in this century was One Two Thirty-four, and there won't be another till One Twenty-three Forty-five."

She hugged him, pressed her face into his shirtfront, and reckoned blissfully. "But then the next one comes later that same year: December Third!"

He touched her breast; she did not move his hand away.

"We give up," her good-natured parents declared that fall. Their daughter was back at the normal school, their future son-in-law back in his high-school classroom, and the pair still not actually dating, but telephoning each other daily and seeing each other casually as often as manageable on the weekends. "You're obviously meant for each other."

But it pleased the couple, perversely, to let their reciprocal desire ripen through that winter without further intimacies until the agreed-upon date, meanwhile reinforcing their bond with the exchange of Reverse Sequentials (3/2/10, 4/3/21, etc.) and the touching observation — Pamela's, when Frank happened to recount to her in more detail the story of his father's suicide — that the date of that sad event was not as "meaningless" as he had supposed, for while it might be tempting to regard 3/3/33 (Frank's "career change" day) as marking the end of the century's first third, the actual "33 percent date" of 1933 — i.e., its 122nd day — would be May 2, when Mr. Parker died. Indeed, since 365 divided by 3 gives not 122 but 121.666 ... n, it was eerily appropriate that the poor man shot himself on the evening of May 1 and died the following morning.

Much moved, "The fraction is so *blunt*," Frank almost whispered: "*One-third*, and that's that. But *point-three-three et cetera* goes on forever."

"Like our love," Pam declared or vowed, thinking *infinite isodigitality* — and herself this time placed his hand, her own atop it, where it longed to go.

On the appointed date, March 9, 1939, they declared their affiancement. In deference to Pam's parents' wishes, however, they postponed their marriage nearly a full two years: not quite to her baccalaureate in May 1941, but to the first day of the month prior, trading off their friends' April Fools' Day teasing for the satisfaction of the American-style Alternator plus European-style Palindrome. Moreover, just as Frank felt his "true" eleventh and twenty-second birthdays to have been not the November Elevenths of those years but 2/22/22 and 3/3/33 respectively, so the newlywed Mr. and Mrs. Parker resolved to celebrate their wedding anniversaries not on the actual dates thereof but on the nearest Alternator thereafter: 4/2/42, 4/3/43, etc.

And so they did, though not always together, for by the arrival of that first "true" anniversary the nation was at war. Not to be conscripted as cannon fodder, thirty-year-old Frank enlisted in the Navy and after basic training found himself assigned to a series of logistical posts, first as a data organizer, later as an instructor, finally as an administrator. Her profession and the couple's decision to put off starting a family "for the duration" made Pam fairly portable; although they missed their first True Anniversary (Frank couldn't get leave from his Bainbridge boot camp) and their fourth (story to come), they celebrated 4/3/43 at his base in San Diego and "the big one," 4/4/44—their third True Anniversary, Frank's thirty-third True Birthday, and their first Congruence of Samers and Alternators, a sort of calendrical syzygy—at his base in Hilo, Hawaii, where Pam happily taught seventh-grade math to the "Navy brats." Whether owing to the tropical ambiance, the poignancy of wartime, the specialness of the date, or the mere maturation of their love, she experienced that night her first serial orgasm; it seemed to her to extend like the decimal equivalent of one-third, to the edge of the cosmos and beyond.

4/5/45 saw them separated again, this time by a special assignment that Frank was dispatched to in the South Pacific. Forbidden to mention to her even the name of his island destination, much less the nature of his duty there (it will turn out to do with logistical support for the atom-bombing of Hiroshima and Nagasaki four months later), all Frank could tell her was that while the first of that year's two Sequentials (1/23/45) saw the war still raging in both the European and the Pacific theaters, he wouldn't be surprised if the show was over by the second. And did his dear Pammy remember first flagging that notable date during their non-date in that little park near Camp Poke-Her-No-No?

How swiftly a good life runs. By their first "irregular" or "corrective" anniversary (4/1/50: The zero in any decade-changing year will spoil their romantic little game, but remind them of their wedding's actual date) they were resettled in Pam's hometown, Frank as assistant superintendent of the county school system, Pam as a teacher in that same system on open-ended leave to deliver—on an otherwise "meaningless" date in May—their first and, it will turn out, only child, Frank Jr. He grew; she returned to teaching; sister Jan's husband deserted her in Syracuse for a younger woman; all hands aged. Some calendar-markers along their way, other than their always-slightly-later True Anniversaries: 7/6/54, a Reverse Sequential on which Frank Jr.'s baby sister miscarried and the Parkers called it a day in the reproduction department; 5/5/55, their Second Syzygy (fourteenth True Anniversary and Frank's forty-fourth True Birthday), when thirty-five-year-old Pam enjoyed by her own account the second best orgasm of her life; November 23, 1958, when Frank came home from the superintendent's office (he had been promoted the year before) to find his wife smiling mysteriously, his third-grade son bouncing with excitement as Pam had once done on her parents' front-porch glider, and on the cocktail table before their living-room fireplace, champagne cooling in a bucket beside a plate of ... dates. The occasion? "One One Two Three Five Eight," she told him happily when he failed to guess: "the only six-number Fibonacci in the century." "Get it, Dad?" Frank Jr. wanted to know: "One and one makes two, one and two makes three, two and three makes five, and three and five makes eight!" "You can pop *my* cork later," Pam murmured into his ear when he opened the bottle, and they happily fed each other the hors d'oeuvres.

By their Third Syzygy — Frank's fifty-fifth True Birthday, their Silver True Anniversary (a full two months later now than their Actual), and the twenty-second of the bloody D-Day landings of Allied invasion forces in Normandy — Frank Jr. was a high-school sophomore less interested in the Fibonacci series or any other academic subject than in getting his driver's license, his girlfriend's attention, and the Beatles' latest album; Pam was recovering from a hysterectomy; Frank Sr. had taken up golf and looked forward already to retirement in Florida, like Pam's parents. No orgasms that night, but contented toasts to "the Number of the Beast and then some" and the True end of their century's second third (its Actual .6666 ... n point, they would have enjoyed pointing out to young Frank if he ever stayed both home and still long enough to listen, was not 6/6/66 but the year's 243rd day, the last of August).

Life. Time. The Parkers subscribed to both, enjoying the former much more than not while the latter ran in any case. 7/7/77 ought to have been their luckiest day: The expense of their son's lackluster college education was behind them (Business Administration at the state university), as was the suspense of his being drafted for service in Vietnam. Now twenty-seven, the young man was employed as an uncertified accountant at, of all history-repeating places, a large Chevrolet-Buick dealership — across Chesapeake Bay in Baltimore, where he lived with his wife and baby daughter. Frank himself was retired and in good health though somewhat potbellied, eager to move south (Pam's parents, alas, had died) but resigned to waiting four more years for his wife's retirement and Social Security eligibility at sixty-two. They doted on their grandchild, wished that Baltimore weren't so long a drive and that their daughter-in-law weren't so bossy, their son so submissive. In the event, nothing special happened in their house that July Thursday except that Frank Sr. managed a usable morning erection despite his hypertrophic prostate; aided by a dollop of personal lubricant to counteract Pam's increasing vaginal dryness, they made pleasurable love — after which, lying in each other's arms three dozen years into their marriage, they agreed that every day since 3/8/38 had been a lucky day for them.

8/8/88 already! Frank's seventy-seventh T.B., the couple's forty-fourth T.A., Pam's sixty-ninth year! They've settled in a modest golf-oriented retirement community in southwest Florida and would normally be back north at this time of year, escaping the worst of the heat and hurricane season and visiting their granddaughter (now twelve) and her maritally unhappy dad. But Frank Sr. is in the hospital, pre-opping for removal of a cancerous kidney (he'll recover), and so they're toughing out their Fifth Syzygy on location. Pam limps in at Happy Hour (arthritic hip) with a smuggled split of Piper-Heidsieck and a zip-lock plastic bag of dates; they kiss, nibble, sip, sigh, hold hands, and reminisce about that Big One in Hilo back in '44, when she went Infinitely Isodigital.

"I wonder what ever happened to that handsome senior counselor at Po-Ko-No," she teases him, and crosses her heart: "the one that never laid a digit on me."

"Maybe he ran off with my alternative Alternator," Frank counters: "Arlene Whatsername. Did I ever tell you she was born on One Six Sixteen?"

In their latter age, Pam busies herself volunteering at the county library and playing bridge with other women in their retirement-community clubhouse. Frank, as his body weakens, has in his son's words "gone philosophical": He reads more than he ever did since college — nonfiction these days, mostly, of a speculative character, and *Scientific American* rather than *Time* and *Life* — and reflects upon what he reads, and articulates as best he can some of those reflections to his mate. His considered opinion (he endeavors to tell her now, lest he happen not to survive the impending surgery) is that like the actual alignment of planets, these calendrical syzygies and other date-patterns that he and she have taken such playful pleasure in remarking are as inherently insignificant as they are indeed remarkable and attractive to superstition. Human consciousness, Frank Parker has come to understand — indeed, animal consciousness in general — has evolved a penchant for noting patterns, symmetries, order; in the case of *Homo sapiens*, at least, this originally utilitarian penchant (no doubt a great aid to survival) tends to acquire a non-utilitarian, "gee-whiz" value as well: Certain patterns, symmetries, and coincidences become fascinating in themselves, aesthetically satisfying. Even non-superstitious folks like himself and Pam, if they have a bit of the obsessive-compulsive in their makeup, may take satisfaction in noting correspondences between such patterns and their significant life-events, and be tempted to jigger such correspondences themselves into a pattern — which may then become causative, influencing the course of their lives in the same way that superstition would maintain, but for opposite, non-mystical reasons.

"You know what?" said Pam (for so swiftly does time run, this pre-op tête-à-tête is already past tense): "Frank Junior is right."

Operation successful, but along with his left kidney the patient lost much of his appetite for both golf and food. Pam underwent a hip replacement, also reasonably successful. Frank Jr.'s wife's heart without warning infarcted; she died cursing God and her milquetoast husband. The latter within the year remarried (a divorcée five years his senior, with two teenagers of her own) and moved the "blended family" to Santa Fe, New Mexico, where he took a job in his new bride's father's accounting firm. Granddaughter Kimberly pleaded with her paternal grandparents to rescue her from her stepfamily; aside from their increasing frailty, however, they thought it best for the girl to accommodate to her new situation. In just a few short years, they reminded her, she would be off to college with their financial assistance and virtually on her own.

"Are we aware," Pam asked Frank on April Fools' Day, 1990 — their "corrective" forty-ninth anniversary — "that our Golden True Anniversary will also be my very first True Birthday?" For so indeed 9/1/91 would be, within the parameters of their game: a syzygy of a different stripe! They would celebrate it, they decided, by taking fifteen-year-old Kimberly to Paris, the first trip abroad for any of them if one discounts a Caribbean cruise the February past. The girl was thrilled, her grandparents if anything more so; the three made plans and shared their anticipatory excitement by telephone and email, crossing their fingers that the Persian Gulf War wouldn't spoil their adventure. More charmed by the date-game than her father had ever been, Kim proudly announced her "discovery" that the Golden Alternator 9/1/91 would in France become a Golden Palindrome: 1.9.91.

"That girl will amount to something," Frank proudly predicted. Amended Pam, "She already does." In mid-August, however, on the virtual eve of Kim's joining them in Florida for their departure from Miami to Paris, Pam suffered the first of what would be a pair of strokes. It left the right side of her body partially paralyzed, impaired her speech, canceled all happy plans, and constrained the "celebration" of her True seventy-second birthday and their Golden T.A. to a grim reversal of 8/8/88: Pam this time the pale and wheelchaired patient; Frank the faux-cheery singer of "Happy Birthday," their granddaughter harmonizing by long-distance telephone.

Through that fall and winter she regained some range of motion, but never substantially recovered and had little interest in continuing so helpless a life solely on the grounds of their surpassing love. Together they discussed, not for the first time, suicide. Neither had religious or, under the circumstances, moral objections; their impasse, which Pam declared unfair to her, was that Frank made clear his resolve to follow suit if she took her life, and she couldn't abide the idea of, in effect, killing him.

"Couldn't you have lied," she complained, "for my benefit?"

Her husband kissed her hand. "No."

On the last day of February, her second and fatal stroke resolved the issue for them before it could harden into resentment. The widower postponed his own termination to see the last rites through, for which his son and granddaughter, but not the rest of that family, flew out from Santa Fe (sister Jan was ten years dead of breast cancer; her grown children had never been close to their Aunt Pam and Uncle Frank). Kimberly, tears running, hugged her grandpa goodbye at the airport afterward and pointed out that by European notation, it being a leap year, Nana Pam had died on a five-digit Palindromic Alternator: 29.2.92. Frank wept gratefully into her hair.

Through half a dozen hollow subsequent "anniversaries," mere dumb habit has kept him alive after all, though ever more dispirited and asocial. Frank Jr.'s second marriage has disintegrated. Feeling herself well out of that household, Kim attends a branch of Florida State University, in part to be near her grandfather, and in fact their connection, though mainly electronic, remains the brightest thing in the old man's life. Hefty and sunny, more popular with her girlfriends than with the boys, she discusses with him her infrequent dates and other problems and adventures; she visits him on school holidays, tsks maternally at his bachelor housekeeping, and briskly sets to work amending it. And without fail she has noted and telephoned him on 9/2/92, 9/3/93, 9/4/94, 9/5/95, 9/6/96— not to wish him, grotesquely, a happy anniversary, but merely to let him know that she remembers.

It is the expectation of her sixth such call that has delayed Frank's calm agenda for this evening, his and Pam's fifty-sixth True Anniversary. The man is eighty-five, in pretty fair health but low on energy and no longer interested in the world or his protracted existence therein. His son and namesake, nearing fifty, currently manages a General Motors dealership back in the tidewater Maryland town where he was born and raised; the two exchange occasional cordial messages, but seldom intervisit. Granddaughter Kim, having spent the summer waitressing at a South Carolina beach resort and the Labor Day holiday with her bachelor father ("a worse housekeeper than you, Grandpa!"), should be returning to Orlando about now to begin her junior year in Hotel Management; as a special treat from her grandfather she'll spend part of this year as an exchange student in France. Usually she telephones in the early evening, just after the rates go down. Last September, though, come to think of it, she merely emailed him a hurried THINKING OF YOU, GRANDPA!!! KIM :-) XOXOXOX 9/6/96.

He has eaten, appetiteless, his microwaved dinner, cleaned up after, poured himself a second glass of red wine, made his preparations as aforenoted, and rechecked the computer (YOU HAVE NO NEW MAIL). Kim's recent messages have spoken of a boyfriend, one of her co-workers at the resort, whom she'll "miss like crazy" when they return to their separate colleges and has hoped to touch base with between her visit home and her rematriculation; perhaps in the unaccustomed excitement of romance she has lost track of the date. She knows that he goes to bed after the ten o'clock TV news; he'll give her till then, although his self-scheduled exit-time was 9:19. A touch muzzy-headed from the wine, as that hour approaches he changes into pajamas (wondering why), wakes the computer one last time, then shuts it down for good — a touch worried, a touch irritated. Call Frank Jr.? No need to worry him; he'll know nothing that Kim's grandfather doesn't. Call the college? She has no new phone number there yet. Her summer workplace, then. But this is silly; she simply though uncharacteristically forgot the date, or remembered but got somehow side-tracked.

Now it's half past nine, and he's annoyed: If he ends his life per program, the girl may blame herself for not having telephoned. So he'll leave her a message, reassuring her of his love and her non-responsibility for his final life-decision. All the same, she'll feel guilty for not having spoken with him one last time. So what? Life goes on, and on and on.

It's just a senseless pattern, he reminds himself: He doesn't have to turn himself off on 9/7/97 or any other "special" date. He can wait to be sure that Kim's okay, tease her for forgetting her old gramps, then do his business when he's sure she won't in any way blame herself — on 9/20, 10/2, whenever. *Not* doing himself in tonight simply for the sake of repudiating the Pattern, he recognizes, would be a backhanded way of acknowledging the thing's ongoing hold on him; but he has these other, perfectly reasonable reasons for delay . . .

Or is he merely temporizing, rationalizing the Pattern's grip? Mightn't his freedom be better demonstrated (to himself, as no one else will know or care) by going ahead now as planned, following the Pattern precisely in order to prove (to himself) that he's under no compulsion either to follow it or not?

Our Frank is sleepy: the uncustomary wine, the hour, the weight of these considerations. He could get a good night's sleep and kill himself *mañana*, with a clear head. He could do it next May, the sixty-fifth anniversary of his father's suicide. He could put it off till 9/9/99, his and Pam's fifty-eighth True Anniversary, his eighty-eighth True Birthday, and his brother's one hundredth Actual. He could for that matter put it off till the next 11/11/11, the ultimate full cycle, and be the first centenarian ever to autodestruct.

Sitting up in his half-empty bed at ten past eleven, with his left foot he pushes off and lets fall to the hardwood floor his right bedroom slipper, the better to scratch a little itch on his starboard instep. 9/9/99, he wearily supposes, would after all be the aptest date for his final Date: just before life's odometer rolls up straight zeroes, as the calendar's never does.

Or he could do the damned thing right now.

TENTH NIGHT

Inquired Graybard Storyteller of his enigmatic muse on the "evening" of Tuesday, September 20, 2001, as fleets of U.S. bombers and warships moved toward Afghanistan in pursuit of Osama bin Laden, his Al Qaeda camps and caves, and any more-or-less-innocent bystanding Afghans mistakable them for,

Can we talk?

Calm, cloudy, and cooler today in Tidewaterland, with off-and-on showers, the first rain since Fourth Night in that drought-stressed venue. On the deck of Ms. Wysiwyg's bright Imaginarium, our chap, attired as usual, sat under an overhang to stay warm and dry while his seemingly weather- and water-proof colleague took her pensive ease in a transparent toga out in the wet, her legs crossed openly in the masculine style, and watched raindrops drip from her laurel-wreathed brow into her wine.

Retsina, tonight's drink is, less resinous than most such but still too turpentinish for GB's taste, much as he appreciates its significance: a symbolic progress from the New World's vineyards to the Old's, from California, Maryland, and upstate New York through France, Iberia, and Italy to the muses' home turf and "a beaker full of the warm South," in Keats's phrase (though the retsina is chilled), "full of the true, the blushful Hippocrene" (though in hue the stuff more resembles, to Graybard's eyes, a urine specimen).

"Sure." She shook water from her hair and looked up brightly: "Last night's story filled the bill in most respects — plenty of numbers but no ball-busting math; lots of nines for Ninth Night Nine Nineteen, and even a Nine Nineteen in the story: that Pam character's birthdate in Nineteen Nineteen, which means she'd've been, let's see, eighty-two yesterday if she weren't a fictional character and hadn't died in Ninety-two. So okay, that Frank fellow's wine was a *rouge* like Keats's blushful beaker with its quote *purple-stainèd mouth*, instead of a nice crispy-clear *blanc*; that's certainly the guy's last-glass privilege, though even on my deathbed I'd want a wine that I can see through clearly." Twiddling a wreath-leaf: "My only complaint is that it was all so bloody *depressing*, Geeb — to which of course your reasonable reply will be What's cheery about Life's Last Act? We agree that autumn hath its splendors — Q.E.D. at asterisk-time last night! But winter? Blah. And while it goes without saying that *anything* may be grist for the muse's mill, this particular Saltyfresh Serviceable Surrogate guesses she's just about had it now with Autumnality, even, not to mention Terminality! Hence her sixth and last Ultimatum, to wit: *One more Falling-Leaf tale and she's out of here.* Okay?"

Responded Graybard when her speech was done, Yes, well: We'll just see — to himself reflecting that from his original ten-tale backlog only one item remained in any case; how they'd manage on Eleventh Night was anybody's guess. But none of that's what I meant, Wys, when I asked Can we talk?

"I think I know what you meant, mate. Drop a couple of those kalamata olives in your retsina, and let's drink up."

It would no longer surprise him, her still-dry visitor allowed, if she *did* know in advance what was on his mind, given her track-record in the Prescience way. Inasmuch as Reader most likely doesn't share her foreknowledge, however, and not even Teller himself is 100 percent sure of his present feelings, with her indulgence he'll have a go at articulating same in an Aside.

She shrugged permission, if any was needed, and raised her glass: "To the Patient Gentle Reader?"

Indeed: Here's looking at you, PGR.

Click of wineglasses. Sip of presumably potioned Hellenic paint-thinner, not bad once one's in the spirit of it, and further enhanced now by a light surface film of kalamata oil. Wysiwyg then contemplated by turns the drizzle-misted evening marsh and the tidy navel under her see-through toga while her client unburdened himself of the following

First-person aside to Patient Gentle Reader:

What was on my mind back there, see, Reader — when I asked her Can we talk? and she sidetracked me pronto with all that natter about nines and wines and No more Autumnality, even — was this, as we suspect *she* knows already but you maybe don't and no wonder, as I scarcely know how to put it into words myself even though putting stuff into words is my guy's line of work: That over the nine nights past and now this tenth of this so-called Hendecameron, with its serial *tête-à-têtes* and *cul-à-culs*, Intimate Inspirational Congresses, incremental asterisks and metaphorical whatevers, your Present Teller of these several tales has come to admire, trust, depend upon, eagerly anticipate the company of, relish his association with, and in general, uh, *feel strongly*, shall we say, for the shall-we-say idiosyncratic Ms. Wysiwyg, with not the foggiest notion of who she "really" is and has been, beyond her exotic current-and-doubtless-temporary role as Storyteller's Sexy Helper. That the woman's quirky combination of fetishistic transparency and programmatic opacity he finds both intriguing and frustrating, alluring and annoying, as she no doubt intends. In short — as she likely knew even before Yours Truly realized it himself — that self finds itself on the verge of *falling in love* with this kinky conundrum of a muse-figure, and while that state of affairs poses no moral problems, Q.E.D., it sure makes a chap wonder what he's getting into, so to speak, and where things go from Tenth Night, after which my guy's current inventory is exhausted. Not to mention after the night after that, assuming there'll be one as implied by this project's working title.

Just thought I'd get that said, mate. I mean, *look* at her, would you? Trim and fit, downright edible to behold, tack-sharp and bright as this wacko Imaginarium of hers or whomever's; independent-spirited and yet at one's service, provisionally and temporarily at least; laying on the asterisks with one hand, so to speak, and those serial nuisance ultimata with the other. I mean, like, wow! And yet there's something plaintive in this muse's numbers, no?, as in Will Wordsworth's aforecited Reaper's: something dark under all these lights, something hiding under all this transparency, don't you reckon?

Just thought I'd get that said.

"Get it said you did," said she
when the above Aside had gotten itself said, although in the nature
of Asides it'd not been said for her to hear, "and I'm much touched,
moved, flattered — *honored*, even, Geebs, that you feel what your Aside
said you feel."

Though of course (our man put in promptly here, anticipating what
she'd say next) it goes without saying that nothing necessarily *follows*
from your feelings about my said feelings . . .

"Correct." She downed her retsina, rose wetly from her chair, and
held out her left hand to him. "But that nothing *necessarily* follows
doesn't necessarily mean that nothing follows. What follows now, e.g.
and s.v.p., is our little creek-dip, okay? Followed by asterisks either in
or out of water, your call, followed by Something It's Time I Told You,
followed by a story that, whatever its other merits, will happen to meet
all six of the wench's damned-nuisance specifications." Which, as Reader may or may not recall, are that it be (1) reasonably recently written,
unlike Night One's *Help!* and *Landscape*; (2) 100 percent fiction, unlike
Night Two's *Ring* and Three's *Dead Cat, Floating Boy*; (3) having naught
to do, at least explicitly, with Ground Situations, Dramatic Vehicles,
and / or Stuck Storytellers, unlike Night Four's *Detective and Turtle*,
among others; (4) free of Sudden Recollection of Repressed-Memory Peccadillos in Protagonist's Long-Past Earlier Incarnations, unlike
Night Five's *The Rest of Your Life*; (5) no Stunts, Costumes, or Gimmicks indeed, devoid of even Totally Innocent Marital Guilt, unlike
Night Six's *Big Shrink*; and, finally, (6) unflavored by Autumnality, not
to mention Terminality, unlike several of the above plus Night Seven's
Extension, Eight's *And Then There's the One*, and Nine's *9999*. A tall
order, one might suppose, given Graybard's track record; but he rose
unhesitatingly at her beck, tossed off his own retsina, and saluted her
empty glass with his.

Clink.

Or, more precisely — the stemware being not glass but clear acrylic for outdoor use — *click*. She then shed her sopping toga and dripping wreath, he his still-dry usuals, and he joined her in the goose-
bump-raising drizzle and the still-warm saltyfresh creeklet — where,
however, they did not consummate their Metaphorical *Et Cetera* as on
the previous night, but at his bidding drew deep breath, ducked under,
and held on to the ladder's low steps and each other for as long as they

could, face to face and eyes wide open in what light came down from her bright HQ, as if to see who'd have to come up first for air ... until either want of same or the silliness of the contest fetched them up as one, gasping, coughing, laughing at themselves.

Well, now, said he when he could: *There's* a metaphor for you. For me, anyhow: In over my head?

"For us." She then waited for him to take his asterisked pleasure, whether then and there or elsewhen elsewhere; he her hers ditto, until with chuckle, sigh, and bearded chin-chuck she led the way up-ladder, cross-deck, and onto a double layer of large thick beach-towels spread conveniently under the overhang, out of the wet. Sprawled then thereupon at her elbow-propped and water-beaded ease, knees raised and feet some feet apart, with a level look that belied her faux-hearty barroom tone, "Anybody for a beakful of the Warm South?" she called as if to the room. "Snort o' the True Blushful?" Then, to him, in a voice that matched that look, "All yours, mate."

* * * * * * * * *

Somewhile later:
> Wuff! Whew.
> "Wuff and whew indeed."
> Wumpf.

And somewhile later yet,
speaking into the fine space between her shoulderblades: Something it's time you told me, I believe you said?

"Mm."

Had he entertained the hope that that something might prove to be that she quite reciprocated those feelings that he'd acknowledged Aside to the PGR, as her deportment — particularly in recent Nights and most especially in the course of their Intercourse — quite suggested? If so, *tant pis,* for "Never mind my feelings," she bade him now: "My feelings don't come into it." What it was time he knew, she went on, smiling sidelong at him (and Reader can imagine Present Teller's breath-bated suspense), was that for the several Nights past, never mind how many, there had been no capital-P Potion or -E Elixir in his wine. That whether she had secretly weaned him from it by reducing the dosage as their asterisks incremented, beginning maybe as early as Night Two or Three, or whether indeed there had *ever been* a literal Upgrade Elixir instead of the mere potent idea thereof—a notion-Potion, an inspiring metaphor for Inspiration that did the job and was *ipso facto* as good as real (like herself?), maybe *better* than real because free of side effects, ditto—none of that mattered. "The bottom line—"

Dearest daintiest deliciousest bottom line from here to Parnassus!

"If you say so. As *I* was saying, the bottom line"—she closed her eyes tight, gave her head a shake—"is the bottom line. Story?"

Story? Yes. Well. Collecting himself, no easy task: Here's one that *has* no bottom line—a circumstance with a whole new voltage on it now.

"Maybe. Title?"

Title. Yes. Well: As our plastic wineglasses said to each other earlier this evening,

Click

"Click?"

So reads their computer monitor when, in time, "Fred" and "Irma" haul themselves out of bed, wash up a bit, slip back into their undies, and — still nuzzling, patting, chuckling, sighing — go to check their email on Fred's already booted-up machine. Just that single uppercase imperative verb or sound-noun floating mid-screen, where normally the "desktop" would appear with its icons of their several files: HERS, HIS, SYSTEM, APPLICATIONS, FINANCES, HOUSE STUFF, INTERNET, ETC (their catch-all file). Surprised Irma, having pressed a key to disperse the screen-saver program and repeated aloud the word that oddly then appeared, calls Fred over to check it out, but the house cybercoach is as puzzled thereby as she. Since the thing's onscreen, however, and framed moreover in a bordered box, they take it to be a command or an invitation — anyhow an option button, like SAVE or CANCEL, not merely the name of the sound that their computer mouse makes when . . . well, when clicked.

So they click (Irm does) on CLICK, and up comes a familiar title, or in this case maybe subtitle — The Hypertextuality of Everyday Life — followed this time by a parenthesized and italicized instruction: (*Click on any word of the above*).

"Your turn," declares our Irma. That's not the woman's real name, any more than the man's is Fred; those are their "online" names, in a manner of speaking, for reasons presently to be made clear. Never mind, just now, their "real" names: They would involve us in too much background, personal history, all the stuff that real names import; we would never get on with the story. Sufficient to say that although these two are unmarried, they're coupled housemates of some years' standing, a pair of Baby-Boomer TINKs (Two Incomes, No Kids) of some ethnicity or other, not necessarily the same, and profession ditto — but never mind those, either. Sufficient to say that what they've just rolled out of the sack from (one of them perhaps more reluctantly than the other) is an extended session of makeup sex after an extended lovers' quarrel, the most serious of their coupleship: a quarrel currently truced but by no means yet resolved and maybe inherently unresolvable, although they're really working on it, fingers crossed.

A bit of background here, perhaps? That's Fred's uncharacteristic suggestion, to which Irma, uncharacteristically, forces herself to reply "Nope: Your turn is your turn. On with the story."

And so her friend — partner, mate, whatever — reaches from behind her to the mouse and, kissing her (glossy auburn) hair, clicks on <u>Hypertextuality</u>. (This parenthesized matter, they agree, is stuff that might be left out of or cut from The Fred and Irma Story — see below — but that they've agreed to put or leave in, at least for the present.) (In the opinion of one of them, there could be much more of it.) (In the opinion of the other, much less — but never mind.)

No surprise, Fred's selection: <u>Hypertextuality</u> is that (sub)title's obvious topic word, modified by the innocuous-seeming article before it and the homely prepositional phrase after (containing its own unexotic substantive [<u>Life</u>] with adjectival modifier [<u>Everyday</u>]). The man of them, one infers correctly, is the sort who gets right down to business, to the meat of the matter. Everybody knows, after all (or believes that he/she knows), what "everyday life" is, different as may be the everyday lives of Kuwaiti oil sheiks and of American felons serving life sentences in maximum-security prisons without possibility of parole (different, for that matter, as may be the everyday lives of FWFs [Friends Who Fornicate] when they're at their separate businesses). The term "hypertextuality" itself may or may not interest our Fred; he's computer-knowledgeable, but not computer-addicted. The phrase "everyday life," however, most certainly doesn't, in itself. The fellow's too busy *leading* (perhaps being led by?) his everyday life to be attracted to it as a subject. With the woman it's another story (possibly to come). But precisely because he hasn't associated something as fancy-sounding as "hypertextuality" with something as ordinary as "everyday life," the juxtaposition of the two piques Fred's curiosity. Not impossibly, for the man's no ignoramus (nor is his companion), he hears in it an echo of Sigmund Freud's provocatively titled 1904 essay *The Psychopathology of Everyday Life*. Everyday life psychopathological? (Try asking Irma, Fred.) (He will — another time.) Everyday life hypertextual? How so? In what sense? To find out, Fred has clicked on the implied proposition's most prominent but least certain term.

There are those (the computer script now declares in effect, along with most of the paragraph above) who out of mere orneriness will select one of the phrase's apparently insignificant elements — the The, for example, or the of — as if to say, "Gotcha! You said 'Click on any word ...'" The joke, however, if any, is on them: A good desk dictionary will list at least eight several senses of the homely word "the" in its adjectival function plus a ninth in its adverbial ("the sooner the better," etc.): twenty lines of fine-print definition in all, whereas the comparatively technical term just after it, "theanthropic," is nailed down in a mere three and a half. As for "of": no fewer than nineteen several definitions, in twenty-five lines of text, whereas the fancy word "oeuvre," just before it, is dispatched in a line and a half. Try "as," Fred, as in "As for 'of'"; try "for," Irm, or "or": The "simple" words you'll find hardest to define, while such technoglossy ones as "hypertextuality" ...

Well. F and friend have just been shown an example of it, no? The further texts that lie behind any presenting text. Look up (that is, click on) the innocent word "of," and you get a couple hundred words of explanation. Click on any one of those or any one of their several phrases and clauses, such as "phrases and clauses," and get hundreds more. Click on any of *those*, etc. etc. — until, given time and clicks enough, you will have "accessed" virtually the sum of language, the entire expressible world. That's hypertext, guys, in the sense meant here (there are other senses; see Hypertext): not the literal menus-of-menus and texts-behind-texts that one finds on CD-ROMs and other computer applications, but rather the all-but-infinite array of potential explanations, illustrations, associations, glosses and exempla, even stories, that may be said to lie not only behind any verbal formulation but behind any real-world image, scene, action, interaction. Enough said?

(If so, click EXIT; otherwise select any one of the four fore-going—image, scene, etc.—for further amplification.)

Restless Fred moves to click on <u>action</u> but defers to Irma (their joint mood is, as mentioned, still tentative just now; he's being more deferential than is his wont), who clicks on <u>scene</u> and sees what the Author/Narrator sees as he pens this: a (white adult male right) hand moving a (black MontBlanc Meisterstück 146 fountain) pen (left to right) across the (blue) lines of (three-ring looseleaf) paper in a (battered old) binder on a (large wooden former grade-school) worktable all but covered with the implements and detritus of the writer's trade. (Parenthesized elements in this case = amplifications that might indeed be cut but might instead well be "hypertexted" behind the bare-bones description, to be accessed on demand, just as yet further amplifications [not given, but perhaps hypertexted] might lie behind "white" "adult male," "MontBlanc" "Meisterstück," etc.) For example, to mention only some of the more conspicuous items: miscellaneous printed and manuscript pages, (thermal) coffee mug (of a certain design) on (cork) coaster, (annotated) desk calendar (displaying MAY), notebooks and notepads, the aforeconsulted (*American Heritage*) desk dictionary open to the "the" page (1333) on its (intricately handcarved Indian) table-stand, (Panasonic auto-stop electric) pencil sharpener (in need of emptying), (Sunbeam digital) clock (reading 9:47 AM), (AT&T 5500 cordless) telephone (in place on base unit), Kleenex box (Scott tissues, actually) half full (half empty?) ... *et cetera.* Beyond the table one sees the workroom's farther wall: two (curtained and venetian-blinded double-hung) windows, between them a (three-shelf) bookcase (not quite filled with books, framed photos, and knickknacks and) topped by a wall mirror. The mirror (left of center) gives back a view not of the viewer—fortunately, or we'd never get out of the loop and on with the story—but of the workroom door (presently closed against interruption) in the wall behind. (The two windows are closed, their figured curtains tied back, their blinds raised. Through them one sees first the green tops of foundation shrubbery [from which Irm infers, correctly, that it's a ground-floor room], then assorted trees [L] and a sward of lawn [R] in the middle distance, beyond which lies a substantial body of water, currently gray. Two wooded points of land can be seen extending into this waterway from the right-hand window's right-hand side, the first perhaps half a mile distant, an uncamouflaged gooseblind at its outboard end, the second perhaps a mile distant and all but obscured now by a light drizzle that also blurs the yet-more-distant horizontal where [gray] water meets [gray] sky.)

(Click on any of these items, including those in brackets.)

But "Enough already," says nudgy Fred, and commandeers the mouse to click action, whereupon some of the leaves on some of those trees move slightly in some breeze from some direction, the water-surface ripples, and across it a large waterfowl flaps languidly left to right, just clearing some sort of orange marker-float out there on his/her way . . . upstream, one reasonably supposes, given that the stretch beyond that bird and those two points seems open water.

"That's action?" Fred scoffs, and moves to click again, but determined Irma stays his mouse-hand with her free right (Irm's a southpaw) while she registers yet a few further details. Atop that bookcase, for example (and therefore doubled in the mirror), are (L to R:) a (ceramic-based) lamp, the carapace of a (medium-size horseshoe) crab, and a (Lucite-box-framed) photograph of three (well-dressed) people (L to R: an elderly man, a middle-aged man, and a younger woman) in (animated) conversation (at some sort of social function).

(Click on any detail, parenthesized or non-, in this scene.)

Irma springs for well-dressed — not nearly specific enough, by her lights, as a description of three people "at some sort of social function" in the photograph on the bookcase in the not-yet-fully-identified scene on their computer's video display terminal. With a really quite commendable effort of will, "Fred" restrains his impulse to utter some exasperated imprecation and snatch the freaking mouse from his freaking partner to freaking click Fast Freaking Forward, On with the Story, EXIT, QUIT, Whatever. Instead, he busses again his lover's (glossy) (auburn) hair, bids her "Have fun; I'll be futzing around outside, okay?," and (having slipped into jeans and T-shirt) clicks with his feet, so to speak, on the scene beyond his own workroom window.

Which twilit scene happens to be a small suburban back yard near the edge of the nation's troubled capital city, where this occasionally dysfunctional pair pursue their separate occupations: Mark the Expediter, as he has lately come to call himself; Valerie the Enhancer, ditto. Those are their "real" given names, if not really the real names of their jobs, and with the reader's permission (because all these digressions, suspensions, parentheses, and brackets are setting this Narrator's teeth on edge as well as Mark's) we'll just follow him out there for a bit while Val explores to her still-bruised heart's content the hypertextuality of everyday life.

Okay. How they got into that "Fred and Irma" business (Mark and I can reconstruct less distractedly now as he waves to a neighbor-lady and idly deadheads a few finished rhododendron blooms along their open side-porch) was as follows: They having pretty well burned out, through this late-May Sunday, their scorching quarrel of the day before — enough anyhow to make and eat together a weary but entirely civil dinner — after cleanup Mark had volunteered to show Valerie, as he had several times previously promised, some things he'd lately learned about accessing the Internet for purposes other than email; more specifically, about navigating the World Wide Web, and in particular (Valerie being Valerie, Mark Mark) about the deployment of "bookmarks" as shortcuts through that electronic labyrinth, the black hole of leisure and very antidote to spare time. Mark is, as aforenoted, no computer freak; the PC in his Expediter's office, their Macintosh at home, are tools, not toys, more versatile than fax machine and phone but more time-expensive, too, and — like dictionaries, encyclopedias, and hardware stores (this last in Mark's case; substitute department stores and supermarkets in Val's) — easier to get into than out of. Tactfully, tactfully (by his lights, anyhow) (the only lights he can finally steer by) — for they really were and are still burned, and their armistice is as fragile as it is heartfelt — he led her through the flashy homepage of their Internet service provider's program, actually encouraging her to sidetrack here and there in the What's New? and What's Cool? departments (she trying just as determinedly to blind her peripheral vision, as it were, and walk straight down the aisles, as it were, of those enticing menus) and then sampling a curious Web site that he had "bookmarked" two days earlier, before their disastrous Saturday excursion to the National Aquarium in Baltimore.

http://www.epiphs.art, it was addressed: the homepage of an anonymous oddball (Net-named "CNG") who offered a shifting menu of what he/she called "electronic epiphanies," or "e-piphs." On the Friday, that menu had comprised three entrees: (1) <u>Infinite Regression v. All-but-Interminable Digression</u>, (2) "<u>Flower in the Crannied Wall</u>," and (3) <u>The Hypertextuality of Everyday Life</u>. Mark had clicked on the curious-sounding second option and downloaded a spiel that at first interested but soon bored him, having to do with the relation between a short poem by Tennyson —

> Flower in the crannied wall,
> I pluck you out of your crannies,
> I hold you here, root and all, in my hand,
> Little flower — but *if* I could understand
> What you are, root and all, and all in all,
> I should know what God and man is.

— and the virtually endless reticulations of the World Wide Web. This time (that is, on this post-meridianal, post-prandial, post-quarrel but ante-makeup-sexual Sunday) the menu read (1) <u>The Coastline Measurement Problem and the Web</u>, (2) "<u>The Marquise went out at five</u>" (CNG seemed to favor quotations as second entries; this one was familiar to neither of our characters), and (3) <u>The Hypertextuality of Everyday Life</u>. That third item being the only carryover, M suggested they see what was what. V clicked on it — the entire title, as no option was then offered to select from among its component terms — and they found themselves involved in a bit of interactive "e-fiction" called "<u>Fred</u> and <u>Irma Go Shopping</u>," of which I'll make the same short work that they did:

Onscreen, the underlined items were "hot": i.e., highlighted as hypertext links to be clicked on as the interacting reader chose. Methodical Mark would have started with <u>Fred</u> and worked his way L to R, but Valerie, left-handing the mouse, went straight for <u>Irma</u>:

> Irma V., 43, <u>art-school</u> graduate, <u>divorced</u>, <u>no children</u>, currently employed as <u>enhancer</u> by small but thriving <u>graphics firm</u> in <u>Annapolis MD</u> while preparing show of her own computer-inspired <u>fractal art</u> for small but

well-regarded gallery in Baltimore. Commutes to work from modest but comfortable and well-appointed row-house in latter city's Bolton Hill neighborhood, 2 doors up from her latest lover, Fred M.

(*more on Irma*) (*on with story*)

"My turn?" Mark had asked at this point, and clicked on Fred M. before Valerie could choose from among divorced, no children, enhancer, latest, well-appointed rowhouse, and more.

Fred M., software expediter and current lover of Irma V.

(*more on Fred*) (*on with story*)

"That's the ticket," in Mark's opinion: "Who cares how old the stud is or where he majored in what? On with their story already."

"My friend the Expediter," Val had murmured warningly, having raised her free hand at his "Who cares?" Whereat her friend the Expediter (it was from here that they borrowed those job-titles for themselves: Valerie in fact does interior design and decoration for a suburban D.C. housing developer; Mark, a not-yet-successful novelist, does capsule texts on everything under the sun for a CD-ROM operation in College Park, distilling masses of info into style-free paragraphs of a couple hundred words), duly warned, had replied, "Sorry there: Enhance, enhance."

But she had humored him by clicking on on, whereupon the title reappeared with only its last term now highlighted: "Fred and Irma Go Shopping."

"Off we go," had invited M. But when the clicked link called up a three-option menu — Department Store, Supermarket, Other — V said "Uh-oh," and even Mark had recognized the too-perilous analogy to their debacle of the day before. Expediter and Enhancer in Supermarket, he with grocery list in one hand, pencil in other, and eye on watch, she already examining the (unlisted) radicchio and improvising new menu plans down the line . . .

"Unh-unh," he had agreed, and kissed her mouse-hand, then her mouth, then her throat. By unspoken agreement, bedward they'd headed, leaving the Mac to its screen-saver program (tropical fish, with bubbly sound effects). Somewhere later Valerie / Irma, re-undied, had returned to check for email; the marine fauna dispersed into cyberspace; there floated CLICK in place of CNG's unpursued interactive e-tale — and here we all are.

Rather, here's Valerie at Mark's workstation in their (detached suburban) house (V's studio is across the hall; unlike those FWFs Irma and Fred, our couple are committed [though unsanctified and unlegalized] life-partners, each with half equity in their jointly owned [commodious, well-appointed, 1960s-vintage] split-level in Silver Spring [MD]), and here are Mark and I out on the dusky porch, deadheading the rhodos while thinking hard and more or less in synch about certain similarities among (1) the sore subject of their Saturday set-to, (2) a certain aspect of their recent makeup sex, (3) the so-called Coastline Measurement Problem afore-optioned by CNG, (4) an analogous problem or aspect of storytelling, and (5) how it is, after all, to be a Self, not on the World Wide Web but in the wide web of the world. Can M think hard about five things at once? He can, more or less expeditiously, when his attention's engaged, plus (6) Zeno's famous paradox of Achilles and the Tortoise, plus (7) the difference between Socrates's trances and the Buddha's. Our chap is nothing if not efficient — a phrase worth pondering — and I'm enhancing his efficiency as worst I can, by impeding it. Valerie, meanwhile (at my off-screen prodding), has reluctantly torn her attention away from that photograph on that bookshelf in that creekside workroom in that onscreen scene hypertexted behind the word "scene" in the definition hypertexted behind Hypertextuality in CNG's menu-option (3) The Hypertextuality of Everyday Life, itself hypertexted the second time up behind the word CLICK. Twenty-year-old wedding-reception photo, she has learned it is, of (present) Narrator with (present) wife and (late) father at (post-)wedding do for (now-divorced) daughter and (then-) new son-in-law — and nothing accessible therebeyond. Interactivity is one thing, restless Reader; prying's another. Having lingered briefly on the shrub outside the RH window (*Viburnum burkwoodii*: grows to 6 ft [but here cropped to 4 for the sake of view and ventilation], clusters 3 in. wide, blooms in spring, zone 4, and it's a lucky wonder her professional eye didn't fix on those figured curtains, or we'd never have gotten her outside) and then on that waterfowl (great blue heron [*Ardea herodias*, not *coerulea*]) flapping languidly up-creek (off Chesapeake Bay, on Maryland's Eastern Shore, where Narrator pens these words as he has penned many others), she's "progressing" unhurriedly toward those two intriguing points of land in the farther distance but can't resist clicking en route on that orange marker-float out yonder near the creek channel:

> Marks an eel pot, 1 of 50 deployed in this particular tidal creek at this particular season by waterman Travis Pritchett of nearby Rock Hall MD in pursuit, so to speak, of "elvers": young eels born thousands of miles hence in the Sargasso Sea and now thronging instinctively back to the very same freshwater tributaries of the Chesapeake from which their parents migrated several years earlier to spawn them in mid-ocean: one of nature's most mysterious and powerful reproductive phenomena. Pritchett's catch will be processed locally for marketing either as seafood in Europe and Japan or as crab bait for Chesapeake watermen later in the season.

Travel-loving Val goes for Sargasso Sea, and there we'll leave her to circulate indefinitely with the spawning eels and other denizens of the sargassum while we click on item (1) some distance above: the sore subject of their Saturday set-to:

They love and cherish each other, this pair. Although neither is a physical knockout, each regards the other and her- or himself as satisfactorily attractive in face and form. Although neither can be called outstanding in his or her profession, both are entirely competent, and neither is particularly career-ambitious in her or his salaried job. Both enjoy their work and take an interest in their partner's. Most important, perhaps, although neither has a history of successful long-term relations with significant others, both have enough experience, insight, and un-arrogance to have smoothed their rougher edges, tempered their temperaments, developed their reciprocal forbearance, and in general recognized that at their ages and stages neither is likely to do better than they've currently done in the mate-finding way; indeed, that despite their sundry differences (at least some of which they've learned to regard as compensations for each other's shortcomings: See below), they are fortunately well matched in disposition, taste, and values. Neither drinks more than an occasional glass of wine at dinner, or smokes tobacco, or sleeps around, or fancies house-pets; both are borderline vegetarian, environmentally concerned, morally serious but unsanctimonious secular unenthusiastic Democrats. Mark has perhaps the quicker intelligence, the duller sensibility, the more various knowledge; Valerie perhaps the deeper understanding, the readier human insight, the sounder education. They've never quarreled over sex or money. Both wish they had children, but neither finally wants them. (Etc.— though that's really enough background for their Saturday set-to, no?)

They do have differences, of course: M enjoys socializing with others more than V does; she enjoys traveling more than he. He's the more liberal (or less frugal) with money; she's the more generous in the good-works way. He's less ready to take offense but also slower to put their occasional tiffs behind him. She leaves closet and cabinet doors ajar and will not learn how to load their dishwasher properly (by *his* standards) (and the user's manual's); he wears his socks and underwear for two days before changing (turning his briefs inside out the second day!) and often makes no effort to stifle his burps and farts when it's just the two of them. (Etc., although [etc.]) These lapses or anyhow disharmonies they've learned to live with, by and large. The difference that really drives each up her or his wall is the one herein amply hinted at already, if scarcely yet demonstrated: at its mildest, a tease- or sigh-provoker, a prompter of rolled eyes and of fingertips drummed on dashboard, chair arm, desk- or thigh-top; at its sorest . . .

Saturday. Their week's official work done and essential house-chores attended to, they had planned a drive up to nearby Baltimore to tour that city's Inner Harbor development, which they hadn't done in a while, and in particular the National Aquarium, which they'd never. After a not unreasonable detour to an upscale dry-goods emporium in the vast shopping complex at Four Corners, a quick shot from their house — where Val really did need to check patterns and prices of a certain sort of figured drapery material for a job-in-the-works (and, having done so, pointed out to Mark that there across the mall was a Radio Shack outlet where he could conveniently pick up the whatcha-callit-adapter that he, not she, insisted they needed for their sound system's FM antenna [while she popped into the next-door Hallmark place for just a sec to replenish their supply of oddball greeting cards, which was running low]) — they zipped from the D.C. Beltway up I-95 to Baltimore and reached Harbor Place in time for a pickup lunch about an hour past noon (no matter, as they'd had a latish breakfast)— hour and a half past noon, more like, since the main parking lots were full by that time, as Mark had fretsomely predicted, and so they had to park (quite) a few blocks away, and it wouldn't've made sense not to take a quick look-see at the new Oriole Park at Camden Yards that was such a hit with baseball fans and civic-architecture buffs alike, inasmuch as there it stood between their parking garage and the harbor and since their objective, after all (she reminded him when he put on his Fidget Face), wasn't to grab a sandwich, see a fish, and bolt for home, but to *tour* Harbor Place, right? Which really meant the city's harbor area, which surely included the erstwhile haunts of Babe Ruth and Edgar Allan Poe. They were on no timetable, for pity's sake!

Agreed, agreed — but he *was* a touch hungry, was Mr. Mark, and therefore maybe a touch off his feed, as it were, especially after that unscheduled and extended stop at Four Corners; and it was to be expected that the ticket line at the Aquarium might well be considerable, the day being both so fine and so advanced . . .

"So we'll catch the flight-flick at the IMAX theater in the Science Center instead," Val verbally shrugged; "or I'll stand in the Aquarium line while you fetch us something from the food pavilion, and then you stand while I do The Nature Company. What's the problem?"

The problem, in Mark's ever-warmer opinion, was — rather, the problems were — that (a) this constant sidetracking, this what's-the-rush digression, can take the edge off the main event by the time one gets to it, the way some restaurants lay on so many introductory courses and side dishes that one has no appetite for the entrée, or the way foreplay can sometimes be so protracted that (etc.). Having no timetable or deadlines doesn't mean having no agenda or priorities, wouldn't she agree? And (b) it wasn't as if this were just something that happened to happen today, or he'd have no grounds to grouse; it was the way certain people went at *everything*, from leaving for work in the morning to telling an anecdote. How often had he waited in their Volvo wagon to get going in time to drop her off at her Metro stop on the way to his office and finally gone back into the house and found her with one earring and one shoe on, making an impulsive last-minute phone call while simultaneously revising her DO list with one hand and rummaging in her purse with the other? (Valerie is a whiz at cradling the phone between ear and shoulder, a trick Mark can't manage even with one of those gizmos designed for the purpose.) How often had he been obliged to remind her, or to fight the urge to remind her, in mid-narrative in mid-dinner party, that the point of her story-in-regress was their little niece's *response* to what Val's sister's husband's mother had said when the tot had walked in on her in the guest-bath shower stall, not what that widow-lady's new Cuban-American boyfriend (whom she hadn't even met yet at the time of the incident) apparently does for a living? And (c) . . .

But he never reached (c) (*click on it if you're curious*), because by this time V was giving as good as she got, right there on the promenade under the old USS *Constellation*'s bowsprit, where their progress toward the distant tail of the National Aquarium ticket line caesura'd for this exchange. As for (a), damn it to hell, if in his (wrongheaded) opinion she was a Gemini who preferred appetizers to entrées both at table and (as he had more than once intimated) in bed, then *he* was a bullheaded whambamthankyouma'amer of a Taurus whose idea of foreplay was three minutes of heavyweight humping to ejaculation instead of two; and (b) who, because he himself had his hands full thinking and breathing simultaneously, couldn't imagine anyone's doing five things at once better than he could manage one; for the reason that (c) . . .

But she never reached (c), for the reason that (b) (now [b1]) reminded her that (b2) *his* idea of a joke was the punchline, his idea of a whodunit the last page, revealing who done it (no wonder he couldn't place his Middle-less novels even with an agent, much less with a publisher); and (a2) if she might presume to back up a bit, now that it occurred to her, his idea of a full agenda was a single item, his top priority always and only the bottom line, his eternal (and infernal) *Let's get on with the story* in fact a *Let's get* done *with the story*, for the reason that — (b3), she guessed, or maybe (a3), who gave a damn? — his idea of living life was the same, *Let's get done with it*, and every time she saw him ready and fidgeting in the car a full ten minutes earlier than he knew as well as she they needed to leave for work, she was tempted to suggest that they drive straight to the funeral parlor instead and *get done with it* (etc., okay? On to the freaking fish already!).

But they never reached the FF ticket line, far less the marine exhibits themselves, and that's a pity, inasmuch as in the 2.5 million recirculating gallons of scrupulously monitored exhibit-water in the National Aquarium's 130-odd tanks and pools are to be found some 10,000 specimens (eels included), concerning every one of which much of natural-historical interest might be said. Under the volatile circumstances, however, it is no doubt as well they didn't, for how could they imaginably have moved and paused harmoniously through the exhibits (Valerie tranced at the very first of them, Mark glancing already to see what's next, and next after that) without re-opening their quarrel? Which quarrel, mind, was still in noisy progress, if that's the right word, there under the *Constellation*'s mighty bowsprit — which bowsprit, at the time I tell of, extended halfway across the promenade from the vessel's prow toward the second-floor Indian restaurant above the first-floor Greek one in Harbor Place's Pratt Street pavilion, but which at the time of this telling is alas no longer there, nor are those restaurants, nor is the formidable frigate-of-war (sister ship of Boston's legendary Old Ironsides) whose bow that bowsprit sprits, or spritted, said vessel having been removed indefinitely for much-needed, long-overdue, and staggeringly expensive major overhaul — to the glancing amusement of passersby (the lovers' spectacular, hang-it-all-out quarrel, I mean, of course, not the *Constellation*'s shifting to some marine-repair Limbo) including Yours Truly, who happened just then to be passing by and sympathetically so saw and heard them, or a couple not unlike them, toe-to-toeing it, and who then or subsequently was inspired to imagine (etc.).

Embarrassed, wasted, desperate, and sore, tearfaced Valerie anon turned her back on the dear, congenitally blinkered bastard whom she so loves and just then despised and stomped off back toward the Light Street food pavilion and their parking garage, no objective in mind except breathing space and weeping room. Mark was damned if he'd go chasing after the beloved, indispensable, impossible, darling bitch, but he did so after all, sort of; anyhow trudged off in the same general direction, but made himself pause — Valerie-like, though in part to spite her — to half attend a juggling act in progress at the promenade's central plaza. Although he was as aware as was V (and no less alarmed) that the heavy artillery just fired could never be unfired and that it had perilously, perhaps mortally, wounded their connection, he nonetheless registered with glum admiration the jugglers' so-skillful routine: their incremental accumulation of difficulties and complications at a pace adroitly timed to maximize dramatic effect without straining audience attention past the point of diminishing returns, a business as tricky in its way as the juggling itself—and now he couldn't refind Valerie among the promenaders. Well, there was The Nature Company yonder; she had mentioned that. And beyond it were the food concessions; she must have been as hungry by then as he, but probably as appetiteless, too, from their wring-out. And somewhere beyond or among those concessions were the public restrooms, whereto she might have retreated to collect herself (V's better than M at self-collection), and beyond them the parking ramp. Did she have her car keys? Probably, in her purse; anyhow there were spares in a magnetic holder under the rear bumper-brace. Would she drive off without him, for spite? He doubted it, although she seemed more hurt and angry than he'd ever known her to be; anyhow the ramp-ticket was in his wallet— not that she mightn't pay the hefty lost-ticket fee just to strand him or, more likely, just to get out of there, with no thought of him either way. Most probably, however, she would just collapse in furious tears in the Volvo's passenger seat, poor sweetheart, and then lay into him with more of her inexcusable even if not wholly off-the-mark insults when he tried to make peace with her, the bitch.

Well, she wasn't in The Nature Company, where among the coruscating geodes and "Save the Rain Forest" stuff his attention was caught by one of those illuminated flat-projection earth-map clocks that show which parts of the planet are currently daylit and which in darkness (the East Coast of North America was just then correctly mid-afternoonish; darkness was racing already across Asia Minor, dawn approaching Kamchatka and Polynesia). What (momentarily) arrested him in this instance was not that vertiginous reminder of on-streaming time and the world's all-at-onceness, but rather the profusion of continental coastlines, necessarily much stylized in so small-scale a rendering, but considerably articulated all the same. Chesapeake Bay, for example—180-some miles in straight-line length, but with upward of 9,600 miles of tidal shoreline in its forty major rivers and their all-but-innumerable creeks and coves—was a simple nick up there between Washington and Philadelphia, yet quite distinguishable in shape and position from Delaware Bay, just above it; even the Delmarva Peninsula between them, no bigger here than a grain of rice, had overall its characteristic sand-flea shape. Framed nearby, as if to invite speculation on the contrast, was a large-scale, fine-grained aerial-photo map of Baltimore's Inner Harbor, every pier and building sharply resolved, including the no-longer-present-as-I-write-this *Constellation*: One could distinguish not only individual small watercraft paddling about or moored at the harbor bulkheads but their occupants as well, and strollers like varicolored sand-grains on the promenade.

One could not, however (Mark duly reflected, looking now for the exit to the food courts and/or for a glimpse of Valerie's ... yellow blouse, was it? Yes, he was almost certain: her yellow whatchacallit blouse with those thingamajigs on it and either a white skirt or white culottes; he couldn't recall which and saw no sign of either), even with so fine a resolution, distinguish male from female, for example, or black from white from Asian; much less identify himself and Valerie having it out under the frigate's bowsprit if they'd happened to be there doing that at that moment; much less yet see the thingumabobs on her whatchacallits and much less yet the individual whatsits on each thingumabob (etc.)—any more than the most finely drawn map of the Chesapeake could show every barnacle on every pile of every pier on every creeklet (etc.): the famous Coastline Measurement Problem afore-referred-to, in terms whereof the estuary's shore-length could as well be put at 96,000,000 miles as 9,600 (etc.). Which-all led him to, but not yet across, the verge of recognizing ...

Yellow blouse? Yes, out there by the Polish-sausage stand, but minus thingumajiggies and blousing a red-faced matron whose steatopygous buttocks were hugely sheathed in pink cotton warm-up pants (though there might, to be sure, he reminded himself, be a truly saintly spirit under all that [maybe helplessly genetic] grossness). *No Middles to his novels*, V had told him! His eye ever on the destination, not the getting there! Already figuring the server's tip while she lingered over the appetizer! No greater evidence of the degree of Pal Val's present pissed-offness than that she had been sidetracked neither in The Nature Company, as even he had briefly been, nor in the food court (where she would normally have been provisioning the pair of them, bless her, with goodies both for present consumption and for future relishment at home), nor on the pedestrian overpass to the parking ramp, where in other circumstances she was entirely capable of dawdling to contemplate at length the vehicular traffic below, the cumulus formations overhead, the observation elevators up-and-downing the Hyatt Regency façade nearby. Unless she had indeed withdrawn into a women's room (he had forgotten to locate the WCs; couldn't've done anything in that precinct anyhow except dumbly stand by), she must have beelined for the car, as did he now finally too.

No Valerie. Well, she was more liable than he to forgetting the level- and pillar-number of their parking slot. Not impossibly, in her present turbled state, she was wandering the ramps in a weepy rage. Plenty turbled himself, he walked up one level and down one, gave up the search as counterproductive, leaned against the Volvo's tailgate for some minutes, arms crossed, then trudged back, *faute de mieux*, toward the walkway / footbridge / overpass / whatever. Halfway across it he stopped, disconsolate, and simply stood — facing uptown, as it happened, but really seeing nothing beyond his distress.

Which let's consider himwith for just a paragraph. A physically healthy, mentally sound, well-educated, (usually) well-fed, comfortably housed and clothed, gainfully employed, not-unattractive early-fortyish middle-class male WASP American is at least temporarily on the outs with his housemate / girlfriend, a comparably advantaged and not-unattractive professional who has declared her opinion that he hasn't the talent to achieve his heart-of-hearts career aim and that this deficit is of a piece with one general characteristic of his that she finds objectionable. So Mr. Mark's pride is bruised, his self-respect ruffled, the future of his closest and most valued personal relationship uncertain indeed. *So what?* he has asked himself before any of us can ask him. The world comprises approximately 4.7 zillion more mattersome matters, from saving the tropical rain forests to finding money enough in the chaotic post-Soviet Russian economy to bring their fiscally stranded cosmonauts back to earth. Not that love and loss, or commitment and (potential) estrangement, aren't serious even among Volvo-driving yuppies, but really, what of real consequence is at stake here? If this were fiction (the wannabe writer asked himself), a made-up story, why should anyone give a damn?

Well, it *wasn't* fiction, from Mark's perspective, although out of aspirant-professional habit he couldn't help considering (as he resumed his troubled path-retracement back to and through the Light Street pavilion in search of his dear damned Valerie) how, if it were, it ought properly to end. Reconciliation? On what terms? Uneasy armistice? Virtual divorce? In each case, signifying what of interest to a reader who presumes the characters and situation to be imaginary?

From *our* point of view, of course, they *are* imaginary, and so these questions immediately apply (in a proper story they would never have come up; bear in mind that it was heart-hurt Mark who raised them) and shall be duly though not immediately addressed. Even their alleged-ly Middle-challenged poser understood, however — as he rescanned in vain the food concessions and monitored for a fruitless while the traffic to and from the women's room after availing himself of the men's — that more's at stake here than the ups and downs of early-middle-aged Baby-Boomer love. Not until "tomorrow" (the Sun. following this sore Sat.) will CNG's interactive e-fiction serendipitously supply them the terms "Expediter" and "Enhancer" to shorthand the characterological differences that erupted under the *Constellation*'s awesome bowsprit; but already back there on the footbridge Mark sensed that the conflict here is larger than any temperamental incompatibility between "Fred" and "Irma" or himself and Val: It's between fundamentally opposite views of and modes of dealing with the infinitely complex nature of reality.

Valerie sensed that, too; she was, indeed, already deep into the pondering thereof when, almost simultaneously, she espied him ap-proaching from the second-level fooderies and he her at a railing-side table on the open deck out there overlooking the promenade. So far from roaming the ramps in a weepy blind rage or storming off alone in the Volvo (Val's better than Mark, we remember, at shrugging off their infrequent blowups; he himself tends to forget that and to project from his own distress), our yellow-bloused Enhancer, her chair tipped back and feet propped on balcony rail, was finishing off a chocolate-choco-late-chip frozen-yogurt waffle cone while simultaneously (a) teaching her sumbitch lover a lesson by neither fleeing nor chasing after him; (b) facilitating their reunion by staying put, as her mother had taught her to do in little-girlhood if "lost" in, say, a department store or su-permarket; and (c) calming her still-roused adrenaline with a spot of yogurt while keeping an eye out for friend M and at the same time considering, in a preliminary way, his criticisms of her and the differ-ences, as she saw them, between Socrates's famous occasional "tranc-es," the Buddha's, and her own. They had in common, those trances, a self-forgetfulness, a putting of circumambient busyness on hold in favor of extraordinary concentration. But Buddha under the bo tree was transcendently *meditating*, thinking *about* nothing in particular while subsuming his ego-self into the cosmic "Buddha self"; Socrates, tranced in the agora or come upon by his protégés stock-still in some Athenian side street, was strenuously *contemplating*, presumably in finely honed logical terms, such uppercase concepts as Knowledge, Reality, Justice, and Virtue. Herself, however — beguiled indefinitely by ... by the hypertextuality of everyday life, we might as well say, as encountered in the very first fish tank in the National Aquarium, or in the book beside the book up-shelf from the book that she had gone to fetch from the library stacks, or on the counter across from the counter in the department en route to the department that she had been vectored toward in the Wal-Mart next door to the supermarket that she was finally aiming for — was not so much meditating or contemplating as *fascinating*: being bemused and fascinated by the contiguities, complexities, interscalar resonances, and virtually endless multifariousness of the world, while at the same time often doing pretty damned efficiently several things at once.

"*Damn*," said Mark, hands on hips on deck beside her. "Damn and damn."

"The same," came back his unfazed friend. "That said, is it on with our day or on with our spat?"

"Spat!" had all but spat more-than-ever-now-pissed-off M.

"Pity." Val gave her (glossy auburn) hair a toss and licked a drip from her (waffle) cone. "I thought *you* were the big mover-onner and I was the overdweller-on-things. Lick?"

"No, thank you. There's a difference between moving on and hit-and-run driving, Val."

"Shall we discuss that difference?" More a challenge than a cordial invitation.

"No, thank you. Because what happened back there was no accident."

"So let's discuss *that*: its non-accidentality."

"No, thank you very much," the fire gone out of him. "Because there'd be no bloody end to it. Let's go the hell home."

But "Not so fast, buster," had countered Ms. Valerie, and although they did in fact then go the hell home after all, they ventilated reciprocally all the way, each charging the other now with spoiling the day. Through that evening, too, they had kept scarifyingly at it, heartsick Mark from time to time declaring, "What it all comes down to . . .," and tearful Valerie being damned if she'd let him shortcut to that bottom line before he'd had his nose thoroughly rubbed en route in this, that, and the other. Exhausted half-sleep, as far apart as manageable in their king-size bed; then a grumpy, burned-out Sunday, both parties by that time more saddened and alarmed than angry, each therapeutically pursuing her or his separate business till Happy Hour — which wasn't, but which at least brought them civilly together as was their custom for their (single) glass of wine with a bit of an hors d'oeuvre, over which they exchanged tentative, strained apologies, then apologies less strained and tentative. Through dinner prep, each guardedly conceded a measure of truth in the other's bill of complaints; through dinner itself (with, uncharacteristically, a second glass of wine, much diluted with club soda), a measure less guarded and more generous. Thereafter, by way of goodwill respite from the subject, M had offered to show V that business he'd mentioned sometime earlier about navigating the World Wide Web. She had welcomed the diversion; they had booted up Mark's Macintosh, shortcut to CNG's e-piphanies homepage with its e-tale of Expediter Fred and Enhancer Irma; had aborted it early in favor of makeup sex (etc.) — and here they are.

Mm-hm. And where is that, exactly?

That exactly is in separate rooms of their (jointly owned, jointly tenanted) Silver Spring house and likewise in their extraordinarily strained but by no means severed connection. More exactly yet, it is (a) in Mark's case, on their pleasant, now-dark side porch, where — having thought hard and efficiently about those five or seven inter-related matters aforelisted (Saturday set-to, makeup sex, Coastline Measurement Problem, analogous aspect of storytelling, selfhood in the world's wide web, etc.) — in a sudden access of loving appreciation of his companion and their indispensable differences he turns from his idle rhododendron-tending to hurry herward with the aim of em-bracing her and ardently reaffirming that she is not only to him indis-pensable but by him treasured, and that he is determined to temper his maddening get-on-with-itness with as much of her wait-let's-explore-the-associationsness as his nature permits. And (b) in Valerie's case, in Mark's workroom, where — having floated a fascinated while in the Sargasso Sea of everyday life's virtual hypertextuality (but at no time so bemused thereby as to lose sight of the subject of their Saturday set-to) — in a sudden access of loving etc. she bolts up from Mark's Mac to hurry himward with corresponding intent. The physical halfway point thembetween happens to be the fourth-from-bottom step of the staircase connecting their house's ground floor (living room, dining room, kitchen/breakfast room, lavatory, front and rear entry halls, side porch, attached garage) and its second (main bedroom and bath, V's and M's separate workrooms with hallway and #2 bath between, library-loft [accessible from main BR] over garage) (additionally, in basement and thus irrelevant to their projectable rendezvous: TV/guestroom, workshop, utility room). Where they'll actually meet is another matter, perhaps suspendable while Narrator tidies a few loose ends. To wit:

— Any reasonable reader's suspicions to the contrary notwithstanding, "CNG" stands in this context not for Compressed Natural Gas, but rather for Center of Narrative Gravity: in a made-up story, the author's narrative viewpoint; in real life-in-the-world, however, the self itself, of which more presently, unless it's clicked on now ...

— Presently, then. Meanwhile, as to the aforedemonstrated essential difference between Ms. Valerie's sensibility and Mr. Mark's, it is nowhere more manifest than in the way each, in the other's opinion, tells a story. "Anna train squish" is how Val claims Mark would render Leo Tolstoy's *Anna Karenina*; indeed, given the man's Middle-challengedness, she suspects he might skip the train. She, on the other hand (claims he, whether teasingly or in their Saturday Set-To mode), would never get beyond Count Tolstoy's famous opening sentence — "Happy families are all alike," etc. — indeed, would never get through, much less past it, inasmuch as she would need to pause to explore such counter-evidence as that her family and Mark's, for example, while both prevailingly quite "happy," are as different in nearly every other respect as aardvarks and zebras; and once having clicked on Mark's family, or equally on hers (or, for that matter, on aardvarks

or zebras), she would most likely never get *back* to Tolstoy's
proposition, not to mention on to its second half and the
eight-part novel therebeyond.

— Myself, I'm on both their sides in this matter, not only because M and V seem equally reasonable, decent, harmless
souls, but also because their tendencies represent contrary
narrative impulses of equal validity and importance. A satis-
fyingly told story requires enough "Valerie"— that is, enough
detail, amplification, and analysis — to give it clarity, texture,
solidity, verisimilitude, and empathetic effect. It requires
equally enough "Mark"— i.e., efficiently directed forward
motion, "profluence," on-with-the-storyness — for coher-
ence, anti-tedium, and dramatic effect. In successful instances, a right balance is found for the purpose (and adjusted for
alternative purposes). In unsuccessful instances ...

Friend of Valerie and Mark's: So, how'd your vacation go, guys?

M: Cool: Spain in ten days.

V: Really terrific, what little we got to see. The very first morning, for example, in Ávila — Do you know Ávila? Saint Teresa and all
that?— we were in a Parador Nacional, just outside the old city wall.
You've stayed in the Spanish *paradores*, right? So, anyhow, the one in
Ávila's this fifteenth-century palace called Piedras Albas ('cause that's
what it's made of, white stones from [etc., *never getting past the breakfast* churros, *inasmuch as "hypertexted" behind them, for Valerie, lies
all of Spanish history, culture, geography, and the rest, inseparable from
the rest of Europe's and the world's. Mark had had practically to drag the
rapt, protesting woman out of that stern and splendid place, to get on
with their itinerary*]) ...

— So what? you ask, unless one happens to take some professional interest in storytelling, which you, for one, do not?
Thanks for clicking on that Frequently Asked Question,
reply CNG and I: The "so what" is that that same right-bal-
ance-for-the-purpose finding applies to the measurement of
coastlines, the appropriate scaling of maps, and — hold that
clicker — not only interpersonal relations, Q.E.D., but *intra*-
personal ones as well.

<u>Intrapersonal relations?</u>

Thanks again, and yes indeed. For what is Valerie, finally, what is Mark, what are you and what am I — in short, what is <u>the self itself</u>, if not what has been aptly called a "posited center of narrative gravity" that, in order to function in and not be over-whelmed by the chaotically instreaming flood of sense-data, continuously notices, ignores, associates, distinguishes, categorizes, prioritizes, hypothesizes, and selectively remembers and forgets; that continuously spins trial scenarios, telling itself stories about who it is and what it's up to, who others are and what they're up to; that finally *is*, if it is anything, those continuously revised, continuously edited stories. In sum, what we're dealing with here is no trifling or merely academic matter, friends: Finding, maintaining, and forever adjusting from occasion to occasion an appropriate balance between the "Mark" in each of us and the "Valerie" ditto is of the very essence of our selfhood, our being in the world. We warmly therefore hope, do CNG&I (click on that & and see it turn into an =, + much <u>more</u> on intrapersonal relations), that that couple work things out, <u>whenever</u> and <u>wherever</u> they recouple.

<u>When</u>. One short paragraph from now, it will turn out, although given the infinite subdivisibility of time, space, and narrative (not to mention <u>The Hypertextuality of Everyday Life</u>), it could as readily be ten novels hence or never. See <u>Zeno's paradoxes</u> of time and motion; see swift <u>Achilles</u> close forever upon the tortoise; see <u>Spot run</u> . . .

<u>Where</u>. Not on that fourth-step-from-the-bottom *Mittelpunkt*, it turns out, but back where this story of them started. Mark (inescapably himself even when determined to be more Val-ish) is off the porch and through the dining room and up the staircase and into the upstairs hallway by the time Valerie (who, decidedly herself even after deciding to be more Mark-like, has stepped from M's workroom first into the #2 bathroom to do a thing to her hair or face before hurrying porchward, then into their bedroom to slip a thigh-length T-shirt over her undies in case the neighbor-lady's out there gardening by streetlight, then back into M's workroom to exit the Internet so that their access-meter won't run on while they finish making up, which could take a happy while), hearing him hurrying herward, re-rises from Mark's Macintosh to meet its open-armed owner with open arms.

To her (glossy) (auburn) hair he groans, "I love you so damned much!"

To his (right) collarbone she murmurs, "I love you more."

They then vow (etc.), and one thing sweetly segues to another right there on the workroom's (Berber) wall-to-wall, while the screen saver's tropical fish and seahorses burble soothingly per program themabove.

— *The Marquise Went Out at Five* (*La Marquise Sortit à Cinq Heures*) is the title of a 1961 novel by the French writer Claude Mauriac and a refrain in the Chilean novelist José Donoso's 1984 opus *Casa de Campo* (*A House in the Country*). The line comes from the French poet and critic Paul Valéry, who remarked in effect that he could never write a novel because of the *arbitrariness*, the vertiginous *contingency*, of such a "prosaic" but inescapable opening line as, say, "The Marquise went out at five"—for the rigorous M. Valéry, a paralyzing toe-dip into what might be called the hypertextuality of everyday life.

Not too fast there, Mark. Not too slow there, Val. That's got it, guys; that's got it . . . (so "CNG" [= I / you / eachandallofus] encourages them from the hyperspatial wings, until agile Valerie lifts one [long] [lithe] [cinnamon-tan] leg up and with her [left] [great] toe gives the Mac's master switch a

ELEVENTH NIGHT

"Endings,"
the male character here called Graybard imagines the female character
here called Wysiwyg saying, with distaste, when that pair re-rendez-
vouses in her see-through dwelling-space at 9:11 "PM" on Friday, September 21, 2001—the eleventh and presumably final "night" of their
Hendecameron: "Blah."

Mm?

Toss of elaborately blond-wigged head. Frown at dark breezeless
night-marsh. "Dénouements, wind-ups, finales—blah. That was my
favorite thing about last night's *Click* story: no proper ending, just a
mid-sentence click-off. Amen!"

Yes, well. But not just *any* old mid-sentence, right? The sentence
that would've been the closing sentence anyhow, as we daresay you noticed. He salutes her with his bubbled champagne-flute. Much obliged
for your assistance, Miz Muse, as always. Click?

Passive. Distracted. "I guess. Yeah, sure: click. To eleven nights
without chardonnay?"

Better yet, how about *to us?*

Regarding him across their tipped glasses as they sip: "And who
might *that* be, Geeb?"

Aha: the Big Question. Stalling for time (he says aloud, as if reading from text while stalling for time), he compliments his inspirer on
her smashing Eleventh Night costume, with the frills whereof she has

been fidgeting through this dialogue: Art Nouveau gauze draperies and Gibson Girl hair-thing with tastefully scattered red leaves, like the "Autumn" panel of an Alphonse Mucha *Seasons* series, circa 1910.

"She begs his pardon?"

Turn-of-last-century poster-artist, Prague and London, as she doubtless knows, having quite possibly inspired and maybe even modeled for him in one of her earlier luscious incarnations. Or are you strictly a lit-lady?

Unlipsticked lips compressed; fine unplucked eyebrows shrugged. "You tell me."

"You understand what a fix we're in, yes?"
his dispatcher had asked him, in effect, that cloudywarm "morning" (i.e., less than half an hour past, at 9:00 AM by the clock on Original Author's writing-table. "What a narrative corner we've painted ourselves into, with a little help from your peekaboo pal?"

Without replying, Graybard stood by: his job-description.

"All I wanted, all we needed, was a bit of a frame-tale to connect those eleven miscellaneous items and make them into a *book* instead of a mere collection, right? So we come up with this wacko Wysiwyg/Muse/Imaginarium idea and decide to give it a spin, see whether it'll fly, never mind the mixed metaphor—but then *wham!*, along comes Nine Eleven, and suddenly it's a whole nasty new world out there, and how're we supposed to float a butcher's dozen irrelevant stories about Autumnality and Innocent Marital Guilt and Stuck Storytellers et cet., now that big-time shit has hit the national fan and Apocalypse has moved in just around the corner?"

Butcher's dozen?

"Baker adds one for good measure; butcher lops off excess lard. So Miss Wys comes to our rescue by defending the relevance of Irrelevance and proposing an eleven-night Hendecameron, but then with her other hand she ups the ante by disqualifying *Help!* as a story, which left us with ten tales for eleven nights; but la-dee-da, we figured we'd cross that narrative bridge when we came to it, so along you guys go with the Come-and-Get-It costumes and serial No-Nos and saltyfresh skinnydips and incremental asterisks and occasional teasers like those Fourth Night *Shabbos* candles, and never mind who the chick Really Is and where she came from and what she's up to in that flaky *pied-à-mer* of hers with its see-through everythings and whether she grocery-shops and cooks and cleans and does laundry in there or just pours white wine and spreads her Metaphorical legs at story-time: Let's go along for the ride, so to speak, we figure, and see where it takes us. So the nights go by and the wines get sipped and the muse gets shagged and the tales get told, and next thing we know it's Eleventh Night! Summer's over and so's the party; the Empire's at war again, with no well-defined enemy and a clutch of ever-uneasier allies; orgies of flag-waving and budget-busting, but not a clue to when where and how the next terrorist mega-shoe will drop on the US of A — any more than you and I have a clue how to wind this gig up and get offstage without egg on our faces. Ayiyi! End of uncharacteristic Authorial Outburst."

Mm-hm. Ten Nights and Good Night, maybe?

"Very funny. Getcherass out of here now, s.v.p., and go save ours — and a good *Shabbos* to Miz Whoeversheis."

Shabbat, I'm told one says nowadays: Sephardic instead of Ashkenazi?

"*Shabbat* shmabbat: Pen's filled, mate; computer's booted up; *hasta la vista* and may the Force be with you. Go fetch us a finale, okay?"

Tall order, but one does what one can, and so — while an uncomfortable alliance is forged between outraged America, volatile Pakistan, and our former enemies in the Afghan Northern Alliance; and bombs are readied for dropping on the noxious Taliban (our once-upon-a-time Afghan allies) and on Osama bin Laden's cave-dwelling Al Qaeda terrorists; and prospects for any sort of Israeli-Palestinian accord go up in smoke and down the drain; and life in the USA becomes less convenient, more constrained and anxious, for what bids to be a *very* long time to come, now that its vulnerability has been so painfully exposed — our Graybard treks once more (and finally?) next door, in a manner of speaking, to his muse's sanctum, reflecting gravely as he treks that it is, after all, perhaps not the worst of times to have most of one's life behind one; to be on one's actuarial Home Stretch; to be, in a word, *Autumnal* . . .

As if privy to all the above,
his odd collaborator awaits him in the aforedescribed Art Nouveau get-up on her storied and once again Sabbath-candled deck, an inverted champagne-flute beside each candlestick and an unopened bottle

of Mumm's *brut* ice-bucketed beside — the whole scene garnished, like her gown and hair, with red and yellow leaves.

Sweetgum, he'd guess.

"My favorite leaf." She twirls one idly between thumb and forefinger, gestures with it at the champagne: "Why can't they put this stuff in clear glass bottles? Anyhow, pop my cork whenever you're ready, Geeb — over the railing, please."

Her mirthless tone and expression belie the feeble double-entendres. Aiming marshward, our man obligingly works the mushroom-shaped cork with his thumbtips until the bottle fires like a sunset gun and arcs its stopper out into the dusk. Biodegradable, he supposes as it plicks into the creek.

"Like the rest of us." She holds out her glass for filling. "I notice we've switched to narrative present tenses."

I noticed that, too. My guess would be that that's because past-time narration implies a present from which Narrator can retrospect, and *that* implies that he's aware of what happened next back then and how the story ended. It's all history already except the telling. Whereas in *our* case . . . but hey, I just work here: What do I know?

"Same here, and thanks for the lecture." Frowning at her glass, at the nightscene, "*Endings,*" she then complains as aforenarrated, and goes on to declare her dissatisfaction with the wind-ups of, e.g., those three first-magnitude narrative navigation stars invoked in this Hendecameron's Invocation: Homer's *Odyssey*, "Scheherazade's" *Thousand Nights and a Night*, and Boccaccio's *Decameron*: "So okay: The big Wandering Hero gets back to his faithful missus and grown-up son after a decade of whacking Trojans and burning their city and another decade trying to get home — thousands dead and the world turned upside down, just because his neighbor-king's wife dropped her drawers for visiting royalty! So much for the yarn's beginning, and no wonder the word *Trojans* makes most folks think of a brand of condoms. But never mind all that, and never mind that most of the guy's ten-year trek consists of wandering from the marital straight and narrow: one whole year in the sack with Circe and seven with Calypso, so only two of actually sailing from Troy to Ithaca and losing all his shipmates along the way, while Faithful Wifey keeps her legs together and stalls her lamebrain suitors with that weaving-unweaving trick, which they'd've caught on to in three days instead of three years if they hadn't been drinking up the winecellar and humping the housemaids. No: What bugs me is that after Mister Trickydick gets his free ride home from Phaeacia to Ithaca—about which I could say plenty, but never mind—and strings his big macho bow that those wussy suitors couldn't even bend, it's not enough for him to slaughter them all for partying hard at his expense: He has to hang the poor serving-pussies as well—a round dozen of them, just on old Rat-Fink Eurycleia's say-so: no Due Process, not even any questions asked! Strings 'em up like thrushes in a net, Homer says, and I quote: *They held their heads in a row, and about them all / There were nooses, that they might die most piteously. / A little while they struggled with their feet, but not for long*—the cruelest lines in the whole bloody epic, for my money—all so Big O can give his long-time-no-see bed-mate the first big O she's had in twenty years. I swear! I swear!"

Well . . .

"And some say the Odyssey was composed by a woman? Not bloody likely!"

Yes, well . . .

"And okay, so your pal Scheherazade puts her life on the line and fucks the Sultan to keep him from raping and butchering a virgin per night as he's been doing for three years already, and she spins her thousand nightsworth of stories and bears him three sons no daughters and finally pleads for her life on their behalf—"

I believe we've covered this ground already, Wys: no particular sign that she *loves* the guy, et cet. (although it's pretty clear that Shahryar has come to love *her*), and not a hint of remorse for his having popped her thousand predecessors . . .

"Worse! They marry off her kid sister to his kid brother, the Butcher of Samarkand, who'd been matching Shahryar virgin for virgin before Scheherazade came onstage and has gone on popping 'em right through the Thousand and One Nights because Big Bro hasn't bothered to spread the news of his own moratorium; so poor Dunyazade gets to be the blushing bride of an even more monstrous serial rapist-murderer than her big sister's bridegroom! And we're supposed to applaud their double wedding as a happy ending? It makes me want to puke!"

Refill?

"Fuck Homer! Fuck Scheherazade! Fuck Boccaccio and his fucking rich lords and ladies who don't give a flying fuck about the Black Death that's killing half of Florence, as long as they can play their flirty little games and tell their naughty little stories and be waited on hand and foot by their lucky servants, and then la-dee-da, wasn't that *fun*, guys; let's do it again next time the world ends! Jee-*sus*, excuse the expression!"

Yes, well, Wys . . .

Glass extended: "Hit me again, Sam. Yes well what?"

He has never seen her so *agitato* — and that not only, as it seems to him, from her exception to those literary monuments, which he suspects of being more the occasion than the cause of her distress. Refilling her glass (he has not yet half finished his own), Well, he protests in those old taletellers' defense, *autres temps, autres moeurs*, for one thing; it's to be expected that texts from a patriarchal time and place will have their patriarchal aspects — or, in Boccaccio's case, their aristocratic aspects.

She slugs her champagne. "Do tell."

What's quite wonderful, I needn't remind you, is that gallery of formidable women, especially in Homer: Penelope obviously, but also spunky Princess Nausicaa and her mom, Queen Arete, not to mention Circe and Calypso, right on up to the goddess Athene.

"Always subservient to Boss-Man Zeus."

Well, yes, but on a *very* long leash. And Scheherazade of course takes on the bloody patriarch with the only weapons in her arsenal, sex and storytelling, and while she can't turn the place into a feminist utopia or even bring the beastly brothers to justice, at least she and Dunyazade defang them.

"For the time being. How long will sex and storytelling keep them distracted?"

A lot longer than ten nights and a night, we bet. As for Boccaccio, those ladies of his are no wussies either, as I remember: The whole gig is Pampinea's idea, and as the make-pretend crown passes from head to head, the queens- and kings-for-a-day rule with equal authority and match each other story for story. Granted that the servants are servants and the gentry gentry, you'll admit that genderwise it's an egalitarian aristocracy, making the best of a horror show that they can do absolutely nothing about.

"Well: They could at least *acknowledge* it from time to time, for pity's sake, the way we've acknowledged what's been going on Out There while we futz around here." More calmly, "But I know what you mean, Geeb."

Of course you do; and I know what *you* mean, Wys. But it's you who taught *me* about the relevance of Irrelevance in these situations. If we're going to fuck Homer and Scheherazade and company, I say let's do it gratefully, not dismissively. You take the two gents and I'll take the lady — if she's so inclined?

To his most agreeable surprise,
"She's so inclined," replies the female entity here called Wysiwyg. She sets down her flute, holds out her hand to him, and for the first time this evening smiles. "Help me out of this silly rig, if *you're* inclined, and let's rack up the asterisks — after which, you and I have serious narrative business to take care of."

Indeed: serious enough, one would think, that its anticipation might, if not unman our man, at least prove materially distracting from Intimate Metaphorical Congress. Be it once again remembered, however, that their incremental asterisks are not performance ratings; at the same time, be it remarked that the spectacle of Ms. Wys stepping out of her leaf-strewn autumn finery like a rebirth of tenderluscious spring may go far toward dispelling all thought of 9/11 *et sequitur ad nauseam*, not to mention all thought of the story — *her* story, surely? — yet to be somehow dreamed up and told at last.

$$* \quad * \quad * \quad * \quad * \quad * \quad * \quad * \quad * \quad *_!$$

Whereafter,
intertwined and pleasurably spent on the marsh-nymph's storied (and internally lighted) waterbed —

"Scratch that." Her lips against his portside ear: "She's not a marsh-nymph."

Just a manner of speaking, Wys, but have it your way: ... *on his muse's* et cetera?

"She's not his muse, either."

Up on one elbow: I deny that! Not *merely* his muse, for sure. Not *his muse exclusively*, no doubt. But His Muse she has most certainly been being, for which he's most grateful indeed.

"Have it your way, for the time being. But there's no quote *storied and internally lighted waterbed*."

There isn't?

"Nope. You guys just dreamed that up."

We did? Then what ...?

But suddenly there isn't, in fact, any Storied *Et Cetera* — and don't ask Narrator what, in that case, the couple are coupled upon in post-metaphoricoital lassitude. I just work here.

"Nor no see-through bed-work-playroom *pied-à-mer*, as you charmingly called it, with all that transparent furniture and stuff. No deck. No ladder. No creek. No saltyfresh tidemarsh."

Hey, come *on*, now! But just as suddenly there are no longer those now-so-familiar surroundings: only two intertwined bare bodies suspended as if in lightless space.

"No *interwined bare bodies as if* et cet.," and the entity here called Graybard feels himself reduced to an incorporeal consciousness attending a disembodied, female-timbred voice.

"... whose presumably final words to him, he hears that voice say now," he hears that voice say now, "are that *none of the above-mentioned items ever existed* outside a certain party's imagination. Bye-bye, dear Geeb; thanks for the ride."

And with that she's gone, as indeed is he, and their narrative page is blank

... until something or someone inspires our chap to exclaim *Only in a certain party's imagination?* All *right!* Whereupon there they all are, as before: buck-naked Wysiwyg and ditto Graybard; the internally lighted waterbed on which the pair now sit chastely side by side, their backs to the see-through wall; the bright Imaginarium round about and above and below them; the laddered deck; the dark marsh out there with its moon-tugged brackish tides; and beyond all those a "real" world wherein Muslim militants plot sundry horrors against a less-than-blame-free United States of America.

"That was a close one ..."

Says the muse-nymph, her bedmate adds, *with just a hint of smile in her voice?*

"Likewise in his."

To which he responds ...?

Taking his hand in hers, "On with the story, friend."

Story, dot dot dot question mark?

"Yup. *Her* story, s.v.p.: *Wysiwyg.*"

WYSIWYG?

So what's a nice girl like her doing in a place like this?
her story's teller might well begin by asking. Whence her obsession
with transparencies literal and figurative, and with narrowing as far
as possible the unclosable gap between Appearance and Reality — an
obsession extending even to her acronymic *nom de guerre, de plume,
de sport*, whatever?

"A *nom*, be it remembered, not of her own choosing. You had to
explain it to me, back in our Invocation. But go on: She's all ears."

By no means, but never mind. This marsh, Reader, this night, this
moon, these tides, are real; likewise humankind's black plagues of religious zealotries, intolerant orthodoxies, and tyrannies of every sort,
not to mention that catastrophic final gift of the Terrible Twentieth
to the Terrifying Twenty-first, the literal global plague of AIDS. All
real. But this glassy Imaginarium is, well, *imaginary* — Q.E.D. a few
pages past. Is its presiding spirit likewise? A spirit pure and total, is she,
dreamed up out of airy Nothing to do the narrative job now ten-elev-
enths done?

Hip to hip beside him, her hand on his upraised knee: "Nothing
pure about her, Geeb. But on with her effing story."

Her effing story indeed. Not every nymph is *ipso facto* nympho-
manic; whence then this full-bloom-summer one's readiness for Intimate Congress with (among who knows how many other interlopers)
a decidedly autumnal and soon-to-be wintry Graybard? Granted,

their asterisked couplings are Metaphorical — but no less so are the couplers, and so within the metaphor their guilt-free intercourse is *as if* literal, no?

"Excuse me? *As if* literal? Figuratively literal? *As good as* literal?"

He considers: *As if* as good as literal, okay? To get right down to it —

"By all means do, the *as-if*-nymphomanic nymph encourages the would-be teller of her story. It's around here somewhere, that *it*: Stop mincing metaphors and get right down to it."

To get right down to it (he presses on), is his frisky friend *merely* a metaphor or *also* a metaphor? If Merely, then why such anomalous specifics as those sundry see-throughs, the Friday-night candles, and her occasionally dark and/or distant moods? "Can no one tell me what she sings?" And if Also, then who is she and has she been, before and beyond her current casting?

"You tell *me*, friend," she challenges with a smile her grateful but cornered Narrator, his back both literally and figuratively against the wall.

"A *glass* wall, mind you," she reminds him: "a *see-through* wall. You can't step through it to the other side, but you can take a shot at telling us what you see back there."

Yes. Well: What I see …

Let's see, now: What I see — "as through a glass, darkly," mind, and more or less reversed, inasmuch as the images beyond the wall that my narrative back is backed up to are reflections in the see-through mirror directly before us, at the foot of this storied waterbed — what I see, let's say, might be, um, e.g. … a Nice (part-)Jewish Girl unaware of that ethnic datum until her thirteenth year? Raised as the much-loved only child of a mild-mannered secular-WASP couple in, um, Bloomington, Indiana, shall we say? Or Madison, Wisconsin? Iowa City? Dad a professor at the university there — Psychology, maybe?

"Close: Cognitive Science."

Cog Sci it is: still a subset of Psychology back then, but nudging toward separate-discipline status. Mom a something-or-other in the university's … Development office, maybe? Like a younger version of Whatsername in our Fifth Night story, *The Rest of Your Life*?

"Julia Fischer. Information Services."

Thankee. Back in the, let's see, Nineteen late Sixties early Seventies, this would've been, our Miz Saltyfresh being presently on or just over the age-thirty threshhold —

"Over."

And we'll skip the period detail, okay? No Johnson / Nixon / Ford / Carter-era stuff; no South Vietnam and Cambodia down history's bloody pipes; no Yom Kippur War and Arab oil embargo: just life as a preschooler, kindergartner, and elementary-school university brat in pleasant Bloomington / Madison / Wherever.

"Sigh: Pleasant it was, Geeb, even in those turbled times, and they the dearest of parents. *Except*, dot dot dot."

Except for their deciding early on to withhold from her, Until She's Old Enough to Understand, the reason for a dark-haired dark-eyed Mediterranean-featured youngster's being the spawn of two stereotypical upper-midwestern Scandinavian Americans named, let's see ... Lars and Helga Lindstrom?

"A bit over the top, but you're in the ballpark."

Gus and Kristina-with-a-K Ullmann, then: Emphasis on the *Krist-*, inasmuch as while the family was programmatically agnostic, both Mom and Dad were long-lapsed Lutherans who respected their former faith as they respected the current or former faiths of their sundry Protestant, Catholic, Jewish, Muslim, Hindu, and Buddhist colleagues, friends, and students. Kristina being alas infertile and the couple desirous of child, they adopted the newborn daughter of one of Doctor Gustav's graduate students by one of her other thesis advisors, a married man who'd sworn to his illicit young lover that no contraceptive precautions need be taken themby, inasmuch as he'd been bilaterally vasectomized years since, and who then disavowed paternity on those grounds, implying that she'd been unfaithful to his unfaithful self with some other stud.

"Heartless, unprincipled shit! But sexy and gentle-mannered, I've been told, until the chips were down."

These being the days before DNA testing, there was no way to resolve the issue, had it been pressed — which it was not, nor ever even made public, Ms. Grad Student preferring to carry the child openly to term as a nine-month reproach to her faithless lover (who indeed left wife, family, and university not long before the infant's birth). She confided her angry secret to none save her dissertation director, Professor Ullmann, who in a second-trimester office conference discreetly broached to her the subject of adoption versus single-parenting and was given the whole tearful tale to believe or not. Ms. Feldman happened to be secular Jewish, her professorial ex-paramour Italian-American *goy-ishe*; whether or not she'd been impregnated by someone else, therefore (the Ullmanns accepted her indignant denials on the grounds of her general honorableness: She would not reveal the adultery to her ex-lover's wife, for example, much less ask her for corroboration of that alleged vasectomy), and, if so, whether that impregnator was Jew or Gentile, her daughter was by Jewish law Jewish — as she let the Ullmanns know upon surrendering the infant to them for adoption. How they elected to handle that fact was strictly their business: She herself meant to emigrate to Tel Aviv upon receipt of her doctorate and would not attempt to communicate with the child or otherwise make her existence and relationship known to her unless both the girl herself and her adoptive parents came to desire such communication — in which case it would be up to them to track down the biological mother, who intended neither to conceal nor to advertise her whereabouts.

And so the tot was raised as Trudy Ullmann — Tru for short, Gertrud for long, the name chosen for its sounding, to Gus and Kristina anyhow, sufficiently North European on the one hand and potentially Jewish on the other to serve its bearer whichever way she might choose to go, if and when: Add an *e* to Gertrud, like the celebrated Ms. Stein, subtract the terminal *n* from Ullmann, maybe one of the *l*'s for good measure, and she's got a passably Jewish name if she wants one, when the time comes.

That time, they decided (against the prevailing wisdom among their Child Psych colleagues, who held it best to apprise adoptees of their status as early as possible, certainly before preschool, cushioning the news with some such bubble-wrap as "Other parents have to take what they get; we *chose* you, because you're special"), would be upon the girl's pubescence, more or less, depending on How Things Went. Unless fiercely principled young Dr. Beth Feldman or her scruple-free ex-lover had a change of heart and unbagged the cat, or some family friend or colleague thoughtlessly did likewise, they would raise young Trudy as their own flesh and blood, attributing the differences in their coloration and physiognomies to the vagaries of genes: "You're the image of your Nana Ullmann's [conveniently deceased] sister Greta!" etc., or perhaps the lucky inheritor of said Greta's splendid pecan-or-maybe-nutmeg hair plus Kristina's Uncle Benjamin's mahogany eyes, which every girl in East Lansing used to swoon over back in the 1930s? Professor Ullmann's switching campuses in Trudy's second year — from Indiana to Michigan or Wisconsin, or vice versa — afforded them some insulation against disclosure by indiscreet old friends and neighbors who knew that Kristina had never been pregnant. Every Trudy-birthday thereafter, the parents agreed, they would review their delayed-disclosure policy in the light of their daughter's development, their own feelings, and the experiences of other adoptive parents whom they might come to know while flying their own false colors, and would change or drop that policy if either came to feel it misguided. If not, they would feed the truth to her in gently calibrated increments as she approached and entered adolescence, even offering her instruction in Judaism, a proper bat mitzvah, and reunion with her biological mother, should she so incline. Meanwhile she was theirs, theirs, theirs; their as-if flesh and blood, and her identity their literal creation.

Such are the follies, here and there, of the highly intelligent and educated, firmly principled, entirely well-meaning, and otherwise sensible — and there's no disputing that the three Ullmanns richly enjoyed Trudy's childhood years.

"*This* Ullmann did, for sure. *Bliss was it in those days to be alive*, et cet. Piano and dance lessons and recitals! Homework-help galore, and class honors ditto! Summer camping trips to Montana, winter ski trips to Colorado, and once all over Europe in a camping trailer!"

Plus team sports and household responsibilities, minor illnesses and accidents, passing spats with best-girlfriends, first crushes on boys —

"*To be young was very heaven*, back there back then."

She loved her parents unreservedly, did our Trudy, and they her; she loved her friends, her schools, her teachers, neighbors, neighborhood, and town. High-percentile bright, though less than highest; accomplished in half a dozen arts, though called unequivocally to none; uncommonly lovely of face and form —

"Though no raving beauty. We get the picture, Geeb."

In every way a delightsome child — until just a month or so before her thirteenth birthday, when in quick succession she experienced her first menstruation, was told by the seventh-grade Bad Boy (following a class discussion of major world religions, in course whereof young Trudy had proudly declared her parents' agnosticism and her own) that

she should haul ass to the nearest synagogue with the kikes she so resembled, and by her closest girlfriend (to whom she had triumphantly
confided the onset of her menses, thus winning the bet between them
which would reach puberty first) that they two were lucky *not* to be
Jewish, inasmuch as Jewish mothers slapped their daughters' faces for
good luck at first menstruation! Duly reporting all this to her mom,
our girl was by her tearfully hugged and kissed, informed that that
face-slapping business was a good-luck custom of the superstitious or
otherwise tradition-bound in sundry cultures, including the Jewish,
and surely most often delivered as a lovingly ceremonious pseudo-slap
rather than an actual wallop. That, as Trudy well knew, the word *kike*
is as offensive an ethnic slur as *nigger, wop, dago, heeb, spic, sheeny,
mick,* and *gringo,* never to be used except perhaps in self-deprecating camaraderie within the respective eths. And — considering that
her thirteenth birthday party would soon be a happy memory like its
dozen predecessors — that the birthday-girlwoman and her parents
were going to have a Quiet Talk About This & That just as soon as Dad
got home from lab: half an hour or so hence, she'd guess. In that brief
meanwhile, Mom suggested (herself just home from her own university office and looking forward to dinner prep with her daughter, a
family custom long enjoyed by both and by Dad as well when he extri-
cated himself from classroom and laboratory and rejoined the family,
no one of whom could have imagined that that pleasant ritual was now
History), Trudy might want to review a certain written statement that
her parents had prepared well in advance of the day they knew must
sooner or later arrive, in the interests of the full, accurate, and fair
accounting that their daughter most certainly deserved of — well, let
Mom just fish the thing out of Dad's home-office files, here it is, and
let Trudy just thumb through it up in her room while she herself just
changes out of office-clothes, and then just as soon as Dad arrives and
fixes their pre-dinner Sip and Nibble, they'll just go over the whole
thing together, answer whatever questions, and just take things from
there. And not to worry: The whole complicated business couldn't've
worked out better for the three of them!

"And some folks thought the world ended on the morning of Nine
Eleven O One! Mine went to hell at five-thirty PM on a fine April Tuesday eighteen years before that. Get me the fuck out of there!"

The fuck out of there she'll get, our pubescent Ms.-Wysiwyg-to-be, but not before Narrator wonders, with her, how two by-no-means-insensitive adults, having concealed The Truth from their daughter for so perilously long, could see fit to break it to her at last in a *written statement*, for pity's sake! What must Kristina Ullmann have been thinking as she exchanged pantsuit for dinner-prep jeans and sweatshirt? What must Gus have felt when he whistled in from campus to find his house in an uproar? Okay, so it was a *lovingly* written statement, the joint effort of loving and articulate parents to get things said Just Right for the record, and no doubt originally meant to follow rather than precede a gentle face-to-face, heart-to-heart disclosure; of course Kristina phoned her husband's office to alert him the minute her fearfully baffled daughter took to her room that manila envelope marked *FOR OUR TRUDY, WITH OUR LOVE*—but found he'd left for home already; and of course she began to question the wisdom of having moved so promptly instead of first discussing with him Trudy's anti-Semitic news from school and reviewing for the thousand-and-first time their longstanding plan of action for When The Day Came But In Any Case No Later Than Her Thirteenth Birthday, so that at least he'd have been there with her when the first hysterics sounded from the other side of the poor girl's door ... But whatever happened to their earlier plan of revealing to her *incrementally*, as she *approached* thirteen, her status as beloved adoptee and, discreetly, the circumstances of her birth and adoption? The case has to have been that by a combination of unspoken denial and comfortable procrastination they had painted themselves into an ever-tighter corner (not unlike Narrator's approach to Eleventh Night): They would cross that bridge when they came to it, they must have gotten the habit of telling themselves — and then found themselves over the edge of a chasm both bridgeless and unbridgeable.

"Something like that. They'd tell me later that they never understood it themselves — and him a psychologist, sort of! They'd gotten so used to living in a fiction, they said, they were afraid to face the facts."

A fiction, yes.

"A fucking *lie*, Geeb. But on with it."

Yes. So the girl's in hysterics — in clinical shock, virtually, smashing up her room, cursing and flailing at her Quote Parents (as she'll call them for a long while after), who, scared witless, simply plead guilty as charged and go literally to their knees to beg a forgiveness that will be years in coming, to the extent that it comes at all.

"Oh, it came, it came — by maybe halfway through college? The poor sweet shmucks meant well, and never forgave themselves. But the years till then are best passed over."

Anyhow summarized: Model daughter becomes delinquent hellion; everything from drugs and sexual promiscuity to shoplifting, indulged and excused by penitent Quote Parents. Is saved from utter self-ruin only by high-school junior-year flirtation with Orthodox Judaism; changes name to Beth Elman after tracking down (with Gus and Kristina's dedicated help) her birthmom and discovering that the luckless Dr. Beth Feldman had succumbed to metastasized uterine cancer not long after immigration to Israel, where she'd worked as a counselor to other Jewish immigrants on a kibbutz in the Negev's Beersheba Basin. Her newly pious daughter and Quote Parents dutifully visit that kibbutz and environs in summer '87 to pay their respects to Gus's late former advisee's grave, upon the starkly simple stone marker whereof Trudy/ Beth reverently places a desert pebble, per custom. Back home, does her catchup Hebrew homework at the local university's Hillel House, where she meets and dates but does not bed a Nice Jewish Freshman. Sustains her Jewhood, as she self-mockingly calls it (though not her Orthodoxy, which softens, semester by semester, from Conservative through Reform to all-but-Non-Observing), into her senior year, when also, to the QPs' vast relief, she repairs her damaged academic standing sufficiently to be admitted the following fall as a freshman pre-med — not at Johns Hopkins, to which she aspired, but as geographically close thereto as she can manage: the University of Maryland's main campus, down near D.C. Her declared ambition is to become a Hopkins M.D. and carry on her birthmother's work by practicing either on a kibbutz or with the selfless Médecins Sans Frontières.

"All an act. *Beth Elman*, for pity's sake!"

Not an act, Narrator protesteth: just desperate-but-honest self-invention. One notes, by the way, that there's been no mention in all this of our young pre-meddie's putative sire . . .

"Oy: Doctor Shithead. We tracked *him* down, too, and found he'd left teaching, or it him, after marrying one of his last students — a girl half his age, upon whom he managed to spawn a son despite his alleged vasectomy — and had gone into private practice in a Milwaukee suburb as guess what? A counselor of at-risk adolescents! Protagonist much inclined to confrontation and exposure of the bastard to wife and child, but asked herself What Would Doctor Mom Do? and wound up giving the prick a free pass for their innocent sake. So never met Half-Brother ..."

Amen. But she can't help wondering, down there in College Park, Maryland, whether she hasn't inherited some of her birthdad's inclination to flying false colors — an unfair self-doubt, in Narrator's opinion, inasmuch as *he* deceived others, whereas *she* was only and earnestly ... not even deceiving herself, really, but *searching* for herself.

"And misleading herself and others by the way, just as Gus and Kris misled her with their self-deceptions or whatever."

Yes, well, maybe — but she's surely more sinned against than sinning, in that department. Commutes often up the turnpike to Baltimore, does our Miz Beth, to breathe the aggressively competitive atmosphere of pre-meds at Hopkins's Homewood campus. *Throats*, I believe they're called?

"Short for Cutthroats, and not my style."

... as she confided to one of their number: a Nice Jewish Boy who took her to a rowhouse party of fellow Throats and turned out to be neither Nice nor Jewish, belying the former by lacing her drinks with whatever was the date-rape pharmaceutical of choice back in the Reagan / Bush late Eighties —

"Mere alcohol in quantity, would be my guess."

— before Throating her indeed, and then some, with what despite her liquored stupefaction she perceived to be a fully foreskinned phallus.

"Oyoyoy. But at least I threw up on the sumbitch."

In retaliation wherefor he roughly took her anal virginity, the vaginal having long since been broadcast to the studs of Bloomington High. This latter violation she inferred only after the fact — upon waking with a three-star hangover on a battered couch in the club basement of a Hopkins Jewish frathouse whereto she'd been gently transported by two bona fide NJB Throats who'd belatedly rescued her from her soused assailant — on evidence of rectal hemorrhaging, which her rescuers (doctors' sons both, carrying on family tradition) had considerately treated with Bacitracin™ and Osco Pantiliners™ borrowed from a sympathetic girlfriend. Who also gave the victim a lift back to College Park, urging en route that criminal charges be brought against the party-crashing date-rapist.

"She being a pre-law at the state U's Baltimore campus."

But our Wys, when recovered at both ends and reasonably sure that the assault had left her neither pregnant, infected, nor hemorrhoidal, found herself less concerned with seeing justice done than with shucking what she now saw to be her desperately improvised identities. She was not Beth Feldman's and Professor Lothario's daughter, except DNAwise; she was Kristina and Gustav Ullmann's, whose grievous but single lapse she presently forgave at least to the extent of removing the quotes from *parents*. She was not "Beth Elman," but Gertrud Ullmann. She didn't really want to be a doctor; maybe she'd go back to painting, for which she'd once been told she had a promising gift. Or if not painting, perhaps art history. Or theater.

"Not theater: No more pretending to be somebody she isn't."

Music, then, maybe; she'd always enjoyed her piano lessons . . .

"Maybe she'd just have herself a nice nervous collapse."

But she didn't. Dropped out of university, yes, and shifted up to the old Maryland Institute of Art in Baltimore on the basis of a hastily cobbled portfolio from junior-high and early high-school days plus a handful of not-bad drawings she'd done in Israel. Quickly realized, among those young seriosos, that hers was at best an amateur flair, not a pre-professional gift — but okay, as long as she pretended to no more than that either to others or to herself. And she found, quite unexpectedly, that what she truly had a gift for, if that's the right word, was modeling for others.

"And here we go."

Especially in the drawing, painting, and sculpture Life Classes . . .

"Here we go: *Au naturel* was second nature to her."

Not even nudity, but *nakedness* in the presence of others: an off-handed nakedness, free of exhibitionism. Even fully dressed, mind, she found that her art-school classmates — male and female, gay and straight, even Representational and Non — were drawn to her as a subject, for reasons not invariably clear to themselves. It was as if her way of holding a pencil or a coffeecup, or brushing her hair, or stepping out of or into her clothes, not only spoke to them as subject-matter (even if the result was an unrecognizable abstraction), but inspired their rendition. And *undressed* . . .

"What You See Is *et cetera*."

The Life Class modeling helped defray her tuition, and when word got around that she grooved on nakedhood there were feelers, so to speak, from lap-dance joints and porn-flick producers, among other entrepreneurs, to all of whom she said

"Fuck off, Charlie."

Or words to that effect — not on account of the nudity and naughti-ty of those pursuits, but because they involved both exhibitionism and imposture of one sort or another, and even in those Life Drawing class-es our Wys never *posed*, in the sense of striking an attitude. She simply sat or stood, being quote *herself*, and even her teachers couldn't resist fetching out their sketchpads. Speaking of words, by the way — "words to that effect," awhile back? — we should note that not only her graphic- and plastic-arts comrades were drawn to her as subject and inspiration for reasons beyond her and often their understanding, but occasionally musician-friends of theirs from the nearby Peabody Conservatory as well, and even the odd poet or aspiring fictionist from up at the Hop-kins Writing Seminars, of whom more presently. By the time she aban-doned any artistic ambitions of her own and went to work full-time, modeling nude for the Institute and clothed for sundry women's-wear photo-ads —

"Nothing phony-sexy or faux-glamorous, mind: just Here It Is, on sale for thirty-nine ninety-five if you're interested."

— her naked face and form had inspired a cello sonata, a quote Meditation for two pianos, a scalp-to-sole sonnet sequence, and —

"Here it comes."

— from her student-architect current lover and first real boyfriend in years, chosen after what one imagines to have been as thorough a vetting as Ms. Ullmann could subject a chap to, and to whom she had confided her only half-humorous growing obsession with Transparen-cy — a sheaf of scale drawings and construction plans for a see-through studio / retreat / love-nest for the pair of them, to be built ASAP on a certain Eastern Shore waterfront property whereof, the fellow de-clared, he sort of owned a share. Glass walls, floors, and ceilings! Clear Lucite and Plexiglas furniture!

"And maybe call it our Transparium! That really spoke to me, Geeb, when I'd come to fool myself that I could never be fooled again. I mean, the guy didn't *fuck* like a sixty-percent-gay bisexual, and his drag-queen boyfriend, who actually owned the marshfront acreage, didn't know his stud was cheating with me any more than I knew *et cetera*. He thought the place was to be for *them!* I give up."

She gave up: quit modeling; quit quote *dating*; almost quit trusting people altogether. Found work with the Maryland attorney general's Consumer Protection office, pursuing complaints of false advertising and suchlike scams. Put off potential friends and Significant Others with her insistence on reciprocal up-front Full Disclosure. Took evening courses here and there toward her uncompleted baccalaureate — including one in Introductory Creative Writing, taught by that young poet-admirer aforementioned: he of the scalp-to-sole Shakespearean sonnet sequence . . .

"Three quatrains and a couplet on the tushie alone."

Two hundred to adore each breast, / But thirty thousand to the rest. No Andrew Marvell, this one, but an apparently principled fellow who encouraged her, after a couple of extracurricular full-disclosure sessions, to try writing a story about her serial hoodwinkings — better yet, a memoir, all the rage in the trade these days. Declared he'd be tempted to an extended poem thereabout, if his vows to the muse didn't prohibit poaching his students' material; he felt much obliged to her already for inspiring those sonnets, and hoped that when the course was done and they were no longer Teacher and Student, he might have the privilege of viewing her undraped person again, inasmuch as even the memory of her navel was enough to inspire a sestina. No need to wait, she replied, and would've peeled off her top then and there, but he demurred on pedagogical principle, and she was so impressed thereat that she actually gave his memoir-suggestion a try.

"Fucking case history was all it was. Tossed it before it even got to her thirteenth birthday. To play the Muse of Inspiration is not *ipso facto* to be inspired."

Toss it she did — but then retrieved it from her Macintosh's Trash icon, copied it to diskette, and urged her instructor to make whatever use of it he would, with her blessing — and of her Undraped Person as well, inasmuch as she was dropping the course forthwith and thereby releasing him from his admirable scruples. Should they start with the aforepraised bellybutton and proceed wherever Inspiration might lead?

Well, maybe, *sure*, her now-former instructor allowed, if she was really thus inclined . . .

"Which she really was: her one inarguable talent."

And although they were lovers for only one ode and two vil-lanellesworth of nights before he shamefacedly confessed that, contrary to his earlier declaration, while he truly never cribbed from his students, he did in fact shag attractive and willing female ones from time to time — but only if the course was Pass/Fail instead of letter-grad-ed, mind, and the shaggee completed all her writing assignments on schedule. He ought to've told her that up front, he supposed …

"As did she, once again deceived and disappointed despite its hav-ing been she, in their case, who took the sexual initiative. Anyhow, no more horizontal tutorials thereafter."

But the good chap conscientiously reviewed that shall-we-say unin-spired memoir-draft —

"That's putting it tactfully: just a synopsis, really, of her Misadven-tures Thus Far."

— and gave it as his professional opinion that the material was more suited to prose fiction than to narrative verse, neither of which was his long suit, he being strictly a lyricist; also that its prolixity deserved, if not a memoir, then a full-fledged novel, or at least some sort of sto-ry-series. Since she herself had abandoned the thing, and it was alas not for him, with her permission he would pass it along to an acquain-tance and sometime colleague of his: a bona fide publishing fictioneer whose project-in-the-works, deponent happened to know — a framed story-collection called *The Book of Ten Nights and a Night* — had been sidetracked by the Nine Eleven terrorist attacks on New York and Washington at least until the author's imagination could come to some sort of terms with that enormous event. Given her consent, he would relay to that fellow her Story Thus Far, or at least the story of that story, together with her *carte blanche* to make what use of it he might, if only as a diversion until his stalled opus got back on track. Permission granted?

"She'd think about it, she said."

And briefly did, and presently with a shrug said, Sure — on one condition. No Horizontal Interviews, her poet-friend supposed, and assured her she needn't worry, as the chap was happily married, dis-inclined to infidelity, and elderly to boot: Together or separately, those three constraints ought to keep things vertical.

"To which Let's-Call-Her-Trudy responded, *Tant pis*: Verticality wasn't the condition she had in mind."

Forget about manuscript review and approval, her advisor advised: No self-respecting fictionist would likely allow that. Due credit given on acknowledgments page? Some share of no-doubt-modest royalties?

"*None of the above*, she declared," she declared. Her condition was simply that her poet-pal tell his novelist-pal that he'd *invented the whole story himself:* just an odd incidental inspiration about a woman so often and consequentially deceived by appearances that *et cetera.* He'd thought there might be a poignant lyric somewhere in there: *Can no one tell me what she sings?*, or some such. So far, however, no one had, and so if Pal Novelist had any use for it, there it was. As for Ms. Anonymous: She and her hang-ups seem to have inspired a clutch of apprentice painters and sculptors, a couple of wannabe composers, one gifted though unprincipled architect, and a well-meaning if less than utterly up-front poet. If they happen to inspire a storyteller too, so be it: Maybe she'd check the Help Wanteds for Muses . . .

So, then: Did he do it?

The poet-chap, we mean? Pass her story along to his alleged novelist-acquaintance, we mean? Or was that fictionist in fact the poet's fiction, a rather elaborate diplomatic device for disengaging himself from his comely but kinky sometime inspirer? Whatever the case, Abracadabra and Allakazam! Next thing we know of her is that she finds herself here on the tale-spinning page, installed in a weirdo see-through pad not unlike the one suggested by that earlier, not-quite-straight inspiree of hers and being there visited eveningly, in the role of Saltyfresh Serviceable Surrogate Muse, by the Graybard embodiment of some scrivener's Narrative Imagination. Sipping wine himwith by mid-September sunset; peeling out of her peekaboos or whatever to dunk in the murky-but-noctilucent tidewater prior to Metaphorical Intimate Congress; prompting and sometimes critiquing his recycled tales . . .

"And, as she understands it, no harm done to anyone."

Not only no harm!, Graybard here vigorously protests. Granted that nothing we've done since Nine Eleven has any relevance whatsoever to that disaster and whatever may follow it —

"Only the relevance of Irrelevance, as I believe we established . . ."

Establish it we did, thanks, and lo and behold: Ten nights and a nightsworth of tales now framed and told! Our Hendecameron done!

"He wishes." She picks herself up, fetches from her deck their empty champagne-flutes, tips into them the last of the Mumm's (just a splash apiece, no doubt at world temperature by now), and returns to sit cross-legged before him on the waterbed. Having handed him his, however, she does not yet raise hers either in salute or to sip.

Problem?

But of course he knows what the problem is, and knows that she knows that he knows: Tale Eleven — *Wysiwyg?* — remains incomplete. So Ms. Let's-Call-Her-Trudy, serially misled by appearances, comes to devote herself quixotically to narrowing, in her fashion, the onerous gap between What One Sees (in others and so, by extension, in herself) and What One Gets — in the course whereof she is interloped upon by Present Company, assists in a musely way his Dispatcher's narrative project, and here they are. So now what? Where's the dénouement? How does Wys's story end, and theirs?

"That's Problem One," his grave colleague affirms, and considers her wine-flute. "Problem Two is that the more he gives her a quote *real* identity and case history, like this Gertrud Ullmann story-in-progress, the less she can really be Wysiwyg the Accommodating Muse. Your Trudy is just another Four-Tees fuck-up: one more more-or-less-piti-ful real-life loser. You forgot, by the way, to give her the grandma from Minsk that somebody mentioned back in our Invocation."

So I did. Four Tees?

Gesturing toward the relevant areas with her glass, "Two Tits, a Tush, and a Twat. Screw her."

Yes, well: *Been there, done that,* a chap could say, but doesn't. Says instead, As to Problem One, dear Wys, you're jumping the gun: We're *in* the story's ending, right here right now, sentence by sentence; its dénouement is whatever you and I do from this page forward. As for Problem Two: Forget about Gertrud Ullmann, cobbled up by Yours Truly (minus the grandma; sorry about that) for the purpose of getting Wysiwyg to where she and Graybard are now. Here. Together. About to wind up this story, this Hendecameron, and the last of this wine.

"Maybe."

Poor Blinkered Four-Tees Trudy, in this taleteller's estimation, comes to be the *inverse* of Wysiwyg: What she gets, after a certain point, is pretty much what she's come to *see*, including the way she's come to see herself.

"With a little tutoring in the School of Hard Knocks."

Granted. But we here declare her to be a Fictional Character: one possibility among many. My Wysiwyg is no Trudy Ullmann; she's you. *You're* you.

"Me, dot dot dot."

You. The woman who discoursed so relevantly on the relevance of Irrelevance, with glosses both pertinent and eloquent on Homer, Scheherazade, and Boccaccio. The woman whose No-Nos and Yes-Yeses navigated this Hendecameron from *Help!* through *Click* to Here and Now. Whose nightly potions re-leaded her Graybard's narrative pencil. *That's* you, Wys: Here's looking at you!

"Not yet. I mean, *look* all you want to, of course. But no toasts just yet."

And why not? he asks, he asks — taking private hope from that Not *Just* Yet.

"Because . . ." Fiddling with flute: "Because. *Your* Wys, you say. And *her* Graybard . . ."

And *our* dénouement. Since the ontological order of things precludes your going back with me to my guy's Scriptorium and its circumambient Real Life, I'm staying here with you, Wys, in this Imaginarium of ours, till this book's last period and beyond. Here's to Us.

Considers. Shakes head. "Not yet."

I, uh, *love* you? As they say?

"Yeah, right. They do say that."

GRAYBARD LOVES WYSIWYG, Reader: TRUE LOVE.

"Mm-hm. And suppose you *were* to stay here — "

Yes! But only with your Yes, of course.

"— if *we* stayed here — a notion that she acknowledges to be not without its appeal — where does that leave Whatsisname?"

The bloke who sent me? No problem: It leaves him cuddling with *his* one and only, back in Literalville. Here's to 'em.

"Not just yet. What I mean is, without you, what does he do for an encore after this all-but-done Hendecameron?"

That's *his* problem, mate. We half suspect he's just something you and I dreamed up anyhow. Like Trudy Ullmann?

"And me."

And me — to the end of encountering you. To us?

This time she actually half raises her glass, and her extraordinary eyes as well — though only to said glass, not yet to him. As if turning his words into a counter-toast, *"To the end,"* she says in italics — and now at last, grave still but smiling, she lifts those eyes to him. "Are you sure you know what you're getting into here, Geeb?"

Of course I'm not sure, any more than you are. But I know what I've seen and what I see. Enough said?

" . . . "

Correction, Love: * * *, yes?

"Yesyesyes: * * * * * * * * * *!"

Et cetera, *ad in* —

"Finis."

AFTERWORDS

9:11 9:21,

that odd clock-calendar flashes: *9:11 9:21,* until one or the other of our imagined couple uncouples to pull its plug. Whereupon, by some odd circuitry, not only that digital distraction goes dark, but the whole Imaginarium: no moon or stars, even, to be seen through tonight's cloud cover; no will-o'-the-wisps flickering in the marsh round about; not even (when at some point they rinse their love-sweat in the warm tidewater) those phosphorescing algae that on nights past had made their bodies sparkle. Whatever from here on out these lovers may Get, neither they nor we can See, except with the mind's eye.

Embracing the darkness and each other, "Right and proper," they agree: Transparency hath its merits — especially in the Forthrightness way, Q.E.D. — but readerly voyeurism is another story.

"Another what?" one half teases.

Responds the other, We'll just see. Meanwhile, a recess from Time and Narrative alike, in the full understanding that although stories end (or, sometimes, merely cease), the Big T famously does not. Its passage, however, may perhaps be ignored — at least for a time?

"So to speak."

And *in* time, so to speak, one or the other of them will remark this night's recentest conjunction to have been their twelfth. Further, that while by their reckoning it's still Eleventh Night, enough They-Know-What has surely passed to put the hour past midnight (*her* time, which is their time now — not that they're attending its passage, mind): by their agreed-upon calendar, the early hours of "Saturday," "September 22," "2001."

Autumnal Equinox, yes? Unless that was yesterday.

"Yesterday, today, tomorrow — in any case, even shorter days ahead from here on out."

The shorter our days, Love, the longer our nights. On to the Twelfth?

"When and if it comes." For we do not imagine the orchestrators of 9/11 to be resting on their bloody laurels. "Meanwhile, if it must be On with anything, let's on with Eleventh Night, and Our Story."

In which,
limbs twined still in metaphoric post-Congressional lassitude, the pair speak quietly of that *other* Twelfth Night — Twelfth Day Eve, to be precise, in the Christian calendar: the merrymaking night before the Feast of Epiphany, dozenth day after Christmas, when tradition has it that the infant Jesus was shown forth to the Magi for certification of His Messiahhood.

"Four days after the kid's *bris*, presumably."

Which ritual circumcision gets passing mention in Luke Two Twenty-one, as we recall, though not the identity of the *mohel* who on His eighth day did Him snip. In any case (back to Twelfth Night), a time of whoopee-making borrowed from the Roman Saturnalia; occasion of Will Shakespeare's play on opposite-sex twins and cross-dressing doubles, wherein Viola's disguising herself as a man will have been vertiginously compounded by the Elizabethan custom of assigning female roles to male actors: a man playing the part of a woman disguising herself as a man.

"And beloved by another quote *woman*, Olivia, who marries Viola's look-alike brother thinking he's quote *she*, whom she takes for a him..."

All which reminds one that in Shakespeare, as in most art and no small measure of life, what you see, at first glance at least, is *not* what you get. But this present Twelfth Night eve, we were saying: Sept Twenty-two O One, the Neverlasting Now ...

"Hardly a time for antic revelry, while smoke still rises from the innocent dead at Ground Zero. Irrelevant stories, yes. Partying, no."

Anyhow, the buck-naked can't cross-dress like Will's Olivia / Viola /

Voilà: What they *feel* is what they get.

"You Graybard male, on the tactile evidence; me Wysiwyg feem. There's revelry enough."

But we *have* had an epiphany or two, you and I, have we not? For which thankee, Wys.

"We have. For which thank*ee*, Geeb. Yom Kippur, our Day of Repentance, is just a few nights down the road, and whatever I have to repent, it isn't Us."

Amen to that. Tomorrow, next week, next month, who knows what? Nerve gas in the subways, smallpox in the reservoirs —

"Anthrax in the mail. Bull market gelded . . ."

All painfully possible. One of us recalls wondering four decades ago, in the wake of JFK's assassination, whether one would ever laugh again, and being told —

"*Oh yes, we'll laugh again — but we'll never be young again.* Something like that?"

Mirabile dictu, her very words. Nor middle-aged again, for that matter, this time around. Nor innocently secure-feeling again, one supposes, to the extent that we-all seem to have been, more or less, till Nine Eleven.

"So . . ."

So our question is, Will there be a story henceforward to go on with?

Some moments' pause. Then:
"A story . . ."

And presently: "We'll just see, Love. In the dark. Together."
We'll see.

The Development (2008)

Peeping Tom

Don't ask me (as my wife half teasingly did earlier this morning) who I think is reading or hearing this. My projected history of our Oyster Cove community, and specifically the season of its Peeping Tom, is barely past the note-gathering stage, and there's nobody here in my study at 1010 Oyster Cove Court except me and my PC, who spend an hour or three together after breakfast and morning stretchies before Margie and I move on to the routine chores and diversions of a comfortably retired American couple in the dawn of the new millennium and the evening of their lives. Maybe our CIA/FBI types have found ways to eavesdrop on any citizen's scribbling? Or maybe some super-shrewd hacker has turned himself into a Listening Tom, the electronic equivalent of Oyster Cove's peeper, even when I'm talking to myself?

Don't ask me (but in that case you wouldn't need to, right?); I just work here. For all I know, "You"—like the subject of this history, in some folks' opinion—may not actually, physically exist. Unlike him, however (and we all assume our P.T., whether real or imagined, to have been a Him, not a Her), you're an invited guest, who- and whatever You are, not an eavesdropper. Welcome aboard, mate, and listen up!

As I was saying, I just work here, more or less between nine and noon most mornings, while Margaret the Indispensable does her ex-businesswoman business in her own workspace upstairs: reviews and adjusts our stock-and-bond accounts and other assets; pays the family bills and balances our checkbook; works the phone to line up service people; schedules our errands and appointments; plans our meals, vacation trips, grandkid visits . . . and Next Big Moves.

Which last-mentioned item prompts this whatever-it-is-I'm-doing. Margie and I have pretty much decided (and she'll soon email the news to our middle-aged offspring, who'll be Sad But Relieved to hear it) that what with my ominously increasing memory problems and her near-laming arthritis, the time has come for us to list this pleasant "villa" of ours with a realtor and get ready to get ready to shift across and down the river from good old Heron Bay Estates (of which more presently) to TCI's assisted-living establishment, Bayview Manor.

Even Margie — a professional real-estate agent herself back in our city-house / country-house days, when she worked the suburban D.C. residential market while I taught history to fifth- and sixth-formers at Calvert Heights Country Day School — even Margie rolls her Chesapeake-green, macularly degenerating eyes at all that developers' lingo. Heron Bay Estates, now approaching the quarter-century mark, was the first large gated-community project of Tidewater Communities, Inc.: a couple thousand acres of former corn and soybean fields, creeper-clogged pinewoods, and tidewater wetlands on Maryland's river-veined Eastern Shore. By no means "estates" in any conventional sense of that term, our well-planned and "ecologically sensitive" residential development is subdivided into neighborhoods — some additionally gated, most not — with names like Shad Run and Egret's Crest (low-rise condominiums), Blue Crab Bight (waterfront "coach homes," the developer's euphemism for over-and-under duplexes, with small-boat dockage on the adjacent tidal creek), Rockfish Reach (more of a stretch than a reach, as the only water in sight of that pleasant clutch of mid- to upper-midrange detached houses is a winding tidal creeklet and a water-hazard pond, ringed with cattails, between the tenth and eleventh holes of HBE's golf course, whose Ecological Sensitivity consists of using recycled "gray water" on its greens and fairways instead of pumping down the water table even further), Spartina Pointe (a couple dozen upscale McMansions, not unhandsome, whose obvious newness so belies the fake-vintage spelling of their reeded land-spit that we mockingly sound its terminal *e*: "Spartina Pointey," or "Ye Oldey Spartina Pointey")— and our own Oyster Cove, whose twenty-odd "villas" (on a circular "court" around a landscaped central green with a fountain that spritzes recycled water three seasons of the year) have nothing of the Mediterranean or Floridian that that term implies: In the glossary of HBE and of TCI generally, "villas" are side-by-side two-story duplexes (as distinct from those afore-mentioned "coach homes" on the one hand and detached houses on the other) of first-floor brick and second-floor vinyl clapboard siding, attractively though non-functionally window-shuttered, two-car-garaged, and modestly porched fore and aft, their exterior maintenance and small-lot landscaping managed mainly by our Neighborhood Association rather than by the individual own-ers. Halfway houses, one might say, between the condos and the de-tached-house communities.

Indeed, that term applies in several respects. Although a few of us are younger and quite a few of us older but still able, your typi-cal Oyster Cove couple are about halfway between their busy profes-sional peak and their approaching retirement. Most would describe themselves as upper-middle-incomers — an O.C. villa is decidedly *not* low-budget housing — but a few find their mortgage and insur-ance payments, property taxes, and the Association's stiff maintenance assessments just barely manageable, while a few others have merely camped here until their Spartina Pointe(y) (Mc)Mansions were land-scaped, interior-decorated, and ready for them and their Lexuses, Mercedeses, and golf carts (3.5-car garages are standard in SpPte). An Oyster Cove villa is typically the first second home of a couple like Margie and me fifteen or so years back: empty nesters experimenting with either retirement or a transportable home office while getting the feel of the Heron Bay scene, trying out the golf course and Club, and scouting alternative neighborhoods. The average residency is about ten years, although some folks bounce elsewhere after one or two — up to Spartina Pointe or Rockfish Reach, down to an Egret's Crest condo, more or less sidewise to a Blue Crab Bight coach home, or out to some other development in some other location, if not to Bayview Manor or the grave — and a dwindling handful of us old-timers have been here almost since the place was built.

To wind up this little sociogram: The majority of Heron Bay Estaters are White Anglo-Saxon Protestants of one or another denomination, but there are maybe three or four Jewish families, a few more Roman Catholics, and probably a fair number of seculars. (Who knows? Who cares? Firm believers in the separation of church and estate, we don't pry into such matters.) Politically, we're split about evenly between the two major parties. No Asians or African Americans among us yet — not because they're officially excluded (as they would have been fifty years ago, and popular though the adjective "exclusive" remains with outfits like TCI); perhaps because any in those categories with both the means and the inclination to buy into a gated community prefer not to be ethnic-diversity pioneers on the mostly rural and not all-that-cosmopolitan Eastern Shore.

"Gated": That too is a bit of a stretch in Oyster Cove, and (in Margie's and my opinion, anyhow) an expensive bit of ornamentation for Heron Bay. In a low-crime area whose weekly newspaper's police blotter runs more to underage tobacco and liquor purchases and loud-noise complaints in the nearby county seat than to break-ins and crimes of violence, there's little need for round-the-clock gatekeepers, HBE Resident windshield stickers, phone-ahead clearance for visitors, and routine neighborhood drive-throughs by the white-painted Security car — though it's admittedly a (minor) pleasure not to bother latching doors and windows every time we bicycle over to the Club for tennis or drive into town for medical / dental appointments, a bit of shopping, or dinner. As for the secondary gates at Spartina Pointe, Blue Crab Bight, and Oyster Cove — unmanned (even though some have gatehouses), their swing-gates operated by push-button code and usually closed only at night — pure snobbery, many of us think, or mild paranoia, and a low-grade nuisance, especially on rainycold nights when you don't *want* to roll down your car window and reach out to the lighted control box, or oblige arriving guests (whom you've had to supply in advance with the four-digit entry code) to do likewise. And both gates — Reader / Listener take note — screen motor vehicles only: Bicycles and pedestrians come and go freely on the sidewalks, whether the gates are open or shut. Our own Oyster Cove gates, by near-unanimous vote of the Neighborhood Association, have remained open and inoperative for the past dozen years. We use the attractively landscaped little brick gatehouse for storing lawn fertilizer, grass seed, and pavement de-icer for the winter months: a less expensive alternative to removing the whole structure, which anyhow some residents like for its ornamental (or prestige-suggesting) value. Since, as aforementioned, the average O.C. residency is a decade or less, it's only we old-timers who remember actually having used those secondary gates.

But then, it's only we who remember, for better or worse and as best some of us can, when the neighborhood was in its prime: "built out," as they say, after its raw early years of construction and new planting, its trees and shrubbery and flower beds mature, the villas comfortably settled into their sites but not yet showing signs of "deferred maintenance" despite the Association's best efforts to keep things shipshape. Same goes for HBE generally, its several neighborhoods at first scalped building lots with model homes at comparatively bargain prices, then handsomely full-bloomed and more expensive, then declining a bit here and there (while still final-building on a few acres of former "preserve") as Tidewater Communities, Inc., moved on to newer projects all around the estuary. And likewise, to be sure, for the great Bay itself: inarguably downhill since residential development and agribusiness boomed in the past half-century, with their runoff of nutrients and pollutants and the consequent ecological damage. Ditto our Republic, some would say, and for that matter the world: downhill, at least on balance, despite there having been no world wars lately.

Nor are we-all what we used to be, either.

But this is not about that, exactly. M. and I have quite enjoyed our tenure here at 1010 Oyster Cove Court, our next-to-last home address. Of the half-dozen we've shared in our nearly fifty years of marriage, none has been more agreeable than our "villa" of the past fifteen and sole residence of the past ten, since we gave up straddling the Bay. We've liked our serial neighbors, too: next door in 1008, for example, at the time I'll tell of, Jim and Reba Smythe, right-wingers both, but generous, hospitable, and civic-spirited; he a semiretired, still smoothly handsome investment broker, ardent wildfowl hunter, and all-round gun lover; she an elegant pillar of the Episcopal church and the county hospital board. On our other side back then, in 1012, lively Matt and Mary ("M&M") Grauer, he a portly and ruddy-faced ex-Methodist minister turned all-purpose private-practice "counselor"; she a chubbily cheerful flower-gardener and baker of irresistible cheesecakes; both of them avid golfers, tireless volunteers, and supporters of worthy, mildly liberal causes. And across the Court in 1011, then as now, our resident philosopher Sam Bailey, recently widowered, alas: a lean and bald and bearded, acerbic but dourly amusing retired professor of something or other at an Eastern Shore branch of the state university, as left of center as the Smythes were right, whose business card reads *Dr. Samuel Bailey, Ph.D., Educational Consultant* — whatever *that* is. Different as we twenty-odd Oyster Cove householders were and are — and never particularly close friends, mind, just amiable neighbors — we've always quite gotten along, pitched in together on community projects (most of us, anyhow: What community doesn't include a couple of standoff-ish free riders?), and taken active part in OCNA, our neighborhood association. Indeed, for the past twelve years I've served as that outfit's president; it's a post I'll vacate with some regret when the For Sale sign goes up out front. And despite my having been, please remember, a mere history *teacher*, not a historian, I find myself inclined to set down for whomever, before my memory goes kaput altogether, some account of our little community, in particular of what Margie and I consider to have been its most interesting hour: the summer of the Peeping Tom.

And when was that? Suffice it to say, not many years since. Odd as this may sound from an ex-history teach, the exact dates aren't import-ant. Truth is, I'd rather not be specific, lest some busybody go through the records and think: "Mm-*hm*: Just after the [So-and-Sos] bought [Twelve-Sixteen, say], which they sold a year later and skipped out to Florida. I *thought* there was something fishy about that pair, him espe-cially. Didn't even play golf!" When in fact the poor guy had advanced emphysema and shifted south to escape our chilly-damp tidewater winters. So let's just say that the time I'll tell of, if I manage to, was well after "Vietnam," but before "Iraq"; more specifically, after desktop and even laptop computers had become commonplace, but before hand-held ones came on line; after cordless phones, but before everybody had cellulars; after VCRs, but before DVDs.

Okay? The name's Tim Manning, by the way — and if You've got the kind of eye and ear for such things that Matt Grauer used to have, You'll have noted that in all four of the families thus far introduced, the men are called by one-syllable first names and their wives by two-, with the accent on the first (Sam Bailey's late mate, a rail-thin black-haired beauty until cancer chemotherapy wrecked her, was named Ethel). So? So nothing, I suppose, except maybe bear in mind Dr. Sam's wise cau-tion that a Pattern — of last names, happenings, whatever — doth not in itself a Meaning make, much as we may be programmed by evolu-tion to see patterns in things, and significance in patterns.

Okay?

Okay. "It all began," as stories so often start (and if I were a storyteller instead of a history-teller, I'd have started this tale right here, like that, instead of where and how I did), late one mid-May evening in 19-whatever: already warm enough here in Chesapeake country to leave windows open until bedtime, but no AC or even ceiling fans needed yet. After cleaning up the dinner dishes, Margie and I had enjoyed a postprandial stroll around Oyster Cove Court, as was and remains our habit, followed by an hour's reading in 1010's living room; then we'd changed into nightclothes and settled down in the villa's family room as usual to spend our waking day's last hour with the telly before our half-past-ten bedtime. At a commercial break in whatever program we were watching, I stepped into the kitchen to pour my regular pale-ale nightcap while Margie went into the adjacent lavatory to pee — and a few moments later I heard her shriek my name. I set down bottle and glass and hurried herward; all but collided with her as she fled the pissoir, tugging up the underpants that she wears under her shortie nightgown on warm end-of-evenings.

"Somebody's *out* there!" In all our years of marriage I'd seldom seen my self-possessed helpmeet so alarmed. "*Looking* at me!"

I flicked off the light and hurried past her to the open lavatory window, near the toilet. Nothing in sight through its screen except the Leyland cypresses, dimly visible in the streetlight-glow from O.C. Court, between us and the Smythes, which give both houses privacy enough to make closing our first-floor window blinds unnecessary. "Call Security," I said (Heron Bay's main gatehouse); "I'll go have a look outside." Hurried back into the kitchen, grabbed the big flashlight from atop the fridge, and headed for the back door.

"Do you think it's safe to go out there?" Margie worried after me. "In your PJs?"

"Not safe for that snooping bastard," I told her, "if I get my hands on him." Though what exactly I would have done in that unlikely event, I'm not sure: haven't been in a physical scuffle since third grade; never served in the military or had any other form of hand-to-hand-combat training; hope I'm not a coward, but know I'm not the macho sort either. Was maybe a bit surprised myself, not unpleasantly, at my impulsive readiness to go unarmed out into the night for a possible-though-unlikely confrontation with a prowler. Went anyhow, adrenaline-pumped, through laundry room and garage to night-lighted rear driveway and around to side yard — shining the flashlight prudently ahead to warn of my approach.

No sign of anyone. The night was sweet; the air moist, mild, bree-zeless, and bug-free. The grassy aisle between those cypresses and our foundation planting of dwarf junipers wasn't the sort to show foot-prints; nor was the shredded-hardwood mulch around those junipers obviously disturbed under the lavatory window, as far as I could tell. Standing among them, I verified that a six-footer like myself could just see over the shoulder-high sill into the lavatory and (with a bit of neck-craning) over to the toilet area. I shrugged a "Who knows?" or "Nobody in sight" sign to Margie, standing inside there with cordless phone in hand, then stepped back onto the grass and checked with the flashlight to see whether *my* footprints were visible. Couldn't say for certain, but guessed not.

"Well, I damned sure didn't imagine it," Margie said a bit defensive-ly when — having inspected the length of our side of the duplex and as much of the front and rear yards as I could without attracting the neighbors' attention — I was safely back indoors.

"Nobody said you did, hon." I gave her a hug, and to lighten things up added, "Great night for prowling, by the way: no moon or mosqui-toes. You called Security?"

"They're sending the patrol car around for an extra check and keeping an eye out for pedestrians leaving the grounds this late in the evening. But they're not armed, and they don't go into people's yards except in emergencies. They offered to call 911 or the sheriff's office for us, but I said we'd call them ourselves if you saw anything suspicious out there. What do we think?"

We considered. What *she'd* seen was certainly suspicious — alarm-ing, even — but was it worth involving the county sheriff and the state police? On the one hand, the prowler might for all we knew have been armed and dangerous, scouting the premises with an eye to Breaking and Entering, as it's called in the crime reports, and been spooked when Margie caught sight of him. On the other hand, he might have been some Oyster Cover out looking for a strayed house pet and mortified to find himself glimpsing Margaret Manning in mid-urination . . .

In either case, "A white guy," she affirmed, her pulse and respiration returning to normal as we brushed our teeth and made ready for bed.

"No eyeglasses or mustache or beard as far as I could tell, though I couldn't see his face clearly out there through the screen. High forehead but not bald, unless he maybe had some kind of cap on. It was just a glimpse, you know? Kind of a pale moon-face that popped up and looked in and then ducked and disappeared when he saw I'd seen him and heard me holler for you."

So what did we think? In the end — maybe partly because by then it was past eleven and neither I nor the main-gate security guys (who phoned us after their pass through the neighborhood) had seen anything amiss — we decided not to notify the sheriff's office, much less call the 911 emergency number, until or unless something further turned up. I would take another look around in the morning, and we would definitely alert our neighbors, ask them to pass the word along and keep an eye out.

"Sonofabitch peeps in on *my* wife," Jim Smythe growled, "I'll blow his damn head off." He had a way, did swarthy Jim, of making those less belligerent than himself seem reprehensible, wimpy: a habit at which Reba, to her credit, rolled her fine brown eyes. Ethel Bailey, on the other hand, was impressed that I'd gone out there alone and unarmed in the dark. She would *never* have let Sam do that, Margie said she'd said — characteristically admiring husbands other than her own while implying that their wives were less appreciative of them than was she. Sam himself good-naturedly questioned my "risk-benefit analysis" while freely admitting that he'd be too chicken to do what I'd done even if he judged it the best course of action, which he didn't. Matt Grauer, too, as fond of proverbs as of patterns, reminded me that discretion is the better part of valor, but jokingly declared himself envious of the Peeping Tom. "Margie on the can!" he teased the two of us. "What an eyeful!" To which his plump Mary added, "If it'd been me, he'd've gotten a different kind of eyeful: I'd've wet my pants." "Not likely," Margie reminded her, "when you've already dropped them to do your business. Anyhow, guys, they don't say 'scared shitless' for nothing: I here report that it applies to Number One as well as Number Two." Whereupon Sam and Matt, our neighborhood eggheads (though only Sam was bald), bemusedly wondered whether the colloquialisms "It scared me shitless" and "It scared the shit out of me" are two ways of describing the same reaction or (understanding the former to mean "It scared me out of shitting" and the latter to mean "It scared me into shitting my pants") descriptions of two opposite, though equally visceral and involuntary, manifestations of fear.

Thus did we banter the disconcerting event toward assimilation, agreeing that the prowler / peeper was in all likelihood a onetime interloper from "outside": some bored, beered-up young redneck, we imagined, of the sort who nightly cruised the shopping-plaza parking lots in their megabass-whumping, NASCAR stickered jalopies and smashed their empty Coors bottles on the asphalt. Until, less than two weeks later, Becky Gibson (with her husband, Henry, the new owners of 220 Bivalve Bend, one of several saltily named side streets off Oyster Cove Court) glimpsed a pale face pressed to the glass of their back-porch door as she passed by it en route through their darkened house to turn off a kitchen light inadvertently left on when the couple retired for the night. Like my Margie, she called for her husband; unlike me (but this was, after all, the second such incident), he unhesitatingly dialed 911. Although the responding officer considerately didn't sound his siren at one in the morning, a number of us noticed the patrol car's flashers even through our closed eyelids and bedroom-window curtains. As OCNA's president, I felt it my responsibility to slip as quietly as I could out of bed and into my pajama bottoms (which Margie and I have always slept without, originally for romantic reasons, latterly out of long habit and urinary convenience in our three-pees-a-night old age) and to step outside and see what was what.

Another fine May night, still and moonless. I could see the distant flashers pulsing from somewhere around the corner on Bivalve Bend, but couldn't tell whether they were from one of the county's multipurpose emergency vehicles or a sheriff's patrol car. Not a fire truck, I guessed, or there'd have been sirens. Lest I be mistaken for a prowler myself, I ventured no farther along the curb than the edge of our property, tempting as it was to continue past the next two duplexes to the corner. Other folks were quite possibly looking out their front windows, and anyhow one had to draw some line between being a concerned neighbor and a prying one. As I turned back, I saw the Heron Bay security patrol car — an "environmentally sensitive" hybrid bearing the Blue Heron logo of HBE — turn into Oyster Cove Court through our ever-open gate and head for Bivalve Bend. Rather than hailing or waving it down in my pajamas to ask what was happening,

I stepped behind a nearby large boxwood (standard walkway-flanking shrub around our circle) and crouched a bit for better cover until the vehicle hummed past.

"Looks like we have ourselves a problem," all hands agreed next day, after details of the past night's alarm had circulated through the community. Like Margie, silver-curled Becky Gibson could say only that the figure at her back-door window had been a beardless adult white male, either dark-haired or wearing a black bill cap backwards; whether it was the same intruder or another, two Peeping Tom incidents in successive weeks in the same small neighborhood obviously spelled trouble. As had been the case with us, neither the Gibsons nor in this instance the sheriff's deputies had found any trace of the prowler, who'd presumably vanished as soon as he knew himself to have been seen. Mary Grauer, wakened like me by the reflected flashes, was almost certain she'd seen from their living room window somebody skulking in our joint front-walk shrubbery: probably the Gibsons' peeper beating a retreat from Oyster Cove. I was tempted to explain and laugh it off, but held my tongue lest anyone get the wrong idea. Even to Margie I said only that I'd stepped outside to have a look, not that I'd walked to the curb in my PJs and ducked for cover when Security came by.

The third incident, just two nights later, was less equivocal than its forerunners: Reba Smythe, looking from a window just after dark as we all seemed to be doing now with some frequency, *thought* she might have glimpsed a furtive figure in the Baileys' front yard, and phoned to alert them. Her husband hurried over, nine-millimeter pistol in hand, just in time to quite frighten Sam Bailey, who deplored handgun ownership anyhow, as he stepped out to see whether anyone was there. The two men then did a perimeter check together, and found nothing. Reba acknowledged that she might have been mistaken: She'd recently suffered what ophthalmologists term a vitreous separation in her left eye, in consequence of which her vision was pestered by black "floaters" that she sometimes mistook for flying insects or other UFOs, as she liked to call them. But she was equally insistent that she might *not* have been mistaken; she just couldn't say for sure, although whatever she'd seen was certainly larger than her usual dark specks.

At a sort-of-emergency meeting of the Neighborhood Association the following afternoon (at our place, with jug wines and simple hors d'oeuvres), we decided to reactivate the Oyster Cove secondary entrance and exit gates as a warning and possible deterrent, even though our P.T., as we'd begun to call him for short, was pretty clearly a pedestrian. And we would press HBECA, the overall community association, for additional nighttime security patrols, even if that entailed an increase in everyone's annual assessment; for it needed no Matt Grauer to point out that three such incidents constituted an alarming pattern, and while they'd been confined thus far to Oyster Cove, it was to be expected that the peeper might try other Heron Bay venues, particularly now that ours was on a geared-up lookout for him.

As we most certainly were: unpleasantly on edge, but reassuringly drawn together by a common nuisance that, while not yet quite an overt threat, was definitely scary.

"Not a threat?" Mary Grauer protested when I described our problem in those terms. "You don't think we feel threatened when some creep might be peeking at us in the shower?"

Posing like a Jazz Age flapper with her glass of chablis in one hand and a brie-smeared cracker in the other, "Speak for yourself, dear," Ethel Bailey teased. "*Some* of us might find it a turn-on."

Less publicly, Matt Grauer and Jim Smythe shared with me the disturbing possibility — just theoretical, mind, not a genuine suspicion yet — that our P.T. might actually be *one of us*: if not an Oyster Cover, maybe some unfortunately perverted resident of an adjacent neighborhood. Or somebody's kinky visiting son, perhaps, or adolescent grandson, out on the prowl unbeknownst to his hosts?

No way to check on that last, really: Nearly all of us being empty-nesters and most of us retirees, there was a constant stream of visiting progeny and out-of-town friends in Heron Bay. But the One of Us hypothesis was reinforced, amusingly though ambiguously, a week or so later, when by early-June full moonlight both Bob and Frieda Olsen (in 1014, on the Grauers' other side from us) spotted a stocky, hatless somebody in dark shorts and shirt crossing stealthily, as it seemed to them, from their backyard into "M&M's." The alarm was quickly passed by telephone from the Olsens to the Grauers to us. We all clicked our backyard lights on, and while Margie rang up the Smythes, we three husbands stepped out back to investigate — and interrupted Jim Smythe, pistol in one hand again and flashlight in the other, completing what he unabashedly declared to us (even as Reba was confirming it by phone to Margie) was the first of the one-man armed patrols of Oyster Cove that he intended to make nightly until either HBECA increased the frequency of its security rounds or he caught and apprehended our P.T. in the act — or, better yet, gunned the sick bastard down as he fled. Not a ready acknowledger of his mistakes, Jim was dissuaded from this self-appointed mission only by our unanimous protest that it was at best more likely to trigger false alarms than to prevent real ones, and at worst might lead to his shooting some innocent neighbor out stargazing or merely enjoying the spring air. "Yeah, well, all right then," he grudgingly conceded (while Reba, who'd joined us along with our wives, did her signature eye-roll). "But they'd better stay in their own backyard, 'cause anybody I catch mooning around in mine, I intend to plug."

"Gun nuts, I swear," Sam Bailey sighed to me next day, when we shook our heads together over the fellow's presumption and short-sightedness. "Doesn't he realize that if one of *us* happened to be a guy like him, he'd have gotten himself shot last night?"

"Maybe *he's* been the P.T. all along," I ventured — not seriously, really, and none of us cared to tease Jim with that proposition.

Less alarming, if we count the foregoing as Peeper Incident #4, was the one that followed it the very next evening, as reported by its perpetrator and sole witness, Sam himself, when I happened to walk out to fetch our morning newspaper off the front walk at the same time as he, the pair of us still in robe and slippers before breakfast and Sam wearing the French beret that he'd affected ever since teaching a Fulbright year in Nanterre three decades past. "So at nine last night Ethel turns on one of those TV sitcoms that I can't stand, okay?" he tells me. "So I step into the library," as the Baileys like to call their book-lined living room, "to read for an hour till bedtime, and I catch sight of some movement just outside the picture window," which, flanked by smaller double-hung windows, overlooks the front yard, the street, and the commons beyond in all Oyster Cove Court villas. "So I cross the room to check it out — in my robe and PJs, same as now?— and the guy comes at me from out there on the porch as I come at him from inside, and I'm thinking, Isn't *he* a brazen bastard, and traipsing around there in his nightclothes too! Until I realize it's my own reflection I'm looking at. So I stand there contemplating myself in the picture window and feeling foolish while my pulse calms down, and then I experiment a bit with different lights on and off — table lamps, reading lamps, the track lights over the bookshelves — to see how a person inside might be fooled by his own reflection in different amounts of light from different angles. Because it's occurring to me that our Peeping Tom might be not only *one* of us, but *each* one of us who's seen him. In short" — he touched his beret — "*Monsieur Voyeur, c'est moi.*"

Nonsense, all hands agreed when Sam's report and theory made the rounds: What had so alarmed Margie at our bathroom window and Becky Gibson at her back door had been a youngish, medium-built man, not the reflection of a gracefully aging though less-thin-than-she-used-to-be woman. And it was Jim Smythe on his reckless neighborhood patrol that the Olsens had spotted behind 1014, not Bob and Frieda's joint reflection.

"On the other hand," Ethel Bailey pretended to consider seriously, squinting over-shoulder at her husband, "that beret of Sam's *could* be mistaken in the dark for a backwards bill cap, *n'est-ce pas?* Do you suppose our Oyster Cove pervert might turn out to be the guy I've been sharing a bed with for forty-three years?" Come to think of it, though, she added, the ladies' P.T. had been *sans* eyeglasses, and Doc Sam couldn't find his own weenie without his bifocals. No fun being a voyeur if you can't see what you're peeping at!

"Seriously though, people," Sam bade us consider while all this was being reviewed, with edgy jocularity, at our next OCNA meeting. "Granted that what the Olsens saw was our pistol-packing Jim-boy, and that whatever Margie and Becky saw, it wasn't *literally* their own reflection. Same with these new reports from Blue Crab Bight and Rockfish Reach . . ." in both of which neighborhoods by then, one resident had reported a peeper / prowler sighting to the HBE Community Association.

"They're just jealous of us Oyster Cove women getting all the attention," Reba Smythe joked, to her husband's nonamusement.

"Better pickings over there, d'you suppose?" Matt Grauer pretended to wonder — and added, despite Mary's punching his shoulder, "Guess I'll have to give it a try some night."

"What *I* worry," Jim Smythe here growled, "is we might have a copycat thing going: other guys taking their cue from our guy."

Ethel Bailey tried to make light of this disturbing suggestion: "Another Heron Bay amenity, maybe? One peeper for each neighborhood, on a rotating basis, so we don't have to undress for the same creep week after week?" But a palpable *frisson* of alarm, among the women especially, went through the room.

With a gratified smile, "You're all making my point for me," Doc Sam declared.

"Your *pointey*," I couldn't resist correcting, and felt Margie's elbow in my ribs. "P-O-I-N-T-E, as they spell it up the road."

But there was a nervousness in our joking. He was not maintaining, Sam went on in his mildly lectorial fashion, that every one of these half-dozen or so sightings had literally been the sighter's own reflection, although his own experience demonstrated that at least one of them had been and raised the possibility that some others might have been too, it being a well-established principle of perceptual psychology that people tend to see what they expect to see. No: All he meant was that to some extent, at least, the P.T. might be — might *embody, represent*, whatever — a projection of our own fears, needs, desires. "Like God," he concluded, turning up his palms and looking ceilingward, "in the opinion of some of us, anyhow."

"Objection," objected Matt Grauer, and Sam said, "Sorry there, Reverend."

"Are you suggesting," Becky Gibson protested, "that we *want* to be peeped at on the potty? Speak for yourself, neighbor!"

More edgy chuckles. Sam grinned and shrugged; his wife declared, "I don't know about you-all, but I've taken to checking my hair and makeup before I undress, just in case."

But scoff though we might at Sam's "projection" theory, at least some of us (myself included) had to acknowledge that for Jim Smythe, say, the P.T. could be said to have addressed a macho inclination to which Jim welcomely responded — as perhaps, changes changed, had been the case with Ethel Bailey's touch of exhibitionism. And we were, as a neighborhood, agreeably more bonded by our common concern than we had been before (or would be after), the way a community might become during an extended power outage, say, or by sharing cleanup chores after a damaging storm. Thanks to our Peeping Tom, we were coming to know one another better, our sundry strengths and shortcomings, and to appreciate the former while accepting the latter. Matt Grauer might tend to pontificate and Sam Bailey to lecture, but their minds were sharp, their opinions not to be taken lightly. Jim Smythe was a bit of a bully, and narrow-minded, but a man to be counted on when push came to shove. Ethel Bailey was a flirt and a tease, but she had put her finger on an undeniably heightened self-consciousness in all of us — perhaps especially, though not merely, in the Oyster Cove wives — as we went about our after-dark domestic routines. And when some days later, for example, it was reported that a fellow from over in Egret's Crest, upon spotting or believing he'd spotted a face at the bathroom window of his first-floor condo as he zipped his fly after urination, had unzipped it again, fished out his penis, marched to the by-then-dark window saying "*Eat* me, cocksucker!" and afterward boasted openly of having done so, his account told us little about the interloper (assuming that there had in fact been one) and rather much about the interlopee, if that's the right word.

For all our shared concern and heightened community spirit, however, by July of that summer we Heron Bay Estaters could be said to be divided into a sizable majority of "Peeping Tommers" on the one hand (those who believed that one or more prowlers, probably from Outside but not impossibly one of our own residents, was sneak-peeking into our domiciles) and a minority of Doubting Thomases, convinced that at least a significant percentage of the reported incidents were false alarms; that, as Sam Bailey memorably put it, we had come collectively to resemble an oversensitive smoke alarm, triggered as readily by a kitchen stove burner or a dinner-table candle as by a bona fide blaze. My wife was among the true believers — not surprisingly, inasmuch as her initial "sighting experience" (Sam's term, assigning our P.T. to the same ontological category as UFOs) had started the whole sequence. I myself was sympathetic both to her conviction and to Sam's "projection" theory in its modified and expanded version set forth above — in support of which I here recount for the very first time, to whoever You are, the next Oyster Cove Peeper Incident, known heretofore not even to Margie, only to Yours Truly.

Hesitation. Deep breath. Resolve to Tell All, trusting You to accept that Tim Manning is not, was never, the P.T. per se. But . . . :

On a muggy tidewater night toward that month's end, while Margie watched the ten o'clock TV news headlines from Baltimore, I stepped out front to admire a planetarium sky with a thin slice of new moon setting over by the gatehouse, off to westward, from where also flickered occasional sheet lightning from an isolated thunderstorm across the Chesapeake. Although our windows were closed and our AC on against the subtropical temperatures, the night air had begun to cool a bit and dew to form on everything, sparkly in the streetlamp light. In short, an inviting night, its southwest breeze pleasant on my bare arms and legs (not this time in my usual after-nine pajamas, I happened to be still wearing the shorts and T-shirt that I'd donned for dinner after my end-of-afternoon shower). No problem with mosquitoes: The Association sprays all of Heron Bay Estates regularly, to the tut-tuts of the ecologically sensitive but the relief of us who enjoy gardening, backyard barbecues, and the out-of-doors generally. Time was, as I may have mentioned, when the two of us and others would take an after-dark stroll around Oyster Cove Court, to stretch our legs a bit before turning in for the night. Since the advent of the Peeping Tom, however, that pleasant practice had all but ceased, despite Jim Smythe's reasonable urging of it as a deterrent; one didn't want to be mistaken for the P.T., and most would prefer not to encounter him in mid-peep, lest he turn out to be not only real but armed and dangerous.

So I had the Court to myself, as it were — or believed I did, until I thought I saw some movement in the corridor between Sam and Ethel's 1011 and the villa to its right. A little flash of light it was, actually, I realized when I turned my head that way, which to my peripheral vision had looked like someone maybe ducking for cover over there, but which I saw now to be either the shadow of movement from inside one of the Baileys' lighted windows or else light from that window on some breeze-stirred foliage outside. More and more of us, as the P.T. incidents persisted, had taken to keeping all blinds and draperies closed after sunset; it was unusual to see light streaming from an uncurtained window of what was evidently an occupied room — the Baileys' main bathroom, in fact, by my reckoning, our Oyster Cove floor plans being pretty much identical. It occurred to me then to check our own bathroom window, to make certain that with its venetian blinds fully lowered and closed nothing could be seen — through some remaining slit at the sill, for example, or at the edges of the slats. Creepy as it felt to be spying on oneself, so to speak, I was able to verify that nothing could be seen in there except that the light was on; no doubt Margie making ready for bed.

What must it be like, I couldn't help wondering, to be that sicko bastard snooping on unsuspecting people as they washed their crotches and wiped their asses? I found myself — I'm tempted to say *watched* myself — returning to the street and strolling as if casually across the Court toward that light from 1011, assuring myself that in good-neighborly fashion I was making certain that nothing was amiss over there, but at the same time realizing, with a thrill of dismay, that what I might really be about to do was . . .

Wearing only her underpants, slim Ethel Bailey stood at her bathroom window, facing its curtained and unlighted counterpart across the shrubberied aisle in 1013 (its floor plan the mirror image of 1011's). Eyes closed, thin lips mischievously smiling, head turned aside like an ancient-Egyptian profile and chin out-thrust in amused, faux-modest challenge, she cupped her small breasts in her hands as if in presentation and swiveled her upper torso slightly from side to side, the better to display them. As I watched from behind a small cypress, she then slid one hand down across her flat belly and into the front of her jay-blue undies, moved it around inside there, and twitched her pelvis as if to the beat of some silent music. Turned herself hind-to; flexed and unflexed her skinny buttocks practically on the windowsill as she worked her panties down! Hot-faced with appall at both of us, I beat as hasty a retreat as prudence allowed. Was relieved indeed to see no one else out enjoying the night air. Hoped to Christ Jim Smythe wasn't checking for prowlers from his front window.

Already in bed, sitting propped against its king-size headboard and working her Sunday *Times* crossword puzzle while she waited for me to join her, "Where've *you* been?" Margie asked, in a tone of mock-petulant amusement, when I came in. "Out peeping on the neighbors?"

"Nobody out there worth peeping at," I declared as lightly as I could manage, and moved past her to the bathroom to hide my flushed face. "All the hot stuff's right here in Ten-Ten."

"Yes, well," she called back — playfully, to my immeasurable relief. "It *is* a bit sticky in here. Maybe turn the ceiling fan on when you come back in?"

I did, having undressed, washed up, brushed teeth, peed (uncomfortably conscious of the window virtually at my elbow), and donned a short-sleeved pajama top — and found that Margie had already shed hers and set aside her puzzle, expectantly. At that period of our lives, we Mannings still made love at least a couple of times a week (the so-clinical phrase "had sex" was not in as general use back then as nowadays, and never between ourselves), most often in the mornings, but also and usually more ardently at bedtime or even on a foul-weather weekend afternoon. That night, as the low-speed overhead fan moved light air over our skin and I was simultaneously stirred and shamed by the unexpungeable image of Sam Bailey's naked wife, we came together more passionately than we had done for some while. Entwined with her then in spent contentment, guilty-conscienced but enormously grateful for our happy and after-all-faithful marriage, I wondered briefly — and unjealously — whom my wife might have been fantasizing as *her* lover while we two went at it.

But "Wow," she murmured in drowsy languor. "That night sky of yours must've been some turn-on. You'll have to try it more often."

"*You're* my turn-on," I assured her — dutifully, guiltily, but nonetheless sincerely as we disconnected our satisfied bodies and turned to sleep.

And there You pretty much have it, make of it what You will. Relieved both as self-appointed chronicler and as a prevailingly moral man to put that discreditable aberration behind me, I wish I could follow it now with a proper dramatic climax and dénouement to this account of the Oyster Cove Peeping Tom: Some rascally local teenager, say, or migrant worker, is caught red-handed (red-eyed?) in the disgusting act and turned over to the Authorities, unless gunned down *in flagrante delicto* by Jim Smythe or some other Oyster Cover, several of whom had seen fit to arm themselves as the sightings multiplied. Or better yet, for dramatic effect if not for neighborhood comity, the P.T. turns out indeed to have been one of us, who then swears he was only keeping an eye out for prowlers, but fails to convince a fair number of us despite his mortified wife's indignant and increasingly desperate defense of him. More or less ostracized, the couple list their villa for sale, move somewhere down south or out west, and divorce soon after.

Et cetera. But what You're winding up here, if You happen to exist, is a history, not a Story, and its "ending" is no duly gratifying Resolution nor even a capital-E Ending, really, just a sort of petering out, like most folks' lives. No further Oyster Cove P.T. sightings reported after July, and only one more from elsewhere in Heron Bay Estates — from an *arriviste* couple just settling into their brand-new Spartina Pointey mansion and, who knows, maybe wanting in on the action?

The late-summer Atlantic hurricane season preempted our attention as usual; perhaps one of its serial dock-swamping, tree-limb-cracking near misses blew or washed the creep away? Life in the community reverted to normal: New neighbors moved in, replacing others moving up, down, sideways, or out. Kitchens and bathrooms were remodeled, whole villas renovated, older cars traded in for new. Grandchildren were born (never on grandparental location, and often thousands of American miles away); their parents — our grownup children — divorced or didn't, remarried or didn't, succeeded or failed in their careers or just muddled through. Old Oyster Covers got older, faltered, died — Ethel Bailey among them, rendered leaner yet in her terminal season by metastasized cervical cancer and its vain attendant therapies; Jim Smythe too, felled by a stroke when Democrats won the White House in '92. We re-deactivated our secondary security gates, and some of us resumed our evening *paseos* around the Court. Already by Halloween of the year I tell of, the P.T. had become little more than a slightly nervous neighborhood joke: "Peekaboo! I see you!" By Thanksgiving, the OCNA membership bowed heads in near unison (the outspokenly atheist Sam Bailey scowling straight ahead as always) while ex-Reverend Matt Grauer gave our collective thanks that that minor menace, or peace-disturbing figment, had evidently passed.

"I can't help wondering," Mary Grauer declared just a month or so ago, when something or other reminded her and Margie of the Good Old Days, "whether that's because there's nothing in Oyster Cove these days for a self-respecting pervert to get off on. Who wants an eyeful of *us*?"

Her husband loyally raised his hand, but then with a wink acknowledged that the likeliest candidates for voyeuring the current femmes of Oyster Cove Court were the geezers of TCI's Bayview Manor, were it not too long a round-trip haul for their motorized wheelchairs. Margie and I exchanged a glance: We had just about decided to make our "B.M. Move," as we'd come to call it between ourselves, but hadn't announced our decision yet.

"You know what?" my wife said then to the four of us (Sam Bailey having joined our Friday evening Old Farts Happy Hour in 1010's family room, with cheese canapés provided by Mary Grauer). "Sometimes I almost *miss* having that sicko around. What does that say about Margaret Manning?"

"That she enjoyed being sixty," Sam volunteered, "more than she enjoys being seventy-plus? Or that for a while there we were more of a neighborhood than before or since? Life in Oyster Cove got to be almost *interesting*, Ethel liked to say."

"I do sort of miss those days," Margie said again to me at that evening's end, as we clicked off the TV and room lights and made our way bedward. "Remember how we'd go at it some nights after you came in from checking outside?"

Replied I (if I remember correctly), "I do indeed," and gave her backside a friendly pat.

Indeed I do.

Toga Party

If "Doc Sam" Bailey — Dick Felton's longtime tennis buddy from over in Oyster Cove — were telling this toga party story, the old ex-professor would most likely have kicked it off with one of those lefty-liberal rants that he used to lay on his Heron Bay friends and neighbors at the drop of any hat. We can hear Sam now, going "Know what I think, guys? I think that if *you* think that the twentieth century was a goddamn horror show — two catastrophic world wars plus Korea and Vietnam plus assorted multimillion-victim genocides, purges, and pandemics plus the Cold War's three-decade threat of nuclear apocalypse plus whatever other goodies I'm forgetting to mention — then you ain't seen nothing yet, pals, 'cause the twenty-first is gonna be worse: no 'infidel' city safe from jihadist nuking, 'resource wars' for oil and water as China and India get ever more prosperous and supplies run out, the ruin of the planet by overpopulation, the collapse of America's economy when the dollar-bubble bursts, and right here in Heron Bay Estates the sea level's rising from global warming even as I speak, while the peninsula sinks under our feet and the hurricane season gets worse every year. So really, I mean: What the fuck? Just as well for us Golden Agers that we're on our last legs anyhow, worrying how our kids and grandkids will manage when the shit really hits the fan, but also relieved that we won't be around to see it happen. Am I right?"

Yes, well, Sam: If you say so, as you so often did. And Dick and Susan Felton would agree further (what they could imagine their friend adding at this point) that for the fragile present, despite all the foregoing, we Heron Bay Estaters and others like us from sea to ever-less-shining sea are extraordinarily fortune-favored folks (although the situation could change radically for the worse before the close of this parenthesis): respectable careers behind us; most of us in stable marriages and reasonably good health for our age (a few widows and widowers, Doc Sam included at the time we tell of; a few disabled, more or less, and/or ailing from cancer, Parkinson's, MS, stroke, late-onset diabetes, early-stage Alzheimer's, what have you); our children mostly middle-aged and married, with children of their own, pursuing their own careers all over the Republic; ourselves comfortably pensioned, enjoying what pleasures we can while we're still able — golf and tennis and travel, bridge games and gardening and other hobbies, visits to and from those kids and grandkids, entertaining friends and neighbors and being by them entertained with drinks and hors d'oeuvres and sometimes dinner at one another's houses or some restaurant up in nearby Stratford — and hosting or attending the occasional party.

There now: We've arrived at our subject, and since Sam Bailey's *not* the one in charge of this story, we can start it where it started for the Feltons: the late-summer Saturday when Dick stepped out before breakfast as usual in his PJs, robe, and slippers to fetch the morning newspaper from the end of their driveway and found rubber-banded to their mailbox flag (as would sundry other residents of Rockfish Reach to theirs, so he could see by looking up and down their bend of Shoreside Drive) an elaborate computer-graphic invitation to attend Tom and Patsy Hardison's *TOGA PARTY!!!* two weeks hence, on "Saturnsday, XXIV Septembris," to inaugurate their just-built house at 12 Loblolly Court, one of several "keyholes" making off the Drive.

"Toga party?" Dick asked his wife over breakfast. The house computer geek among her other talents, between coffee sips and spoonfuls of blueberry-topped granola Susan was admiring the artwork on the Hardisons' invitation: ancient-Roman-looking wild-party frescoes scanned from somewhere and color-printed as background to the text. "What's a toga party, please?"

"Frat-house stuff, I'd guess," she supposed. "Like in that crazy *Animal House* movie from whenever? Everybody dressing up like for a whatchacallum . . ." Pointing to the fresco shot: "Saturnalia?"

"Good try," Doc Sam would grant her two weeks later, at the party.

"Especially since today is quote 'Saturnsday.' But those anything-goes Saturnalia in ancient Rome were celebrated in December, so I guess Bacchanalia's the word we want — after the wine god Bacchus? And the singular would be bacchanal." Since Sam wasn't breakfasting with the Feltons, however, Dick replied that he didn't know beans about Saturnalia and animal houses, and went back to leafing through the *Baltimore Sun.*

"So are we going?" Sue wanted to know. "We're supposed to RSVP by this weekend."

"Your call," her husband said or requested, adding that as far as he knew, their calendar was clear for "Saturnsday, XXIV Septembris." But the Feltons of 1020 Shoreside Drive, he needn't remind her, while not recluses, weren't particularly social animals, either, compared to most of their Rockfish Reach neighborhood and, for that matter, the Heron Bay Estates development generally, to which they'd moved year-round half a dozen years back, after Dick's retirement from his upper-mid-level-management post in Baltimore and Susan's from her office-administration job at her alma mater, Goucher College. To the best of his recollection, moreover, their wardrobes were toga-free.

His wife's guess was that any wraparound bed sheet kind of thing would do the trick. She would computer-search "toga party" after breakfast, she declared; her bet was that there'd be a clutch of websites on the subject. "It's all just *fun*, for pity's sake! And when was the last time we went to a neighborhood party? Plus I'd really like to see the inside of that house of theirs. Wouldn't you?"

Yeah, well, her husband supposed so. Sure.

That less-than-eager agreement earned him one of Sue's see-me-being-patient? looks: eyes raised ceilingward, tongue checked between right-side molars. Susan Felton was a half-dozen years younger than Richard — not enough to matter much in her late sixties and his mid-seventies, after forty-some years of marriage — but except for work he inclined to be the more passive partner, content to follow his wife's lead in most matters. Over the past year or two, though, as he'd approached and then attained the three-quarter-century mark, he had by his own acknowledgment become rather stick-in-the-muddish, not so much *depressed* by the prospect of their imminent old age as *subdued* by it, de-zested, his get up and go all but gotten up and gone, as he had observed to be the case with others at his age and stage (though by no means all) among their limited social acquaintance.

In sum (he readily granted whenever he and Sue spoke of this subject, as lately they'd found themselves doing more often than formerly), the chap had yet to come to terms with his fast-running mortal span: the inevitable downsizing from the house and grounds and motorboat and cars that they'd taken years of pleasure in; the physical and mental deterioration that lay ahead for them; the burden of caregiving through their decline; the unimaginable loss of life-partner ... The prospect of his merely ceasing to exist, he would want it understood, did not in itself much trouble him. He and Sue had enjoyed a good life indeed, all in all. If their family was less close than some that they knew and envied, neither was it dysfunctional: Cordially Affectionate is how they would describe the prevailing tone of their relations with their grown-up kids and growing-up grandkids; they could wish it better, but were gratified that it wasn't worse, like some others they knew. No catastrophes in their life story thus far: Dick had required bypass surgery in his mid-sixties, and Sue an ovariectomy and left-breast lumpectomy in her mid-menopause. Both had had cataracts removed, and Dick had some macular degeneration — luckily of the less aggressive, "dry" variety — and mild hearing loss in his left ear, as well as being constitutionally over-weight despite periodic attempts at dieting. Other than those, no serious problems in any life department, and a quite satisfying *curriculum vita* for each of them. More and more often recently, Richard Felton found himself wishing that somewhere down the road they could just push a button and make themselves and their abundant possessions simply disappear — *poof!* — the latter transformed into equitably distributed checks in the mail to their heirs, with love ...

These cheerless reflections had been center-staged lately by the business that he readdressed at his desk after breakfast: the periodic review of his and Susan's Last Will and Testament. Following his routine midyear update of their computer-spreadsheet Estate Statement, and another, linked to it, that Susan had designed for estimating the distribution of those assets under the current provisions of their wills, it was Dick's biennial autumn custom, in even-numbered years, to review these benefactions, then to call to Sue's attention any that struck him as having become perhaps larger or smaller than they ought to be and to suggest appropriate percentage adjustments, as well as the addition or deletion of beneficiaries in the light of changed circumstances or priorities since the previous go-round: Susan's dear old all-girls prep school, e.g., had lately closed its doors for keeps, so there went Article D of Item Fifth in her will, which bequeathed to it three percent of her Net Residual Estate after funeral costs, executors' fees, estate taxes, and other expenses. Should she perhaps reassign that bequest to the Avon County Public Library, of which she and Dick made frequent use? Estate lawyers' fees being what they were, they tried to limit such emendations to codicil size, if possible, instead of will-redrafting size. But whatever the satisfaction of keeping their affairs in order, it was not a cheery chore (in odd-numbered-year autumns, to spread out the morbidity, they reviewed and updated their separate Letters to Their Executors). The deaths in the year just past of Sam Bailey's so-lively wife, Ethel (cervical cancer), and of their own daughter Katie's father-in-law out in Colorado (aneurysm)—a fellow not even Dick's age, the administration of whose comparatively simple estate had nevertheless been an extended headache for Katie's husband—contributed to the poignancy of the current year's review. Apart from the dreadful prospect of personal bereavement (poor old Sam!), he had looked in vain for ways to minimize further the postmortem burden on their grown-up daughter and son, whom they most certainly loved, but to whom alas in recent years they'd grown less than ideally close both personally and geographically. Dick couldn't imagine, frankly, how he would survive without his beloved and indispensable Susan: less well than Sam Bailey without Ethel, for sure, whose lawyer son and CPA daughter-in-law lived and worked in Stratford, attentively monitored the old fellow's situation and condition, and frequently included him in family activities.

For her part, Susan often declared that the day Dick died would be the last of her own life as well, although by what means she'd end it, she hadn't yet worked out. Dick Junior and Katie and their spouses would just have to put their own lives on hold, fly in from Chicago and Seattle, and pick up the pieces. Let them hate her for it if they chose to; she wouldn't be around to know it, and they'd be getting a tidy sum for their trouble. "So," she proposed perkily when the couple reconvened at morning's end to make lunch and plan their afternoon. "Let's eat, drink, and be merry at the Hardisons' on X-X-I-V Septembris, since tomorrow *et cetera*?"

"Easy enough to say," her grave-spirited spouse replied. "But whenever I hear it said, I wonder how anybody could have an appetite for their Last Supper." On the other hand, he acknowledged, here they were, as yet not dead, disabled, or devastated, like the city of New Orleans by Hurricane Katrina just a week or so since: No reason why they *shouldn't* go to the party, he supposed — if they could figure out what to wear.

Over sandwiches and diet iced tea on their waterside screened porch, facing the narrow tidal creek of Rockfish Reach agleam in end-of-summer sunshine, "No problem," Sue reported. She'd been on the Web, where a Google search of "toga party" turned up no fewer than 266,000 entries; the first three or four were enough to convince her that anything they improvised would suffice. It was, as she'd suspected, an old fraternity-house thing, made popular among now-middle-aged baby boomers by John Belushi's 1978 film *Animal House*. One could make or buy online "Roman" costumes as elaborate as any in such movies as *Ben-Hur* and *Gladiator*, or simply go the bed-sheet-and-sandals route that she mentioned before. Leave it to her; she'd come up with something. Meanwhile, could they be a little less gloom-and-doomy, for pity's sake, and count their blessings?

Her husband thanked her wholeheartedly for taking charge of the matter, and promised her and himself to try to brighten up a bit and make the most of whatever quality time remained to them.

Which amounted (he then honored his promise by *not* going on to say), with luck, to maybe a dozen years. No computer-adept like his wife, Dick nonetheless had his own desktop machine in his study, on which, between his more serious morning desk chores, it had occurred to him to do a little Web search himself. "Life expectancy," entered and clicked, had turned up nearly fourteen *million* entries (more than a lifetime's worth of reading, he'd bet), among the first half-dozen of which was a questionnaire-calculator — age, ethnicity, personal and family medical histories, etc.— that, once he'd completed it, predicted his "median quartile" age at death to be 89.02 years. In (very!) short, fourteen to go, barring accident, although of course it could turn out to be more or fewer.

Only a dozen or so Septembers left. How assimilate it? On the one hand, the period between birth and age fourteen had seemed to him of epochal extent, and that between fourteen and twenty-eight scarcely less so: nonexistence to adolescence! Adolescence to maturity, marriage, and parenthood! But his thirties, forties, and fifties had passed more swiftly decade by decade, no doubt because his adult life-changes were fewer and more gradual than those of his youth. And his early sixties — when he'd begun the gradual reduction of his office workload and the leisurely search for a weekend retreat somewhere on Maryland's Eastern Shore that could be upgraded to a year-round residence at his and Sue's retirement — seemed the day before yesterday instead of twelve-plus years ago.

So: Maybe fourteen years left — and who knew how many of those would be healthy and active? Eat, drink, and be merry, indeed! About what?

Well, for starters, about not being a wiped-out refugee from the storm-blasted Gulf Coast, obviously, or a starving, gang-raped young African mother in Darfur. "God's only excuse is that He doesn't exist," Sam Bailey liked to quote some famous person as having said (Oscar Wilde? Bertrand Russell? Don't ask Dick Felton, who anyhow regarded it as a pretty lame excuse). But here they were, he and his long-beloved, on a warm and gorgeous mid-September afternoon in an attractive and well-maintained neighborhood on a branch of a creek off a river off a bay luckily untouched (so far) by that year's busier-than-ever Atlantic hurricane season; their lawn and garden and crape myrtles flourishing; their outboard runabout, like themselves, good for a few more spins before haul-out time; their immediately pending decisions nothing more mattersome than whether to run a few errands in Stratford or do some outdoor chores on the property before Sue's golf and Dick's tennis dates scheduled for later in the day.

So they would go to the goddamn party, as Dick scolded himself for terming it out of Susan's hearing. Some hours later, at a break in whacking the yellow Wilson tennis balls back to Sam Bailey on the Heron Bay Club's courts (since Ethel's death, Sam had lost interest in playing for points, but he still enjoyed a vigorous hour's worth of back-and-forthing a couple of times a week, which had come to suit Dick just fine), he mentioned the upcoming event: that it would be his and Sue's first toga party, and that they'd be going more to have a look at their new neighbors' Loblolly Court mansion and get to know its owners than out of any interest in funny-costume parties. To his mild surprise, he learned that Sam — although an Oyster Cover rather than a Rockfish Reacher — would be there too, and was in fact looking forward to "XXIV Septembris." As a longtime board member of the Club, Sam had met Tom and Patsy Hardison when they'd applied for membership, even before commencing their house construction. And while he himself at age eighty could do without the faux-Roman high jinks, his Ethel had relished such foolery and would have loved nothing more than another toga party, if the goddamn nonexistent Almighty hadn't gifted her with goddamn cancer.

They resumed their volleying, until Sam's right arm and shoulder had had enough and the area behind Dick's breastbone began to feel the mild soreness-after-exertion that he hadn't yet mentioned either to Susan or to their doctor, although he'd been noticing it for some months. He *had* shared with both his life partner and his tennis partner his opinion that an ideal way to "go" would be by a sudden massive coronary on the tennis court upon his returning one of Sam's tricky backhand slices with a wham-o forehand topspin. "Don't you *dare* die first!" his wife had warned him. All Sam had said was "Make sure we get a half-hour's tennis in before you kick."

"So tell me about toga parties," Dick asked him as they packed up their racquets and balls, latched the chain-link entrance gate behind themselves, and swigged water from the drinking fountain beside the tennis court restrooms. "What kind of high jinks should we expect?"

The usual, Sam supposed: like calling out something in Latin when you first step into the room . . .

"Latin? I don't know any damn Latin!"

"Sure you do: *Ave Maria? Tempus fugit?* After that, and some joking around about all the crazy getups, it's just a friendly cocktail-dinner party for the next couple hours, till they wind it up with some kinky contest-games with fun prizes. Susan will enjoy it; maybe even *you* will. *Veni, vidi, vici!*"

"Excuse me?"

"You're excused. But *go*, for Christ's sake. Or Jove's sake, whoever's." Thumbing his shrunken chest, "*I'm* going, goddamn it, even though the twenty-fourth is the first anniversary of Ethel's death. I promised her and the kids that I'd try to maintain the status quo as best I could for at least a year — no major changes, one foot in front of the other, *et cetera* — and then we'd see what we'd see. So I'm going for her sake as much as mine. There're two more passwords for you, by the way: *status quo* and *et cetera.*"

Remarkable guy, the Feltons agreed at that afternoon's end, over gin and tonics on the little barbecue patio beside their screened porch. In Dick's opinion, at least, that no-major-changes-for-at-least-the-first-year policy made good sense: Keep everything as familiar and routine as possible while the shock of bereavement was so raw and overwhelming.

But "Count me out," said Sue. "Twenty-four hours tops, and then it's So long, Susie-Q. But what I *really* want is the Common Disaster scenario, thanks"—a term they'd picked up from their estate lawyer over in the city, who in the course of this latest revision of their wills had urged them to include a new estate-tax-saving gimmick that neither of them quite understood, although they quite trusted the woman's professional advice. Their wills had formerly stipulated that in the event of their dying together (as in a plane crash or other "common disaster"), in circumstances such that it could not be determined which of them predeceased the other, it would be presumed that Dick died before Susan, and their wills would be executed in that order, he leaving the bulk of his estate to her, and she passing it on to their children and other assorted beneficiaries. But inasmuch as virtually all their assets — cars, house, bank accounts, securities portfolio — were jointly owned (contrary to the advice of their lawyer, who had recommended such tax-saving devices as bypass trusts and separate bank and stock accounts, not to the Feltons' taste), the Common Disaster provision had been amended in both wills to read that "each will be presumed to have survived the other." It would save their heirs a bundle, they'd been assured, but to Dick and Sue it sounded like Alice in Wonderland logic. How could each of them be presumed to have survived the other?

"Remind me to ask Sam that at the party, okay? And if he doesn't know, he can ask his lawyer son for us."

And so to the party they-all went, come "XXIV Septembris," despite the unending, anti-festive news reports from the Louisiana coast: the old city of New Orleans, after escaping much of the expected wind damage from Hurricane Katrina, all but destroyed by its levee-busting storm surge and consequent flooding; and now Hurricane Rita tearing up the coastal towns of Mississippi even as the Feltons made their way, along with other invitees, to the Hardisons'. The evening being overcast, breezy, and cool compared to that week's earlier Indian-summer weather, they opted reluctantly to drive instead of walk the little way from 1020 Shoreside Drive to 12 Loblolly Court — no more than three city blocks, although Heron Bay Estates wasn't laid out in blocks — rather than wear cumbersome outer wraps over their costumes. The decision to go once made, Dick had done his best to get into the spirit of the thing, and was not displeased with what they'd improvised together: for him, leather sandals, a brown-and-white-striped Moroccan caftan picked up as a souvenir ten years earlier on a Mediterranean cruise that had made a stop in Tangier, and on his balding gray head a plastic laurel wreath that Susan had found in the party-stuff aisle of their Stratford supermarket. Plus a silk-rope belt (meant to be a drapery tieback) on which he'd hung a Jamaican machete in its decoratively tooled leather sheath, the implement acquired on a Caribbean vacation longer ago than the caftan. Okay, not exactly ancient Roman, but sufficiently oddball exotic — and the caesars' empire, as they recalled, had in fact extended to North Africa: Antony and Cleopatra, *et cetera*. As for Sue, in their joint opinion she looked Cleopatralike in her artfully folded and tucked bed sheet (a suggestion from the Web, with detailed instructions on how to fold and wrap), belted like her husband's caftan with a drapery tieback to match his, her feet similarly sandaled, and on her head a sleek black costume-wig from that same supermarket aisle, with a tiara halo of silver-foil stars.

Carefully, so as not to muss their outfits, they climbed into her Toyota Solara convertible, its top raised against the evening chill (his car was a VW Passat wagon, although both vehicles were titled jointly) — and got no farther than halfway to Loblolly Court before they had to park it and walk the remaining distance anyhow, such was the crowd of earlier-arrived sedans, vans, and SUVs lining the road, their owners either already at the party or, like the Feltons, strolling their costumed way toward #12.

"Would you look at that?" Dick said when they turned into the tree-lined keyhole drive at the head whereof shone the Hardisons' mega-McMansion: not a neo-Georgian or plantation-style manor like its similarly new and upscale neighbors, but a great rambling beige stucco affair — terra-cotta-tiled roof, great arched windows flanked by spiraled pilasters — resplendent with lights inside and out, including floodlit trees and shrubbery, its *palazzo* design more suited in the Feltons' opinion to Venice or booming south Florida than to

Maryland's Eastern Shore. "How'd it get past Heron Bay's house-plan police?" Meaning the Community Association's Design Review Board, whose okay was required on all building and landscaping proposals. Susan's guess was that Tidewater Communities, Inc., the developer of Heron Bay Estates and other projects on both shores of the Chesapeake, might have jiggered it through in hopes of attracting more million-dollar-house builders to HBE's several high-end detached-home neighborhoods, like Spartina Pointe. She too thought the thing conspicuously out of place in Rockfish Reach, but "You know what they say," she declared: "*De gustibus non est disputandum*"— her chosen party password, which she was pleased to have remembered from prep school days. "Is that the Gibsons ahead of us?"

It was, Dick could affirm when the couple — she bed-sheet-toga'd like Susan, but less appealingly, given her considerable heft; he wearing what looked like a white hospital gown set off by some sort of gladiator thing around his waist and hips — passed under a pair of tall floodlit pines flanking the entrance walkway: Hank and Becky Gibson, Oyster Covers like Sam Bailey, whom the Feltons knew only casually from the Club, Hank being the golfer and Becky the tennis player in their household.

"*Et tu, Brute!*" Sue called out (she really had been doing her homework; that "Bru-tay" phrase sounded familiar, but Dick couldn't place it). The Gibsons turned, laughed, waved, and waited; the foursome then joked and teased their way up the stone walk beside the "Euro-cobble" driveway to #12's massive, porte-cochèred main entrance: a two-tiered platform with three wide, curved concrete steps up to the first marble-tiled landing, and another three to the second, where one of the tall, glass-paned, dark-wood-paneled double doors stood open and a slender, trim-toga'd woman, presumably their hostess, was greeting and admitting several other arrivals.

"A miniskirted toga?" Hank Gibson wondered aloud, for while the costume's thin white top had a fold-and-wrap toga look to it, below the elaborately figured multipaneled belt were a short white pleated skirt and sandal lacings entwined fetchingly almost to her knees. "*Amo amas amat!*" he then called ahead. The couple just entering turned and laughed, as did the hostess. Then Sam Bailey — whom the Feltons now saw stationed just inside the door, in a white terry-cloth robe of the sort provided in better-grade hotel rooms, belted with what appeared to be an army-surplus cartridge belt and topped with a defoliated wreath that looked a bit like Jesus' crown of thorns — called back, "*Amamus amatis amant!*" and gestured them to enter.

Their sleek-featured hostess — more Cleopatran even than Sue, with her short, straight, glossy dark hair encircled by a black metal serpent-band, its asplike head rising from her brow as if to strike — turned her gleaming smile to them and extended her hand, first to Susan. "Hi! I'm Patsy Hardison. And you are?"

"Sue and Dick Felton," Sue responded, "from around the bend at Ten-Twenty Shoreside? What a beautiful approach to your house!"

"And a house to match it," Dick added, taking her hand in turn.

"I *love* your costumes!" their hostess exclaimed politely. "So *imaginative!* I know we've seen each other at the Club, but Tom and I are still sorting out names and faces and addresses, so please bear with us." As other arrivals were gathering behind them, she explained to all hands that after calling out their passwords to Sam Bailey, whom she and Tom had appointed to be their Centurion at the Gate, they would find nametags on a table in the foyer, just beyond which her husband would show them the way to the refreshments. "Passwords, please? Loud and clear for all to hear!"

"*De gustibus non est disputandum!*" Sue duly proclaimed, hoping her hosts wouldn't take that proverb as any sort of criticism. Dick followed with "*Ad infinitum!*" — adding, in a lower voice to Sam, who waved them in, "or *ad nauseam*, whatever. Cool outfit there, Sam."

"The Decline and Fall of the You Know What," their friend explained, and kissed Sue's cheeks. "Aren't *you* the femme fatale tonight, excuse my French. Ethel would've loved that getup."

"I can't *believe* she's not in the next room!" Sue said, hugging him. "Sipping champagne and nibbling hors d'oeuvres!"

"Same here," the old fellow admitted, his voice weakening, until he turned his head aside, stroked his thin white beard, and cleared his throat. "But she couldn't make it tonight, alas. So *carpe diem*, guys."

Although they weren't certain of the Latin, its general sense was clear enough. They patted his shoulder, moved on to the nametag table on one side of the marble-floored, high-ceilinged entry hall, found and applied their elegantly lettered and alphabetically ordered stick-on labels, and were greeted at the main living room step-down by their host, a buff and hearty-looking chap in his late fifties or early sixties wearing a red-maned silver helmet, a Caesars Palace T-shirt from Las Vegas, a metallic gladiator skirt over knee-length white Bermuda shorts, and leather sandals even higher-laced than his wife's on his dark-haired, well-muscled legs. With an exaggeratedly elaborate kiss of Susan's hand and a vise-hard squeeze of Dick's, "*Dick and Susan Felton!*" he announced to the room beyond and below, having scanned their name stickers. "Welcome to our humble abode!"

"Some humble," Dick said, his tone clearly Impressed, and Sue added, "It's *magnificent!*"

As indeed it was: the enormous, lofty-ceilinged living room, its great sliding glass doors open to a large, roofed and screened terrace, beyond which a yet larger pool / patio area extended, tastefully landscaped and floodlit, toward the tidal covelet where the Hardisons' trawler yacht was docked. A suitably toga'd pianist tinkled away at the grand piano in one corner of the multi-couched and -cocktail-tabled room; out on the terrace a laureled bartender filled glasses while a minitoga'd, similarly wreathed young woman moved among the guests with platters of hors d'oeuvres.

"Great neighborhood, too," Dick added, drawing Sue down the step so that their host could greet the next arrivals. "We know you'll like living here."

With a measured affability, "Oh, well," Tom Hardison responded. "Pat and I don't actually *live* here, but we do enjoy cruising over from Annapolis on weekends and holidays. Y'all go grab yourselves a drink now, and we'll chat some more later, before the fun starts, okay?"

"Aye-aye, *sir*," Dick murmured to Susan as they dutifully moved on. "Quite a little weekend hideaway!"

She too was more or less rolling her eyes. "But they seem like a friendly enough couple. I wonder where the money comes from."

From their husband-and-wife law firm over in the state capital, one of their costumed neighbors informed them as they waited together at the bar: Hardison & Hardison, very in with the governor and other influential Annapolitans. What was more, they had just taken on their son, Tom Junior, as a full partner, and his younger sister, just out of law school, as a junior partner: sort of a family 4-H Club. And had the Feltons seen the name of that boat of theirs?

"Not yet."

"Stroll out and take a look." To the bartender: "Scotch on the rocks for me, please."

Susan: "White wine spritzer?" And Dick: "I'll have a glass of red."

The barman smiled apologetically. "No reds, I'm afraid. On account of the carpets?" And shrugged: not *his* house rule.

"Mm-*hm*." The living room wall-to-wall, they now noted, was a gray so light as to be almost white. Poor choice for a carpet color, in Sue's opinion — and for that matter, what color *wouldn't* be stained by a spilled merlot or cabernet? But *de gustibus, de gustibus.* "So make it gin and tonic, then," Dick supposed.

"*Ars longa!*" a late-arriving guest called from the hallway.

Sam Bailey, behind them, asked the bartender for the same, predicted that that new arrival was George Newett, from the College, and called back "*Vita brevis est!*" His own *vita* without Ethel, however, he added to the Feltons, had gotten *longa* than he wanted it to be. Raising his glass in salute, "Fuck life. But here we are, I guess. *E pluribus unum.* Shall we join Trimalchio's Feast?"

The allusion escaped them, but to make room for other thirsters they moved away from the bar, drinks in hand, toward the groups of guests chatting at the hors d'oeuvres tables at the other end, and out on the pool deck, and in what Susan now dubbed the Great Room. As Sam had foretold, once the admission ritual was done, the affair settled into an agreeable Heron Bay neighborhood cocktail party, lavish by the standards of Rockfish Reach and Oyster Cove if perhaps not by those of Spartina Pointe, and enlivened by the guests' comments on one another's costumes, which ranged from the more or less aggressively noncompliant (the bearded fellow identified by Doc Sam as "George Newett from the College" wore a camouflage hunting jacket over blue jeans, polo shirt, and Adidas walking shoes; his wife an African dashiki), to the meant-to-be-humorous, like Tom Hardison's casino T-shirt and Dick Felton's caftan-cum-machete, to the formally elaborate, like Patricia Hardison's and some others' store-bought togas or gladiator outfits. Although not, by their own acknowledgment, particularly "people" people, husband and wife found it a pleasant change from their customary routines to chat in that handsome setting with their neighbors and other acquaintances and to meet acquaintances of those acquaintances; to refresh their drinks and nibble at canapés as they asked and were asked about one another's health, their former or current careers, their grown children's whereabouts and professions, their impression of "houses like this" in "neighborhoods like ours," their opinion of the Bush administration's war in Iraq (careful stepping here, unless one didn't mind treading on toes), and their guesses on whether Chesapeake Bay, in places still recovering from the surge floods of Tropical Storm Isabel two years past, might yet be hurricaned in the current hyperactive season.

"Just heard that Rita's blowing the bejesus out of Gulfport and Biloxi. I swear."

"Anybody want to bet they'll use up the alphabet this year and have to start over? Hurricane Aaron? Tropical Storm Bibi?"

"As in B. B. King?"

"C. C. Ryder? Dee Dee Myers?"

"Who's that?"

"E. E. Cummings?"

"Who's *that*?"

"I can't get over those poor bastards in New Orleans: Why didn't they get the hell out instead of hanging around and looting stores?"

"Did you hear the one about Bush's reply when a reporter asked his opinion of *Roe versus Wade*? 'I don't care how they get out of New Orleans' says W, 'as long as it doesn't cost the government money.'"

"*George Newett*, is it? At my age, I wish *everybody* wore nametags."

"On their foreheads. Even our grandkids."

"*Love* that headband, by the way, Pat. Right out of *Antony and Cleopatra*!"

"Why, thanks, Susan. Tom's orders are that if some joker says I've got my head up my *asp*, I should tell them to kiss it. Now is that nice?"

"Some cool djellaba you've got there, Dick."

"Caftan, actually. Some cool yacht you've got out there! Is that your RV too, the big shiny guy parked down by your dock?"

It was, Tom Hardison readily acknowledged. In simple truth, he and Pat enjoyed *owning* things. Owning and doing! "What the hell, you only get one go-round."

George Newett's wife (also from the College, and with a last name different from her husband's) explained to Susan, who had asked about Sam Bailey's earlier reference, that Trimalchio's Feast is a famous scene in the first-century *Satyricon* of Petronius Arbiter: an over-the-top gluttonous orgy that became a sort of emblem of the Roman Empire's decadence. "The mother of all toga parties, I guess. But talk about over the top ..." She eye-rolled the sumptuous setting in which they stood. The two women agreed, however, that Patricia Hardison really did seem to be, in the best sense, *patrician*: upscale but good-humored, friendly, and without affectation; competent and self-assured but no-wise overbearing; as Amanda Todd (i.e., Mrs. George Newett, poet and professor, from Blue Crab Bight) put it, superior, but not capital-S Superior.

"I like her," Susan reported to her husband when they next crossed paths in their separate conversational courses. "First poet I ever met. Is her husband nice?"

Dick shrugged. "Retired from the College. Describes himself as a failed-old-fart writer. But at least he's not intimidating."

"Unlike . . .?"

Her husband nodded toward their host, who was just then pro-claiming to the assembled "friends, Romans, countrymen" that the dinner buffet (under a large tent out beside the pool deck) was now open for business, and that Jove helps those who help themselves. "Af-ter dinner, game and prize time!"

En route past them toward the bar, "Me," Sam Bailey said, "I'm go-ing to have me another G and T. D'ja see their boat's name? Bit of a mouthful, huh?"

Sue hadn't. She worried aloud that Doc Sam was overdoing the booze, maybe on account of his wife's death-day anniversary; hoped he wouldn't be driving home after the party. "I doubt if he cares," Dick said. "*I* sure wouldn't, in his position." The name of the boat, by the way, he added, was *Plaintiff's Complaint*. Which reminded him: Since both Hardisons were lawyers, maybe he'd ask Emperor Tom about that "each survives the other" business in their wills, and Sue could ask her new pal Cleopatra. Or was it Sheba?

"Come on," his wife chided. "They're friendly people who just hap-pen to be rich as shit. Let's do the buffet."

They did it, Sue chatting in her lively/friendly way with the people before and after them in the help-yourself line and with the caterers who sliced and served the roast beef au jus and breast of turkey; Dick less forthcoming, as had lately more and more become his manner, but not uncordial, and appreciative of his mate's carrying the conver-sational ball. Time was when they'd both been more outgoing: In their forties and fifties they'd had fairly close *friends*, of the sort one enjoys going out with to a restaurant or movie. By age sixty, after a couple of career moves, they had only office lunch-colleagues, and since their retirement not even those; just cordial over-the-fence-chat neighbors, golf / tennis partners, and their seldom more than annually visited or visiting offspring. A somewhat empty life, he'd grant, but one which, as afore-established, they enjoyed more than not, on balance — or *had* enjoyed, until his late brooding upon its inevitably approaching decline, even collapse, had leached the pleasure out of it.

So "I'll fetch us another glass of wine," he said when they'd claimed two vacant places at one of the several long tables set up under the tent. And added in a mutter, "Wish they had some *red* to go with this beef."

"Shh. Mostly club soda in mine, please." Then "Hi," she greeted the younger couple now seating themselves in the folding chairs across from theirs: "Dick and Sue Felton, from down the road."

"Judy and Joe Barnes," the man of them replied as they scanned one another's nametags: "Blue Crab Bight." He extended his hand first to seated Susan and then to Dick, who briefly clasped it before saying "Going for a refill; back in a minute."

Speaking for him, "Can he bring you-all anything?" Sue offered. "While he's at it?"

They were okay, thanks. He ought to have thought of that himself, Dick supposed, although he'd've needed a tray or something to carry four glasses. Anyhow, screw it. Screw it, screw it, screw it.

Some while later, after they'd fed themselves while exchanging get-acquainted pleasantries with the Barneses — Sue and Judy about the various neighborhoods of Heron Bay Estates, Dick and Joe about the effects of global warming on the Atlantic hurricane season and the ballooning national deficit's impact on the stock market (Joe worked in the Stratford office of a Baltimore investment-counseling firm)— "Aren't *you* the life of the party," Susan half teased, half chided her husband, who on both of those weighty questions had opposed Joe Barnes's guardedly optimistic view with his own much darker one. The two couples were now on their feet again, as were most of the other guests, and circulating from tent to pool deck and lanai.

"Really sorry about that, hon." As in fact he was, and promised her and himself to try to be more "up." For in truth he had enjoyed meeting and talking with the Barneses, and had had a good post-dinner conversation with young Joe out by the pool while Susan and Judy visited the WC— "on the jolly subject of that Common Disaster provision in our wills."

"You didn't."

"Sure did — because *he* happened to mention that his clients often review their estate statements with him so he can help coordinate their investment strategies with their estate lawyer's advice, to reduce inheritance taxes and such."

"O joy."

"So naturally I asked him whether he'd heard of that 'each survives the other' business, and he not only knew right off what I was talking about but explained it simply and clearly, which Betsy Furman" — their estate lawyer — "never managed to do." What it came down to, he explained in turn to not-awfully-interested Susan, was that should they die "simultaneously," their jointly owned assets would be divided fifty-fifty, one half passing by the terms of his will, as if he had outlived her, and the other half by hers, as if she'd outlived him. "So you make us up another computer spreadsheet along those lines, and we can estimate each beneficiary's take."

"O very joy." But she would do that, she agreed, ASAP — and she appreciated his finally clarifying that little mystery. Nor had she herself, she would have him know, been talking only girlie stuff: When Pat Hardison had happened to speak of "her house" and "Tom's boat," upon Sue's questioning their hostess had explained that like most people she knew, the Hardisons titled their assets separately, for "death tax" reasons: Their Annapolis place was in Tom's name, this Stratford one in hers; same with the boat and the RV, the Lexus and the Cadillac Escalade, their various bank accounts and securities holdings. *So* much more practical, taxwise: Why give your hard-earned assets to the government instead of to your children? Weren't Sue and her husband set up that way?

"I had to tell her I wasn't sure, that that was your department. But my impression is that everything we own is in both our names, right? Are we being stupid?"

Any estate lawyer would likely think so, Dick acknowledged. Betsy Furman had certainly encouraged bypass trusts, and had inserted that "each survives the other" business into their wills as the next best thing after he'd told her that they were uncomfortable with any arrangement other than joint ownership, which was how they'd done things since Day One of their marriage. He was no canny CPA or estate lawyer or investment geek, one of those types who tell you it's foolish to pay off your mortgage instead of claiming the interest payments as a tax deduction.

Probably they knew what they were talking about, but it was over his head and not his and Susan's style. "If the kids and grandkids and the rest get less of the loot that way than they'd get otherwise, they're still getting plenty. Who gives a shit?" What he really cared about, he reminded her, was not their death, much less its payoff to their heirs, but their Last Age and their dying. It required the pair of them in good health to maintain their Heron Bay house and grounds and the modest Baltimore condo that they'd bought as a city retreat when they'd retired, sold their dear old townhouse, and made Stratford their principal address. The day either of them joined the ranks of the more than temporarily incapacitated would be the end of life as they knew and enjoyed it; neither of them was cut out for long-term caregiving or caregetting. A Common Disaster, preferably out of the blue while they were still functioning, was the best imaginable scenario for The End: Let them "each survive the other" technically, but neither survive the other in fact — even if that meant making the necessary arrangements themselves.

"My big bundle of joy," Susan said, sighing, and hugged him to put a stop to this lately-so-familiar disquisition.

"Sorry sorry sorry, doll. Let's go refill."

"Hey, look at the lovebirds!" Sam Bailey hollered, too loudly, across the deck from the terrace bar. The old fellow was pretty obviously overindulging. A few people paused in their conversation to glance his way, a few others to smile at the Feltons or raise eyebrows at the old fellow's rowdiness. By way of covering it, perhaps, Tom Hardison, who happened to be standing not far from Sam, gave him a comradely pat on the shoulder and then strode behind the bar, fetched out a beribboned brass bugle, of all things, that he'd evidently stashed there, blew a single loud blast like an amplified, extended fart, and called "Game and prize time, everybody!" The "Great Room" pianist underscored the announcement with a fortissimo fanfare. When all hands were silent and listening, perky Pat Hardison, holding a brown beer bottle as if it were a portable microphone, repeated her husband's earlier "Friends, Romans, countrymen," politically correcting that last term to country-*folk*, "lend me your ears!"

"You want to borrow our *rears?*" Sam Bailey asked loudly.

"We've got those covered, Sam," the host smoothly replied; he too now sported a beer-bottle mike in one hand, while with the other placing the bugle bell-down on his interrupter's head, to the guests' approving chuckles. "Or maybe I should say *uncovered*, since tonight's Special Olympics consist of Thong-Undie Quoits for the ladies, out on the pool deck, and for the gents, Bobbing for Grapes wherever you see them, as you very soon will. I'll be refereeing the quoits"—he held up a handful of bikini briefs for all to see—"and Pat'll oversee the grapes, which every lady is invited to grab a bunch of and invite the bobber of her choice to bob for."

"Here's how it's done, girls," Pat explained. Out of the large bowl of dark grapes the bartender had produced from behind his station, she plucked a bunch and nestled it neatly into her cleavage. "You tuck 'em in like so, and then your significant other, or whoever, sees how many he can nibble off their stems—without using his hands, mind. The couple with the fewest grapes left wins the prize." Turning to her husband: "Want a no-grope grape, sweetie-pie?"

"Yummy! Deal me in!" Doffing his helmet, he shmushed his face into his wife's fruited bosom and made loud chomping sounds while she, with a mock what-are-you-going-to-do-with-men? look at the laughing bystanders, uplifted her breasts with both hands to facilitate his gorging, and one of the hors d'oeuvre servers began circulating with the bowl among the female guests. A number of them joined in; as many others declined, whether because (like Susan's) their costumes were non-décolletaged, or they preferred watching the fun to joining it, or chose the quoits contest instead. More disposed to spectate than to participate, the Feltons moved with others out to the far side of the pool deck to see how Thong-Undie Quoits was played. Tom Hardison, his grape-bobbing done for the present ("But save me a few for later!" he called back to Patricia), led the way, carrying a white plastic bin full of varicolored thong panties in his left hand while twirling one with his right. On the lawn just past the deck, a shrubbery light illumined a slightly tipped-back sheet of plywood, on the white-painted face of which were mounted five distinctly phallic-looking posts, one at each corner and one in the center: six-inch tan shafts culminating in pink knobs and mounted at a suggestively upward angle to the backboard.

"Here's how it's done, ladies," Tom explained; "not that you didn't learn the facts of life back in junior high . . ." Holding up a robin's-egg-blue underpant by its thong, from behind a white-taped line on the deck he frisbeed it the eight feet or so toward the target board, where it landed between pegs and slid to the ground. With a shrug he said, "Not everybody scores on the first date," and then explained to the waiting contestants, "Three pairs for each gladiatrix, okay? If you miss all three, you're still a virgin, no matter how many kids and grandkids you claim to have. Score one and you get to keep it to excite your hubby. Two out of three and you're in the semifinals; *three* out of three and you're a finalist. All three on the same post and you win the Heron Bay Marital Fidelity Award! Who wants to go first?" Examining the nametag on one middle-aged matron's ample, grapeless bosom, "*Helen McCall*," he announced, "*Spartina Pointe*. How about it, Helen?"

The lady gamely handed her wineglass to her neighbor, pulled three panties from the bin, called out "We who are about to *try* salute you!" and spun the first item boardward, where it fell two feet short. "Out of practice," she admitted. Amid the bystanders' chuckles and calls of encouragement she tossed her second, which reached the board but then slid down, as had the host's demonstration throw.

Somebody called, "Not everybody who drops her drawers gets what she's after," to which someone else retorted, "Is that the Voice of Experience speaking?" But Ms. McCall's vigorous third toss looped a red thong undie on the board's upper left peg, to general cheers. Tom Hardison retrieved and presented it with a courtly bow to the contestant's applauding husband, who promptly knelt before her, spread the waistband wide, and insisted that she step into her trophy then and there.

"What fun." Susan sighed and took Dick's hand in hers. "I wish *we* were more like that."

"Yeah, well, me too." With a squeeze, "In our next life, maybe?" He glanced at his watch: almost nine already. "Want to hang around a while longer, or split now?"

Incredulously, "Are you *kidding*? They haven't awarded the prizes yet!"

"Sorry sorry sorry." And he was, for having become such a party-pooping partner to the wife he so loved and respected. And it wasn't that he was having an unenjoyable evening; only that — as was typically the case on the infrequent occasions when they dined out with another couple — he reached his sufficiency of good food and company sooner than Susan and the others did, and was ready to move on to the next thing, to call it an evening, while the rest were leisurely reviewing the dessert menu and considering an after-dinner nightcap at one or the other's house. To his own surprise, he felt his throat thicken and his eyes brim. Their good life together had gone by so fast! How many more so-agreeably-routine days and evenings remained to them before ... what?

Trying as usual to accommodate him, "D'you want to watch the game," Sue asked him, "or circulate a bit?"

"Your call." His characteristic reply. In an effort to do better, "Why not have a go at the game yourself?" he proposed to her. "You'd look cute in a thong."

She gave him one of her looks. "Because I'm *me*, remember?" Another fifteen minutes or so, she predicted, ought to wind things up, gamewise; after the prizes were handed out they could probably leave without seeming discourteous. Meanwhile, shouldn't he maybe go check on Doc Sam?

Her husband welcomed the errand: something to occupy him while Susan made conversation with their hostess, a couple of her golf partners, and other party guests. He worked his way barward through the merry grape-bobbers, their equally merry encouragers and referees ("How many left down there? Let me check." "No, me!" "Hey hey, no hands allowed ..."), and the occasional two or three talking politics, sports, business. Couldn't immediately locate his tennis pal, in whose present position he himself would ... well, what, exactly? Not hang around to *be* in that position, he hoped and more or less re-vowed to himself. Then he heard the old fellow (but who was Dick Felton, at age five-and seventy, to call eighty "old"?) sing out raucously from the living room, to the tune of "Oh Holy Night":

"O-O-Oh ho-ly shit! ..."

Sam stumbled out onto the terrace, doing the beer-bottle-microphone thing as the Hardisons had done earlier, but swigging from it between shouted lines:

"The sky, the sky is fall-ing! ..."

Smiling or frowning people turned his way, some commenting behind their hands.

"It is the end ... of our dear ... U-S-A! ..."

Dick approached him, calling out as if in jest, "Yo, Sam! You're distracting the thong-throwers, man!"

"And the grape-gropers, too!" someone merrily added. Thinking to lead him back inside and quiet him down, Dick put an arm around the old fellow's bony shoulders. He caught sight of Pat Hardison, clearly much concerned, heading toward them from the food tent. But as he made to turn his friend houseward, Sam startled him by snatching the machete from its sheath, pushing free of its owner, raising it high, and declaring, "If there's no red wine, I guess I'll have a bloody mary."

"Sam Sam Sam . . ."

Returning to his carol parody, "*Fall . . . on your swords!*" Sam sang. "*Oh hear . . . the angels laugh-ing! . . .*"

Too late, Dick sprang to snatch back the blade, or at least to grab hold of its wielder's arm. To all hands' horror, having mock-threat-ened his would-be restrainer with it, Sam thrust its point into his own chest, just under the breastbone. Dropped the beer bottle; gripped the machete's carved handle with both hands and pushed its blade into himself yet farther; grunted with the pain of it and dropped first to his knees, then sideways to the floor, his blood already soaking through his robe front onto the terrace deck. Pat Hardison and other women screamed; men shouted and rushed up, her husband among them. An elderly ex-doctor from Stratford — whose "toga" was a fancied-up set of blue hospital scrubs and who earlier had complained to the Feltons that the ever-higher cost of medical malpractice insurance had pres-sured him into retirement — pushed through the others and took charge: ordered Tom Hardison to dial 911 and Pat to find a bunch of clean rags, towels, anything that he could use to stanch the blood flow; swatted Sam's hands off the machete handle (all but unconscious now, eyes squint shut, the old fellow moaned, coughed, vomited a bit onto the terrace, and went entirely limp); withdrew and laid aside the bloody blade and pressed a double handful of the patient's robe against the gushing wound.

"Bailey, you idiot!" he scolded. "What'd you do *that* for?"

Without opening his eyes, Sam weakly finished his song: "*It was the night . . . that my dear . . . Ethel died . . .*"

"We should call his son in Stratford," Sue said, clutching her hus-band tearfully.

"Right you are." Dick fished under his caftan for the cell phone that he almost never used but had gotten into the habit of carrying with him. "Where's a goddamn phone book?"

Pat hurried inside to fetch one. "Tell him to go straight to the Avon Health Center!" the doctor called after her.

Men led their sobbing mates away. A couple of hardy volunteers applied clean rags to the blood and vomit puddled on the terrace; one considerately wiped clean the machete and restored it to its owner when Dick returned outside from making the grim call to Sam Junior.

"Jesus," Dick said, but gingerly resheathed the thing. The EMS ambulance presently wailed up, lights flashing; its crew transferred the barely breathing victim from floor to stretcher to entranceway gurney to vehicle without (Susan managed to notice) spilling a drop of his plentifully flowing blood onto the carpeting. The ex-doctor — *Mike Dowling*, his nametag read, *Spartina Pte* — on familiar terms with the emergency crew from his years of medical practice, rode with them, instructing his wife to pick him up at AHC in half an hour or so. The Feltons then hurried to their car to follow the ambulance to the hospital, promising the Hardisons (who of course had their hands full with the party's sudden, unexpected finale and the postparty cleanup) that they would phone them a report on Sam's condition as soon as they had one.

"I can't believe he'll live," Sue worried aloud en route the several miles into Stratford, the pair of them feeling ridiculous indeed to be approaching the hospital's emergency wing in their outlandish costumes. "So much blood lost!"

"Better for him if he doesn't," in Dick's opinion. The sheathed machete, at least, he left in the convertible, cursing himself for having included it in his getup but agreeing with Susan that in Sam's desperate and drunken grief he'd have found some other implement to attack himself with, if not at the party, then back at his house in Oyster Cove. Their headdresses, too, and any other removable "Roman" accessories, they divested before crossing the parking lot and making their way into the brightly lit ER lobby. The few staff people they saw did a creditable job of keeping straight faces; the visitor check-in lady even said sympathetically, "Y'all must've been at that party with Doctor Dowling..." The patient's son, she informed them, had arrived already and was in a special standby room. They should make themselves comfortable over yonder (she indicated a couch-and-chair area across the fluorescent-lighted room, which they were relieved to see was unoccupied); she would keep them posted, she promised.

And so they sat, side by side on one of the dark gray plastic-cushioned couches, Sue's left hand clasped in Dick's right; they were too shocked to do more than murmur how sad it all was. On end tables beside them were back issues of *Time, Fortune, People, Chesapeake Living, Sports Illustrated, Field & Stream*. The sight of their covers, attention-grabbing reminders of the busy world, made Dick Felton wince: Never had he felt more keenly that All That was behind them. If Dr. Dowling's wife, per instructions, came to retrieve her husband half an hour or so after he left the toga party, Sue presently speculated, then there must be a special entrance as well as a special standby room, as more time than that had passed since their own arrival at Avon Health Center without their seeing any sign of her or him. Eventually, however, the receptionist's telephone warbled; she attended the message, made some reply, and then called "Mister and Miz Felton?" There being no one else to hear, without waiting for them to come to her station she announced Dr. Dowling's opinion that there was no reason for them to stay longer: Mr. Bailey, his condition stabilized, had been moved to intensive care, in serious but no longer critical condition. He had lost a great deal of blood, injured some internal organs, and would need further surgery down the line, but was expected to survive. His son was with him.

"Poor bastard," Dick said—meaning either or both of the pair, he supposed: the father doomed to an even more radically reduced existence than the one he had tried unsuccessfully to exit; the dutifully attentive but already busy son now saddled with the extra burdens of arranging the care of an invalid parent and the management of that parent's house until he could unload it and install the old fellow in Bayview Manor, across and downriver from Heron Bay Estates, or some other assisted-living facility.

"Loving children *do* those things," Sue reminded him. "Sure, it's a major headache, but close families accept it."

Lucky them, they both were thinking as they drove back to HBE, through the main entrance gate (opened by the night-shift gatekeeper at sight of the Resident sticker on their Toyota's lower left windshield-corner), and on to their Rockfish Reach neighborhood, Sue having cell-phoned her promised report to the Hardisons as they left the AHC parking lot. How would either of themselves manage, alone, in some similar situation, with their far-flung and not all that filially bonded son and daughter?

"We wouldn't," in Dick's opinion, and his wife couldn't disagree.

All the partygoers' cars were gone from Loblolly Court, they observed as they passed it, but lights were still on in #12, where cleanup no doubt continued. By the time they reached their own house's pleasantly night-lighted drive and entranceway, the car's dashboard clock read the same as their Shoreside Drive house number: 1020. Noting the coincidence, "Now *that* means something," Susan said — a Felton family joke, echoing Dick's late mother (who'd fortunately had a devoted or anyhow dutiful unmarried middle-aged daughter to attend her senile last years in western Maryland). But her effort at humor was made through suddenly welling tears: tears for herself, she explained when her husband remarked them as he turned into their driveway; tears for them both, as much as for poor Sam Bailey.

Dick pressed the garage door opener button over the rearview mirror, turned their convertible expertly into the slot beside their station wagon, shifted into Park, clicked off the headlights, and pressed the remote button again to roll the door back down. Instead of then shutting off the engine and unlatching his seat belt, however, after a moment he pushed the buttons to lower all of the car's windows, closed his eyes, and leaned his head back wearily against the driver's headrest.

"What are you doing?" There was some alarm in Susan's voice, but she too left her seat belt fastened, and made no move to open her door. "Why'd you do that?"

Without turning his head or opening his eyes, her husband took her hand in his as he'd done back in the hospital waiting room, squeezing it now even more tightly. "Shit, hon, why not? We've had a good life together, but it's done with except for the crappy last lap, and neither of us wants that."

"*I* sure don't," his wife acknowledged, and with a sigh back-rested her head, too. Already they could smell exhaust fumes. "I love you, Dick."

"I love *you*. And okay, so we're dumping on the kids, leaving them to take the hit and clean up the mess. So what?"

"They'll never forgive us. But you're right. So what?"

"We'll each be presumed to have survived the other, as the saying goes, and neither of us'll be around to know it."

The car engine quietly idled on.

"Shouldn't we at least leave them a note, send them an email, something?"

"So go do that if you want to. Me, I'm staying put."

He heard her exhale. "Me too, I guess." Then inhale, deeply.

If Doc Sam Bailey were this story's teller, he'd probably end it right here with a bit of toga-party Latin: *Consummatum est; requiescat in pacem* — something in that vein. But he's not.

The overhead garage light timed out.

Teardown

In large gated communities like our Heron Bay Estates development, obsolescence sets in early. The developers knew their business: a great flat stretch of former pine woods and agribusiness feed-corn fields along the handsome Matahannock River, ten minutes from the attractive little colonial-era town of Stratford and two hours from Baltimore/Washington in one direction, Wilmington/Philadelphia in another, and Atlantic beach resorts in a third, converted in the go-go American 1980s into appealingly laid-out subdevelopments of condos, villas, coach homes, and detached-house neighborhoods, the whole well landscaped and amenitied. The first such large-scale project on the Eastern Shore end of Maryland's Chesapeake Bay Bridge, it proved so successful that twenty years later it was not only all but "built out" (except for a still controversial proposal for midrise condominiums in what was supposed to remain wood-and-wetland preserve), but in its "older" subcommunities, like Spartina Pointe, already showing its age. In Stratford's historic district, an "old house" may date from the early eighteenth century; in Heron Bay Estates it dates from Ronald Reagan's second presidential term. More and more, as the American wealthy have grown ever wealthier and the original builder-owners of upscale Spartina Pointe (mostly retirees from one of those above-mentioned cities, for many of whom Heron Bay Estates was a weekend-and-summer retreat, a second or even third residence) aged and died or shifted to some assisted-living facility, the new owners of their twenty-year-old "colonial" mini-mansions commence their tenure with radical renovation: new kitchen and baths, a swimming pool and larger patio / deck area, faux-cobblestone driveway and complete relandscaping — all subject, of course, to approval by the HBE Design Review Board.

Which august three-member body, a branch of our Heron Bay Estates Community Association, had reluctantly approved, back in the 1980s, the original design for 211 Spartina Court, a rambling brick-and-clapboard rancher on a prime two-acre lot at the very point of Spartina Point(e), with narrow but navigable Spartina Creek on three sides. It was a two-to-one decision: None of the three board members was happy to let a ranch house, however roomy, set the architectural tone for what was intended as HBE's highest-end neighborhood; two- and three-story plantation-style manses were what they had in mind. But while one of the board folk was steadfastly opposed, another judged it more important to get a first house built (its owners were prepared to begin construction immediately upon their plan's approval) in order to help sell the remaining lots and encourage the building of residences more appropriate to the developer's intentions. The third member was sympathetic to both opinions; she ultimately voted approval on the grounds that preliminary designs for two neighboring houses were exactly what was wanted for Spartina Pointe — neo-Georgian manors of whitewashed brick, with two-story front columns and the rest — and together should adequately establish the neighborhood's style. The ranch house was allowed, minus the rustic split-rail fence intended to mark the lot's perimeter, and with the provision that a few Leyland cypresses be planted instead, to partially screen the residence from street-side view.

The strategy succeeded. Within a few years the several "drives" and "courts" of Spartina Pointe were lined with more or less imposing, more or less Georgian-style homes: no Cape Cods, Dutch colonials, or half-timbered Tudors (all popular styles in easier-going Rockfish Reach), certainly nothing contemporary, and no more ranchers. The out-of-synch design of 211 Spartina Court raised a few eyebrows, but the house's owners, Ed and Myra Gunston, were hospitable, community-spirited ex-Philadelphians whom none could dislike: organizers of neighborhood parties and progressive dinners, spirited fund-raisers for the Avon County United Way and other worthy causes. A sad day for Spartina Pointe when Myra was crippled by a stroke; another, some months later, when a For Sale sign appeared in front of those Leyland cypresses.

All the above established, we may begin this teardown story, which is not about the good-neighbor Gunstons, and for which the next chapter in the history of their Spartina Point(e) house, heavily foreshadowed by the tale's title, is merely the occasion. We shift now across Heron Bay Estates to 414 Doubler Drive, in Blue Crab Bight, the second-floor coach home of early-fortyish Joseph and Judith Barnes — first explaining to non-tidewater types that "doubler" is the local watermen's term for the mating stage of *Callinectes sapidus*, the Chesapeake Bay blue crab. The male of that species mounts and clasps fast the female who he senses is about to molt, so that when eventually she sheds her carapace and becomes for some hours a helpless "softcrab," he can both shield her from predators and have his way with her himself, to the end of continuing the species: a two-for-one catch for lucky crabbers, and an apt street name for a community of over-and-under duplexes, whose owners (and some of the rest of us) do not tire of explaining to out-of-staters.

Some months have passed since the space break above: It is now the late afternoon of a chilly-wet April Friday in an early year of the twenty-first century. Ruddy-plump Judy Barnes has just arrived home from her English-teaching job at Fenton, a small private coed junior-senior high school near Stratford, where she's also an assistant girls' soccer coach. This afternoon's intramural game having been rained out, she's home earlier than usual and is starting dinner for the family: her husband, a portfolio manager in the Stratford office of Lucas & Jones, LLC; their elder daughter, Ashleigh, a Stratford College sophomore who lives in the campus dorms but often comes home on weekends; and Ashleigh's two-years-younger sister, Tiffany, a (tuition-waived) sixth-form student at Fenton, who's helping Mom with dinner prep.

Osso buco, it's going to be. While Judy shakes the veal shanks in a bag of salt-and-peppered flour and Tiffany dices carrots, celery, onions, and garlic cloves for preliminary sauteing, Joe Barnes is closing his office for the weekend with the help of Jeannine Weston, his secretary, and trying in vain to stop imagining that lean, sexy-sharp young woman at least half naked in various positions to receive in sundry of her orifices his already wet-tipped penis. *Quit that already!* he reprimands himself, to no avail. *Bear in mind that not only do you honor your marriage and love your family, you also say amen to the Gospel According to Mark, which stipulates that Thou Shalt Not Hump the Help.* "Mark" being Mark Matthews, his boss and mentor, first in Baltimore and then, since Lucas & Jones opened their Eastern Shore office five years ago, in Stratford. That's when the Barneses bought 414 Doubler Drive: a bit snug for a family of four with two teenagers, but a sound investment, bound to appreciate rapidly in value as the population of Avon and its neighboring counties steadily grows. The girls had shared a bedroom since their babyhood and enjoyed doing so right through their adolescence; the elderly couple in 412, the coach home's first-floor unit, were both retired and retiring, so quiet that one could almost forget that their place was occupied. In the four years until their recent, reluctant move to Bayview Manor, they never once complained about Ashleigh's and Tiffany's sometimes noisy get-togethers with school friends.

Perhaps Reader is wincing at the heavy New Testament sound of "Mark Matthews Lucas and Jones"? "Thou shalt not wince," Mark himself enjoys commanding new or prospective clients in their first interview. "Why do you think Jim Lucas and Harvey Jones [the firm's cofounders] hired me in the first place, if not to spread the Good Word about asset management?" Which the fellow did in sooth, churning their portfolios to the firm's benefit as well as theirs and coaching his protégé to do likewise. That earlier gospel-tenet of his, however, he formulated after breaking it himself: In his mid-fifties, coincident with the move from Baltimore to Stratford, he ended his twenty-five-year first marriage to wed the striking young woman who'd been his administrative assistant for three years and his mistress for two. "Don't hump the help," he then enjoyed advising their dinner guests, Joe and Judy included, in his new bride's presence. "You should see my alimony bills!" "Plus he had to find himself a new secretary," trim young Mrs. Matthews liked to add, "once his office squeeze became his trophy wife"—and his unofficial deputy account manager, handling routine portfolio transactions from her own office in their Stratford house, "where unfortunately I can't keep an eye on him."

But "*Eew*, Mom!" Tiffany Barnes is exclaiming in the kitchen of 414 Doubler Drive, where she's ladling excess fat off the osso buco broth. "Even without this glop, the stuff's so *greasy!*"

"Delicious, though," her mother insists. "And we only have it a couple times a year."

"We have it *only* a couple times a year," her just-arrived other daughter corrects her. An English major herself, Ashleigh likes to catch her family's slips in grammar and usage, especially her English-teacher mother's. Patient Judy rolls her eyes. "Dad says I should open a cabernet to breathe before dinner," the girl then adds. "He'll be up in a minute. He's doing stuff in the garage."

"Just take a taste of this marrow," Judy invites both girls, indicating a particularly large cross-section of shank bone in the casserole, its core of brown marrow fully an inch in diameter, "and tell me it's not the most delicious thing you ever ate."

"*Ee-e-ew!*" her daughters chorus in unison. Then Tiffany (who's taking an elective course at Fenton called The Bible As Literature that her secular mother frowns at as a left-handed way of sneaking religion into the curriculum, although she quite respects the colleague who's teaching it) adds, "Think not of the marrow?" Judy chuckles proudly; Ashleigh groans at the pun, musses her sister's hair, and goes to the wine rack to look for cabernet sauvignon, singing a retaliatory pun of her own that she'd seen on a bumper sticker earlier in the week: "*Life is a ca-ber-net, old chum . . .*"

Sipping same half an hour later with a store-bought duck pâté in the living room, where a fake log crackles convincingly in the glass-shuttered fireplace, "So guess who just bought that house at the far end of Spartina Court?" Joe Barnes asks his wife. "Mark and Mindy Matthews!"

"*Mindy,*" Ashleigh scorns, not for the first time: "What a lame name!" Though only nineteen, she's allowed these days to take half a glass of wine with her parents at cocktail time and another half at dinner, since they know very well that she drinks with her college friends and believe that she's less likely to binge out like too many of them on beer and hard liquor if, as in most European households, the moderate consumption of wine with dinner is a family custom. Tiffany, having helped with the osso buco, has withdrawn to the sisters' bedroom and her laptop computer until the meal is served.

"That ranch house?" Judy asks. "Why would the Matthewses swap their nice place in Stratford for a run-of-the-mill ranch house?"

Her husband swirls his wine, the better to aerate it. "Because, one,

Mark's buying himself a cabin cruiser and wants a waterfront place to go with it. And, two, by the time they move in it'll be no run-of-the-mill ranch house, believe me. Far from it!"

Judy sighs. "Another Heron Bay remodeling job. And we can't even get around to replacing that old Formica in our kitchen! But a renovated rancher's still a rancher."

Uninterested Ashleigh, pencil in hand, is back to her new passion, the sudoku puzzle from that day's *Baltimore Sun*. She has the same shoulder-length straight dark hair and trim tight body that her mother had when Joe and Judy first met as University of Maryland undergraduates two dozen years ago, and that Jeannine Weston (of whose tantalizing figure Joe is disturbingly reminded lately whenever, as now, he remarks this about his eldest daughter) has not yet outgrown. He and Judy both, on the other hand, have put on the pounds — and his hair is thinning toward baldness, and hers showing its first traces of gray, before they even reach fifty . . .

"Never mind remodeling and renovation," he says. "That's not Mark's style." He raises his glass as if in toast: "Heron Bay Estates is about to see its very first teardown!"

. . . plus her generous, once so fine, firm breasts are these days anything but, and "love handles" would be the kindest term for those side rolls of his that, like his belly, have begun to lap over his belted trouser top. Men, of course, enjoy the famously unfair advantage that professional success may confer upon their dealings with the opposite sex: Unsaintly Mark, e.g., is hardly the tall / dark / handsome type, but his being double-chinned, pudgy, and doorknob bald didn't stand in the way of his scoring with pert blond Mindy — and what in God's name is Joe Barnes up to, thinking such thoughts at Happy Hour in the bosom of his family?

Thus self-rebuked, he takes it upon himself to clean up the hors d'oeuvres and call Tiffany to set the table while Judy assembles a salad and Ashleigh pops four dinner rolls into the toaster oven. As is their weekend custom when all hands are present, they then clink glasses (three wines, one diet Coke) and say their mock table-grace — "Bless this grub and us that eats it"— before settling into the osso buco. *I love you all, goddamn it!* lump-throated Joe reminds himself.

"So what do the Matthewses intend to put up in place of their teardown?" Judy asks. "One of those big colonial-style jobs, I guess?"

"Oh, no." Her husband grins, shakes his head. "Wait'll you see. You know that fancy new spread on Loblolly Court, over in Rockfish Reach?" Referring to an imposing Mediterranean-style stucco-and-tiled-roof house built recently in that adjacent neighborhood despite the tsk-tsks of numerous homeowners there.

"Ee-e-ew," comments Tiffany.

"Well, this morning Mark showed me their architect's drawings for what he and Mindy have in mind — Mindy especially, but Mark's all for it — and it makes that Loblolly Court place look as humble as ours."

"Ee-e-ew!" Ashleigh agrees with her sister: a putdown not of their coach home, which she's always happy to return to from her dorm even though their bedroom has become mainly Tiffany's space these days, but the pretentiousness, extravagance, and inconsiderate arrogance, in her liberal opinion, of even the Loblolly Court McMansion, which at least was built on an unoccupied lot.

A month or so later, on a fair-weather AM bicycle ride through the pleasantly winding bike and jogging paths of Heron Bay Estates, Judy and the girls and a couple of Tiffany's Fenton classmates pedal up Spartina Court to see what's what (Joe's in Baltimore with his boss and secretary at some sort of quarterly meeting in the Lucas & Jones home office). Sure enough, the Gunstons' rambling rancher and its screen of trees have been cleared away completely and replaced by a building-permit board and a vast shallow excavation, the foundation footprint of the Matthewses' palatial residence-in-the-works.

"A perfectly okay house," indignant Ashleigh informs her sister's friends, "no older than ours and twice as big, and *wham!* They just knock it down, haul it to the dump, and put up Buckingham Palace instead!"

"More like the Alhambra," in her younger sister's opinion (Tiff's art history course at Fenton includes some architecture as well).

"Or Michael Jackson's Neverland?" offers one of her companions.

"Dad showed us the latest computer projections of it last week?" Ash explains with the rising inflection so popular among her generation. "Ee-e-*ew!* And he thinks it's just fine!"

"Different people go for different things," her mother reminds them all. "*De gustibus non est disputandum?*"

"See what I mean?" Tiffany asks her friends, and they seem to, though what it is they see, Judy prefers not to wonder.

"Anyhow," Ashleigh adds, "whatever's right by our dad's boss is fine with our dad."

"Ashleigh! Really!"

Tiffany's exaggerated frown suggests that on this one she sides with her mother, at least in the presence of nonfamily. To Judy's relief, Ashleigh drops the subject, and they finish their bike ride.

Over their early Sunday dinner, however — which Joe, as promised, has returned from Baltimore in time for, before Ashleigh goes back to her dorm — the girl takes up her cudgel again. It's one thing, she declares, to build a big pretentious new house like that eyesore in Rockfish Reach, if that's what a person wants? But to tear down a perfectly okay quote-unquote *older* one to do it is, in her opinion, downright obscene — like those people who order a full-course restaurant meal and then just nibble at each course, leaving the rest to be tossed out. Gross!

"Weak analogy," her teacher mother can't help pointing out. "Let's think up a better one."

"Like those people who buy a new car every two years?" Tiffany offers. "When their quote *old* one's in perfectly good condition with maybe ten thousand miles on it?"

"No good," in her sister's opinion, "because at least the old car gets traded in and resold and used. This is more like if every time they buy a new one they *junk* their perfectly okay old one."

"Good point," Judy approves.

"Or like Saint Mark Matthews," bold Ashleigh presses on, "dumping the mother of his kids for a trophy blond airhead half his age."

Alarmed, Tiffany glances from sister to mother to dad. But Joe, who until now has seemed to Judy still to have city business on his mind, here joins the conversation like the partner she's loved for two dozen years. "Beg to disagree, guys? Not with your analogies, but with your judgment, okay? Because what the heck, Ash: The ranch-house people weren't evicted or dumped; they put their place up for sale and got close to their asking price for it. Seems to me the whole business calls for nothing more than a raised eyebrow — more for the new house's design, if you don't happen to like it, than for the replacement idea itself."

"I think I second that," his wife decides.

"And Mindy Matthews, by the way, is no *airhead*," Joe informs his daughters. "She's sharp as a tack."

"Hot in bed, too, I bet," Tiffany makes bold to add. Her father frowns disapproval. Judy declares, "That's none of our business, girls."

"But what still gets me, Dad," Ashleigh persists, less belligerently, "is the *extravagance* of it! We learned in poly sci this week that if Earth's whole human population could be shrunk to a village of exactly one hundred people—with all the same ratios as now?—only thirty of us would be white people, only twenty would live in better than substandard housing, only eight would have some savings in the bank as well as clothes on our back and food in the pantry, and only *one* of the hundred would have all that plus a college education! And you're telling us that this teardown thing isn't disgraceful?"

"That's exactly what I'm telling you," her father amiably agrees. "We live in a prosperous free-enterprise country, thank God. Mark Matthews—whom I happen to very much admire—earned his money by brains and hard work, and he and Mindy are entitled to spend it as they damn well please. And their architect, builder, and landscaper are all local outfits, so they'll be putting a couple million bucks into Avon County's economy right there, along with their whopping property taxes down the line." He turns up his palms. "Everybody benefits; nobody gets hurt. So what's your problem, Lefty?"

This last is a family tease of a couple years' standing. Ashleigh Barnes was in fact born left-handed, as was Judy's mother, but the nickname dates from her ever more emphatic liberalism since her fifth- and sixth-form years at Fenton. It's a tendency that her younger sister has lately been manifesting as well, although apart from their mother and a few of Judy's colleagues, the school, its faculty, and its students' families are predominantly center-right Republicans.

Her problem, Ashleigh guesses with a sigh, is that she just doesn't like fat cats.

"Mindy Matthews *fat?*" Tiffany pretends to protest. "She's downright anorexic! Speaking of which," she adds to her father, "at least one person sure got hurt when Saint Mark changed horses: Sharon Matthews." Mindy's predecessor.

Judy looks to her husband with a smile and raised eyebrows, as if to ask, How d'you answer *that* one? But Joe merely shrugs and says, "With the alimony payments she's getting for the rest of her life, that woman can cry all the way to the bank. So let's enjoy our dinner now, okay?"

His wife sees their daughters give each other their we-give-up look. She does likewise, for the present, and the family returns to enjoying, or at least making the best of, one another's company.

Later that evening, Ashleigh drives back to campus in her hand-me-down Honda Civic, Tiffany busies herself in her room with homework and computer, Judy takes a preliminary whack at the Sunday *New York Times* crossword puzzle before prepping her Monday lesson plans, Joe scans that newspaper's business section while pondering what Mark Matthews told him that morning en route back from Baltimore in Mark's new Lexus (Mark and his secretary in the front seat, Joe and Jeannine Weston in the rear) and that he hasn't gotten around yet to sharing with Judy — and the new downstairs neighbors' little Yorkshire terrier starts the infernal yip-yipping again that's been driving them batty ever since the Creightons moved into 412 a month ago. They're a pleasant enough younger couple, he an assistant manager at the Stratford GM dealership, she a part-time dietitian at Avon Health Center and busy mother of their four-year-old son. But the kid is noisy and the dog noisier — a far cry from the unit's previous owners! — and although the Creightons respond good-naturedly to the Barneses' tactful complaints, promising to see what if anything they can do about the problem ("You know how it is with kids and pets!"), it gets no better.

He slaps the newspaper down in his lap. "We've got to get out of this fucking place, hon."

"I'm ready." For rich as it is with five years' worth of family memories — the girls' adolescence, their parents' new jobs — the coach home has never really been big enough. No home-office space; no TV/family room separate from the living room; a dining area scarcely large enough to seat six. No guest room even with Ashleigh in the dorm; no real backyard of their own for gardening and barbecuing and such. But the place has, as they'd predicted, substantially appreciated in value, and although any alternative housing will have done likewise, by Joe's reckoning they're "positioned," as he puts it, to move on and up. What Judy would go for is one of the better Oyster Cove villas, a side-by-side duplex instead of over-and-under: three bedrooms, of which one could be her study/workroom and another a combination guest room/den once Tiffany's off to college; a separate family room with adjacent workshop and utility room; and their own small backyard for cookouts, deck lounging, and as much or little gardening as they care to bother with. But what Joe has in mind lately is more ambitious: to buy and renovate one of those older detached houses in Rockfish Reach. A dining room big enough for entertaining friends and colleagues in style, as well as Ash and Tiff and *their* friends; a *real* yard and patio; maybe a pool and some kind of outboard runabout to keep at their own private dock. And they should finally cough up the money to join the Heron Bay Club on a golf membership and take up the game, without which one is definitely *out* of the social scene (so Mark told him, among other things, in the car that morning).

Judy's flabbergasted. "Are you *kidding*? A twelve-thousand-buck initiation fee plus, what, two-hundred-a-month dues? Plus a house to renovate and two college tuitions coming up, dot dot dot question mark?" It's a thing she does now and then.

"Leave that to me, hon," her husband suggests, in a tone she's been hearing him use lately. "I've learned a thing or two from Master Mark about estate building." *Among other things*, he silently adds and she silently worries — not without cause, although "Tennis, maybe, but count me out on the golf" is all she says aloud. "Not this schoolmarm's style."

Amiably, not to alarm her, "Folks can change their style, you know," he says — and then shares with her part of what's been distracting him all day, since Mark announced it on the drive home. Jim Lucas, one of the firm's founding partners, intends to retire as of the fiscal year's end. Mark Matthews will be replacing him as senior partner and codirector of the company's home office (he and Mindy are buying a condo on the city's Inner Harbor to supplement their Spartina Pointe weekend-and-vacation spread). "And Saint Mark's successor as chief of our Stratford office will be . . . guess who? Whoops, sorry there, Teach: Guess *whom*."

"Oh, *sweetie!*" She flings aside her crossword and lays on the congratulatory cries and kisses; calls for Tiffany to come hear Daddy's big news; asks him why in the world he didn't announce it while Ashleigh was there to hear it too; but laughingly agrees with him that the girl will scornfully assign them to the *crème de la crème* of her hypothetical hundred-person village — and refrains from pointing out to him that the nominative-case "guess who" is in fact correct, the pronoun being the transposed subject of the verb "will be" rather than the object of "guess." No champagne in the house to toast his promotion with;

they'll get some and raise a glass to him when Ashleigh's next with them. And in their *new* house, maybe he can have the wine cellar he's always yearned for! Meanwhile . . .

"Congratulations, Dad!" cheers Tiffany, piling onto his lap to kiss him. And when Mom and Dad retire not long afterward to their bedroom for the night, Judy gives her crotch a good wash-cloth-wipe after peeing, to freshen it in case he goes down there in the course of celebratory sex. Since the commencement of her early menopause, she's been bothered by occasional yeast infections, with accompanying vaginal discharge and sometimes downright painful intercourse — not that they go at it as often or as athletically as in years past.

But this night they do, *sans soixante-neuf* and such but vigorously *a tergo* and, to her mild surprise, in the dark. Normally they leave Joe's nightstand light dimmed during lovemaking, to facilitate his finding, opening, and applying their personal lubricant and to enjoy the sight of each other's so familiar naked bodies. Tonight, however, it's only after he clicks off the light and snuggles up to say goodnight (also to her surprise) that Joe seems to change his mind. He places his right hand on his partial erection and raises himself on one elbow to lift her short nightie, kiss her navel and nipples, and begin fingering her vulva — all the while scolding himself for imagining a certain younger, leaner body responding to his caresses. In the car that afternoon, when Mark broke the big news of his own and Joe's promotions, Jeannine Weston had squealed with excitement, flung her arms around her boss (those fine breasts of hers pressing into his right upper arm), and planted a loud wet kiss on his cheek. Alice Benning, Mark's secretary since Mindy's promotion to wifehood, had then declared to all hands that she'd asked Jeannine earlier whether she'd be interested in shifting to Baltimore to become the hot-stuff new front-desk receptionist for Lucas & Jones, LLC, and that the girl had replied, "As long as Joe Barnes wants me, I'm his." "Tattletale!" Jeannine had mock-scolded the older woman, and squeezed her chief's right hand in both of hers and leaned her head fondly on his shoulder. Mark, winking broadly at the couple in his rearview mirror, had teased, "Don't forget Rule Number One, Joe," and when Jeannine asked what *that* might be, Alice turned in her seat to whisper loudly, "It's *Hands off the help* — a good rule to live by, says I." So "Shoo, girl!" Joe had duly then bade his young assistant with a broad wink of his own—and to his startlement, in the spirit of their sport, she had slid laughing over to her side of the seat, crossed one arm over those breasts, and with her other hand cupped her crotch as if protectively. It is those body parts that Joe Barnes helplessly finds himself picturing now, and that tight little butt of hers, bare and upraised for him to clutch in both hands while he thrusts and thrusts and thrusts and *ahhh! . . .* collapses atop his accommodating spouse in contrite exhilaration.

Now: This teardown story could proceed from here in any of several pretty obvious directions, e.g.: (1) Joe Barnes "comes to his senses," his love for Judy and the family reaffirmed by that short-lived guilty temptation. While his office relationship with Jeannine Weston retains an element of jocular flirtation, no adultery follows. A year later the young woman is reoffered that receptionist post in the Baltimore office, and this time she takes it. Her replacement in Stratford is a married woman slightly older than Joe: amiable and competent, but not the stuff of lecherous fantasies. Alternatively, (2) somewhat to his own appall, Joe does indeed succumb to temptation and "humps the help," either in what used to be Mark Matthews's office but is now his or in some motel far enough from town for anonymity. The imaginable consequences range from (a) Next to None (adultery goes undiscovered; both parties, ashamed, decide not to repeat it; Jeannine meets and soon after marries a young professor at Stratford College who eventually moves to a better-paying academic post in Indiana), to (b) Considerable (Joe confesses to Judy and asks for divorce with generous settlement. She brokenheartedly agrees to what she condemns as a "marital teardown." Joe and Jeannine then wed and do a modified Mark-and-Mindy, renovating a large house in Rockfish Reach. The girls, both in college by that time, are shocked, embarrassed, and angry, but in time come more or less to terms with the family's disruption. Judy remarries—an estate lawyer from her southern Maryland hometown—and all parties get on with their lives' next chapter, neither unscarred nor, on balance, unhappy), to (c) Disastrous (Judy discovers the affair, goes ballistic, sues for divorce, and bars Joe from the house. Their daughters turn against him for life. The small-town scandal obliges Jeannine to quit her job and Joe to shift, under a cloud, to Lucas & Jones's far-western-Maryland office. "What'd I tell you?" Mark scolds triumphantly.

Judy stays on at her Fenton post and in the Blue Crab Bight coach house, where the downstairs dog yips maddeningly on to the tale's last page and beyond).

My personal inclination (George Newett here, Reader, who's been dreaming up this whole story: Tale Teller Emeritus [but no tale bearer] in Stratford College's Department of English and Creative Writing and, like "Joe and Judy Barnes," resident with my Mrs. in Blue Crab Bight) is to go with (3) None of the Above. This being, after all, a teardown story, I'm deciding to tear the sumbitch down right about here, the way people like "Mark and Mindy Matthews" might decide to tear down not only the Gunstons' "old" ranch house on Spartina Court but also the barely started *hacienda grande* that they're in the costly process of replacing it with. Mindy, let's say, has been belatedly persuaded by her longtime friend and fellow Stratford alumna Faye Robertson (now on the Fenton Day School faculty, Judy Barnes's colleague and Tiffany's art history teacher) that a mission-style *palacio* in Spartina Pointe will be as in-your-face and out of place as that neo-Neapolitan *palazzo* of Tom and Patricia Hardison's in Rockfish Reach, and that for the sake of Heron Bay Estates' "aesthetic ecology," the Matthewses really ought to have considered a Williamsburg-style manse instead. "Never too late to reconsider," I imagine bold Mindy declaring to her astonished friend with a Just You Watch sort of laugh and then announcing her mind-change to "Saint Mark," who wonders whether *he'd* better reconsider what he's gotten himself into with this woman. Maybe time for a midstream change of horses on *that* front too? But he then decides it'd be a better demonstration of upscale panache just to shrug, chuckle, and say, "Whatever milady desireth . . ."

You see how it is with us storytellers — with some of us, anyhow, perhaps especially the Old Fart variety, whereof Yours Truly is a member of some standing. Our problem, see, is that we invent people like the Barneses, do our best to make them reasonably believable and even simpatico, follow the rules of Story by putting them in a high-stakes situation — and then get to feeling more responsibility to *them* than to you, the reader. "Never too late to reconsider," we end up saying to ourselves like Mindy Matthews, and instead of ending their teardown tale for better or worse (sorry about that, guys), we pull its narrative plug before somebody gets hurt.

Here's how:

The Bard Award

Of the many tidal rivers on Maryland's Eastern Shore of Chesapeake Bay, most bear Indian names, as does the great Bay itself; names antedating the fateful arrival of white colonists four centuries ago, but filtered through those English ears into their present form and spelling: Pocomoke, Wicomico, Nanticoke, Choptank — and the handsome Matahannock, near whose ever-less-wooded shores I write these lines. A mile wide where it ebbs and flows past our Heron Bay Estates, the Matahannock (like these opening sentences of this would-be story) then winds on and on: another dozen-plus miles upstream, ever narrower and shallower, northeastward through the agribusiness corn and soybean fields and industrial-scale chicken farms of our table-flat Delmarva Peninsula to its petering out (or in) at its marshy headwaters somewhere near the Delaware state line, and about the same distance downstream from here, ever wider and somewhat deeper, southwestward past marinas, goose-hunting blinds, crab- and oyster-boat wharves, former steamboat landings, eighteenth-century estates, twenty-first-century mega-mansions, and more and more waterfront developments, until it joins our planet's largest estuarine system, which itself flows from and ebbs into the Atlantic and thence all the other oceans. Although no Heron Bay Estater has yet done so or likely ever will (we being mostly Golden Agers), one could theoretically set out from HBE's Blue Crab Marina Club, sail down the Matahannock, under the Bay Bridge and on south into Virginia waters, then hang a left at Cape Charles and cruise on to the Azores, Cape Town, Tahiti — right round the world!

The region's counties, on the other hand, like the state they subdivide, have Anglo names — not surprisingly, since they didn't exist as geographical entities until the natives' dispossessors claimed, mapped, and laid them out: Dorchester, Talbot, Avon, Kent — most of them boundaried by the above-mentioned rivers. Ditto those counties' seats and other towns, their American characters quite out of synch with their historic English names. Cambridge and Oxford, for example, on opposite shores of the broad Choptank, are pleasant small towns both, but absent anything remotely like their Brit counterparts' venerable universities.

Likewise "our" Avon County's Stratford (the gated community of Heron Bay Estates is five miles downriver, but Avon's county seat is our P.O.). A colonial-era customs port on the slightly wider river-stretch where Stratford Creek joins the Matahannock, it's now a comfortable town of six or seven thousand that nowise resembles its famed English antecedent: not a thatched roof or half-timbered gable-end to be found in our Stratford's red-brick-Georgian historic district. Unlike those Choptank towns aforenoted, however, it does in fact boast a modest institution of higher learning. Stratford College is no Oxford or Cambridge University, but it's a good small liberal-arts college, old by American standards like the town itself. We currently enroll some fifteen hundred students, mainly from our tri-state peninsula, with a double handful from across the Bay and nearby Pennsylvania and half a handful from remoter venues. As might be expected of a Stratford in, if not quite on, an Avon, the college gives particular emphasis and budgetary support to its Department of English and Creative Writing. *Who'll be our Shakespeare?*, our student-recruitment ads ask prospective applicants: *Maybe you!* — adding that many a potential bard not *born* in Stratford has been *re*born in the College's Shakespeare House, headquarters of the writing program, "under the benignly masterful tutelage of experienced author-professors on the faculty and distinguished visitors to the campus." What's more (those ads bait their hook by declaring further), every budding playwright, poet, and prose writer in the program has a shot at winning the College's Shakespeare Prize, awarded annually to the graduating senior with "the most impressive body of literary work composed in his or her courses."

And this is where Yours Truly comes in, eventually. Stratford's "Bard Award," as everybody on campus calls it, is a hefty prize indeed, endowed some decades ago by a wealthy alumnus who had aspired unsuccessfully to playwriting but later flourished as the CEO of Tidewater Communities, Inc., his family's real-estate development firm. His munificent Shakespeare Fund pays the honoraria and travel expenses of an impressive series of visiting lecturers, maintains Shakespeare House and its associated quarterly lit mag, *The Stratford Review*, and annually showers one lucky apprentice writer with a cash award currently twice the size of—get this—the Pulitzer Prize, the National Book Award, and PEN's Faulkner Prize combined: the equivalent of at least two years' tuition at the College or the annual salary of one of its midrange professors! Little wonder that competition is intense among the ten to fifteen seniors who submit portfolios (StratColl.edu is a small operation, remember), and the pressure considerable on the half-dozen of us faculty folk who review and, to the best of our ability, judge them.

That "us" and "our" ... After thirty-some years of teaching at Stratford, I'm newly retired from academe these days, but I still enjoy hanging out at Shakespeare House with new students and old colleagues (my wife among them, who has a couple of years yet to go before joining me in geezerdom) and serving on the Prize Committee. Mandy and I are a pair of those "experienced author-professors" mentioned in the school's ads, who out of teacherly habit here remind you that Experienced doesn't necessarily mean Good, much less Successful. Not likely you'll have heard of the "fictionist" George Newett or his versifying spouse Amanda Todd, even if you're one of those ever scarcer Americans who still read literature for pleasure (as you must be if you're reading this, if it ever gets published, if it ever gets written). Oh, I scored the occasional short story once upon a time, and Mandy the occasional lyric poem, mainly in serious quarterlies not much more widely read than our *Stratford Review*: little magazines that we ourselves rarely glance at unless something of ours or our colleagues is in them, which was never often and, in my case anyhow, is now nearly never. *The New Yorker? Harper's? Atlantic Monthly?* Neither of us ever made it into those prestigious (and better-paying) glossies. I did manage to place a novel forty years ago—not with one of the New York trade houses, alas, but with my midwestern alma mater's university press. On the strength of that modest publication plus three or four lit-mag stories, an M.F.A. from the Iowa Writers' Workshop, and two years of assistant-professoring at one of our state university's branch campuses, I was hired at Stratford, where then-young Mandy was already an instructor with an M.A. from Johns Hopkins and a comparably promising track record in poetry. A fine place to raise kids, she and I were soon happily agreeing in and out of bed — and so the town and its surroundings proved to be. Over our wedded decades, however, our separate and never loquacious muses more or less clammed up here in Oyster and Blue Crab Land, as they doubtless would have in any other venue, and we learned to content ourselves with trying to help others do better than their coaches were doing. The circumstance that as of this writing no Stratford alum has managed that not-so-difficult achievement does not prove our pedagogical labors fruitless, at least in our and most of our colleagues' opinion. Our program's graduates are better writers by baccalaureate time than they were at matriculation: more knowledgeable about language, literary forms and genres, and the achievements of three thousand years' worth of their predecessors. If they then become law clerks, businesspeople, schoolteachers, or whatever else, rather than capital-W Writers — well, so did their profs, and we don't consider *our* careers wasted.

Do we?

We don't, really, most of us more-or-less-Failed Old Farts, at least not most of the time. For one thing, showing all those apprentice scribblers what wasn't working in *their* works (that worked so well in the works of the great ones they were reading) showed us FOFs, on another level, the same thing vis-à-vis our own, if you follow me, and our consequent self-silencing spared posterity a lot of second- and third-rate writing, no? Though, come to think of it, most of our never-finished-if-ever-even-started stuff wouldn't have found a publisher anyhow, and most of what managed to find one would've mostly gone unread. So what the hell.

That being the case, why in the world am I writing *this*, and where, and to whom? The *where*, at least, I can answer: I'm in my office-cum-guest-room in our empty-nest coach home in Blue Crab Bight, a neighborhood of over-and-under duplexes in the sizable community of Heron Bay Estates, itself one of several extensive developments — residential and commercial, urban/suburban/exurban — built by the virtual patron of Stratford's Shakespeare Prize Fund, the afore-mentioned Tidewater Communities, Inc. Indeed, inasmuch as our house purchase made its tiny contribution to TCI's profitability and thus to the wealth of its philanthropical CEO, we Newett-Todds feel triply linked to that problematical award: as coaches of its candidates, as judges of their efforts, and as (minuscule, indirect) contributors to the winner's outsized jackpot.

It's a jackpot that Stratford's apprentice writing community regards, only half humorously, as jinxed: Shakespeare's Revenge, they call it, or, if they know their *Hamlet*, the Bard's Petard ("For 'tis the sport to have the enginer/Hoist with his own petard," the Prince observes grimly in act 3)—as if, having hit the literal jackpot on some gargantuan slot machine, the unlucky winner then gets crushed under an avalanche of coins. Much as our Public Information Office welcomes the publicity attendant on every spring's graduation exercises, when the Shakespeare Prize routinely gets more press than the commencement speaker, its ever more embarrassing side is that of the nearly two-score winners over the decades since the award's establishment, nearly none so far has managed to become "a writer"—i.e., a more or less established and regularly publishing poet, fictionist, essayist, screenwriter, journalist, or scholar—even to the limited extent that their coaches did. Worse yet, some who aspired simply to additional practice in one of our Republic's numerous master of fine arts programs have had their applications rejected by the more prestigious ones despite their not needing a teaching assistantship or other financial aid. And the few of our B.A.s who *have* gained admission to those top-drawer graduate programs happen not to have been among our Shakespeare laureates: a circumstance in itself no more surprising than that a number of the world's finest writers—Joyce, Proust, Nabokov, Borges, Calvino—never won the Nobel Prize, while not a few of its winners remain scarcely known even to us lovers of literature. *C'est la vie, n'est-ce pas?* But awkward, all the same, for the Bard awardees and awarders alike.

In vain our efforts to reduce the pot to some more reasonable though still impressive size—four or five thousand dollars, say, or even ten—and divert the surplus to other of our program's amenities: more munificent honoraria to attract eminent visitors, better payment for contributors to *The Stratford Review*, upgrades of Shakespeare House's facilities, larger salaries for the writing faculty ... Our benefactor's team of canny lawyers saw to it that the terms of the endowment are un-fiddle-withable. In vain too what I thought to be Mandy's and my inspired suggestion to a certain noted novelist on whom the College conferred an honorary Litt.D. ten years ago: that once the doctoral hood was hung on her, just before the awarding of the Prize, she announce, "By the authority invested in me by the Muse of Story and the Trustees of Stratford College, I declare that what I've been told is called Shakespeare's Curse is hereby lifted, both henceforward and retroactively. My warm congratulations to whoever may be this year's winner: May your efforts bear rich fruit! And my strong encouragement to all previous winners: May the Muse reward with future success your persistence in the face of past disappointment! Amen."

The audience chuckled and applauded; the media were duly amused; that year's prizewinner (a high-spirited and, we judges thought, quite promising young African-American poet from Baltimore) hip-hopped from the podium over to the seated dignitaries, check in hand, to bestow a loud kiss on his would-be savior—and returned triumphantly after the ceremony to his ghetto 'hood across the Bay, only to be killed later that summer in a "drug-related" drive-by shooting. Nor did his forerunners' and successors' fortunes appreciably improve, although several of my thus-far-luckless novel-writing protégés from commencements past have kept on scribbling vainly with their left hands, so to speak, while pursuing nonliterary careers with their right, their old coach having warned them that unlike violinists, mathematicians, theoretical physicists, and even lyric poets, for example—all of whom tend to blossom early or never—many novelists don't hit their stride until middle age.

Or later.

"So am I there yet?" one such perennially hopeful thirty-five-year-old asked me not long ago in a cover note to the typescript of her opus-still-in-progress, which she'd shipped to Blue Crab Bight for my perusal and comments despite my standing request to our graduates that they pass along all their future *publications*, to warm their old coach's heart and encourage his current coachees, but show me *no more unpublished writings ever*, please. A few pages plucked grudgingly from the thick pile's opening, middle, and closing chapters attested that their author wasn't, alas, "there yet." To spare her that blunt assessment, I emailed my praise for her persistence, reminded her of my No More Manuscripts policy ("We'd be shortchanging our present students if we kept on critiquing our alumnae"), and reminded her further always to enclose a self-addressed stamped envelope with any manuscript that she wanted returned to her. No reply, and so after a fair-enough interval I recycled her eternally gestating opus through my word processor, using its pages' bare white backside for next-draft printouts of my own work-in-regress at the time.

Namely? Well, since you asked: a "story" provisionally titled "The Bard Award," not by Yours Truly, George Newett, but by "Yours Falsely, George Knewit"—a.k.a. a certain Ms. "Cassandra Klause" (quotes hers), beyond question the most troublesome, gifted, and all-round problematical coachee that "Yours Falsely" and his colleagues (my wife included) ever had the much-mixed privilege of coaching, and of being coached by.

Those quotation marks; that saucy sobriquet and *nom de plume*, as openly provocative as the "bare white backside" of a few lines back (all typical Klause touches) ... Who knows how a youngster born to and raised by stolid Methodist parents on an Eastern Shore poultry farm and educated in marshy lower Delmarva's public school system came by age eighteen to be the unpredictably knowledgeable, aesthetically sophisticated, shyly brash and unintimidatable "literary performance artist" (her own designation) who, even as a Stratford freshman, was signing her term papers and exam bluebooks (always in quotes) "Sassy Cassie," "Sandy Claws," or "[in]Subordinate Klause," and contrived on her driver's license and other official documents to have her true name set between quotes? ("It's like that on my birth certificate," "C.K." once declared in class with her puckish smile. "My folks thought it looked more *official* that way.")

"And anyhow," she added this time last year in my old Shakespeare House office, "what's in a name?, as Uncle Will has that poor twat Juliet ask her hot-pants boyfriend. Best way to find out is to try on different ones for size, right? Like pants or penises. Now then, Boss: my final exam. *Ta-da!*" Whereupon she turned her back to me, bent forward, and yanked down her low-cut jeans to display, on her unpantied bare white *et cetera*, the marker-penned title and opening lines of her latest composition: *A BODY OF WORDS, by Nom D. Plume.* I didn't seriously believe, by the way, did I (she nattered calmly on as I hurried to reopen the office door, which she herself had closed before displaying her let-

tered derrière, and call for my across-the-hall colleague, the FOF poet
Amanda Todd, to please come verify that if anyone in the House was
Behaving Inappropriately, it was our student, not her teacher), that that
bumpkin of a glover's son from the Stratford boondocks actually wrote
those plays himself? About as likely as a down-county chicken farmer's
hatchling's winning next year's Bard Award!

Which in fact, however, she added as my wife came to my rescue,
she was dead set on doing, this time next year. "C'mon, Doc, *examine
me!*"

"Ms. Klause is up to her old tricks," said I with a sigh to Professor
Todd, and gestured toward our saucy pupil's "final exam."

"*New* tricks, guys." She turned her (plumpish) "text" to the pair of
us — and to the open door, which my wife quickly reclosed behind herself. "Just call me Randy Sandy, Mandy."

A calmer hand than her spouse in situations involving bare-assed
coeds bent over one's office desk, my Mrs. granted briskly, "Very amusing, Cass. And we get your point, I think: all that feminist/decon-
structionist blather about Writing the Body? Up with your pants now,
please, or you get an Incomplete for the semester."

Undaunted, "Cass my ass, Teach," the girl came back, and maintained her position: "If y'all don't read Cassie's Ass, her semester's incomplete anyhow."

Said I, "Excuse me now, everybody?" and consulted my wife's eyes
for her leave to leave: "Professor Todd will review and evaluate your
final submission, Ms. Klause — "

To my desktop she retorted, "*Semi*final submission. You ain't seen
nothing yet."

I'd seen more than enough, I declared. I would wait in Professor
Todd's office while its regular tenant examined and evaluated the rest
of the text for me. "Your title and pen name pretty well establish the
general idea."

To my departing back, as with a headshake I thanked Mandy and
got out of there, "No fair, Chief. You read 'em out of cunt-text!"

Some while later, over lunch at a pizzeria just off campus, my wife
and I shook heads over this latest, most outrageously provocative bit
of *Klauserie*. What she had seen further of A BODY OF WORDS, she
reported (feet, arms, belly, back, and neck had been enough for her),
confirmed her opinion of its being a not-unclever assemblage of quotes

from all over the literary corpus, having to do literally or figuratively with the various anatomical items upon which they were inscribed: Virgil's "I sing of arms" on her forearms, the Song of Solomon's "Thy belly is like a heap of wheat set about with lilies" encircling her navel, etc. "She said she'd intended to 'perform the whole text,' quote-unquote, in class, but then decided to hear your editorial suggestions first."

"Very considerate of her. What a handful that wacko kid is!"

"A *figurative* handful, we presume you mean?" Because though no beauty by fashion-mag standards, the ample-bodied Ms. Klause, we agreed, was a not unclever, not unattractive young woman, not unpopular with her classmates both male and female.

"Listen to us," I said to my spinach-mozzarella stromboli: "'Not unclever, not unattractive, not unpopular' . . . The girl's extraordinary! One tour de force after another, while everybody else in the room is still doing 'It was a dark and stormy night.' She *deserves* a fucking prize!"

"Better one of those than the Bard Award, we bet."

A certain small voltage had built across the table during this dialogue; it dispersed, if that's what voltages do, when I here declared, "The PITA Prize is what she deserves: Pain In The Ass." Back to being the dedicated, indeed impassioned teacher/colleague/wife I loved, "The girl's amazing," my wife enthused (a verb that she hates, but that her husband sometimes finds convenient). And "While we're talking about writing," she went on, although we hadn't been, exactly, "Ms. PITA Prize suggested to me that you should, and I quote, 'get some *description* done in that lame Bard Award story that he and I are supposedly collaborating on,' close quote. By which she meant you and her. Question mark?"

"*What?*"

That afore-noted small voltage resurged. "Her very words, George." Raising two fingers to make a quote mark, "'Like give the Gentle-Ass Reader some idea of how things feel, smell, sound, and *look*, for pity's sake, beyond Cassie's Bare White *Et Cetera* and Ms. Mandy's Jealous-Green Eyes, don't you think?' End of quote — and *what the fuck story is she talking about*, please? What's this *collaboration*?"

I was damned if I knew, and energetically swore so, adding that of course Ms. Klause and I had spoken in conference about the much coveted but problematical Shakespeare Prize, I being after all her faculty adviser, and that (partly as a result of that discussion) it had in fact oc-

curred to me that there might be a George Newett short story in there
somewhere: about an eccentrically gifted student "writer," say, whose
"texts" are collages, rearrangements, pastiches of the words of others.
But despite a few notebook notes and a false-start draft page or two,
I had yet to work out what that story might be — and most certainly,
to my knowledge, hadn't discussed it with "Cassandra Klause." When
a potential story of mine is still that nebulous, she might remember, I
don't speak of it even to my beloved fellow-writer spouse, much less
to my students. And "Could we please change the subject now, hon?
Enough voltage already!"

We duly did: spoke of our distant pair of adult children and of our
grandchild, already high school age, up in Vermont; of our plans for
the weekend; of some of our other, less troublesome Stratford students.
But my mind remained at least half on "Cass Klause"'s editorial suggestion, with which I found myself so in accord that I itched to get
back to my desk at home and experiment with a bit of sensory detail
(never my strongest writerly suit) in that story-not-quite-yet-in-em-
bryo: to "flesh out," for example, such lame lines as *"The girl's amazing,"
my wife enthused* with enhancements like *My wife closed her* [Ma-
tahannock-green-brown?] *eyes, shook her* [uh, very attractive? rud-
dy-cheeked? short-walnut-hair-framed?] *head, and* [um, enthused?]
"The girl's amazing!"

Better yet, maybe go back and cut out all that river-name and gated-community stuff at the tale's front end and get right to the action:
the day when a certain budding prankster / performance *artiste* proposed to her writing coach that instead of submitting to the class a
manuscript of his own for *them* to criticize (as she'd heard I'd done
once or twice in the past, half in jest, at semester's end), I should let
her submit one of mine under *her* name — as if for a change she was
making up her own sentences and paragraphs, characters and scenes,
instead of rearranging and "performing" other people's, when in fact
she wouldn't be! That way I'd get some *really* objective feedback, right?
As could scarcely be expected otherwise, except from her outspoken
self ("Too many parentheses and dashes, in this reader's opinion; not
enough *texture,*" etc.). Plus maybe submit as mine a story of hers: She'd
try to hack out something conventional, maybe about life in a tacky
gated community like Heron Bay Estates, or about a professor whose
maverick student puts an additional small strain on his prevailingly

quite happy marriage by teasing him with her "corpus" . . . that sort of thing. Which is pretty much what Ms. "Cassandra Klause" did, Reader, at the time here told of — and here we go, almost.

Additional small strain, somebody just said, on a *prevailingly* happy marriage. Mandy's and mine has been that, for sure; keenly aware of each other's strengths and shortcomings, we feel much blessed in each other, on balance. But of course there've been trials, strains, bumps in our road: the undeniably disappointing atrophy of our separate literary talents, to which however we feel we have, on the whole, commendably accommodated; one serious temptation apiece, somewhere back there, to adultery — which however we each take credit for candidly acknowledging and, we swear, resisting; never mind the details. And our inevitably mixed feelings, as we've approached or reached the close of our academic careers, not to mention of our lives, about what each and the other have accomplished, professionally and personally: about what we've done and not done, who we've been and not been, separately and together, during our joint single ride on life's not-always-merry-go-round. Hence those occasional small voltage surges above-noted: nothing that our coupled domestic wiring can't handle, as I'm confident we'd agree if we spoke of it, which we seldom do. Why bother? It's an electrical field potentiated over the past year by "Cassandra Klause" at one pole and at the other by my Shakespeare House "replacement," Professor Franklin Lee — who would've been introduced earlier into this "story" if its "author" didn't have a chip on his shoulder with respect to that smug sonofabitch. That tight-assed, self-important asshole. That . . .

Oh, that not untalented, not unhandsome, undeniably dedicated, generally quite capable and personable forty-five-year-old who joined the Stratford faculty half a dozen years ago upon the publication, two years before *that*, of his first (and eight years later still his only) novel — as utterly conservative, conventional, and unremarkable an item as its corduroy-jacketed author, but (to give the devil his due) not a bad job, really: issued by a bona fide New York trade house, not an academic press, and politely enough received by its handful of reviewers. Long since out of print, of course, but who among us isn't? A second novel allegedly still "going the rounds" up in Manhattan, and its author altogether mum about what, if anything, he and his strait-laced muse have been up to since.

In short and for better or worse, the guy's one of us, toward whom Mandy feels less animus and more colleagueship than does her spouse. "Frank Lee?" she'll tease when I get going like this on the subject. "Frank-*ly*, my dear, I don't give a damn, and neither should you." She's right, as usual, and I probably wouldn't, so much, except that it's been "Miz Klause's mizfortune," as that young woman herself puts it, to have Professor Lee as her official senior-year adviser, coach, and critic — and there, in her workshop mates' no doubt relieved opinion, go any hopes she might have entertained of so much as a long shot at this year's Shakespeare Prize.

But not in her own irrepressible estimation, nor in that of her FOF former coach. Shit, Reader (as Franklin Lee would never say): I'm no avant-gardist; would anytime rather read (or have written) the works of Ernest Hemingway, John Steinbeck, or Scott Fitzgerald, e.g., than those of Gertrude Stein or the later James Joyce. About contemporary "experimental" fiction — interactive electronic hypertext and the like? — I have only the most dutiful, professorial curiosity. Or used to, anyhow, back in my professoring days: used to urge my Stratford charges to keep an open mind and interested eye on the edges of their medium's envelope, reminding them that like the highest and lowest octaves on the classical eighty-eight-key piano — which, though rarely used, may be said to give a sort of resonant *optionality* to the middle octaves, making their use the composer's or performer's choice rather than a constraint — so likewise *et cetera*, you get the point. I therefore welcomed into my last year's workshop, after my initial startlement, the flagrantly unconventional "submissions" (misleading term!) of the apparently unscrupulous but actually strong-principled *faux-naïve provocateuse* "Cassandra Klause." The academic year that culminated last spring in A BODY OF WORDS, *by Nom D. Plume* had kicked off in the previous autumn with such unconventionalities as the opening pages of *Don Quixote* over the name "Pierre Menard" ("Borges's story, you know?" she had to explain to her baffled classmates. "About the guy who recomposes Cervantes's novel word for word?" They didn't get it); cribbed pages of a Joyce Carol Oates story signed "Toni Morrison," and vice versa (the "point" being that those two eminent Princeton colleagues must surely feel some rivalry, and might mischievously [etc.]); followed by other pointed or pointless but always transparent "plagiarisms" signed "The Grace of God," "The Way," "A

Long Shot," "Extension," or "Bye Baby," leaving the reader to supply the missing "by." Never a sentence of her own composing, but invariably a presentation more original than anything else in the room, even when flagrantly cribbed, chopped, and reassembled from the previous week's workshopped efforts of her classmates and re-presented as [by] "D. Construction" or "Tryst'em Sandy!" And then that *BODY OF WORDS*, which she openly declared to be her trial run for the Bard Award ("Hey, it's for the quote 'most impressive *body* of work' unquote, right?") and "performed" for a handful of fellow workshoppers in her dorm room after its preview by me and Mandy. And the "author" of these brazen stunts, mind, was an invariably unassuming, perky but shy-mannered young woman who also happened to be the most astute and candid yet diplomatic critic in the room (except perhaps for her coach) of her colleagues' literary efforts, so earnest but clunkily unimaginative by comparison.

One can readily imagine how less than edifying, instructive, or even entertaining Professor Franklin Lee found this sort of thing. In conference before the opening classes of her senior fall semester (my ex-student reported to me by email), he pleasantly but firmly let her know that *his* Advanced Fiction Writing seminar, "unlike some," was no theater for avant-garde gimmickry, but a serious workshop in "the millennia-old art of rendering into language the human experience of life": more specifically, in the less ancient art of "inventing and constructing short dramatic prose narratives for print, involving Characters, Setting, Plot, and Theme, in the noble tradition of Poe and Maupassant through Hemingway and Faulkner, Eudora Welty and Flannery O'Connor, to such contemporary masters of the form as Jorge Luis Borges and John Updike." If she found too constraining for her unconventional tastes a genre so splendidly various and accommodating (though rigorous), he advised, she should drop his course and sign up for something in the way of Experimental Theater, perhaps.

And when I pointed out to him that the Stratford catalogue doesn't offer any such courses [her e-message went on], *he smirked that tweedy little smirk of his and said, "Maybe Professor Emeritus Newett will be willing to do some sort of Independent Study project with you in his retirement, unless his wife objects. If he isn't willing, or if she says no, it might just be that Stratford isn't really the right venue for you." In his class, however, while we were free to write in the comic or non-comic*

mode, the realistic or the fantastic, the traditional or the innovative, what
we were going to make up and set down was STORIES, not "marginally
interesting aesthetic points presented by non-narrative means."

So HELP!!!!! (me, God) (And why wd yr wife object to a few extra-
curricular sessions, just you&me&my rambunctious muse, either some-
where on campus or maybe @ yr place, while Ms. Todd's meeting her
classes?) (Just kidding, Ma'am ;-)

Adieu[10]/0 (=Much Ado Over Nothing),
Yrs (truly), "CK"

"I personally think Frank has a point," opined Mandy when I showed
her this message (she and I have no secrets from each other, that I
know of). "And damn straight I object! She's so obviously coming on to
you, whether she means it seriously or not." If I chose to celebrate my
academic retirement by humping a coed forty-five years my junior, she
added, thereby dishonoring our longtime solemn vow to keep hands
off our students, I should go right the hell ahead, and there'd be "much
adieu" indeed: adieu to our marriage and to my academic reputation,
for starters. My call.

This-all said no more than half seriously, she crediting me with no
such intentions. And of course I abandoned the notion of any such
tête-à-tête tutorials, if I'd ever really half entertained it. But I maintained Cassie's and my email connection, offering to show my wife any
and all such communications if she wished to monitor them — which
she hoped I was kidding even to suggest. Because, truth to tell, my
previous year's exposure to "Nom D. Plume"'s "rambunctious muse"
showed signs of stirring my own muse from her extended hibernation.
During Klause's second junior-year semester with me, and over the
following summer, I had found myself reviewing two decades' worth of
George Newett story-scripts (most of them rejected after serial submissions), including a half-dozen comparatively recent ones that I hadn't
bothered to show Mandy. After my experience of "CK"'s freewheeling,
no-holds-barred imagination, they all struck me as, well, earnest but
clunky; "not untalented" but nowise exceptional; the sort of stuff that
a Franklin Lee might produce, with none of the sparkle that marked
Cassie's more imaginative perpetrations. Pallid rehashes, they were,
of "the 3 Johns" (her dismissive label for Messrs. Cheever, O'Hara,
and Updike): the muted epiphanies and petty nuances of upper-mid-

dle-class life in a not-all-that-upscale gated community on Maryland's endearingly funky Eastern Shore. Not impossibly, I had come to feel, some infusion of "CK"ish radicality might goose that muse of mine into rejuvenated action in my Golden Years, and George Newett would be remembered as a once-conventional and scarcely noticed writer who, in his Late Period, produced the refreshingly original works that belatedly made his name.

Meanwhile, however (not having lost my marbles altogether), I respected Frank Lee's ultimatum, sort of, or at least his right to declare it, as Amanda most certainly did as well. But I was determined to come to my former student's aid somehow or other. With some misgivings, therefore, I confided all the above to her by email as her senior-year registration date approached, and we came up with a plan, mostly but by no means entirely hers, to kill several birds with one stone. So to speak? I would supply her with drafts of those unpublished and abandoned later stories of mine: the ones that not even Mandy had seen. She would then edit, revise, and / or rewrite them as much or as little as she chose and submit them to Professor Lee's workshop as her own, perhaps over such Klausean pen names as "John Uptight," "(Over A-) Cheever," "Scareless O'Hara"— surely Professor Lee wouldn't object to *that!* The payoff for me would be fresh input (including his) on those old efforts, for whatever that might be worth, which I could perhaps then re-revise and present to some book publisher as a story collection. For "Sandy," the reward would be her baccalaureate and a shot after all at the Shakespeare Prize (one of whose judges I still was, along with Mandy, Frank Lee, another literature professor, and the head of the English Department). In competition for which she would submit ... what? Perhaps a "body of work" comprising specimens of her provocative junior-year stunts, her senior-year experiments with conventional forms and straightforward realism, and some sort of capstone piece embodying both, to demonstrate her "Hegelian evolution" as a writer (her term for it), from Thesis versus Antithesis to a Synthesis triumphantly combining and transcending both.

Yes, well, reader of these strung-out pages: We did that, my star ex-coachee and I — unbeknownst to my wife, to Franklin Lee, and to my other Stratford ex-colleagues — and all parties were impressed. Ms. Klause had been, remember, the ablest critic in my workshop; now she showed herself to be by far the best editor / rewriter as well. Those ho-hum scribblings of mine took on a resonance, texture, and sparkle that they'd formerly manifested only here and there, if at all — on the strength of which example I dared hope to return to my long-abandoned second novel and CPR it back to new life. "Best damned writing student I ever had," Frank Lee marveled to Amanda and me over a colleaguely lunch one April day in the Stratford Club, "by a factor of several!" He would never have guessed, he went on, that those jim-dandy stories that she had come up with for his workshop were Crazy Cassie's, if not for their jokey pen names — "which of course we will get rid of before she sends them off to *Harper's* and *The New Yorker*."

That winking, almost conspiratorial "we": So surprised and delighted was Fussy Frank by "our problem child's metamorphosis" that he generously included among its causes my earlier patient encouragement of her, along with his own "less permissive" standards. "Like Thesis and Antithesis, right?" he actually remarked to Mandy. "And she's our Synthesis." Hence the lunch-in-progress (his suggestion), to which he'd also invited my wife on the strength of her having rescued me a year ago from that *BODY OF WORDS*, by now a campus legend.

"I'll drink to that," she allowed, and raised her glass of faculty-club merlot to mine and to our colleague's de-alcoholized chardonnay (he had a class to teach that afternoon, he explained — but then, so did Mandy). As we nibbled our smoked-turkey-and-bean-sprout wraps, he even hinted, shyly, that if our joint protégée needed some extra cash this summer, he might actually hire her to review the typescript of his second novel and make editorial suggestions, so impressed was he by her acumen in that line. "Not that she'll likely be short on funds," he added with a chuckle — inasmuch as he would soon be presenting to the Prize Committee her assembled portfolio, which in his candid, considered, and confidential opinion need consist of nothing more than those half-dozen first-rate contributions to his senior seminar to make her a shoo-in for the Bard Award. "Who'd've thought, last September, that I'd hear myself saying that?"

I could have raised my hand, but of course did not. Among the things of which my lunchmates were unaware was that our Triumphantly Synthesizing student's senior-year output included two items that would not appear in her portfolio: a story of mine that she had submitted under her name to three good quarterlies simultaneously, without editing or revising it, as what she termed a "control" (all three had rejected it, as then had she), and one of her own under *my* name, programmatically imitative of my style, subject matter, and thematic preoccupations, but evidently superior to her model, as it was promptly accepted for publication by a lesser but still worthy periodical.

Consider it a thank-you for all you've done for me, the girl explained by email when I (1) received the lit mag's baffling acceptance letter (she'd supplied my Heron Bay Estates address on the obligatory self-addressed stamped envelope), (2) made a puzzled inquiry of the editor, (3) quickly surmised what was afoot, (4) canceled the publication (at least under my name), (5) provided the actual author's name and address in case the magazine was still interested (it was, but would need to Inquire Further), and (6) demanded from that author an explanation of this latest jawdropper. *XOXO Mwah!,* her message signed off, *cklause2@stratcoll.edu.*

Mwah my fat ass! I messaged back, demanding now both apology and cross-her-heart promise of no further such embarrassments — and at once regretted that angry imperative, to which she responded, *Just name the time and place, Coach. (And yours isn't all that fat, by the way: You shd see mine these days! ;-)*

Aiyiyiyiyi: How to get out of this me-made mess, and this mess of a nonstory about it by Who Knows Whom: a "story" that opened so George Newett-like, with a serene little disquisition on Eastern Shore river and place names; that proceeded smoothly through a half-dozen pages on Stratford College and its problematical Bard Award, establishing en route its newly retired narrator / protagonist and his not-yet-retired wife / colleague — and that then derailed just when it ought really to have got going, with the introduction of Conflict in the form of Troublesomely Brilliant Student "Cassandra Klause"? Should FOF Newett now commit his maiden adultery, so to speak, by humping one of his not-quite-ex students — at her initiative, to be sure, but still . . . — thereby blighting both his long happy marriage and his academic retirement, disgusting his colleagues and grown-up children, but perhaps reactivating (for what they're worth) his so-long-quiescent creative energies? And if so, so what? Or ought we to have the guy come to his moral senses (if necessary, since we've seen thus far no incontestable sign of his being *seriously* tempted by "CK"'s flagrances) and not only decline her seductive overtures but terminate altogether their somewhat sicko connection, make a clean breast of it to his faithful, so-patient Amanda before that breast gets irrevocably soiled, and content himself with his writerly Failed-Old-Farthood and his inarguably good works as teacher and coach of future FOFs? But again: If so, so what?

Or could/should it turn out to be at least possibly the case that *nothing thus far here narrated has been the* (actual, nonfictive) *case?* And if so...?

"Well of *course* it hasn't been, dumdum!" he imagines his frisky new sex mate teasing as he mounts her latest cleverly lettered performance piece, *BARTLETT'S DEFAMILIARIZED QUOTATIONS,* [by] "*Gosh & Golly,*" the two of them on all fours on the faux-oriental living room rug in her new apartment, rented with a bit of her Shakespeare Prize money and her earnings as editorial assistant to Professor Franklin Lee. "Do I need to remind *you,* of all people, that this whole she-bang is a made-up story? There *is* no 'Cassie-Ass Klause' or Georgie-Boy Newett! No you, no me, no Frankie-Pank Lee! No StratColl dot e-d-u, nor any Bard Award! All just freaking fictions! So sock it to me, Coach! *Unh! Unh!*"

Yes, well: No thanks, *chérie*; not even in an Effing Fiction. And as for the question with which you're now about to pull the rug from under your narrator — How to wrap up a longish story that has no proper plot development anyhow? A story that for all one knows (or cares) may be being written by Not-Yet-Failed Fictionist Franklin Lee, say: beneath his corduroy camouflage a less straitjacketed writer than some mistake him to be, ha-ha, and longtime secret lover of a certain poet-colleague of his, ha-ha-ha, as well as of her pathetic husband's ex-protégée "CK," ha-ha-ha-ha! ...?

No problem, mate (ha-ha-ha-ha-ha & *UNH!*) ...:

THE END
Respectfully submitted to the Shakespeare Prize Committee [by]
"Hook R. Crook"
(Copywrong ☺Twenty-Something [G.I. Newett])

Progressive Dinner

1. HORS D'OEUVRES AND APPETIZERS

"Hey, Rob! Hey, Shirley! Come on in, guys!"

"And the Beckers are right behind us. Hi-ho, Debbie! Hi-ho, Peter!"

"Come in, come in. Nametags on the table there, everybody. Drinks in the kitchen, goodies in the dining room and out on the deck. Yo there, Jeff and Marsha!"

"You made your taco dip, Sandy! Hooray! And Shirley brought those jalapeño thingies that Pete can't keep hands off of. Come on in, Tom and Patsy!"

> TIME: *The late afternoon / early evening of a blossom-rich late-May North Temperate Zone Saturday, half-a-dozen-plus springtimes into the new millennium. Warm enough for open doors and windows and for use of decks and patios, but not yet sultry enough to require air conditioning, and still too early for serious mosquitoes.*

"So, did you folks see the Sold sign on the Feltons' place?"

"No! Since when?"

"Since this morning, Tom Hardison tells us. We'll ask Jeff Pitt when he and Marsha get here; he'll know what's what."

"The poor Feltons! We still can't get over it!"

"Lots of questions still unanswered there, for sure. Where d'you want this smoked bluefish spread, Deb?"

"In my mouth, just as soon as possible! Here, I'll take it; you guys go get yourself a drink. Hey there, Ashtons!"

> *PLACE: 908 Cattail Court, Rockfish Reach, Heron Bay Estates, Stratford, Avon County, upper Eastern Shore of Maryland, 21600: an ample and solidly constructed two-story hip-roofed dormer-windowed Dutch-colonial-style dwelling of white brick with black shutters and doors, slate roof, flagstone front walk and porch and patio, on "Rockfish Reach," off Heron Creek, off the Matahannock River, off Chesapeake Bay, off the North Atlantic Ocean, etc.*

"So, Doctor Pete, what's your take on the latest bad news from Baghdad?"

"You know what I think, Tom. What all of us ivory-tower-liberal academics think: that we had no business grabbing that tar baby in the first place, but our president lied us into there and now we're stuck with it. Here's to you, friend."

"Yeah, well. Cheers? Hey, Peg, we all love our great new mailboxes! You guys did a terrific job!"

"Didn't they, though? Those old wooden ones were just rotting away."

"And these new cast-metal jobs are even handsomer than the ones in Spartina Pointe. Good work, guys."

"You're quite welcome. Thanks for *this*, Deb and Pete and everybody. *Mmm!*"

"So where're the Pitts, I wonder?"

"Speak of the devil! Hi there, Marsha; hi-ho, Jeff! And you-all are . . . ?"

> *OCCASION: The now-traditional season-opening progressive dinner in Heron Bay's Rockfish Reach subdivision, a pleasantly laid out and landscaped two-decade-old neighborhood of some four dozen houses in various architectural styles, typically three-bedroom, two-and-a-half-bath affairs with attached two-car garage, screened or open porches, decks and/or patios, perhaps a basement, perhaps a boat dock, all on low-lying, marsh-fringed acre-and-a-half lots. Of the nearly fifty families who call the place home, most are*

empty- or all-but-empty-nesters, their children grown and flown. About half are more or less retired, although some still work out of home offices. Perhaps a third have second homes elsewhere, in the Baltimore/Washington or Wilmington/Philadelphia areas where they once worked, or in the Florida coastal developments whereto they migrate with other East Coast snowbirds for the winter. Half a dozen of the most community-spirited from the Reach's Shoreside Drive and its adjacent Cattail and Loblolly Courts function as a neighborhood association, planning such community events and improvements as those above-mentioned dark green cast-metal mailboxes (paid for by a special assessment), the midsummer Rockfish Reach BYOB sunset cruise down the Matahannock from the Heron Bay Marina, and the fall picnic (in one of HBE's two pavilioned waterside parks) that unofficially closes the season unofficially opened by the progressive dinner, here in early progress.

As usual, invitation notices were distributed to all four dozen households a month before the occasion, rubber-banded to the decorative knobs atop those new mailboxes. Also as usual, between fifteen and twenty couples signed on and paid the $40-per-person fee. Of the participating households (all of whom have been asked to provide, in addition to their fee, either an hors d'oeuvre/appetizer or a dessert, please indicate which), six or seven will have volunteered to be hosts: one for the buffet-and-bar opening course presently being enjoyed by all hands, perhaps four for the sit-down entrée (supplied by a Stratford caterer; check your nametag to see which entrée house you've been assigned to), and one for the all-together-again dessert buffet that winds up the festive occasion. The jollity of which, this spring, has been somewhat beclouded—as was that of last December's Rockfish Reach "Winter Holiday" party—by the apparent double suicide, still unexplained, of Richard and Susan Felton (themselves once active participants in these neighborhood events) by exhaust-fume inhalation in their closed garage at 1020 Shoreside Drive, just after Tom and Patsy Hardison's elaborate *toga party last September to inaugurate their new house on Loblolly Court. Recommended dress for the progressive dinner is "country club casual": slacks and sport shirts for the gentlemen (jackets optional); pants or skirts and simple blouses for the ladies.*

"Hi there. Jeff insists that we leave it to him to do the honors."

"*And* to apologize for this late addition to the guest list, *and* to cover the two extra plate charges, *and* to fill in the nametags — all courtesy of Avon Realty, guys, where we agents do our best to earn our commissions. *May I have your attention, everybody?* This handsome young stud and his blushing bride are your new about-to-be neighbors Joe and Judy Barnes, formerly and still temporarily from over in Blue Crab Bight but soon to move into Number Ten-Twenty Shoreside Drive! Joe and Judy, this is Dean Peter Simpson, from the College, and his soulmate Deborah, also from the College."

"Welcome to Rockfish Reach, Joe and Judy. What a pleasant surprise!"

"Happy to be here . . . Dean and Mrs. Simpson."

"Please, guys. We're Debbie and Pete."

"*Lovely* house, Debbie! And do forgive us for showing up empty-handed. Everything happened so *fast!*"

"No problem, no problem. If I know Marsha Pitt, she's probably brought an hors d'oeuvre *and* a dessert."

"Guilty as charged, Your Honor. Cheesecake's in the cooler out in our car for later at the Greens'; I'll put these doodads out with the rest of the finger food."

"And *your* new house is a lovely one too, Judy and Joe. Pete and I have always admired that place."

"Thanks for saying so. Our daughters are convinced it'll be haunted! One of them's up at the College, by the way, and her kid sister will be joining her there next year, but they'll still be coming home most weekends and such."

"We hope!"

"Oh my, how *wonderful* . . . Excuse me . . ."

"So! Go on in, people. Jeff and Marsha will introduce you around, and we'll follow shortly."

"Aye-aye, Cap'n. The Barneses will be doing their entrée with us, by the way. We've got plenty of extra seating, and they've promised not to say that our house is the Pitts."

"*Ai*, sweetheart, you promised not to resurrect that tired old joke! Come on, Joe and Judy, let's get some wine."

("You okay, hon?"

"I'll make it. But that daughters thing really hit home."

"Yup. Here's a Kleenex. On with the party?")

> HOSTS: The "associates": Deborah Clive Simpson, fifty-seven, associate librarian at Stratford College's Dexter Library, and Peter Alan Simpson, also fifty-seven, longtime professor of humanities and presently associate dean at that same quite good small institution, traditionally a liberal-arts college but currently expanding its programs in the sciences, thanks to a munificent bequest from a late alumnus who made a fortune in the pharmaceuticals business. The Simpsons are childless, their only offspring, a much-prized daughter, having been killed two years ago in a multicar crash on the Baltimore Beltway during an ice storm in the winter of her sophomore year as a premedical student at Johns Hopkins. Her loss remains a trauma from which her parents do not expect ever to recover; the very term "closure," so fashionable nowadays, sets their teeth on edge, and the coinciding of Julie's death and Peter's well-earned promotion to associate dean has leached much pleasure from the latter. Nevertheless, in an effort to "get on with their lives," the Simpsons last year exchanged their very modest house in Stratford — so rich in now-painful memories of child-rearing and of the couple's advancement up the academic ladder from relative penury to financial comfort — for their present Rockfish Reach address, and they're doing their best to be active members of both their collegiate and their residential communities as well as generous supporters of such worthy organizations as Doctors Without Borders (Médecins Sans Frontières), to which it had been Julie's ambition to devote herself once she attained her M.D.

"So we bet those new folks — what's their name?"

"Barnes. Joe and Judy. He's with Lucas and Jones in Stratford, and she teaches at the Fenton School. They seem nice."

"We bet they got themselves a bargain on the Feltons' place."

"More power to 'em, *I* say. All's fair in love, war, and real estate."

"Don't miss Peggy Ashton's tuna spread, Rob; I'm going for another white wine spritzer."

"Make that two, okay? But no spritz in mine, please. So, Lisa: What were you starting to say about the nametags?"

"Oh, just that looking around at tonight's tags reminded me that friends of ours over in Oyster Cove told us once that nine out of ten husbands in Heron Bay Estates are called by one-syllable first names and their wives by two-syllable ones: You Rob-and-Shirley, we Dave-and-Lisa, *et cetera*."

"Hey, that's right. I hadn't noticed!"

"And what exactly does one make of that sociocultural info bit, *s'il vous plâit?*"

"I'll let you know, Pete-and-Debbie, soon's I figure it out. *Meanwhile . . .*"

"What *I* notice, guys — every time I'm in the supermarket or Wal-Mart? — is that more and more older and overweight Americans — "

"Like us?"

"Like some of us, anyhow — go prowling down the aisles bent forward like *this*, with arms and upper body resting on their shopping cart as if it was some kind of a walker . . ."

"And their fat butts waggling, often in pink warmup pants . . ."

"Now is that nice to say?"

"It's what Pete calls the American Consumer Crouch. *I* say 'Whatever floats your boat . . .'"

"*And* keeps the economy perking along. Am I right, Joe Barnes?"

"Right you are, Jeff."

"So, Deb, *you* were saying something earlier about a long letter that Pete got out of the blue from some girl in Uganda?"

"Oh, right, wow: *that . . .*"

"Uganda?"

"I should let Pete tell you about it. Where are you and Paul doing your entrée?"

"Practically next door. At the Beckers'."

"Us too. So he'll explain it there. Very touching — but who knows whether it's for real or a scam? Oh, hey, Pat: Have you and Tom met the

Barneses? Joe and Judy Barnes, Tom and Patsy Hardison from Loblolly Court."

"Jeff Pitt introduced us already, Deb. Hello again, Barneses."

"Hi there. We've been hearing great things about your Toga Party last fall! Sounds cool!"

"All but the ending, huh? We can't *imagine* what happened with Dick and Susan Felton that night . . ."

"Has to've been some kind of freak accident; let's don't spoil this party with that one. Welcome to Rockfish Reach!"

"Joe and I love it already. And your place on Loblolly Court is just incredible!"

"Jeff pointed it out to us when we first toured the neighborhood. Really magnificent!"

"Thanks for saying so. An eyesore, some folks think, but it's what we wanted, so we built it. You're the new boss at Lucas and Jones, in town?"

"I am — and *my* boss, over in Baltimore, is the guy who stepped on lots of folks' toes with that teardown over in Spartina Pointe. Maybe you know him: Mark Matthews?"

"Oh, we know Mark, all right. A man after my own heart."

"Mine too, Tom. Decide what you want, go for it, and let the chips fall where they may."

"Well, now, people: Excuse me for butting in, but to us lonely left-wing-Democrat dentist types, that sounds a lot like our current president and his gang."

"Whoa-ho, Doctor David! Let's not go there, okay? This is Lisa Bergman's husband Dave, guys. He pulls teeth for a living."

"And steps on toes for fun. Pleased to meet you, folks."

"Entrée time in twenty minutes, everybody! Grab yourselves another sip and nibble, check your tags for your sit-down-dinner address, and we'll all reconvene for dessert with the Greens at nine!"

"So, that Barnes couple: Are they golfers, d'you know?"

2. ENTRÉE

The assembled now disperse from the Simpsons' to shift their automobiles or stroll on foot to their various main-course addresses, their four host-couples having left a bit earlier to confirm that all is ready and to be in place to greet their guests. Of these latter, four will dine with George and Carol Walsh on Shoreside Drive; six (including the newcomer Barneses) with Jeff and Marsha Pitt, also on Shoreside; eight (the Ashtons, Bergmans, Greens, and Simpsons) with Pete and Debbie's Cattail Court near-neighbors Charles and Sandy Becker; and ten with Tom and Patsy Hardison over on Loblolly Court. Stratford Catering's entrée menu for the evening is simple but well prepared: a caesar salad with optional anchovies, followed by Maryland crabcakes with garlic mashed potatoes and a steamed broccoli-zucchini mix, the vegetables cooked in advance and reheated, the crabcakes prepared in advance but griddled on-site, three minutes on each side, and the whole accompanied by mineral water and one's choice of pinot grigio or iced tea.

The Becker group all go on foot, chatting together as they pass under the streetlights in the mild evening air, their destination being just two houses down from the Simpsons' on the opposite side of the cul-de-sac "court." To no one in particular, Shirley Green remarks, "Somebody was wondering earlier whether the Barneses got a bargain price on the Feltons' house? None of our business, but *I* can't help wondering whether the Beckers' house number affects *their* property value."

"Aiyi," Peggy Ashton exclaims in mock dismay. "*Nine-Eleven* Cattail Court! I hadn't thought of that!"

If *he* were Chuck Becker, Rob Green declares to the group, he'd use that unfortunate coincidence to appeal their property-tax assessment. "I mean, hell, Dick and Susan Felton were just two people, rest their souls. Whereas, what was it, three *thousand* and some died on Nine-Eleven? That ought to count for something."

His wife punches his shoulder. "Rob, I *swear!*"

Walking backward to face the group, he turns up his palms: "Can't help it, folks. We accountants try to take everything into account."

Hisses and groans. Peter Simpson takes his wife's hand as they approach their destination. He's relieved that the Barneses, although certainly pleasant-seeming people, won't be at table with them for the sit-down dinner to distress Debbie further with innocent talk of their college-age daughters.

The Beckers' house, while no *palazzo* like the Hardisons', is an imposing two-story white-brick colonial, its columned central portico flanked by a guest wing on one side and a garage wing on the other, with two large doors for cars and a smaller one for golf cart and bicycles.

The eight guests make their way up the softly lighted entrance drive to the brightly lit main entry to be greeted by ruddy-hefty, bald-pated, silver-fringed Charles Becker, a politically conservative septuagenarian with the self-assured forcefulness of the CEO he once was, and his no-longer-sandy-haired Sandy, less vigorous of aspect after last year's successful surgery for a "growth" on her left lung, but still active in the Neighborhood Association, her Episcopal church in Stratford, and the Heron Bay Club. Once all have been welcomed and seated in the Beckers' high-ceilinged dining room, the drinks poured, and the salad served, their host taps his water glass with a table knife for attention and says, "Let's take hands and bow our heads for the blessing, please."

The Simpsons, seated side by side at his right hand, glance at each other uncomfortably, they being nonbelievers, and at the Bergmans, looking equally discomfited across the table from them. More for their sake than for her own, Debbie asks, as if teasingly, "Whatever happened to the separation of church and dinner party?" To which Charles Becker replies smoothly, "In a Christian household, do as the Christians do," and takes her left hand in his right and Lisa Bergman's right in his left. David shrugs his eyebrows at Pete and goes along with it, joining hands with his wife on one side and with Shirley Green on the other. Peter follows suit, taking Debbie's right hand in his left and Peggy Ashton's left in his right; but the foursome neither close eyes nor lower heads with the others while their host intones: "Be present at our table, Lord. / Be here and everywhere adored. / These mercies bless, and grant that we / May feast in Paradise with Thee. Amen."

"*And*," Paul Ashton adds at once to lighten the little tension at the table, "grant us stomach-room enough for this entrée after all those appetizers!"

"Amen and *bon appétit*," proposes Sandy Becker, raising her wineglass. "Everybody dig in, and then I'll do the crabcakes while Chuck serves up the veggies."

"Such appetizers they were!" Lisa Bergman marvels, and then asks Paul whether he happens, like her, to be a Gemini. He is, in fact, he replies: "Got a birthday coming up next week. Why?"

"Because," Lisa declares, "it's a well-known fact that we Geminis prefer hors d'oeuvres to entrées. No offense intended, Sandy and Chuck!"

Her husband winks broadly. "It's true even in bed, so I've heard — no offense intended, Paul and Lisa."

Sipping their drinks and exchanging further such teases and pleasantries, all hands duly address the caesar salad, the passed-around optional anchovy fillets, and the pre-sliced baguettes. Although tempted
to pursue what she regards as presumption on their host's part that
everyone in their community is a practicing Christian, or that because
the majority happen to be, any others should join in uncomplainingly,
Debbie Simpson holds her tongue — as she did not when, for example,
the Neighborhood Association proposed Christmas lights last winter
on the entrance signs to Rockfish Reach (she won that one, readily
granting the right of all residents to decorate their houses, but not
community property, with whatever religious symbols they cared to
display), and when the Heron Bay Estates Community Association put
up its large Christmas tree at the development's main gatehouse (that
one she lost, and at Pete's request didn't pursue it, they being new residents whom he would prefer not be branded as troublemakers). She
gives his left hand a squeeze by way of assuring him that she's letting
the table-grace issue drop.

"So tell us about that strange letter you got, Pete," Peggy Ashton proposes. "From Uganda, was it? That Deb mentioned during appetizers?"

"Uganda?" the hostess marvels, or anyhow asks.

"*Very* strange," Peter obligingly tells the table. "I suppose we've all
gotten crank letters now and then — get-rich scams in Liberia and like
that?—but this one was really different." To begin with, he explains, it
wasn't a photocopied typescript like the usual mass-mailed scam letter, but a neatly handwritten appeal on two sides of a legal-size ruled
sheet, with occasional cross-outs and misspellings. Polite, articulate,
and addressed to "Dear Friend," it was or purported to be from a seventeen-year-old Ugandan girl, the eldest of five children, whose mother had died in childbirth and whose father had succumbed to AIDS.
Since their parents' death, the siblings have been lodged with an uncle,
also suffering from AIDS and with five children of his own. Those he
dresses properly and sends to school, the letter writer declares, but
she and her four brothers and sisters are treated harshly by him and
his wife, who "don't recognize [them] as human beings." Dismissed
from school for lack of fee money and provided with "only two clothes
each" to wear and little or nothing to eat, they are made to graze the
family's goats, feed the pigs, and do all the hard and dirty housework
from morning till night. In a few months, when she turns eighteen,

she'll be obliged to become one of some man's several wives, a fate she fears both because of the AIDS epidemic and because it will leave her siblings unprotected. Having (unlike them) completed her secondary education before their father's death, she appeals to her "dear Friend" to help her raise 1,500 euros to "join university for a degree in education" and 1,200 euros for her siblings to finish high school. Attached to the letter was a printed deposit slip from Barclays Bank of Uganda, complete with the letter writer's name and account number, followed by the stipulation "F/O CHILDREN."

"How she got *my* name and address, I can't imagine," Pete concludes to the hushed and attentive table. "If it was in some big general directory or academic Who's Who, how'd she get hold of it, and how many hundreds of these things did she write out by hand and mail?"

"And where'd she get paper and envelopes and deposit slips and postage stamps," Lisa Bergman wonders, "if they're so dirt poor?"

"And the time to scribble scribble scribble," Paul Ashton adds, "while they're managing the goats and pigs and doing all the scutwork?"

Opines Rob the Accountant, "It doesn't add up."

"It does seem questionable," Sandy Becker agrees.

"But if you could see the letter!" Debbie protests. "So earnest and articulate, but so unslick! Lines like 'We do not hope that our uncle will recover.' And 'I can't leave my siblings alone. We remained five and we should stick five.'"

Taking her hand in his again and using his free hand to make finger quotes, Pete adds, "And, quote, 'Life unbearable, we only pray hard to kind people to help us go back to school, because the most learnt here is more chance of getting good job,' end of quote."

"It's heartbreaking," Shirley Green acknowledges. "No wonder you-all have so much of it memorized!"

"But the bottom line is," Chuck Becker declares, "did you fall for it? Because, believe me, it's a goddamn scam."

"You really think so?" Dave Bergman asks.

"Of course it is! Some sharpster with seven wives and Internet access for tracking down addresses sets his harem to scribbling out ten copies per wife per day, carefully misspelling a few words and scratching out a few more, just to see who'll take the bait. Probably some midlevel manager at Barclays with a PC in his office and a fake account in one of his twelve daughters' names."

"How can you be so *sure*?" Lisa Bergman wants to know.

With the air of one accustomed to having his word taken, "Take my word for it, sweetie," their host replies. Down-table to his wife then, "Better get the crabcakes started, Sandy?" And to the Simpsons, "Please tell me you didn't send 'em a nickel."

"We didn't," Debbie assures him. "Not yet, anyhow. Because of course we're leery of the whole thing too. But just suppose, Chuck and everybody—just *suppose* it happens to be authentic? Imagine the courage and resourcefulness of a seventeen-year-old girl in that wretched situation, with all that traumatic stuff behind her and more of it waiting down the road, but she manages somehow to get hold of a bunch of American addresses and a pen and paper and stamps and deposit slips, and she scratches out this last-chance plea for a *life* ... Suppose it's for real?"

"And we-all sit here in our gated community," Lisa Bergman joins in, "with our Lexuses and golf carts and our parties and progressive dinners, and we turn up our noses and say, 'It's a scam; don't be suckered.'"

"So what *should* we do?" Paul Ashton mildly challenges her. "Bet a hundred bucks apiece on the *very* long shot that it's not a shyster?"

"I'm almost willing to," Shirley Green admits. Her husband shakes his head no.

"What we *ought* to do," Dave Bergman declares, "is go to some trouble to find out whether the thing's for real. A *lot* of trouble, if necessary. Like write back to her, telling her we'd like to help but we need more bona fides. Find out how she got Pete's name and address. Ask the American consulate in Kampala or wherever to check her story out. Is that in Uganda?"

"You mean," his wife wonders or suggests, "make a community project out of it?"

Asks Debbie, "Why not?"

"Because," Rob Green replies, "I, for one, don't have time for it. Got a full plate already!" He checks his watch. "Or soon will have, won't we, Shirl?"

"Same here," Dave Bergman acknowledges. "I know I ought to *make* time for things like this, but I also know I won't. It's like demonstrating against the war in Iraq, the way so many of us did against the war in Vietnam. Or even like working to get out the vote on Election Day. My hat's off to people who act that strongly on their convictions, and I used to be one of them, but I've come to accept that I'm just *not* anymore. Morally lazy these days, I guess, but at least honest about it."

"And in this case," Chuck Becker says with ruddy-faced finality, "you're saving yourself a lot of wasted effort. Probably in those other cases too, but never mind that."

"Oh my goodness," his wife exclaims. "Look what time it is! I'll do the crabcakes, Chuck'll get the veggies, and Paul, would you mind refreshing everybody's drinks? Or we'll never get done before it's time to move on to Rob and Shirley's!"

3. DESSERT

The Greens' place on Shoreside Drive, toward which all three dozen progressive diners now make their well-fed way from the several entrée houses to reassemble for the dessert course, is no more than a few blocks distant from the Becker and Simpson residences on Cattail Court — although the attractively winding streets of Heron Bay Estates aren't really measurable in blocks. Chuck and Sandy Becker, who had earlier walked from their house to Pete and Debbie Simpson's (practically next door) for the appetizer course, and then back to their own place to host the entrée, decide now to drive to the final course of the evening in their Cadillac Escalade. The Greens themselves, having left the Beckers' a quarter-hour earlier to make ready, drove also, retrieving their Honda van from where they'd parked it in front of the Simpsons'. The Ashtons, Paul and Peggy, walk only far enough to collect their Lexus from the Simpsons' driveway and then motor on. Of the five couples who did their entrée at 911 Cattail Court, only the Simpsons themselves and the Bergmans decide that the night air is too inviting not to stroll through it to Rob and Shirley's; they decline the proffered lifts in favor of savoring the mild westerly breeze, settling their crabcakes and vegetables a bit before tackling the dessert smorgasbord, and chatting among themselves en route.

"That Chuck, I swear," Lisa Bergman says as the Beckers' luxury SUV rolls by. "So *sure* he's right about everything! And Sandy just goes along with it."

"Maybe she agrees with him," Peter suggests. "Anyhow, they're good neighbors, even if Chuck can be borderline insufferable now and then."

"I'll second that," Dave Bergman grants. Not to walk four abreast down a nighttime street with no sidewalks, the two men drop back a bit to carry on their conversation while their wives, a few feet ahead, speak of other things. Charles Becker, David goes on, likes to describe himself as a self-made man, and in considerable measure he is: from humble beginnings as a small-town carpenter's son —

"Sounds sort of familiar," Peter can't help commenting, "except our Chuck's not about to let himself get crucified."

"Anyhow, served in the Navy during World War Two; came home and went to college on the G.I. Bill to study engineering; worked a few years for a suburban D.C. contractor in the postwar housing boom; then started his own business and did very well indeed, as he does not tire of letting his dentist and others know. No hand-scrawled Send Me Money letters for *him*: 'God helps those who help themselves,' *et cetera*."

"Right: the way he helped himself to free college tuition and other benefits not readily available to your average Ugandan orphan girl. Hey, look: Sure enough, there's Jeff Pitt's latest score."

Peter means the Sold sticker on the For Sale sign (with *The Jeff Pitt Team* lettered under it) in front of 1020 Shoreside Drive, the former residence of Richard and Susan Felton. The women, too, pause before it — their conversation having moved from the Beckers to the Bergmans' Philadelphia daughter's latest project for her parents: to establish a Jewish community organization in Stratford, in alliance with the College's modest Hillel club for its handful of Jewish students. Lisa is interested; David isn't quite convinced that the old town is ready yet for that sort of thing.

"The Feltons," he says now, shaking his head. "I guess we'll never understand."

"What do you mean?" Debbie challenges him. "I think *I* understand it perfectly well."

"What do *you* mean?" David cordially challenges back. "They were both in good health, comfortably retired, no family problems that anybody knows of, well liked in the neighborhood — and *wham*, they come home from the Hardisons' toga party and off themselves!"

"And," Peter adds, "their son and daughter not only get the news secondhand, with no advance warning and no note of explanation or apology, but then have to put their own lives on hold and fly in from wherever to dispose of their parents' bodies and house and belongings."

"What a thing to lay on your kids!" Lisa agrees. The four resume walking the short remaining distance to the Greens." And you think that's just fine, Deb?"

"Not 'just fine,'" Debbie counters: "*understandable*. And I agree that their kids deserved some explanation, if maybe not advance notice, since then they'd've done all they could to prevent its happening." What she means, she explains, is simply that she quite understands how a couple at the Feltons' age and stage — near or in their seventies after a prevailingly happy, successful, and disaster-free life together, their children and grandkids grown and scattered, the family's relations reportedly affectionate but not especially close, the parents' careers behind them along with four decades of good marriage, nothing better to look forward to than the infirmities, losses, and burdensome caretaking of old age, and no religious prohibitions against self-termination — how such a couple might just decide, Hey, it's been a good life; we've been lucky to have had it and each other all these years; let's end it peacefully and painlessly before things go downhill, which is really the only way they can go from here.

"And let our friends and neighbors and children clean up the mess?" David presses her. "Would you and Pete do that to us?"

"Count *me* out," Peter declares. "For another couple decades anyhow, unless the world goes to hell even faster than it's going now."

"In our case," his wife reminds the Bergmans, "it's friends, neighbors, and *colleagues*. Don't think we haven't talked about it more than once since Julie's death. I've even checked it out on the Web, for when the time comes."

"On the *Web?*" Lisa takes her friend's arm.

Surprised, concerned, and a little embarrassed, "The things you learn about your mate at a progressive dinner!" Peter marvels to David, who then jokingly complains that he hasn't learned a single interesting thing so far about *his* mate.

"Don't give up on me," his wife says. "The party's not over."

"Right you are," Debbie agrees, "literally and figuratively. And here we are, and I'll try to shut up."

The Greens' house, brightly lit, with a dozen or more cars now parked before it, is a boxy two-story beige vinyl-clapboard-sided affair, unostentatious but commodious and well maintained, with fake-shuttered windows all around, and on its creek side a large screened porch, open patio, pool, and small-boat dock. Shirley Green being active in the Heron Bay Estates Garden Club, the property is handsomely landscaped: The abundant rhododendrons, azaleas, and flowering trees have already finished blossoming for the season, but begonias, geraniums, daylilies, and roses abound along the front walk and driveway, around the foundation, and in numerous planters. As the foursome approach, the Bergmans tactfully walk a few paces ahead. Peter takes his wife's arm to comfort her.

"Sorry," Debbie apologizes again. "You know I wouldn't be thinking these things if we hadn't lost Julie." Her voice thickens. "She'd be fresh out of college now and headed for med school!" She can say no more.

"I know, I know." As indeed Peter does, having been painfully reminded of that circumstance as he helped preside over Stratford's recent commencement exercises instead of attending their daughter's at Johns Hopkins. Off to medical school she'd be preparing herself to go, for arduous but happy years of general training, then specialization, internship, and residency; no doubt she'd meet and bond with some fellow physician-in-training along the way, and Peter and Debbie would help plan the wedding with her and their prospective son-in-law and look forward to grandchildren down the line to brighten their elder years, instead of Googling "suicide" on the Web . . .

Briefly but appreciatively she presses her forehead against his shoulder. Preceded by the Bergmans and followed now by other dessert-course arrivers, they make their way front-doorward to be greeted by eternally boyish Rob and ever-effervescent Shirley Green.

"Sweets are out on the porch, guys; wine and decaf in the kitchen. Beautiful evening, isn't it?"

"Better enjoy it while we can, I guess, before the hurricanes come."

"Yo there, Barneses! What do you think of your new neighborhood so far?"

"Totally awesome! Nothing like this in Blue Crab Bight."

"We can't wait to move in, ghosts or no ghosts. Our daughter Tiffany's off to France for six weeks, but it's the rest of the family's summer project."

"So enjoy every minute of it. Shall we check out the goodies, Deb?"

"Calories, here we come! Excuse us, people."

But over chocolate cheesecake and decaffeinated coffee on the torch-lit patio, Judy Barnes reapproaches Debbie to report that Marsha Pitt, their entrée hostess, told them the terrible news of the Simpsons' daughter's accident. "Joe and I are *so* sorry for you and Peter! We can't *imagine* ..."

All appetite gone, "Neither can we," Debbie assures her. "We've quit trying to."

And just a few minutes later, as the Simpsons are conferring on how soon they can leave without seeming rude, Paul and Peggy Ashton come over, each with a glass of pale sherry in one hand and a chocolate fudge brownie in the other, to announce their solution to that Ugandan orphan girl business.

"Can't wait to hear it," Peter says dryly. "Will Chuck Becker approve?"

"Chuck shmuck," says Paul, who has picked up a few Yiddishisms from the Bergmans. "The folks who brought you your dandy new mailboxes now propose a Rockfish Reach Ad Hoc Search and Rescue Committee. Tell 'em, Peg."

She does, emphasizing her points with a half-eaten brownie. The informal committee's initial members would be the three couples at dinner who seemed most sympathetic to Pete's story and to the possibility that the letter was authentic: themselves, the Bergmans, and of course the Simpsons. Peter would provide them with copies of the letter; Paul Ashton, whose legal expertise was at their service, would find out how they could go about verifying the thing's authenticity, as David Bergman had suggested at the Beckers'. If it turned out to be for real, they would then circulate an appeal through Rockfish Reach, maybe through all of Heron Bay Estates, to raise money toward the girl's rescue: not a blank check that her uncle and aunt might oblige her to cash for their benefit, but some sort of tuition fund that the committee could disburse, or at least oversee and authorize payments from.

"Maybe even a scholarship at Stratford?" Paul Ashton suggests to Peter. "I know you have a few foreign students from time to time, but none from equatorial Africa, I'll bet."

"Doesn't sound impossible, actually," Peter grants, warming to the idea while at the same time monitoring his wife's reaction. "*If* she's legit, and qualified. Our African-American student organization could take her in."

"And our Heron Bay Search and Rescue Squad could unofficially adopt her!" Lisa Bergman here joins in, whom the Ashtons have evidently briefed already on their proposal. "Having another teenager to keep out of trouble will make us all feel young again! Whatcha think, Deb?"

To give her time to consider, Peter reminds them that there remains the problem of the girl's younger siblings, whom she's resolved not to abandon: "We remained five and we should stick five," *et cetera*. Whereas if she "went to university" in Kampala for at least the first couple of years, say, she could see the youngsters into high school and then maybe come to Stratford for her junior or senior year . . .

"Listen to us!" He laughs. "And we don't even know yet whether the girl's for real!"

"But we can find out," David Bergman declares. "And if we can make it happen, or make something *like* it happen, it'll be a credit to Heron Bay Estates. Make us feel a little better about our golf and tennis and progressive dinners. Okay, so it's only one kid out of millions, but at least it's one. I say let's do it."

"And then Pete and I officially adopt her as our daughter," Debbie says at last, in a tone that her husband can't assess at all, "and we stop eating our hearts out about losing Julie, and everybody lives happily ever after."

"Deb?" Lisa puts an arm around her friend's shoulder.

"Alternatively," Debbie suggests to them then, "we could start a Dick and Susan Felton Let's Get It Over With Club, and borrow the Barneses' new garage for our first meeting. Meanwhile, let's enjoy the party, okay?" And she moves off toward where the Pitts, the Hardisons, and a few others are chatting beside the lighted pool. To their friends Peter turns up his palms, as best one can with a cup of decaf in one hand and its saucer in the other, and follows after his wife, wondering and worrying what lies ahead for them — tonight, tomorrow, and in the days and years beyond. They have each other, their work, their colleagues and friends and neighbors, their not-all-that-close extended family (parents dead, no siblings on Debbie's side, one seven-years-older sister of Peter's out in Texas, from whom he's been more or less distanced for decades), their various pastimes and pleasures, their still prevailingly good health — for who knows how much longer? And then. And then. While over in Uganda and Darfur, and down in

Haiti, and in Guantánamo and Abu Ghraib and the world's multitudi-
nous other hellholes ...

"They had *nothing* like this back in Blue Crab Bight, man!" he hears
Joe Barnes happily exclaiming to the Greens. "Just a sort of block party
once, and that was it."

"Feltons or no Feltons," Judy Barnes adds, "we've made the right
move."

Nearby, florid Chuck Becker is actually thrusting a forefinger at David Bergman's chest: "We cut and run from I-raq now, there'll be hell
to pay. Got to *stay the course.*"

"Like we did in Nam, right?" unintimidated Dave comes back at
him. "And drill the living shit out of Alaska and the Gulf Coast, I guess
you think, if that's what it takes to get the last few barrels of oil? Gimme
a break, Chuck!"

"Take it from your friendly neighborhood realtor, folks," Jeff Pitt
is declaring to the Ashtons: "Whatever you have against a second Bay
bridge — say, from south Baltimore straight over to Avon County?—
it'll raise your property values a hundred percent in no time at all, the
way the state's population is booming. We won't be able to build condos and housing developments fast enough to keep up!"

Peggy Ashton: "So there goes the neighborhood, right? And it's bye-
bye Chesapeake Bay ..."

Paul: "*And* bye-bye national forest lands and glaciers and polar ice
caps. Get me outta here!"

Patsy Hardison, to Peter's own dear Deborah: "So, did you and Pete
see that episode that Tom mentioned before, that he and all the TV
critics thought was so great and I couldn't even watch? I suspect it's a
Mars-versus-Venus thing."

"Sorry," Debbie replies. "We must be the only family in Heron Bay
Estates that doesn't get HBO." Her eyes meet Peter's, neutrally.

Chuckling and lifting his coffee cup in salute as he joins the pair,
"We don't even have *cable*," Peter confesses. "Just an old-style antenna up on the roof. Now is that academic snobbishness or what?" He
sets cup and saucer on a nearby table and puts an arm about his wife's
waist, a gesture that she seems neither to welcome nor to resist. He has
no idea where their lives are headed. Quite possibly, he supposes, she
doesn't either.

Up near the house, an old-fashioned post-mounted school bell clangs: The Greens use it to summon grandkids and other family visitors in for meals. Rob Green, standing by it, calls out, "Attention, all hands!" And when the conversation quiets, "Just want to remind you to put the Rockfish Reach sunset cruise on your calendars: Saturday, July fifteenth, Heron Bay Marina, seven to nine PM! We'll be sending out reminders as the time approaches, but *save the date*, okay?"

"Got it," Joe Barnes calls back from somewhere nearby: "July fifteenth, seven PM."

From the porch Chuck Becker adds loudly, "God bless us all! And God bless America!"

Several voices murmur "Amen." Looking up and away with a sigh of mild annoyance, Peter Simpson happens at just that moment to see a meteor streak left to right across the moonless, brightly constellated eastern sky.

So what? he asks himself.

So nothing.

Us / Them

To his wife, his old comrades at the *Avon County News*, or his acquaintances from over at the College, Gerry Frank might say, for example, "Flaubert once claimed that what he'd *really* like to write is a novel about Nothing." In his regular feature column, however — in the small-town weekly newspaper of a still largely rural Maryland county — it would have to read something like this:

> *FRANK OPINIONS, by Gerald Frank*
> *Us / Them*
>
> The celebrated 19th-century French novelist Gustave Flaubert, author of *Madame Bovary*, once remarked that what he would *really* like to write is a novel about Nothing.

After which he might acknowledge that the same was looking to be the case with this week's column, although its author still hoped to make it not quite about Nothing, but rather ("as the celebrated Elizabethan poet/playwright William Shakespeare put it in the title of one of his comedies") about Much *Ado* About Nothing.

There: That should work as a lead, a hook, a kick-start from which the next sentences and paragraphs will flow (pardon Gerry's mixed metaphor) — and voilà, another "Frank Opinions" column to be emailed after lunch to Editor Tom Chadwick at the *News* and put to bed for the week.

But they *don't* come, those next sentences — *haven't* come, now, for the third work-morning in a row — for the ever-clearer reason that their semiretired would-be author hasn't figured out yet what he wants to write about what he wants to write about, namely: Us(slash)Them. *In Frank's opinion*, he now types experimentally in his column's characteristic third-person viewpoint, *what he needs is a meaningful connection between the "Us/Them" theme, much on his mind lately for reasons presently to be explained, and either or all of (1) a troubling disconnection, or anyhow an increasing distinction/difference/whatever, between, on this side of that slash, him and his wife — Gerald and Joan Frank, 14 Shad Run Road #212, Heron Bay Estates, Stratford, MD 21600 — and on its other side their pleasant gated community in general and their Shad Run condominium neighborhood in particular; (2) his recently increasing difficulty — after so many productive decades of newspaper work! — in coming up with fresh ideas for the F.O. column; and/or (3) the irresistible parallel to his growing (shrinking?) erectile dysfunction* [but never mind *that* as a column topic!].

Maybe fill in some background, to mark time while waiting for the Muse of Feature Columns to get off her ever-lazier butt and down to business? Gerry Frank here, Reader-if-this-gets-written: erstwhile journalist, not quite seventy but getting there fast. Born and raised in a small town near the banks of the Potomac in southern Maryland in World War Two time, where and when the most ubiquitous Us/Them had been Us White Folks as distinct from Them Coloreds, until supplanted after Pearl Harbor by Us Allies versus Them Japs and Nazis (note the difference between that "versus" and the earlier, more ambivalent "as distinct from," a difference to which we may return). Crossed the Chesapeake after high school to Stratford College, on the Free State's Eastern Shore (B.A. English 1957), then shifted north to New Jersey for the next quarter-century to do reportage and editorial work for the *Trenton Times*; also to marry his back-home sweetheart, make babies and help parent them, learn a few life lessons the hard way while doubtless failing to learn some others, and eventually — at age fifty, when those offspring were off to college themselves and learning their own life lessons — to divorce (irreconcilable differences). Had the immeasurably good fortune the very next year, at a Stratford homecoming, to meet alumna Joan Gibson (B.A. English 1967), herself likewise between life chapters just then (forty, divorced, no children, copyediting for her hometown newspaper, the *Wilmington* [Delaware] *News Journal*). So hit it off together from Day (and Night) One that after just a couple more dates they were spending every weekend together in her town or his, or back in the Stratford to which they shared a fond attachment — and whereto, not long after their marriage in the following year, they moved: Gerry to associate-edit the *Avon County News* and Joan ditto the College's alumni magazine, *The Stratfordian*.

And some fifteen years later here they are, happy with each other and grateful to have been spared not only direct involvement in the nation's several bloody wars during their life-decades, but also such personal catastrophes as loss of children, untimely death of parents or siblings, and devastating accident, disease, or other extraordinary misfortune. Their connection with Gerry's pair of thirty-something children, Joan's elder and younger siblings, and associated spouses and offspring is warm, though geographically attenuated (one couple in Oregon, another in Texas, others in Vermont and Alabama). Husband and wife much enjoy each other's company, their work, their modest TINK prosperity (Two Incomes, No [dependent] Kids), and their leisure activities: hiking, wintertime workouts in the Heron Bay Club's well-equipped fitness center and summertime swimming in its Olympic-size pool, vacation travel to other countries back in more U.S.-friendly times, and here and there in North America since 9/11 and (in Gerald Frank's Frank Opinion) the Bush administration's Iraq War fiasco (U.S./ "Them"?). Also their, uh . . . friends?

Well: No F.O. column yet in any of *that*, that Gerry can see. While typing on from pure professional habit, however, he perpends that paragraph-ending word above, flanked by suspension points before and question mark after: something to circle back to, maybe, after avoiding it for a while longer by reviewing some other senses of that slash dividing Us from Them. Peter Simpson, a fellow they know from Rockfish Reach who teaches at the College and (like Joan Frank) serves on the Heron Bay Estates Community Association, did a good job of that at one of HBECA's recent open meetings, the main agenda item whereof was a proposed hefty assessment for upgrading the development's entrance gates. As most readers of "Frank Opinions" know, we are for better or worse the only gated community in Avon County, perhaps the only one on Maryland's Eastern Shore. Just off the state highway a few miles south of Stratford, Heron Bay Estates is bounded on two irregular sides by branching tidal tributaries of the Matahannock River (Heron and Spartina Creeks, Rockfish and Oyster Coves, Blue Crab Bight, Shad Run), on a third side by a wooded preserve of pines, hemlocks, and sweet gums screening a sturdy chain-link fence, and on its highway side by a seven-foot-high masonry wall atop an attractively landscaped berm, effectively screening the development from both highway noise and casual view. Midway along this side is our entrance road, Heron Bay Boulevard, accessed via a round-the-clock manned gatehouse with two exit lanes on one side, their gates raised and lowered automatically by electric eye, and two gated entry lanes on the other: one on the left for service vehicles and visitors, who must register with the gatekeeper and display temporary entrance passes on their dashboards, and one on the right for residents and non-resident Club members, whose cars have HBE decals annually affixed to their windshields. So successful has the development been that in the twenty-odd years since its initial layout it has grown to be the county's second-largest residential entity after the small town of Stratford itself—with the consequence that homeward-bound residents these days not infrequently find themselves backed up four or five cars deep while the busy gate-keepers simultaneously check in visitors in one lane and look for resident decals in the other before pushing the lift-gate button. Taking their cue from the various E-Z Pass devices commonly employed nowadays at bridge and highway toll booths, the developers, Tidewater Communities, Inc., suggested to the Association that an economical alternative to a second gatehouse farther down the highway side (which would require expensive construction, an additional entrance road, and more 24/7 staffing) would be a third entry lane at the present gatehouse, its gate to be triggered automatically by electronic scansion of a bar-code decal on each resident vehicle's left rear window.

Most of the Association members and other attendees, Joan and Gerry Frank included, thought this a practical and economical fix to the entrance-backup problem, and when put to the seven members for a vote (one representative from each of HBE's neighborhoods plus one at-large tie-breaker), the motion passed by a margin of six to one. In the pre-vote open discussion, however, objections to it were raised from diametrically opposed viewpoints. On the one hand, Mark Matthews from Spartina Pointe — the recentest member of the Association, whose new weekend-and-vacation home in that high-end neighborhood was probably the grandest residence in all of Heron Bay Estates — declared that in view of HBE's ongoing development (controversial luxury condominiums proposed for the far end of the preserve), what we need is not only that automatic bar-code lane at the Heron Bay Boulevard entrance, but the afore-mentioned second gated entrance at the south end of the highway wall as well, and perhaps a third for service and employee vehicles only, to be routed discreetly through the wooded preserve itself.

In the bluff, down-home manner to which he inclined, even as CEO of a Baltimore investment-counseling firm, "Way it is now," that bald and portly, flush-faced fellow complained, "we get waked up at six AM by the groundskeepers and golf course maintenance guys reporting for work with the radios booming in their rusty old Chevys and pickups, *woomf woomf woomf,* y'know? Half of 'em undocumented aliens, quote unquote, but never mind *that* if it keeps the costs down. And then when we-all that live here come back from wherever, the sign inside the entrance says Welcome Home, but our welcome is a six-car backup at the gate, like crossing the Bay Bridge without an E-Z Pass. I say we deserve better'n that."

"Hear hear!" somebody cheered from the back of the Community Association's open-meeting room: Joe Barnes, I think it was, from Rockfish Reach. But my wife, at her end of the members' table up front, objected: "Easy to say if you don't mind a fifty percent assessment hike to build and staff those extra entrances! But I suspect that many of us will feel the pinch to finance just that automatic third entry lane at the gatehouse — which I'm personally all for, but nothing beyond that unless *it* gets backed up."

A number of her fellow members nodded agreement, and one of them added, "As for the racket, we just need to tell the gatekeepers and the maintenance foremen to be stricter about the no-loud-noise rule for service people checking in."

Mark Matthews made a little show of closing his eyes and shaking his head no. The room in general, however, murmured approval. Which perhaps encouraged Amanda Todd — a friend of Joan's and an Association member from Blue Crab Bight — to surprise us all by saying "Gates and more gates! What do we need *any* of them for, including the ones we've got already?"

Mild consternation in the audience and among her fellow members, turning to relieved amusement when Joan teased, "Because we're a gated community?" But "Really," Ms. Todd persisted, "those TCI ads for Heron Bay are downright embarrassing, with their 'exclusive luxury lifestyles' and such. Even to call this place Heron Bay *Estates* is embarrassing, if you ask me. But then to have to pass through customs every time we come and go, and phone the gatehouse whenever we're expecting a visitor! Plus the secondary nighttime gates at some of our neighborhood entrances, like Oyster Cove, and those push-button driveway gates in Spartina Pointe . . . Three gates to pass through, in an area where crime is practically nonexistent!"

"Don't forget the garage door opener," Mark Matthews reminded her sarcastically. "That makes *four* entrances for some of us, even before we unlock the house door. Mindy and I are all for it."

"Hear hear!" his ally called again from the back of the room, where someone else reminded all hands that we weren't *entirely* crime-free: "Remember that Peeping Tom a few years back? Slipped past the main gatehouse and our Oyster Cove night gates too, that we don't use anymore like we did back then, and we never did catch him. But still . . ."

"You're proving my point," Amanda argued. Whereupon her husband — the writer George Newett, also from the College — came to her support by quoting the Psalmist: "Lift up your heads, O ye gates! Even lift them up, ye everlasting doors, and the King of Glory shall come in!"

"Amen," she said appreciatively. "And *leave* 'em lifted, I say, like those ones at Oyster Cove. No other development around here has gates. Why should we?"

"Because we're *us*," somebody offered, "with a community pool and tennis courts and bike paths that aren't for public use. If you like the other kind, maybe you should move to one of *them*."

Mark Matthews seconded that suggestion with a pleased head-nod. But "All I'm saying," Ms. Todd persisted, less assertively, "— as Robert Frost puts it in one of his poems? — is, quote, 'Before I built a wall, I'd ask to know what I was walling in and walling out, and to whom I'm likely to give offense,' end of quote. Somebody just mentioned *us* and *them*: Who exactly is the Them that all these walls and gates are keeping out?"

To lighten things a bit, I volunteered, "That Them is Us, Amanda, waiting at the gate until we get our Heron Bay E-Z Pass gizmo up and running. Shall we put it to a vote?"

"Not quite yet, Gerry," said Peter Simpson — also from the College, as has been mentioned, and chairman of the Association as well as its member from Rockfish Reach. "Let's be sure that everybody's had his / her say on the matter. Including myself for a minute, if I may?"

Nobody objected. A trim and affable fellow in his fifties, Pete is popular as well as respected both in the Association and on campus, where he's some sort of dean as well as a professor. "I'll try not to lecture," he promised with a smile. "I just want to say that while I understand where both Mark and Amanda are coming from, my own inclination, like Joan's, is to proceed incrementally, starting with the bar-code scanner gate and hoping that'll do the trick, for a few years anyhow." He pushed up his rimless specs. "What's really on my mind, though, now that it's come up, is this Us-slash-Them business. We have to accept that some of us, like Amanda, live here because they like the place *despite* its being a gated community, while others of us, like Mark, live here in part precisely *because* it's gated, especially if they're not fulltime residents. The great majority of us, I'd bet, either don't *mind* the gate thing (except when it gets backed up!) or sort of like the little extra privacy, the way we appreciate our routine security patrols even though we're lucky enough not to live near a high-crime area. It's another Heron Bay amenity, like our landscaping and our golf course. What we need to watch out for (and here comes the lecture I promised I'd spare you) is when that slash between Us and Them moves from being a simple distinction — like Us Rockfish Reach residents and Them Oyster Cove or Spartina Pointers, or Us Marylanders and Them Pennsylvanians and Delawareans — and becomes Us not merely *distinct* from Them, but more or less *superior* to Them, as has all too often been the case historically with whites and blacks, or rich and poor, or for that matter men and women."

Up with the glasses again. Mark Matthews rolled his eyes, but most present seemed interested in Pete's argument. "At its worst," he went on, "that slash between Us and Them comes to mean Us *versus* Them, as in race riots and revolutions and wars in general. But even here it's worth remembering that *versus* doesn't always necessarily mean inherently superior: It can be like Us versus Them in team sports, or the Yeas versus the Nays in a debating club, or some of the town/gown issues at the College that we try to mediate without claiming that either side is *superior* to the other."

Here he took the glasses off, as if to signal that the sermon was approaching its close. "I'm sure I'm not alone in saying that some of Debbie's and my closest friends live outside these gates of ours."

"Amen," Joan said on his behalf. After which, and apologizing again for nattering on so, Pete called for a vote authorizing the Association to solicit bids and award a contract for construction of an automatically gated HBE Pass third lane at our development's entrance. When the motion passed, six to one, Amanda Todd good-naturedly reminded Mark Matthews, the lone dissenter, that "Us versus You doesn't mean we don't love you, Mark." To which that broad-beamed but narrow-minded fellow retorted, "You College people, I swear."

"Objection!" Amanda's husband called out.

"Sustained," declared Peter Simpson, rising from his chair and gathering the spec sheets and other papers spread out before him. "No need to pursue it, and thank you all for coming and making your opinions known." Offering his hand to Matthews then, with a smile, "Here's to democracy, Mark, and parliamentary procedure. Agreed?"

"Whatever."

And that had been that, for then. But en route back along sycamore-lined Heron Bay Boulevard to our condominium in "Shad Row," as we like to call it (punning on that seasonal Chesapeake delicacy), we Franks had tsked and sighed at Mark Matthews's overbearing small-mindedness versus Pete Simpson's more generous spirit and eminently reasonable review of the several senses of Us/Them. "Like when people born and raised in Stratford talk about 'us locals' and 'them c'meres,'" Joan said, using the former's term for out-of-towners who "come here" to retire or to enjoy a second home. "Sometimes it's a putdown, sometimes it's just a more or less neutral distinction, depending."

"And even when it's a putdown," her husband agreed, "sometimes it's just a good-humored tease between friends or neighbors — unlike Lady Broad-Ass's Us/Thems in our condo sessions," he added, referring to his Shad Run Condominium Association colleague Rachel Broadus, a hefty and opinionated widow-lady who, two years ago, had vehemently opposed the sale of unit 117 to an openly gay late-middle-aged couple from D.C., early retired from careers in the federal government's General Services Administration — even letting the prospective buyers know by anonymous letter that while it was beyond the Association's authority to forbid the sale, homosexuals were not welcome in Heron Bay Estates. A majority of the Association shared her feelings and had been relieved when the offended couple withdrew their purchase offer, although most agreed with Gerry that the unsigned letter was reprehensible; he alone had spoken on the pair's behalf, or at least had opposed the opposition to them. When in the following year Ms. Broadus had similarly inveighed against the sale of unit 218 to a dapper Indian-American pharmacist and his wife ("Next thing you know it'll be Mexicans and blacks, and there goes the neighborhood"), he'd had more company in objecting to her objection, and the Raghavans had come to be well liked by nearly all of their neighbors. "Even so," Gerry now reminded his wife, "Broad-Ass couldn't resist saying 'Mind you, Ger, I don't have anything against a nice Jewish couple like you and Joan. But *Hindus?*'"

Joan groaned at the recollection — who on first hearing from Gerry of this misattribution had said, "You should've showed her your foreskinned shlong already. Oy." Or, they'd agreed, he could have quoted the Irish-American songwriter George M. Cohan's reply to a resort-hotel desk clerk in the 1920s who refused him a room, citing the establishment's ban on Jewish guests: "You thought I was a Jew," said the composer of "The Yankee Doodle Boy," "and I thought you were a gentleman. We were both mistaken." Rachel Broadus, they supposed, had heard of Anne Frank and had readily generalized from that famed Holocaust victim's last name, perhaps pretending even to herself that the Them to which she assigned the Shad Run Franks was not meant pejoratively. It was easy to imagine her declaring that "some of her best friends," *et cetera*. Gerry himself had used that edged cliché, in quotes — "Some of Our Best Friends . . ." — as the heading of a "Frank Opinions" column applauding the progress of Stratford's middle-class African Americans from near invisibility to active representation on the Town Council, the Avon County School Board, and the faculties not only of the local public schools but of the College and the private Fenton Day School as well.

All the above, however, is past history: the HBECA lift-gate meeting and us Franks' return to Shad Run Road for a merlot nightcap on our second-story porch overlooking the moonlit creek (where no shad have been known to run during our residency) before the ten o'clock TV news, bedtime, and another flaccid semi-fuck, Gerry's "Jimmy" less than fully erect and Joan's "Susie" less than wetly welcoming. "Never mind that pair of old farts," Joan had sighed, kissing him goodnight before turning away to sleep: "They're Them; we're still Us." Whoever *that's* getting to be, he'd said to himself—for he really has, since virtual retirement, been ever more preoccupied with his approaching old age and his inevitable, already noticeable decline. To her, however, he wondered merely, "D'you suppose they're trying to tell us something?"

"Whatever it is." she answered sleepily, "don't put it in the column, okay?"

The column: Past history too is his nattering on about all the above to his computer for four work-mornings already, and now a fifth, in search of a "Frank Opinions" piece about all this Us/Them stuff. By now he has moved on from Joan's "Us Franks" as distinct from "Them body parts of ours," or the singular "I-Gerry/Thou-'Jimmy,'" to Gerry's-Mind/Gerry's-Body and thence (within the former) to Gerry's-Ego/Gerry's-Id+Superego, and while mulling these several Us/Thems and I/Thous of the concept Mind, he has duly noted that although such distinctions are *made* by our minds, it by no means follows that they're "all in our minds."

Blah blah blah: Won't readers of the *Avon County News* be thrilled to hear it?

Yet another Us/Them now occurs to him (just what he needed!): It's a standing levity in Heron Bay Estates that most of its male inhabitants happen to be called familiarly by one-syllable first names and their wives by two-: Mark and Mindy Matthews, Joe and Judy Barnes, Pete and Debbie Simpson, Dave and Lisa Bergman, Dick and Susan Felton—the list goes on. But while we Franks, perhaps by reflex, are occasionally fitted to this peculiar template ("Ger" and "Joanie"), we're normally called Gerry and Joan, in exception to the rule: an Us distinct from, though not opposed to, its Them.

So? So nothing. Has Gerald "Gerry" Frank mentioned his having noticed, years ago, that his normal pulse rate matches almost exactly the tick of seconds on his watch dial, so closely that he can measure less-than-a-minute intervals by his heartbeat? And that therefore, as of his recent sixty-eighth birthday, he had lived for 24,837 days (including

17 leap days) at an average rate of 86,400 pulses per day, or a total of 2,145,916,800, give or take a few thousand for periods of physical exertion or unusual quiescence? By which same calculation he reckons himself to have been mulling these who-gives-a-shit Us/Thems for some 440,000 heartbeats' worth of days now, approaching beat by beat not only his ultimate demise but, more immediately, Tom Chadwick's deadline, and feeling no closer to a column than he did five days ago.

Maybe a column about that? Lame idea.

Tick. Tick. Tick. Tick. Tick.

He believes he did mention, a few thousand pulses past, that the Shad Run Franks, while on entirely cordial terms with their workmates and with ninety-nine percent of their fellow Heron Bay Estaters, have no *friends*, really, if by friends one means people whom one enjoys having over for drinks and dinner or going out with to a restaurant, not to mention actually vacation-traveling together, as they see some of their neighbors doing. They used to have friends like that, separately in their pre-Us lives and together in the earliest, pre-Stratford period of their marriage. Over the years since, however, for whatever reasons, their social life has atrophied: annual visits to and from their far-flung family, lunch with a colleague now and then (although they both work mainly at home these days), the occasional office cocktail party or HBE community social — that's about it. They don't particularly *approve* of this state of affairs, mildly wish it were otherwise, but have come to accept, more or less, that outside the workplace that's who they are, or have become: more comfortable with just Us than with Them.

As if his busy fingers have a mind of their own, *To be quite frank, Reader,* he now sees appearing on his computer screen, *old Gerry hasn't been being quite Frank with you about certain things. E.g.:*

— He and his mate share another, very different and entirely secret life, the revelation whereof would scandalize all Stratford and Heron Bay Estates, not to mention their family.

— Or they *don't*, of course, but could sometimes half wish they did, just for the hell of it.

— Or they *don't* so wish or even half wish, for God's sake! Who does this nutcase columnist take us for, that he could even *imagine* either of them so wishing?

— Or he has just learned that the precious, the indispensable Other Half of our Us has been diagnosed with . . . oh, advanced, inoperable pancreatic cancer? While *he* sits scared shitless on his butt counting his heartbeats, her killer cells busily metastasize through that dearest of bodies. Maybe less than a million ever-more-wretched tick-ticks to go, at most, until The End — of her, therefore of Us, therefore of him.

— Or he's just making all this crap up. Trying it out. Thinking the unthinkable, perhaps in vain hope of its exorcism, or at least forestallment. But such tomfoolery fools no one. While his right hand types *no one*, his left rummages in a drawer of the adjacent inkjet-printer stand for the reassuring feel of the loaded nine-millimeter automatic pistol that he keeps in there for "self-defense": i.e., for defending Joan and Gerry Frank yet a while longer from murder / suicide — which they agree they'd resort to in any such scenario as that terminal-cancer one above-invoked by reminding himself that they have the means and the will to do it, if and when the time comes.

But they don't — have the means, at least; at least not by gunfire. There is no pistol, never has been; we Franks aren't the gun-owning sort. Should push come to shove *chez nous*, in our frank opinion we'd go the route that Dick and Susan Felton went last year: double suicide (nobody knows why) by automobile exhaust fumes in the closed garage of their empty-nest house in Rockfish Reach, with not even a goodbye note to their traumatized, life-disrupted offspring.

Well, we guess we'd leave a note.

Maybe this is it?

Nah. Still . . .

Deadline a-coming: Tick. Tick.

Deathline? Tick.

FRANK OPINIONS: Us / Them
or,
Much Ado About

Assisted Living

Like any normal person, Tim Manning (speaking) used to think and speak of himself as "I" or "me." *Don't ask me*, the old ex-history teacher would start off one of his "His-Stories" by typing on his computer, *who I think is reading or hearing this* — and then on he'd ramble about his and Margie's Oyster Cove community in Heron Bay Estates, and the interesting season when they and their neighborhood were bedeviled (or at least had reason to believe they were) by a Peeping Tom. Stuff like that. *I grabbed the big flashlight from atop the fridge*, he would write, *told Margie to call Security, and stepped out back to check.* Or "*I do sort of miss those days," Margie said to me one evening a few years later...*

That sort of thing.

But that was Back Then: from the Depression-era 1930s, when Timothy Manning and Margaret Jacobs were born, a few years and Chesapeake counties apart, through their separate childhoods and adolescences in World War Two time, their trial romances and (separate) sexual initiations in late high school and early college years, their fortuitous meeting and impulsive marriage in the American mid-1950s, their modest contributions to the post war baby boom, and their not unsuccessful careers (he guesses they'd agree) as high school teacher (him), suburban D. C. realtor (her), and life partners (them!). Followed, in their sixties and the century's eighties, by their phased retirement to Heron Bay Estates: at first Bay-Bridge-hopping between their city house near Washington and their new weekend/vacation duplex in Heron Bay's Oyster Cove neighborhood, then swapping the former for a more maintenance-free condominium halfway between D.C. and Annapolis (where Margie's real-estate savvy found them a rare bargain in that busy market), and ultimately — when wife joined husband in full retirement — selling that condo at a healthy profit, unloading as best they could whatever of its furnishings the new owners had no interest in buying, and settling contentedly into their modest villa at 1010 Oyster Cove Court for the remainder of their active life together.

Amounting, as it turned out, to a mere dozen-plus years, which feels to Tim Manning as he types these words like about that many months at most. Where did the years go? He can scarcely remember — as has been becoming the case with more and more things every year. Where'd he put the car keys? Or for that matter their old station wagon itself, parked somewhere in the Stratford shopping plaza that he still manages to drive to now and then for miscellaneous provisions? As of this sentence he hasn't yet reached that classic early-Alzheimer's symptom of forgetting which keys are for what, or which car out there is their Good Gray Ghost (excuse him: *his* GGG, damn it, now that Indispensable Margie — his "better two-thirds," he used to call her — is no more), but he sure forgets plenty of other things these days.

E.g., exactly what "Tim Manning" was about to say before this particular His-Story wandered. Something having to do with how — beginning with the couple's reluctant Final Move three years ago from dear "old" Oyster Cove to Bayview Manor and especially since Margie's unassimilable death just one year later — he has found himself standing ever more outside himself: prodding, directing, *assisting* Tim Manning through the increasingly mechanical routines of his daily existence. Talk about Assisted "Living". . .

And who, exactly, is the Assistant? Not "I" these days, he was saying, but old T.M.: same guy who'll get on with telling this story if he can recollect what the hell it is.

Well, for starters: In a way, he supposes, "T.M." is replacing (as best he can't) irreplaceable Margie as Tim Manning's living-assistant. In the forty-nine and eleven-twelfths years of their married life, she and he constantly assisted each other with everything from changing their babies' diapers to changing jobs, habitations, outworn habits, and ill-considered opinions as their time went by. In more recent years, as her body and his mind faltered, he more and more assisted her with physical matters — her late-onset diabetes, near-crippling arthritis and various other -itises, their attendant medicos and medications — and ever more depended on *her* assistance in the memory and attention departments as his Senior Moments increased in frequency and duration. While at the same time, of course, they continued to assist each other in the making of life decisions.

Such as . . .

Ahem: *Such as?*

Sorry there: got sidetracked, he guesses, from some sidetrack or other. *Such as*, he sees he was saying, their no-longer-avoidable joint recognition — after some years of due denial, so unappealing were the alternatives — that what with Margie now all but wheel-chaired and her husband sometimes unable to locate the various lists that he'd come to depend on to remember practically everything, even the housekeeping of their Oyster Cove duplex was becoming more than they could manage. Time to check out Assisted (ugh!) Living.

Not long after the turn of the new millennium, they apprised their two grown children of that reluctant intention, and both the Son in St. Louis and the Daughter in Detroit (that alliteration, their father was fond of saying, helped him remember which lived where) dutifully offered to scout suitable such operations in their respective cities. But while the elder Mannings quite enjoyed their occasional visits to Bachelor-girl Barbara and Married-but-childless Michael, they felt at home only in tidewater country, where they still had friends and former workmates. Dislocation enough to exchange house and yard, longtime good neighbors, and the amenities of Heron Bay Estates for a small apartment, communal meals, and a less independent life, most probably across the Matahannock Bridge, in another county. Although they went through the motions of collecting brochures up and down the peninsula from several "continuing care retirement communities" whose advertisements they'd noted in the weekly *Avon County News* ("Quality retirement lifestyles! Gourmet dining! On-site medical center! A strong sense of caring and community!"), and even took a couple of Residency-Counselor-Guided Personal Tours, they agreed from the outset that their likeliest choice would be Bayview Manor. Situated no farther from the town of Stratford on the river's east side than was Heron Bay Estates on its west, Bayview was a project of the same busy de-

veloper, Tidewater Communities, Inc. It was generally regarded as being at least the peer of any similar institution on the Shore, and among
its residents were a number of other ex-HBE dwellers no longer able
or inclined to maintain their former "lifestyles" in Shad Run or Oyster Cove, much less in the development's upper-scale detached-house
neighborhoods. Depending upon availability — and one's inclinations
and financial resources — one could apply for a one- or two-bedroom
cottage there (with or without den) or choose from several levels of
one- and two-bedroom apartments, all with a variety of meal plans.
Standard amenities included an indoor pool, a fitness center, crafts
and other activities rooms, a beauty salon, gift shop, and branch bank
office, and periodic shuttle service to and from Stratford; also available
were such extra-cost options as linen and personal laundry service,
weekly or biweekly housekeeping, a "professionally staffed" Medical
Center, and chauffeured personal transportation. For a couple like the
Mannings who didn't yet require *fully* assisted living, the then-current
"base price entry fees" ranged from $100,000 for a small one-bedroom
apartment (refundable minus two percent for each month of occupancy) to just under $500,000 for a high-end two-bedroom cottage
with den (ninety percent refundable after reoccupancy of unit by new
resident when current occupants shift to Med Center residence or to
grave). Housekeeping and other service fees ranged from $2,000 to
$4,000 monthly, and meal plans from individual dining room meal
charges for those who preferred to continue preparing most of their
own meals at home to about $800 monthly for a couple's thrice-daily
feed in the dining hall.

"Jesus," Tim wondered. "Can we even consider it?"

They could, his wife (the family investment manager) assured him.
But what about the fact that Bayview, no less than the other places
they'd checked out, got its share of bad reviews as well as good? On the
one hand were those happy Golden Agers in the brochure photos, duly
apportioned by gender and ethnicity and handsomely decked out in
"country club casual" attire while bird-watching or flower-arranging,
painting and quilting and pottery-making, or smiling at one another
across bridge and dining tables. On the other, such Internet chatroom
grumbles both from some residents and from their relatives as *The food
sucks, actually, if you've been used to eating* real *food,* and *Be warned:
It's college dorm life all over again — at age eighty!,* and *Frankly, it's the*

effing pits. The best Margie and Tim could guess was that temperamentally upbeat, outgoing, people-enjoying types were likely to find their continuing-care situation at least as much to their liking as what had immediately preceded it in their *curriculum vitae*, while the more easily dissatisfied were, well, dissatisfied. They themselves, they supposed, fell somewhere between those poles.

"May we not fall on our geriatric asses between them," they more or less prayed; then gave each other a determinedly cheerful high-five over white wine and champignon cheese at Happy Hour on their screened porch overlooking Oyster Cove, and took the plunge: what they'd come to call the Old Farts' B.M. Move. Given the ever-rising value of Heron Bay real estate, Margie figured they could list for $400K the free-and-clear villa for which they'd paid slightly more than half that amount fifteen years ago, take out a $300K mortgage on it to finance either a midrange Bayview cottage or one of those high-end apartments, pay off the mortgage shortly thereafter when good old 1010 Oyster Cove Court sells for, say, $375K, and shift across the river with most of their present furnishings at a tidy profit — the more since ex-realtor Margie would be handling the sale and saving them the seven percent agent's commission.

Thus the plan, and thus it came to pass — even a bit better than their projection, but at their age a wrench and hassle all the same. In a mere five months, the villa found a buyer for $380K, and between its sale and closing dates a high-end Bayview apartment became available, its widowed and emphysemic tenant obliged to move into the Manor's Medical Center. While they'd thought that "transitioning" to one of the cottages might be less of a jolt, they took the apartment, reminding themselves that they had, after all, rather enjoyed that interim condominium over near Annapolis, and that as they grew older and less able than presently, the apartment would be more convenient — to that same Medical Center, among other things. So okay, they would miss gardening, outdoor barbecuing, and the relative privacy of a house. But what the hell, they had adjusted readily enough back in the '80s from detached house to duplex living; they could hack it in a comfortable apartment.

So hack it they did: quite admirably all in all, given Margie's physical limitations. As their nation enmired itself in Afghanistan and Iraq, the

Mannings bade goodbye to their Oyster Cove neighbors and other Heron Bay friends (who were, after all, a mere thirty-minute drive from Bayview), scaled down from two cars in a garage to just Old Faithful in a designated parking-lot space, and packed and unpacked their stuff for what must surely be the last time. Over the next year-and-a-bit—from late summer 2003 to mid-autumn '04—they repositioned their furniture and knick-knacks, rehung their wall art, reshelved as many of their books as they had room for, donated the rest to the Avon County Library, and gamely set about making new acquaintances, sampling the Manor's sundry activities, and accustoming themselves to their start-out meal plan: breakfasts and lunches together in the apartment, dinners in the dining hall except now and then in a Stratford restaurant. Pretty lucky they were, T.M. supposes in retrospect, to have made their "B.M. Move" when they did, before the nationwide housing-market slump just a few years later, not to mention before the recent, all-but-total destruction of Heron Bay Estates by that spinoff tornado from Tropical Storm Giorgio in an otherwise eventless hurricane season. And most certainly not to mention . . . the Unmentionable, which however is this His-Story's defining event and therefore *must* be mentioned, to say the least, not far hence.

And a pretty good job they did, all in all (he believes he was saying), of making the best of their new life. Okay, so they shook their heads occasionally at the relentless professional cheeriness of some of the Bayview staff; and they had no taste for the bridge tournaments, square-dance and bingo nights, and some other items on the Activities menu; and the dining hall fare, while it had its fans, was in their opinion mostly blah. But on the plus side were some of the Manor's sightseeing excursions to places like the du Pont estate's Winterthur Garden, up near Wilmington, and the Chesapeake Bay Maritime Museum down in St. Michaels (the Mannings had got out of the habit of such touring), the Happy Hour and dinnertime socializing in the Blue Heron Lounge and dining hall, which one could do as much or little of as one chose (sipping from one's personal wine supply at the bar), and the comforting-indeed knowledge that, if needed, assistance was as near at hand as the Help Alarm button conveniently located in every residence unit. They were doing all right, they assured their children and their Heron Bay Estates friends; they were doing all right . . .

Until, on a certain chill-but-sunny midmorning in November 2004, as suddenly and without warning as that above-mentioned fluke tornado two years later, out of nowhere came the End of Everything. After a late breakfast of orange juice, English muffins, and coffee (they'd been up past their usual bedtime the night before, watching with unsurprised dismay the presidential election returns on TV), Tim had withdrawn to his computer desk in the apartment's guest-bedroom/study to exchange disappointed emails with Son and Daughter, who shared their parents' stock-liberal persuasion. Margie, still in her nightclothes, lingered at table over a second coffee to read the *Baltimore Sun*'s painful details of John Kerry's unsuccessful bid to thwart George W. Bush's reelection — a disaster for the nation, in the Mannings' opinion — after which she meant to move as usual to *her* computer in their little den/office/library to do likewise and attend to some family business before lunch and whatever. But he had no sooner sat down and booted up than he heard a crash out there and, bolting kitchenward, found his without-whom-nothing life partner, his bride of half a century minus one month, his Margie!Margie!Margie! face-down and motionless on the breakfast-nook floor tiles, coffee from the shattered porcelain mug staining her nightgown and the crumpled pages of the *Sun*. With a half-strangled cry he ran to his fallen mate, her eyes open but not moving, her face frozen with alarm. Some years previously, the Mannings had signed up at the Heron Bay Estates Community Activities Center for a half-day course in Cardiopulmonary Resuscitation and Warning Signs of Stroke and Cardiac Arrest, and had vowed to review the various drills together at least annually thereafter — but never got around to doing so. Now he desperately felt for a pulse, put his face near hers to check for respiration, and detected neither; dashed to locate and press that Help button (on the wall beside the main-bath toilet); dashed back to try whether he could recollect anything whatever of the CPR routine; pressed his mouth to Margie's in what was meant to be some sort of forced inhalation but dissolved into a groaning kiss and then collapsed into a sobbing, helpless last embrace.

Helpless, yes: He still damns Tim Manning for that. Not that anything he or anyone else might have done would likely have saved her, but had their situations been reversed — had the thitherto undetected and now fatally ruptured aneurysm (as the Cause of Death turned out to be: not, after all, the news of Bush and Cheney's reelection) been his instead of hers — Margie Manning, for all her alarm and grief, would no doubt have taken some charge of things. She'd have dialed 911, he bets, and / or the establishment's Medical Center; would have shouted down the hallway for help and pounded on their neighbors' doors — all the usual desperate things that desperate people in such situations typically do, even if in vain. And would then have somehow collected herself enough to deal as needed with Med Center and other Bayview functionaries; to notify children and friends, comfort and be comforted by them, handle the obligatory farewell visits, and manage the disposition of the Departed's remains and estate and the rearrangement of the Survivor's life. But except back in his high school history-teaching classroom before his retirement and in a few other areas (tending their former lawn and shrubbery, making handyman repairs, presiding over their Oyster Cove cookouts), Margie was ever the more capable Manning — especially in emotionally charged situations, which tended to rattle and de-capacitate her husband. Now (i.e., then, on Election Day + 1, 2004) he lay literally floored, clutching his unbelievably dead mate's body as if he too had been stroke-stricken, which he desperately wished he *had* been. Unable to bring himself even to respond to the Manor's alarm-bell First Responder (from the nurses' station over in Assisted Living) when she presently came knocking, calling, doorbell-ringing, and doorknob-twisting, he lay closed-eyed and mute while the woman fetched out her passkey, turned the deadbolt, and pressed in with first-aid kit and urgent questions.

Don't ask T.M. how things went from there. Death is, after all, a not-unusual event in elder-care establishments, whose staff will likely be more familiar with His visitations than will the visited. As it happens, neither Tim nor for that matter Margie had had any prior Death Management experience: Their respective parents' last days, funeral arrangements, and estate disposition had been handled by older siblings, whose own life closures were then overseen by competent grown offspring who lived nearby and shared their parents' lives. The Bayview responder — an able young black woman named Gloria, as Tim sort of remembers — knelt to examine the pair of them, spoke to him in a raised voice, cell-phoned or walkie-talkied for assistance, spoke to him some more, asking questions that perhaps he answered or at least endeavored to, and maybe did a few nurse-type things on the spot. After a while he was off the floor: in a chair, perhaps mumbling apologies for his helplessness while Margie's body was gurneyed over to the Med Center to await further disposition. Although unable to take action, not to mention taking charge, he eventually became able at least to reply to questions. *To be notified?* Son in St. Louis, Daughter in Detroit. *Funeral arrangements?* None, thankee. *None?* None: Both Mannings preferred surcease *sans* fuss: no funeral, no grave or other marker, no memorial service. *You sure of that?* Sure: Organs to be harvested for recycling if usable and convenient; otherwise forget it. Remaining remains to be cremated — and no urn of ashes or ritual scattering, *s.v.p.*; just ditch the stuff. All her clothes and other personal effects to the nearest charity willing to come get them. Oh: and if Nurse happened to have in her kit a shot of something to take him out too, they could do a two-for-one right then and there and spare all hands more bother down the road.

Because what the fuck (as he explained to S-in-S and D-in-D when both were "B-in-B": Billeted, for the nonce, in Bayview): He and Margie had been fortunate in their connection and had relished their decades together. Unlike their Oyster Cove neighbor Ethel Bailey, for example, with her metastasized cervical cancer, Margie had been spared a lingering, painful death; she'd gone out in one fell swoop, a sort of Democrat parallel to their other O.C. neighbor Jim Smythe's fatal stroke in '92 upon hearing of Bill Clinton's defeat of George Bush *père*. Better yet — so he can see from his present perspective — would've been for the two of them to go out together like George and Carol Walsh over in Rockfish Reach last year, when T.S. Giorgio's freak tornado flattened most of Heron Bay Estates. On second thought, though, that must have been scary as shit: Best of all (if they'd only known that that goddamn aneurysm was about to pop) would've been to take matters into their own hands like those other Rockfish Reachers Dick and Susan Felton, who for no known reason drove home one fine September night from a neighborhood party, closed their automatic garage door, left their car's engine idling and its windows down, and snuffed themselves. Way to go, guys! Yeah: Pour Margie a glass of her pet pinot grigio and himself a good ripe cabernet, crank up the Good Gray Ghost, hold hands, breathe deep, and sip away till the last drop or last breath, whichever.

Whoops, forgot: no garage these days over here in Geezerville. Nor much get-it-done-with gumption either, for that matter, in this lately overspacious apartment, where T.M. pecks away at his word processor *faute de* fucking *mieux* (but No thankee, Barb and Mike: Dad'd rather stay put than change geographies this late in the day). Left to himself, Yours Truly Tim Manning is ... well ... *left to himself,* making this minimal most of his hapless self-helplessness by chewing on language like a cow its cud.

Assisted Living? Been there, done that.

So?

Well. Somewhere on this here QWERTYUIOP keyboard — maybe up among all those *F1-F12, pg up/pg dn, num lock/clear* buttons?— there ought to be one for Assisted Dying ...

Like, hey, one of these, maybe: *<home? end>*?

help

Worth a try:

enter

The End

We Delmarvans ... Delmarva Peninsulars? Anyhow, we dwellers on this flat, sand-crab-shaped projection between the Atlantic Ocean and Chesapeake Bay, comprising the state of Delaware and the Eastern Shores of both Maryland and Virginia, are no strangers to major storms. Even before global warming ratcheted up our Atlantic hurricane season — pounding the Caribbean, the Gulf of Mexico, and the East Coast of the USA from July into November with ever more numerous and destructive tropical tempests — there had been slam-bangers every decade or so for as long as anybody can remember. The nameless Big One of 1933, for example, cut a whole navigable inlet through our peninsula's coastal barrier islands, decisively separating the resort town of Ocean City, on Fenwick Island, from undeveloped Assateague Island, below it. Hurricane Connie in 1955 roared over the Outer Banks of North Carolina into Chesapeake Bay, sent crab boats through second-story windows in our marshy lower counties, and sank the three-masted tourist schooner *Levin J. Marvel* in mid-Bay, with considerable loss of life. Even in George and Carol Walsh's dozen and a half years in Heron Bay Estates, at least three formidable ones have "impacted" that gated community and environs: Hugo in '89, which downed trees and power lines hereabouts after ravaging the Carolinas; Floyd in '99, with its humongous basement-flooding downpours; and Isabel in 2003 — a mere tropical storm packing less wind and rain than those hurricanes, but piling a record-breaking eight-foot storm surge into the upper Bay that tore up countless waterfronts and flooded historic riverside houses in nearby Stratford that had been dry, if never high, since the eighteenth century. Nothing so catastrophic hereabouts to date as the great Galveston hurricane of 1900 or Katrina's wipeout of New Orleans in 2005, but we tidewater Marylanders keep a weather eye out and storm-prep list handy from Independence Day to Halloween.

That earlier holiday, with its traditional patriotic fireworks display upriver in Stratford and Heron Bay's own smaller one off our Blue Crab Marina Club pier (rebuilt after T.S. Isabel), was just a few weeks behind us when Tropical Storm Antonio fanfared this year's season by fizzling out north of Puerto Rico after sideswiping the Leeward Islands with minimal damage. On Antonio's Latino heels a fortnight later came his *gringuita* sister Becky, who during her transatlantic passage rapidly graduated from Tropical Depression to Named Tropical Storm (sustained winds between 50 and 73 miles per hour on the Saffir-Simpson scale) to Category 1 Hurricane (74-95 mph) before turning north-northwest in midocean, passing harmlessly east of Bermuda as if en route to Nova Scotia, but dissipating long before she got there. To all hands' surprise then — not least the National Hurricane Center's, which had predicted another busier-than-average season — there followed the opposite, an extraordinarily stormless summer: fewer-than-normal ordinary thundershowers, even, along our mid-Atlantic Coast, and a series of tropical depressions only a handful of which achieved named-storm status, much less hurricanehood. In vain through August and September the severe-weather aficionados (of whom the afore-mentioned George Walsh was one) daily checked Weather.com for signs of the promised action. The autumnal equinox passed without a single hurricane's whacking Florida and points north or west — a far cry indeed from '05's record-breaking season, which in addition to wrecking the Gulf Coast had exhausted that year's alphabet of storm names and obliged the weather service to rebegin in October with the Greek alphabet. This year Columbus Day came and went, Halloween approached, and we were no farther down the list than Tropical Storm (T.S.) Elliott, with the inevitable lame jokes about its name's proximity to that of the author of *The Waste Land*.

But then — *ta-da!* — after Elliott fizzled in the Windward Islands and then Frederika, right behind him, petered out off the Leewards, there materialized in midocean the tempest that might have been dubbed George if that name hadn't been used already, but since it had been (1998), was dubbed Giorgio instead, in keeping with the Weather Service's storm-naming policies of ethnic diversity and gender alternation. And now, perhaps, this non-story called "The End" can begin.

"*Giorgio?*" I imagine George Walsh wondering aloud to his wife, who's at her computer, as is he his, in the adjoining workrooms of their ample Georgian-style house on Shoreside Drive, in Rockfish Reach. "Is that me in Spanish?"

"In Spanish you'd be J-o-r-g-e," I hear Carol call back through the open door between His and Hers — in which latter she's checking out the websites of various resort accommodations on the Hawaiian island of Kauai, where they hope to vacation next February: "Pronounced *Hor*-hay. Giorgio's Italian. Wherefore ask ye, prithee?"

She talks that way sometimes. Her husband then explains what he's just seen on Weather.com: that a tropical depression near the Cape Verde Islands off West Africa, which he's been monitoring for the past several days, has organized and strengthened into the seventh named storm of the season as it crossed toward the Antilles, and is currently forecast to escalate in the Caribbean from Tropical Storm Giorgio to a Category 1 hurricane.

"O joy," Mrs. W. would likely respond, her tone the auditory equivalent of a patient eye-roll, and go back to her Internet chatroom on the pros and cons of those vacation lodgings, as does Mr. to his storm-tracking.

So meet the Walshes, Reader, as I reconstruct them — who, despite prevailingly robust health in their seventh decade of a successful life and fourth of a good marriage, have only eight remaining days of both until The End. Longtime Stratfordians before they shifted the five miles south to Heron Bay Estates, like the majority of their neighbors they're more or less retired at the time of this "story." Carol, sixty-five, is the ex-vice principal of Avon County High School, where for years she'd been a much-loved teacher of what the curriculum called Literature & Language and she called Reading & Writing. Outgoing and athletic (though less trim and more fatigue-prone nowadays, I'd bet, than she's used to being), she still enjoys tennis, swimming, and bicycling, and "to keep her hand in" coaches a number of college-bound ACHS seniors for their SATs as well as presiding over weekly meetings of the Heron Bay Book Club. Her husband, sixty-eight, was born and raised in Stratford, where his father directed a local bank. After graduation from the county high school at which his future wife would later teach and administrate, he crossed the Bay to take a baccalaureate in business at the University of Maryland, where Carol (from the Alleghenies of western Maryland) happened to be working toward her degree in education. By happy chance among so many thousands of College Park undergraduates, in her freshman and his senior year they met, introduced by a fraternity brother of George's who happened to be an old high school friend of Carol's and who, shortly after her graduation three years later, would be best man at their wedding. The bridegroom being by then busily employed at Stratford Savings & Loan, the newlyweds set up housekeeping in his hometown. While George — on his own merits, be it said — rose rapidly in the ranks of his father's firm, Carol completed at Stratford College the requisite postgrad credits for teacher certification. The two then thrived in their chosen fields, moving through the decades to high, though never top, positions in each (George would no doubt have succeeded his father as president of SS&L had he remained there rather than shifting in the early 1980s to a promising position with the Eastern Shore wing of Tidewater Communities, Inc., just breaking ground for its Heron Bay Estates project). Although less extroverted and community-spirited than Carol, he got along easily with colleagues and business associates, and in his retirement still enjoys attending Rotary Club and TCI board meetings. Husband and wife agree that like their differing genders, their differing temperaments, interests, and even metabolisms enhance rather than detract from their connection (despite his hearty appetite, George's body has shrunk with age, and his posture is becoming bent already, as was his father's). Their one child — a sometimes difficult but much-loved daughter with her mother's smile and her father's frown — went off to college in Ohio and never returned to Tidewaterland except to visit her parents. Now forty, lesbian, childless, and currently companionless as well, Ellen Walsh works in the editorial offices of the *Cleveland Plain Dealer* to support herself while pursuing, thus far without success, what she believes or anyhow hopes is her true vocation, the writing of serious literary fiction. Her parents content themselves with their hobbies and household routines: the pleasures and activities above-mentioned plus some gardening and small-scale renovation projects. Also, of course, household chores, errands, and dealings with maintenance-and-service people — yard crew, housecleaner, roofer and plumber and painter and electrician — all more frequent as their house gets older by HBE standards. To which must be added visits to the sundry doctors, dentists, and pharmacists who tend to their similarly aging bodies.

In all, a comfortable, fortune-favored life, as they well appreciate: ample pensions, annuity income, and a solid, conservative investment portfolio; not-bad health; no family tragedies; few really close friends (and no house pets), but no enemies. To be sure, they fear the prospect of old age and infirmity; can't help envying neighbors with married children and grandkids near at hand to share lives with and eventually "look after" them. Over their seven decades, separately and together, they've done this and that if not *this* or *that*; traveled here and there though not there and there; succeeded at A, B, and C if not at D, E, and F. No extraordinary good luck beyond their finding each other and being thus far spared extraordinary bad luck. Could wish for some things they never had, but feel graced indeed with each other, with their family (siblings and nieces and nephews in addition to their daughter), their neighbors and neighborhood, and the worthy if unremarkable accomplishments of their past and present life. They wish it could go on for a long while more! And have, after all, no reason to expect that it won't, for at least another decade or so.

But it won't.

"Yup," George reports next morning, or maybe the morning after that. "We've got ourselves a Cat. One hurricane. Looks like old Giorgio's going to pass under Puerto Rico and smack southern Haiti."

His wife sighs, shakes her head, adjusts her reading glasses. "Just what that poor miserable country needs."

I see them at breakfast in their nightclothes, George scanning the *Sun*'s weather page while Carol reads with sympathetic indignation an op-ed criticism of the Bush administration's ill-funded public-education program called No Child Left Behind: all show and no substance, in her and the columnist's opinion. The news from Iraq, as usual, is all bad: Husband and wife agree that their government's preemptive invasion of that country was unnecessary, poorly planned, and disastrous, but neither has a firm opinion on what's to be done about the resulting debacle. Things aren't going well in Afghanistan either, and the news from sub-Saharan Africa remains appalling. After breakfast, stretching exercises, and an hour or so at their desks, Carol will change into warmup clothes for her tennis date at the Club while George attends to some errands in town. They'll kiss goodbye as usual, remeet for lunch — perhaps out on their pleasant screened porch, the day being sunny and unseasonably warm for late October — and plan their afternoon: a bit of autumn yard cleanup, maybe, before next month's major leaf-fall from the neighborhood's maples, oaks, and sycamores; some cricket spray around the house foundation before the first frosts bring the critters indoors. Then perhaps a bicycle ride on Heron Bay's bike and jogging paths, if they're not too tired, before cocktails and hors d'oeuvres on the patio, a shower, dinner prep (still good weather for barbecuing), and after dinner their customary hour or so of reading and/or Internet stuff, a nightcap hour of television, and to bed after the ten o'clock news and a check of the Weather Channel.

So?

So nothing, really. In a proper Story, one would by now have some sense of a Situation: some latent or overt conflict, or at least some tension, whether between the Walshes themselves or between them on the one hand and something exterior to them on the other (a neighbor, a relative, a life problem, whatever); then some turn of events to raise the dramatical stakes. In short, a story-in-progress, the action of which is felt to be building strategically to some climax and satisfying denouement. The narrative thus far of this late-middle-aged, upper-middle-class, early-twenty-first-century, contented exurban North American married couple, however, its teller readily acknowledges to be no proper Story, only a chronicle: Its Beginning now ended, its Middle has begun, and its End draws nearer, sentence by sentence, as Hurricane Giorgio, after hitting Haiti with 90-mile-per-hour winds, turns northwest, crosses eastern and central Cuba (diminishing inland to Tropical Storm force and then restrengthening to Category 1 in the warm Florida Straits), veers north-northwest, and at a leisurely forward speed of 8 mph approaches landfall between the Keys and Miami. But an End is not the same as an Ending.

Just wanted to get that clear. Over the several days following, while Carol and George carry on with their drama-free lives,

Tropical-Storm-again Giorgio drenches southeast Florida, turns north-northeast into the Atlantic below Cape Canaveral, and re-regains hurricane force before his next landfall, between Capes Fear and Lookout in North Carolina's Outer Banks; he then weakens yet again from Cat. 1 to Borderline T.S. as he makes his way toward Norfolk and the mouth of the Chesapeake, leaving the usual trail of flash floods and power outages. Closely following his progress, the Walshes and their fellow Delmarvans hope he'll turn out to sea or at worst pass just offshore; instead, at bicycle speed he moseys straight up our peninsula, his sustained winds diminishing to 35-40 mph with occasional higher gusts, before his disorganized remnants pass up into Pennsylvania and New Jersey. Much (welcome) rain to relieve a droughty autumn, and overall not a lot of damage: some roads temporarily flooded; relatively few trees and power lines down, the ground having been abnormally dry; the routine handful of casualties (macho teenager drowned in flash flood while trying to cross rushing stream; elderly couple killed in collision with skidding SUV on I-95 between Baltimore and Wilmington); some messed-up basements and damaged boats at docks and marina slips, but nothing like '03's shoreline-wrecking Isabel.

Except that, as happens on rare occasions, the system spun off a single, short-lived but *very* strong tornado, watches for which had been posted for much of Maryland's Eastern Shore but generally ignored beyond the typical storm-prep stuff, our Tidewater land being non-twister-prone. Subsequently rated a high-end F3 on the Fujita scale (winds just above 200 mph), the thing touched down here in Avon County a few miles south of Stratford, fortunately sparing that colonial-era college town but bull's-eyeing instead, not one of those mobile-home parks that such tempests seem to favor, but handsome Heron Bay Estates.

I.e., us. Established by TCI during the Reagan administration as the area's first gated community. Successfully developed through the George Bush Senior and Bill Clinton years from blueprints and promotional advertisements to built-out neighborhoods of detached and semidetached houses and low- and mid-rise condos, all generously landscaped and tastefully separated from one another by tidal creeks and wetland ponds, winding roads, golf-course fairways, and small parkland areas. Amenitied with grounds- and gatekeepers, security patrols, clubhouses, tennis courts, marina facilities, pool and fitness center and activities building, community and neighborhood associations, website, and monthly calendar-magazine; also with sightseeing excursions to D.C., Baltimore, Philadelphia, and various Atlantic beach resorts; interest groups ranging from contract bridge, book discussion, gardening, and investment-strategy clubs to political, religious, and community-service organizations; Internet and foreign-language classes; neighborhood picnics, progressive dinners, and holiday parties. Populated by close to a thousand mostly white Protestant, mostly late-middle-aged, mostly middle- and upper-middle-class families, nearly all empty-nesters, many retired or semiretired, a considerable percentage with other homes elsewhere, plus a few quite wealthy individuals and a sprinkling of Catholics, Jews, Asians, and other minorities — even a half-dozen school-age children. Our lack of such urban attractions as museums, concert halls, nightclubs, and extensive restaurant and shopping facilities largely offset both by our reasonable proximity to those afore-mentioned cities and by nearby Stratford College, with its public lecture and concert series, continuing-education programs, and varsity sports events. In sum, a well-conceived and admirably executed project — nay, *community* — developed to completion over two dozen years and then, in half that many minutes, all but obliterated.

Not for the first time in these pages, "So?" one might reasonably inquire: on the scale of natural catastrophes, a trifle compared to Hurricane Katrina or the 2004 Southeast Asian tsunami, with its death toll of some 230,000. Indeed, although Heron Bay Estates was effectively wrecked, the human casualties of that spinoff tornado were remarkably low: only two deaths (one fewer than the earlier-mentioned toll of Giorgio's unhurried movement up the peninsula) plus numerous bone fractures and assorted lacerations, sprains, and contusions from flying debris, several of which injuries required emergency room treatment.

Indeed, that so many dwelling places and other structures could be destroyed with so comparatively few people seriously hurt, not to mention killed, would seem as fluky a circumstance as the twister itself — the more so since, unlike hurricane warnings, tornado watches hereabouts don't prompt evacuation. Granted, it was the forenoon of a late-October weekday: Those half-dozen youngsters were in school, their working parents and other office-going adults at their jobs in Stratford or elsewhere, and others yet doing various errands beyond our gates. Many of the snowbirds had migrated already to their winter quarters in more southern climes; numerous of those for whom Heron Bay was a weekend / vacation retreat were at their primary residences in the Washington-to-Philadelphia corridor, and some of our year-round resident retirees were off traveling. Even so, not a few HBEers were at home in their Egret's Crest or Shad Run condos, their Oyster Cove villas or Blue Crab Bight coach homes, their detached houses in Rockfish Reach or Spartina Pointe — at work in home offices, fiddling with their computers, or doing routine chores — while some others were enjoying bridge games at the Club, workouts at the fitness center, etc. And our staff, of course, were about their regular employment at the entrance gates, the golf course and grounds maintenance depots, the Community Association office, and the Heron Bay and Blue Crab Marina clubhouses. Bit of a miracle, really, that so many survived such devastation so little scathed — collapsed buildings ablaze from leaking propane lines or flooded by ruptured water pipes (in some cases, both at once)— and that only a couple were killed.

"A couple" in both senses: M / M George and Carol Walsh, of what used to be 1110 Shoreside Drive in what used to be the Rockfish Reach neighborhood of what once was Heron Bay Estates, in what manages to go on being Avon County, upper Eastern Shore of Maryland, USA 21600. Crushed and buried, they were, in the rubble of that not-un-handsome residence: two red-brick-sided, white-trimmed, black-shut-tered-and-doored, slate-roofed stories, of which only the far end of one chimneyed exterior wall remained standing after the tornado had roared through the community into Heron Bay proper, where it wa-terspouted and then quickly dissipated in the adjoining Matahannock River. Their bodies (his more or less atop hers) not excavated there-from until quite a few days later, when stunned survivors managed to tally the injured, review the roster of those known or thought to have been in residence, note the unaccounted-for, and attempt to contact next of kin while salvaging what they could of their own possessions, assessing their losses, and scrambling to make at-least-temporary new living arrangements for themselves. A traumatic business, especially for the elderly among us and most particularly for those without a sec-ond home or nearby relatives to take them in. No makeshift Federal Emergency Management Agency trailers for us Heron Bay Estaters, thanks!

"So?" you not unreasonably persist: Why should you care, other than abstractly, as one tsks at the morning newspaper's daily report of disasters large and small around the globe? And while you're at it, who's this "I," you might ask, the presumptive teller of this so-called tale, who speaks of "we" Delmarvans and "our" HBE? Am I perhaps, for example, Dean Peter Simpson of Stratford College, a Rockfish Reacher like the Walshes and, with my Ms., one of the hosts of that neighborhood's annual progressive-dinner parties, as were George and Carol? Or maybe I'm another George: that self-styled Failed-Old-Fart Fictionist George Newett, also from the College once upon a time and, with *my* Ms., erstwhile resident of what used to be HBE's Blue Crab Bight? George Newett, sure, why not, who ... let's see ... let's say ... once upon a dozen-years-ago time permitted himself, to his own surprise and likely hers as well, a one-shot adulterous liaison with ... guess who: Carol Walsh! In her early fifties she was back then, his fellow Heron Bay Estates Community Association member and, shall we say, ardent community servicer? Never mind the details. Or wait: Maybe I'm that Miz of his, the poet Amanda Todd, who (you know how it is with us poets) upon her husband's shamefacedly confessing his uncharacteristic lapse, sought poetic justice, shall we say, by bedding George Walsh in turn — or would have so done, except that that astonished and out-of-practice chap couldn't get it up even to the point of consenting to let her try getting it up for him?

Good tries yourself there, Comrade Reader — to which you might add the possibility that I'm *Ellen Walsh*, George and Carol's errant, Sapphic daughter! Ellen Walsh, sure: Early wire-service reports of that freak Delmarva tornado reach my office at the *Plain Dealer*, followed by more specific accounts of a certain gated community's near-total destruction. I repeatedly phone both "home" and the HBE Community Association office, in vain: All phones in the area are out. No point in calling Uncle Cal and Aunt Liz in Virginia or Uncle Ray and Aunt Mattie in Delaware yet, who're no doubt making the same anxious, fruitless inquiries; soon enough they'll be phoning me, to hear what I've learned of Mom and Dad's situation. It occurs to me to try the offices of the *Avon County News* in Stratford, or maybe just hop the next flight to Baltimore / Washington International, rent a car, and get my butt over the Bay Bridge to HBE, since no matter what my parents' fate, I ought surely to be there to aid and comfort them, pick up the pieces, whatever. But — paralyzed, maybe, by some combination of anxiety, denial, anticipatory grief, self-pity, and who knows what else — to my own dismay I find myself staying put for a day, and then another and another. I turn off my phone-answering machine and decline even to answer the caller-ID'd attempts of aunts, uncles, and others to reach me, with whatever tidings, though for all I know some of the *unidenti-fied* calls could be from my folks themselves, reassuring me that they're safe somewhere but needing my help. I go through the motions of my work, my "life," steering clear of the few officemates and "friends" who know where I grew up (i.e., in Stratford, back before HBE was built) and who might be wondering . . .

Nay, more, now that I think of it: I find myself staying put in the little apartment that I share with a ten-gallon tropical-fish tank and a past-its-prime computer and *losing* my fucked-up self in what I've long wished, to no avail, had been my true vocation, the writing not of inter-office memos but of serious-type fiction stories. Like maybe one about an only-child daughter who, coming to realize that she's a lez, leaves small-town Maryland after high school, goes to university somewhere Midwest, and returns thereafter only for dutiful visits to her parents — unlike the tale's author, who never left "home" but often wishes she had, instead of winding up as a sexless spinster in an entry-level Egret's Crest condo partly financed by her folks and miraculously spared by Giorgio's tornado. A tornado that never actually occurred, it occurs to her to imagine, except in her heartbroken, wish-granting imagina-tion — wherein, while she's at it, she fancies that she's only *fancying* that she "stayed behind" in Avon County! Or, on the contrary, that she long ago left it and never moved back . . .

Thus do I find myself by losing myself: While the directors of Tidewater Communities, Inc., at their next board meeting, observe a moment's silence in honor of their late colleague and his Mrs., and then debate the pros and cons of rebuilding Heron Bay Estates — weighing the projected (and environmentally ruinous) ongoing population surge in the Chesapeake Bay region against the recent nationwide slump in new and existing home sales and the predicted hyperactive hurricane seasons, with their attendant steep hikes in H.O. and flood-insurance premiums —"I" invent a pleasant, "eco-sensitive" gated community called Heron Bay Estates, replete with a natural preserve, recreational facilities, good neighbors and Peeping Toms, toga parties and progressive dinners, neighborhood- and community-association meetings, house renovations and teardowns, adulteries and suicides — the works. Sometimes I almost get to thinking that the place is real, or used to be; even that *I* am, or once was. Other times, that I dreamed both of us up, or anyhow that *somebody* did.

In whichever case (as happens), B followed A, and C B, et seq., each perhaps the effect, at least in part, of its predecessors, until . . .

Rebeginning

Where in the world to begin, and how? Maybe with something like *In the beginning, Something-or-Other created Creation* — including what became our local galaxy and solar system . . .

On whose third-from-the-sun planet, a primordial land mass divided over the eons into a clutch of continents . . .

Along the eastern coast of one of which (named "North America" by a certain subset of an animal genus that evolved together with the geography), the off-and-on glaciations and other geological morphings developed that particular planet's largest estuarine system — called "Chesapeake Bay" by the "English" colonizers who displaced its aboriginal human settlers after appropriating many of their place names along with their place . . .

Which those newcomers then named "Maryland" . . .

In what their descendants would call "the USA" . . .

And lo, on the "Eastern Shore" of this same river-intricated Bay, near the small college town of "Stratford" in ever-less-rural "Avon County," an enterprising outfit trade-named "Tidewater Communities, Inc." developed in the "1980s" a soon-thriving gated community called by its developers "Heron Bay Estates" . . .

Which project prospered just long enough for its thousand-and-some inhabitants to begin to feel that their variously laid out and well-shrubberied neighborhoods constituted not only a successful residential development but a genuine community . . .

Until, a mere two dozen years after its inception, that development was all but totally flattened in fewer than two dozen minutes by an F3-plus tornado, rare for these parts, spun off from an ever-less-rare tropical storm — the one called "Giorgio" in the "October" of "2006," during that year's annual hurricane season — and here we refugee-survivors of that freak twister freaking *are*, and that's more than enough already of this strung-out, quote-mark and hyphen-laden blather, the signature stylistic affliction of Failed-Old-Fart Fictionist George I. Newett, emeritus professor of more-or-less-creative writing @ the above-alluded-to Stratford College, who here hands the figurative microphone to his former colleague and fellow displaced Heron Bay Estatesman Peter Simpson, just now clearing his throat to address the first postapocalyptic meeting of the Heron Bay Estates Community Association (HBECA, commonly pronounced "H-Becka"), convened *faute de mieux* in a StratColl chemistry lecture hall thanks to Chairperson Simpson's good offices as associate dean of said college and open to all former residents of that former development. Your podium, Pete, and welcome to it: Rebegin, sir, *s.v.p.*!

"Yes, well," Dean Simpson said to the assembled — then paused to reclear his throat and adjust with experienced hand the microphone clamped to the lectern perched between lab sinks and Bunsen burners on the small auditorium's chemistry-demonstration rostrum: "Here we-all are indeed — or *almost* all of us, anyhow, and thanks be for that!" He shook his balding but still handsome late-fiftyish head and sighed, then with one forefinger pushed up his rimless bifocals at the nose piece, smiled a tight-lipped smile, and continued: "And the question before us, obviously, is *Do we start over?* And if so, how?"

"Excuse me there, Pete," interrupted one of the six official neighborhood representatives seated together in the lecture hall's front row — plump Mark Matthews from Spartina Pointe, Heron Bay's once-most-upscale detached-house venue — "*I* say we oughta start over by starting this here *meeting* over, with a prayer of thanksgiving that even though Heron Bay Estates was wrecked, all but a couple of us survived to rebuild it."

"Amen to that," some fellow gruffed from an upper rear row — beefy-bossy old Chuck Becker, Pete saw it was, from Cattail Court, in his and Debbie's own much-missed Rockfish Reach neighborhood — and there were other murmurs of affirmation here and there in the well-filled hall. But "Objection," a woman's voice protested from elsewhere in the room — the Simpsons' friend and (former) neighbor Lisa Bergman: Dr. Dave the Dentist's wife and hygienist-partner, and HBECA's trim and self-possessed rep from their late lamented subdivision. "If we're going to bring Gee-dash-Dee into this meeting," she went on, "—which I'm personally opposed to doing?—then before we thank Him-slash-Her, at least let's ask Her-slash-Him to explain why He / She killed George and Carol Walsh and wrecked all our houses, okay?"

"Hear hear!" agreed her swarthy-handsome husband and several others, including Pete's afore-mentioned Debbie, the Stratford po-et-professor Amanda Todd, and *her* spouse, Yours Truly, the off-and-on Narrator of this rebegun Rebeginning. Enough present objected to the objection, however — both among the official representatives from what used to be HBE's Shad Run, Egret's Crest, Oyster Cove, Blue Crab Bight, et al., and among the general attendees of this ad hoc open meeting from those several neighborhoods — that Peter was obliged to restore order by tapping on the microphone before proposing that in the interests of all parties, a few moments' silence be observed forthwith, during which those inclined to thank or supplicate the deity of their choice would be free to do so, and the others to reflect as they saw fit upon the loss of their homes and possessions and the survival of their persons. "All in favor please raise your hands. Opposed? Motion carried: Half a minute's silence here declared, in memory of our late good neighbors the Walshes and our much-missed Heron Bay Estates."

While all hands prayed, reflected, or merely fidgeted, their chairperson could pretty well tell who was doing what by raising his eyes while lowering his head, stroking his short-trimmed beard, and noting the lowered heads with *closed* eyes (Spartina Pointers Mark Matthews and his self-designated trophy wife, Mindy; Mark's investment-counseling protégé Joe Barnes from Rockfish Reach; and his afore-mentioned cheerleaders Chuck and Sandy Becker, among others), the defiantly raised heads and wide-open eyes (notably Pete's own wife, Debbie, of whom more anon; the afore-noted Bergmans; the weekly *Avon County News* columnist Gerald Frank from Shad Run; and us Newett / Todds, late of Blue Crab Bight), and other somewhere-betweeners like Pete himself (e.g., Joe Barnes's wife, Judy; Gerry Frank's Joan; the tirelessly upbeat party hosts Tom and Patsy Hardison from Annapolis and Rockfish Reach; and, somewhat surprisingly, the Oyster Cove expastor Matt Grauer, whose conversion from Methodist minister to educational consultant perhaps reflected some weakening of faith?). As Dean Pete makes his unofficial tally, your *pro tem* Narrator will take the opportunity to stretch this thirty-second Moment of Silence into a more extended patch of what in the trade we call Exposition before getting on with the business at hand and this story's Action, if any — rather like that other windbag, our Giorgio tornado, expanding its few-minute life span into what seemed an eternity to us hapless and terrified HBEers huddled in our basements and walk-in closets while windows and skylights blew out and trees and walls came a-tumbling down.

Okay, okay: weak analogy; scratch it. But whether or not this Moment of Silence helps any present to decide where we go from here, both as individuals and as a community, there's no doubting that those other moments of horrifying wind-roar changed the lives of most of us who survived it (not to mention the Walsh couple who didn't) and of many others lucky enough to have been in Stratford or elsewhere at the time but unlucky enough to have lost their primary or secondary dwelling place.

E.g., in that latter category, those Matthewses, Mark and Mindy, whose weekend-and-vacation establishment — an imposing faux-Georgian McMansion in Spartina Pointe — had scarcely been finished and landscaped when F3 all but wrecked it. The pair were over in Baltimore at the time, Mark in his downtown office at Lucas & Jones, LLC, whereof he is CEO, and his ex-secretary Mindy in their nearby harborfront penthouse condominium. Thanks to its no-expense-spared construction, enough of their Heron Bay house remains standing to make its restoration feasible, but for Mark the question is whether to rebuild at all in a community that may or may not follow suit, or to take what insurance money he can get, claim the rest as a casualty-loss tax deduction, clear the ruins, list the lot for sale, kiss HBE bye-bye, and build their *second* second home on higher ground somewhere less flood- and hurricane-vulnerable, like maybe the Hunt Valley horse country north of the city or the Allegheny hills of western Maryland. With their well-diversified equities portfolio, their Baltimore condo plus a couple of other "investment units" here and there, and a certain offshore account in the Cayman Islands, they're in no great pain. Indeed, for pert and upbeat Mindy the wreck of 211 Spartina Court is as much opportunity as setback: Long and hard as she'd worked with architect, designers, and decorators on that house's planning and construction — including radically changing its original "design concept," at no small cost, from mission-style *hacienda grande* to Williamsburg colonial — they had enjoyed the finished product just long enough for her to wish that she'd done a few things differently: better *feng shui* in the floor plan, especially in the mansion's wings, and maybe one of those "infinite edge" swimming pools instead of the conventional raised coping right around. Something to be said for going back to Square One, maybe, whether with TCI in a redesigned and even better-amenitied Heron Bay or with some other architect/ builder elsewhere ...

No such temptations for the Hardisons, among others: those pros-perous, high-energy Annapolis lawyers whose Rockfish Reach *palazzo* was the second most expensive casualty of the storm. They want the *status quo ante* restored as quickly as possible, not only at their Loblolly Court address but in all of Heron Bay Estates, so that they can get back to their weekend golf and tennis, their costume parties, progressive dinners, and Chesapeake cruising on their forty-foot trawler yacht, *Plaintiff's Complaint*. While for the elderly Beckers (who have flown up from their winter retreat on Florida's Gulf Coast to attend this meet-ing), the question isn't whether to rebuild what had been their primary residence on Rockfish Reach's Cattail Court or to build or buy another elsewhere in the area, but whether instead to give up altogether their annual snowbird migrations between two houses, shift their primary domicile to state-income-tax-free Florida, and escape its sweltering summer season on cruise ships, Elderhostel tours, and such — includ-ing, for Sandy Becker especially, frequent Stratford revisits to keep in touch with her many Episcopal church and Heron Bay Club friends.

Nor any such options and luxurious dilemmas for us reasonably well-off but by no means wealthy Simpsons, Bergmans, Greens, Franks, and Newett/Todds, whose wrecked houses and ruined possessions were our *only* such, and who've been reduced to making shift as best we can in generally inadequate temporary lodgings — motel rooms, in some instances — in small-town Stratford while still reporting daily to our company workplaces, our college or other-school classrooms, or our improvised laptop-and-cell-phone "home" offices. For pity's sake, cry we, let's get old HBE up and running, however rudimentary its resurrection! And the same goes in spades for those elderly widows and widowers like Rachel Broadus, Reba Smythe, and Matt Grauer, who had been managing well enough, all things considered, in their Shad Run condos or Oyster Cove villas, but are now renting unhappily like us or squatting with their grown children, and in either case wondering whether the time has come for them to pack it in as homeowners and shift across the Matahannock River to TCI's Bayview Manor Continuing Care Community.

End of overextended Exposition. Back to you, Peter?

"Okay," that ever-reasonable fellow declared to the assembled, glancing at his agenda notes and tapping the microphone again to end their memorial Moment of Silence: "Let's start again — which of course is this meeting's agenda exactly." Comradely grin; stroke of close-cut gray-black beard. "The questions are Where, and How, and To What Extent, and In What Order we do whatever we end up deciding to do." Sympathetic head-shake. "I quite understand that most of you have your hands as full as Debbie and I do, squatting in temporary quarters while we deal with insurance adjusters"— boos and hisses from here and there, not directed at the speaker — "and scrabble around to make do while trying to keep up with our jobs and all. It's overwhelming! I want to emphasize that what each of you does with your damaged or destroyed property is entirely up to you, as long as you bear in mind HBE's covenant and building codes. All rebuilding plans for detached houses need to be cleared with our Design Review Board, obviously, just as they were back when those neighborhoods were first built. The condominium and villa and coach-home communities we presume will be rebuilt pretty much as before — assuming they *are* rebuilt — by a general contractor selected by each of the neighborhood associations, and the plans passed along to H-Becka, whose unenviable job it'll be to coordinate and monitor the several projects. Reconstruction of the Heron Bay Club and the Marina Club and piers will be up to each one's board of governors, subject to the same review protocols. And TCI, I'm happy to report, will be standing by to advise and consult on HBE's infrastructure and on any changes we may want to make in its overall layout — even though it's our baby these days, not its original developer's."

He paused, glanced around the hall, readjusted his eyeglasses, and returned to his notes. "I know that several of you have ideas and proposals for a 'new' [*finger quotes*] Heron Bay Estates, while others of you would be more than content to have things put back as much as possible the way they were before. It's important for you to understand that this meeting is *for preliminary input only*, not for any final decisions. And some kinds of things can be put off till we get our homes rebuilt and reoccupied — may the day come soon! But even in that department there may be some suggestions that we ought to be considering as we plan our repairs and reconstruction. So the floor's open, folks: We'll make note of any and all proposals, talk 'em over in committee, and report back to you at our next open meeting. Let me remind you that you can also make written suggestions and comments on the H-Becka website." Smile of invitation. "Who wants to go first?"

Several hands went up at once, among the neighborhood representatives (my wife's, for one) and in the general audience (among them, mine). Before the chair could call on any, however, Mark Matthews heaved to his feet, turned his ample dark-suited back to Peter Simpson, and loudly addressed the hall: "Friends and neighbors! Mark Matthews here, from Spartina Pointe and the Baltimore office of Lucas and Jones — an outfit that knows a thing or two about turning setbacks into opportunities, as Joe Barnes yonder, from our Stratford office, can testify. Am I right, Joe and Judy?"

In a fake darkie accent, "Yassuh, boss," the male of that couple called back. A few people chuckled; his wife, sitting beside him, did not. Nor did Pete, who raised his eyebrows and stroked his chin but evidently decided not to interrupt, at least for the moment, this interruption of normal meeting procedure.

"Now, then! Mindy and I personally haven't made up our minds yet whether or not to rebuild our Spartina Court place, but I can tell you this, folks: The current downturn in the housing market — all those contractors hungry for work? — is such a golden opportunity for all hands present that if TCI isn't interested, Charlie Becker and I might just get into the construction racket ourselves! You with me there, Chuck?"

That elderly Becker (in fact the retired CEO of a Delaware construction firm) grinned and cocked his white-haired head as if considering the suggestion. And "Hear hear!" duly seconded Joe Barnes.

"But if we do," Matthews went on, "it won't be just to get back to where we were. No sirree! It'll be to build a *bigger and better* Heron Bay Estates! And here's how." Raising his stout right thumb: "First off, we buy us a couple hundred more acres of cornfields and woodlots, either next door or across the highway or both, for an *HBE Phase Two!*" Now his thick forefinger: "Then we build us a couple more mid-rise-or-higher condominium complexes and detached-house neighbor-hoods — *to raise our base*, know what I mean?" Middle finger: "Plus we build ourselves an Olympic-size *indoor* pool and spa complex at the Club to use in the cooler months, and maybe even a second golf course on some of that useless preserve acreage of ours that just *sits* there. *Et cetera et cetera*: a whole new ball game!"

Tom Hardison it was, for a change, who said, "Sounds about right to me, Mark." Joe Barnes, of course, echoed assent, and there were approving or at least worth-considering nods from Chuck Becker and Stratford realtor Jeff Pitt as Matthews, clearly much pleased with himself, plumped back into his seat and beamed almost defiantly up at Peter Simpson. But "It sure sounds anything but right to *me*," my Amanda objected, also rising as if to address the gathering at large, but then turning to the podium: "However, instead of just grabbing the floor, I'll ask the chair's permission before I sound off."

Obviously welcoming the return to parliamentary procedure, "Permission granted," Simpson said at once. "Let's hear what you have to say, Amanda."

In her firm but gentle professorial voice, "What I have to say," she declared to the assembly, "is just about a hundred and eighty degrees from what you've just heard." Tucking a lock of gray-brown hair behind her ear, she smiled down at Matthews, who appeared to be studying the spread fingers of his left hand. "I agree with Mark that the catastrophe we-all have suffered can be turned into an opportunity. But in my opinion — and I'm not alone in this — what it's an opportunity *for* is not to *destroy* our precious preserve land and adjacent acreage and grow bigger-bigger-bigger, like too many already-overweight Americans — "

"*Ob*jection," Mark Matthews complained, and seemed about to rise again from his seat, but didn't.

"Noted but overruled, Mark," Peter declared, and nodded to Amanda to continue.

"Let's imagine instead a very *different* kind of Heron Bay makeover," my wife proposed. "Given what we all know the future has in store for us with global warming and such, and the critical importance of reducing our carbon emissions and foreign-oil dependency, here's our chance to make HBE a model 'green' community!" The adjective in finger quotes. "Solar panels on every building, plus whatever other energy-saving technologies we can deploy — expensive to start with, but they soon pay for themselves in lower utility bills, and what's bad news for Delmarva Power and Light is good news for the environment. *Fewer* grass areas to be fertilized and irrigated, instead of more; *more* preserve instead of less, and natural 'xericulture' landscaping wherever possible, instead of high-maintenance flower beds and shrubbery. Energy-efficient houses and condos, and propane-powered shuttle buses to Stratford and back every hour, like the ones they use in some of our national parks, to cut down on gasoline consumption and car-exhaust emissions every time we need to get into town. What an example we could set for twenty-first-century America!"

"I'll second that," called Debbie Simpson.

"And I'll third it," added Joan Frank. "We might just want to reconsider the whole gated-community concept too, while we're at it, as Mandy suggested last year."

"Whoa-ho-*ho!*" Jeff Pitt protested, rising from his seat in the audience and, like Mark, not waiting for acknowledgment from the chair: "Excuse me, ladies, but you take this tree-hugging stuff far enough and next thing we know you'll be telling us to donate the whole shebang to the Nature Conservancy instead of rebuilding at all!"

Uneasy chuckles here and there. Unfazed, "Don't think I haven't considered that option, Jeff," Amanda replied: "Collect our insurance payouts and take our casualty-loss deductions and then buy or build in an already-existing population center like Stratford: smart growth instead of suburban sprawl! But I'm trying to be less radical than that: We keep our entry gates and our golf course; we rebuild our beautiful Heron Bay Estates and even keep that pretentious last word of its name, if that's what most of us want; but we rebuild it more green and eco-friendly, for our own good as well as the planet's! Thank you all for hearing me out."

Your Narrator applauded, proud as usual of his spunky mate, though disinclined to go quite so far as she in the extreme-makeover way. What *I'd* settle for, frankly, at my age and stage, is to be back with my dear high-mileage Apple desktop in my snug little study in our snug little coach home in HBE's snug little Blue Crab Bight subdivision exactly as it was before Mister Twister hit the Delete button, pecking away my Old-Fart-Emeritus autumn mornings at yet another rambling prose piece while Amanda, in *her* snug little *et cetera*, invokes the Muse of Less-Than-Immortal Versifiers but Damned Good Teachers to see her through yet another StratColl.edu semester or three before she joins her gin-and-tonic-slurping mate out in the pasture. Yes indeedy, Cap'n Gawd: Get us back Just Where & As We Were, Sir, *s. V.p.*— rolling our fortune-favored eyes at the word "Estates" and the 24/7 entrance gates and security patrols in our all-but-crime-free neck of the tidewater Maryland woods; tsking our liberal tongues at the U.S. fiasco in Iraq and at sundry other disasters around the world; shaking our snotty-intellectual heads at our community's toga parties and old-fashioned socials while at the same time quite enjoying them.

O bliss!

But no such luck, of course. Fabulator though G.I. Newett by vocation may willy-nilly be, the subject of these present fumbling fabulations is (anyhow *was*) a subdivision of the Real World — wherein, as Reader may have had occasion to note, nothing once truly whacked is ever quite restorable to What It Was Before. Best one can do is bid Mister Chairperson to tap the old microphone/gavel and proceed with our proceedings. Okay, Pete?

"Okay," declared Peter Simpson, and did just that: tapped the mic and thanked Amanda for her input, which he pronounced most certainly worth serious consideration even by those who — like himself and no doubt numerous others present ("Not including my wife," he acknowledged with a small smile: "She's with *you*, Amanda")— inclined to a more conservative conservationism, so to speak: the reconstruction of Heron Bay Estates as expeditiously as possible and as close as possible to what it was before, perhaps with "green" enhancements where convenient and cost-effective. Reduced community-assessment fees, say, for energy-efficient and/or eco-sensitive building and landscape designs?

"Right on," somebody agreed — Gerry Frank, I'd guess, or Dave Bergman — and there was a general rustle of approbation in the hall. No need for motions and seconds, Pete reminded us, since this wasn't a formal meeting, just a sort of solidarity and opinion-gathering session for us lucky-but-hard-hit survivors. "Your neighborhood reps and I will be getting together as often as we can to review and approve rebuilding proposals from individual homeowners, as well as from the condo and villa and coach-home associations and the Club and Marina Club boards, and we'll green-light as many as we possibly can in keeping with HBE's covenant, using what we've heard from you today as our guidelines." Deep exhale; stroke of beard. "So: The floor's open now to any others who want to be heard."

A few more did, mainly to affirm one or another already-voiced position, after which the aspiring teller of this would-be tale took it upon himself to thank our Association chairman for his good offices on our behalf. "No call for that," Dean Pete modestly replied, gathering up his notes. And then, to the house, "On behalf of H-Becka, it's I who thank *you*-all for coming to this get-together and making your opinions known. We're all plenty stressed out, for sure. But one way or another, by George . . ." As if just realizing what he'd said, he grinned meward. "One way or another, we'll *rebegin!*"

Yeah, right. And while we're about it, friends and neighbors, let's rebegin our derailed lives, okay? Taking a more or less alphabetical clutch of us as we've appeared in the Faltering Fables of G.I. Newett, let's have Sam Bailey's wife Ethel *not* die of cervical cancer this time around, so bereaving my old ex-colleague and Oyster Cove neighbor that he skewers himself (unsuccessfully) with a borrowed machete at the Hardisons' toga party in Rockfish Reach. Okay? And let those other RRers Dick and Susan Felton *not* feel so prematurely finished with their lives' prime time that they drive home from that same bloodily disrupted fest and off themselves with auto exhaust fumes in their garage, *sans* even a farewell note to their distant kids! Let good Pete and Debbie Simpson's daughter, Julie — their much-prized only child, on track to graduate from Johns Hopkins, go on to med school, and thence to service in some selfless outfit like Doctors Without Borders — *not* be car-crashed to death in her sophomore year by a drunken driver on the Baltimore Beltway, so traumatizing both parents (but Deb in particular) that they haven't enjoyed a truly happy hour in the several years since! Let George and Carol Walsh *not* be crushed to a bloody mush in the rubble of their house on Shoreside Drive (Rockfish Reach again) by that fucking five-minute F3 funnel-cloud! *Et cetera*? And while we're about all *that*, let's rebegin us Newett/Todds, making my Mandy this time around *not* merely an okay Poet + Damned Fine Teacher, but the Essential Lyric Voice of Early-Twenty-First-Century America + DFT!

And her husband?

Yes, well. *In the beginning* (that chap believes he was saying once upon a time) there was this place, this "development." There were these people: their actions, inactions, and interactions, their successes and failures, pleasures and pains, excitements and boredoms, in a particular historical time and geographical location. Nothing very momentous or consequential in the larger scheme of things: one small tree-leaf in the historical forest, its particular spring-summer-and-fall no doubt to be lost in Father Time's vast, ongoing deciduosity. But just as, now and then, one such leaf may happen against all odds to be noticed, picked up, and at least for some while preserved—between the leaves of a book, say—and may with luck outlast its picker-upper as the book may outlast its author and even its serial possessors, so may this verbal approximation of the residential development called Heron Bay Estates and of sundry of its inhabitants survive, by some fluke, that now-gone place and its fast-going former denizens—whether or not it and they in some fashion "rebegin," and even if this feeble reimagining themof, like the afore-invoked leaf-pressed leaf, itself sits pressed and scarcely noted in Papa T's endless, ever-growing library—

Or, more likely, his recycling bin.

—[Good]By[e] George I. Newett